SISTERHOOD OF
DUNE

THE DUNE SERIES

BY FRANK HERBERT

Dune
Dune Messiah
Children of Dune
God Emperor of Dune
Heretics of Dune
Chapterhouse: Dune

BY FRANK HERBERT, BRIAN HERBERT, AND KEVIN J. ANDERSON

The Road to Dune (includes the original short novel *Spice Planet*)

BY BRIAN HERBERT AND KEVIN J. ANDERSON

Dune: House Atreides
Dune: House Harkonnen
Dune: House Corrino

Dune: The Butlerian Jihad
Dune: The Machine Crusade
Dune: The Battle of Corrin

Hunters of Dune
Sandworms of Dune

Paul of Dune
The Winds of Dune
Sisterhood of Dune

BY BRIAN HERBERT

Dreamer of Dune
(biography of Frank Herbert)

SISTERHOOD OF
DUNE

Brian Herbert

and

Kevin J. Anderson

TOR®

A TOM DOHERTY ASSOCIATES BOOK

NEW YORK

SISTERHOOD OF DUNE

A Tor Book
Published by Tom Doherty Associates, LLC
175 Fifth Avenue
New York, NY 10010

www.tor-forge.com

Tor® is a registered trademark of Tom Doherty Associates, LLC.

Library of Congress Cataloging-in-Publication Data

Herbert, Brian.
    Sisterhood of Dune / Brian Herbert, Kevin J. Anderson. — 1st ed.
        p. cm.
    "A Tom Doherty Associates book."
    ISBN 978-0-7653-2273-9
    1. Dune (Imaginary place)—Fiction.   2. Life on other planets—Fiction.
I. Anderson, Kevin J., 1962–   II. Title.
    PS3558.E617S57 2012
    813'.54—dc22

                                                                        2011025167

First Edition: January 2012

Printed in the United States of America

0 9 8 7 6 5 4 3 2 1

This book is dedicated to the legions of Dune fans worldwide. Your tremendous support has made this remarkable universe possible.

Thanks to Frank Herbert's enthusiastic readers, *Dune* became the first novel ever to win both of science fiction's highest honors, the Hugo Award and the Nebula Award. Later, as the number of fans grew, *Children of Dune* became the first science fiction novel ever to appear on the *New York Times* bestseller list. When David Lynch's film version was released in 1984, the novel *Dune* hit #1 on the *New York Times*.

Today, nearly fifty years after the original publication of *Dune*, the fans have kept Frank Herbert's magnificent legacy alive, continuing to read all of his original chronicles as well as our new novels.

ACKNOWLEDGMENTS

As with all our books, we owe a tremendous debt of gratitude to our wives, Janet Herbert and Rebecca Moesta Anderson, for their love and creative support. We would also like to express our gratitude to Tom Doherty at Tor Books, our editors Pat LoBrutto (Tor) and Maxine Hitchcock (Simon & Schuster UK), and our agent, John Silbersack (Trident Media Group). In addition, Kim Herbert and Byron Merritt have worked tirelessly to help raise awareness of the Dune novels through promotional efforts, convention appearances, and website work. Kevin would also like to thank Mary Thomson for her many hours of transcription, and test readers Diane Jones and Louis Moesta.

It was a time of geniuses, of people stretching the limits of their imagination and wondering about the possibilities for their race.
—HISTORY OF THE GREAT SCHOOLS

One might think that humanity would have peace and prosperity after the defeat of the thinking machines and the formation of the Landsraad League to replace the old League of Nobles, but the battles had just begun. Without an external enemy to fight, we began to fight ourselves.
—ANNALS OF THE IMPERIUM

SISTERHOOD OF
DUNE

It has been eighty-three years since the last thinking machines were destroyed in the Battle of Corrin, after which Faykan Butler took the name of Corrino and established himself as the first Emperor of a new Imperium. The great war hero Vorian Atreides turned his back on politics and flew off to parts unknown, aging only imperceptibly because of the life-extension treatment given to him by his notorious father, the late cymek general Agamemnon. Vorian's one-time adjutant, Abulurd Harkonnen, was convicted of cowardice during the Battle of Corrin and exiled to the gloomy planet Lankiveil, where he died twenty years later. His descendants continue to blame Vorian Atreides for the downfall of their fortunes, although the man has not been seen for eight decades.

On the jungle planet Rossak, Raquella Berto-Anirul, who survived a malicious poisoning that transformed her into the first Reverend Mother, has adapted methods from the near-extinct Sorceresses to form her own Sisterhood, featuring a school that trains women to enhance their minds and bodies.

Gilbertus Albans, once the ward of the independent robot Erasmus, has established a different sort of school on the bucolic planet of Lampadas, where he teaches humans to order their minds like computers, making them into Mentats.

The descendants of Aurelius Venport and Norma Cenva (who remains alive, although in a highly evolved state) have built a powerful commercial empire,

Venport Holdings; their spacing fleet uses Holtzman engines to fold space and mutated, spice-saturated Navigators to guide the vessels.

Despite the time that has passed since the defeat of the thinking machines, antitechnology fervor continues to sweep across the human-settled planets, with powerful, fanatical groups imposing violent purges. . . .

After being enslaved for a thousand years, we finally overwhelmed the forces of the computer evermind Omnius, yet our struggle is far from ended. Serena Butler's Jihad may be over, but now we must continue the fight against a more insidious and challenging enemy—human weakness for technology and the temptation to repeat the mistakes of the past.

—MANFORD TORONDO, *The Only Path*

Manford Torondo had lost count of his many missions. Some he wanted to forget, like the horrific day that the explosion tore him apart and cost him the lower half of his body. This mission, though, would be easier, and eminently satisfying—eradicating more remnants of mankind's greatest enemy.

Bristling with cold weapons, the machine warships hung outside the solar system, where only the faintest mist of dwindled starlight glinted off their hulls. As a result of the annihilation of the scattered Omnius everminds, this robot attack group had never reached its destination, and the population of the nearby League star system never even realized they had been a target. Now Manford's scouts had found the fleet again.

Those dangerous enemy vessels, still intact, armed, and functional, hung dead in space, long after the Battle of Corrin. Mere derelicts, ghost ships—but abominations, nonetheless. They had to be dealt with accordingly.

As his six small vessels approached the mechanical monstrosities, Manford experienced a primal shudder. The dedicated followers of his Butlerian movement were sworn to destroy all vestiges of forbidden computer technology. Now, without hesitation, they closed in on the derelict robot fleet, like gulls on the carcass of a beached whale.

The voice of Swordmaster Ellus crackled over the comm from an adjacent ship. For this operation, the Swordmaster flew point, guiding the Butlerian hunters to these insidious robot vessels that had drifted unnoticed for decades. "It's an attack squadron of twenty-five ships, Manford—exactly where the Mentat predicted we'd find them."

Propped in a seat that had been specially modified to accommodate his leg-less body, Manford nodded to himself. Gilbertus Albans continued to impress him with his mental prowess. "Once again, his Mentat School proves that human brains are superior to thinking machines."

"The mind of man is holy," Ellus said.

"The mind of man is holy." It was a benediction that had come to Manford in a vision from God, and the saying was very popular now with the Butlerians. Manford signed off and continued to watch the unfolding operation from his own compact ship.

Seated next to him in the cockpit, Swordmaster Anari Idaho noted the position of the robot battleships on the screen and announced her assessment. She wore a black-and-gray uniform with the emblem of the movement on her lapel, a stylized sigil that featured a blood-red fist clenching a symbolic machine gear.

"We have enough weaponry to destroy them from a distance," she said, "if we use the explosives wisely. No need to risk boarding the ships. They'll be guarded by combat meks and linked fighting drones."

Looking up at his female attendant and friend, Manford maintained a stony demeanor, though she always warmed his heart. "There is no risk—the evermind is dead. And I want to gaze at these machine demons before we eliminate them."

Dedicated to Manford's cause, and to him personally, Anari accepted the decision. "As you wish. I will keep you safe." The look on her wide, innocent face convinced Manford that he could do no wrong in her eyes, make no mistakes—and as a result of her devotion, Anari protected him with ferocity.

Manford issued brisk orders. "Divide my followers into groups. No need to hurry—I prefer perfection to haste. Have Swordmaster Ellus coordinate the scuttling charges across the machine ships. Not a scrap can remain once we're finished."

Because of his physical limitations, watching the destruction was one of the few things that gave him pleasure. Thinking machines had overrun his ancestral planet of Moroko, captured the populace, and unleashed their plagues, murdering everyone. If his great-great-grandparents had not been away from home, conducting business on Salusa Secundus, they would have been trapped as well, and killed. And Manford would never have been born.

Though the events affecting his ancestors had occurred generations ago, he still hated the machines, and vowed to continue the mission.

Accompanying the Butlerian followers were five trained Swordmasters, the Paladins of Humanity, who had fought hand-to-hand against thinking machines during Serena Butler's Jihad. In the decades after the great victory on Corrin, Swordmasters had busied themselves with cleanup operations, tracking down and wrecking any remnants of the robotic empire they found scattered throughout the solar systems. Thanks to their success, such remnants were getting more and more difficult to locate.

As the Butlerian ships arrived among the machine vessels, Anari watched the images on her screen. In a soft voice, which she used only with him, she mused, "How many more fleets like this do you think we'll find, Manford?"

The answer was clear. "I want all of them."

These dead robotic battle fleets were easy targets that served as symbolic victories, when properly filmed and broadcast. Lately, though, Manford had also become worried about the rot, corruption, and temptation he observed within the new Corrino Imperium. How could people forget the dangers so quickly? Soon enough, he might need to channel his followers' fervor in a different direction and have them perform another necessary cleansing among the populations. . . .

Swordmaster Ellus took care of the administrative details, sorting the robotic ships onto a grid and assigning teams to specific targets. The five other ships settled in among the derelict machines and attached to individual hulls. Then the respective teams blasted their way aboard.

Manford's team suited up and prepared to board the largest robotic vessel, and he insisted on going along to see the evil with his own eyes, despite the effort it entailed. He would never be content to stay behind and watch; he was accustomed to using Anari as his legs, as well as his sword. The sturdy leather harness was always close by in case Manford needed to go into battle. She pulled the harness onto her shoulders, adjusted the seat behind her neck, then attached the straps under her arms and across her chest and waist.

Anari was a tall and physically fit woman and, in addition to being faultlessly loyal to Manford, she also loved him—he could see that every time he looked into her eyes. But *all* of his followers loved him; Anari's affection was just more innocent, and more pure than most.

She hefted his legless body easily, as she had done countless times before, and settled his torso onto the seat behind her head. He didn't feel like a child when he rode on her shoulders; he felt as if Anari were part of him. His legs had been blown off by a deluded technology-lover's bomb that had killed Rayna Butler, the saintly leader of the anti-machine movement. Manford had been blessed by Rayna herself, in the moments before she died of her injuries.

The Suk doctors called it a miracle that he'd survived at all, and it was that: *a miracle*. He'd been meant to live on after the horrifying day. Despite the physical loss, Manford had seized the helm of the Butlerian movement, and led them with great fervor. *Half a man, twice the leader.* He had a few fragments of pelvis left, but very little remained below his hips; nevertheless, he still had his mind and heart, and did not need anything else. Just his followers.

His curtailed body fit neatly into the socket of Anari's harness, and he rode high on her shoulders. With subtle shifts of his weight, he guided her like part of his own body, an extension below his waist. "Take me to the hatch, so we can be the first to board."

Even so, he was at the mercy of her movements and decisions. "No. I'm sending the other three ahead." Anari meant no challenge in her refusal. "Only after they verify there is no danger will I take you aboard. My mission to protect you outweighs your impatience. We go when I have been advised that it is safe, and not a moment sooner."

Manford ground his teeth together. He knew she meant well, but her overprotectiveness could be frustrating. "I expect no one to take risks in my stead."

Anari looked up and over her shoulder to gaze at his face, with an endearing smile. "Of course we take risks in your stead. We would all lay down our lives for you."

While Manford's team boarded the dead robotic ship, searching the metal corridors and looking for places to plant charges, he waited aboard his own vessel, fidgeting in his harness. "What have they found?"

She did not budge. "They'll report when they have something to report."

Finally, the team checked in. "There are a dozen combat meks aboard, sir—all of them cold and deactivated. Temperature is frigid, but we've restarted the life-support systems so you can come aboard in comfort."

"I'm not interested in comfort."

"But you need to breathe. They will tell us when they're ready."

Though robots did not require life-support systems, many of the machine vessels had been equipped to haul human captives in the cargo bays. In the final years of the Jihad, Omnius had dedicated all functional vessels to the battle fleet, while also building huge automated shipyards to churn out new war vessels by the thousands.

And still the humans had won, sacrificing everything for the only victory that mattered. . . .

Half an hour later, the atmosphere in the machine ship reached a level where Manford could survive without an environment suit. "Ready for you to come aboard, sir. We've located several good places to plant explosive charges. And human skeletons, sir. A cargo hold, at least fifty captives."

Manford perked up. "Captives?"

"Long dead, sir."

"We're coming." Satisfied, Anari descended to the connecting hatch, and he rode high on her back, feeling like a conquering king. Aboard the large vessel, the air was still razor-thin and cold. Manford shuddered, then grasped Anari's shoulders to steady himself.

She gave him a concerned glance. "Should we have waited another fifteen minutes for the air to warm up?"

"It's not the cold, Anari—it's the evil in the air. How can I forget all the human blood these monsters spilled?"

Aboard the dim and austere ship, Anari took him to the chamber where the Butlerians had pried open the sealed door to reveal a jumble of human skeletons, dozens of people who had been left to starve or suffocate, likely because the thinking machines didn't care.

The Swordmaster wore a deeply troubled and hurt expression. For all her hardened fighting experience, Anari Idaho remained astonished by the offhand cruelty of the thinking machines. Manford both admired and loved her for her innocence. "They must have been hauling captives," Anari said.

"Or experimental subjects for the evil robot Erasmus," Manford said. "When the ships received new orders to attack this system, they paid no further attention to the humans aboard." He muttered a silent prayer and blessing, hoping to speed the lost souls off to heaven.

As Anari led him away from the human-cargo chamber, they passed an angular, deactivated combat mek that stood like a statue in the corridor. The arms sported cutting blades and projectile weapons; its blunt head and optic threads were a mockery of a human face. Looking at the machine in disgust, Manford suppressed another shudder. *This must never be allowed to happen again.*

Anari drew her long, blunt pulse-sword. "We're going to blow up these ships anyway, sir . . . but would you indulge me?"

He smiled. "Without hesitation."

Like a released spring, the Swordmaster attacked the motionless robot; one blow obliterated the mek's optic threads, more blows severed the limbs, others smashed the body core. Deactivated for decades, the mek didn't even spurt a stream of sparks or lubricant fluid when she dismembered it.

Looking down, breathing heavily, she said, "Back at the Swordmaster School on Ginaz, I slew hundreds of these things. The school still has a standing order for functional combat meks, so trainees can practice destroying them."

The very thought soured Manford's mood. "Ginaz has too many functional meks, in my opinion—it makes me uneasy. Thinking machines should not be kept as pets. There is no useful purpose for any sophisticated machine."

Anari was hurt that he had criticized her fond recollection. Her voice was small. "It's how we learned to fight them, sir."

"Humans should train against humans."

"It's not the same." Anari took out her frustration on the already battered combat mek. She bludgeoned it one last time, then stalked toward the bridge.

They found several other meks along the way, and she dispatched each one, with all the ferocity that Manford felt in his heart.

On the robotic control deck, he and Anari met up with the other team members. The Butlerians had knocked over a pair of deactivated robots at the ship's controls. "All the engines function, sir," one gangly man reported. "We could add explosives to the fuel tanks just for good measure, or we can overload the reactors from here."

Manford nodded. "The explosions need to be big enough to eradicate all the nearby ships. These vessels are still operational, but I don't want to use even the scrap metal. It's . . . contaminated."

He knew that others did not have such qualms. Beyond his control, groups of corruptible humans were scouring the space shipping lanes to find intact fleets like this for salvage and repair. Scavengers without principles! The VenHold Spacing Fleet was notorious for this; more than half of their ships were refurbished thinking-machine vessels. Manford had argued with Directeur Josef Venport several times over the issue, but the greedy businessman refused to see reason. Manford took some consolation in the knowledge that at least these twenty-five enemy warships would never be used.

Butlerians understood that technology was seductive, fraught with latent danger. Humanity had grown soft and lazy since the overthrow of Omnius. People tried to make exceptions, seeking convenience and comfort, pushing the boundaries to their perceived advantage. They wheedled and made excuses: *that* machine might be bad, but *this* slightly different technology was acceptable.

Manford refused to draw artificial lines. It was a slippery slope. One small thing could lead to another, and another, and soon the downgrade would become a cliff. The human race must never be enslaved by machines again!

Now he swiveled his head to address the three Butlerians on the bridge. "Go. My Swordmaster and I have one last thing to do here. Send a message to Ellus—we should be away within fifteen minutes."

Anari knew exactly what Manford had in mind; she had, in fact, prepared for it. As soon as the other followers returned to their ship, the Swordmaster removed a small gilded icon from a pouch in her harness, one of many such icons that Manford had commissioned. He held the icon reverently, looked at the benevolent face of Rayna Butler. For seventeen years now, he had followed in that visionary woman's footsteps.

Manford kissed the icon, then handed it back to Anari, who placed it on the robotic control panel. He whispered, "May Rayna bless our work today and make us successful in our critically important mission. The mind of man is holy."

"The mind of man is holy." At a brisk trot, breathing out warm steam in the frigid air, Anari hurried to their ship, where the team sealed the hatch and disengaged from the dock. Their vessel drifted away from the rigged battle group.

Within the hour, all the Butlerian strike vessels rendezvoused above the dark robot ships. "One minute left on the timers, sir," Swordmaster Ellus transmitted. Manford nodded, his gaze intent on the screen, but he spoke no words aloud. None were necessary.

One of the robot ships blossomed into flame and shrapnel. In rapid succession, the other ships detonated, their engine compartments overloading or their fuel ignited by timed explosions. The shock waves combined, swirling the debris into a soup of metal vapor and expanding gases. For a few moments, the sight was as bright as a new sun, reminding him of Rayna's radiant smile . . . then it gradually dissipated and faded.

Across the calm, Manford spoke to his devout followers. "Our work here is done."

We are barometers of the human condition.
—REVEREND MOTHER RAQUELLA BERTO-ANIRUL,
remarks to third graduating class

Out of necessity, Reverend Mother Raquella Berto-Anirul took a long view of history. Because of the wealth of unique ancestral memories in her mind—history personified—the old woman had a perspective of the past that was not available to anyone else . . . not yet.

With so many generations to draw from in her thoughts, Raquella was well equipped to see the future of the human race. And the other Sisters in her school looked to their sole Reverend Mother to be their guide. She had to teach that perspective to others, expanding the knowledge and objectivity of her order, the physical and mental skills that set members of the Sisterhood apart from average women.

Raquella felt a drizzle of rain on her face as she stood with other Sisters on a cliff balcony of the Rossak School, the formal training facility of the Sisterhood. Dressed in a black robe with a high collar, she gazed solemnly down from the edge of the cliff at the purplish jungle below. Though the air was warm and humid for the somber ceremony, the weather was hardly ever uncomfortable at this time of year, because of breezes that blew regularly along the cliff faces. The air had a faint sour smell, a brimstone aftertaste from distant volcanoes mixed with the stew of environmental chemicals.

Today they were enduring another funeral for a dead Sister, one more tragic death from poison . . . another failure to create the second Reverend Mother.

More than eight decades ago, the dying and bitter Sorceress Ticia Cenva had given Raquella a lethal dose of the most potent poison available. Raquella should have died, but deep in her mind, in her cells, she had manipulated her biochemistry, shifting the molecular structure of the poison itself. Miraculously she survived, but the ordeal had changed something fundamental inside her, initiating a crisis-induced transformation at the farthest boundaries of her mortality. She had emerged whole but different, with a library of past lives in her mind and a new ability to see herself on a genetic level, possessing an intimate understanding of every interconnected fiber of her own body.

Crisis. Survival. Advancement.

But in all the years afterward, despite many attempts, no one else had achieved the same result, and Raquella didn't know how many more lives she could justify losing in order to reach the elusive goal. She knew only one way to push a Sister over the brink: driving her to the edge of death where—possibly—she could find the strength to evolve. . . .

Optimistic and determined, her best trainees continued to believe in her. And they died.

Raquella looked on sadly as a black-robed Sister and three green-robed acolytes took positions on top of the canopy of trees and lowered the corpse down into the humid depths of the silvery-purple jungle. The body would be left there for predators as part of the eternal circle of life and death, recycling human remains back into the soil.

The valiant young woman's name had been Sister Tiana, but now her body was wrapped in pale fabric, anonymous. The jungle creatures stirred deep below, as the thick canopy swallowed up the platform.

Raquella herself had lived for more than 130 years. She had witnessed the end of Serena Butler's Jihad, the Battle of Corrin two decades later, and the years of turmoil afterward. Despite her age, the old woman was spry and mentally alert, controlling the worst effects of aging through moderate use of melange imported from Arrakis and by manipulating her own biochemistry.

Her ever-growing school was comprised of outside candidates recruited from the best young women in the Imperium, including the special last descendants of the Sorceresses who had dominated this planet in the years before and during the Jihad; only a scant eighty-one of them remained. In total, eleven hundred Sisters trained here, two-thirds of them students; some were children from the nurseries, daughters from Raquella's missionaries who became pregnant by acceptable fathers. Recruiters sent hopeful new candidates here, and the training continued. . . .

For years the voices in her memory had urged her to test and enhance more Reverend Mothers like herself. She and her fellow proctors devoted their lives to showing other women how to master their thoughts, their bodies, their own future. Now that the thinking machines were gone, human destiny demanded that people become more than they had ever been before. Raquella would show them the way. She *knew* that a skilled woman could transform herself into a superior person, under the proper conditions.

Crisis. Survival. Advancement.

Many of Raquella's Sisterhood graduates had already proved their worth, going offworld to serve as advisers to noble planetary rulers and even at the Imperial Court; some attended the Mentat School on Lampadas, or became talented Suk doctors. She could feel their quiet influence spreading across the Imperium. Six of the women were now fully trained Mentats. One of them, Dorotea, served as a trusted adviser to Emperor Salvador Corrino back on Salusa Secundus.

But she desperately wanted more of her followers to have the same understanding, the same universal view of the Sisterhood and its future, and the same mental and physical powers as she did.

Somehow, though, her candidates could not make the leap. And another promising young woman had died. . . .

Now, while the women continued the oddly businesslike disposal of the dead Sister's remains, Raquella worried about the future. Despite her long life span, she harbored no illusions of personal immortality, and if she died before anyone else learned to survive the transformation, her skills could be forever lost. . . .

The fate of the Sisterhood, and their extensive works, was much more important than her own mortal fate. Humanity's long-term future depended on careful advancement, improvement. The Sisterhood could no longer afford to wait. She had to groom her successors.

As the funeral ended with the disposal of the body, the rest of the women turned back to the cliff school, where they would continue their classroom exercises. Raquella had chosen a fresh new candidate, a young woman from a disgraced family with little future, but someone who deserved this opportunity.

Sister Valya Harkonnen.

Raquella watched Valya leave the other Sisters and proceed toward her along the cliff-side path. Sister Valya was a whiplike young woman with an oval face and hazel eyes. The Reverend Mother observed her fluid movements, the confident tilt of her head, the carriage of her body—small but significant details adding up to the whole of the individual. Raquella did not doubt her choice; few other Sisters were as dedicated.

Sister Valya had joined the Sisterhood at the end of her sixteenth year, leaving her backwater planet of Lankiveil to go in search of a better life. Her great-grandfather, Abulurd Harkonnen, had been banished for cowardice after the Battle of Corrin. During her five years on Rossak, Valya had excelled in her training and proved to be one of Raquella's most faithful and talented Sisters; she worked closely with Sister Karee Marques, one of the last Sorceresses, studying new drugs and poisons to be used in the testing process.

When Valya presented herself to the old woman, she did not seem overly upset by the funeral. "You asked to see me, Reverend Mother?"

"Follow me, please."

Valya was clearly curious, but she kept her questions to herself. The two walked past the administration caves and domicile warrens. In its heyday in past centuries, this cliff city had supported thousands of men and women, Sorceresses, pharmaceutical merchants, explorers of the deep jungles. But so many had died during the plagues that the city was mostly empty, housing only members of the Sisterhood.

One entire section of caves had been used for the treatment of the Misborn, children who suffered birth defects as a result of toxins in the Rossak environment. Thanks to careful study of the breeding records, such children were born only rarely, and those who survived were cared for in one of the cities to the north, beyond the volcanoes. Raquella did not permit any men to live in her school community, although they occasionally came here to deliver supplies or perform repairs or other services.

Raquella guided Valya past barricaded cliff-side entrances that had once led to large sections of the hivelike cave city, but were now abandoned and blocked off. They were ominous places, devoid of all life, the bodies having been removed years ago and laid to rest in the jungle. She pointed to the treacherous path that led steeply along the cliff face to the top of the plateau. "That is where we're going."

The young woman hesitated for a flicker of an instant, then followed the Reverend Mother past a barricade and signs that restricted access. Valya was both excited and nervous. "The breeding records are up there."

"Yes, they are."

During the years of horrific plagues spread by Omnius, while entire populations were dying, the Sorceresses of Rossak—who had always kept genetic records to determine the best breeding matches—began a far more ambitious program to keep a library of human bloodlines, a far-reaching genetic catalog. Now, tending that wealth of information fell to Raquella and her chosen Sisters.

The path rose in sharp switchbacks along the rock face, a solid cliff wall on one side of them, a sheer drop-off to the dense jungle on the other. The drizzle had stopped, but the rocks remained slick underfoot.

The two women reached a lookout point where wisps of fog encircled them. Raquella looked out at the jungle and smoldering volcanoes in the distance— little had changed in that landscape since she'd first arrived decades ago, a nurse accompanying Dr. Mohandas Suk to treat victims of the Omnius plague.

"Only a few of us ever go up here anymore—but you and I are going farther." Raquella was not one for small talk, and kept her emotions tightly controlled, but she did feel an excitement and optimism to be introducing another person to the Sisterhood's greatest secret. A new ally. It was the only way the Sisterhood could survive.

They stopped at a cave opening set amid blocky boulders near the top of the plateau, high above the fertile, teeming jungles. A pair of Sorceresses stood guard at the entrance. They nodded to the Reverend Mother, allowed them to pass.

"The compilation of the breeding records is perhaps the Sisterhood's greatest work," Raquella said. "With such an enormous database of human genetics, we can map and extrapolate the future of our race . . . perhaps even guide it."

Valya nodded solemnly. "I've heard other Sisters say it's one of the largest data archives ever compiled, but I never understood how we could possibly manage so much information. How do we digest it all and make projections?"

Raquella decided to be cryptic, for now. "We are the Sisterhood."

Inside the high caves, they entered two large chambers filled with wooden tables and writing desks; women bustled about, organizing reams of permanent paper, compiling and stacking immense DNA maps, then filing documents that were reduced and stored in dense near-microscopic text.

"Four of our Sisters have completed Mentat training under Gilbertus Albans," Raquella said. "But even with their advanced mental abilities, the project is overwhelming."

Valya struggled to control her awe. "Such an immensity of data here . . ." Her bright eyes drank in the new information with fascination. She felt great honor and pride to be allowed into the Reverend Mother's inner circle. "I know more women of our order are training on Lampadas, but this project would require an army of Sister Mentats. The DNA records from millions and millions of people on thousands of planets."

As they passed deeper into the restricted tunnels, an elderly Sister emerged from a file room wearing the white robe of a Sorceress. She greeted the two visitors. "Reverend Mother, is this the new recruit you have decided to bring to me?"

Raquella nodded. "Sister Valya has excelled in her studies and has proved her dedication in aiding Karee Marques in her pharmaceutical research." She nudged the young woman forward. "Valya, Sister Sabra Hublein was one of the original architects of the expanded breeding database during the plagues, long before I ever came to Rossak."

"The breeding records must be maintained," the other old woman said. "And watched."

"But . . . I'm not a Mentat," Valya said.

Sabra led them into an empty tunnel and looked over her shoulder, making certain they were not seen. "There are other ways to help us, Sister Valya."

They stopped near a curve in the passageway, and Raquella faced a blank stone wall. She glanced at the younger woman. "Are you afraid of the un-known?"

Valya managed a small smile. "People always fear the unknown, if they are truthful about it. But I can face my fears."

"Good. Now come with me and tread on territory that is largely unexplored."

Valya looked uneasy. "Do you want me to be the next volunteer to try a new transformative drug? Reverend Mother, I don't think I'm ready for—"

"No, this is something else entirely, though no less important. I am old, child. It makes me more cynical, but I have learned to trust my instincts. I've watched you carefully, seen your work with Karee Marques—I want to bring you into this plan."

Valya did not look fearful, and she kept her questions to herself. *Good,* Raquella thought.

"Take a deep breath and calm yourself, girl. You are about to learn the Sister-hood's most closely guarded secret. Very few in the order have ever seen this."

Taking the young woman's hand, Raquella pulled her toward the seemingly solid wall. Sabra stepped forward beside Valya, and they passed entirely through the rock—a hologram—and entered a new chamber.

The three of them stood in a small anteroom. Blinking in the bright light, Valya struggled to hide her surprise, using her training to maintain her compo-sure.

"This way." The Reverend Mother led them into a large, brightly lit grotto, and Valya's eyes widened as they encompassed the sight.

The chamber was filled with humming and clicking machines, constellations of electronic lights—banks and banks of forbidden *computers* on levels that rose high along the curving stone walls. Spiral stairways and wooden ramps con-nected them all. A small number of white-robed Sorceresses bustled back and forth, and machine noises throbbed in the air.

Valya stammered, "Is this . . . Is this . . . ?" She couldn't seem to phrase the question, then exclaimed, "Thinking machines!"

"As you suggested yourself," Raquella explained, "no human, not even a trained Mentat, can store all the data the women of Rossak have compiled over the gen-erations. The Sorceresses used these machines secretly for many generations, and some of our most trusted women are trained to maintain and service them."

"But . . . why?"

"The only way we can keep such vast amounts of data, and make the neces-sary genetic projections over successive descendants, is with the aid of computers—which are strictly forbidden. Now you see why we need to keep these machines secret."

Raquella studied Valya carefully, noted the calculating expression as her gaze moved around the chamber. She seemed overwhelmed, but intrigued, not horrified.

"There is much for you to learn," Sabra said. "For years we have studied the breeding records, and we fear that the true Sorceresses are going to die out. Few enough of us remain, so there is little time left. This may be the only way we can understand what's happening."

"And find alternatives," Raquella said. "Such as the creation of new Reverend Mothers." She was careful not to let her desperation, or her hope, creep into her voice.

One of the Sorceress workers spoke briefly to Sister Sabra about a breeding matter, then returned to her work after giving Valya a brief curious glance. "Sister Esther-Cano is our youngest pureblood Sorceress," Raquella said, "barely thirty years of age. The next youngest, however, is more than ten years older. The telepathic characteristic of Sorceresses occurs only rarely in native daughters now."

Sabra continued, "The school's breeding records include information from people on thousands of planets. Our database is vast, and the goal—as you already know—is to optimize humankind through personal improvement and selective breeding. With the computers, we can model DNA interactions and project breeding possibilities from a near-infinite number of bloodline pairings."

Valya's brief, automatic terror had been replaced by a more intense interest. She looked around the chamber and said in a practical tone, "If the Butlerians ever find out about this, they will raze the school and kill every last Sister."

"Yes, they will," Raquella said. "And now you understand the amount of trust we have placed in you."

I have already contributed more than my share to history. For more than two centuries I influenced events and fought the enemies that were defined for me. Finally I turned my back and walked away. All I wanted was to fade quietly into memory, but history refuses to let me alone.
—VORIAN ATREIDES, *The Legacy Journals*, Kepler period

When he returned from his solitary hunt in the Thornbriar Ridges, Vorian Atreides saw greasy pillars of unexpected smoke curling into the sky. The thick plumes rose from the village where his family lived and the surrounding farmlands.

He began to run.

Vorian had spent five days away from his country home, his wife, his extended family, and his neighbors. He liked to hunt the plump flightless gornet birds, one of which could feed a family for more than a week. Gornets lived high in the dry ridges, away from the fertile settled valley, and loved to dive for shelter into the razor-sharp thornbriars.

More than the hunt itself, though, Vor enjoyed the solitude, a chance to feel quiet and peace inside. Even alone in the wilderness, he could draw upon several lifetimes of personal memories, relationships formed and lost, things to regret and things to celebrate . . . friends, loves, and enemies—sometimes all reflected in the same person, over the course of time. His current wife, Mariella, had lived decades in happy contentment with him; they had a large family—children, grandchildren, and great-grandchildren.

Though reluctant at first, given his past, Vor had settled into this bucolic life on planet Kepler like a man slipping into old, comfortable clothes. Many decades ago, he had two sons on Caladan, but they were always distant, estranged, and he hadn't seen them or their family line since the Battle of Corrin.

A long time ago, his father, the notorious cymek general Agamemnon, had granted him a secret life-extension treatment, never guessing that Vorian would decide to fight against the thinking machines. Generations of bloodshed had been physically exhausting and hard on his soul. When the war hero Faykan Butler formed the new Imperium, Vor began to feel a lack of interest. He took his ship and a generous reward from the new Emperor, turned his back on the League of Nobles, and headed off into the frontier.

After wandering alone for years, though, he met Mariella, fell in love again, and settled down here. Kepler was quiet and satisfying, and Vor took the time to create a new home, a place he actually wanted to stay. He'd raised three daughters and two sons, who married other Kepler villagers, and gave him eleven grandchildren and more than two dozen great-grandchildren who were now growing old enough to have families of their own. He enjoyed simple pleasures, quiet evenings. He had changed his surname, but now, half a century later, he didn't much bother to keep the secret. What did it matter anymore? He wasn't a criminal.

Though Vor had aged very little physically, Mariella showed her years. She liked nothing more than to be with her family, but she let Vor go off into the hills and hunt as often as he wished. After two centuries, he knew how to fend for himself. He rarely thought about the outside Imperium, though he was still occasionally amused to see old Imperial coins that carried his likeness. . . .

Now, however, when he came back from the hunt to find smoke rising from the farmhouses, Vor felt as if a door to his past had blown open in a storm. He dumped twenty kilos of fresh wrapped gornet meat from his pack, then sprinted down the trail, taking only his old-fashioned projectile rifle. Ahead, Vor saw the valley's patchwork of croplands, now besmirched with brown and black scars as orange flames raced along the rows of grain. Three large spaceships had landed in the fields rather than on the designated landing field: not attack craft, but blunt torpedo-shaped vessels designed to hold cargo or personnel. Something was terribly wrong.

A large vessel lumbered into the air, and moments later a second vessel blasted dust clouds and exhaust as it, too, heaved itself off the ground. Swarms of crewmen scurried around the third ship, preparing to depart.

Though Vor had never seen this type of craft here on Kepler, he knew from long experience what slave-raiders looked like.

He ran headlong downhill, thinking about Mariella, about his children, grandchildren, all their spouses, their neighbors—this place was his *home*. Out of the corner of his eye, he saw the farmhouse where he had lived for many years. The roof was smoldering, but the damage was not nearly as bad as several of the other homes. The outbuildings around his daughter Bonda's house were aflame; the small town hall was an inferno. Too late—too late! He knew all these people, every one of them connected to him by bonds of blood, marriage, or friendship.

He was breathing too hard to manage a shout. He wanted to bellow for the slavers to stop, but he was just one man, and they would never listen to him. The raiders had no idea who Vorian Atreides was, and after so long a time they might not even care.

The remaining handful of slavers dragged their human cargo aboard the third ship, hauling limp forms. Even from a distance, Vor recognized his son Clar with his long ponytail and purple shirt; he was obviously stunned, and the invaders took him aboard. One of the slavers lagged behind, bringing up the rear while four of his companions carried their last victims up the ramp to the open hatch.

When he was in range, Vor dropped to one knee, raised the projectile rifle, and aimed. Though his heart was pounding and he couldn't catch his breath, he forced a moment of calm, focused carefully, and shot at the foremost slaver. He didn't dare hit one of his own people. He thought for certain his aim was true, but the slaver only flinched, looked around, and then shouted. His comrades began to run, searching for the source of the shot.

Vor aimed carefully, fired again, and the second shot also caused only panic, not injuries. Then he realized that the two men wore personal shields, nearly invisible barriers that stopped fast projectiles. Concentrating, he swung the rifle toward the man lagging behind, squinted, and squeezed off another shot—striking the muscular slaver in the lower back. The man pitched forward and fell onto his face. So, they didn't all have shields.

As soon as the third rifle shot sounded, Vor was up and running toward the slaver craft. The fallen man's companions had seen him drop, and they began to shout, looking in all directions. As he sprinted, Vor raised the rifle again and fired another shot, more carelessly this time. The projectile ricocheted off the metal hull near the hatch, and the slavers yelled. Vor shot again, hitting the open hatch door.

Over the course of his life, Vor had killed people under various circumstances, usually with good reason. Now, he couldn't think of a better justification. He actually felt more regret for the gornet bird he had killed the previous evening.

Slavers were fundamentally cowards. Protected by shields, the rest of them rushed inside and sealed the hatch, abandoning their fallen comrade. The big vessel's thrusters belched exhaust, and the last slaving craft staggered into the air, taking its cargo of captives. Though Vor ran as fast as he could, he couldn't reach the ship in time. He raised the rifle and fired two more impotent shots at the underbelly, but the craft raced away over smoldering fields and homes.

He could smell the smoke in the air, saw the buildings burning, knew that his people had been decimated. Were they all captured or killed? And Mariella, too? He longed to run from house to house, find *anyone* . . . but he also had to rescue the captives. Before the ships got away, he needed to know where they were going.

Vor stopped by the man he had shot. The slaver lay on the ground, his arms twitching. He wore a yellow cloth tied around his head, and a thin black line was tattooed from his left ear to the corner of his mouth. A moan escaped from his lips, along with a trickle of blood.

Still alive. Good. With a wound like that, though, the man wouldn't last long. "You are going to tell me where those captives are being taken," Vor said.

The man groaned again and gurgled something that sounded like a curse. Vor didn't consider it an acceptable answer. He glanced up, saw the fire spreading along the roofs of the houses. "You don't have much time to answer."

Receiving no cooperation from the man, Vor knew what he would have to do next, and he wasn't proud of it, but this slaver was far down on the list of people for whom he felt sympathy. He drew his long skinning knife. "You *are* going to tell me."

WITH THE INFORMATION secured and the man dead, Vor ran past the outbuildings around his big house, calling out for anyone who might be alive. His hands and arms were covered with blood, some of it from the gornet bird he had butchered, some from the slaver he had questioned.

Outside, he found two old men, Mariella's brothers, who helped bring in the harvest each year. Both were groggy, returning to consciousness. Vor guessed that the slaving ships had flown over the settlement and sprayed the houses and fields with stun beams to knock everyone unconscious, then they'd simply hauled off anyone who looked young and strong. Mariella's brothers did not make the cut.

The healthier candidates—his sons and daughters, grandchildren, neighbors—had been taken from their homes and dragged aboard the ships. Many of the town buildings were now on fire.

But first, his wife. Vor burst into the main house, yelling, "Mariella!" To his vast relief, he heard her voice calling back, from upstairs. In the second-story guest room, she was using a compression fire-suppressant canister to fight the smoldering roof by leaning out a high gable. As he rushed into the room, Vor was giddy to see her aged but beautiful face—seamed and careworn features, her hair like spun silver. He was so glad to find her safe and alive that he almost wept, but the fire demanded his attention. He took the canister from her and sprayed at the flames through the window. The fire had traveled along the edge of the rooftop, but the house was not yet fully involved.

"I was afraid they'd take you with all the others," Mariella said. "You look as young as our grandsons."

The flames began to flicker out under the dispersed spray. He set the canister aside and pulled her close, holding her as he had done for more than half a century. "And I was worried about you."

"I'm way too old for them to be interested in me," Mariella said. "You would have realized that, if you stopped to think."

"If I'd stopped to think, I wouldn't have gotten there before all the ships lifted off. As it is, I managed to kill only one of the slavers."

"They took almost everyone else who could perform manual labor. A few might have hidden, and a few were just killed, but how are we . . ." She shook her head and looked down at her hands. "It's not possible. They're all gone."

"I'll get them back."

Mariella responded with a sad smile, but he kissed the familiar lips that had been part of his life, his family, his home for so long. She was much like his previous wife, Leronica Tergiet, on another world, a woman with whom he had also stayed as she bore him children, then grew old and died, while he never changed.

"I know where they're going," Vor said. "The ships are taking them to the slave markets on Poritrin. The slaver told me."

HE AND MARIELLA'S brothers went to the other homes, searching for survivors. They found a number of them, scattered, and rallied them to control the spreading blaze, help the injured, tally the missing. Only sixty of the valley's several hundred inhabitants had been left behind, and most were either old or infirm. Ten had fought back and were killed. Vor dispatched messages to the other settled valleys on Kepler, warning them to be on guard for slavers.

That night, Mariella got out photos of their children, their families, their grandchildren, and spread them around the table, on the shelves. So many faces, so many people needing to be rescued. . . .

She found him in the smoky-smelling attic of their home, where he had uncovered a storage trunk. Opening it, Vor removed a pressed and folded old uniform, crimson and green, the familiar colors of the Army of Humanity, formerly the Army of the Jihad.

The package had been sealed away for many, many years.

"I'm going to Poritrin to get our people back." He held up the uniform shirt and ran his fingers over the smooth fabric of the sleeves, musing about how many times the uniform had been patched, how many bloodstains had been removed. He had hoped never to go into battle again. But this was different.

"And after I save them, I need to make sure it never happens again. I'll find some way to protect this planet. The Corrinos owe me that."

It is easy to look backward and cast blame on others, but more difficult to gaze ahead and take responsibility for your own decisions and your own future.

—GRIFFIN HARKONNEN, final dispatch from Arrakis

It was a hard winter on Lankiveil, but the Harkonnens had to make do. For generations—since Abulurd Harkonnen's exile here for his actions in the Battle of Corrin—the once powerful family had been left to forget about their lost glory on Salusa Secundus.

And most of them had indeed forgotten.

Relentless sleet streamed down, then froze to a glassy coating of ice each night. In their wooden homes huddled on the shores of the fjord, the locals had to thaw and kick their doors open every morning just to face the blustery cold. Sometimes they would glance at the choppy waters and cloudy skies, and then close the doors again, deciding it was too dangerous to venture out on the water. The fur-whale fleets had been trapped in port for the past month, and they could not harvest the planet's only commodity valued by the rest of the Imperium.

Even the short-range fishing boats rarely managed to make it out to deep waters, and the catch was sparse. The people often had to resort to eating last year's salted fish and preserved whale meat. In comparison to the glory and riches of the old days, the Harkonnens had few prospects.

Griffin Harkonnen—the elder son of Vergyl, who was the ostensible Land-sraad League ruler on Lankiveil—hated this planet, as did his younger sister, Valya. The two of them had an arrangement, a plan, by which they hoped to pull the family out of the pitiful existence that had been left for them because of the mistakes of their great-grandfather, Abulurd, and the treachery committed against him by Vorian Atreides. Their parents and the rest of the family did not share their ambitions, but indulged their determination, and allowed Griffin and Valya to see what they could do, despite their youth.

While Valya was away, seeking to advance herself in the Sisterhood (and thereby gain power and influence for House Harkonnen), Griffin remained behind, working to build the family's commercial assets, extend their investments, and step out of their isolation. Each day he spent long hours at his studies, intent on learning the family business and improving the standard of living for the people of this backwater planet. It was not a comfortable world, but he refused to allow himself to be beaten down by it, and was as determined as his sister to see their fortune and influence in the Imperium restored. His part of their agreement was an ambitious one, including the management of family assets and seeing that they were invested properly, as well as developing a business plan that went beyond the parochial goal of merely surviving in difficult weather conditions.

Griffin was twenty-three years old with a lean frame, an even-keeled disposition, and a pragmatic way of thinking. Where his sister was the more mercurial of the two, and could no longer tolerate living on Lankiveil, he was calmer, like a captain steering his ship through icy waters, plowing ahead as he looked for better seas, and the sunshine he knew was out there, beyond the clouds.

Despite his young age, Griffin already had a good knowledge of history, mathematics, commerce, and government, as he intended to make himself a qualified and competent leader of the planet someday . . . thus paving the way for future Harkonnen generations to return to prominence in the Imperium.

Already Griffin knew more than his father about the intricacies of whale-fur commerce, profit-and-loss ratios, and Imperial regulations. Despite his inherited title, Vergyl Harkonnen simply had no interest in it, and left much of the hard work and thinking to his son. Vergyl was content to wield power comparable to that of a town mayor rather than a Landsraad leader. He was a good father, though, and gave plenty of attention to his younger children, Danvis and Tula.

Griffin and his sister Valya had greater dreams for the family, even if they were the only ones who did. Once, during a particularly vigorous sparring match with her brother on a rocking wooden raft out in the cold harbor, Valya had said she thought they were the only true Harkonnens on the planet.

Valya was only a year younger, and their mother had limited ("realistic," the woman said) expectations for her, assuming the girl would marry a local man, perhaps an owner of a whaling boat or two, have children, and carry on. However, after speaking with a missionary Sister who had visited Lankiveil five years ago, Valya found her opportunity to leave, and went to be trained among the adept women on Rossak. But she had not departed before having several long conversations with Griffin, and reaching an agreement with him about how both of them could best improve the fortunes of the family.

Now, Griffin's father came up behind him as he deciphered paragraphs of opaque bureaucratic language and history, much of which was desperately dry. The young man worked at the documents like a careful surgeon, dissecting the sections until he understood the labyrinthine nuances of government.

Vergyl seemed amused to see his son so intent. "I used to study history when I was your age, and my grandfather Abulurd told me his stories, but I couldn't bear how the official Corrino records talked about our family. I decided just to live my life. Best if those days are not revisited."

Griffin gestured toward the documents. "I've read enough about that particular past, Father, but now I'm analyzing something on a larger scale. Imperial politics is important to our future." He stroked his chin. The pale brown hair of his mustache and goatee matched the hair on his head. He thought the facial hair made him look distinguished, giving him the appearance of someone to be taken seriously. "I'm studying the structure of the Landsraad, reading the charter. I want to take the test and be certified as Lankiveil's official representative to the Landsraad Council."

Vergyl chuckled. "But we already have a proxy. There's no need for you to travel all the way to Salusa Secundus for meetings."

Griffin fought back a flush of annoyance and stopped himself from snapping at his father. "I studied the trade agreement that was arranged by our purported proxy. It involves ninety-two planets, including Lankiveil—believe me, the agreement does not benefit *us*. It is going to cost Lankiveil and eighty-four other planets additional taxes, while eight planets that are already well-off are receiving real benefits. It looks to me like the proxy was paid off."

"You don't know that for sure. I've met Nelson Treblehorn, and he seems like a nice fellow."

"Charming, yes. Effective on our behalf, no. Father, the first step in regaining respect for our family is to have direct representation in the Landsraad. I intend to journey to Salusa Secundus, where I can see the Landsraad Hall and look into the eyes of my beloved cousin, *the Emperor*."

Several generations back, the Harkonnens and the Butler/Corrinos had been the same family, but now the leaders of the Imperium considered the Harkonnen name an embarrassment and never spoke of it. Griffin knew how his sister longed to remove the blot of shame caused by Vorian Atreides. Griffin felt the weight of the injustice committed against the family, too, and each of them played a part in the planned restoration. In addition to his business goals, Griffin was working to build political alliances, and one day he would travel to Salusa to claim Lankiveil's rightful seat in the Landsraad Hall. He intended to *earn* Harkonnen importance.

Now that all the League worlds and former Unallied Planets had been drawn together in the same net, the combined Imperium encompassed more than thirteen thousand worlds. But no business could possibly get done if that many separate planetary representatives had to address every bureaucratic measure before a vote could be taken. Proxies designated by Emperor Salvador collected dozens of loosely related worlds under a single umbrella and cast votes on behalf of their populations. It was considered a convenience (earning Imperial subsidies or other benefits), but not mandatory, and exceptions were allowed, at the expense of the benefits. As far as Griffin was concerned, the Imperial favors Lankiveil gained in exchange for the proxy relationship were so minimal as to be nonexistent.

On Salusa Secundus, Griffin intended to speak for his planet, and for his family. Personally. With Valya becoming one of the skilled Sisters from the respected school on Rossak, and Griffin soon to be serving as an official representative to the Landsraad League, while also managing and expanding the family's commercial operations, the prospects for House Harkonnen were brightening.

"Well, I'm sure it's the right decision then." Vergyl seemed amused by his son's grand ideas. Though Griffin had taken over much of the business work and decisions, his father still thought of him as a naïve young man.

For an ambitious new merchant venture that Griffin and Valya had brainstormed together, he had asked their uncle Weller to travel from planet to planet representing the family and arranging whale-fur contracts. Though Weller was an excellent salesman and everybody liked him, he did not have a very good head for business, and his brother Vergyl was even more out of touch with important issues affecting the family. At least Uncle Weller understood commercial tactics and goals, wanted to do something, and was willing to contribute his time and talents; Vergyl had basically given up. If Griffin's father ever had any ambitions at all when he was younger (and Griffin was not sure about that), he certainly did not have any now.

In the year previous, investing and planning for the expanded market, Griffin had arranged to dispatch hundreds of additional ships to secure the largest single fur-whale harvest the planet had ever produced. Then he had brokered a transportation and cargo-hauling deal with the low-end shipping company Celestial Transport, to take Uncle Weller and his wares across the Imperium.

The League's dominant transportation line was the VenHold Spacing Fleet. Its safety record was impeccable, because their ships were guided by mysterious— some said inhuman—Navigators who could foresee hazards and accidents before they occurred. But VenHold charged prohibitively high fares, and House Harkonnen had invested a significant portion of their family profits into this expansion. Griffin could not justify the additional expense; though Celestial Transport was slower and did not use Navigators, they did offer very favorable terms. So, with all the details arranged, Griffin's uncle had departed with a huge cargo of silky whale fur, hoping to establish a demand and then lock down lucrative distribution deals with other planets.

Meanwhile, Griffin dove into his studies to take the qualification exam to become Lankiveil's official representative to Salusa Secundus. He glanced up at his father. "I need to finish studying—I'm required to dispatch my test packet on the next outbound ship."

Vergyl Harkonnen gave him an offhanded compliment, meant as encouragement. "You'll do fine, son." He left Griffin to his studies.

I am a generous man, when my largesse is earned. But I see a difference between generosity to those who deserve it, and charity to those who would take advantage of my wealth.

—DIRECTEUR JOSEF VENPORT,
standard response to donation request

Narrowing his blue eyes, Josef Venport regarded the nervous crew chiefs who waited to deliver their reports in the environmentally controlled conference room at VenHold's headquarters on planet Arrakis. "Make no mistake. I will do whatever is necessary to protect my holdings."

The directeur paced the room to burn off energy, attempting to keep his anger under control. His thick cinnamon hair was brushed back from his forehead, and he sported a bushy mustache above thin lips that rarely smiled. His heavy brows drew tighter as he looked at the managers. "My great-grandmother, Norma Cenva, sacrificed most of her space fleet, not to mention countless human lives, to defeat the thinking machines. Guarding my own business interests may not seem as dramatic, but I advise you not to test my resolve."

"We have never doubted your resolve, sir," said Lilik Arvo, overseer of the company spice-harvesting operations on Arrakis. His voice quavered. Arvo's skin was tanned dark and leathery, like an old raisin. The other two men, section heads of production teams in the deep desert, flinched, also fearing Josef's wrath. Only a dusty woman sitting at the back showed no fear. She scowled as she watched the proceedings.

"I did not want to come here in the first place," Josef continued. "I prefer that these operations run independently, but if another company is stealing my spice— *my spice!*—I need to stop it. Immediately. I want to know who is behind the other harvesting operations here, who is funding them, and where the damn spice is going."

Anyone who had worked his or her way to a position of authority in VenHold understood that when anyone failed Josef, he insisted on balancing the books. And if his overseers and administrators did not want to become targets of his wrath, they had better find a more appropriate recipient for punishment.

"Give us your instructions, sir, and we'll take care of it," said the woman in the conference room, whose dusty rags covered a well-fitted and maintained reclamation suit. "Whatever you need." Among those here, she was the only one he considered competent. She was also the only one who didn't like to be in the cool, humidified air.

The cracks and wrinkles around her eyes suggested age, though the desiccating desert environment, as well as the life-prolongation properties of melange, made any guess of age problematic. Her eyes were the eerie blue-within-blue that indicated constant spice consumption, even addiction.

Josef regarded her with satisfaction. "You know the situation, Ishanti. Tell us what you recommend." He shot a withering glance at the crew chiefs who had made excuses rather than suggestions.

She shrugged. "It should not be too difficult to find a name or two."

"But how?" said Arvo. "We have to find the poachers first. Their machinery is unmarked, and the desert is vast."

"One simply needs to know where to look." Ishanti smiled, without showing her teeth. She had rich brown hair bound in a colorful scarf. She wore two pendants of a typical Buddislamic design, no surprise since most of the sheltered deep-desert tribes were Zensunni, primarily refugees from slavers.

Though she held no formal position in Venport Holdings or its commercial subsidiary Combined Mercantiles, Josef paid her well for her useful services. Ishanti came from the deep desert, moving easily from isolated tribal caves to the spaceport and the surrounding settlements. She kept an eye on Venport's spice-harvesting operations, traded with merchants in Arrakis City, and then vanished like a dust-devil into the dunes again. Josef had never tried to follow her, and he'd given the others strict instructions to let Ishanti have her privacy.

He addressed the listeners. "I want you all to send out messages. Spread bribes if you need to, dispatch spotters to search the desert. Combined Mercantiles will offer a large reward to any spice team that exposes an off-the-books operation out there. I will not leave this planet until I have answers." His eyebrows drew together. "And I do not want to remain here long."

Ishanti smiled at him again, and Josef wondered what standards of beauty the Zensunnis used out here. Was she trying to flirt with him? He didn't find the hard-bitten desert woman attractive at all, but he did respect her skills. He had his own wife to get back to on Kolhar, an intelligent Sisterhood-trained woman named Cioba—the only person he trusted to watch the conglomerated VenHold business operations while he was away.

"We'll make your stay as short as possible, sir," Arvo said. "I'll get on it right away." In truth, Josef put more stock in Ishanti.

He lectured them all. "My ancestor, Aurelius Venport, saw the potential in spice-harvesting operations and risked much, invested much, to make it profitable." He leaned forward. "My family has generations of blood and money on this planet, and I refuse to let any upstart competitor dance on the foundation the Venports have laid. Thieves must be dealt with." He drank from his tall glass of cool water, and the others gratefully did the same. He would have preferred to be drinking a triumphant toast, but that was premature.

JOSEF SEALED HIMSELF in private quarters in Arrakis City, ate the food that was brought to him without noticing it, and pored over his business records. Cioba had already prepared a summary of the most vital matters relating to the company's numerous investments, and she appended a personal note about the progress of their two young daughters, Sabine and Candys, who were being trained on Rossak.

Over the past few generations, VenHold had grown so incredibly wealthy that Josef needed to split off their cargo-distribution arm and create a separate entity, Combined Mercantiles, which traded in melange from Arrakis as well as other high-value goods. He had also established numerous large financial institutions on important planets, where he could divest, invest, and hide VenHold's profits. He did not want anyone—particularly the crazed antitechnology fanatics—to have an inkling of how much power and influence he really possessed. But among the numerous threats and challenges that he faced, the short-sighted Butlerian barbarians were invariably at or near the top of his list. They routinely destroyed perfectly viable derelict robot ships that could have been incorporated into the VenHold Spacing Fleet.

As soon as he returned to Kolhar, he had much work to do. He was also expected on Salusa Secundus soon for an important Landsraad meeting. But he couldn't leave Arrakis until he had resolved a certain problem. . . .

Ishanti had indeed located a competitor's illegal spice-harvesting operation out in the isolated desert. (Josef couldn't understand why his better-equipped scout flyers had been unable to find anything.) By the time Lilik Arvo sent a response team to the location, the poachers had escaped. Nevertheless, Arvo intercepted a small cargo ship before it could leave the planet. The hold was filled with contraband melange. Josef had, of course, confiscated the cargo and added it to his own supplies.

VenHold engineers scoured the unmarked craft, analyzed component serial numbers, and found indications that it belonged to Celestial Transport. That did not make Josef happy. Arjen Gates was once again meddling where he did not belong.

CT was Josef's only real competition in the space-transportation industry, and he did not look kindly on that intrusion. From secret information he had obtained (at great cost), he knew that Celestial Transport lost up to one percent of its vessels—a ridiculously high failure rate. But it was caveat emptor. For choosing a low price and unreliable transportation, the CT passengers and shippers got what they deserved. . . .

Arvo and Ishanti came to Josef's private rooms, escorting a bound and gagged man dressed in an unmarked flight suit. Arvo looked pleased with himself, as if he took credit for the operation. "This man was the only person aboard the black-market ship. We'll get to the bottom of this, sir, but so far he refuses to talk."

Josef raised his thick eyebrows. "He needs to be encouraged, then." He turned to the captive, who perspired heavily. *Wasting water,* as the desert people would think of it. "Who is in charge of your operations here on Arrakis? I would like to speak with that person."

When Ishanti removed the captive's gag, the man folded his lips in distaste. "This is a free planet. You have no more rights to melange than anyone else does. Hundreds of operations worked on Arrakis during the plagues. The spice is just there for us to harvest off the ground! We made our own investment. Our work doesn't interfere with your trade."

"It is *my* spice." Josef didn't raise his voice, but the anger behind it roiled like a building thunderstorm. He made a dismissive gesture. "Ishanti, learn what you can from him. It's well within your talents. In fact, you can keep his water as the price of your service."

Now Ishanti smiled enough to show teeth, and she partially drew the milky-white dagger at her waist. "Thank you, sir." She placed the gag back on the captive's mouth, muffling his protestations, and led the struggling man away.

It will never be possible to explain my motives to anyone, with the exception of Erasmus. We understand each other, despite our obvious differences.

— GILBERTUS ALBANS, private journal notes

To encourage Mentat concentration, Headmaster Gilbertus Albans had built his school on the least populated continent of Lampadas. Though this was already a pastoral world, he needed a place where his instructors and students could focus on the demanding curriculum and not be distracted by external concerns.

When choosing this world as the home of his Mentat School, he had erred by underestimating the continued strength of the Butlerian movement after the defeat of Omnius. The antitechnology fervor should have waned quickly, sputtering out through lack of passion and need, but Manford Torondo was more powerful than ever. Gilbertus had to walk a fine line.

In the main instruction theater he stood on the stage, the focus of attention. The seats encircled him and rose steeply up to the rear. The amphitheater's surrounding walls and ceiling were of dark, stained wood, with an artificial patina that made them look very old, with a weight of importance. Clever amplifiers carried his calm, reserved voice to all of his attentive students.

"You must look past initial appearances." The Headmaster gestured down to the two bodies that rested on autopsy slabs at the center of the stage. One table held a pale, naked human cadaver, head upturned and eyes closed; the dead man's arms were extended straight at the sides. On the other table lay a deactivated combat mek, its fierce weapon arms and bullet-shaped head positioned in a similar arrangement.

"A human and a thinking machine. Note the parallels. Study them. Learn from them, and ask yourselves: Are they really so different after all?"

Gilbertus wore a tweedy waistcoat and trousers, and round spectacles on his narrow face, because he preferred these to medical treatments that could have improved his eyesight. His hair was thin but still the natural straw-yellow of his youth. He had to keep up appearances, and took great care to hide the fact that he was more than 180 years old now, thanks to the life-extension treatment he'd received from the independent robot Erasmus. Not a single one of the Mentat students suspected how important the machine mentor had been in his life; it would be dangerous if the Butlerians were to discover the truth about Gilbertus's past.

"The Jihad proved that humans are superior to thinking machines, true. But upon closer inspection, one can see the similarities."

Because Mentats were the human answer to computers, the antitechnology Butlerians supported his school. Gilbertus, however, had entirely different experiences with the thinking machines. He kept his opinions to himself for his own safety, especially here on Lampadas.

Gilbertus lifted the smooth head of the combat mek and disengaged it from the neck anchor mechanism. "The robot you see here is a remnant of that conflict, and we received special dispensation to use it as a teaching tool." (The Imperial government had posed no problems, but Manford Torondo had not been so easily convinced.)

He lifted the cadaver's pale right arm. "Note the musculature, compare it to the mechanical anatomy of the combat robot."

As the silent students watched, some intrigued and some displaying obvious horror, Gilbertus methodically removed organs from the prepped cadaver, then took out the roughly equivalent parts from the combat mek, step by step, showing the parallels. He displayed all the parts on trays next to each body, performing the autopsies simultaneously.

For half an hour, he dissected the fighting robot, explaining how the components fit together and functioned, how the mek's built-in weapons systems worked, expounded on their capabilities, and tied each point back to the human analog.

His senior student, Draigo Roget, who also served as a teaching assistant, made an adjustment to the simple projector, which displayed the details of his operation to the audience. Draigo wore black clothing from head to toe, which accentuated his long, jet-black hair, black eyebrows, and dark eyes.

The skull of the cadaver had been opened up in preparation for the class and its brain removed, and now Gilbertus exposed the combat robot's computer processing unit. He placed the mek's gelcircuitry core in a tray: A soft-looking metallic sphere was the counterpart to the convoluted human brain that sat in its own pan. He prodded the computer core with a fingertip. "Thinking machines have efficient memories and high-speed processing, but their capacity is a finite thing, limited by the specifications that were manufactured into it."

Gilbertus dissected the brain. "The human brain, on the other hand, has no known set of manufacturer's specifications. Note the complex arrangement in this cutaway: cerebrum, cerebellum, corpus callosum, diencephalon, temporal lobe, midbrain, pons, medulla—you are all familiar with these terms. Despite the physical mass of the brain, most of the thinking and computing capacity was never used by its owner."

He looked up at them. "Each of you must learn to tap into what we all possess. There may be no limit to how much information our memories can hold—if we order and store it properly. At this school, we teach each student to emulate the organization and efficient calculation methods of thinking machines, and we have found that humans can do it *better*."

The students muttered, some of them uneasy. In particular, he noted the sour expression of Alys Carroll, a talented but close-minded young woman who had been raised among the Butlerians. She was one of the students Manford Torondo had assigned here; surprisingly, on a mental-skill level, Alys had done rather well.

To build his Mentat School on Lampadas, Gilbertus had made certain sacrifices. As part of his agreement with Manford, which granted him support for the school, each year Gilbertus had to admit a specified number of trainees selected by the Butlerians. Although the Butlerians were not the best candidates, and took vital slots that might have been better suited for more talented and objective individuals, it was a concession he'd had to make.

Gilbertus took a step back from the two specimens on the autopsy tables. "My objective is to send you out of this school with your thoughts organized and your memory capabilities expanded so that you will be more than the equal of any computer." He gave them a paternal smile. "Is that a goal worthy of your efforts?"

"Yes, sir!" The wave of assent traveled around the theater.

THOUGH THE PHYSICAL environment around the Mentat School was unpleasant—vast wetlands, swampy canals, and dangerous predators—Gilbertus knew that difficult surroundings honed the most proficient humans. Erasmus had taught him that.

The school complex was a large cluster of interlocked, floating platforms anchored on a huge marsh lake, surrounded by undeveloped, unpopulated land. A warding shield system kept away the bothersome disease-carrying swamp insects, creating a sort of oasis for the Mentat students.

Gilbertus crossed a floating walkway over the swamp, hardly noticing the dark-green water below. He passed a floating sport court and one of the free-standing auditoriums, then entered the administration building on the perimeter of the complex, which held offices for the deans and tenured Mentat professors. The school already had more than two hundred instructors and four thousand students, a remarkable success among the many learning centers that had sprung up after the defeat of the thinking machines. Due to the rigors of Mentat instruction, the failure rate approached thirty-five percent even among the very best candidates who were accepted into the school (not counting the required Butlerian candidates), and only the best of those would advance to become Mentats.

The biosene lamps in Gilbertus's office emitted a faint but not unpleasant odor. The large room was appointed with a dark koagany floor and rugs woven from the leaves and bark of swamp willows. Very faintly, he heard classical music playing, some of the compositions he and Erasmus had once enjoyed in the robot's contemplation gardens on Corrin.

Out of nostalgia, he had made his office resemble features of the home of Erasmus on Corrin, with the same plush purple drapes and ornate furniture style. He had to be very careful, but he knew no one would ever make the connection. Gilbertus was the only human alive who remembered the lavish trappings of the independent robot's private villa.

Bookshelves rose to the high ceiling, built from polished wood that looked ancient; nicks and scrapes had been added during assembly to give the illusion of age. When establishing his school, Gilbertus had wanted to create the impression of a long-standing institution with gravitas. Everything about this office, the building, and the school complex had been laid out with a good deal of thought.

And that is only appropriate, he mused. *After all, we are Mentats.*

The deans and professors developed and improved innovative instructional programs to push the boundaries of the human mind, but the essence of the Mentat curriculum had come from a source known only to Gilbertus—a source that, if revealed, would put the entire school in extreme danger.

After verifying that he was alone, Gilbertus locked the door behind him and drew down each of the wood-and-fabric blinds. Removing a key from his waistcoat pocket, he unlocked a solid wood cabinet built into one set of shelves. He reached inside and touched a panel in a precise place, causing the shelves to rearrange, spin around, and then open like the petals of a flower.

On a shelf rested a shimmering memory core, and he said to it, "I am here, Erasmus. Are you ready to continue our conversation?"

His pulse quickened, partly due to the emotions he felt, partly because of the risk. Erasmus was the most notorious of all independent robots, a thinking machine as hated as the evermind Omnius itself. Gilbertus smiled.

Before the catastrophic fall of Corrin, he had removed the core from the doomed robot and smuggled it away as he mingled with countless human refugees. In the intervening years, Gilbertus had created an entirely new life for himself, a false past. He had used his talents to develop this Mentat School—with the clandestine assistance of Erasmus, who provided him with ongoing advice.

The gelcircuitry sphere throbbed with activity, and the independent robot spoke in a familiar erudite voice through small amplifiers. "Thank you—I was beginning to feel claustrophobic, even with the hidden spyeyes you've allowed me."

"You saved me from a life of ignorance and squalor, and I saved you from destruction. A fair exchange. But I apologize that I can't do more—not yet, anyway. We have to be very cautious."

Years ago, Erasmus had selected one child from the miserable slave pens on the machine world, an experiment to see if it was possible to civilize one of the feral creatures through careful training. Over the years, the independent robot became a father figure and mentor who taught Gilbertus how to organize his thoughts, and how to enhance his brain so that he could think with an efficiency formerly reserved for computers. How ironic, Gilbertus thought, that his school for maximizing human potential had its roots in the world of thinking machines.

Erasmus was a hard but excellent teacher. The robot would likely have had success with any young human he tried to train, but Gilbertus was deeply grateful that fate had chosen him. . . .

The two spoke in low tones, always apprehensive about being discovered. "I know the risks you are already taking, but I grow restless. I need a new framework, a functional body that allows me to be mobile again. I am constantly thinking of innumerable test scenarios that would yield interesting results with your cadre of students. I am certain that humans continue to do fascinating, irrational things."

As always, Gilbertus sidestepped the issue of creating the new body that the robot desired. "They do, Father—and unpredictable, violent things. That's why I must keep you concealed. Of all the secrets in the Imperium, your existence is perhaps the greatest."

"I long to interact with humans again . . . but I know you are doing your best." The machine voice paused, and Gilbertus could imagine the shifting expression on the robot's old flowmetal face, on the body left behind on Corrin. "Take me for a walk around the room. Open one of the shades a bit so that I might peek out with my sensors. I need input."

Always alert, Gilbertus lifted out the lightweight core and cradled it in his hands, taking great care not to drop or otherwise damage it. He brought the sphere to one of the windows that faced the broad, shallow lake—a direction from which observers were unlikely to be watching—and lifted the blinds. He could not deny Erasmus this small favor; he owed the independent robot too much.

The memory core chuckled, a gentle cachinnation that reminded Gilbertus of peaceful, idyllic times on Corrin. "The universe has changed much," Erasmus mused. "But you've adapted. You've done what you needed to do to survive."

"And to protect you." Gilbertus held the memory core close. "It's difficult, but I will keep up the masquerade. You'll be safe while I'm gone, Father."

Soon, Gilbertus was due to depart from Lampadas with Manford Toronado, both of them going to Salusa Secundus to address the Landsraad Council and Emperor Salvador Corrino. It was a delicate, dangerous balancing act on Gilbertus's part . . . a form of acrobatics that always made him uneasy.

Life is complicated, regardless of the circumstances into which we are born.

— HADITHA CORRINO, letter to her husband, Prince Roderick

Pulled by four golden lions, the royal carriage led a procession through the Salusan capital city of Zimia. It was a city of monuments, honoring the numerous heroes of the long Jihad. Everywhere, Emperor Salvador Corrino saw images of Serena Butler, her martyred baby, Manion, and the Grand Patriarch Iblis Ginjo—on fluttering banners, on the sides of buildings, on statues, on storefronts. Ahead, the great golden dome of the Hall of Parliament was a reassuring presence, itself a site of epic, historical events.

Under cloudy skies, they rolled past a towering cymek walker on display, a dented and rusting monument as high as the tallest buildings. The fearsome machine had once been guided by a human brain, part of an enemy attack force during the first Battle of Zimia. Now, the immense form was lifeless, a relic standing as a reminder of those dark days. After more than a century of Serena Butler's Jihad, the thinking-machine forces had been entirely defeated at Corrin, and humans were no longer slaves.

Zimia had been severely damaged twice by machine attacks in the Jihad, and on both occasions the city had been rebuilt—a testimonial to the unrelenting spirit of humanity. Out of the carnage and rubble of the Battle of Corrin, the Butler family changed their name to Corrino and rose to lead the new Imperium. The first Emperor was Salvador's grandfather, Faykan, and then his son, Jules. The two men had ruled for a combined total of seventy-one years, after which Salvador assumed the throne.

Inside the royal carriage, the Emperor felt irritated at the interruption to his morning schedule, but he'd received word of a grim discovery that he needed to see for himself. He had hurried from the Palace along with his entourage of royal guards, assistants, advisers, and full security (because the restless people always found something to protest). A Suk School doctor rode in the carriage behind his, just in case something went wrong. Salvador worried about a lot of things and wore his apprehension like an ill-fitting garment.

As the procession continued, the Emperor did not particularly want to see the gruesome discovery to which they were escorting him, but it was his obligation. The lion carriages made their way toward the center of the city, past other carriages, groundcars, and trucks that pulled over to let the royal party pass.

His ornate carriage stopped smoothly in the large central plaza, and liveried attendants hurried to open the enameled door. As they helped the Emperor out, he could already smell the stench of burned flesh in the air.

A tall, muscular man approached in a scarlet tunic and gold trousers, the colors of House Corrino. Roderick was the Emperor's demi-brother, sharing the same father but a different mother; the two also had a troubled half-sister, Anna, by yet another mother. (Emperor Jules had been very busy, although he'd never sired a child from his actual wife.)

"Over here," Roderick said in a quiet voice. He had a full head of thick, blond hair, unlike Salvador, who—two years older at forty-seven—had only a patch of wispy brown hair on top. Both men wore activated shield belts as casual items of clothing, enveloping them in a barely discernible field. The men hardly gave the ubiquitous technology any thought.

Roderick pointed toward a statue of Iblis Ginjo, the charismatic but complex religious leader of the Jihad who had inspired billions to fight against the machine oppressors. Salvador was horrified to see a burned, mutilated body dangling from the statue. A placard was attached to the roasted, unrecognizable corpse, identifying him as "Toure Bomoko—Traitor to God and Faith."

Salvador knew the name very well. Twenty years ago, during his father's reign, the Commission of Ecumenical Translators had caused a horrendous uproar with their release of a new holy book that was ostensibly for all religions, the *Orange Catholic Bible*. Toure Bomoko had been chairman of the CET delegates who spent seven years in isolation in a domed compound on the radioactive wasteland of Old Earth. The CET had compiled a compromise summation of the basic tenets of religion, then presented their masterpiece with giddy triumph. The cobbled-together holy text was intended to solve all of humanity's religious differences, but actually accomplished the opposite.

Rather than being celebrated as a triumph of unification and the cornerstone of wider understanding, the book and the hubris behind it inspired a violent backlash across the Imperium. Bomoko and his fellow delegates fled from the mobs; many delegates were lynched, while others vehemently recanted to save their skins. Some of them committed suicide, often under suspicious circumstances, while others, like Bomoko, went into hiding.

Later, after being granted sanctuary in the Imperial Palace by the grace of Emperor Jules, Chairman Bomoko admitted in public that his commission had erred in trying to create new religious symbols, which only served to "introduce uncertainties into accepted belief" and to "stir up controversy about God." After a scandal at the palace involving the chairman and the wife of the Emperor, Bomoko had escaped—the second time he was forced to flee. He had never been found.

Now Roderick stood at his brother's side, studying the charred, faceless corpse strung up on the statue. "Do you think they really found him this time?"

Unimpressed with the mutilated body, Salvador rolled his eyes. "I doubt it. This is the seventh supposed 'Bomoko' they've killed. But run the genetic tests anyway, just to make sure."

"I'll take care of everything."

Salvador knew he didn't have to worry. Roderick had always been the cooler, calmer brother. The Emperor let out a slow sigh. "If I knew where Bomoko was, I'd hand him over myself, just to keep the mobs happy."

Roderick's lips pulled together in a frown. He looked seriously at his brother. "I assume you'd talk it over with me first."

"You're right, I wouldn't do anything that serious without your advice."

Over the years, protests had ebbed and flowed, though no major riots had occurred in more than a decade, not since Salvador took the Corrino throne. Soon, he would announce a revised (and somewhat sanitized) edition of the OC *Bible*, and *that* was bound to incense some people, as well. The new edition would bear Salvador's own name, and at first that had seemed like a good idea. Through his religious scholars, Salvador had tried to solve some of the problematic text, but extremists wanted the consolidated holy book burned, not modified. He could not be too careful around religious zealots.

Roderick gave crisp orders to two officers of the palace guard. "Remove the body and clean up the scene."

As the burned corpse was taken down, some of the reddened meat on the shoulders and torso slipped off the bone, and the guards recoiled with exclamations of disgust. One of the men brought Salvador the placard, and he squinted to read the small print on the back. The lynch mob felt they needed to explain that the victim's body had been mutilated in precisely the same way that the thinking machines had done to Serena Butler—their justification for a horrendous act.

As he walked back to the royal carriage with his brother, the Emperor grumbled, "After a thousand years of machine enslavement, and more than a century of the bloody Jihad, you'd think people would be tired of it all by now."

Roderick gave a quiet, knowing nod. "They do seem addicted to the clash and frenzy. The mood of the people is still raw."

"Humanity is so damned impatient." The Emperor stepped into the carriage. "After Omnius fell, did they really expect all problems would be solved in an instant? Eighty years after the Battle of Corrin, things should not still be in turmoil! I wish you could just fix it, Roderick."

His brother gave him a thin smile. "I'll do what I can."

"Yes, I know you will." Salvador pulled shut the door to the carriage, and the driver urged the lions to a fast pace as the rest of the entourage scrambled to follow.

THAT EVENING, RODERICK delivered the genetic results to his brother at his country estate. Salvador and the Empress Tabrina were in the midst of one of their loud arguments, this time over her desire to take a minor role in the government, rather than her customary ceremonial duties.

Salvador adamantly opposed the request. "It is not traditional, and the Imperium needs stability more than anything else." The royal couple was in the trophy room, where a frozen menagerie of mounted fish and wild animals adorned the walls.

Fortunately, having heard the argument before, Prince Roderick marched into the trophy room, oblivious to their shouts. "Brother, I've brought the results. I thought you'd like to see them yourself."

Salvador grabbed the paper from Roderick's hands, pretending to be annoyed by the interruption, but he secretly gave his brother a grateful smile. While Tabrina seethed, sitting by the fireplace and drinking wine—too polite to keep quarreling in front of a guest—Salvador read the one-page report. Satisfied, he rolled it into a ball and tossed it in the fire. "Not the real Bomoko—just as I thought. The mobs string up anyone who arouses their suspicions."

"I wish they'd string you up," the Empress muttered under her breath. She was a strikingly beautiful woman with dark, almond-shaped eyes, high cheekbones, and a lithe body wrapped in a long, formfitting dress. Her auburn hair was arranged in elaborate coiffure.

Salvador considered snapping back that he'd let them do it, just to get away from her, but he was in no mood to be funny. He turned his back on her and sauntered out of the room. "Come, Roderick. There's a popular new card game I'd like to teach you. I learned it from my newest concubine."

At the mention of the concubine, Tabrina let out an annoyed snort, which Salvador pretended not to hear.

Roderick gave a peremptory bow. "If you command it."

Salvador raised his eyebrows. "Do I need to?"

"No." The two made their way to the parlor.

During the Jihad, Rossak was defended by the psychic powers of the Sorceresses. They were powerful living weapons who could annihilate the mind of a cymek, though at the cost of their own lives. Alas, those days are gone! Today, fewer than a hundred pureblood Sorceresses remain, and those do not have the powers of their predecessors.
        —preface to *The Mysteries of Rossak*, Sisterhood textbook

While the many acolytes and Sisters continued their instruction inside the cliff city, and youth proctors taught the children in the nursery chambers, Valya descended into the thick jungles for her daily assignment. An important assignment.

The creaking, wooden lift-car dropped through the thick canopy into the murky, twilight world. As she emerged from the wooden cage and stepped onto the moist ground, Valya inhaled the mixture of rich odors from the soil, plants, and animal life. She followed a path into the dense, silvery-purple foliage. Giant ferns curled and uncurled around her, as if flexing their muscles. From far overhead, thin shafts of filtered sunlight changed from moment to moment as the branches stirred. The leaves rustled, and something skittered through the underbrush; a predatory vine thrashed like a cracked whip, stunning a hairy rodent, then encircling it. Down here, she knew always to be alert.

She arrived at a black metal door mounted in an immense tree. As she had done every day for many months, Valya used a passkey to slide open the entrance, revealing a dim passageway beyond, lit only by yellowish glowglobe lamps. She descended a curving staircase that went beneath the tree's root system, and presently the passage opened into a series of rooms that had been hewn from the bedrock. In the largest chamber, the old Sorceress Karee Marques performed pharmaceutical experiments with electroscopes, jars of powder, tubes of fluids, centrifuges.

The chambers reminded Valya of the mysterious laboratories of a hermit alchemist, with beakers of bubbling liquids and distillations from obscure jungle fauna, fungi, plants, and roots. Sister Karee was unfathomably ancient, almost as old as Reverend Mother Raquella, but she did not have the same precise control over her body's biochemistry, so the years hung on her small bony frame like a heavy garment. Karee's large eyes, however, were a strikingly beautiful green that seemed undiminished by age. She had white hair and high cheekbones.

The old woman acknowledged Valya's arrival without turning from the chemical studies. Excitement tinged her voice. "I've had an idea this morning—a breakthrough, I think. We can use a distillation from the mucus secreted by bur-rowing slugs. It has deadly paralytic qualities, but if we can mitigate the effects, this compound might be the correct balance to send a Sister to the brink of death, freezing her body's systems, while still allowing her mind to remain active and focused until the last moment."

Valya had seen the plump, segmented slugs burrowing through the rotting forest detritus—yet another dangerous creature from Rossak. "An interesting possibility. It might have the correct qualities." Valya, though, did not feel unre-alistic confidence. *Haven't we tried everything else over the decades?* She was not eager to die in another hopeless test.

Bins held harvested leaves and mushrooms, lichen scraped from rocks, venom milked from large arachnids, squashed pupae of jungle moths. "How soon do you think we'll be ready to test another volunteer?" Valya asked. Sister Tiana had died, and most unpleasantly, only a week earlier.

The old Sorceress raised her eyebrows, misinterpreting her question. "Are you stepping forward yourself? Do you finally believe you are ready, Sister Valya? I agree that you are more prepared than most of the previous volunteers. If any-one were to have a chance—"

"No, that's not what I meant," Valya said quickly. "I merely wanted to point out that we should proceed with the greatest care, or the Sisters will lose hope, given the number of deaths . . . the failures over the years."

"Any true Sister will always believe there is hope in human potential," Karee said, moving a beaker off a warming plate.

Valya had undergone instruction here on Rossak for five years, seeing the Rossak School of the Sisterhood as a way to emerge from the trap of her exiled family, and over the course of her training she had attracted the attention of the Reverend Mother. Valya was always looking for ways to advance herself in the order of women, and now that the Reverend Mother had let her into the inner circle, revealing the tremendous and terrifying secret of the breeding-record computers, she believed that many more doorways were opening for her.

How she wished she could tell Griffin!

Secretly, Valya was also keeping alert for opportunities throughout the Impe-rium. Normally, her disgraced family name would have slammed those doors shut in her face, but maybe, through the Sisterhood, she would be viewed differently. In the meantime, focusing on her studies here on Rossak, she continued her intensive mental and physical training.

The Reverend Mother hoped Valya would remain on the homeworld of the Sisterhood and devote herself to the order, but the young woman had no intention of remaining trapped here. That would not help House Harkonnen. One option she was considering would be to become one of the missionary Sisters like Sister Arlett, who had recruited her. Perhaps Valya could find a place in a nobleman's household, or even at the Imperial Court on Salusa Secundus, just like Sister Dorotea—Sister Karee's previous assistant here.

In the labs, Valya had watched volunteer after volunteer go into the medical beds with clenched jaws and determined gazes, as well as the hubris to believe that they could achieve the impossible and become Reverend Mothers like Raquella, when all others had failed before them. Most died in the ordeal, and those who survived fell into comas, lost memories wholesale, or suffered other forms of brain damage. No, Valya would not volunteer for that.

"We already have more candidates than we need," Karee Marques said, "but there will be a delay until I am satisfied that a potential drug has a good chance of success."

Fortunately, the Sorceresses of Rossak had kept the detailed pharmaceutical studies compiled by Aurelius Venport. Back in the days before the Jihad, Venport had amassed a fortune selling unique drugs and chemicals derived from the exotic flora and fauna on Rossak. Because the only apparent way for a Sister to cross the barrier and become a Reverend Mother required a direct mental confrontation at the farthest boundaries of mortality, Karee Marques had diligently set about testing the deadliest drugs that were found in the pharmacopeia.

Valya kept her expression blank, unreadable. *And I do not intend to be one of the volunteers.*

She moved to the laboratory equipment, stood beside Karee. "I will do anything to help, you know that," she said, but she didn't mean it.

"Somewhere here is the secret," Karee said. "We just need to keep testing."

BY NOW, REVEREND Mother Raquella no longer felt quite so awkward when the head of the Suk Medical School visited. Even though Dr. Ori Zhoma had been dismissed from the Sisterhood in disgrace, the stern woman had certainly proved her worth in the forty years since, graduating with honors from Suk training and working her way up through the hierarchy of Suk doctors.

Though she was a skilled medical practitioner, Zhoma's true abilities lay in administration, hard decisions based on emotionless assessments. Since the strange suicide of her predecessor years before, Dr. Zhoma had run the old flagship school in the Imperial capital city, and now she oversaw the expansion of the school's primary independent campus and headquarters on Parmentier.

Raquella went to meet the Suk administrator personally as her shuttle landed on the polymerized forest canopy. As a young woman, Zhoma had trained on Rossak for two years, and Reverend Mother Raquella had seen great talent and ambition in her. At the time, Zhoma had been interested in the potential of various Rossak drugs to increase strength, speed, endurance, mental acuity. But—a fact that was not discovered until much later—Zhoma also saw the profit potential, and she had started supplying black-market merchants with rare extracts and intensely potent drugs, selling them at exorbitant prices . . . until she was caught.

When facing the Reverend Mother, Zhoma had tried to rationalize the extracurricular activities by asserting that her actions benefited the Sisterhood. But the voices in Raquella's head had been skeptical. Zhoma claimed that she had added all the profits to the school's coffers (and indeed she had), but even that did not excuse her primary transgression: performing an illegal activity in the name of the Sisterhood without Raquella's knowledge. That could not be tolerated.

Thus, the Reverend Mother had had no choice but to send Zhoma away, though as a courtesy she had not made the reasons public. Because the woman had such potential, Raquella had allowed her to keep her reputation, and Zhoma's career had not been affected. She had applied to the Suk School, excelled there, and made herself an important and influential person. However, even after all these years, Zhoma craved the acceptance and forgiveness of the Reverend Mother whom she had so disappointed.

The shuttle disembarkation door opened, and a gruff, compact woman in her early sixties emerged. Representing the Suk doctors, Ori Zhoma was humorless, all business; she took care of her body like a factory owner maintained a valuable piece of machinery. She had never been vain and did not see any purpose in making herself attractive; Raquella knew the woman had trouble making friends and doubted she had any romantic ambitions. If not for her indiscretion, Zhoma would have made a talented Sister, in large part because of her control over her emotions.

Zhoma regularly came to Rossak to treat (but more likely, to *study*) the damaged Sister volunteers who had survived unsuccessful attempts to become Reverend Mothers. Raquella refused to let the comatose or brain-damaged women be sent away to Parmentier, where Suk researchers could prod and analyze them as test subjects, but as a concession, she allowed Zhoma to come here personally. The doctor took samples and ran her tests, but so far she had not been able to cure any of the failed Reverend Mother candidates.

Raquella greeted her in a cordial voice, "Welcome again to Rossak, Dr. Zhoma.

The condition of the damaged Sisters remains unchanged, but we appreciate the attention you give them."

Stepping down the ramp, the doctor hesitated, as if all the rehearsed words had flowed out of her mind. Finally, she said, "The Suk doctors and the Sisterhood have much in common." Zhoma stepped forward and extended a hand to clasp Raquella's with brusque formality. "We all work toward the betterment of humanity."

"The alliance makes sense. I am always open to suggestions as to how the Sisterhood and your doctors can achieve our common goals," Raquella said. "My connection to Mohandas Suk dates back to before our schools were formed."

Raquella led the doctor up the path to the cliff city. Inside a special section of caves used as the Sisterhood's infirmary, she guided Dr. Zhoma to a private ward where four young women lay in vegetative states; in adjacent rooms, five more mentally afflicted women lived in varying states of awareness and normalcy. Two of them spoke in languages that no one could understand, not even Raquella with the countless generations of past memories inside her mind. Two were haunted by terrible nightmares. One, Sister Lila, lived in stony, affectless silence most of the time, but became perfectly lucid for no more than ten minutes each day, during which time she excitedly tried to explain what she had seen and experienced. As soon as her memories began to crystallize, however, Lila fell back into her blank state.

Now, Dr. Zhoma knelt by the four comatose patients, studied their eyes, their pulses, their skin tones. She was competent, efficient, but had no bedside manner; the victims' vegetative state allowed her to work without distractions. Zhoma took blood samples and moved about as if going through a detailed checklist in her mind.

This section of the caves had been used to care for the Misborn, the children of Rossak Sorceresses who had suffered severe birth defects—which were once common because of the planet's pervasive mutagens and environmental contaminants. Thinking of the Misborn, Raquella felt a pang for the young deformed Jimmak Tero, a child of Sorceress Ticia Cenva. A long time ago, when Raquella had suffered from the plague, Jimmak took her out to the jungle, tended her, and kept her alive by a miracle. He was dead now—most of the people Raquella had known in those days were long gone, as were so many Sister volunteers who tried to find the same uncharted path that she had traveled.

So many dead . . . and so little hope of achieving the goal.

As she looked at these victims, she spoke her thoughts to Zhoma, "Could it be I am just an anomaly? What if it's not possible for anyone else to repeat my transformation? Such an agonizing process, so much death and injury." She sighed. "Is it worth the risk? Maybe I should stop."

Zhoma's cool expression hardened, showing true determination. "Reaching our human potential is always worth the risk, Reverend Mother. Now that our race is free of machine domination, we must improve ourselves, stretching our abilities of mind and body in every possible direction. That is what the Suk doctors believe. That is what your Sisterhood believes, and also the Mentats on Lampadas, and the Swordmasters. And even—if I understand correctly—the mutated Navigators used by the VenHold Spacing Fleet. We can't back away now. We can't let our resolve fail. It is our common destiny."

Raquella's heart warmed as she heard this, and she smiled at the stocky woman. "Ah, Ori, maybe you should have stayed in the Sisterhood after all."

It is a trivial thing to say you agree with certain beliefs, but a far greater challenge to have the conviction to act on them.

—MANFORD TORONDO, address to the Landsraad Hall

Normally, whenever Manford appeared before a crowd of loyal supporters on Lampadas, the cheers buffeted him like the winds of a cleansing storm. Today, however, when two bearers carried his palanquin into the Landsraad Hall on Salusa Secundus, the reception was much cooler.

The sergeant-at-arms announced him in a booming voice filled with pretentious formality, though surely everyone recognized the leader of the Butlerian movement. The responding applause from the nobles was polite and anticipatory, but not overwhelming, not ecstatic. Manford chose not to notice. Sitting on the palanquin, rather than on his Swordmaster's shoulders, he straightened his back. His own shoulders were broad, his arm muscles well developed from compensating for the loss of his legs by using his arms to get about, and from regular, vigorous exercise. As the bearers carried him forward to the speaking podium, Anari Idaho walked alongside, an intimidating, protective presence.

Manford looked around the immense hall. The dizzying rows of seats looked like ripples that extended outward from a rock thrown into a placid pond. The benches held representatives from important planets and proxies from groups of lesser worlds, along with countless observers and functionaries, many of them bureaucrats. Emperor Salvador Corrino sat in his ornate box, attending the proceedings, although he appeared bored. His brother, Roderick, occupied the companion chair in the Emperor's box, and he leaned over to say something to the balding Salvador. The two men didn't seem to be paying much attention to him.

The bearers stopped when his palanquin was properly positioned in the amplification field. A brilliant light shone down on him, and he raised his face, basking in it, as if to receive a blessing from heaven.

The Speaker's voice resounded, bringing him back to the matter at hand. "Manford Torondo, representative of the Butlerian movement, you have asked to address the Landsraad Council. Please state your business."

Manford noted the many empty seats in the huge chamber. "Why are there so many absences? Was there no announcement of my appearance? Don't you know that my words are vitally important?"

The Speaker seemed impatient. "There are always absences in our meetings, Leader Torondo. Nevertheless, we have a quorum."

Manford drew a deep breath, let it out as a sigh. "I am sorry to see that the seats are not full. May I have a list of the attendees who are actually here?" He was really more interested in who had chosen *not* to attend.

"It is a matter of public record. Now, please state your business."

Manford was taken aback by the man's abruptness, but he dredged strength from the darkest corners of his heart and decided to be reasonable, for the moment.

He spoke as if to equals. "Very well. I come here to report on the good works of my followers, and to request a demonstration of unity. Butlerians continue to discover, and destroy, outposts and robot ships. While that is part of our legitimate work, those vessels are merely symbols of what the thinking machines did to us, remnants of the past. The real threat is more insidious . . . and you bring it upon yourselves."

He twisted on the palanquin so that he could sweep a demonstrative arm around the Landsraad Hall. His bearers remained motionless, like statues. Anari stared at the audience.

"The main reason I have come here is because you need to be *reminded*. My people are prevalent throughout the Imperium, and I receive reports of how your planets have gone soft, how you make excuses and exceptions for your populations, how you pretend that centuries of oppression can be ignored after only a few decades."

He heard muttering from the seated representatives. Emperor Salvador now perked up in his private box, paying close attention to him. Roderick Corrino looked deep in thought.

Manford continued, "You allow machines into your cities and homes. You tell yourselves the devices are harmless, that *this* little piece of technology can't hurt anyone, or *that* convenient machine should be allowed, or *this* particular device is an exception. But have you all forgotten?" He raised his voice to a shout. "*Have you forgotten?* How many little steps does it take before you step over the brink? The enslavement of humanity did not happen overnight, but after a succession of bad decisions, as people put an increasing amount of trust in thinking machines."

The legless man inhaled deeply. "Despite these errors, we defeated the evil machines, and now we again have our chance to march proudly down the right path. The *only* path. We dare not waste this opportunity, so I call upon you to follow us now! The Butlerians have found the true path that can keep us safe, and keep us *human*."

"The mind of man is holy," Anari murmured in benediction.

He pointed to one of the guest seats. "Gilbertus Albans traveled here from the Mentat School on my own planet. He and his students have proved that we don't need computers. Truly, the mind of man is holy!"

Seeming embarrassed to be singled out, the bespectacled Mentat headmaster rose to his feet reluctantly and spoke. "Yes, esteemed representatives. By careful application of our efforts, through practice and mental exercise, certain candidates have the ability to order their minds in the proper way. They can complete calculations and make detailed second- and third-order projections. A fully trained and qualified Mentat can perform the functions of a computer. Many of my graduates have already entered into service in noble households."

Manford turned in the direction of the Imperial box. "Sister Dorotea from Rossak is one of several members of the Sisterhood who advises the Imperial Court. She can attest to this truth."

A black-robed woman sitting near Emperor Salvador bowed her head, as the audience turned toward her. Salvador looked at Dorotea in surprise; apparently he had not expected to find a Butlerian sympathizer in his own court. The woman had done her work well, while concealing that detail.

The lanky Dorotea stood, continued to bow, and announced, "The purpose of our Sisterhood is to maximize human potential. Our own bodies are the greatest machines ever created. Through the application of physical and mental skills, we can develop and rely on our *humanity*. We have no need for machines."

A gruff voice called out, booming across the great chamber. "So will you barbarians dispose of everything, then? Send us back to the Stone Age?"

All eyes turned toward the visitors' gallery, and Manford frowned in disgust. With his cinnamon-colored hair and prominent mustache, Directeur Josef Venport was quite distinctive. The ambitious businessman was willing to adopt any form of technology he could turn to a profit.

Venport sniffed. "You would have us discard all medical advances? All transportation? All the hallmarks of human civilization? Look at you there, using an amplification field to deliver your words! You are inconsistent and hypocritical, Torondo—not to mention ignorant."

"Please, we mustn't take this to absurd lengths," cried another man from the delegate stands. He was identified as Ptolemy, representative of the planet Zenith, a smallish man with a professorial demeanor. "On my world we have a collegial atmosphere and countless projects to use science for the benefit of humankind. Technology, like people, can be good or bad."

"Technology is *not* like people." Manford's voice was cold and hard. "We know the evils of rampant science, discoveries that never should have been made. We know the pain and suffering that unfettered technology has caused our race. Look at the radioactive ruins of Earth and the destruction of Corrin, look at a thousand years of human enslavement by the cymeks and by Omnius." He became quieter and more paternal, as well as more threatening. "Haven't you learned your lesson? You are playing with fire."

Directeur Venport called out sarcastically, "And you are trying to have us *undiscover* fire!" A mutter of uneasy laughter rippled across the audience.

Anari Idaho took offense, but Manford controlled his anger. He ignored Venport's outburst and continued, "Many of you have made glib promises to shun technology, but as soon as our attention is diverted, you slip back to your conveniences. Know this and take caution: My Butlerians are watching."

Sounding annoyed, Emperor Salvador spoke into his own amplifier. "This is an old argument, Leader Torondo, and it will not be settled today. The Landsraad has business to conduct. What exactly do you want here?"

"A vote," he said. If this had been one of his rallies, the people would be screaming and weeping by now. "In fact, I *demand* a vote. Every representative must state publicly, on the record, whether or not he or she adheres to the principles taught by Rayna Butler. Will you follow the Butlerian guidelines and forever cast aside all advanced technology?"

He expected applause. Instead, the muttering from the stands rose to an uneasy rumble. Manford couldn't understand why they would delay, or resist what they knew was right, but these rich, fat, and comfortable people would not give up the things that made their lives easier.

In the Imperial box, a concerned Roderick Corrino whispered to his brother, who also looked flustered. Gathering himself, Salvador announced, "This is an issue that must be discussed at great length. Each planetary representative or proxy has a right to speak, and each person should go back to his or her planet and determine the wishes of the populace."

Manford said, "With a word, I can summon tens of thousands of my followers to fill the streets of Zimia, and command them to smash every piece of technology down to the smallest pocket watch. I would advise you not to stall." A fearful susurration passed among the delegates. They were offended by his threat, but they knew full well that he could carry it out. "We cannot let a new age of thinking machines appear."

"And I will not be bullied by a Neanderthal thug," Venport bellowed, "even if he threatens to summon a mob of ignorant fools."

"Please, this is nonsense! It's a specious argument. We can discuss—" insisted Ptolemy from Zenith, still trying to negotiate in a reasonable tone. He was shouted down.

Roderick Corrino slipped away from the Emperor's box. Salvador appeared panicked.

"I demand a vote," Manford repeated. "Every representative here must state for the record whether their planet sides with human freedom or with eventual enslavement."

"A point of order," said one of the delegates who did not identify herself. "Manford Torondo is merely a guest speaker. He has no authority to make demands of this Landsraad meeting. He cannot call for a vote."

Five people from the stands, official delegates of planets that were controlled by the Butlerians, stood up and shouted (exactly as instructed) to call for a formal vote. Manford had many allies, and he had planned ahead. "I think we've dispensed with your points of order. I will remain here all day if necessary. Well, Emperor Salvador? Will you call a vote?"

The balding leader of the Imperium clearly did not like to be forced into a corner. His face was red. He looked from side to side as if for advice, but Roderick wasn't there. Sister Dorotea whispered to him, but he shook his head.

Shrill alarms ratcheted through the Landsraad Hall, causing a wave of panic. Roderick Corrino reappeared in the Imperial box, said something urgent to his brother, and then took the Emperor's amplifier. "Ladies and gentlemen, we have just received a credible bomb threat. The Landsraad Hall may be in danger. Please evacuate as quickly as possible."

The rush and rumble of voices grew louder. Delegates began to stream away from their seats, and pandemonium reigned as they escaped into the streets. Anari barked orders to Manford's bearers, and they rushed from the Hall, whisking the legless man to safety.

Manford cried out, "But there must be a vote!"

The Swordmaster trotted beside him, always alert. "If there's even a possibility that a bomb might explode, I must get you safely from this place. Now."

Manford clenched his fists. Who would have threatened the Landsraad during his speech? Years ago, an assassin's explosion had killed Rayna Butler and cost Manford his legs. He knew he had enemies, but this didn't seem like their tactics.

"They will reschedule the meeting," Anari said as they raced out the door. "You can address them another time."

"I shall insist upon it." Manford was so enraged that his body trembled. He was convinced that the timing of this "bomb threat" was all too convenient.

What one person sees as contributing to a loss of humanity, another might view as an improvement on the human condition.
— NORMA CENVA, Kolhar shipyards internal memo

After the turmoil and nonsense of the recent Landsraad League meeting, Josef Venport returned to the primary VenHold headquarters on Kolhar and continued to stew over what he had seen and heard. Manford Toronto and his barbarians wanted to seize the controls of the great ship of human civilization and crash it!

Legless "Half-Manford" was a bizarre spokesperson, but the odd man, along with Rayna Butler before him, and the revered Serena Butler preceding both of them, bore the mystique of martyrdom, which held a certain guilty attraction for some.

In establishing and expanding Venport Holdings, Josef and his predecessors strove to lay down a viable commercial network to raise the Imperium from the ashes after defeating Omnius. He wanted to lift humanity to the glorious heights they had been denied under the domination of thinking machines.

The Butlerians, on the other hand, wanted to drag populations into a dark swamp of hardship and ignorance. He had firmly, perhaps naïvely, believed that the Butlerian silliness would peter out in time, and he couldn't fathom how the movement had gained so much momentum. He considered it a personal affront: Logic and progress should automatically trump superstition.

With all that on his mind, Josef was in a surly mood when he returned home, but his wife, Cioba, and six advisers met him as he disembarked at the spaceport, and he felt a sense of stability returning. She was a bastion of organization. Cioba, with her rigorous Sisterhood training, was a perfect match for him, helping to run the numerous components of Venport Holdings—both the public ones and the secret ones—like a well-choreographed dance.

She was a striking woman, beautiful and intense, with prominent dark eyebrows, pale skin, and very long brunette hair that she kept pinned up under a practical scarf during the business day, but when she loosed the tresses and brushed them in the evening, they fell down below her waist.

Josef was not a romantic man, and he had approached the marriage from a business perspective, knowing that he had to plan for the future of the Venport line. Having one of their graduates marry into VenHold was an obvious boon for the Rossak School, due to Venport's wealth and political power, and the Sisterhood had offered several candidates for him to consider; Cioba had scored highest when Josef assessed his options. In the twelve years of their marriage, Cioba had been an incomparable partner in running the business.

As the granddaughter of Karee Marques, she also had a hint of Sorceress blood. Josef traced his own lineage back to Rossak as well, through Norma Cenva—whose mother, Zufa Cenva, had been one of the most powerful Sorceresses in history. Cioba's two young daughters with Josef had enormous potential, according to the Sisterhood bloodline analysis, and both had been sent off to Rossak to be raised and trained there.

He walked forward from the shuttle, giving a formal greeting to his wife and the advisers. He did not kiss her, nor did she expect it; that would come later—they filled different roles now, in public. She had her report ready, and delivered a rapid-fire summary of urgent matters, crises she had already solved, other emergencies that required his intervention. What he appreciated most was that Cioba did not waste his time; she sorted out only the items that genuinely required his attention.

She talked as he set the pace, always moving, and the advisers chimed in, adding necessary details and opinions. Although Josef paid attention to the many VenHold operations and investments, he tried to remain above the nitty-gritty details, not unlike his great-grandmother Norma Cenva, who remained in mental isolation, engrossed in her own concerns and barely able to communicate with mere humans like him. Returning here from Salusa Secundus, he felt secure and stable, knowing that VenHold was in good hands, and he could forget the outside chaos . . . for a while.

Around him, the landing fields were a blur of movement, shuttles rising and landing, cargo pods dropping into place, refueling tankers racing up to docked vessels. Support workers, engineers, and designers filled cylindrical administrative complexes like drones in a hive.

By the time they reached his office in the giant admin building, Cioba had finished delivering her summaries. Josef turned to the advisers and dismissed them before closing the door so he could be alone with his wife. Both of them took seats, relaxing but still focused on business. "So, which things are time-critical?" he asked. "Exactly what needs my signature, and what can wait until tomorrow?"

"I believe the last thing I mentioned is the most time-critical," Cioba said. "As we discussed before you left, I stepped up efforts to watch three more exiles from the CET. One of them was exposed by the mobs and killed. The other two renegades are ready to go to ground under the terms we proposed."

"I have no patience for mobs." His face took on a pinched expression. "Although the CET delegates caused their own troubles, I'm willing to help protect them from the foolish religious hordes." The riots over the *Orange Catholic Bible* were only peripherally connected with the Butlerian movement, but they shared a similar basis in superstition and ignorance. Peasants bearing torches.

Cioba said in an even voice, "Remember, the delegates were misguided fools, too—the whole Commission of Ecumenical Translators, in fact. They started with the false premise that they could apply a single rational order to all of humanity's diverse and contradictory religious beliefs. No wonder people revolted against them."

Josef had established a hidden refuge on a near-forgotten planet, Tupile, offering it as a sanctuary for anyone who wanted to vanish—including the reviled Toure Bomoko, who had fled there immediately after that unpleasant incident in the Imperial Palace with the wife of Emperor Jules Corrino, and the subsequent bloodbath. Only the spacing fleet Navigators knew how to reach that planet, so its location was completely secure.

"Very well, ship them off to Tupile—no one will find them there. If you agree?"

"I agree that would be best."

Josef signed the authorization document, then asked his wife to accompany him out to see Norma Cenva in her tank.

UNDER THE CLOUDY Kolhar sky, the broad paved field was crowded with sealed tanks. Insulated plaz portholes were designed to allow external inspectors to peer inside rather than for the tanks' inhabitants to look out. Workers with suspensor-levitated canisters moved from tank to tank, pumping in fresh melange gas. Inside the numerous individual tanks, embryonic Navigators swam in dense brownish-orange clouds, their physical bodies languid while their thoughts stampeded down uncharted paths.

Atop a mound that had been built and ornamented like an acropolis sat the largest and oldest chamber, the tank that held Norma Cenva. Accompanied by Cioba, Josef ascended the marble steps, feeling like a supplicant approaching an idol. His great-grandmother had been immersed in spice gas, never breathing fresh air, never emerging in more than eight decades, while her thoughts traveled through an esoteric tapestry of mathematics and physics. By most measures, she was no longer human.

Norma was freakishly intelligent, with an evolved body and an ever-expanding mind, and her need for spice was insatiable. The Navigators, the VenHold Spacing Fleet—indeed, the whole concept of Holtzman shields and spacefolding engines—would have been impossible without her incredible breakthroughs.

"No one can tell what she's really thinking about," Josef said to his wife, "but she's made it clear to me that she longs to add many more ships to the VenHold Spacing Fleet. I told her that tens of thousands of vessels would be necessary to adequately service all the planets in the Imperium."

"Maybe she just wants more Navigators," Cioba said. "More like herself."

He smiled as he reached the top step. "She's creating Navigators as quickly as she can, but for that she requires extraordinary quantities of spice. I pointed out to her that the more ships we possess, the more melange we can transport around the Imperium . . . and thus the more Navigators she can create. Everyone benefits."

From the hill, they could see the busy spaceport and shipyards. Each hour, a newly refitted vessel lifted off. Launch towers were great spires in the sky, needles pointing toward the heavens. Simply keeping track of all the scheduled spacefaring flights that connected and serviced the Imperium's thousands of planets was an administrative nightmare, but Josef had thousands of people to work on the task, all of them housed in a single building complex.

Fortunately, not all of his ships required Navigators. Slow-haulers were adequate for transporting noncritical cargo from planet to planet on traditional routes, using old-style pre-Holtzman engines. Even though the trip took months, it was less expensive and perfectly safe.

Spacefolders could make the passage almost instantaneously, but for years they had flown blindly; the pilots had charted their courses and prayed that no hazards lay along the path. Currently, low-budget carriers like Celestial Transport still risked blind travel, usually without informing their hapless passengers of the dangers. Years ago, during Serena Butler's Jihad, Aurelius Venport had provided spacefolders for the war effort on condition that only his company had the right to use the technology after the thinking machines were defeated. And yet, within two decades of the Battle of Corrin, Emperor Jules had amended the agreement to "allow competition."

Josef remained incensed that his family's risk and hard work had been brushed aside, but he had also changed with the new rules. Only VenHold knew the secret of creating and training Navigators, who could actually encompass the cosmos in their minds and envision safe pathways through foldspace.

Saturated with melange gas, floating in suspensor fields, the Navigator-candidates turned their thoughts inward to a landscape of surreal physics and mathematics. As their minds changed and expanded, their need for spice became insatiable. Just as Josef's need for more Navigators was insatiable.

Although Cioba could occasionally get through to her, talking about their common Rossak connections, Josef was the only one who could regularly communicate with Norma. Originally, her son Adrien Venport—one of the key figures in establishing the Venport commercial empire—had served as Norma's liaison with the outside world for many years. In his later days, when his body was failing, Adrien had finally let his mother convince him to go into a spice tank himself where he hoped to transform into a similarly evolved creature, but Adrien was too old and his body too inflexible, and he had drowned in the melange gas. Grieving and withdrawn, Norma Cenva hadn't been close to another human in years . . . until Josef had gotten through to her.

Now he stood before her tank, addressed the speakerpatch, then waited, knowing that it sometimes took minutes for her attention to shift so that she noticed him. When Norma finally replied from within the tank, her voice was ethereal, drifting, synthesized. He had no idea what her actual vocal cords sounded like now, or even if they still functioned. "Have you brought more ships?" she asked. Sometimes Norma was perfectly articulate and comprehensible, sometimes distant and obtuse. It all depended on how much attention she gave him.

"We've had some successes and some setbacks."

"Need more ships, more Navigators, more spice. The universe is waiting."

In response, he said, "We don't have Navigators for all the vessels currently online. We need more Navigators to guide the ships to haul the spice to create more Navigators."

Norma paused for a moment, pondering. "I see the conundrum."

"And more volunteers to undergo the transformation," Cioba added. That was the true bottleneck. "Few are willing to pay the price."

"The reward is the entire universe," Norma said.

"If only it were that simple," Josef said. She truly didn't understand.

As more and more vessels were added to the Venport fleet, the greatest need was finding enough volunteers to attempt the Navigator transformation—and having enough of them survive—to serve aboard the new ships. Someday, Josef hoped that all of the Navigator-candidates would be *willing* volunteers; as it was, he needed to work with the material he had available.

He and Cioba had discussed the problem at length, and she had even presented the offer to Reverend Mother Raquella, but so far none of the Sisters had volunteered to transform themselves. How did one induce an intelligent candidate to enclose himself in a small prison filled with toxic amounts of spice gas, and undergo an extreme physical and mental transformation? It was a tough sell.

"I'm doing what I can," he said. "Please be patient."

"I am patient," Norma said. "I can wait forever." She fell silent, pondering, then said, "I am guiding these candidates through their mental exercises. They will be good Navigators." Her enlarged eyes and flattened features drifted close to the smeared porthole. "For all the technology that drives our spacefolder ships, the fleet still depends upon a human brain." Her thoughts wandered, and Josef thought he had lost her attention, but then Norma spoke up again. "Need more ships. Need more Navigators. Need more spice. Therefore, we need more ships."

Although she understood seemingly impossible things, Norma didn't grasp the sprawling business interests that Josef had established. Not surprisingly, she also no longer cared about the nuances of politics, which was why Josef had to watch over her.

He spoke up. "There are many ships—former machine ships—that VenHold can refit as passenger and cargo vessels. Whole fleets drift abandoned in space, but it's a race to find the available ships before the Butlerians do. They destroy the robot craft whenever they find them—vandals and terrorists in the name of their cause." His voice rose with anger.

"Then stop them," Norma said. "They should not destroy ships we need."

"Even Emperor Salvador turns a blind eye when the fanatics destroy the ships," Cioba said. "I think he's afraid of the Butlerians."

"The Emperor should stop them." Norma fell silent, drifting in her tank. Josef sensed she was deeply troubled. Finally, in her alien voice, she said, "I shall ponder this." Then she drifted back into the thickening cinnamon mist.

Whether you see mankind's future as light or dark depends upon how you filter the flow of data streaming back to you.

—NORMA CENVA

S alvador Corrino was not having a good day; in fact, he could not recall the last day he'd considered even acceptable. Much of that was his own fault, since his phobias were excessive compared to those of an average person, but the ruler of the vast Imperium was not an ordinary person; everything about him was supposed to be larger than life. While the Emperor suffered for his concerns, he wished he could be as calm and even-keeled as his brother, Roderick.

Today, Salvador was plagued by an infernal, unrelenting headache. He desperately needed to find a reliable doctor, one who did not make him suspicious. No one could match the attentive Dr. Elo Bando, former head of the Suk Medical School, who had truly understood the Emperor's pains and worries, a medical expert who had offered so many beneficial (though expensive) treatments. If only the damned man hadn't committed suicide. . . .

Though the famed school had moved its new headquarters to Parmentier, their old school building remained nearby in Zimia. Salvador requested their best doctors to tend him, but they sent someone different for each of his ailments, each time he experienced a twinge or imagined a new dire physical problem. Doctor after doctor, and none of them could find anything wrong with him. Incompetents! Salvador still hadn't found a new doctor he liked . . . and this one—he couldn't even remember the man's name—seemed no better than the rest.

He knew the guests would all be waiting in the Banquet Hall for the evening meal, but the Corrino Emperor was not ready, and they would just have to be patient. He couldn't be expected to attend a tedious banquet with his head pounding his thoughts to distraction.

In his dressing room, Salvador slumped back in a plush chair while the latest Suk doctor leaned over him, humming an annoying tune as he affixed probe strips to the ruler's balding pate. The doctor's long reddish hair was secured in a silver ring at the shoulder. He read signals on his handheld monitor, and the tone of his humming changed. "That's quite a headache you have."

"A brilliant diagnosis, Doctor. I don't need you to tell me that! Is it serious?"

"No need to be unduly concerned yet, though you do look rather thin and emaciated, Sire. Your skin seems pale."

"You're here to see about my headache, not my complexion."

When Salvador's father was seventy, a Suk doctor had diagnosed him with a brain tumor, but Emperor Jules refused to submit to high-tech medical procedures. Although Roderick, ever the voice of reason, had urged their father to seek the best treatment, Emperor Jules publicly supported the antitechnology Butlerian movement and shunned sophisticated doctors. And he had died.

Salvador did not want to make the same mistake.

"Here, let's see how this works for you." Still humming, the doctor adjusted the monitor, and Salvador felt massaging vibrations permeate his skull, as if his brain were immersed in a soothing liquid . . . like a cymek brain in a preservation canister. Instantly, he began to feel better.

The doctor smiled at his important patient's relieved expression. "Is that an improvement?"

"It will have to be good enough, for now. There's a banquet to attend." Salvador had been through this before. The headache might recede for now, but the tide would return soon. The Emperor got up and left without thanking him; this doctor would be gone before long, like all the rest.

As he suspected, the other dinner guests were already seated around the table, looking at their empty plates in anticipation of the first course. Salvador exchanged gazes with his brother, and noted that Roderick's auburn-haired wife, Haditha, sat farther down the table, talking with the slender Empress Tabrina. Good; she would keep the troublesome Tabrina occupied.

Despite the promise of tight security around the Emperor, some guests wore personal shields that shimmered faintly in the air. As was their custom, the entire royal family did as well, with the exception of Salvador's reclusive stepmother, Orenna, who had a personal dislike for many aspects of technology.

Down the table, Orenna sat straight-backed, willowy and haughty, a woman of sharp edges rather than soft curves, although she had been considered a great beauty in her day. The people still called her the Virgin Empress, because Emperor Jules had made it clear that he never consummated his marriage to her. Chatty Anna, the younger half-sister of Salvador and Roderick, sat next to Orenna; she and her stepmother had an oddly close relationship, often spending time together, sharing their secret thoughts.

Anna Corrino had short brown hair and a narrow face like the Emperor's; her eyes were small and blue. Though twenty-one, she seemed much younger, mentally and emotionally. Her moods swung like a pendulum on a storm-rocked boat, and she hadn't been entirely stable since suffering an emotional trauma as a child. But she was a Corrino, the Emperor's royal sister, and her flaws were overlooked.

Anna glared at Salvador as soon as he entered, her expression full of hurt and accusation. Knowing exactly why she was miffed, he sighed and felt his headache already coming back. Acting as her eldest brother, and as the Emperor, Salvador had put an end to the girl's inappropriate romance with a palace chef, Hirondo Nef. For some months now, Anna had allowed no one but Nef to prepare and deliver her food, but Salvador's spies had discovered that the chef was delivering more than dinner to his sister. What had the girl been thinking?

Entirely unfazed by the family drama that simmered beneath the surface of the social gathering, Roderick talked easily with Sister Dorotea, a lanky woman with a sensual feline face. A few days earlier, during Manford Torondo's alarming demands in the Landsraad Hall, Roderick had been surprised to discover that Dorotea sympathized with the Butlerians, unlike most of the Sisters of Rossak. Thankfully—with swift thinking, as usual—he had staged the bomb threat and disrupted the silly but dangerous vote.

Salvador didn't like the antitechnology fanatics; they were so intense, single-minded zealots who caused a lot of trouble. But he could not ignore their ever-growing numbers, their fervor, and their potential for violence. He had to tolerate them at least. Maybe Dorotea could act as a liaison, a buffer between himself and the charismatic leader. . . .

He certainly couldn't deny the benefits that Dorotea and the ten Sisters like her brought to the Imperial Court. The women who graduated from Rossak had extraordinary powers of observation and analysis, and Dorotea had indeed impressed him with her perceptiveness ever since she'd come to the Palace. Maybe *she* could talk some sense into his little sister before Anna got herself into more embarrassing trouble. . . .

Struggling to feign an aura of glowing health, the Emperor arrived at the head of the table. His guests rose to their feet (even Anna, grudgingly), but not his overdressed stepmother, who claimed to suffer from severe pains in her joints. Salvador had learned to ignore Lady Orenna's quirks and passive disrespect; she was his father's widow, after all, and deserved consideration for that, though in

Imperial matters she remained irrelevant. Since Jules's three children were all illegitimate, born from different mothers and none of them from his actual wife, Salvador supposed the old woman's annoyance could be excused.

He took his seat, and the other guests dutifully sat back down. Instantly, servants burst like spring-loaded projectiles from where they had been waiting in the wings. They served an appetizer in a flurry, a salad of blova-shrimp and savory hepnuts, presented on star-shaped leaves of lettuce. An attendant took up his position to taste the Emperor's food, in case it had been poisoned.

Roderick, though, waved the man away and leaned over to take a bite from the salad on his brother's plate. "I'll take care of this." Salvador reached out in alarm to stop him, but it was too late. Roderick chewed and swallowed. "The salad is very good." The blond, muscular man smiled, and everyone began to eat as he whispered to Salvador, "You're silly to worry so much about your food. It makes you look weak and frightened. You know I'd never let anything happen to you."

With a sigh of exasperation, Salvador began eating. Yes, he did know that Roderick would give his life to protect him, would risk poison or throw himself in front of an assassin's projectile. Alas, Salvador knew that he wouldn't do the same were the circumstances reversed. Roderick was a better person in almost every way.

Down the table, Empress Tabrina let out a loud laugh, and Haditha nodded, pleased by some amusing comment. Salvador looked wistfully at his brother's wife, not out of lust but out of envy for their relationship. Roderick's marriage to Haditha was stable, happy, and had produced four well-behaved children, while Salvador's marriage to Tabrina was as loveless as it was childless. Without doubt, the Empress was a great beauty, but lurking under that lovely exterior was a disagreeable, demanding personality.

Tabrina's wealthy mining family was a key supplier of strong, lightweight construction materials that were vitally needed for government projects, and Salvador had signed an agreement guaranteeing dire financial repercussions if the Emperor ever divorced her; there were even severe contractual penalties in the event of her premature death. Salvador had no way out now. It was a lousy contract and a lousy marriage.

Fortunately, he had eight concubines . . . not so many for a man of his position, and his father had certainly had plenty of lovers besides Empress Orenna. Tabrina might not approve, but it was established tradition, providing the rulers with other options than a loveless bed.

The other diners conversed in low tones, occasionally glancing in his direction. They were waiting for him to establish the subject of conversation, which he customarily did. His headache was already coming back.

Roderick noted the cue and took the lead to put his brother at ease, which Salvador appreciated. As they waited for the soup course, he raised a glass of white wine to the woman from Rossak. "Sister Dorotea, your school is mysterious, but quite impressive. Perhaps you can share some of your learning with us?"

"And perhaps not." Her brown feline eyes sparkled. "If we told our secrets, what need would there be for the Sisterhood?" Chuckles circled the table.

Roderick tipped his glass to her, conceding the point, and the discussion turned to the merits of the plethora of schools that had arisen since the end of the Jihad. "We are living in very exciting times, a renaissance of learning—so many schools specializing in the potential of the human mind and body."

Dorotea agreed. "It is imperative that humans see how far we can advance without oppression of thinking machines."

The Emperor received regular reports from across his vast realm. Schools were springing up like weeds around the Imperium, each one with a particular specialization, a focus on various mental or physical disciplines. The Emperor could not keep track of all the philosophies, although he assigned functionaries to monitor them. In addition to the Sisters of Rossak and the Suk doctors, Mentats were being taught on Lampadas, and adept Swordmasters continued to emerge from Ginaz. He had also just learned of a well-financed new Academy of Physiology on Irawok that included studies of kinesiology, anatomical functions, and nervous systems. And there were literally hundreds of other crackpot disciplines. *Educational cults*, he considered them.

Salvador took every opportunity to show public appreciation for his brother. "Roderick, unlike me, you are a fine physical specimen. Perhaps you could be an instructor at the new physiology academy, or even a recruiter!"

Roderick laughed and addressed Dorotea, while all the diners listened. "My brother doesn't mean it. I have too many important governmental duties."

"Quite true," Salvador said with not-so-feigned embarrassment. "Too often he needs to clean up after my mistakes."

Nervous laughter. Roderick made a dismissive gesture, continuing to focus on Dorotea. "And your advice has been invaluable as well, Sister."

Finally, servants began laying out the soup course. "As women complete their training," she said, "Reverend Mother Raquella sends the majority of our graduates out to assist noble families in the Landsraad League. We think the Sisterhood has much to offer. As for my own skills, I am particularly adept at determining truth from falsehood." She smiled at the two Corrino men. "Such as when one brother is lovingly teasing another."

"My family relationships are not so playful or loving," Anna blurted out, causing a hush to fall. "In fact, Salvador doesn't know much about love at all. He has no love in his own marriage, so he's determined to deny me a chance at romance." The young woman sniffed, obviously expecting a show of commiseration from her companions. Lady Orenna gave the girl a sympathetic pat on the shoulder. Empress Tabrina wore a completely stony expression.

Anna sat straighter, her eyes flashing at Salvador. "My brother shouldn't order me around in my personal life."

"No, but an *Emperor* can." Sister Dorotea's crisp voice filled the shocked lull at the table.

Good response, Salvador thought. *Now, how to get Anna out of here gracefully?* He exchanged glances with Roderick, and his brother rose to his feet. "Lady Orenna, would you be so kind as to take our sister back to her rooms?"

Anna remained petulant. Refusing to look at her stepmother or at Roderick, she kept her eyes focused on Salvador. "Separating me from Hirondo will not prevent us from loving each other! I'll find out where you've sent him, and I'll go there."

"Not tonight, though," Roderick said calmly and motioned to his stepmother again. After a brief hesitation, Orenna straightened from her chair, displaying the excellent posture of her station. Salvador noted that the older woman showed no apparent pain in her joints now as she took Anna's arm. The younger woman acquiesced at her touch, and the two departed the banquet hall with exaggerated dignity.

One guest dropped a silver fork on a charger plate with a loud clatter in the awkward silence. Salvador wondered how he was going to salvage the evening and hoped Roderick might say something clever to lighten the mood. Anna was proving to be an unruly embarrassment. Maybe she would have to be sent away somewhere. . . .

Just then, the air popped in the hall, and a large armored chamber materialized in the open area that was occasionally used by court musicians. A rush of wind swirled around the banquet table. Diners scrambled away, and palace guards ran forward in alarm, surrounding the Emperor to protect him. Automatically, he activated his personal shield.

Through clearplaz windows in the tank, Salvador saw orange gas and the shadowy silhouette of a mutated creature with an oversize head. He recognized the figure immediately, though she was rarely seen in public anymore. Over many decades Norma Cenva had evolved into a form that no longer looked human.

Ignoring the uproar among the diners in the hall, Salvador stood and faced the tank. At least it wasn't the drama of his little sister's romantic indiscretions. "This is a most unorthodox visit."

Silence fell in the hall when Norma's eerie voice emanated through speakers, as if from far across space. "I no longer require a spacefaring vessel. I can now fold space with my mind." She sounded fascinated by the very idea. The spice gas in her tank became agitated, making a storm of swirls.

Salvador cleared his throat. He had spoken with this mysterious woman only twice in the twelve years of his reign. She awed and intimidated him, but to his knowledge she had never harmed anyone with her extraordinary powers, "You are welcome in my court, Norma Cenva. Your contributions to our victory over the thinking machines are immeasurable. But why have you come here tonight? It must be something very important."

"I no longer relate to others. Bear with me as I attempt to express myself." Her large midnight eyes stared through the tank at Salvador, sending a chill of fear down his spine. "I see parts of the future, and I am concerned." She drifted in her tank, and Salvador remained silent and tense, waiting for her to continue. "To bind the Imperium, we must have a network of transportation and commerce. And for that we must have starships."

Salvador cleared his throat. "Yes, of course. We have the VenHold Spacing Fleet, Celestial Transport, and countless other enterprises."

Everyone remained hushed in the banquet hall. Then Norma said, "Thousands of machine vessels were abandoned in space. They are still intact. Those ships can be used for commerce, for civilization. But other groups destroy these vessels wherever they are found. Mobs cause great harm. I am very disturbed by this."

Salvador's throat went dry. "The Butlerians." Manford Toronto took pride in sending reports to enumerate the machine ships that his people ransacked and exploded. "They act on their convictions. Some would call their fervor admirable."

"They destroy valuable resources that could be used to strengthen human civilization. You must stop them." The rusty swirls of gas cleared away, revealing Norma with all of the hideous, deformed details of her body—the stunted torso, the tiny hands and feet, the grossly large head and eyes, the nearly invisible mouth, nose, and ears. "Or your Imperium will fragment and die."

Salvador was left entirely without a response. He had no idea how he could stamp out the Butlerian movement, even if he wanted to. Before he could come up with excuses, however, Norma Cenva folded space, and her tank vanished from the banquet hall, leaving only a *pop* of displaced air.

Emperor Salvador shook his head and muttered with forced levity, "Amazing what those Navigators can do."

A quiet observer may learn countless secrets, but I prefer to be an active participant.

—ERASMUS, secret laboratory notebooks

In order to keep his thoughts and memories in precise, accessible order, a Mentat required a certain amount of meditation and mental practice every day, uninterrupted hours of quiet contemplation. As the headmaster of the school, Gilbertus Albans kept his office private, an isolated sanctuary where he could wall himself off and focus on improving his mind. Students, fellow instructors, and school administrators knew not to disturb him when he was inside his sealed office chamber.

No one guessed what he was really doing there.

The Erasmus memory core sat exposed on its stand, completely engaged in conversation. When Gilbertus paced around the office, the independent robot spoke up. "Do you realize you taunt me just by moving about, flaunting your freedom by pacing back and forth?"

Gilbertus took a seat at his desk, pushed a wisp of hair out of his eyes. "I'm sorry. I'll stay seated."

Erasmus chuckled. "You realize that does nothing to solve the problem."

"And yet it keeps you alive. You must accept certain sacrifices and limitations in order to continue to exist. I saved you from Corrin."

"And I appreciate that, but you speak of eighty years ago."

Gilbertus enjoyed sparring and debating with his old mentor. "Weren't you the one to tell me that machines have infinite patience?"

"True, but I was not made to be a passive observer. I have too many experiments to perform, too much to learn about the intriguing inconsistencies in human behavior."

"I understand your predicament, Father, but you will have to content yourself with studying the material I provide—until we find some other solution. I can't stay here forever." Gilbertus had already reached the limit where casual observers had begun to wonder about his perfect health, how he seemed quite young for his years, though he altered his appearance to look older. In order to keep secret the life-extension treatment he'd received from Erasmus, Gilbertus had fostered the rumor that he consumed melange regularly, and the geriatric properties of spice gave him a youth and vigor beyond his years. Although he kept records of his spice purchases, he never consumed the substance. The last thing Gilbertus Albans needed was something to make him look even younger.

The robot spoke up again. "If I am to be a scholar, then I must study human interactions. Despite this frustrating isolation, I have been able to tap into the school's power conduits and ventilation systems. With the materials at hand, I created an even more extensive network of optic fibers, tiny remote spyeyes, so I can watch the day-to-day activities of your school. It is fascinating."

"If your spyeyes are discovered, the Butlerians might burn down the school."

"Illogical but interesting," Erasmus said. "I will trust your conclusion, after my experiences with provocative and shockingly unpredictable human behavior."

From his desk, Gilbertus withdrew a printed document that had been submitted for the library at the Mentat School. "I have obtained a new history released by the Butlerians, which focuses on destroying your reputation."

"Another one?"

"See the title, *The Tyranny of the Demon Robot Erasmus*." He raised the book, and the optic threads implanted in the room's walls and ceiling drank in the cover of the tome.

Erasmus chuckled again. "That does not sound objective."

"I thought you enjoyed the propaganda aspects of historical accounts."

"It always amuses me how a person with no firsthand knowledge of events can distort the facts with such vehemence. When I read Agamemnon's memoirs, I saw how the cymek general distorted history. It took me a long time to discover that humans do not appreciate or even want the truth. Machines, on the other hand, would be at a great disadvantage if they knowingly used false data to draw their conclusions."

Gilbertus let out a bright laugh. "I think you enjoy being so reviled."

The robot pondered this. "I was hated for many centuries by my labor crews, my household slaves. Even Serena Butler despised me, and she was one of my favorite humans of all time. You, Gilbertus, are the only one who has ever seen my true worth."

"And even I am still learning," Gilbertus replied. In fact, he had read the histories himself and knew from his own observations that the robot had indeed committed most of the horrors attributed to him.

Erasmus sounded impatient. "Open the book. I want to read what the Butlerians say about me."

Gilbertus dutifully turned page after page so that Erasmus could scan and absorb the words. "Ah, I was not aware that the Butlerians had access to my laboratory notebooks. One of the volumes was recovered from Corrin after the battle? I'm so glad the records were preserved, although I am disturbed that this author—and presumably the readers of this volume—could draw such ridiculous conclusions from my carefully researched data. I believe I understand more about human suffering than humans themselves do," Erasmus said. Gilbertus could imagine him shaking the smooth and beautiful flowmetal head he used to have. "However, if you would find a way to provide me with a sophisticated body again, I could continue my important work."

"You know that wouldn't be wise at this time." Although he loved the independent robot for all of the tremendous opportunities he'd given him, Gilbertus was wary and protective. Despite his mental acuity, Erasmus wasn't fully cognizant of the dangers he would face if ever he emerged from hiding. And Gilbertus didn't entirely trust what the robot might do.

"I wish the humans hadn't made such a mess of things," Erasmus said, simulating a long sigh. "The thousand years of machine rule were quite efficient and well organized. I fear the galaxy will never be the same."

Gilbertus closed *The Tyranny of the Demon Robot Erasmus.* "I don't disagree, but you may be overlooking a key insight."

"A key insight?" Erasmus sounded delighted. "Share it with me."

"It serves no purpose for you to criticize the humans for their rebellion, when you yourself were the catalyst. You personally were the direct cause of the downfall of the machine empire."

Erasmus sounded offended. "How so? I might have inadvertently contributed in some small way by dropping Serena's baby from the tower—"

"In every way," Gilbertus countered. "None of the machine defeat would have happened without you. *You* posed the challenge to Omnius, deciding to question the loyalty of the human slaves who had previously shown no evidence of organized resistance. *You* suggested that you could trick some of your slavemasters into turning against the machines. *You* planted the hints of a human rebellion."

"It was an interesting experiment," Erasmus said.

"And it destroyed the Synchronized Empire. Without *you,* Iblis Ginjo would never have organized his rebel cells, would never have considered overthrowing the Omnius worlds. When you killed the infant son of Serena Butler by throwing him off a balcony in front of a great crowd, *you* touched a spark to the tinder that you yourself had laid."

"An unusual conclusion." Erasmus sounded hesitant, then admitted, "When viewed in that light, perhaps I was responsible."

Gilbertus stood from his desk. "Ponder that, Father, when you're feeling restless and isolated here. If you had been more careful, the machine empire would never have fallen. And because you're all that's left, and because I worry about you, I don't intend to be careless."

He closed the robot's memory core back in its hidden cabinet, making sure all the locks and seals were in place. Then he went off to instruct his students on how to order their minds more like those of thinking machines.

History may remember me with awe, terror, or hatred. I don't care, so long as I am not forgotten.

—GENERAL AGAMEMNON, *New Memoirs*

L eading a small group of Butlerian hunters, Swordmaster Ellus felt more like a scavenger than a predator. Omnius and his robotic forces had been utterly defeated, and even their deactivated remnants could pose no threat; the rebellious cymeks had also been wiped out, leaving dead walker bodies and obscure empty outposts.

But cleanup remained to be done.

In the icy ruins of the last cymek stronghold on Hessra, human investigators had discovered a database compiled by the notorious Titan Juno, records listing the locations of many secret cymek bases, and Manford had commanded that each one be destroyed before the bases fell into the hands of corruptible humans like Josef Venport. Methodically, Ellus and his hunters were going to each set of coordinates in the Hessra records and leaving the machine bases in smoldering ruins. The mission would last for six months or longer, and he would be out of contact with Butlerian headquarters except to submit occasional progress reports.

During their years of ruthless physical training on Ginaz, Ellus and Anari Idaho—comrades, rivals, occasional lovers—had been fascinated by the legends of Serena Butler's glorious Jihad. Captivated by stories of those heroic days, he and Anari wished they could have been fighting armies of combat robots or ferocious cymek walkers, but they had been born a century too late. All that remained now was a mop-up operation to eradicate the leftovers . . . but it was a job that needed to be done.

His scout ship arrived at the next location—a cratered, airless rock that barely met the definition of a planet. Robots had no need for an atmosphere, and cymek brains, protected inside their preservation canisters, could live anywhere. If this system hadn't been noted in the secret cymek records, no one would have bothered to go there.

"Scan closely and keep your eyes open," Ellus said to his Butlerian comrades. "Look for artificial structures. There's got to be something here."

Ellus had spent years on Ginaz learning how to fight with a pulse-sword against salvaged combat meks. He and Anari had done well, killing many of their machine opponents and feeling like gladiators in an ancient arena. But it was all for show. The thinking machines had been long defeated.

The Swordmaster fantasized about finding a still-functioning base crowded with evil thinking machines—worthy opponents at last for a man of his fighting skills. It would be like turning over a rock and discovering an infestation of tiny black beetles. That, however, was a private thought that he did not dare discuss with anyone. Not even dear Anari.

Ellus felt driven, but also calmly confident. Each step brought the Butlerians closer to eradicating all vestiges of thinking machines, though no closer to forgetting them. What would they do when there was nothing left? When the thinking machines were completely gone, the movement would lack focus and purpose. *If there is no enemy, do we just create a new one?* Manford's followers couldn't just go around smashing everything that contained electronics or moving parts—that would be foolish and misguided, and would inevitably force them to shun even the workings of their own spacecraft.

The ship cruised over the stark landscape, where distant, unfiltered sunlight cast the crags and canyons into sharp relief. Ellus's team members—six Butlerians and two more Swordmasters—peered through the windowports and scanned the surface before erupting into chatter. "There it is, sir! On the left side of that crater."

"By God and Saint Serena, it looks like the war's already been fought here," said Alon, one of the two other Swordmasters with the team.

Ellus caught a glint of metallic domes and habitation chambers—clearly an outpost or a base. Several of the outpost domes were smashed, and the rocky landscape was pocked with divots and craters surrounded by black starbursts of debris—clearly the result of recent explosions rather than ancient impacts. Mangled cymek walkers lay strewn about, their crablike legs smashed and bent. Robot attack ships had crashed on the crater floor.

"This must have occurred during the civil war between the cymeks and Omnius," Ellus said. "This was a secret cymek base, and the combat robots fought them here." He gazed intently at the view below. "Looks like the two sides wiped each other out."

"Let's hope they left something for us to trash," Swordmaster Alon said with a chuckle. "Otherwise this was a long and wasted trip."

"If there's anything left, we'll get rid of it." Ellus turned to his pilot. "Find a place to land so we can make our way inside."

They found the core of the laboratory facility still intact, and the ship managed to dock with an access hatch. The atmosphere inside read as frigid, but surprisingly breathable. The power was still on and life-support systems functioning. "Everyone, join us inside and assist with the operation," Ellus announced. They would all want their chance.

"They must have conducted experiments with humans here," said Kelian, the third Swordmaster, "or they wouldn't have bothered with heat and air."

"If we find records inside, maybe we can discover what the cymeks were doing and what happened during this battle," said one of the Butlerians. Ellus had not bothered to learn all of their names.

He raised his voice, brisk and businesslike. "Such answers don't concern us. We just have to get rid of this place, for it is inherently dangerous." He shuddered to think what might happen if some ambitious person, such as Josef Venport, were to find this site and try to recreate the abominable work of the cymeks.

Once the entire team crossed over to the outpost, the Butlerians began to move through the chambers, ransacking and destroying. They needed no explicit orders.

Swordmaster Alon discovered experimental logs kept in a set of nonsentient computer databases, but the Butlerians pummeled the machines into wreckage without reading them. Specimens, frozen tissue samples, dissected brains, gelcircuitry patterns, and reservoirs of vibrant-blue electrafluid filled shelves and storage lockers.

The full destruction took hours. Ellus could have bombarded the whole outpost from the hunter ship, but he believed in doing things properly, providing him and his comrades with emotional satisfaction that they could pass on to their superior. Ellus included as many details as he could remember in his reports to Manford, so that the Butlerian leader could imagine that he had participated.

As the destruction continued, Ellus and the other two Swordmasters made their way to the center of the complex, a nightmarish chamber filled with glistening, forbidden machinery and computer technology. Looking like an intaglio etched in the glass, frost covered the inner window of a thick door that led to a sealed vault. Ellus bent closer, wondering what further horrors the cymeks might have been working on, and peered through the frost-dusted window into the armored vault. Was there some specific reason the thinking machines had come to eradicate this secret cymek place?

Inside, he saw two standing forms: the slender human figures of a man and a woman. The two had no wristbands or shackles holding them prisoner. Both were petrified, sheathed in a thin coating of frost.

Ellus summoned Alon and Kelian to his side while he studied the chamber controls, trying to determine the most likely way to unseal the door. With only clubs, battering rams, and pry bars, the three Swordmasters would never get through that massive hatch. Fortunately, even though he knew little about technology, the controls were intuitive, perhaps even willingly cooperative, as if some small demon still lived within the computer system and wanted to cause mischief. In only a few minutes, the vault door hissed open with a gasp of roiling, chemical-scented air. Ellus held his breath for fear the gas might be poison, but it dissipated quickly.

A small glow of station lights lit the cold vault without flickering, illuminating the preserved man and woman. They were about twenty years old, trim and perfect in appearance, with dark hair, delicate features, and a line of frost on their eyebrows and lips. Both were naked.

Ellus felt disgust like a heavy weight inside. "These poor people. They must have been victims of experiments."

Kelian said, "Manford would want us to give them a respectful burial."

"The mind of man is holy," Alon intoned.

In seeming disagreement with the assessment of their deaths, the young man and woman simultaneously opened their eyes, gray orbs that stared unfocused, then sharpened. The duo shivered, twitched their shoulders, and inhaled a loud drowning-person's breath. With a shout, Ellus rushed to catch the young woman before she could collapse, but she brushed aside the assistance with unexpected strength and went ramrod straight.

The young man stepped forward, gave a cobweb-clearing shake of his head. "That was a long time waiting. Has it been decades . . . or centuries?"

"We've released you now. You're safe," Ellus said. "Who are you?"

The young woman spoke up. "I am Hyla, and this is my twin Andros."

"Are we free now?" the man asked.

The Swordmasters led them out of the cold chamber. "Yes, you're free—we saved you," Ellus said.

Kelian added, "Omnius and the thinking machines are no more. The cymeks have all been destroyed, every last one of them. We were victorious! You are safe—your long nightmare is over."

The twins looked at each other, cocking their heads to listen. In other chambers of the complex, Ellus could hear wanton smashing as the Butlerians destroyed the machinery, the computers.

"Fortunately, we found you in time," Ellus said. "We will soon finish demolishing this base."

Andros's eyes narrowed, and his face went tight. "They shouldn't be doing that."

"We travel to every known machine base and erase all vestiges of the cymek reign of terror," said Swordmaster Alon. "That is our mission. Once we grind everything under our heels, those dark memories will never bother us again."

A ripple of rage swept like a dust storm across the strange young man's face. His skin flickered, the pale flesh tone taking on a metallic cast, as if mercury flowed just beneath the skin. Andros flattened his hand, which became as rigid as steel, and he slashed sideways in an effortless karate chop that cleanly decapitated the Swordmaster.

Even before blood could spurt from the stump of Alon's neck, the young woman sprang into motion. Hyla shoved her fist through Kelian's chest, crushing his sternum and pushing all the way through his spine.

Swordmaster Ellus had just enough time to bring up his sword, and Hyla parried the blade with her armored-skin forearm. A metallic sound rang out, and the unexpected jarring nearly dislocated Ellus's arm. He had fought against the most sophisticated combat meks on Ginaz; his sensei-instructor had challenged him with the highest and fastest settings in the battle robot's memory. But none of that had prepared him for these twins.

The young woman grasped Ellus's sword with both hands and snapped the blade in half, then struck a hard blow on the base of his neck, crushing his spine and paralyzing him. The last Swordmaster dropped to the floor, still awake, still aware.

Three flushed and giddy Butlerians entered the room just as Ellus fell. Grinning, Andros leaped forward and began tearing them limb from limb.

Hyla stood over the paralyzed Ellus, gazing down at him, her face young, beautiful, and inhuman. The Swordmaster heard screams as her brother finished murdering the three Butlerians in the chamber, then bounded down the connecting passages to hunt the rest of them. None of those people stood a chance.

Hyla leaned closer to Ellus and said, "We are the children of Agamemnon. My brother and I have been awake here for decades with nothing to do but wonder, and question, and wait. Now, before I finish killing you, tell me exactly what has happened in the intervening years. We need to know."

The Swordmaster clamped his mouth shut.

In the adjoining module, another set of horrified screams rang out, echoing off the curved metal walls.

"*Tell me.*" Hyla bent down, extended a forefinger, and began to toy with his eye.

Slavery can take many forms. Some are overt, while others are discreet.
All are reprehensible.

　　　　　　—VORIAN ATREIDES, *The Legacy Journals*, Kepler period

The slave markets on Poritrin covered a vast area of the muddy and humid Isana River plain. Vorian felt discouraged to see the clutter of ships landing and departing, the burgeoning crowds in the marketplace. Locating one group of captives in all this would be nearly impossible, yet he had led the generations-long fight against Omnius—and the human race had won, beating all odds. Yes, he would find his people.

But it was going to take some effort.

Poritrin had long engaged in the buying and selling of slaves. During the crusade against the thinking machines, many planetary populations had refused to join the fight, hiding from the most important battle mankind had ever faced. For that reason, other humans had felt justified in forcing the pacifists to work for the greater good.

Now, however, the Jihad was over and the thinking machines defeated. As Vor walked among the jostling people, he could no longer imagine any rationale for slavery, but the practice continued anyway. Too much money and power was involved in the operations, and some of Imperial society still depended on these slave markets. Morally obsolete, but still profitable. He knew, however, that a new justification had developed as an unexpected side effect of the antitechnology fervor. With many planets naïvely abandoning sophisticated machinery in the wake of the growing Butlerian movement, they required a large labor pool to do the work. To some people, he supposed, slaves were more palatable than machines. . . .

Vor had been to many planets in his life, more than he could remember offhand. In his early years, he had accompanied the robot Seurat all across the Synchronized Worlds in an update ship, delivering copies of the Omnius ever-mind. Once he switched his loyalties to the League Worlds, he had fought the thinking machines on planet after planet, for more than a century. Here, on Poritrin, he had carried out an ambitious scheme of building a gigantic fleet of faux warships—a massive bluff that had intimidated the Omnius fleet, a wonder-fully successful trick.

He hadn't been to Poritrin in many, many years.

As a sideshow in the middle of Serena Butler's Jihad, a massive slave upris-ing on this planet had wrought great devastation. A pseudo-atomic explosion annihilated much of the city of Starda and killed the legendary scientist Tio Holtzman, a great blow to humanity's defenses.

But the explosion had merely cleared a crowded section of town. The low-lands were now paved over, the ground fused, the pooling waters constrained within rigid canals. A kaleidoscope of temporary structures crowded the open areas where slavers brought their cargos, offered them for sale, then took down the tents and flew away as new flesh merchants swooped in to grab the opened space. Catering to them, vendors offered lodging, food, drugs, massage services, prostitutes, and moneylending.

In a sad way, he realized that not much had changed.

Keeping his eyes open and forming a plan for his search, Vor found himself swallowed in a stew of humanity as he moved through New Starda, absorbing the size and structure of the place. He was surrounded by grit and odors and city noises, and just walking along the streets and alleys felt like making his way through a pitched battle against combat meks.

Vor longed for the quiet and peace of isolated Kepler, hunting gornet birds in the hills. Now he had to hunt for his family, friends, and neighbors, and bring them home. They were captives here—surely still alive because dead slaves had no value. He needed to find them quickly before they were split up and sold off to dozens of different buyers. He would free them at whatever cost, take them back with him . . . and find some way to protect the world he had adopted as his own for the past half century.

During his flight from Kepler, recalling all the photos Mariella had spread around in their home, Vor had painstakingly assembled a list of his sons and daughters, his adult grandchildren, their spouses, the neighbors, the fellow farmers in the valley, missing friends, anyone he could remember. He had to make certain he left no one behind.

As he walked through the slave market, he found a roly-poly slave vendor setting up a stand. When Vor showed him the list of names, the man pursed his lips, looked at him in surprise. "Your first mistake, sir, is thinking that we keep track of individual names. The items offered for sale are not individuals with separate identities. They are mere tools to do a task." He raised his eyebrows. "Would you name a pry bar or a hammer?"

Remembering how Xavier Harkonnen would have laid out a detailed battle plan, Vor next went to a Poritrin tourism office, where guides advertised tours of the canyons upriver or zeppelin flights over the open plains. He expected the government-sponsored office to know the layout of the slave markets, perhaps offering a map or guide, but the smiling official was no help at all.

Vorian Atreides made further inquiries and paid bribes. Over the centuries, he had amassed quite a fortune, now dispersed in various far-flung accounts around the Imperium. The wealth meant little to him, since he had everything he needed and did not live an extravagant lifestyle. Fortunately, the new banking system offered by VenHold linked those accounts, so Vor had access to his funds. He could be generous with his inducements, but simple questions raised too many questions of their own.

Despite his increasing sense of urgency, haunted by the faces of all the people he had lived with on Kepler, the social tapestry that had made his life feel so complete, he decided to take a different tack, thinking like a businessman rather than an aggrieved party. Vorian Atreides had deceived entire armies of thinking machines; he could certainly outwit a few slavers.

Among the crowded stalls, the tall, dark-haired man spoke to one of the dragoon police guards who patrolled the markets. "I'm willing to pay for solid, verified information. I have a large construction project in a particularly hot and humid area of my planet. Surely, you keep track of where the slaves come from? I don't want to buy a workforce from a cold world, or an arid one. I've done my research, and I need people accustomed to the climate, or I'll lose half of my workers in a week."

The guard pursed his lips. "I take your meaning, sir. New Starda is in the process of instituting records to help match certain kinds of slaves to compatible environments. Alas, the formal system is caught up in committee right now and not readily available." He shrugged.

Vor recognized the tantalizing hint and hesitation as a subtle request for a bribe. So, he offered money, and the dragoon scratched the side of his face, as if thinking through the problem, although he already had a solution. "I know a woman in spaceport administration who has access to landing and cargo records. Such information is not normally open to inspection, but if you give her my name and pay her a . . . discretionary fee, she will let you inspect the records of all slaving ships that have arrived recently."

Vor maintained his cool expression, though his pulse began to race. He had seen the three slaving ships that preyed upon Kepler; hopefully he would find them in the documentation.

The dragoon pocketed his payment with a deft movement. "It may require some homework on your part, but maybe you can look at the source planet information and find workers to your liking."

AT THE SPACEPORT, Vor had to pay three more bribes just to find the woman he was supposed to meet, then another large sum to gain access to the landing records. The money didn't matter; he would pay whatever was necessary. In his brash earlier years, he and Xavier might have tried to coerce the information, fighting for justice, but this method was, ironically, more civilized, though more expensive.

He couldn't overthrow an entire world or a long-standing way of life. Seeing the long lists of human cargo tore at his heart. All those captives had been torn from their homes on hundreds of poorly defended planets, leaving behind families who were just as distraught as he was. But Vorian Atreides was only one man, and he was done crusading. His personal crusade now was to save the people he loved.

When he reviewed the extensive records, the sheer number of vessels surprised him. Even back in the heyday of Salusa Secundus, he doubted the League's capital city had ever experienced so much traffic. So, slavery was definitely not on the wane.

After several hours, he discovered what he was looking for: a notation of a group of three ships whose previous destination was listed as *Kepler*. The records showed images of the vessels for security purposes, and he recognized the ships that had landed on the croplands after blasting the village with widespread stun fields.

He clenched his jaw to contain his anger, wishing the one captive slaver had lived just a little longer so Vor could have learned more details about the captains and crews. But he developed his plan with the information he knew.

Highest priority: To get his people back safely, all of them. His secondary, and more enjoyable, mission was to hurt the slavers. If he planned well enough, he could accomplish both.

He took the time to purchase a new formfitting suit and assumed the identity of a wealthy businessman from Pirido. He even bought a small well-trained lapdog with a jewel-studded collar, who trotted happily beside his new master as Vor strolled through the slave markets to the appropriate grid location. There, he hired four young men and purchased similar clothing for them, so they could accompany him as his entourage, with strict instructions that they were not to say anything.

Following the grid map he had purchased, they then marched off to the specific landing slots and the holding areas where the ships kept their human cargo. When Vor spotted the three hulking vessels near the holding area, he remembered them clearly, having seen them lift off from the valley on Kepler, laden with captives.

Yes, he had found exactly the right place.

Getting in character, he put on a haughty air and gave a withering frown to the thick-lipped but thin-voiced man who prevented him from marching directly to the holding pens. "You aren't allowed to get close to the slaves, sir. They're valuable merchandise."

"Then you, my good man, don't know how things are done here." Vor sniffed. He knew his people were there, just on the other side of the holding fence, and he tensed, willing to kill this man if necessary. But if he broke the captives free and tried to escape, he knew he would not get far . . . not here on Poritrin. So he remained in character. "If I intend to bid on the whole lot of these new arrivals, I want to inspect their health. I'm not going to buy any weak, sick, or dirty slaves. They would soil my entire planet! How do I know they're not infested with Chusuk tapeworms? Or blood boils?"

The slaver's fleshy lips tugged downward in a frown. "They'll have full medical clearance, don't you worry. We take good care of them—lost only two during the flight here from Kepler."

"*Only* two? Hmm." Vor had to fight to keep the look of disgust from his face. Which two? Was it Bonda? His grandson Brandis? The names rolled across his mind. That meant two more dead, plus the ten who had died resisting the initial raid . . . people he knew and loved. His sneer was not feigned. "Sounds shameful to me. I don't recall VenHold Spacing Fleet or Celestial Transport routinely losing passengers on any voyage."

With a grunt, the slaver ran his eyes up and down Vor's fastidious garments, his four silent followers, and the prissy dog. "In any business operation involving cargoes, there's a certain amount of damage in shipment. Those people go on sale tomorrow morning. We'll have them cleaned up by then."

"And well fed, I assume?"

"They'll be ready for sale."

The slaver was obviously not going to let him get any closer, so Vor drank in the visible security measures around the ships. He nodded to his entourage, gave a slight tug on the leash, and the dog turned about and trotted faithfully beside him. "I'll be back in the morning."

He rented a room, promised the four followers another payment if they joined him the following day, and then hunkered down inside the room to continue his planning. The dog sat on his lap, perfectly content. Although twice Vor found himself absently petting the small creature while he strategized, he refused to give it a name—it, too, was merely a tool.

Once landed on Poritrin in the New Starda markets, slavers used security measures to manage and protect their human cargoes, but the empty ships themselves were easy targets. In his younger days, he and Xavier Harkonnen would have staged a military operation, bringing in armed soldiers to attack the slaver ships. Vor would have had no qualms about killing the captain and crew, seizing their captives, and perhaps even freeing hordes of other slaves as well. Swashbuckling mayhem, using more brawn and testosterone than brains.

But that was a foolish idea, and not the most effective means to secure his loved ones. Vor wondered how he and Xavier had ever survived back then. He didn't dare attempt anything so bold now—too many of his own people might be harmed—so he thought of a more practical, mature solution instead.

Only after he was certain he could get his family and friends back, would he cause a little extra mayhem. . . .

The next morning, he and the pampered-looking dog, followed by four earnest-looking young men in Pirido clothing, arrived at the start of the appropriate auction. They worked their way to the front of a swelling crowd of spectators, investors, and even a few hecklers who had nothing better to do than jeer at the miserable slaves, trolling from one auction to the next. In the New Starda slave market, numerous similar auctions were being held this morning; the people around him saw nothing special in this particular sale.

The auction master called the crowd to order, and the burly slave hunters prodded the ranks of captives onto a levitating stage two meters above the ground. Vor watched the forlorn group file up, all of them bound and dispirited looking. His appearance was so different now, though, that he didn't expect any of them to recognize him. The dog barked, then fell silent in the hubbub.

Emotions roiled inside him as he recognized so many faces. He was angry to see his people this way, yet overjoyed to see them alive, and determined to get them back home to their normal lives. They were indeed clean, but gaunt. He noted a few bruises on pale skin, but no overt signs of brutalization. He saw Deenah, a beloved niece who was herself a mother now, his sons Oren and Clar, daughter Bonda and her husband Tir, and dozens of others. He would have to compare them all against his list of missing persons from Kepler—he would track down any stragglers if necessary, but he hoped he had arrived in time.

"We have an opening bid of six thousand Solaris," said the auction master, after someone shouted out the amount. A second customer bid seven thousand. Another jumped to ten thousand amidst a ripple of admiring mutters. Vor said nothing, just waited. The bidding gradually rose to fifteen thousand, then twenty thousand. Then someone requested that the slaves be divided into smaller lots and that the bidding be continued by specified groups. The bidder promised to pay a premium but only for the healthy males.

Vor knew he had to act. He raised his voice before the auctioneer could consider the proposal. "Thirty thousand Solaris for the whole lot, with immediate delivery." He could have paid less, but he wanted to make a point.

A rush of indrawn breath rippled through the crowd. The four young men in his entourage looked at him with surprise; one wore an impish grin, sure that this was part of a larger scam.

"Could you repeat that, sir?" said the auction master, with a great deal of respect.

"Thirty thousand Solaris, but only if I can take possession of them right away. All of them." The amount was enough to buy an entire continent on some small planets. "Or do you want to waste my time?"

The Kepler captives on the platform stirred, whispering to one another, looking at the man who had made such a bid . . . the man who would be their master. His daughter Bonda had recognized Vor as soon as he made his bid. He could see it in her eyes.

The auction master hesitated, though no one expected the bid to be topped. "Sold, to the gentleman with the dog—the entire lot of slaves from planet Kepler."

After the smattering of applause died away and Vor paid for the slaves, he knew he had to make his point. "Now, free them—remove their bonds." The slavers hesitated, but he remained firm. "They are my property, and I can do with them as I choose."

"That may be dangerous, sir." The auction master raised a hand to summon a dragoon guard. "These are fresh slaves, not yet broken or trained."

Handing the dog to one of the young men in his entourage, Vor strode to the edge of the hovering platform and swung himself onto the stage. "I'll clip the bonds myself if I must."

He didn't care about the angry grumbling as he used his own dagger to cut the nearest two prisoners free, his two overjoyed sons, Oren and Clar. "Do I have to do all this myself? Maybe I'll withhold part of my fee as compensation for the inconvenience." The burly slavers moved quickly to cut the rest of the captives free.

Vor turned to shout out at the audience. "For centuries, the thinking machines enslaved our men and women, and we sacrificed half of the human race for liberty. And yet you—all of you—perpetuate this. You should understand more about freedom by now."

The other captives rushed forward—friends, family, neighbors, some weeping with relief, others shaking, disbelieving. The whole group moved off the hovering platform and stood together, apart from the uneasy audience.

His sons embraced him; his neighbors were sobbing. Vor dismissed the four young men he had hired, then handed the dog's leash to Bonda. "Here, I got you a new pet."

THOUGH THE PEOPLE of Poritrin did not agree with Vor's philosophy on slavery, the money from his accounts solved any problems the merchants might have had. He arranged rooms for his people in a temporary lodging house, so all of them could rest, wash themselves, and celebrate while he studied spaceport schedules and secured passage back to Kepler. A VenHold spacefolder was due to depart in two days, and he bought cabins for all of them. They would be back home in a week.

He gave Bonda the task of verifying all the names on his list, after sadly marking off the two people who had died in transit—a husband and wife who had lived in a farm adjacent to Mariella's house.

Even in the midst of so much joy and hugging, Vor remained disturbed. When he'd left public life behind, he had wanted only solitude and peace. Now he had more work to do. He slipped out at night after checking to be sure that all of his people were safe and secure.

HE ACCOMPANIED THE freed slaves to the spaceport, wanting to watch with his own eyes as they boarded, so he could know they were on their way. He felt grimly satisfied.

The spaceport was in turmoil from a bad accident the night before, but most of the fires on the field had been extinguished. The trio of slaver ships that had preyed on Kepler had filed departure papers and lifted off shortly after sunset, their cargo holds empty and ready to be refilled. Unfortunately, due to bizarre and simultaneous engine malfunctions and an improper explosive mix of fuel, all three ships then exploded in the sky above New Starda. An appalling freak accident.

Vor had been there, alone, to observe. As the people on the ground stared, aghast, he was the only one smiling. . . .

Now, one of the last to board the transport ship, Bonda cradled the dog, already adoring it. Vor turned to her, lowered his voice. "Tell your mother I'll be back as soon as I can."

She blinked in surprise. "What? You're not coming with us? We need you on Kepler!"

Her husband Tir stood beside her. "What if more slavers come?"

"That's exactly what I hope to prevent. I have something else to do before I can come home. Maybe it'll keep Kepler safe."

"But . . . where are you going?" Bonda asked. The dog wriggled in her arms and licked her cheek.

"To Salusa Secundus," he said. "I intend to speak to the Emperor himself."

The only good machine is a dead machine.
—MANFORD TORONDO,
excerpt from a speech on Lampadas

Zimia had many prominent memorials made from the wreckage of cymek warrior forms, but the Emperor had to post constant guards to prevent them from being vandalized by the Butlerians. Even though such displays celebrated the defeat of the machines, the antitechnology movement wanted to erase all vestiges . . . all "temptations," as they called them.

Although the Jihad had been won a century ago, Roderick Corrino understood the public's continuing need to vent its anger, and so he convinced his brother to create a formalized event, a pressure release. Each month, champions from the people were allowed to attack some representation of the onerous machines. Salvador loved the idea, and each "rampage festival" grew more popular than the last.

Now, Roderick rode with his sullen sister in a coach drawn by two roan Salusan stallions. The latest spectacle would take place on the outskirts of Zimia, between the white spires of the capital city and the rolling hills where nobles maintained their estates, vineyards, and orchards.

It was midday, and the gathering crowd was in a festive mood. Citizens had set up picnic areas in a wide perimeter around the thinking-machine relics that were the subject of today's rampage: a small robotic scout ship and the shell of a plague capsule that had been launched by Omnius. Neither one of the objects had originally fallen here, but were among many that had been salvaged after the war and warehoused for these monthly celebrations. Considering the scope of the Synchronized Worlds, machine remnants were not difficult to find, more than enough to keep holding the popular rampage festivals for many years to come.

Already, gleeful children were bouncing rocks off the metallic objects, making loud clangs. Soon it would be the turn of the adults, to do even more damage.

Inside the coach, Roderick sat cool and professional, a dutiful representative of the Imperial Court, but Anna did not seem to be in the mood for festivities. Throughout the procession from the Palace, the girl had been crying about Hirondo Nef, begging Roderick to help her find him (which, of course, he would not do). She was so delicate, so sheltered, so easily bruised; Roderick was torn between toughening her by allowing her to be hurt, and continuing to protect her from heartache.

"Hirondo's dead!" she said. "I just know it! Salvador had him murdered!"

The coach jolted to a stop, and Roderick placed an arm around his trembling sister, consoling her as best he could. "Our brother wouldn't do that. I promise, he's just reassigned the man to a safe place where he can start a new life—and you can, too. We're trying to protect you."

Roderick had, in fact, prevented Salvador from having the chef killed on the spot. He had intervened just in time and put the young man under arrest, primarily for his own safety. Then, taking his own brother aside, Roderick advised, "An Emperor can't help but have blood on his hands, but you should never kill when you don't have to." Fortunately, Salvador had listened to him, as he usually did. Nef was sent away, reassigned to one of the noble estates outside the city, where he would never take advantage of Anna again.

His sister looked up at him, her small blue eyes filled with tears. "I don't want to be protected—I want my Hirondo!"

Roderick hated to see such pain on his sister's face. It seemed Anna didn't even remember that she'd been just as smitten with a young guard four months earlier. She had such a need for acceptance and love that her emotions were like a high-pressure hose, uninhibited and uncontrolled.

"I'm so sorry you're hurt, Anna."

"Do you know where Hirondo is? I love him—I need to see him."

"The Emperor does not consider him appropriate for you. Hirondo should have known better than to put you in such a position. It's an unfortunate fact of life, but you need to find someone of your own station. We are Corrinos, and certain things are expected of us."

He and Salvador would have to discuss marrying her off soon. It shouldn't be difficult to find some nobleman whom she could love just as overwhelmingly. Unless she decided to be contrary for the sake of being that way.

She wiped tears from her cheeks. "Am I not entitled to love? On his deathbed, our father said he wanted us all to marry well."

"You are entitled to love, dear sister, if you can find it in the right place: Emperor Jules was not referring to us marrying *chefs*." He kissed her forehead.

"Salvador took no joy in what he did. He was performing his duty—as you must do. Please listen to me, as your brother—forget about Hirondo."

"But they just ripped him away from me! We didn't even have a chance to say goodbye. I need to see him, just one last time. How can I live with myself if I don't know he's all right, if I can't see it with my own eyes? I promise, if you tell me where he is, I'll face my responsibilities from now on."

Roderick shook his head, but she would not stop begging him. "We must face our responsibilities regardless of whether we get what we want." He opened the door of the coach. "Now, let's go out there and perform another duty. The people are waiting. They all love you."

The Corrinos went to a flag-decked platform that had been erected for the occasion, and looked out at the crowd. The stone-throwing children were removed to a safe distance from the machine replicas, watched by guards and nannies so that their parents could participate in the festivities. The crowd surged forward, energized by the arrival of the Emperor's brother and sister. Most of the people in the throng carried clubs, cudgels, sledgehammers, crowbars.

"I'll let you do the honors this time," Roderick said to his sister. "Unleash the energy of the people." *Before it unleashes itself.*

Red-eyed, Anna went to the front of the platform, and the gathered people fell into a hush, holding their collective breath like a pack of hunting hounds waiting to be loosed upon a hare. The robot ship and the plague capsule waited there, intact, symbolic reminders of the horrific machine tyranny . . . which few people alive could remember. But they knew what they had been taught, and they knew what to hate.

Anna raised her hand, and the crowd tensed. She had done this before, knew the words, but Roderick was ready to take over if his sister should surrender to renewed misery over Hirondo. She drew a hitching breath, glanced at him, and he nodded in reassurance.

Anna said, "We defeated the thinking machines, but we will never forget what they did to humanity." The gathered people grumbled and hissed, brandishing their simple but destructive weapons. "Let this day serve as a reminder to us and to our children of our victory against the machines that enslaved us." She brought her hand down in a chopping motion, and the crowd surged forward.

The clamor was deafening as metal bars, clubs, and sledgehammers pounded down on the capsule, on the robotic ship. Hull plates buckled, controls smashed, plaz shattered. The people cheered and laughed, some screamed in wordless anger, pummeling the nightmarish, symbolic enemy.

The frenzy lasted half an hour, and by the time the people were sated, the remnants of the machine objects had been beaten into shapeless, unrecognizable shrapnel.

When tears streamed down Anna Corrino's cheeks, the people thought she wept for the victory of humanity, but Roderick knew better.

THOUGH BOTH OF her brothers did their best to hide Hirondo from her, the love-struck young man still found a way to get a message to the Princess. He managed to smuggle a note revealing his whereabouts to Lady Orenna, and Anna's old stepmother was sympathetic to the young lovers. She might seem cold and loveless to others, but the Virgin Empress had a soft spot in her heart for the girl, and she arranged for Anna to slip away, to say one last goodbye.

Thus, Anna and Hirondo had an unexpected and glorious reunion in the servants' quarters of the manor house where he had been exiled. She knew in her soul that they were meant to be together.

Anna had fallen deeply in love with this man and could not envision spending her life without him, despite his lowly station. Now that they were together again, the two spoke in hushed voices about running away to Harmonthep, Chusuk, or some other backwater world. "It doesn't matter where, as long as we're together," she whispered, snuggling close to him on the bed.

Hirondo was olive-skinned with a solid physique and brown eyes that always held a hint of sadness. She touched his bare chest, wanted to make love to him again, but he looked troubled. "I'd like to go away with you more than anything, Anna, but we'd never make it. I have no money, no resources, no contacts."

"I have all that, my darling. Somehow, some way, I'll do it." She didn't have any doubts; they were in love, and everything would work out. "I *have* to do it."

He shook his head. "Your family will hunt us down. It'll never work. They're too powerful. This will have to be our farewell . . . but I'll never forget you."

She glowered at him for being so pessimistic, wondering why everyone was so adamant against letting her be happy. Suddenly self-conscious of her nakedness, Anna swung out of bed and pulled her clothes back on, wondering if she'd made a mistake. She had longed for Hirondo so desperately, and now he seemed to have no backbone. Very well, she would make the arrangements herself without his agreement, and prove to Hirondo that it could be done.

Without warning, the door to the servants' quarters burst open, and uniformed Imperial guardsmen rushed in, shouting commands, grabbing Hirondo as he tried to scramble away. They were more gentle when they seized Anna, but kept a secure hold on her nevertheless.

Shaking his head with sad disappointment, Roderick entered behind the guards. "Anna, I tried hard to help you, but it's out of my hands now."

She struggled, trying to run to Hirondo, but she couldn't break free. "How did you know?"

"It's my job to know. And you leave a wide trail."

They brought Anna back to the Imperial Palace and escorted her directly to the Emperor in his private suite. Roderick stood to one side with his arms folded across his chest. Salvador wore a gold-and-white robe of state and looked as if he'd been to a session in the Landsraad Hall. He regarded his sister with a sour face.

Anna fell to her knees in front of him, grabbed his robe. "Please, Salvador! Let me give up my title and run away with Hirondo. I won't ask for money. I'll change my name. We're destined to be together!"

Salvador looked heavenward, as if pleading for help, then steadied his gaze on her. "That will never happen. You're a Corrino and will always be a Corrino. Our father told us to watch out for you." Then he spoke as if issuing a decree. "You'll never see Hirondo Nef again."

"Don't kill him! Please don't hurt him."

Salvador pursed his lips, leaned back in his chair. "That would be the easiest solution, but he is beneath my notice. Besides, you would just find some other inappropriate dalliance. Killing Hirondo Nef doesn't solve the core problem, dear sister, when *you* are the problem. Our brother has a much more sensible idea."

Roderick frowned, as if he disliked being given the credit for the idea. Or the blame. "We're quite impressed with Dorotea and the other Sisters in the royal court. They are women of refinement and wisdom, and the Rossak School is one of the best in the Imperium. The solution is obvious."

Salvador yanked his robe from Anna's grip, pushed her away. "We're sending you to the Sisterhood, where I believe you will find a purpose in life. Maybe with their training you'll do something valuable and meaningful, instead of wasting your time in delusions and aimless pursuits. You have to grow up. We can no longer handle you here at court."

Anna looked to Roderick for help, but he shook his head and told her, "This is for the best. You may not know it now, but one day you'll thank the Emperor for his kindness."

Adaptability is the essence of survival.
—from the *Azhar Book*

U nless you follow instructions carefully, some of you may perish during today's exercise," the Reverend Mother said to the acolytes assembled on the rolling surface of the polymerized treetop. Her smile carried no humor. "The same can be said of many aspects of life: If you are careless, you may die."

While the young students wore pale green, Reverend Mother Raquella had on a black leotard, as did Valya and the other assistant proctor, Sister Ninke—a stocky and muscular woman with a stern face and flecks of gray in her auburn hair, though she was only thirty-four years old.

Ninke held a bound copy of the Sisterhood's recently compiled manual of philosophies and religions, the *Azhar Book*. Sometimes, the Reverend Mother liked to quote from the Book during classroom instruction. Even though she surely knew every word in the text, Raquella also believed in the power of formality and rites, helping to cement the profound importance of the philosophical compilation.

Sisterhood scholars had assembled the *Azhar Book* in the midst of the CET riots and the uproar over the imposition of the far-reaching *Orange Catholic Bible*. The compendium of beliefs and esoterica was their private response to the *OC Bible*, though the women denied any religious ties.

Rossak was more than a school, with long-established spaceports and old cliff cities that had since been commandeered by Raquella and her followers. By now their graduates numbered in the tens of thousands. After the Sisters finished training, a number of them returned to their original homeworlds to apply their new abilities, demonstrating the worth of Raquella's training. Some Sisterhood-trained women actively traveled throughout the Imperium to recruit for the school, keeping their eyes open for worthy new students. Most Sisters, however, remained on Rossak to join the ever-growing ranks of advanced women in what had become not just a school but a strengthening order of adherents to a new way of life.

When Valya had first entered the Rossak School as a sixteen-year-old acolyte, many of the words in the Sisterhood's lexicon had sounded so mystical to her, rooted in the witchcraft of the original Sorceresses. She remembered finding it all exciting and mysterious . . . unlike anything in her dull life on Lankiveil.

Trapped on that backwater planet with little hope of advancement, Valya Harkonnen had made up her mind to become a superior fighter, so that she could stand strong against threats. She and her dear brother, Griffin, had engaged in traditional boxing, wrestling, and martial arts matches. He was taller and stronger, but she had speed, trickery, and unpredictability, so that she defeated him more often than not . . . which helped him improve, as she did. Neither Valya nor Griffin looked like formidable fighters, but they were deceptively skilled, and the "normalness" of their appearance often put opponents off guard. Since joining the Sisterhood, Valya had learned even more techniques of controlling her body, muscles, and reflexes. She knew that the next time she sparred with Griffin, he would be quite surprised.

Now the new group of acolytes stood close together on the paved treetops. They looked down at the sheer precipice cut into the high canopy, like a canyon carved through the interlocked branches and leaves.

"For today's demonstration, we will show you how powerful we women can be," the gray-haired Raquella said, looking up as Karee Marques and three other pureblooded Sorceresses prepared to impress the acolytes. Valya had seen the demonstration many times before; she would be awed and saddened, as always.

These last few survivors of Rossak's most powerful women exhibited remarkable talents, in many ways superior even to Reverend Mother Raquella's ability to focus control over her body down to the smallest cell. Valya felt disappointed and discouraged because *she* could never have such powers without risking the transformative process. And so far, the testing to create new Reverend Mothers had been a dead end.

Karee Marques said, "Once, the Sorceresses of Rossak were greatly feared, the most powerful women in the old League of Nobles. Without our mental powers, the human race might not have survived the war against the cymeks."

The three Sorceresses next to her curled their hands into loosely balled fists. Their hair began to waft freely about, energized with static electricity. The silvery-purple leaves on the edge of the flattened forest canopy began to stir as if alive . . . as if fleeing. Valya's head began to pound with the pressure. Disturbed by the building wave, two birdlike moths flew away squawking, beating their iridescent wings.

"The Sorceresses were able to kill cymeks with psychic powers, boiling their brains inside their preservation canisters. Though shielded, they could not withstand us," Karee's face was drawn, the strain pulling the sinews on her neck tight. "But each victory against the cymeks cost the life of a Sorceress. The most powerful ones caused the greatest damage, but by the end of the Jihad, most of the living Sorceresses had sacrificed themselves. The bloodline grew diluted . . . and those of us here in the School are all who remain."

Together in eerie silence, the group of Sorceresses levitated themselves, rising up from the paved canopy as if borne on suspensors, but they did it all with their minds, keeping their eyes closed.

Valya remained silent, staring in wonder. She heard the acolytes gasp.

"This is just a hint of the potential in every human being," Reverend Mother Raquella said. "Through careful study of the genetic records in our breeding database, we were able to eliminate the potential for many horrific birth defects. Once, large numbers of Misborn were cast out into the jungles, genetically inferior, horribly deformed. That doesn't happen anymore." The old woman's lips turned in a frown. "But Sorceresses are rarely born, either."

Karee and the other Sorceresses drifted back down to the canopy and relaxed, releasing their intense concentration that had built up to a telepathic thrumming in the air. Valya felt the pain inside her skull recede.

She noted that all the Sorceresses had their eyes open now, and they emitted a simultaneous sigh. "You must each attain your own potential," Raquella said to the fascinated acolytes. "You must work with us to find it."

"Without machines—we use only what is in our own hearts and minds," said a new acolyte named Ingrid, who had arrived from the Butlerian stronghold of Lampadas. She had been recommended by Sister Dorotea, who now served Emperor Salvador Corrino himself.

Raquella paced around the gathered acolytes. Her blue eyes were watery as she looked from face to face. "Answer this—in what ways are humans better than machines?"

"Creativity," one of the acolytes answered immediately.

"Adaptability."

"Foresight."

Ingrid piped up, "Love?"

Valya wasn't sure she liked this new Sister. Ingrid was intense and didn't seem to listen well. She had arrived at the school with far too many inflexible opinions and had a tendency to blurt out whatever was on her mind. And, now that

Reverend Mother Raquella had entrusted Valya with the secret of the breeding-record computers, it made the young woman suspicious of anyone with such close ties to the Butlerians.

The Reverend Mother stood squarely in front of the naïve new acolyte. "You consider *love* to be a human advantage?"

"Yes, Reverend Mother." Ingrid looked nervous.

Without warning, Raquella slapped her hard across the face. At first Ingrid looked confused, shocked, and hurt—then her face reddened with fury. Heat flared in her eyes as she tried to control her temper.

With a chuckle, Raquella relaxed and said, "Love may set us apart from thinking machines, but it is not necessarily an advantage. During the Jihad, we didn't defeat Omnius with *love*! Hatred, now, that's another matter, isn't it?" She leaned closer. "We all saw it on your face when I struck you. *Hatred!* That's the emotion that enabled us to defeat the machines. Controlled hatred. That's a concept to be understood, but it's risky."

Ingrid was not afraid to speak up. "And faith. With all due respect, Reverend Mother, hatred alone did not lead us to victory. We had faith in our righteous cause, and love made all those martyrs willing to sacrifice for their families, their friends, and even for strangers. Faith, Reverend Mother, *faith*. And love."

Raquella seemed disappointed in the young woman. "That may be what Manford Torondo teaches his followers, but you are in the Sisterhood now. Your perspective must change from blind acceptance of whatever the Butlerians say."

Ingrid jerked her head back, as if she'd heard sacrilege, but the question about human advantages was a rehearsed springboard for what Raquella wanted to teach. She addressed the group of acolytes. "You must set aside beliefs you held before arriving on Rossak. Allow your minds to become a receptive slate upon which we will inscribe new beliefs, new ways. You must be *Sisters* first, and anything else second."

"Are we not *humans* first?" Ingrid asked. Valya decided that she definitely disliked this annoying young woman.

"*Sisters* first."

At a nod from Raquella, Sister Ninke opened the *Azhar Book* and read a prearranged passage. " 'The first question to ask each day when we arise, and the last question each evening when we retire, is this: *What does it mean to be human?* These seven words form the basis of all our behavior and endeavor. If we do not seek to answer this, what purpose is there to breathing or eating or going about one's daily life?' "

THAT EVENING, A supply ship arrived at Rossak bearing a message from Salusa Secundus, wrapped in ostentatious packaging.

Valya was attending the Reverend Mother in her private, stone-walled chamber when the message cylinder arrived. Raquella's quarters were in the oldest section of caves, in a chamber that had once belonged to the legendary Sorceress Zufa Cenva.

Valya had been listening to the old woman describe how the voices of past memories had guided her plans to utilize the computerized breeding records to shepherd the human race. Her voice droned on. "Women have always been the driving force behind society, whether or not men wear the mantles of leadership. We have the innate genetic power to create, and even though the Imperium is still stumbling in its first steps, if we in the Sisterhood can extend our influence, sending out even more of our well-trained Sisters as advisers, confidantes, or wives, then we can provide a more stable foundation for the great houses of the Landsraad League." Raquella drew a long, wistful breath. "Ah, if only you could see it yourself, Valya. Countless generations are contained in my memory, life upon life, extending across the rugged landscape of human history. The perspective is . . . breathtaking!"

Valya watched curiously as a young Sister delivered the ornately embossed package to the Reverend Mother. Raquella dismissed the girl, curious to study the sealed message cylinder; Valya offered to leave as well, but the Reverend Mother made an offhanded gesture for her to stay. Valya sat perfectly still, holding her silence as Raquella read the tightly rolled sheet. "It is from Sister Dorotea."

"News from the Imperial Court?" Though she felt very close to Reverend Mother Raquella, Valya still anxiously awaited the day when she could leave Rossak. She hoped someday to be assigned to Salusa Secundus, where she could make vitally important connections with influential nobles and Imperial officials and help House Harkonnen regain its standing. She might even marry into a powerful noble family. Barring that, maybe she could obtain a position with Venport Holdings. The Sisterhood provided her with a menu of options. . . .

Raquella's brow furrowed like pale parchment as she digested the coded message; she didn't seem to know whether to smile or frown. "Emperor Salvador wants his sister, Anna Corrino, to join the Sisterhood. Something to do with a scandal at the court. Our school has been instructed to accept the girl as an acolyte." The old woman looked at Valya, raised her eyebrows. "She is your age."

Valya blinked in surprise. At twenty-one, she was hardly more than a girl herself. "The Emperor's sister?" she asked. "If she joins us, our school would gain visibility and prestige . . . but is Anna Corrino qualified to become an acolyte?"

"It is not a request." The Reverend Mother set aside the message. "We need to make arrangements to depart on the next spacefolder for Salusa. As Reverend Mother, I will travel there myself to receive the Corrino princess into our care. Her rank demands that we go to great lengths to make her feel valued and welcome." She looked at Valya, considering, and perhaps listening to unheard voices inside her head. Reaching a decision, she smiled. "And I want you to accompany me."

One can draw maps of planets and continents with extreme accuracy, but the map of a life contains unchartable terrain.

—ABULURD HARKONNEN, *Memoirs from Lankiveil*

By midafternoon, the sleet stopped and the skies cleared, a taunting reminder of how pleasant Lankiveil could be. Muffled in his warm whale-fur jacket, Griffin Harkonnen watched fishermen haul their craft out of the boathouses; he knew it would take them until nightfall to get the vessels ready, but he admired them for trying.

He had gone over the budget and the tax projections, and knew how much the hard winter had hurt the economy. Several docks needed to be repaired, and an avalanche had closed one of the roads through the mountains. Someday, through his own efforts, he hoped the planetary treasury would grow strong enough to allow his people to do more than eke out a living in difficult times.

He looked up as a smoky roar split the sky: a shuttle coming down from orbit, the regular delivery ship that bore packages of expensive supplies, formal documents, mail dispatches, and news releases from Salusa Secundus. He didn't expect a response yet from the governmental examination he had taken, since bureaucracy and approvals ground slowly through the administrative red tape. But soon—when he received the results of the tests he knew he had passed—he would become a full-fledged Landsraad representative, and the distasteful proxy relationship could be ended.

After the shuttle landed, Griffin went to sign for the delivery, although some of the new captains specifically wanted Vergyl Harkonnen's mark. By now, though, most of the starship captains knew the young man by sight. Griffin made a point of meeting each of them, never wanting to ignore possible connections.

Some of the vessels that came to outlying planets such as Lankiveil were operated by the VenHold Spacing Fleet, but Celestial Transport made more frequent stops in this sector. After the shuttle landed in the small, paved spaceport, local cargo handlers emerged from their homes, ready to help unload and distribute the offworld shipments.

Griffin was professional and cordial as he went to greet the shuttle captain, but the offworlder sounded annoyed as he held out the manifest sheet. "Miserable planet! I've been in orbit since early yesterday, but the storm clouds were thick as a planetary shield. Didn't think I'd ever be able to land." He seemed to be blaming Griffin. "Your deliveries and dispatches aren't worth crashing my ship over."

"It wasn't my choice to live on this forsaken place," Griffin said, biting back his long-held resentment. "We're glad you made it, Captain. The weathersats say the storms will close in again tomorrow."

"Oh, I'll be long gone by then—I'm already behind schedule because of the delays here." With a brusque gesture, the captain handed Griffin a packet of diplomatic papers and letters.

While the crew and local porters unloaded supplies from the shuttle's cargo hold, Griffin checked items off the manifest, then transferred funds from the treasury to pay for the municipal deliveries. He offered hospitality to the captain, but the man wanted to be off again the moment his hold was empty. Gray clouds began congealing overhead after only an hour of clear weather.

As soon as the shuttle had lifted into the sky and he finished overseeing the cargo crates sent to the harbor warehouses, Griffin took the documents back to the dark-wood house he shared with his family. In the study by a warm fire, he sat back and sorted through the packets, expecting to spend the rest of the day conducting business.

Because Lankiveil felt so isolated, he was always happy for news dispatches from the Imperium. He longed for, but didn't expect, a letter or holorecording from his sister; she was rarely allowed to write. A quick sorting of the packages led to disappointment—nothing from her, and no approval document that named him Lankiveil's planetary Landsraad representative. Nor did he find a dispatch from his uncle Weller with an update of his progress from planet to planet, making new trade agreements for whale fur.

With growing displeasure, he saw that the stack contained only government reports, a few commercial inquiries, and an official-looking document from the offices of Celestial Transport. Coming into the room to say hello, his father glanced through the correspondence, saw nothing that interested him, and went off to consult the chef about dinner.

Griffin worked his way through the pile. Then, when he opened the CT dispatch, he felt a chill like a wash of icy spray curling up over the bow of a fishing boat. The letter began with five words that had signified catastrophic news throughout history. "We regret to inform you . . ."

The commercial spacefolding vessel bearing the passenger Weller Harkonnen, along with the entire cargo of whale fur from Lankiveil, had been lost en route to Parmentier. Due to a navigational hazard, all goods and passengers had vanished somewhere in deep space. They were considered unrecoverable.

The letter went on. "Space travel over such vast distances and poorly charted routes has always been a risky venture, and accidents inevitably happen. Celestial Transport is attempting to work through this difficulty, and we appreciate your patience in the matter. Please allow us to express our sincerest personal sympathies."

The letter bore the replicated signature of Arjen Gates, head of the company. Griffin knew there must be over a thousand similar letters to the next-of-kin of the other passengers. An attachment referenced a waiver and disclaimer statement on the original shipping documents that Griffin had signed when engaging the transport.

Weller was gone, and the cargo with him. At first, Griffin thought more about the loss of his beloved uncle, then, as he read the dispatch again, he also began to grasp the severity of the blow to the Harkonnen treasury. There would be very little compensation, only a minimal payment that was described in the fine print of the bill of lading. Griffin had invested much of their family wealth into the whale-fur business venture, and House Harkonnen would be decades recovering from this. His carefully orchestrated plan to expand Harkonnen commercial influence had just collapsed into the vacuum of uncharted space.

As if in a dream, Griffin heard his father cheerfully whistling in the kitchen. Vergyl and the family chef had such good rapport. The young man sat stunned and silent for a long time, unwilling to destroy his father's happiness. He would wait until the following day before telling anyone.

When Valya learned the news, she would no doubt find some way to trace the blame back to Vorian Atreides. Griffin, though, began to wonder if the Harkonnen family was cursed.

A storm in the desert leaves many scars and erases many others.
—a saying of the Freemen of Arrakis

After she had extracted all the information the black-market pilot could give, Ishanti spent two weeks quietly investigating the desert activities. Soon she found the illicit spice-harvesting operations.

The chief of the poachers, Dol Orianto, had made boastful comments in Arrakis City bars. He seemed to think there was nothing to be worried about. "This planet is big enough for competition—there were plenty of independent melange operations during the spice rush. Venport doesn't own the whole world!" Orianto had laughed, and his workers chuckled with him.

The small industrial outpost in the mountains above Carthag was obvious and undefended, and the VenHold teams moved in. The attack was over quickly, and Ishanti and her forty attack skimcraft flew away from the industrial outpost, leaving the smoking ruins of habitation buildings behind and charred bodies strewn on the rocks. The spice-storage silos remained intact—Directeur Venport had been adamant that the contraband melange was much too valuable to be discarded in a fit of pique.

At first, Ishanti considered letting one or two of the poachers live so they could send a grim report to Arjen Gates and Celestial Transport. Instead, she recorded images of the attack, deciding that a simple message pack would do the job. That way they could control the message.

Now, inside the noisy passenger compartment of the skimcraft, Ishanti shouted to her companions—many of them female Freemen warriors—above the thrum of articulated wings. "Once we finish here, we'll salvage the equipment and retrieve the spice as a special gift." Secretly, she would also send an immediate message to Naib Sharnak out in the deep desert settlement, informing her people that if they moved quickly they could take away all the bodies to reclaim the water before anyone knew the difference.

Ishanti had been careful to capture Dol Orianto alive, so that the appalled man could watch the slaughter of his crew. Tied up and tossed on the deck like a piece of discarded cargo, Orianto squirmed and struggled, but every time he thrashed, the shigawire bindings contracted around his wrists, legs, and throat, drawing lines of blood in the flesh.

"There is nothing you can say to save yourself," Ishanti said in a cool voice, squatting next to him. "Think carefully now on the only decision you have left, your most important decision: How will you die—bravely, or as a coward?"

He didn't answer. Tears were pouring out of his eyes . . . a waste of water, she thought, but his whole body was a waste of water. Still, some messages were necessary and, in the larger scheme of things, more important than a few liters of water.

She had already given the pilot her course, and the skimcraft flew high above the gathering dust clouds. Ishanti had studied weathersat readings to find the nearest Coriolis storm. It was less than an hour away.

When Dol Orianto did not answer her question, she sat back and rode in silence. The chief poacher whimpered but did not beg for his life; she gave him credit for that.

The pilot, an expert on Arrakis weather patterns, guided them over a whirlpool of clouds and dust. From the sealed, scratched ports, the passengers could look down into a frightening maw. The vortex of howling winds struck fear into all desert people. Viewing the gigantic storm now from above, even at a safe altitude, Ishanti found it awe-inspiring, intimidating, and beautiful in a way.

But not beautiful for Dol Orianto.

When they were directly above the sand hurricane, the pilot circled and signaled from the cockpit. Ishanti stood up from her hard metal bench, grabbed the poacher by his shoulders and dragged him to his feet. He was trembling.

"Some things have to be done," she said, by way of apology. Josef Venport had made his wishes very clear. "Others would call this a glorious death."

She and her companions clipped their harnesses to the interior wall so they would not be sucked out when the hatch opened. Orianto squirmed harder, tried to get away; the tightening shigawire sliced through his wrists, and his veins gushed blood.

Ishanti closed her eyes, uttered a quick prayer, and heaved him out through the hatch.

The man tumbled headfirst into the sky, toward the yawning mouth of the Coriolis storm. He dwindled to a tiny speck long before the vortex swallowed him up. Yes, some would call that a glorious death.

She closed the skimcraft hatch and signaled to the pilot. "We have all the images we need. Now back to Arrakis City—I have a report to make."

The elite Mentat School accepted only the most gifted candidates, and in the decades that Gilbertus Albans had run the facility, a number of his students had excelled in the rigorous programs, advancing faster than their peers. Their minds were efficient and organized, advanced, sharp . . . true human computers.

Erasmus was very proud to see his influence.

Currently, the school's best student, arguably the best ever, was Draigo Roget. Draigo surpassed even most of the Mentat instructors in his skills—a fact that did not escape the young man himself, who at times displayed too much ego. Just five years ago, Draigo had arrived on Lampadas, passed the qualification tests and entry examination, and paid for his considerable tuition with a gift from an unnamed benefactor.

Gilbertus had never met anyone quite so brilliant, and now Draigo was nearly finished with everything the Mentat School could teach him. He would graduate with the next group in a month, and Gilbertus had asked him to consider remaining on Lampadas as an instructor, but Draigo was noncommittal.

This morning they met in an oval war-game chamber; the room was large enough to accommodate hundreds of students, but now it contained only the two of them. Windows around the perimeter of the room showed part of the blue-walled administration building and glimpses of the greenish waters of the marsh lake, sparkling in sunlight.

The pair of Mentats, though, were intent on far-off, imaginary space battles. They sat in tall chairs and engaged in a competition, each controlling a holographic war fleet through a tactical obstacle course of asteroids, gravity wells, foldspace mishaps, uncertain targets. Their minds intent, Gilbertus and Draigo conducted a skirmish, throwing simulated war fleets against each other, prosecuting an imaginary war at the speed of thought.

Barely moving in their chairs, they made finger movements that were interpreted by motion sensors and transmitted into the mechanism. Gilbertus would never demonstrate the system to Manford Torondo even though, technically, this was not forbidden technology, because it could not function without human guidance.

Simulated space battles flurried in the air between them, ship movements so swift that the images were blurred. The war vessels were like game pieces, tangled inside a crowded solar system. The complex engagements took place among moons or gas giants, close to inhabited planets, or out in the distant cometary cloud. Color codes distinguished the sides, red against yellow, battles within battles.

Over the course of an hour, speaking hardly a word, Gilbertus and Draigo had already fought eleven battles, and now the tempo increased. Other than in his intense exercises with Erasmus, the Mentat teacher had never faced such a challenge. He still held a substantial advantage over Draigo, but his student was catching up.

On the compressed timescale of the simulation, entire solar systems could be lost in seconds. Each Mentat could envision battle plans, unfolding how every second-, third-, and fourth-order consequence would play out in their minds. Gilbertus had taught such techniques, but few of his students grasped the broad field of view of Gestalt philosophy—a restructuring of perception to encompass the whole, instead of its individual parts.

Drops of perspiration formed on Gilbertus's forehead.

Unseen, the memory core of Erasmus watched the proceedings via concealed sensors. The restless robot's gelcircuitry core needed a small measure of freedom. Gilbertus planned to construct a physical form so that the independent robot could become mobile again. Someday. With his exceptionally high intellect, Erasmus required constant stimulation. The robot core had offered to help him in the war-game simulations against Draigo, but Gilbertus refused to cross that moral line. "Cheating," he had called it.

"Improving your odds," Erasmus countered. "Increasing your advantage."

"No. You will watch—that's all."

As he witnessed the rapid progress of his star pupil playing the game with him, however, Gilbertus began to have second thoughts. . . .

While the men remained intent on their simulation, sitting across from each other, Gilbertus spoke to his pupil, "You continue to improve, but never forget that there are always unforeseen elements in battle. Seemingly small and insignificant factors, but possibly of great importance—things you cannot plan for. Be alert, assess each situation rapidly, and take appropriate action."

"You are trying to distract me, sir." Draigo's black eyebrows knitted together in concentration, and his dark gaze studied the simulated space conflict.

Loud conversation interrupted the competitors as students pulled open the chamber doors and entered for their scheduled class. Startled by the disruption, Draigo twitched, scattering his projected fleet around the virtual battlefield. Gilbertus could have seized the opportunity to secure a victory then, but he froze the game instead.

"Unforeseen elements such as that, for example," he said.

Draigo recovered. "I understand. Shall we finish?"

"Very well. A Mentat must learn to concentrate under all circumstances."

Gilbertus resumed the simulation as Mentat students gathered around to observe the show, but his conscience urged him to end this private battle and give the other trainees the attention they deserved. In the thick of the battle, Gilbertus intentionally slacked off and waited for his opponent to move in for the kill.

Noticing his instructor's change of mind-set, however, Draigo sat back in his tall chair with a disgusted look. He let his own forces collapse and get hit by Gilbertus's hamstrung force. With a sigh, the young man disengaged himself from the war-game controls. "I don't want to win that way."

Gilbertus stood and stretched. "Soon you won't have to."

The young man had won nearly forty percent of the engagements.

From a tiny seed can grow a mighty tree, able to withstand the most severe of storms. Remember, Rayna Butler was just a sickly, fever-struck girl when she began her crusade—and look what has grown from it! I am but another tree in the forest of steadfast belief that Rayna planted. My followers will not bend to the whims of nonbelievers who fight against us.

—MANFORD TORONDO, *The Only Path*

Though his important work carried him across the Imperium, Manford enjoyed rare moments of peace in his own home in the company of Anari. The simple, wholesome people of Lampadas had established small farms, growing their own food, making their own fabrics, and living a contented existence without artificial monstrosities: without enslavement by machines or dependence upon the crutches of technology.

The mind of man is holy.

Manford's cottage had been built out of fieldstone and mortar, framed with timbers cut by hand and shaped with hand tools. His followers had erected the house for him; if he'd asked for it, they would have built him a palace more magnificent than the Emperor's, but the very idea was so contrary to Manford's philosophy and desires that he upbraided anyone who dared to suggest it. His cozy cottage was perfect, lovingly decorated with handcrafted quilts, adorned with paintings done by his followers. Volunteers planted flowers in front of the cottage; gardeners trimmed his hedges; landscapers laid down stone paths. People baked and cooked for him, bringing such bounty that he could never eat it all, and so he shared it.

It made his heart swell to see proof positive that humans could be happy without gadgets, computers, or sophisticated—and evil—technology. The Butlerians worked harder, ate better, and were generally healthier than those who sought constant treatment from doctors and medicines.

The Imperium had too few worlds like this, and his movement still had much to do. Beyond simply smashing the vestiges of combat robots and thinking-machine ships, he had to do constant battle against a *mind-set* of dependency.

But not tonight. He sent his followers away, thanking them for their company, but insisting that he needed to rest and meditate. Only Anari Idaho remained with him, as always.

He sat propped up on his cushions, watching her go about her tasks. He knew that if he snapped his fingers, countless others would rush to meet his every need: They would carry him on a palanquin, feed him, maintain his home, and tend him with obsessive attention. But no one was like Anari. Manford would not have survived without her. She took such good care of him.

The Swordmaster added another split log to the fire from the woodpile outside the house (which held enough firewood to last a hundred people for a year). In the chill autumn evenings, Manford liked to have the windows open for fresh air so Anari kept the fire burning; she even woke herself to add logs throughout the night. In the kitchen she had already put kettles of water on the stove to heat for Manford's bath. Anari never complained about the menial chores; in fact, she occasionally hummed because she was so pleased with her life, so happy to take care of him.

She walked past him now, carrying the second brass kettle. He could smell the resinous aromatic leaves she had steeped in it. "Your bath is almost ready. I'll be back for you."

"I can make it to my bath myself," he said.

"I know. But I love to do things for you." She smiled softly and left the room.

While Anari was gone, he sprang up on his powerful arms and used them like legs to walk across the room upside down, where he grabbed one of the numerous parallel bars that had been installed at his height, to help him steady himself when moving around the house on his own. Though he had lost half the height of his body, he exercised regularly with what remained. He would never surrender to helplessness, but he also made certain he looked dignified in public. He let people help him when it was necessary, but he wasn't as crippled as people believed him to be.

He heard Anari pour the kettle into the tub in the next room, after which she came back out to where he had been sitting on his cushions. Anari saw that he had crossed the room without her, gave him a brief disapproving expression, then bent down and extended an arm.

He slipped into her strong embrace, wrapping one arm around her shoulders to hold himself upright. Anari carried him along, their hips touching like a lovestruck couple walking down the street, except she did all the walking for both of them. Propping him against her, she bent over and sloshed her palm in the water to check the temperature. Finding it adequate, she removed Manford's shirt and wrappings, then placed him in the tub.

He closed his eyes and sighed. Anari took up a frayed rag and began washing him. She never gave any indication that it was a chore. He let her continue. He did not feel uncomfortable to be the focus of Anari's ministrations, because she made him feel that he was in a safe place with her, that he could trust her completely. He let his thoughts drift away, but the nightmares were always there . . . that terrible day of the explosion that had killed Rayna Butler.

Manford would always wonder if he could have moved faster, could have saved her somehow. He'd made a heroic attempt, and failed—and it had cost him his legs. He would have been willing to sacrifice anything for her.

Even after the defeat of Omnius, Rayna Butler had continued her antitechnology movement, which was then called the Cult of Serena. After launching her crusade when she was just a girl, having miraculously survived the machine plagues that killed her whole family, Rayna never swerved from her mission—until an assassin's bomb killed her at the age of ninety-seven.

The CET riots were an added flash point to her followers. The uproar against the *Orange Catholic Bible* was not precisely the same as Rayna's desire to stifle technology, but the two movements had similar goals. Rayna Butler had been old, but still sharp and charismatic, and she had not relied on medical technology or melange or drugs; she had lived to such a great age because she was *pure*.

Manford had joined the Butlerians as an enthusiastic, idealistic fifteen-year-old after running away from home. He knew that the machines had wiped out the population on his family's home planet long ago, and even though Omnius and the cymeks had been defeated decades before his birth, Manford still held a grudge. He was an impassioned young man who wanted to fight long after the battles had ended.

Fitting in among the Butlerians, he loved being close to Rayna, listening to her, watching her. He adored her like a student with a crush on an elderly teacher, admiring the sparkle and gleam in her eyes, the radiance of her ivory-pale skin. Although she had lost all of her hair as a child due to the machine-induced plague, Manford still saw immense beauty in her.

She had noticed him among her followers; and once, she'd even told Manford that she expected great things from him. When he gave the embarrassed response that he was much too young to become a real leader, Rayna answered, "I was only eleven when I received my calling."

As the fledgling Imperium expanded, there were those who resisted Rayna's efforts—the protechnology forces, business interests, planetary populations who refused to surrender their conveniences. During one of her rallies on Boujet, a planet that was trying to build an industrial and technological base, a protechnology fanatic planted a bomb, intending to kill her.

Manford had discovered the bomb at the last minute, raced to protect Rayna, and been caught in the explosion. Old Rayna had died in his arms, torn apart and yet beatific. She'd lifted a bloody finger to bless him, telling Manford with her dying breath to carry on her good work.

Now the thought made him shudder in the warm bath. He still had nightmares of how he'd watched the light fade from Rayna's eyes as he held her, briefly envisioning her as a young woman again. He was so enraptured as she died—and so much in shock—that he didn't even notice his own grievous wounds, his lower body blown off. . . .

Afterward, Butlerian mobs stormed the cities and factories of Boujet, burning most of it to the ground and leaving the people there with no technology, no conveniences, only ashes. They reverted the planet to the Stone Age.

Manford had astonished the doctors by surviving the trauma, and he took Rayna's blessing as his armor and sword. One of his holiest possessions was a scrap of bloodstained cloth removed from her body on the day of her death. He carried the torn fabric with him at all times; it gave him strength.

Anari began working his knotted muscles with her fingers, massaging his shoulders. Gazing down at Manford as he stirred in the herb-infused water, she asked, "You're thinking about Rayna again. I can tell by the look on your face."

"Rayna is always with me. How can I stop thinking of her?"

Anari removed him from the water and gently toweled him off, then dressed him again. As she held him up with her strong arms, he leaned his head on hers. "Put me by my desk near the bed. And light a candle. I'd like to read before I go to sleep."

"As you wish, Manford."

When she left him alone, he sat before copies of the bound printed journals and laboratory notebooks written by the heinous robot Erasmus. The dangerous backup documents had been found in the wreckage of Corrin and salvaged, but kept locked away. Appalling journals, providing a window into the mind of a monster. Now Manford studied the pages, sickened by what the twisted robot had written. It was like confronting the words of a demon, and the more he read the more horrified he became. The thinking machine's pride in his tortures and crimes showed through in the pedantic accounts. The comments chilled Manford's soul.

"Machines have patience that humans can never achieve," Erasmus had written. "What is a decade, a century, a millennium to us? We can wait. And if they think they have defeated us, I remain confident. Humans created thinking machines in the first place, and we became their masters. Even if they succeed in eradicating every computer mind in this war, I know what will happen. I know them. Given enough time, they will forget . . . and will create us all over again. Yes, we can wait."

Disturbed by the passage, Manford felt stinging tears in his eyes, and he swore it must never happen. He closed the volume, but knew he would not sleep for a long time. Some things were too terrifying for him to share with his followers.

Life! If only we could revisit our pasts and make wiser choices.
　　　　　　　　　　　　　　—anonymous lament

On the rare occasions when Raquella Berto-Anirul had visited Salusa Secundus, the weather was always exceptional—clear, warm days with gentle breezes fluttering the colorful flags of the Landsraad League and the golden Corrino lion crest. From the crowded historical lives in her mind, she could recall this planet over the centuries, a gem among all the settled worlds of humanity.

As Raquella and her delegation of Sisters arrived this afternoon, however, the sky was leaden and the air as still as a bated breath, so that the colorful banners hung slack on their poles. Zimia had grown somber, as if it knew that Raquella had come to take Anna Corrino away.

She had wanted to impress Emperor Salvador with the Sisterhood's professionalism, to prove that his decision to send his sister to Rossak was correct. According to the established schedule, Raquella and her companions should have landed the evening before, but a last-minute delay in the VenHold spacefolder had prevented their timely arrival. Now the group of women were hours overdue for their meeting at the Imperial Palace. Not an auspicious beginning, she thought.

The chartered groundcar pulled to a halt in the bustling drop-off loop in front of the multi-spire Corrino Palace, as if Reverend Mother Raquella, Sister Valya, and the two other Sisters were guests at a glamorous reception. A pair of liveried footmen opened the groundcar door and helped Raquella out, treating her like a fragile old woman. She let them feel useful, though she was still nimble and did not require any assistance.

When Valya Harkonnen emerged from the vehicle, the young woman looked around, clearly impressed by the glory of the capital, before remembering herself and marshaling her emotions. The footmen hurriedly moved on to another ambassadorial car to welcome more representatives, not giving a second glance to the women from Rossak. No one paid much attention to their arrival.

As they made their way to the palace, Raquella and her party became lost in the flow of dignitaries, bureaucrats, and representatives that streamed in and out of the gigantic Palace. Exuding confidence, she presented herself to a uniformed escort who waited at the base of the long waterfall of stairs leading up to the grand arched entrance. "I am Reverend Mother Raquella Berto-Anirul, from the Sisterhood's school on Rossak. My companions and I have come at the Emperor's request to see Princess Anna Corrino."

Not at all surprised, as if she had merely announced the delivery of a parcel of groceries, the man led them up a seemingly endless succession of white marble steps.

At the Palace entrance, the lanky Sister Dorotea hurried to intercept them, looking breathless. Five other Sister graduates who served in the Imperial Court had joined her. All of them bowed with respect before the Reverend Mother; even Sister Perianna, assigned as personal secretary to Roderick Corrino's wife, had broken away from her duties to greet the visitors.

Dorotea dismissed the palace escort and guided Raquella and her companions through the echoing, arched hallways. "I apologize for not arranging a more organized reception, Reverend Mother. We were uncertain when you would arrive."

"The vagaries of space travel," Raquella said, acting as if it didn't matter. "VenHold Spacing Fleet is quite reliable, but this delay was out of our control. I hope Emperor Salvador is not terribly upset."

"I rearranged the appointments on his calendar," Dorotea said. She had been raised among the Sisterhood, and had no idea that she was actually Raquella's granddaughter. "He won't notice the difference, and Anna is certainly in no hurry to leave."

Raquella allowed warm pride to creep into her voice. "You have always been one of my most competent Sisters. I am impressed with what you've done here in the Palace." She paused. "I expect you were instrumental in the choice of our school for Anna Corrino?"

"I may have suggested it." Dorotea gave a slight bow. "Thank you for coming in person to receive the Princess as a new acolyte. The gesture means a great deal to her family."

"It's a tremendous honor that the Emperor has entrusted her to us. With so many new schools springing up around the Imperium, he had other options."

Dorotea led the visitors deeper into the sprawling palace. "My Sisters and I have proved our worth and set a good example. Given Anna's predilection for immature choices, the Emperor wants to have Anna trained along the same lines as we were." She looked directly at Valya, assessing. "I've read the reports. You are the one who took over my duties assisting Sister Karee Marques in the pharmaceutical research?"

"Yes. We still have much work to do." She bowed, but could hardly contain her excitement. "Right now, though, I am grateful for this opportunity to see the Imperial capital."

Dorotea gave her a faint smile. "Then we have much in common."

Raquella interrupted. "I have confidence in Sister Valya. She has proven herself in many ways. For now, I have added befriending Anna Corrino to her list of duties."

Valya's eyes were bright with excitement at being on Salusa Secundus, giving Raquella pause about the young woman's priorities. She did not find Valya's humble tone convincing as she said, "I'll try to make her feel welcome during her difficult transition to the Sisterhood."

"You two are the same age, so she may warm to you." Dorotea seemed skeptical, too, perhaps because she viewed Valya as a personal rival. "However, the Emperor asked me to accompany his sister, so that she might have a familiar face on a strange world. My work on Salusa Secundus is concluded by Imperial command, so I'll be returning to Rossak myself."

Though she would have preferred to leave Dorotea where she was, Raquella could not countermand Emperor Salvador's wishes. "Very well, you can return to your work with Sister Karee, and I will reassign Sister Valya. I'll be sad to lose you as our representative at the Imperial Court, but we still have four Sisters here." Inside Raquella, voices whispered with excitement, pointing out that few other Sisters were as advanced in their training as Dorotea, or as ready to attempt the transformation. Maybe she would be next. . . . *My own granddaughter!* But all Sisters must be equal, and family ties hidden.

Shortly after giving birth to Dorotea, Raquella's daughter Arlett had refused to be separated from her baby, insisting that she would take the child, leave the Sisterhood, and find the father. Seeing such weakness in her own daughter, Raquella had reached an important decision, encouraged by all those other insistent and objective voices from history.

The Reverend Mother had gone into the crèche chamber where the newborns rested in their cribs. Without hesitation, Raquella removed all the labels from the babies, then moved the children around, and dispatched every mother elsewhere, including Arlett, with instructions to spread the word about the Rossak School across the Imperium.

From that day on, Raquella maintained the policy that baby daughters born to loyal Sisters and raised on Rossak would have no knowledge of their parentage. Each child would start out with a clean slate and no preferential treatment.

When Dorotea was old enough, Raquella had sent her as a missionary to Lampadas so she could work quietly among the Butlerians, to observe and analyze them. The Reverend Mother intended it to be a unique training experience, immersion in an extremist organization to show her granddaughter how people could be driven to illogical lengths by a perceived cause. From that stepping stone, Dorotea had gone to Salusa Secundus and worked her way into the Imperial Court. Now, after years of successful assignments, she would be coming home. Raquella couldn't admit it aloud, but she would be glad to have Dorotea back.

Valya spoke quickly, "Reverend Mother, if Sister Dorotea is leaving the Imperial Court, might I be allowed to remain on Salusa? I would like the opportunity—"

"No." Raquella didn't have to ponder her decision. Not only did she need Valya's help with the breeding-record computers, but she was also well aware of the young woman's ambitions to restore her family's name. "If you are ever assigned to Salusa, it will be to fulfill *our* goals, not your own. Do not forget, you are in the order now, with responsibilities to the rest of us. The Sisterhood is your only family now."

Valya bowed in contrition. "Yes, Reverend Mother. The Sisterhood is a family unlike any other. Perhaps a missionary assignment someday then, if you find me worthy? I appreciate the promotion you gave me, but I would prefer not to stay on Rossak for the rest of my life."

"Patience is a human virtue, Sister."

Dorotea gestured for them to follow her. "Come, I'll arrange for you to meet Anna Corrino."

The five other Sisters who served at court exchanged brief farewells, then went back to their business in the Palace. With whispering footsteps, Dorotea guided the Reverend Mother and her entourage through a labyrinth of vaulted halls and into a less crowded wing with numerous offices, meeting rooms, and library chambers.

Dorotea paused outside the door to a large room, then escorted the four Sisters inside to a small reception chamber, where the petite Anna Corrino waited for them wearing a petulant scowl on her face. A stern-looking female palace guard stood at the doorway just inside the room, to prevent her from leaving. Though Raquella had never met the Emperor's sister before, her Corrino features were instantly recognizable.

Anna sounded aloof, putting obvious contempt into her voice. "When you didn't arrive last night, I was hoping my brother had changed his mind, but you're here anyway."

But Raquella also detected anxiety in her tone. Trying to be sympathetic, she said, "We didn't mean to cause you any undue stress. The spacefolder was delayed." She took one of the girl's hands in her own. "It may take some adjustment from your life here in the Imperial Palace, but you'll like the Sisterhood."

"I doubt that," she said.

Valya came forward smiling, her demeanor much different than it had been a few moments ago. "I don't doubt it. I'll be your friend, Anna. *Sister* Anna. We'll become great friends."

Seeing someone her own age, the other girl brightened and her emotions shifted slightly. "Maybe it's for the best. Without Hirondo, I don't want to be around this place anymore."

Looking backward may seem a simpler exercise than looking forward, but it can be more painful.

—ORENNA CORRINO, the Virgin Empress, private diary

T*wo days*, Princess Anna thought. Only two days until she would have to join the Sisterhood escorts and go to Rossak . . . exiled because she had dared to love the wrong man, because she made her own decisions, because she refused to follow the rules her brothers imposed. In a sense, it seemed romantic, a demonstration that she had stuck to her principles and followed her heart . . . and now she was being sent to an all-women's school. It was so unfair!

The clock was ticking down. She had imagined running off with Hirondo, but even he had balked at the risk. Now she knew she would never see her lover again. Despite Roderick's assurances, Anna wasn't even convinced he was still alive. Maybe she could run away by herself. . . .

Her heart beat rapidly, and she had trouble catching her breath. How could she not be upset over being taken away from the only home she had ever known? Salvador treated her like a spoiled child. Why should he make all the decisions for her?

And though the Sisters had come here, clumsily trying to make her feel comfortable about her new situation, the insular women seemed strange and ethereal. Even at court, she had never liked the lanky Sister Dorotea who always watched and whispered advice to her brothers. Now she was going to be immersed in a whole school of women like that. Anna had no desire to join them, or to be like them—but she had no choice. The heartless Emperor had commanded it.

Guards would prevent her from leaving the extensive palace grounds; nevertheless, Anna hurried outside, feeling a desperate need to hide somewhere, to escape . . . if only for a little while. She took a flagstone path through the ornamental gardens surrounding the Imperial Palace and crossed over a walking bridge that traversed a flowing brook. Glancing back to be sure no one followed, although hidden monitors no doubt tracked her every move, the young woman quickened her pace and took a side path through a grove of Salusan elms. She sought only a few last minutes of freedom before she was formally taken into custody and carted off to another planet. Anna already felt like a prisoner.

Ahead, she spotted one of the larger cottages on the grounds, now boarded up and long abandoned. The structure straddled the brook, so that the water gurgled underneath and turned a tall waterwheel. A chill ran down her spine. She rarely visited this portion of the gardens, given the bad memories associated with that cottage . . . the place where so long ago she had witnessed the terrible crime against her stepmother, Orenna—a crime that had deeply traumatized her and triggered a cascade of bloody events she could never forget.

Anna had only been a little girl then. In the years since, she had forced herself to return here a few times, approaching the isolated house, trying to get closer each time so she could face her fear. Though panic always swirled around her head like startled blackbirds, she tried to convince herself that setting foot inside would somehow erase the nightmares. But Anna never managed to summon the necessary courage. Now she would never have the chance. The scars would remain. . . .

Leaving the manicured trail, Anna made her way toward a maze of fogwood shrubs where she used to play as a child. The unique Ecazi plants were blue-green now, based on a choice Anna had made years ago, using the power of her mind. And, though she had not done so in a while, she could change the colors of the leaves whenever she wished—and otherwise modify the sensitive plants—when she walked by.

Many fogwood species were responsive to human thoughts and moods, but Anna had a particular affinity for this variety, more so than most of the growers. The palace gardeners considered the ornamental shrubs to be defective, because their thoughts could not penetrate them. As a consequence, she had spent much time here as a little girl, surrounded by the dense knot of plants, sensitizing them to her mind; it was her little secret.

Anna had discovered her affinity for these particular plants even before she'd witnessed Toure Bomoko's brutal attack on her stepmother. The dense fogwood grove was her secret place, a child's hideout where no one else was permitted to go. Now, the stiff branches brushed against her as she pressed through; they parted just enough to let her pass, then closed behind her.

Inside, she took a deep, calming breath and sat upon a small bench of bent branches that she had fashioned with her thoughts; above her, the woven branches let in filtered sunlight. In other nooks and baskets mentally shaped out of living twigs, she kept a stash of tins of food, water, games, and old-style books. She could hide here for days and emerge when it was safe.

Most of the time, no one even noticed that she had disappeared, but with the Rossak shuttle due to depart soon, someone would try to hunt her down. She wondered how long it would be before guards raised the alarm. If she could hide long enough, maybe Salvador would think she had already fled to some distant star system. When she finally emerged, perhaps her brother would be so relieved to see her safe that he would decide to let her stay after all.

Half an hour later she heard voices outside her hideout, palace guards calling her name. She ignored them and settled into reading a historical book, an analysis of the events surrounding the rape of the Virgin Empress and the bloody retribution Emperor Jules had commanded against Toure Bomoko and the CET delegates to whom he had granted sanctuary inside the palace grounds.

Anna had been not quite five years old then, so she hadn't understood any of the politics—she still didn't understand them completely, in fact—but the images had been burned into her brain. Emperor Jules had made his young daughter watch the executions, too, somehow believing that the horrific sight would make her feel better. Her mind had been frayed ever since.

As a mark of courage, Anna tried again to learn the complicated background, to understand the decisions and justifications. If the Sisters were going to drag her to Rossak and brainwash her with their mysterious training, this might be her last chance to set her thoughts right.

She used a mental command that made one of the twig-walled cupboards open for her, and she retrieved a tin of melange chocolate biscuits. Nibbling on a biscuit, she continued to read the dense book.

The violent response following the release of the *Orange Catholic Bible* had taken Emperor Jules by surprise. Three years into the riots, after several delegates had already been murdered, the hounded CET chairman, Toure Bomoko, rushed to Salusa Secundus with his party of refugees and begged the Emperor for sanctuary and protection.

Jules's advisers warned against siding with the delegates, pointing out that eighty million people had already been killed in the unrest against the Commission. Hearing that, the aloof Emperor shrugged and famously said, "You exaggerate the danger—that's only six thousand per planet. I lose more than that to tainted sausages!"

So, by the Emperor's command, thirty-five delegates were given sanctuary on Salusa, along with Chairman Bomoko. Jules still didn't understand what people were so upset about, and he assured Bomoko that he would try to calm the masses.

However, when the Emperor attempted to address a bloodthirsty mob in Zimia, the appearance did not go well, and, for his own safety, he was forced to retreat with his guards. Tensions remained high for more than a month.

At the time, her brother Salvador had been thirty-one and Roderick twenty-nine, while Anna was just a child, pampered and sheltered from all the unrest. One day, while playing on the grounds, she had wandered into the waterwheel cottage, looking for her stepmother. She came upon Orenna in one of the chambers, her clothes torn off, and Chairman Bomoko—also naked—attacking her.

Anna had been much too young to understand, but she screamed. Shocked and terrified, she kept screaming. She remembered Orenna screaming as well, then many other chaotic shouts. The guards raced in—Anna recalled only a blur of images now, and she tried to drive them away as she focused on the words in the historical account, such cool and crisp letters to describe a horrible event. One entire chapter was called "The Rape of the Virgin Empress."

Supposedly, Emperor Jules had never shared a bedchamber with his legitimate wife. Realistically, the historians admitted, their marriage may well have been consummated, but Jules and Orenna simply didn't like each other. He preferred his concubines, with whom he had fathered his three children.

However, the furor over the assault on the Empress—raped by a man to whom Jules had so graciously granted protection—drove the ruler over the edge. The Emperor ordered his guards to seize and execute all members of the delegation.

Anna's heart pounded now as she recalled the desperate hours when Imperial guards hunted down and slaughtered all thirty-five of the delegates, bloodying the palace and the surrounding gardens. Though some of the men and women tried to flee, they were caught, dragged out into the public courtyard, and butchered. Anna's father made her watch; Orenna also stood there, as white as chalk, speaking not a word. One delegate after another fell to the hacking blades, begging for mercy that never came.

And somehow in the turmoil, Chairman Bomoko slipped away. He vanished from the palace, which—to the people—only proved his evil genius. Sure that the rapist had received help from some of the staff, Emperor Jules interrogated fourteen suspects; and although they revealed no information, they did not survive the questioning.

Distraught but steely, Emperor Jules had placed himself before the swelling crowds and addressed them again, this time condemning the CET delegates, telling the mobs that he had been wrong before. That was the same year that an assassin's bomb had killed Rayna Butler, which only inflamed the Butlerian movement. Troubled times. . . .

Traumatized by the event, Empress Orenna went into seclusion for many months, and to this day she refused to talk about those dark days. The remaining five years of Emperor Jules Corrino's reign had been hard and reactionary, but Toure Bomoko was never found, despite countless supposed sightings.

Anna closed the book and ate another one of the melange biscuits. Soon, she would be away from reminders of that part of her past. On Rossak, among the Sisters, very little, and perhaps nothing, would bring the events to mind. Maybe it would be for the best after all. Sometimes she hated being part of the Imperial family.

Though she thought the guards had gone to another part of the grounds to look for her, Anna now heard movement outside her fogwood haven. A woman's voice called out, firm but not unfriendly. "Anna, I know you're hiding in there. Move these branches and let me in, please."

Anna froze like a startled deer; she sat on her wooden bench, held her breath.

"Child, you don't fool anyone. It's Orenna—let me in so we can talk. *Please.* I want to help you. I'm alone."

"I'm not a child," Anna said, surrendering a little.

"I know you're not, and I'm sorry. I've seen you shape the fogwood before, but I never told anyone about your secret hiding place, or your special ability with the plants." The voice was soothing. "Come, let me say goodbye."

Anna did have a special bond with her stepmother. Oftentimes, they would talk about plants and birds, or just walk together, silently admiring the natural beauty around them. Orenna had once confided that she thought the two of them were good for each other, therapeutic in a way that neither could have expected.

Even after all these years, they never discussed the rape Anna had witnessed, but it hung there between them, like another presence.

With a sigh of resignation, Anna sent a thought that parted the fogwood branches. Orenna entered, glancing around. "I've always wondered what your hiding place looked like inside." The older woman wore a white silkine gown, with the golden lion Corrino crest embroidered on one lapel. "This is very nice."

"At least it's peaceful." Anna made a branch bend down to create a seat for her stepmother.

Gathering her skirts, the Virgin Empress sat down. With a wink of her rheumy blue eyes, she said, "You won't pull this out from under me, will you?"

Anna giggled. "That depends on what you say. Are you going to try to convince me that I'll be happy on Rossak?"

Orenna looked closely at the young woman. "We have an understanding between us, a bond of friendship. Do you trust me, Anna?"

She needed several moments to answer, but said, "Yes."

Her stepmother pushed silvery hair out of her eyes. "You must realize that there is nowhere for you to go out there. Other than this small refuge, you cannot hide anyplace on Salusa Secundus, and you cannot get off-planet without alerting the Emperor."

"Then I'll stay right here. You can bring me food and drink." She knew the idea would never work even as she suggested it.

"Sooner or later, I'd be noticed, and you'd be discovered."

"Then I will die here. I prefer that to being sent off to Rossak! My life ended when they took Hirondo away from me anyway."

"But must the lives of others end as well?"

"What do you mean?"

"If you don't turn up soon, Salvador will execute Hirondo, and the entire kitchen staff for helping him keep the secret of your love affair."

Tears streamed down Anna's face. "I hate my brother! He's a monster!"

"He is very traditional, and he knows what the public expects of a royal family. He only wants what is best for you, and for House Corrino."

"You're taking his side, just as Roderick does."

Lady Orenna shook her head. "On the contrary, I'm taking your side, child, and I want you to thrive and grow old. I want you to be as happy as possible—as happy as you can be without the man you love. Just as I've tried to be."

The words made Anna pause, and she asked, "What do you mean? Did you love someone you couldn't have?"

Orenna seemed sad, but she made an unconvincing smile, brushed distractedly at her sleeve. "Oh, that was a long time ago, and none of it matters now. I had to move on, and you must do the same."

Anna wiped the tears from her cheeks, gazed at the older woman through reddened eyes. Whom had she really loved?

"Rossak is where you belong now. It will be your sanctuary, just like this little place. Go with the Sisters, learn from their teachings, and when you return you'll be stronger than ever. I promise. Be the best you can possibly be without Hirondo, and in time your sadness will heal. Let him go somewhere else and find a new life."

"But the Sisters don't believe in love. How can you possibly think that will help me?"

"You must find a new kind of inner strength, one that does not rely on your relationship with any man. I have had to do this over the years, and I am stronger for it, a better person."

Anna sat for several long moments, listening for sounds outside, any noises of searchers waiting for her. She went to the perimeter of her chamber and mentally created an opening to look through. The gardens and the woods were perfectly still.

"All right, I'll try it—for you." She embraced her stepmother, then unfolded a leafy doorway and led the way outside.

Every noble family has its dark secrets.
—REVEREND MOTHER RAQUELLA BERTO-ANIRUL,
Sisterhood records

Valya Harkonnen reveled in every day she and her fellow Sisters spent at the Imperial Court. This was where she and her brother belonged, not Lankiveil. Even though she was just a member of the Reverend Mother's entourage, she was still inside the Imperial Palace in Zimia. It gave her a better idea of what her family deserved.

In the past, the Harkonnens had been at the heart of the old League of Nobles, well respected, with an honored history. But thanks to Vorian Atreides, who disgraced Abulurd all those years ago, they were shut out of the circles of power. The reminder gnawed at her, but she used Sisterhood techniques to calm herself and focus her thoughts. Nevertheless, as she looked around at court, she could see the possibilities.

To everyone else here, even to Anna Corrino, she was merely *Sister Valya*. Her family name was never mentioned. Someday, though . . .

Now, she accompanied the Reverend Mother to an audience of the wealthiest Landsraad leaders. She could not stop thinking that the Harkonnens were nobles, too, even though their bloodline had been pruned from the Imperial family tree.

When Reverend Mother Raquella presented herself and her entourage to the Emperor the first evening, Salvador gave them only a cursory greeting. "I hope your school can help my dear sister. She needs guidance and instruction."

"We will watch her carefully, Sire." Raquella bowed. "And see to it that she reaches her potential."

In the midst of his private meal, the Emperor wiped his mouth with a shimmering napkin, then frowned at the remnants of food on his tray, as if he had lost his appetite. He seemed to be suffering from indigestion. "I am anxious to get Anna away from here, and I trust your discretion to draw as little attention as possible. No need to add fuel to the scandal." Valya could read the embarrassment on his face.

However, the next spacefolder from Salusa to Rossak would not depart for two days, so they remained as guests in the Imperial Palace. Valya didn't mind a bit. She drank in the details of the experience, knowing her ancestors had walked the same halls and slept in the same rooms. Her father would have been a duke or a baron in the Landsraad, if their family heritage had not been stripped away. Such thoughts always angered her, and she calmed herself by thinking instead about her brother and how hard Griffin studied to become Lankiveil's official representative to Salusa Secundus. She was sure he would pass his exams.

Meanwhile, Valya tried to work her way closer to Anna Corrino, but the Emperor's sister had no interest in being social, choosing instead to sulk in her quarters. Once they got to Rossak, though, there would be time enough to make friends with her, under circumstances that were not in the Princess's control. Valya did not intend to waste her time here in the Imperial capital. Feeling like a schoolgirl or a tourist, she had asked the Reverend Mother if they might attend the Emperor's business meeting, so that she could observe and dream about what might have been. When Raquella made the request, Sister Dorotea easily obtained an invitation for them to sit in on the proceedings.

Salvador held his audience in an antechamber of the Palace's Autumn Wing, beneath a dome painted with vivid frescoes of the Butlers fighting heroic battles against thinking machines. Facing the audience, the Emperor sat on a great golden chair atop a dais. This secondary chamber was half empty, and the unoccupied seats had been withdrawn into the stone floor, leaving only the appropriate number of benches for the fifty participants to gather close to the throne.

"Today I've decided to have a more intimate session." Salvador's voice echoed across the speaker system, with the volume adjusted too loud for the small audience. He waited for a court technician to reset the controls, then started over. "We have certain economic issues to discuss, areas where planetary leaders can be more cooperative with one another than in the past—for our mutual benefit, of course. With that in mind, I have brought a number of expert witnesses to testify."

Two men in business uniforms filed onto a platform at the base of the dais; one stepped up to a podium and activated a holo-prompter. For several minutes he droned on about tariffs imposed on materials imported between various star systems, surcharges imposed by Venport Holdings for the transport, and the significantly increased risks of contracting with lower-priced shipping companies that did not use the mysterious Navigators. In spite of her giddiness at sitting in on the special session, Valya found it dull—until the gilded door of the hall's main entrance swung open.

A tall, hawk-featured man strode forward, dressed in an old-fashioned, militaristic costume. Looking closer, Valya thought it might be an authentic Army of Humanity uniform from decades ago, adorned with braids and rank insignia. The other attendees of the meeting turned to look, muttering at the interruption; some even seemed relieved for the break from the tedious speech. Valya thought the visitor looked like an actor from a historical drama of the Jihad. Something about him seemed strangely familiar.

The man's focus was too sharp to be distracted by the din of surprised conversation. He marched straight to the podium like a general capturing a strategic hill, and nudged the startled economist out of the way. "It's been more than eighty years since I was last on Salusa, so some of you might not know who I am." He ran his gaze up and down Emperor Salvador on the throne, as if assessing him. "I can see the Butler in you, Sire, a bit more of Quentin than Faykan."

Salvador bristled on his throne. "I don't recognize you, sir. Explain yourself."

Valya suddenly knew who the man was, or had to be. *He was still alive?* A chill ran down her spine, and loathing kept her speechless. She had spent a great deal of time staring at his image, hating what he had done to her family, to her future. But he was still *alive?* It seemed inconceivable.

Since her arrival, she had seen statues of Vorian Atreides in Zimia, and she had studied records of his adventures with Xavier Harkonnen, memorizing his damning speech at Abulurd's trial, which had brought about the downfall of her whole family. Amazingly, the man's appearance had not changed over the course of the Jihad . . . but that was to be expected. The life-extension treatment given to him by General Agamemnon was a matter of public record.

Throughout her life, Valya had known that Vorian Atreides was the cause of her family's disgrace, but it was always a distant, *theoretical* thing. He had disappeared generations ago. Assuming he must be dead, she had hoped that he'd suffered a horrible, painful death.

Now he was here! Her pulse raced, and her skin felt hot with anger.

"I am Vorian Atreides," he said, as if expecting applause. Others had been muttering his name. Reverend Mother Raquella looked stunned, though she had a most peculiar sparkle in her eyes. Salvador sat up, one of the last in the chamber to grasp the identity of the intruder.

"I'm here to demand protection for my world and the end to an injustice. Raiders recently struck our planet of Kepler, took my people. I just came from the slave markets of Poritrin, where I liberated them."

The Emperor sat forward on his throne, and his voice sounded across the chamber's speaker system, again too loud. "Kepler? Never heard of the place." He looked around, but no adviser stood close to him. "That's where you've been all these years?"

"I had hoped to begin anew there. After all I contributed to the Jihad, this isn't too much to ask, is it, Emperor Salvador?"

"No, of course not. If you truly are who you say, then you deserve it. You retired a hero."

Vorian stood straight, not bowing before the throne. "I am here to request protection for my planet and people. While I would prefer that you shut down the Poritrin flesh markets and outlaw the practice of slavery, I know that will never happen. It's not realistic, because of the entrenched interests." He looked at the befuddled economics expert who still seemed anxious to complete his presentation. "However, Sire, I will accept your guarantee of protection for Kepler, so that slavers never bother us again." He continued to look at Salvador as if the rest of the audience did not exist . . . as if Valya did not exist. "I know you Corrinos can grant that much."

"If you can prove who you are." Salvador stepped down from his throne. His initial confusion had gradually slipped into awe. "I suppose that's a possibility, Supreme Bashar. Do you still hold that rank?"

"Supreme Bashar," Vor said. "Also, Hero of the Jihad, and before that I was Primero. I don't know the ranks of your current military. Because of my honorable service, I was granted permission to use my rank as long as I lived—and in my case, that is a very long time. I will submit genetic proof of my identity, if that's what you require."

Salvador blinked, obviously not sure how to deal with such a legendary figure; mutters of admiration rippled through the crowd. "We need to discuss this further, sir, but for the moment we provisionally welcome you back to Salusa. House Corrino remembers your outstanding service during the Jihad and the great victories you achieved on our behalf. If not for your heroism, Supreme Bashar Atreides, none of us would be here today." He came forward to shake Vorian's hand.

The Emperor's deferential attitude made Valya cringe. She thought she'd be sick.

The chamber erupted in cheers and shouts of approval, but Valya had to restrain herself from screaming. After what this bastard had done, how could the Emperor even consider honoring him? *This* man had crushed House Harkonnen and tossed her family on the garbage heap of history. He should be thrown into the deepest Salusan prison.

She wanted to launch herself toward him and attack with every fighting method she knew—but not now, not yet. She had learned patience and planning during her years in the Sisterhood. Now she was here to assist Reverend Mother Raquella and become a companion to the Emperor's sister. She did not want to throw away the opportunity to restore legitimacy to her family.

Her brother, on the other hand, could take care of the rest. She trusted Griffin, and she knew he would do it for her. Now that Valya knew Vorian Atreides was alive, and which planet he called home, Griffin could track him down and take the revenge that his family honor required.

Sadly, I must admit to myself that I am the pinnacle of my bloodline. All my descendants are disappointments, despite the advantage of their breeding.

—GENERAL AGAMEMNON, *New Memoirs*

The twins had remained imprisoned in their preservation vault, immobile and fully aware, for more than a century. In all that time, Andros and Hyla had nothing to do but think and stew and plan. Having never left the laboratory, they had little grasp of the Jihad or of the League humans who fought against the Synchronized Worlds.

The silence inside the sealed facility now seemed heavy and unnatural, as if the walls still reverberated with screams.

"We killed them all too soon." Andros stood in the laboratory module, studying the interesting red patterns splashed on the walls, the strewn body parts of the Swordmasters and Butlerians who had inadvertently released them. "They might have provided more information."

Swordmaster Ellus had been quite reluctant to divulge any secrets, but he did eventually, though Hyla had been forced to use her fingers to extract several of his teeth.

"We can be forgiven our impatience." She tapped her fingertips together and felt the tackiness of drying blood. "I've been restless, and Juno never allowed us much time to practice the skills she gave us."

Thanks to what Ellus had revealed between his screams, Andros and Hyla knew the basic story of humanity's great purge against Omnius and the final victory at Corrin and how the cymek rebellion had ultimately failed. The battle that had wiped out so many neo-cymeks and robotic battleships at this laboratory outpost had been little more than an unmarked skirmish in the much-larger war. Even so, it had left the twins stranded, preserved inside the vault for year after year after year.

Such a thing might have driven a lesser person mad, Hyla thought.

"We should leave here," Andros said. "We'll take their ship, study their records, and find everything else we need to know."

"Juno created us to be superior specimens." Hyla looked around at the slaughter. "We just proved that, but there is so much more we need to know and see and do."

"Juno never returned after Omnius attacked this outpost, and our preparation was incomplete," Andros said. "We'll have to do the rest ourselves."

The Titan Juno—General Agamemnon's chosen mate for more than a thousand years—had been one of the oldest cymeks. Juno, Agamemnon, and the rest of the Twenty Titans had taken over complacent humanity, ruling as tyrants before surgically shedding their organic bodies and placing their brains in preservation canisters, so they could live for centuries inside machine bodies. First, however, Agamemnon had preserved his own sperm in order to create offspring when he deemed it appropriate, but his other sons had failed him, causing Agamemnon to erase them all.

Juno, however, established this secret test program, where she created Hyla and Andros from Agamemnon's sperm and a slave female's eggs. General Agamemnon knew nothing of the plan. Juno had enhanced the children—impregnated their skin with flowmetal, intensified their reflexes, and saturated their minds with sophisticated combat skills and tactical knowledge—imprinting their pliable brains with all the information they would need to become invincible weapons. Worthy children of Agamemnon.

Juno had hoped to launch a larger-scale breeding program once the twins proved the concept. Stalking back and forth in her bulky combat body in front of their indoctrination chambers, Juno had talked with great anticipation about when she would introduce the twins to their legendary father. The words from Juno's speakerpatch carried genuine sadness and anger when she talked about how Vorian Atreides, Agamemnon's thirteenth son and greatest hope, had betrayed him after all.

The twins had listened to every word, absorbing all of that vengeful spite.

The robot attack on this outpost had destroyed the neo-cymek tenders, the laboratory assistants. Hyla was bitter that the cymek queen had so quickly discarded them. According to Swordmaster Ellus in his last gurgling revelations, Juno was dead, as was Agamemnon—both betrayed by *Vorian Atreides*.

"Will we take anything with us from the laboratory?" Andros asked.

"There's nothing we need here. I'm sick of this place. You and I are sufficient. We'll let the vacuum of space reclaim the outpost."

The two made their way to the docked Butlerian ship and rapidly familiarized themselves with the controls inside the cockpit. The pilot had mounted three prominent religious icons on a makeshift altar: a beautiful woman, an infant child, and an androgynous, hairless woman raising her hands and preaching. Hyla discarded the items.

The vessel's navigation system held charts of prominent worlds in the newly formed Imperium. Hyla also found historical accounts of the Jihad against Omnius, celebrations of the great hero Vorian Atreides . . . their brother.

"We have work to do," Andros said, "and a long journey ahead of us."

"We have time. We've already waited a century. Now let's go find our brother."

Andros activated the ship's engines, and the craft rose from the cratered ground, leaving the haunted outpost behind.

The more he thought about it, the Emperor was deeply troubled by the re-emergence of Vorian Atreides, not to mention the demands he made. A legendary war hero, revered by generations of schoolchildren, a leader who had helped save the human race during its greatest conflict . . . and conveniently back again after eighty years of absence? What did the man really want? A handful of military patrol ships to guard a planet that nobody cared about? That seemed highly suspicious.

Salvador was trying to be cautious in this matter of the Atreides scion and the verification of the man's identity. Yes, the longevity of Vorian Atreides was well known and well documented, but anyone with similar features could *claim* to be the long vanished Hero of the Jihad, based upon statues and images in history books. Nobody alive remembered exactly what Vorian looked like in the flesh, or his mannerisms, or the tone of his voice. Besides, the gullible mobs continued to spot the renegade Toure Bomoko around every corner, so appearances were not exactly reliable.

As Emperor, he needed to be careful. But if the man was who he claimed to be (and Salvador suspected he was), perhaps he could ride on the coattails of Atreides's popularity.

In order to give himself time to think, the Emperor sent away the economic experts, the Landsraad attendees, and the Sisters from Rossak, with strict instructions that they were not to speak of the strange visitor they had seen at court, though he knew rumors would leak out soon enough—and then the uproar!—assuming the man's identity could be genetically verified. Vorian Atreides had accepted, even seemed to anticipate such questions and doubts, and had not objected when the Emperor demanded biological samples for testing. For now, Salvador could only delay something that was probably inevitable.

The man submitted to a hasty medical examination by Dr. Ori Zhoma herself, the head of the Suk School, who had recently returned to Zimia for business at the old Suk headquarters. His blood samples were even now being analyzed.

While waiting for the answers, Salvador didn't know whether to be honored or nervous. He needed to talk with Roderick. In the meantime, claiming urgent Imperial matters, he offered Vorian Atreides temporary guest quarters in the Palace. The man from the past seemed to understand Salvador's reticence, felt the awkwardness of their meeting, and took his leave. "I shall await your summons, Sire."

Rather than attending to other business, though, Salvador sat by himself, wrestling with possible scenarios, and spent the afternoon anticipating Dr. Zhoma's report.

Finally, the doctor walked into the throne room, efficient and all business. She performed a pro forma bow to the throne, straightened, and delivered her results in a crisp, professional voice. "We have run our tests, Sire, comparing the new samples with DNA extracted from historical Jihad artifacts. This man is indeed who he says he is: Vorian Atreides."

The Emperor nodded, though he was not entirely pleased with the news. The hero's appearance might cause instability at a time when the Imperium could least afford it. Salvador and his brother needed to decide what to do.

AFTER NEWS OF Vor's return spread, the people of Zimia sprang up in spontaneous celebration, like drooping flowers awakening after a rain. The greatest hero of the Jihad! The legendary Primero who had fought the thinking machines for more than two life spans, from the start of the conflict to its bloody end! The very idea fired their imaginations, excited them, lifted their minds from their troubled, mundane lives. It was as if he had stepped out of a history tome, magically come to life.

Hauling out banners and reenacting pageantry from the days before the Battle of Corrin, the Butlerians marched and chanted, revering the three martyrs: Serena Butler, her baby son, Manion, and Grand Patriarch Iblis Ginjo.

Emperor Salvador accompanied Vor with great smiles in the midst of public acclaim, welcoming him as a long-lost comrade. As the crowds turned out in the Palace square, the Emperor accepted the applause as partially his own. Vor participated in the spectacle like a man enduring an unpleasant medical procedure.

The people treated him as a savior, begging him to touch their babies, to bless their loved ones. The Butlerians adopted him as one of their own, though he did not encourage them. Their movement seemed even more extreme than Rayna Butler's crusade against all forms of machines and technology back during the darkest days of the Jihad. Rayna's followers had wrought a great deal of damage, especially on Parmentier, where his own granddaughter Raquella had tended those who fell ill from the Omnius plagues, and Rayna Butler's followers had turned on her.

These Butlerians made him uneasy.

Decades had passed since Vor last set foot in the capital city, and as he looked around he saw indications of decrepitude; the level of technology had regressed instead of advancing. Subtle signs: vehicles, instruments, even lighting and sound systems for the grand parade in his honor . . . everything seemed slightly more primitive. But he politely watched as the colorful parade filed past the Imperial viewing stand.

Salvador sat next to him, smiling, while his brother, Roderick, remained behind the scenes arranging the event. As the crowds continued to swell in the Palace square, the cheers and excited voices became deafening. The people called out for Vor, chanting his name and demanding that he give a speech. The Emperor raised his hands and tried to impose order, with little success. But when Vor stood up, the crowd fell into a thunderous hush as swiftly as air rushing from an open airlock.

"I thank you for such a wondrous welcome. It's been such a long time. I fought my battles in Serena Butler's Jihad, and now I see the victory I truly gained—a free Imperium, a vibrant civilization, unhindered by the threat of thinking machines." He smiled with false modesty. "And I'm touched that you haven't forgotten me."

In the lull after his words, someone in the crowd shouted out, "Have you come to take the throne? Are you here to lead us?"

Someone else called, "Are you our next Emperor?"

Voices swelled up in a deafening roar, chanting his name: "Vorian! Vorian!"

Startled, Vor laughed and dismissed the comments. "No, no—I came to protect my people on Kepler, nothing more. The Emperor's throne belongs to the Corrinos." He turned to Salvador and bowed slightly in deference to him, inspiring further applause among the crowd. But he could still hear them chanting *his* name, not Salvador's.

And he could see that the Emperor was not at all pleased.

Superstitious fears are childish, a measure of ignorance and gullibility. Sometimes, however, those fears are well-founded.
                    —Suk Medical School records, *Analysis of Stresses on the Human Psyche*

I taught you to think beyond yourself," the Erasmus sphere said. "Now, like the best thinking machine, you can project far into the future, make plans and estimates. Under my guidance, you formed your school here seventy years ago. We taught many humans to order their minds like computers. We improved them, made them less volatile."

Gilbertus said, "And I am pleased by our seventy years of success, starting a decade after the fall of the Synchronized Empire."

"But we must not give up on Utopia." Erasmus's simulated voice held an undertone of scolding.

Utopia. Gilbertus took a deep breath, didn't say what was on his mind, that he no longer felt as he had in his youth, that a thinking-machine Utopia was the most ideal state of society, better than anything humans could create. That had been one of Erasmus's oft-repeated opinions, and it had become so ingrained in Gilbertus's psyche that he had not doubted a word of what the independent robot said to him.

In the years since the end of the Jihad and the Battle of Corrin, Gilbertus had done his own research, keeping careful secrets even from the independent robot. Living among the freed humans, watching the growth of the new Imperium, Gilbertus had studied aspects of society that Erasmus had never shown him. Back on Corrin, the robot had performed many violent experiments on captives and drawn conclusions based on that isolated data set, but once he read the numerous accounts from the old League of Nobles, Gilbertus saw things differently and understood the true bravery displayed during Serena Butler's Jihad, when humans had risked their entire race to throw off the yoke of the thinking machines.

These unfiltered stories were not the same as those Erasmus had taught him, and Gilbertus began to develop a more balanced perspective. It bothered him to think that his great mentor might not be entirely correct, or objective.

But he could not tell Erasmus.

The robot's voice interrupted his thoughts. "I am helpless and vulnerable in this state, Gilbertus, and I grow concerned. Must it really take so long for you to find me another body? Let me have one of those decommissioned combat meks, if you must. You and I together can then fashion a suitable means for me to return to full functionality." He simulated a sigh. "Ah, what a fine body I used to have!"

"It is not wise to rush, Father. A single mistake could destroy everything, and I don't dare lose you." Nor did he dare admit that he feared what Erasmus might do if given his full capabilities again, the destruction he was likely to wreak across the entire populated galaxy. None of this meant that Gilbertus felt any less affection for the independent robot, who would always be his father, but it made their relationship more complex, and guided the decisions he had to make about what he would allow the mental core to do, and where he needed to draw the line.

"But if anything should happen to you . . ." The robot let his words hang in a pregnant pause.

"You did give me the life-extension treatment, remember? But I suppose I could die in an accident. I have considered bringing my student Draigo in on our little secret. An objective man—the best of all the Butlerian trainees Manford has forced me to allow into the school."

Erasmus sounded excited. "You have spoken much of Draigo Roget. If you are positive he can aid us, then by all means we should indoctrinate him."

"But I'm not yet positive of his unconditional loyalty."

The school had started out small. He had escaped Corrin with the rest of the refugees, and after scraping by for a few years, he went to secret stashes that Erasmus identified and gathered the seeds of a fortune, which he'd used to launch his training center. Gilbertus kept his real name, because no one from Corrin had ever known it.

They had chosen Lampadas for its isolation, a place where his students could organize their mental processes without being disturbed. The planet was unkind to them at first, the marshes inhospitable and the training difficult. But Gilbertus succeeded, with the secret help of the independent robot.

Under the system the two of them set up, some of the Mentat School's graduates remained behind to teach classes, while certain special students worked as teaching assistants. Other graduates recruited new candidates from around the Imperium, who in turn came to Lampadas and departed years later as Mentats themselves. . . .

And in all that time, Draigo was the best student (and teaching assistant) of all, soon to graduate with the highest honors in the history of the school.

"I'll ponder it more thoroughly, Father," he said, then carefully sealed away the memory core.

WHEN GILBERTUS ASKED his student Alys Carroll to assist him in completing an inventory of the robot components kept in the teaching storeroom, she reacted as if he had asked her to join him in the depths of hell. *Predictably.* And exactly why he chose her in the first place.

"It is a menial task, Headmaster." She took one step backward and looked away. "Surely one of the newer students would be more appropriate for the task."

"But I did not ask one of the newer students. I asked you." He narrowed his eyes. "I am the creator and Headmaster of this entire school, yet I am willing to do the task because I see the need. I accepted you into this school as a personal favor to Manford Torondo, promising that I would teach you all I know. I'm sure that arrogance was not one of the teachings in our curriculum."

The young woman still looked tense and pale, and she stammered, "I'm sorry, sir. I didn't mean—"

"When you go out into the Imperium and serve a noble household or a large business or banking operation, will you pick and choose among the assignments your master gives you?"

Alys's reply did not answer the question. "I will work for the Butlerian movement, Headmaster, not for any commercial entity. In fact, I have considered remaining here as a teacher. It is vital and necessary to make sure the students receive proper instruction."

"They receive proper instruction," Gilbertus said, his tone edgy. "Whether you are a Butlerian or not, a Mentat must be objective and thorough. Reality does not change just because you don't like the data."

"But a proper presentation of the data can change how reality is perceived."

"This has the makings of a fascinating debate, young woman, but right now, there's a job to be done. Come with me."

With obvious reluctance, Alys followed him to an austere storeroom. He unlocked the door with a key on the chain at his waistcoat pocket. Motion-sensing glowglobes shone like harsh white stars, casting long shadows.

Inside were several partially dismantled robots that Gilbertus had confiscated and applied for teaching purposes—detached robot heads with burnished faces, dark constellations of optic threads, burly piston-and-cable driven combat-mek arms, grasping claws that had been removed from cylindrical torsos. Three combat meks were intact, except that all of their weapons systems had been extracted as a safety precaution.

Alys hesitated at the threshold, just staring at the machines, then forced herself to enter the storeroom.

"Most of these still have rudimentary power sources," Gilbertus said. "We need to know how many of each model we have, which pieces can still be powered on, and which are just worthless scrap metal, serving no purpose. I want a functional inventory."

Because he often visited here, pondering the potential of all these components, he knew the inventory quite well already. Each robot, each dismantled piece, had been obtained at a dear price and after much argument. The Butlerians wanted every vestige of thinking machines eradicated, but he, as well as the instructors at the Swordmaster School on Ginaz, insisted that the leftover robots were necessary for their schools.

"Must we risk powering them on?"

"Risk?" Gilbertus asked. "Why do you say risk?"

"They are thinking machines!"

"*Defeated* thinking machines. You should take more pride in our accomplishments." Allowing no further argument, he stepped up to a metal shelf that contained four detached robot heads.

He knew that Erasmus was watching him now. Spyeyes had been incorporated cleverly into hidden corners of the storeroom, as well as lecture halls, the dining hall, sports enclosures, and some of the perimeter towers. Incredibly thin circuit paths made out of flowmetal no more than a few molecules thick extended like the growing fibers of a complex forest root network, all tracing back to the robot's isolated memory core.

As he looked at the combat meks and forlorn appendages, Gilbertus stroked his goatee and contemplated the incredibly organized civilization of the Synchronized Worlds—all gone, due to the destructiveness of human fear and hatred. And now civilization was being threatened by a movement that feared technology in all its forms, even down to basic industrial mechanisms. Although it sickened Gilbertus, he had to accept the Butlerians and their support of his school . . . for the time being.

Suddenly the optic threads on two of the robot heads in front of him began to glow, glimmering like asterisms. Next, detached combat-mek arms twitched and bent, the segmented fingers extending and then folding again. On the other side of the room, an intact combat mek swiveled from side to side.

Alys Carroll screamed.

The other detached components began to shudder and jump, awakening. Another combat mek glowed to life, raising one weaponless arm.

"They are possessed!" Alys cried. "They must be destroyed. We need to barricade the chamber!" She backed toward the storeroom door, her face as white as milk.

Gilbertus remained calm. "It's just a random power surge, easily fixed." He walked up to the nearest combat mek, fiddled with the torso casing, and removed the power pack so that the robot slumped, dim and dead once more. "Nothing to worry about."

He was sure she didn't believe him, perhaps couldn't even hear his answer. He deactivated the second combat mek, then went methodically around the room, keeping his face placid, although his own emotions were rising. Gilbertus had no question in his mind who had done this. Erasmus had been growing increasingly restless; Gilbertus would have to do something soon to keep the robot in his place.

He shut down the separated limbs, powered off the machine heads, all the while sure that Erasmus was watching, and no doubt amused. Was it a practical joke intended to frighten or provoke his Mentat student? A way to force Gilbertus to take action? The last robot arm clicked its metal fingers together, as if taunting; Gilbertus shut it down by removing the small power cell.

He looked up at Alys and smiled. "You see, this is trivial, although it's a lesson we must learn. In the future we shall take extra precautions." He guided her out of the storeroom, pulled the door shut and, using the key in his pocket again, locked it securely.

In the hall Alys bolted, and he knew she would talk among the other Butlerian students, possibly even submitting a report to Manford. Gilbertus took measured, unhurried steps back to his office, pretending that he felt no urgency.

AFTER ACTIVATING THE hidden panels to reveal the memory core, Gilbertus did not wait before blurting out, "That was dangerous, and foolish!" Though the doors were locked, he fought to keep his voice low, so that no one might overhear him talking while supposedly alone in his private office. "What did your little trick accomplish, except to increase the superstitious fear of one of my students?"

"Your student has already made her feelings quite clear. Her mind may be organized along the Mentat lines you have taught her, but it is not open to new beliefs."

"You didn't make her any more open-minded with what you did! Now she's even more terrified."

The robot manufactured one of his tinny laughs. "I have analyzed many images of her facial expressions. It was quite amusing."

"It was stupid!" Gilbertus snapped. "And there may be repercussions. People will want explanations. Manford could send Butlerian inspectors here."

"Let them come. They will find nothing. I simply wanted to test my new extensions, and I was able to verify my theory about that woman's reaction. Butlerian sympathizers are so predictable."

Gilbertus felt quite agitated. He still wasn't getting through to the independent robot. "You have to understand, Manford and his followers are *dangerous*! If they find you, they will destroy you, and me, and this entire school."

"I'm bored," Erasmus said. "We should go away from here and find a place where we can work together in peace. We can build our own machine city and fabricate an appropriate new body for me. Things can once again be the way they were."

"Things will never be as they were," Gilbertus said. "I give you updates and news reports, but you don't see all the tiny activities going on throughout the Imperium. You don't feel the mood of the people. Trust me. You'll just have to bide your time."

The robot fell silent for a long moment, then said, "It reminds me of when I was trapped in that crevasse on Corrin, frozen in place, locked there for years and years. Now I'm just as imprisoned, except this is worse, because I can see some of what is going on out there. My son, I so want to participate. Think of how much we could learn, how much we could accomplish!"

"All those years in the crevasse with nothing to do but think and expand your mind turned you into the remarkable being you are now. Use this time to keep evolving and improving."

"Of course . . . but it is incredibly tedious. I so enjoyed my body!"

Gilbertus pushed the metallic core back into its hidden shielded alcove, then closed the interlocking compartment segments. He brushed perspiration from his forehead and realized that his heart was pounding.

Even altruism has business implications.
—JOSEF VENPORT,
VenHold internal memo

As Chief Administrator of the Suk School, Dr. Zhoma could not afford to keep a low profile. Her job was to seek benefactors, highlight the benefits and accomplishments of the Suks—and save the school from its desperate straits. Taking it upon herself to push for the development of advanced medical technology, especially among reactionary populations who viewed science with suspicion, she gave frequent informational speeches to planetary leaders on the League worlds, hoping to inspire them.

Though she was not a woman to panic or overreact, Zhoma took great care to conceal just how shaky and unstable the school's finances were after years of mismanagement and corruption by her predecessor. Suk funding had also been damaged by the baffling and ever-growing tide of Butlerians, who shunned sensible medical treatment and testing in favor of prayer. Through it all, the Suk order had to survive, and Dr. Zhoma was determined to save it, regardless of rules or conventions she might have to bend, or break. Even Reverend Mother Raquella did not know of their budgetary plight, because Zhoma would have been ashamed to admit it to her.

In the year since taking over her position from the charlatan and embezzler Elo Bando, she had spent very little time serving as a physician; instead, she constantly sought funding and promoted the cause of the Suk School. In effect, she had become a solicitor rather than a doctor, but such work was necessary for the survival of the institution, which was widely acknowledged as the best humanity had to offer.

She had been giving investors a tour through the old Suk headquarters building in Zimia when Emperor Salvador called for her to verify the identity of the man who claimed to be Supreme Bashar Vorian Atreides. She had met Salvador numerous times, as he repeatedly requested replacement doctors and she assigned new ones. The Emperor went through many physicians, treating most of them badly; he hadn't liked a Suk doctor since Elo Bando (which, in itself, didn't speak much for the Corrino Emperor's intelligence, because Bando had been a villain and an idiot).

Nevertheless, Zhoma had been eager to demonstrate her personal capabilities to the Emperor himself, proving her competence. If the Corrinos became patrons of the Suk doctors, the school's financial worries would be over. Alas, that was not likely to happen.

And now she was off on another mission for the school—this time a much more private one. Sometimes, out of sheer necessity, she had to operate in gray areas of the law—as she had done during her brief years at the Sisterhood. The Reverend Mother had once scolded her for easy rationalizations and convenient situational ethics, but Zhoma knew that Raquella would have made the same choices if her Sisterhood were at stake.

This time, rather than speaking at a banquet or meeting with treasury representatives, Dr. Zhoma had to hide her movements so that no one could track her. She had already assumed three different false identities on the trip to a distant star system, boarding a VenHold ship under one name, getting off, and embarking on another ship as another person, hopscotching from planet to planet to reach an important rendezvous.

Finally, aboard the appropriate vessel on the appropriate date, she met with Directeur Josef Venport himself.

All his vessels had ultra-secure decks that housed their mysterious Navigators, as well as restricted areas and administrative boardrooms for conducting business. Zhoma was not dressed as a Suk doctor; she had set aside the traditional silver metal ring that bound her dark-brown hair. Here, she was a businesswoman seeking funding.

Venport was a husky man with a prominent mustache, heavy eyebrows, and a thick head of combed-back hair. They had met before, both openly in Landsraad situations, and in secret, like today. He had the resources to keep the school intact.

Now he sat at a flat desk that hovered at exactly the right height, held up by a sturdy suspensor field. Its writing surface was an extremely thin sheet of bloodwood from Ecaz, and the preserved crimson wood grain still flowed and pulsed like a wounded circulatory system.

Venport was a rugged and inflexible man, yet his eyes now held a twinkle of amusement. "You do understand, Dr. Zhoma, that it's futile to work so hard at hiding your movements? Every passenger is monitored and investigated from the moment they board."

A knot coalesced in Zhoma's stomach. She always prided herself on her proficiency. "You keep track of everyone on your ships? *Everyone?*" Considering the number of passengers that moved among the thousands of worlds in the Imperium, she shuddered to think of the sheer recordkeeping capacity that such an effort would require.

"The VenHold Spacing Fleet has sufficient computing power, in addition to Mentats and expert observers who are trained for our purposes." For Venport to admit that he used computers—nonsentient ones, of course—was a provocative statement; perhaps he meant to demonstrate a level of trust in her; perhaps he was simply flaunting his invincibility.

"I hope you don't share the information you acquire," she said.

"Of course not. As a doctor, you also hold a great deal of confidential medical data. We wouldn't want that to get out, either. Hmmm, we are fiduciaries of certain information, you and I."

She straightened. "The Suk School rests on a foundation of trust and reliability. We hold the confidence of our patients to be sacred."

Venport brightened. "You see? Rational people understand rational needs. But all too often we have to deal with irrational people, and in times like these, when headstrong barbarians are intent on plunging us into a new Dark Age, I have to be sure of my own allies. That's why I've been willing to help your school." He folded his hands on top of the bloodwood desktop. The dark red patterns swirled around in an unsettling way.

Dr. Zhoma managed a brittle smile. Venport had been very generous in helping the Suk School through its severe financial difficulties, but he still charged enough interest to cripple their already shaky treasury. She would have to test his generosity now. "I've come to ask a bit more indulgence and understanding from you, Directeur Venport."

A frown flickered across his face, and his demeanor changed ever so slightly. He was not a man who liked when things did not go his way. "Please explain further."

"I'll need more time, or more flexible terms, to make the next few scheduled payments. With all of our new facilities on Parmentier, the Suk School is in a difficult transitional period."

"Still in budgetary chaos, you mean," Venport said.

"That's the legacy of my predecessor, Dr. Bando—as you well know." Zhoma swallowed hard, trying to fight back the flush of shame.

"Fortunately, he is no longer with us." Venport gave her a knowing smile, which only deepened the disgrace she felt for her involvement in his death.

Elo Bando had been found dead in his opulent new headquarters office at the half-constructed school complex on Parmentier. Bando had chosen to move the main school complex from Zimia to the former homeworld of the school founder, Mohandas Suk, where the great man had spent years tending the terminally ill.

Elo Bando's death had been ruled a suicide, a self-inflicted overdose—a conclusion that was absurd to anyone who looked at the record: He had been injected more than fifty times with various poisons, stimulants, and hallucinogens, so that his death was long and agonizing. Dr. Zhoma, the school's secondary administrator at the time, insisted on conducting the pro forma autopsy herself, but she already knew the conclusion she would write in the formal records, and she did not regret what she had done. There could be no excuse for the man's obscene behavior.

The reprehensible Bando had nearly destroyed the fine academic institution that Mohandas Suk had founded decades ago, robbing the students and humanity of an enduring legacy of medicine. But the money was gone, thanks to the self-serving, profligate man, and the numerous training hospitals under construction on Parmentier were on the verge of bankruptcy.

Bando had gained great prominence by worming himself close to Salvador Corrino, gaining the Emperor's trust, preying upon his phobias, and proposing a host of imaginary and expensive treatments—"poison-protection therapy" and bogus life-extension treatments. For his services to the Emperor, Bando had pocketed huge sums, which he then leveraged to expand the Suk facilities far beyond the school's means, so that the organization appeared to be flourishing. It was all an illusion, and the school was greatly in debt, built upon a foundation of eggshells.

Zhoma had caught Elo Bando at his crimes. When she discovered that he had already squirreled away a fortune and was preparing to flee, Zhoma killed the vile man herself, then covered up the matter. It was necessary and she had done it without hesitation, afraid the corruption scandal would expose the school's precarious financial position. But Bando had conducted his con well and managed to fool all outside observers, especially Emperor Salvador.

In order to keep the institution solvent, Zhoma didn't dare reveal to the Emperor how Bando had duped him, so she was forced to turn to alternatives. Foremost among them, Venport Holdings had vast sums of money distributed across numerous enterprises, including interplanetary banking. The tycoon had his own sources of information, and after a careful study of Elo Bando's autopsy report, he easily surmised what Dr. Zhoma had done—and did not hide what he knew.

Oddly, her method of dealing with the quack Bando earned her Venport's delighted respect. He told her that he admired how she'd solved a sticky problem, not to mention the fact that she had gotten away with it. Amused and impressed, he had agreed to loan Zhoma large sums of money. "I do, in fact, understand you very well, Doctor."

At first, Zhoma was concerned he would use the knowledge to blackmail her, but Venport was a man who hoarded interesting information, even when he did not necessarily make use of it. But he could, of course, at any time.

Though murder went against Suk principles, Zhoma knew she had done the right thing, the honorable thing, in killing the charlatan for the sake of the school. She longed to tell the Reverend Mother about it one day, sure the older woman would understand. Even after all these years away from the Sisterhood, Zhoma felt she needed Raquella's acceptance, if not forgiveness.

She sat stonily now, facing Venport's scrutiny. "It's more than just the financial improprieties my predecessor caused," she said. "Our school continues to suffer from the Butlerian attitude, the foolish resistance to basic medical technology. They have ransacked, even shut down, some of our modern treatment facilities on other planets. Many lives have been lost because testing scanners and surgical instruments have been smashed."

His expression darkened. "You don't need to convince me, Doctor."

"I have faith that enlightenment will prevail."

"I wish I could share your faith, Dr. Zhoma, but rabid faith is the biggest problem humanity faces now, and the next Age of Reason will not come easily in this time of magical beliefs and superstitious fear."

"So we must continue the fight. You have thrown our school a lifeline, Directeur Venport, and I'm afraid we'll need it just a little longer."

He cleared his throat and said, "I understand the difficulties you face, but let's discuss practical considerations. As businesspeople."

She swallowed hard, fearing what terms he would impose.

"Here is my solution: I understand that you recently acquired and tested biological samples of Vorian Atreides, on orders from Emperor Salvador? Everyone thought him long dead, but now that he's come back, he hasn't aged a day—and the man is over two centuries old!"

"Due to General Agamemnon's life-extension treatment," Zhoma said. "That's a matter of record in the Annals of the Jihad, but the technique has been lost. Only the cymeks knew how to perform the procedure."

"And wouldn't it be a triumph to find it again? In any event, I want those original samples, Dr. Zhoma. Surely they have not been discarded. Obtain them for me, and I'll accept that as the Suk School's next three payments."

Zhoma's brow furrowed. "Those samples are private, strictly for proving the genetic identity of Vorian Atreides. You spoke of fiduciary responsibility earlier, so you already understand that it is highly unethical to use them in any unauthorized manner." From Venport's expression, she could see that he was not at all interested in her moral dilemma. When he continued to regard her in silence, she asked, "What are you going to do with them?"

"That is not your concern. Just see that it's done."

History is best left in the past, so that legends do not interfere with our daily lives.

—RODERICK CORRINO, private memo to the Emperor

Wearing his old dress uniform from a military force that no longer existed, Vorian Atreides met privately with the Emperor and Roderick Corrino. Despite the lavish surroundings in the Imperial Palace, he preferred his private home with Mariella on quiet Kepler.

Now that he had reappeared with such fanfare in the public eye, however, he feared the people would not leave him in peace. The enthusiastic public reaction during the recent parade had disturbed him as much as it had the Emperor.

As Vor entered the Emperor's personal office, he noted the gilded desk and tables, the priceless paintings on the walls, the ornately woven curtains tied back with gold braids. He remembered his years of fighting in the old League of Nobles; he had been a hero to the people and could easily have crowned himself the first Emperor after the Battle of Corrin. Back then, Faykan Butler had been afraid of Vor's popularity, not understanding that Vor never had imperial ambitions. He had been paid off and sent away . . . which was exactly what Vor wanted.

Now, summoned by Roderick and Salvador Corrino, he could guess that they wanted the same thing. And he would make them pay dearly—again.

The three men sat at a whorled elaccawood table, and Vor opened the discussion by talking about the dark practice of slavery on the fringe worlds, as well as the cruel men who had recently struck Kepler. "Perhaps it's time for me to lead a different crusade." Vor let the anger bubble in his voice, making sure they knew he could cause plenty of trouble if he wished. "Didn't the Jihad teach us that human beings should not be treated in such a way?"

"Slavery is still an important part of the economy out in the frontier," Roderick observed.

"Then frontier planets need to be protected from the slavers."

At the head of the table, Salvador looked unsettled. "There are so many planets, how can we watch them all?"

Vor narrowed his eyes. "You can start by watching Kepler. Protect my world." Leaning forward, forcing himself to remain calm, Vor described the day that many of his people had been taken; he submitted a full roster of their names, as well as his bill of sale to prove that he had purchased them from Poritrin. "I freed them this time, but that doesn't solve the problem. More slavers will prey on my world—and even if they don't strike my valley again, they will go to one of the other settled areas. You must not allow that to happen, Sire."

Roderick's expression was hard. "We hear your passion, Vorian Atreides, but in an Imperium burdened with crises, a few unruly slavers on minimally populated planets are not our predominant concern."

"If I chose to rally the people, I could make it a predominant concern," Vor said.

Salvador's anger flared, but Roderick remained calm. "Perhaps you could use your celebrity to accomplish that—and perhaps we can come to some *reasonable* accommodation. What, precisely, would you like us to do about your situation?"

"You can't ask us to outlaw slavery entirely!" Salvador blurted out.

"I could ask for that, but it would not be practical." His gaze shifted to the Prince. "What can you do in exchange for my silence, you mean?" Vor paused, and provided the answer. "Simple enough. Issue an Imperial decree announcing that Kepler is off-limits to slavers, then give me a dozen or so warships to discourage anyone who doesn't listen."

Salvador rocked back as if he had been slapped. "One doesn't speak to the Emperor in such a manner. It is customary to make requests, not demands."

Vor found that humorous. "I knew your great-great grandfather. I fought at his side, and his son's, and his grandson's—long before you called yourselves Corrinos and long before the Imperium existed at all." He leaned across the table. "Considering the fact that my family was kidnapped and sold into slavery, you will forgive me for skipping a few niceties. I came here to request your help, but I can just as easily call upon the people. You saw their reaction at the parade. They would rally around a living legend. They've seen statues with my face, and coins imprinted with my likeness—just like an Emperor. But I'm sure you would rather they cheered for you than for me."

While Salvador reddened, Roderick made a calming gesture to his brother, then said, "Our Imperium is fragile enough as it is—the CET riots, the Butlerians, so many powerful interests pulling us in all directions." He spoke as if his words were written on fine parchment even before he uttered them. "We shall not tolerate you creating more unnecessary turmoil. Our people must think of the future, not be reminded of the bloody past."

Salvador's voice was darker. "Have you come to set yourself up as the next Emperor? As the people shout out?"

Vorian gave a cold laugh. "I left such personal aspirations behind long ago, and do not intend to revisit them. I have retired and want to be left alone. As I come before you, Sire, I swear my allegiance to you, and swear that I have no interest in taking any role in government or in appearing before the full Landsraad." His gray eyes hardened. "But I do want my family and planet protected. Keep my people safe and you have nothing to worry about. I will slip back into obscurity. You'll never see me again." Vor looked away. "Frankly, I'd rather have it that way, too. I just want to go home and be left in peace."

"Unfortunately," Roderick said, "the people know you are alive now. They will come to you at Kepler, beg you, pester you, ask you to come to the aid of the Imperium by taking up the mantle of a legend. How long will you be able to resist their demands for you to return to public life?"

"As long as necessary."

Vorian understood that Salvador would feel threatened, would never be the center of attention when the great war hero was present. Since the current Emperor was not even the legitimate child of Emperor Jules Corrino, the dynasty was already weakened. Vor could take over the Imperium, if he wanted it. But he didn't.

"I give you my word I will remain on Kepler with my family. You need never see me on Salusa again."

Salvador remained silent, considering the offer. Roderick said, "The solution isn't quite that simple, Supreme Bashar. You have stepped back into the limelight. The people *know* you are still alive after they've assumed you to be long dead. You cannot stay on Kepler. You have to vanish again."

"I prefer to keep a low profile anyway. I'll change my name if I must."

Roderick shook his head. "You won't be able to stay hidden on Kepler. People know you too well there." His face was hard. "This is one guarantee we will require of you as a condition of our help. Leave the planet and Kepler will never need to worry about the threat of slavers again. We'll issue a decree of Imperial protection and provide a few warships in orbit to keep slaver ships away, as you requested. Imperial troops will operate the guard ships initially, but the vessels will eventually be turned over to the control of the local Kepler government. Under this arrangement your people will be safe, your family and friends—but *you* must leave, go to some other planet."

"Vanish back into history, where you belong!" Salvador interjected.

Vor swallowed, but could taste only dust. Leave Kepler? Leave Mariella, their children, and grandchildren? He had been happy there for decades, watching the babies grow up to become parents and his wife grow old. . . . while he had not aged a day.

But he also remembered the lumbering slaver ships, how they had so easily stunned the entire village, whisking away all the captives they wanted and killing a dozen others. He had promised he would find a way to keep them safe. . . .

"My solution repays the Corrino debt of honor, protects your people, saves a whole world," Roderick said. "Just move on and quietly vanish again for the rest of your life, however long that may be."

Before Vor could answer, the Emperor cut in. "That's our offer. Take it or leave it."

Unable to forget the burning fields and buildings on Kepler, or the crowded, stinking slave markets of Poritrin, Vor understood the reality. It was time for him to turn the page and begin the next chapter in his long life.

When he agreed, he saw the Emperor breathe an unmistakable sigh of relief.

On my own planet, I make my own rules. And I have many planets.
—JOSEF VENPORT, VenHold internal memo

With a private space fleet at his command and dedicated Navigators to guide him safely through foldspace, Josef Venport could travel wherever he wanted, whenever he wanted. His wife, Cioba, could easily handle the intricate management activities back on Kolhar, while he went off to deal with other important business. Some of his destinations were unknown to anyone else in the Landsraad League, planetary coordinates held only in the grossly expanded minds of the Navigators. The galaxy was a vast place, and even something as large as a solar system could easily be overlooked.

Many isolated colonies and outposts had been established, and forgotten, during the millennium of thinking-machine rule; Emperor Salvador—and especially the barbarian fanatics—did not need to know about them. The sanctuary planet of Tupile was one such world, the hiding place to some of the Imperium's most-wanted fugitives (after they paid exorbitant fees to VenHold). Josef didn't care much about the people who hid there; it was simply a business transaction.

Dr. Zhoma had come through for him with the genetic samples, as he'd known she would. The Suk School had no other choice, and her little misdeed wasn't, after all, so much to ask.

His own particular interest at the moment was the unpleasant planet Denali, a small, hot world with a thick and poisonous atmosphere, where no human could survive except inside sturdy colony modules. Josef had made a point of establishing his own private outpost in a solar system that no scout would ever notice, on a world where the Butlerians would never discover the research projects funded by Venport Holdings.

A personal Navigator flew him aboard a small spacefolder to the Denali system, after which Josef personally guided the shuttle through the orange-gray clouds that denoted sulfur and chlorine gases. He landed in the paved clearing next to the cluster of garishly lit metal domes, the laboratory modules and living spaces for his scientists.

Josef looked through the cockpit windows into the corrosive murk as the connecting airlock sealed his shuttle to the docking module. Outside, he could see a few discarded skeletal forms of cymek walkers, hulking machine bodies that had once held the brains of near-immortal men and women. Long ago, this harsh planet had been a cymek outpost, and the debris of their mechanical bodies lay strewn about, dumped into a scrap heap for spare parts. *Research materials.* Just one of many projects here on Denali.

Though he visited this secret facility only rarely, he transmitted strict orders that the teams were not to interrupt their work just to greet him with frivolous fanfare. Josef did not want to disturb the individual scientists; there was too much at stake.

As he entered the complex, he drew a breath and caught a sharp whiff of brimstone and harsh chlorine, trace contaminants from the outside air that scrubbers could not remove. Josef supposed his research teams no longer even noticed the odors.

With small hands knotted in front of him, Administrator Noffe greeted Josef. Noffe was a hairless Tlulaxa scientist, the side of his face marred by three startlingly white blotches. Noffe had never explained where the marks had come from, but Josef imagined some kind of laboratory accident, a splashed bleaching chemical that caused permanent damage. VenHold hadn't hired Noffe to be pretty anyway, but to be brilliant.

The Tlulaxa chief of research always sounded breathless. "Even if we had ten times as many facilities and a hundred times as many researchers, Directeur Venport, it would take more than a lifetime just to recreate the progress that's been lost since the end of the Jihad." It was a sobering thought.

Though he was an advocate of progress, Josef was not blind to the dangers raised by some of the research; hence, the other reason for the planet's isolation. Each lab module had a rigorous quarantine system, protective walls, and self-contained fail-safe circuits so that if an experimental plague were to escape or a computer subroutine were to achieve aggressive sentience, the entire module could be isolated and, if necessary, annihilated.

Noffe had been a well-known researcher back on Thalim, where he had dedicated himself to cloning and genetics investigations, determined to create good works to erase the blotch of shame on his race's history. But the Butlerian mobs had not liked that. They had come to the Tlulax system, conquered the planet, demolished the genetic and cloning laboratories (which they didn't understand), and imposed harsh restrictions on all Tlulaxa scientists. Under a new draconian rule, they set up a religious board whose approval was required to conduct even the most basic laboratory tests. Noffe spoke out against the injustice, complaining that the zealots didn't understand how they were harming humanity. And so they arrested and convicted him.

But Josef Venport had recognized the scientist's potential and arranged for Noffe's escape, whisking him to Denali and appointing him administrator, where he had been quite content and productive for several years now. Noffe took a cold pleasure in overseeing avenues of investigation that would make the barbarians squirm and gnash their teeth.

Josef carried a small sealed case of biological samples as he followed the small man into the adjoining module. "I have a new project for you, Administrator. Something close to my heart."

"I'm always open to new ideas. But first let me show you what we've accomplished since my last report." Noffe led him on a cursory inspection of the numerous projects underway at Denali. He was quite proud to guide Josef into a room filled with tanks that held exposed human brains, some swollen and mutated, others shriveled. "The brains of failed Navigators are particularly interesting and responsive," Noffe said. "We've even made preliminary contact with some of the subjects in the preservation canisters."

Josef nodded. "Excellent work. I'm sure they must be proud to provide such a service, after failing to become Navigators."

"We learn from failures as well as successes, Directeur."

Back on Kolhar, Norma Cenva churned through volunteers, expanding and enhancing their minds to make them sophisticated Navigators—but many of the candidates did not survive the transformation, their bodies collapsing, their skulls unable to sustain the physical growth of gray matter. Since the mutated failures would die anyway, Josef dispatched the subjects to Denali so that Noffe's researchers could perform their experiments. It was a fundamental first step in understanding the remarkable changes undergone by a Navigator; someday, it might be possible to reproduce those mental skills without requiring such extreme bodily changes.

When they returned to Noffe's office chamber, the Tlulaxa could no longer hide his eagerness as he looked meaningfully at the case that Josef still carried. "What is it you've brought, sir?"

He set the case on Noffe's metal desk, opening the seal. "These are biological samples from Vorian Atreides." He paused, watching for a reaction on the bald Tlulaxa's face.

"The greatest hero of the Jihad? Have these samples been preserved in stasis all these years?"

"They are fresh. Taken from Vorian himself only weeks ago." Seeing the Tlulaxa's surprise, he continued, "The old warhorse is more than two centuries old and looks as young as I do. His father, General Agamemnon, gave him a life-extension procedure that was common for cymeks."

"I don't think anyone knows how to do that anymore," Noffe said.

"Precisely. I want you to use the cellular history in these samples to rediscover the process. Learn what the cymeks did to prevent Vorian Atreides from aging . . . and how we can reproduce it for ourselves." The Denali administrator took the sample case with sudden reverence, and Josef continued, "With all the work we have ahead of us, we are going to need that procedure. We have to survive if we're going to save humanity."

Vengeance is as difficult to define as it is to deny.
—GRIFFIN HARKONNEN, letter to Valya

After the loss of his uncle Weller and the entire shipment of whale fur, Griffin Harkonnen no longer looked forward to the arrival of the regular Celestial Transport supply ship. The cargo vessels had been his connection with the rest of the Imperium, bearing news and messages to and from Salusa Secundus, documents that made Lankiveil, and himself, a part of the larger governmental landscape.

But now he felt as if a door had been slammed in his face. His sister was well aware of the importance of their uncle's venture, and Griffin didn't know how he was going to tell her. . . .

"It's a setback, not a complete disaster," Griffin said to his father, though he did not truly believe his own words.

Standing next to him in the parlor, his father said, "Of course, you're right. We'll get through this. My brother never should have left the planet, should have just remained here, at home. . . ."

In the latest mail delivery, among the letters and packages, Griffin found a paltry settlement payment from Celestial Transport to compensate for the loss of their "loved one" (the form letter hadn't even included the name of the deceased) as well as payment for the insured amount of the cargo, which was vastly undervalued. Due to the limited distribution, Griffin could not prove how much whale fur was worth away from Lankiveil. If the commercial venture had succeeded and the demand had risen, they would have had plenty of financial data, but as it was, he couldn't prove the case.

"Please accept our deepest sympathies and this respectful attempt to make

things right," the letter continued. "Note that acceptance of these funds consti-
tutes an agreement to hold Celestial Transport blameless and waives the right to
claim further damages against this company or any of its subsidiaries. This agreement is legal and binding upon you, your heirs, and assigns in perpetuity."

Griffin was upset by the callous tone in the letter, and considered the amount
of the check an insult. "This is only a fraction of the cargo's value! How does
that compensate for our loss? I've studied legal precedents in the Salusan code.
We have two years in which to file a dispute and pursue litigation."

Vergyl Harkonnen, though, had neither the heart nor the inclination to
fight. "Chasing after wealth cost Weller his life." Holding the check, he sat down
and shook his head. "Why let greed and vengeance deepen our wound? We must
accept this payment, and make the best of rebuilding our lives."

Griffin let out a bitter sigh of resignation. Although he knew Celestial Transport was cheating them, a legal battle against such a wealthy entity would be like
wading chest-deep through a bog in the Lankiveil highlands. To fight them
for their incompetence he would have to dig deeper into the severely weakened
treasury, devoting all of his attention to the matter while letting other commercial opportunities fall by the wayside. The matter would drag on for years . . .
and even if House Harkonnen won the case, the final balance sheet would show
a loss.

If he received confirmation that he had passed his political examination,
Griffin could go to Salusa Secundus as Lankiveil's official planetary representative,
and address the Landsraad assembly. He could demand tighter regulations, more
oversight on foldspace shipping operations. If he could get appointed to important
committees, he intended to demand an investigation into Celestial Transport's
business practices.

But he could not abandon the family holdings here on Lankiveil. Their treasury was badly diminished, and his parents could not manage or even grasp the
magnitude of the crisis they faced. It would take the greatest finesse for Griffin to
keep House Harkonnen solvent, hoping that someday he could rehabilitate the
stained family name. With the loss of his uncle and the huge monetary setback
of an entire fur-whale harvest, Griffin felt his diminished dreams turning inward, leaving him with little ambition beyond keeping his home and family from
ruin.

A *setback*, he emphasized to himself . . . *not a complete disaster.*

He knew his sister would have clung to her righteous indignation as a weapon,
demanding satisfaction from Celestial Transport rather than peace. Griffin and
Valya had always enjoyed a close bond, while a large gap of age separated them
from their younger siblings, Danvis and Tula.

But Valya had been away on Rossak for years, and he hoped her time with the Sisterhood's intensive studies and meditation had channeled her energies in productive directions. She counted on him here, but he feared he had already let her down. . . .

Ten years ago, when he and his sister were thirteen and twelve, respectively, his father and uncle had taken them out on a boat into the frigid northern waters, tracking a fur-whale pod. Riding into choppy seas, Griffin and Valya both enjoyed the adventure. They had never imagined danger, and their father had ignored the need for life preservers, against the advice of the crew.

Standing on the bow, laughing at the spray, the teenage Griffin failed to see the wave that came from the starboard side and washed him overboard with the casual unexpectedness of someone swatting an insect. Griffin was stunned— plunged into the arctic water and clamped in an impossible vise of cold. In only a few seconds he could barely move, and could barely manage to keep his head above the surface.

As he struggled in the water, he remembered looking up to see his father staring down in horror from the deck rail, and his uncle Weller yelling for ropes and a life preserver. Then Griffin slipped under.

And Valya . . . *Valya* went in after Griffin. With no thought of herself, she dove into the water. Defying the paralyzing cold, she stroked out to him, grabbed him by the shoulders, and lifted his head above water. And then, her adrenaline exhausted, she began to succumb to the icy water, too.

Life preservers and rescue ropes had splashed in the water, and he could barely hold on. Gasping, shivering, cursing, Valya kept him afloat just long enough for the boat to come around again . . . but now she was slipping away. She made certain Griffin had a hold on the life preserver, and then went limp and gray.

Though Uncle Weller shouted for the sailors to haul up the rope, Griffin clutched his sister, refusing to let go. He kept his frozen fingers knotted into her wet blouse. He lost consciousness, but never released his grip.

Afterward, when they were both dry, wrapped in thick blankets and surrounded by heaters in the cabin of the fur-whale boat as it chugged back to their home fjord, Griffin looked at his sister in disbelief. "That was stupid. You shouldn't have jumped in after me."

"You would have done the same for me." And Griffin knew she was right.

"We both could have died," he said.

"But we didn't—because we can count on each other. . . ."

And how true that was. He'd already returned the favor a year after she rescued him, when three drunken fishermen tried to attack her near the docks. She had always been attractive, and the Harkonnen name had meant little to the brutes. Valya could have fended off one of the large men with her speed and surprising strength; three, though, were too formidable. Still, her toughness had bought valuable time, allowing Griffin to sense her peril and rush to her aid. They'd made quick work of the drunken trio, and their father had pressed charges afterward.

Griffin closed his eyes at the recollections. He and his younger sister shared a bond that touched on the paranormal. Whenever either of them felt depressed or had other troubles, they seemed to sense it about each other, even though they were apart.

Now, he missed her terribly. . . .

Uninterested in the rest of the newly arrived packages, letters, and official documents, Vergyl and Sonia Harkonnen took their younger children, Danvis and Tula, out to comb a rocky beach on the main channel, hoping to gather shellfish. They left Griffin to manage the administration activities of Lankiveil, as they had been doing since he was twenty.

Going to the town's business offices, Griffin spent the day overseeing the distribution of the newly arrived items, along with cargo that had been delivered to the municipal warehouses. Then he sat in on a meeting where groups of fishermen argued over the rights to certain deepwater coves.

Just another day on Lankiveil . . . although Griffin wasn't sure he would ever feel normal again after the recent losses.

When he returned home in the late afternoon, the house smelled of rich herbs, pepper oil, sea salt, and the persistent tang of fish. The cook had made a large kettle of her special chowder, as well as fresh-baked rolls. The smell of the chowder began to whet his appetite, but he would wait to eat until his family returned.

In his home office, Griffin sorted through the correspondence the CT ship had delivered, and much to his delight he found a small package from Valya. He was under the impression that the Sisterhood pressured its members to avoid nostalgia, homesickness, and family ties; her letters home were rare, and very special.

Opening the package, he found that it contained a small, old-style memory crystal of a type used only by antique hologram readers—a model that Valya knew her brother had in his possession. The device was old, something Abulurd Harkonnen had brought to Lankiveil in his initial exile. Eager to hear what she had to say, Griffin rummaged through his shelves and drawers until he found the old reader, inserted the crystal, and played it.

A small, shimmering image of his sister appeared—dark-haired, with intense eyes, generous lips, and an attractiveness that would become outright beauty if she softened with age. When he heard Valya's voice, it was as if she had never left Lankiveil.

"I have seen Vorian Atreides," she said without preamble. "The blackheart has returned! Finally, we have a chance for justice." Valya squared her shoulders, as if she imagined her brother reeling back in astonishment.

"He is not dead, as we thought, but has been in hiding, and now he's back. Damn him, he looks as young and healthy as ever! Emperor Salvador fawned over him, celebrated his visit—Vorian Atreides!" Disgust flowed from her words. "You should have seen his face, his attitude, as if he owned the Imperium. . . . By now he must think the Harkonnens have forgotten what he did."

Griffin felt his own mounting rage. His hands gripped the arms of his chair as he listened.

"We've talked about this for years, Brother—*dreamed* about it—and now we have our chance. Atreides will pay for bringing down our whole family, for making us villagers instead of Emperors and Empresses."

As he absorbed this, Griffin thought of their conversations about the injustices committed against their House by Vorian Atreides. Together, they had studied the known records of their family's disgrace, including both the official story from the Annals of the Jihad and the personal pain expressed by Abulurd in his private memoirs. House Harkonnen had been very important in the old days, before and during Serena Butler's Jihad. With sadness and longing, he and Valya had gazed at images of the old family estate on Salusa Secundus, with its great house, vineyards, olive groves, and hunting grounds.

In one discussion, when they were teenagers, an animated Valya had spoken to her brother as if she faced a full audience. "We have inherent greatness, but it was unfairly taken from us through propaganda and distortions—by Vorian Atreides himself. This fundamental injustice has tarnished House Harkonnen for generations!"

Valya had always been explosively angry about this subject, and Griffin's own feelings ran close to hers. Both of them had seen friends and relatives die on the cold and dangerous planet where the family had been exiled. Valya had long imagined how different their history might have been, often obsessing over revenge against a man who had vanished eight decades before. . . .

"I know where he is now, Griffin," she said from the holo-image. "He met with the Emperor and will be departing again. He lives on a planet called Kepler—I have attached the coordinates to this recording. He has a family there, a happy home." She paused. "I want you to take it *all* from him."

Griffin felt cold inside. He had always hoped that revenge would not be necessary, that Vorian Atreides had died on a distant planet, with no fanfare. But the fact that he was still alive, and his location known, changed the entire equation.

"There is a difference between honor and justice," she said. "We must have justice *first* and then begin to rebuild our honor. The festering wound must be lanced and the poison drained, before we can heal. Weller is gone, and you know that our father doesn't have the backbone to accomplish this. I would do it my-self, but my obligations to the Sisterhood prevent me. So . . . it falls to you to avenge our family honor."

His brow furrowed as he listened. He wished he could reach out and touch her, talk with her, but her image continued, gathering vehemence, stirring his emotions.

"It's a simple enough thing. Vorian Atreides will go back to his planet, where he should be an easy target for assassination. He'll suspect nothing. I have never asked anything of you, never needed to, but you know how important this is to our family, to us . . . to me. Revenge pays its own debt. Wipe the slate clean, my brother, and then nothing can stop us. We are true Harkonnens—we can ac-complish anything."

Justice . . . honor . . . revenge. Griffin knew his life would not be the same after this.

Valya's face lit up with a genuine smile now. "Avenge our family honor, Grif-fin. I know I can count on you."

The hologram winked out.

Griffin sat there, feeling as if he'd been knocked overboard again into frigid northern seas. But she had jumped in after him then.

You would have done the same for me, she'd said.

Sitting alone, he brooded for a long time, thinking rationally of all his com-mercial obligations, the family business he could not turn over to his father, the administrative details, the careful expenditures from a very limited treasury. He had to help House Harkonnen rebuild after the loss of the major shipment, had to work with the townspeople to recover from the extremely hard winter.

But in the choppy arctic water, Valya had held him up for the few precious minutes he needed. And when she lost consciousness in the freezing sea, when the life ropes were pulling them to safety, he had never let go of her. . . .

You would have done the same for me.

Now, when his parents and siblings returned to the house, soggy from an unexpected rainstorm, he was startled to realize how many hours had passed. But, logic or no logic, his obligation had been clear to him from the first moment, and he would be leaving soon.

"Have you had dinner yet, Griffin?" his mother called. "We're about to ladle out the chowder."

"I'll be right there." Griffin pocketed the hologram crystal and emerged from the office wearing a forced smile. While Danvis and Tula chattered about their day's adventures, he was caught up in his own thoughts. Griffin barely tasted the savory chowder and finished only half a cup before he blurted out, "I have to leave Lankiveil on an important business trip. I might be gone for some time."

His little brother and sister peppered him with questions, and although their father was surprised, he didn't seem overly curious. "What calls you away?"

"It's something Valya asked me to do."

Vergyl Harkonnen nodded. "Ah! You never could deny her anything."

Standing together, the remaining descendants of the original Sorceresses of Rossak still exhibit mental powers, though not enough to generate the waves of telekinetic energy with which they once defeated powerful cymeks. Even so, the Sorceresses often practice defensive maneuvers, primarily to safeguard the Reverend Mother and the integrity of the Sisterhood's breeding records.

—preface to The Mysteries of Rossak, *Sisterhood textbook*

The Reverend Mother stood at the railing on a cliff-side platform, watching as hundreds of robed Sisters filed along the narrow trail just below, heading for one of the larger cave entrances. It was nearly time for the evening meal, with the sun beginning to set behind the silvery-purple jungle horizon. In the distance, she saw the lights of aircraft above a large clearing favored as a landing zone by people who came to the jungle to harvest pharmaceutical resources unique to Rossak.

Raquella's stomach had been knotted all day, robbing her of appetite. She could feel the tension like a tangible weight. The memory-lives inside her were disturbed, a cacophony of uneasiness that she couldn't understand. However, despite her close understanding of her own body and mind, Raquella could not pinpoint the source of her agitation. She knew of no particular threats, no weighty decisions hanging in the balance. . . .

The surprising return of Vorian Atreides kept turning over in her mind, and she wondered how that story would play out. He was Raquella's maternal grandfather, the sire of her birth mother, Helmina Berto-Anirul, and the great grandfather of Sister Dorotea. He looked young in comparison with Raquella, though he was almost ninety years older than she—an advantage of the life-extension treatment.

But that was not what bothered her now. Vorian had not been in touch with her since he vanished after the Battle of Corrin, and she had always thought it was for the best. Family relationships had a way of bringing out energy-consuming emotions, and of wasting a great deal of time. She did not have time for such things. Even so, from the audience, she had enjoyed seeing him. Raquella had never denied her own feelings; she just needed to keep them in check, so that she could manage the critically important work of the Sisterhood.

Perhaps the recent arrival of Anna Corrino was making her tense. The Emperor's sister was no ordinary acolyte. And, though she could not identify the girl down there among the crowd of new recruits, Raquella was confident Sister Valya would watch out for her.

Although accepting the unorthodox trainee into the Sisterhood was a political necessity, Raquella had no inkling of Anna's basic skills or dedication. She had told Valya in confidence aboard the transport to Rossak, "She will begin as an acolyte, like any other recruit, and there's a very good possibility she might not advance far in her training. Regardless, the Emperor's sister has to be protected at all costs. You know that some of the rigorous school exercises pose risks."

"I'll watch her," Valya assured the Reverend Mother. The young woman had seemed preoccupied, deeply disturbed after seeing Vorian Atreides on Salusa Secundus, and it had not been difficult for Raquella to figure out why, considering Vorian's part in the humiliation of Abulurd Harkonnen. Valya had said nothing of her feelings to the Reverend Mother, and Raquella had not pressed her about it, but it was yet another indication that Valya thought too much about House Harkonnen, when she should be totally dedicated to the Sisterhood.

Even so, Raquella could not help being impressed by Valya's intelligence, power, and steely determination. Raquella believed that Valya would eventually accomplish great things, and the inner voices agreed, but the young woman had to be reined in, and her tendency toward recklessness controlled.

Raquella hoped the connection with Anna Corrino would provide the proper focus and outlet.

The Reverend Mother had spoken with the Emperor's sister that morning at her first training session; Anna was angry at being taken from her lavish home, making her sulky and disinterested in the curriculum or in any of the Sisters. Raquella expected that Valya would prove herself up to the challenge of making friends.

It was time now for the early dinner gathering. The Sisters ate each meal at two communal seatings in a deep cave that had once been part of an extensive cliff-side city network, teeming with population, but was now mostly empty.

So much has been lost here, Raquella thought. She didn't need the overlapping memories to remind her—she had seen Rossak with her own eyes during its glory days.

However, this was a time of rebuilding for Rossak, of starting over without forgetting the lessons of the past. The Rossak School needed to draw upon the talents of the remaining Sorceress descendants, before it was too late. Few enough of the telepathic women remained, as Raquella could see by the smattering of white robes in the crowd below, amidst the pale-green robes of acolytes and the black robes of full Sisters.

On the trail below, she spotted Karee Marques, the oldest remaining Sorceress, who as a young woman had been Raquella's own ward during her work here throughout the Omnius plagues. Sensing the Reverend Mother above, Karee did not enter the dining cave, but climbed the metal staircase to the next level where Raquella stood. Instead of a more traditional robe, Karee wore a white worksuit that she often donned when gathering jungle samples; the collection pouches still hung at her waist, bulging with fungi, variegated leaves, and yellow flowers.

Karee gave a formal, even brusque, greeting, and the edge in her voice told Raquella that something had upset her as well. The old Sorceress regarded her with sharp green eyes, then said without preamble, "You can sense it yourself, can't you?"

Raquella nodded stiffly. "The tension in the air is pervasive."

"I was collecting samples in the jungle, pondering important Sisterhood issues, when suddenly my thoughts took over my body. I stopped where I was, frozen on the trail—I had slipped into Mentat mode. I let my mind follow a cascade of consequences, just as I learned in the Mentat School on Lampadas, but could make no projection! I was so disturbed that I rushed to meet the other Sister Mentats to chart our future, as we often do, and we all felt an urgency in the air."

The Reverend Mother nodded. "A sensation of impending trouble. It has been this way ever since we returned from Salusa Secundus." In her mind, Raquella could not trace the source.

"As a Sorceress, my psychic abilities make me more sensitive than other people. However, this dangerous tension affects the other seven Sister Mentats, too, and none of them are Sorceresses. It affects you as well." Karee gazed out at the smoke-tinged sunset, which was splashing colors over the polymerized treetops. "For some time now, we Sister Mentats have been gathering data, running projections. We've come to the conclusion that the Sisterhood is going to face a terrible schism that will set Sister against Sister."

"A schism over what?"

"The same fracture that runs through all of human society: a dispute over the use of technology. I fear that some Sisters may suspect the nature of our breeding database . . . there are rumors of computers in the Sisterhood."

Raquella swallowed hard. The voices in her head were very concerned, whispering contradictory advice, but after so many years she had learned to control them to a limited extent, pushing them into the background when she needed to concentrate. "My concern is with improving the breeding stock of humanity, filtering out undesirable traits, making our race strong. The urge to harm other human beings, for example, could be eliminated, resulting in more harmonious societies."

"Social engineering at its optimum. I straddle the fence, my old friend—as a Sorceress and Mentat who knows about the breeding-record computers. You speak of molding human traits, but who is to determine what is desirable and what is not? That smacks of what machines do. To meddle with human breeding is dangerous."

Raquella, though, had too much invested in her far-reaching vision, and her other memories had insisted on it. "Not if we do it right. And you are correct—a Mentat cannot make accurate projections with incomplete data. We will have to bring the other Sister Mentats into the secret."

"Be careful," Karee said. "If even one of them has Butlerian sympathies . . ."

"Yes, we must be careful, but if we cannot trust the highest-ranking members of our Sisterhood, what is the future of our project?"

Karee pursed her wrinkled lips. "The situation is complicated. There are many possible futures . . . many of which could result in disaster. The breeding program is the core of the Sisterhood, a noble cause that gives us purpose. We must not abandon it."

The tension in the dusk had grown even sharper, gnawing at the back of Raquella's mind. Her gnarled hands tensed on the rail, and she silently vowed not to lose what she had worked so hard to create.

DEEP INSIDE THE cliff-side maze of tunnels and caverns, two Sisters shared a private meal of bread, wine, cheese, and jungle fruits. Sister Dorotea had not seen the green-robed young acolyte Ingrid in more than a year, and they were anxious to catch up on their friendship. Since arriving back on Rossak, Dorotea had already returned to her work with Sister Karee down in the jungle research chambers, while Valya introduced Anna Corrino to the daily routine of an acolyte.

Over their first glasses of rich red wine, Dorotea told Ingrid all about the Imperial Court on Salusa Secundus, and how she had advised Roderick and Salvador Corrino. Despite the glamour and excitement of the capital world, she was pleased to be home, away from the pettiness of Imperial politics and intrigue.

Preoccupied, Sister Ingrid sat listening, not saying much in response. She swallowed a slice of cheese without the bread and washed it down with wine, both of which were imported from Lampadas. "The news here is not good. Though I don't believe the Sisters recognize it themselves, factions are beginning to develop. It started out as an intellectual conversation over a midday meal, but escalated to real disagreements about the use of forbidden technology. Many of the Sisters are like us—they loathe anything that reminds them of the thinking machines. Others assert that we should preserve some aspects of computer technology to make our lives easier."

"I'm disappointed to hear that." Dorotea's face tightened. "The debate is vehement back in Zimia, but here I would have expected our Sisters to reach the obvious and correct conclusion that such technology is dangerous and unnecessary." Dorotea stared at her nearly empty wineglass. "Human beings can do whatever machines can."

"I have argued about the dangers of technology, but some Sisters will not listen. Sister Hietta, for example, and Sister Parga, both use an ancient saying that we shouldn't throw the baby out with the bathwater. They argue that we should retain some thinking machines to aid humankind, to give people more leisure time for important pursuits. It's nonsense, of course."

"In the few days I've been back, I've heard nothing of this issue." Dorotea set the glass aside. "How widespread are these arguments?"

"Hietta and Parga have perhaps twenty-five women with them—not a large group—and around the same number support our strict view. Most Sisters prefer to stay out of the fray, but no one can avoid this issue forever."

"Some people have short memories, and bad thinking leads to bad decisions," Dorotea said. "But the Sisterhood does not use thinking machines, so it's an irrelevant argument."

Ingrid pinched her face into a scowl. She looked around, lowered her voice: "There are rumors of computers here on Rossak!"

Dorotea nearly choked on the berries she had popped into her mouth. "What?"

"The breeding information maintained by the Sisterhood is vast. No human mind, or combination of human minds—even our Mentats—can encompass it all. Some Sisters have concluded that computers are being used."

"If that is true, we have a problem, a very serious one."

"Back on Lampadas, I heard reports of Butlerian search-and-destroy missions," Ingrid said. "It would be a shame if that were to happen here. . . ."

Dorotea no longer had an appetite. "We must see that it doesn't, then. If there are computers on Rossak, we must find them and destroy them ourselves."

Love endures, but flesh does not. One must grasp any possible happiness in the time allotted to a lifetime.

—VORIAN ATREIDES, private journals

Accompanied by nine surplus military ships provided by Emperor Salvador Corrino, Vorian returned to Kepler feeling triumphant but burdened. Mariella would hate the terms that bound him, but he'd been forced to agree. Besides, after all these years in one place, maybe it was time for Vor to move on.

Given the enthusiastic and hopeful cheers he had received from the crowds on Salusa Secundus, he knew the Emperor had good reason to be worried. Vor had used his own leverage as much as possible, reaching one definition of a reasonable agreement in that both sides were somewhat dissatisfied with the terms, but willing to accept it nonetheless.

At least Kepler would be safe. Vor's loved ones would be safe.

These leftover warships from the Army of Humanity would stand guard in orbit, stationed there indefinitely to frighten away slavers. Within twelve months, the Imperial troops manning the vessels would be recalled to Salusa Secundus, but the ships would remain behind. By then, Vor's people would be trained to mount their own defenses. They would not be caught unawares again, and no longer would human predators see this backwater world as easy pickings.

But he wished he didn't have to leave Kepler, and hoped that Mariella would go with him—though he did not hold out much hope in that regard. She was old, and her children and grandchildren were here; a lifetime of memories were here, and at her stage in life it would not be easy for her to leave it all behind.

After Vor landed his ship on an open, stubbled field in the middle of the valley, his people rushed forward, cheering. They had made welcoming banners and signs for him, and his chest swelled as the applause buffeted him. The locals seemed to consider the liberation of the captives as equivalent to a victory against the thinking machines.

He viewed the smiling faces of people he had last seen in the Poritrin slave markets when he paid for their passage back home. His daughter Bonda stood there holding the small dog he had purchased as part of his disguise in New Starda.

He saw work crews, construction machinery, lumber deliveries. The homes and outbuildings damaged in the slave raid were already being rebuilt or repaired, as the villagers worked together to strengthen their community. And they all cheered him. It meant more to him than all the pageants and parades in Zimia.

Tears sprang to his eyes. Vor loved this world and these people, and he hated the fact that he would have to depart. But he had agreed to the terms in order to keep Kepler safe. A fair trade. Neither Salvador nor Roderick had hinted that they might address the greater problem of rampant slaving operations, but for now Vor's focus was closer to home . . . the home he would soon have to leave behind.

At the front of the crowd, he spotted the face he most longed to see: weathered and lined with age, her hair gray but eyes bright, stood Mariella. And when Vor looked through his heart instead of his eyes, he still saw the beautiful woman he had romanced so many decades before.

Over the centuries, Vorian Atreides had been blessed with a succession of deep and abiding loves. In his youth he had loved the legendary Serena Butler, although chastely . . . and next there was Leronica Tergiet from Caladan. His two sons by Leronica had both gone off to form their own families far away, leaving Caladan. Then Mariella had been the center of his life for more than fifty years.

He remembered them all, still loved them all, and could envision their faces in brief glimpses of memory, but time and a plethora of human lives flowed past him like the waters of a rushing stream, while he remained stuck, a rock in the midst of the cascade. Sometimes, beloved people like Leronica or Mariella splashed up a high spray around him, but eventually they, too, passed on. And he could see how old Mariella was.

In his younger years, Vorian had lived an oblivious, sheltered life, running Omnius updates across the Synchronized Worlds with his closest friend, the independent robot Seurat. Reading Agamemnon's memoirs had led him to believe he understood the feral humans and their squalid lives. He had wanted to please his father.

The other twelve known sons of Agamemnon had been raised, trained, and ultimately killed by the cymek general. From an early age, Vor had dreamed of becoming a cymek one day, of having his brain removed from his weak biological body so he could live indefinitely as a cymek beside Titans like Agamemnon, Juno, Xerxes, and Ajax. But that had never happened.

Instead, after Vor had won a huge victory against humans, General Agamemnon dragged him off to a cymek laboratory, strapped Vor to a table, and tortured him with probes, burning chemicals, and sharp instruments. Thus, through unspeakable pain, Agamemnon bestowed the life-extension treatment that made his thirteenth and best son virtually immortal. "I gave you many centuries," he had told Vor later. "You can't expect that to come cheap."

Afterward, Vor had agreed that enduring the pain was indeed a small price to pay for a vastly extended life, albeit in his original human body. In the long and difficult centuries that followed, however, Vor had his doubts. On Kepler, again he remained unchanged while everyone grew old around him. . . .

Now, ignoring the rest of the crowd, he wrapped his arms around Mariella and drew her close; he wanted to embrace her tightly and never let go. She melted up against him. "I'm so glad you're home. Thank you for what you did."

The crush of people around Vor demanded his attention, and though he was not interested in feasts or celebrations, nevertheless his family and neighbors insisted on it. Bonda and Tir came up, laughing, and lifted their little dog so that it could lick his cheek.

Smiling, Vor raised his hands for silence, and shouted, "All of you will be safe now. I've reached an agreement with Emperor Corrino. The whole Imperium knows that he has issued a decree making this planet off-limits to slavers. A group of armed ships will be stationed in orbit overhead, and I have arranged to provide you with additional weapons for defending your families and homes. No one will ever prey upon this world again."

From their cheers and whistles, they obviously expected little else from the great Vorian Atreides. They would feel obligated to shower him with well-intentioned gifts—helping on his farm, cooking food, making clothing for him, whether or not he needed it. He had never seen the people so happy.

It pained his heart that he would have to leave without telling them . . . except for Mariella.

WHEN THE TWO of them returned home late that night, weary from dancing and conversation and feasting, their ears ringing from music, Vor noted that the roof had been repaired from the fire the slavers had set. The house also had a fresh coat of paint and new shingles.

Mariella looked tired when she entered the drawing room, and sat in a chair, pulling a blanket onto her lap. "Our home has been so lonely, Vor. Just having you back fills it up."

He heated water to make tea and sat next to her, studying her face, eager to preserve every remaining moment with her. "Our family doesn't need to worry anymore. I made sure of that." He hesitated as he sipped his strong herbal tea with a faint hint of melange. His wife held her cup, just staring at the steam that rose from the liquid. Her eyes sparkled as if with a sheen of tears. Did she suspect already? His voice cracked as he said, "But I had to make certain concessions. I had to agree that I would . . . drop out of sight again."

"I was afraid of that," Mariella said with a long sigh. "I know you well, my husband, and I've been sensing a darkness today, something you were having trouble telling me."

Vor swallowed hard. He loved this life on Kepler, wanted to remain here forever, but that was impossible. "I'm an antique, a relic of bygone days. With the Jihad over, the Imperium needs to move on, but I'm a reminder of the past. The Emperor is uneasy to have someone with such great and renewed popularity in the Landsraad League. No matter how much I insist that I have no interest in taking the throne, he will always harbor that doubt. And there would be people coming out of the proverbial woodwork, wanting to use me to accomplish their own agendas." He shook his head and said in a low voice, "Before Salvador Corrino would agree to protect Kepler, he made this his strict condition: I have to go away. Vorian Atreides must seem to disappear—permanently."

She gave him a wan smile, but the tears stayed in her eyes, and in the flood of emotions she seemed to be having trouble coming up with what to say.

He straightened. "I want you to come with me, Mariella. We can move to another world . . . we'll review dozens of possibilities first, if you like. We can bring our children, too. Anyone who wants to go." His words came out in a rush as he began to feel hope again. "It could be a grand adventure for all of us—"

"Oh, Vor! As much as I love you, I can't leave Kepler. This is my home. And you can't uproot our children, our grandchildren, their families, their friends, their spouses from this valley!"

Vor's throat went dry. "I don't want to leave without you. We could go together, just the two of us."

"Don't be foolish. I am an old woman—too old to start a new life. We both know you will have to move on without me sooner or later." She wiped her cheeks self-consciously, then patted her gray hair. "It's time you left anyway, so you don't have to see me grow any older. It's embarrassing to have such a handsome young man in my bed."

"I hadn't noticed you were any less beautiful," Vor said, barely able to form the words, "and I mean that. I'm the one who should be thankful, not you."

He wrestled with his emotions and obligations. He could change his appearance and his name, remain hidden on Kepler in some remote outpost. What difference would it make? A handful of the people would know, but he could swear them to secrecy, and Emperor Salvador would never find out.

Vor sighed in resignation. Such things were always discovered, and if he went back on his word, it could put his family and neighbors in danger.

Mariella said in a musing voice, "You've already given me a happier life and a longer marriage than any woman could hope for, but I know you were born to wander. When we first married, you explained the fact that you don't age. We both knew, and we both *agreed*, that a time would come when you would have to move on."

"But not during your lifetime."

"Maybe it is better this way," she insisted.

He went to her chair, bent down, and kissed her on the cheek, then on the lips, a kiss that reminded him of their first, so long ago. "Leaving you reminds me of just how long I've been alive, Mariella. It's hard to explain how heavily the years can weigh on me."

"Do you know where you'll go? Or does that have to be a secret?"

"I only promised the Emperor I would leave Kepler and never come back—not that I wouldn't tell you where I was. I . . . have in mind a place I'd like to visit," he said. "Arrakis. I need a clean break, and I've heard there are tribes in the deserts there, people with incredibly long life spans—possibly from constant consumption of melange. I doubt they've lived as long as I have, but they might have some insights for me."

"I'll think of you every day," Mariella said. "I'll tell our children so that they know you're out there somewhere, and safe. And you'll know where we are. We won't forget you."

"And I could never forget you," he said. "My love for you is in every breath I take. When I get established, I'll send word. I'll find a way to stay in touch."

I am the real Emperor of the Known Universe, and Salvador Corrino is my puppet.

—MANFORD TORONDO, remarks to Anari Idaho

R oderick Corrino experienced feelings of unease whenever he watched combat robots in the private exhibition fights sponsored by his brother. Elegantly dressed noblemen and their ladies watched from behind safety barriers, cheering for their favorites and booing opponents. It was evening in a small private arena on the grounds of the Imperial Palace, following a sumptuous feast. Many of the nobles wore veils and domino masks to disguise their identities and protect them; the Butlerian influence on Salusa remained strong.

According to the tight legal strictures set out at the end of the Jihad, these reactivated robots had no artificial intelligence whatsoever and were instead programmed to run through a series of fighting maneuvers, which were salted with chance variables—flaws that would cause an unexpected deficiency, or surprise enhancements. Spectators did not know in advance which type of fighter they were getting when they placed their wagers, and the outcome was never predetermined.

Roderick had to admit that it made for interesting, stimulating entertainment, watching these vanquished machine demons duel in the arena, knowing that they would destroy one another. Because it danced so close to the cliff edge of forbidden technology, the carefully selected nobles were titillated by the spectacle. Such events were, of course, kept secret from Butlerian observers.

When his brother first suggested the idea, Roderick had cringed. If Manford Torondo ever found out what the Emperor and his inner circle of nobles did behind the high gates and walls of the private estate . . . But Salvador brushed aside his concerns. "Nobles must have their diversions. It's harmless entertainment, and the end result is to destroy robots, so what is the harm?"

Roderick could imagine a great deal of harm, so without his brother's knowledge, he had doubled security surrounding each private combat exhibition, and made certain that only the most trusted nobles were invited, each of whom was sworn to secrecy—a pledge that the powerful Corrino family could enforce.

Now he watched as two combat robots—one with a deep copper alloy skin and the other shimmering chrome—circled one another, probing with built-in (though limited) weapons that battered each other, knocking their armored bodies to the ground. A small army of palace guards surrounded the ring, bearing heavy weapons and ready to destroy any combat mek that might get out of hand.

Sitting in his private, shaded box beside Roderick, the Emperor spoke with Alfonso Nitta, a wheedling nobleman in search of a favor to curtail the operations of a business adversary. Nitta manufactured expensive ladies' dresses, and an upstart commoner had opened a large rival business on Hagal, after paying bribes to the planetary leader.

"It's dirty business," Nitta insisted. "The Hagals have a grudge against House Nitta because my grandfather reported their grandfather's illegal war-profiteering operations during the Jihad."

Salvador kept his eyes on the clashing robots. "I'll see what I can do." He didn't seem interested, and Nitta was particularly inept in making his request.

Roderick helped the nobleman with a nudge, because he didn't seem to understand how business was conducted at this level. "Investigating the matter will take time and resources, Lord Nitta. The Emperor has to worry about his discretionary budget."

Finally, Nitta's eyes lit up with understanding. "Ah, perhaps as a demonstration of the quality of my product. I'll provide a large sampling of my finest dresses for the Empress Tabrina—lovely gowns, the most lavish wardrobe to make her breathtakingly beautiful for you, Sire. Perhaps even some stylish unmentionables could be arranged."

Roderick sighed. Considering the state of his brother's relationship with Tabrina, it was precisely the wrong thing to say.

Salvador responded coolly. "I said I'll look into the matter."

The nobleman bowed and turned his attention back to the combat event.

After a while, the Emperor leaned closer to Roderick, smiling as one of the combat meks tore a cylindrical arm from its opponent. "This is so appropriate. First we lobotomized the robots, and now we make them destroy each other. I could watch this all day."

Roderick nodded. "It's preferable to having the machines compel humans to do what they command."

In the stands, a rotund new invitee squealed, afraid of the ferocious metallic monsters, then laughed when he realized there was no actual danger.

"I can't remember," Salvador said. "What did we wager today?"

Roderick knew his brother remembered precisely what they had bet against each other. "Our summer villas on Kaitain, of course. Whoever wins gets both."

"Oh, yes. I've always preferred yours."

The copper-skinned robot launched a spiked spear from under its forearm, knocking the other machine down, where it lay on the ground, twitching and sparking. The first mek moved in for the kill.

"It looks as if my robot is winning," Roderick said, "but you know you're always welcome to use my villa if you like."

His elder brother's forehead wrinkled like a folded piece of paper. "What's that? The copper mek is mine. Do you really believe that damaged hulk can fight back?"

"You chose the chrome one, dear brother. Remember, you picked first."

Salvador's blue eyes flashed. He liked to act absentminded when it suited him, but Roderick knew his mind was sharp. The Corrino Emperor was far more intelligent than most people realized. Crafty smart. He knew full well that he had chosen the chrome mek. "Very well, but you should feel guilty the way you always get the better of me."

"It was pure luck this time. We had no way of knowing which robot would win." The Emperor ran a finger along his lips. "I suppose we could cheat."

"Against each other? I wouldn't do that to you."

"As I am so often reminded, you are a better man than I."

Roderick disagreed, as he was expected to, but both men knew it was true.

The chrome robot did rally and lurched to its feet to continue the fight, accompanied by a round of delighted cheers. Another "disguised" nobleman came and whispered a request into Salvador's ear. The thin domino mask did not hide the identity of elderly Tibbar Warik, a prominent real-estate broker who needed a favor. Throughout these gladiatorial combats, inner-circle invitees would make such requests, and Roderick would have to implement them, according to his brother's decisions.

When the copper-skinned mek finally defeated its opponent, battering it into twitching shrapnel, the palace guards stepped forward and blasted the winner down.

Tibbar Warik complained about deferred or defaulted payments from the new Suk Medical School, an extravagant complex under construction on Parmentier. Roderick thought the elite doctors had pretensions of grandeur. However, because Salvador had received a great many expensive (and questionable, in Roderick's opinion) medical treatments from the former head of the Suk School, he often turned a blind eye toward the excesses. Warik was quite upset by the losses, and the Emperor dismissed him with a promise.

When the nobleman was gone, and as staff members dragged the robot debris off the fighting field, Salvador turned to Roderick. "Warik says there's a scandal brewing, involving a Suk doctor who duped a patient. You heard that Lars Ibson of Caladan died recently?" Roderick remembered the wealthy commoner who had built a fishing empire and lived like an emperor himself. "According to Warik, Ibson relied on a Suk doctor and paid a king's ransom for bone-cancer treatments—treatments that turned out to be bogus. Complete placebos. Ibson didn't live any longer, and certainly died poorer."

Roderick didn't comment that he thought many of Elo Bando's prescribed treatments for the Emperor fell into the same category; after Bando's highly suspicious "suicide" on Parmentier, investigations had been closed, but Roderick suspected a more widespread problem among the Suks. "Do you think the Medical School would agree to a detailed audit of their operations? We've heard of investors loaning money to the school, and we know the Suks take in substantial revenues for their services, but it still doesn't seem to add up." Much of the funding for their extravagant expansion had come from the exorbitant sums Salvador himself had paid to the former head of the school.

"A scandal could hamstring their good work," Salvador said. "The Butlerians object to advanced medical treatment, and I wouldn't want to give them the wedge." He rubbed his temples. "Besides, I need another personal physician, and the Suks haven't sent me an acceptable one yet. I miss poor Dr. Bando. The school isn't the same without him."

Despite the corrupt medical practices of some doctors, Roderick knew the Suk School still produced better physicians than any other academy in the Imperium, and he remembered the remarkable good that Mohandas Suk had done during the machine plagues. Unlike Salvador, though, he believed the loss of Elo Bando improved their respectability rather than worsened it. "Let me look into it, Sire. If they're evading Salusan taxes, or defaulting on payments, they will be held to account."

"The school is becoming problematic, too full of its own importance." Salvador was troubled. "I don't want them shut down. At least not yet . . . not before I get my own personal physician."

"At the very least, they should have closer monitoring."

The Emperor nodded, then leaned forward as the next combat meks shambled into the fighting area. "You're right, as usual, little brother. Let's deepen our normal financial investigations of them, and see what we turn up."

*Do we derive our identity, our worth, from our families or from our-
selves?*

— REVEREND MOTHER RAQUELLA BERTO-ANIRUL,
Sisterhood Training Manual

A s Princess Anna's mentor and protector, Valya tried to discover how to
motivate the young woman and make her a stronger person . . . but the
girl had very little drive. Raised and sheltered in the Imperial Palace, Anna was
prone to impulsive, somewhat juvenile decisions and mood swings. Sisterhood
training should eventually teach her how to deal with that, and Anna would
return to Salusa Secundus as a changed woman . . . and Valya's close friend.

Perhaps Anna would ask Valya to accompany her back to Zimia and give her
a position at court. From there, Valya could open political doors for her brother.
His success in the Landsraad League would go a long way toward restoring
Harkonnen wealth.

But that was not all she wanted, not by a long shot. She actually considered
the assassination of Vorian Atreides to be an even higher priority than getting
Griffin to Zimia, which was why she had demanded that he go in search of the
treacherous man who had brought down House Harkonnen. If Griffin cauter-
ized the festering wound that had made generations of Harkonnens so miserable,
their family could finally escape the ignominy they had been forced to endure
for eighty years, the terrible pall of shame that had been covering them like a
Lankiveil ice sheet. Revenge was more important to her than wealth, far more
important.

Back on her cold and barren homeworld, Valya had seen little point in marrying a native fisherman or whale hunter. Her great-grandfather Abulurd had
left the family with no legacy, and her own father had few ambitions, too readily
accepting their drastically reduced state. Her mother, Sonia, was a traditional

local woman who had never been off-planet and was not interested in the rest of the Imperium. Since she had no noble blood, she was willing to accept the pittance of a life she and her family had, not questioning what House Harkonnen's enemies had done to them.

Valya could not be so passive. Once she escaped from Lankiveil and the millstone it represented, she intended to accomplish a great deal for House Harkonnen. For a young woman in her situation, the Rossak School seemed to offer limitless possibilities—as proven by this chance to establish close ties with the Corrinos.

Even so, Valya was quickly losing excitement about her assignment to befriend Anna Corrino. The girl was sweet, with many misconceptions about how others lived, and sometimes the job tested Valya's patience.

Alone now, she hurried down one corridor and then another, calling Anna's name, but getting no response. The girl was so unpredictable! A few minutes ago, as breakfast ended in the great dining chamber and Sisters were milling about or heading for the exits, the green-robed Anna had slipped away, melting into the crowd of women. Did she think this was a game? Muttering, Valya felt a sinking sensation. If anything bad happened to the Corrino Princess, it would not be good for the Sisterhood, nor for Valya's personal ambitions.

As she passed an alcove, she saw Anna peeking out from around a statue of one of the heroes of the Jihad, chortling like a preteen. Valya was the same age, but there was a huge gulf of maturity between them.

"Don't ever do that again," Valya took her by the hand and pulled her out with a little more force than she intended.

"I can take care of myself," Anna said.

Valya controlled her temper, reminding herself of this young woman's connections. "Rossak has dangers, and the Sisterhood has rules. I'm just trying to watch out for you." She kept protectively close to the troublesome young woman while guiding her to an Imperial economics class.

When she released Anna just inside the classroom, the Princess frowned. "You won't sit next to me?" Natural light illuminated the room, entering through slits and crevices in the rock, accompanied by a warm breeze that was redolent with the pungent odors of the jungle.

"This is a class for acolytes, and I have another assignment," Valya said. "I'll come and get you after the lecture."

"Are you my best friend now?" Anna asked. "I haven't had a good friend for a long time."

Valya softened her voice. "Yes, I'm your best friend now. Trust me, once you adjust here, you won't want to go home." She put a gentle hand on the girl's shoulder.

"Hirondo really cared for me." Anna looked dejected and needy. "My stepmother Orenna loved me."

"And now you have me, and we have trust."

Anna looked up at her. "My brothers never trusted me."

"Then you're better off here, with us." Through her own feelings and goals, Valya felt some sympathy for this misfit woman who had suffered from her doomed infatuation with a lowly kitchen worker, but Valya knew emotional attachments might compromise her own mission in life.

She saw plainly that Anna was in desperate need of a friend—and no doubt had been for years. Valya intended to fill that role, partly out of pity, but primarily for her own reasons. She could only hope Griffin would also fulfill his obligations. He should already be on his way to deal with Vorian Atreides.

Logic and reason are deceptive. They can lead a person to lose his soul.
—MANFORD TORONDO, speech on Salusa Secundus

Though the Butlerian movement had spread across the Imperium, their headquarters on Lampadas were modest and unpretentious. Manford felt that the domination of thinking machines should have taught mankind humility at the very least. It was through hubris and ambition that the original Titans had created the computer evermind in the first place.

Propped up in a chair at his desk, which hid his lack of legs from visitors, he pored over lists of planets where his representatives had conducted successful demonstration raids. Occasionally, the local Butlerian leaders dispatched holorecordings, but Manford preferred the more intimate experience of reading words written by a human hand.

Mankind had gotten into a great deal of trouble by looking for shortcuts, speed, and simplification. Devices could be so seductive. He remained haunted by the dark words Erasmus the robot had written in his journal: *Given enough time, they will forget . . . and will create us all over again.*

When vehicles were easily available, lethargic people grew fat because they were too lazy to walk. Calculating machines could provide swift answers to complex sums, but what happened when the human mind atrophied and forgot how to calculate? As proof of human potential and superiority, Mentats from the school of Gilbertus Albans performed all the functions a computer could, and they were far more trustworthy than any calculating machine. . . .

Though Manford longed for a quiet season with Anari, where they could watch the natural pace of the harvest and the changing weather on Lampadas, he knew he had not been made for a normal life, nor had his beloved mentor,

Rayna Butler. She'd survived the horrific Omnius plagues, while her whole family died around her. Forever scarred by the experience, Rayna spent her entire life insisting that humanity expunge its dependence on machines. Following her heroic example, Manford had been through a similar crucible. He was just as scarred, but in a different way, and he was just as driven. He would be traveling again soon. There were always planets that needed to hear his words.

Anari Idaho entered the office wearing her impeccable black-and-gray uniform. Her hair was cut short, her face scrubbed clean to show her rough beauty; the devotion on her expression was as indelible as a tattoo. "Two offworlders are here to request a meeting." The slight downturn of her mouth was a sign of disapproval. "They have brought . . . equipment."

Manford set the documents aside. "Who are they? What kind of equipment?"

"They come from the planet Zenith, scientists of some sort. One of them acts as if he is a person of note."

Now Manford was curious. After asking the man's name and making no connection with it, he said, "What do scientists want here?"

"Shall I interrogate them?" She sounded eager. Manford knew that if he requested it, she would break their necks without batting an eyelash. He didn't know what he'd ever do without her.

"Send them in. I'll talk with these scientists myself. If I need you to do anything, I will ask."

A pair of diminutive men entered the room, pulling a sealed case the size of a small coffin. It floated on suspensors, and the blinking lights of a diagnostic panel shone on the top.

The smaller of the two belonged to the disgraced Tlulaxa race; he had short, dark hair and a pinched expression, and he was obviously subordinate. After the horrific scandal that had brought down the Tlulaxa organ farms during Serena Butler's Jihad, most humans carried an intrinsic animus toward the race, but the Tlulaxa had been subdued and supposedly rehabilitated. In recent decades, zealous Butlerians had established a watchdog presence on the main Tlulaxa worlds, closely monitoring any research being conducted there. Many of their insidious projects had been quashed, much to the consternation of the Tlulaxa Masters. But they had been meek and cooperative; he expected no trouble from them.

The second man, obviously the one in charge, was not a Tlulaxa. Large eyes gave him an owlish look. He had brown hair, a weak chin, and a studious demeanor that made him seem more like an accountant than a researcher. The bookish man came forward briskly, evincing a scholarly and even conciliatory manner. "Thank you for seeing us on such short notice, Leader Torondo. I am Ptolemy, an independent scientist and Landsraad representative from Zenith. This is my good friend and research associate Dr. Elchan."

Manford kept his expression cool. "And what brings you to Lampadas? Very few self-proclaimed scientists offer to join our movement for the preservation of the human soul." He forced a smile. "But I remain optimistic."

Ptolemy blinked his owlish eyes, took a moment to gather his bearings. "That is part of the reason we've come. You may have heard of my planet Zenith, which encourages and funds many research projects designed for the benefit of the human race—medical advances, agricultural developments, automated shelter construction for the poor on primitive worlds. As the official representative from Zenith, I heard the speech you presented at the Landsraad Hall, and I felt compelled to see you in person."

"Ah, now I remember you. You spoke on the record." At the time, the man had seemed weak and unimpressive, as if the fate of the human race could be boiled down to a simple schoolhouse debate.

Ptolemy offered a smile. "Though I admit I did not agree with your argument, I respect your convictions and passion. A man must speak up when he has strong convictions—that is what makes humans great. We can agree on that? A bit of common ground?"

"Only a starting point." Manford wondered what these men intended.

"I have to believe we can talk like reasonable men. Your impassioned speech gave me much food for thought."

"Good." Manford folded his hands together on the desk. "Humans think. Machines don't. The mind of man is holy."

"The mind of man is holy," Anari murmured.

"Our two sides have grown so far apart they no longer hear each other, Leader Toronto. What if you and I could have a frank and logical discussion? The human race would be much more productive, stronger, and happier if we find some kind of compromise. We shouldn't work against one another."

Ptolemy's smile was hopeful, and naïve. Manford did not smile back.

"One does not compromise by cutting a thing in half. They are my core beliefs and principles."

The scientist chuckled nervously. "Oh, I'm not asking for anything like that! Please hear me out. We all know that technology can be abused, but it isn't inherently evil. Some of our early experiments focused on growing sheets of polymer-based tissue to be grafted onto burn victims—Dr. Elchan's work. The Suk doctors already use it extensively. But we have gone far beyond that. My associate and I have brought you a gift created in our laboratories on Zenith." He gestured to the coffin-case that bobbed on its suspensors like a rowboat on a lake. "You'll find it very beneficial."

The quiet Tlulaxa partner did not seem so optimistic; in fact, Manford could sense a deep-seated fear emanating from him, as if he were walking a tightrope across a deep chasm. Ptolemy, though, was like a puppy, smiling encouragement to his friend. After opening the case, the Tlulaxa reached in and removed a flesh-colored object—an amputated leg!

Anari flinched, grabbed for her sword. Elchan blurted out, "No, it's no trick! Please, just *look*." Ptolemy sent his partner a questioning look, surprised at the reaction.

No, Manford realized upon closer inspection, it was a *prosthetic* leg sheathed in a very realistic, skinlike polymer.

Ptolemy continued with unabashed pride in his voice. "On Zenith, we have a separate independent laboratory dedicated to developing lifelike artificial replacement limbs that connect directly with biological nerve endings. In the past, many Jihad veterans were forced to live as amputees. Earlier, before the organ-farm troubles"—he glanced over at Dr. Elchan, then back at Manford—"the Tlulaxa labs provided tank-grown eyes or internal organs, but that work has been all but abandoned for almost a century. Now he and I have created this new bionic system that, when properly attached and configured, can tap into your mind's impulses. The muscle analogs are responsive polymer fibers, and the nerve conductors are thin wires."

He took the flopping false leg from his partner and held it up like a prop, poking at the flesh with his fingertips. "Our gift to you, Leader Torondo—an olive branch to show you the real benefits of properly applied technology. With this, you shall *walk again*! Dr. Elchan and I can give you your legs back, to let you see how science can help humanity and ease the hurt of so many who suffer."

Manford was not the least bit tempted by the offer. "The cymeks used similar principles for their brains to operate machine forms. The human body is not a machine."

Ptolemy looked baffled. "But of course it is—a biological machine. The skeleton is a structural framework, muscle fibers are like cables and pulleys, blood vessels are fluid-transport conduits, nerve endings are like sensors, the heart is the engine and the brain like a memory core—"

"What you say is deeply offensive."

The scientist seemed disappointed by Manford's stony reaction, but he pressed ahead anyway with dogged determination. "Please hear me out. If you will look at my friend and colleague?" He turned to his Tlulaxa partner, though the other man did not at all want the attention. "Through a serious accident, Dr. Elchan lost the use of his left arm, and we have replaced it with one of these prosthetics. I doubt you even noticed it until now."

The other man raised his arm, flexed his fingers, and used his real hand to tug a gray sleeve up to reveal the smooth plastic skin on his left arm. A shiver of revulsion ran down Manford's back. Standing at the doorway of the office, Anari Idaho was also repulsed by the prosthetics.

Still jabbering as if presenting a rosy progress report to a board meeting, Ptolemy removed the second leg from the coffin-container. "After we affix these to your body, you will be a whole man again." He didn't realize that he had stepped over a very important line.

Fighting back his disgust, Manford raised his chin and looked over at Anari. "You know what to do, Swordmaster."

Like a released spring, she drew her sword and shouldered the two scientists aside. With a surprised cry, Ptolemy dropped the artificial leg onto Manford's desk, and Anari swung her blade like a woodsman chopping a log. Lubricants and nutrient fluids spurted, dousing the papers, but Manford didn't flinch. Ptolemy and Elchan cried out in dismay. Anari struck three times before the first leg was mangled beyond repair, then she made quick work of the other. "The mind of man is holy," she said.

Sobbing, Dr. Elchan pulled his left arm tight against his chest, fearing the Swordmaster would hack the artificial limb off his body.

Appalled, Ptolemy said in a hollow voice, as if *he* were the one who had been betrayed, "Why did you do that? Those legs were our gift to you." Manford almost pitied the man. He honestly didn't understand!

"There is a seductive quality to machine technology. It is a slippery slope," Manford said. "If I permit one thing, where do I draw the line? I do not want to open that door."

"But you use machines regularly, sir! Your logic is arbitrary."

Unbelievable—the man was still trying to get through to him! In a way, he admired Ptolemy's dedication to his beliefs, even if they were wrong. "My faith is perfectly clear."

Dr. Elchan was terrified and shuddering, but Ptolemy stuck to his principles. "Please, there must be something! If you won't allow us to give you replacement limbs, then we can create a simple suspensor platform for you to ride in."

"No. A suspensor platform is still technology, a first step on the road to ruin, and I will not allow it. Your temptations won't work on me."

Ptolemy pointed toward the naked sword Anari held. "*Technology* made that blade. Technology drives the starships that you use to travel from planet to planet. You accept it only when it meets your needs?"

Manford shrugged, not willing to concede the point. "I am not perfect, and I make some sacrifices for the greater good. There are many thousands of worlds in the Imperium, and all of them need to hear my words. I can't simply shout across space. It's a necessary compromise. I have to use some forms of technology for the greater good."

"That's a contradiction," Ptolemy said.

"Faith sees through contradictions, while science cannot." He looked down at the mangled prosthetics. "But when it comes to my body, I draw the line. Sacred human flesh was made in God's image, and the only assistance I will accept in place of walking is from another human being. Countless volunteers are willing to carry me on a palanquin wherever I need to go. Anari here"—he gestured to the Swordmaster—"bears me on her shoulders when necessary."

Ptolemy frowned, as if Manford had spoken to him in a foreign language. "So it is your preference to oppress a human being rather than use a simple wheelchair? Don't you see how demeaning it is to use a person as a beast of burden?"

A flare of rage flushed Anari's face. "I consider it an honor."

She raised her sword, stepping toward the two scientists, but Manford stopped her from killing them. "There's no need for violence, my loyal companion. These misguided scientists came here to speak their point of view, and I agreed to hear them."

She muttered under her breath. "I am not a slave. I serve you willingly."

Manford said to the two men, "I will not budge on the matter. I respect your dedication to your delusions, Dr. Ptolemy—but if only you could see the light. Your mission here has been a complete waste of time, and this meeting is at an end. You may leave your equipment rubbish here. We'll see that it's disposed of properly."

As the two scientists left in disgrace, Ptolemy looked back with obvious disappointment, devastated to see the mangled prosthetic legs. He looked so lost and confused; he simply couldn't comprehend a man whose convictions were different from his own.

Manford felt sorry for him, and for what would have to happen next.

Be careful of the knowledge you seek, and the price you must pay for it.
—axiom of the Sisterhood

When Josef Venport returned from Denali, an unpleasant surprise awaited him at the Kolhar headquarters, one far more serious than the usual administrative problems he faced.

His wife met him, accompanied by his security chief, Ekbir. Cioba said nothing at first, but he could read a wealth of concerns in her stolid expression. She let Ekbir deliver the information. "A spy, sir."

Josef went rigid as anger built within him, though he didn't dare show any reaction. The idea seemed utterly preposterous, but was not unexpected. With its space fleet, planetary banking, and mercantile operations, Venport Holdings was much too influential and far-reaching not to attract malicious attention.

"We neutralized him," Cioba said. "Limited the release of information. I have ideas on how to deal with spies, but I thought I should check with you first."

"Where did you find him?" Josef asked.

Ekbir steeled himself, met the Directeur's gaze. "Out in the Navigator fields, sir. The man posed as one of our technicians. He had the proper uniform, identification badge, access codes."

"Find out how he got them."

Ekbir gave a slow nod. "Already working on it, sir."

Josef's thick eyebrows drew together. "All VenHold maintenance technicians are carefully vetted and given specific psychological training. They're a close-knit team. How did he infiltrate them?"

Cioba nodded. "That is exactly how he was caught. Though his credentials appeared to be impeccable, our people sensed something wrong. He was reported in less than an hour."

Josef's face turned warm as he pictured the grassy plain covered with sealed tanks, each containing an embryonic Navigator immersed in mutagenic concentrations of melange gas. "He discovered what we're doing out there, I presume?"

"Yes, sir." Ekbir had no way to deny it.

Josef had known the secret would leak out sooner or later. Norma Cenva was the first to experience the biological enhancements caused by long-term exposure to spice gas—but his great-grandmother's mind had been special in the first place. Only after a great deal of experimentation had another human candidate survived the change. Successes still comprised a relatively small percentage.

"He hasn't revealed much to us yet, though we've only begun the interrogation process," Cioba said. "I monitored it myself, and we've got Scalpel working on it."

"Good." The specially trained torturers in the Suk organization's Scalpel division were efficient at inflicting long-term pain with no visible damage. He looked up at his wife, admired her pale skin, her porcelainlike beauty; Cioba's Sorceress heritage was prominent in her features, but alas she exhibited no telepathic powers. "I wish you could just go into his mind and rip out the information."

She stroked his arm with a brief, electric touch. "Yes, we can wish. But in the meantime we'll have to use other means." Perhaps their two daughters would show greater mental strength, once they grew older and completed their Sisterhood training.

"We assume he was sent by one of the other commercial transport companies, anxious to learn about our Navigators. . . ." Ekbir's voice faltered as he realized he was stating the obvious.

"Arjen Gates already had his company meddling with the spice operations on Arrakis. I put a stop to that, but I still don't believe he's learned his lesson." Josef had taken great pleasure in watching the images Ishanti sent of the capture and destruction of poaching operations near Carthag, hurling the rival chief down into a Coriolis storm.

None of the other space fleets had developed anything similar to Navigators, and his competitors had only the vaguest understanding of why VenHold ships never suffered a mishap, when their own blind flying resulted in high accident rates. Through careful analysis, Cioba had surmised that some of the other companies could be using computerized navigation devices, which were strictly forbidden. Venport had his own spies investigating the matter.

Personally, Josef had no qualms about using mechanical navigation devices, which he considered useful and reliable—he would have used them himself if he didn't have Norma's Navigators—and the restrictions against them were just silly. Nonetheless, if he could prove that one of his rivals used outlawed computers, he wouldn't hesitate to report them, which would result in the confiscation and likely destruction of all ships in the competitor's fleet. It was, after all, only business.

"Let me see this spy," Josef said.

"We're holding him in an interrogation chamber, sir, pending your orders."

Josef scratched his thick mustache, glanced at his wife. "You know what my orders are going to be."

Cioba led him out of the room, walking close beside him. "Don't take any precipitous action."

The security man guided them to the underground levels of the headquarters tower, where they met a gaunt man, who kept his head bowed and displayed a funereal manner. Dr. Wantori had completed specialized training at the Suk School, although his degree was not a matter of public record. Over the course of their studies at the medical institution, certain adepts discovered a penchant for inflicting pain rather than relieving it. Wantori was the best of the surreptitious Scalpel interrogators and torturers that Josef could find.

"This way, sir," said Wantori in a grave voice. "We are beginning to make progress."

They stopped in front of an opaque plaz viewing window. "Is he in there?" Josef asked. "Why is everything dark?"

"There is nothing to see, at the moment." Wantori worked the screen, sliding through the spectrum. An image blurred, then focused as the sensors adjusted the range and mathematically shifted the display to visible light.

A man hung at an angle in the middle of the chamber, arms and legs outstretched, with his head tilted toward the floor. He looked like a lost soul in an old story of limbo. "What have you done to him?"

"He is unharmed, sir. The chamber is devoid of light and sound. Suspensors negate the gravity. The temperature precisely matches his body temperature. In his own perceptions, he is *nowhere*." Wantori looked up, blinked his large eyes as if he didn't like to reveal his techniques. "Often that's enough to break an interrogation subject, but this one hasn't revealed anything yet."

"I wouldn't have expected him to. Any man who could infiltrate my Navigator field is no ordinary spy. He's either very dedicated or very well paid." Josef considered. "I hope he's well paid, because a mercenary can be bought, whereas a man with political or religious convictions is harder to break."

Ekbir pointed out, "He is physically unharmed, except for some contusions and one broken finger, which he received while resisting capture."

"I healed it," Wantori said.

"Maybe you shouldn't have bothered," Josef said.

The interrogator shook his head slightly. "The pain of a broken bone or the ache of bruises decreases the effectiveness of sensory deprivation. It gives the subject something to hold on to, a focus. Now he has nothing, not even the pain. To him, it must seem as if a thousand years have passed. And my procedure is just beginning."

Josef said, "Let me speak to him."

Wantori looked alarmed. "It'll be a setback to our disorientation process, sir."

"Let me speak to him!" Josef barely controlled his temper. The fact that someone would come here like a rapist in a nunnery offended him. For generations the Venports had built their empire, funded research, constructed ships, acquired wealth and power. He found it deeply insulting that anyone would try to take what he had *achieved*.

Cioba nodded to the interrogator. "Do as my husband says. It may yield some interesting results."

Wantori activated a set of controls, gestured toward an input speaker. When Josef spoke, his words boomed into the lightless tank. "My name is Josef Venport." After days of utter silence, without any sensation whatsoever, the captive spy must have thought he sounded like a deity. "I can tell you're a professional at what you do, and I won't insult you by asking detailed questions. Dr. Wantori will take care of that for me. Will you at least do me the courtesy of telling me your name and why you are here?"

The spy twisted as he floated, but did not seem uncomfortable or disoriented. He did not try to find the source of the voice. "I was waiting for someone to ask. My name is Royce Fayed, and I should think my reason for coming here is obvious."

"Who sent you?"

Was that a smile on the spy's face? "I thought you weren't going to ask me detailed questions."

"Indulge my curiosity." Josef's nostrils flared.

"I'm sorry, Directeur Venport, but you'll have to work a little harder than that."

Josef knew better than to be drawn into that game, so he switched off the transmitter, then turned to Wantori. "Find out what you can. Find out everything."

WHEN THE STRANGER named Royce Fayed was brought to Josef Venport's main offices again two weeks later, the spy looked gaunt and significantly changed. His hands and fingers were comically splayed, the joints smashed and then badly re-fused. His head had been shaved, and scars marred his scalp. Dr. Wantori had been very thorough.

Fayed stood sullenly as the VenHold security chief read his report. "He is working for Celestial Transport. Arjen Gates hired him personally. The company is getting desperate after the recent string of accidents and the sudden unavailability of insurance coverage for them. Clever of you to set that up."

Josef allowed himself a smile, glanced at his wife. Another plan that he and Cioba had developed together. It had taken years, but his holding company had bought a controlling interest in most of the insurance companies that covered commercial space transportation. As such, VenHold now possessed accurate data on just how many losses Celestial Transport had suffered in spacefolding mishaps; and, since he owned the insurance carriers, Josef was able to deny coverage to CT outright. He could have charged outrageous premiums, but the money didn't matter to him as much as driving his key competitor out of business.

"Arjen Gates wants to know how you navigate foldspace," Fayed said without a trace of humor. "And I am paying the price for his curiosity. I'm not complaining. I did accept the job."

"We won't even send your body back to him as a warning that his attempt failed. I'll just let him remain curious."

The broken man still had a gleam in his eye. "Don't you want to know why he so urgently needs Navigators?"

"His loss rate answers that question," Cioba pointed out.

"Oh, but he is more desperate now." Royce Fayed did his best to straighten himself, though his body no longer functioned properly.

"Are you trying to make a bargain?" Josef asked. "If I know you have more information, I can just have Dr. Wantori continue the interrogation."

Fayed did not shudder. "That will not be necessary. I take satisfaction in knowing that when I tell you, you'll be even more frustrated." His bruised lips somehow made a smile.

"What is it?" Josef snapped.

"CT scouts recently discovered hundreds of perfectly intact robot ships. Once they are refurbished and retrofitted with Holtzman engines, Celestial Transport's fleet will be four times the size it is now, maybe even larger than your own. Scouts also found the robotic facilities for refueling and manufacturing those vessels— large facilities. Arjen Gates has everything now . . . except Navigators."

Josef sucked in a quick breath, and a hungry excitement filled his eyes. "And where are these ships? How can I find them?" His own scouts had been combing known machine planets for intact facilities like that, hoping to find a key manufacturing yard. He had not expected Celestial Transport's scavengers to be more successful than his people.

Fayed let out a wheezing laugh. "And there's the joke on you, Directeur Venport. I was hired to learn about your Navigators, but I don't know where the facility is. I don't have the coordinates, not even which star system it's in. That is my final trick on you. Your doctor is quite proficient at interrogation, but I genuinely don't know any more than that."

Security Chief Ekbir was startled by the revelation. "I apologize that I didn't get the additional information from him in the first place, sir. I do believe him when he says he doesn't know."

Cioba sat coolly in her chair. She nodded in agreement.

Unfortunately, Josef believed the man as well. His mind was already racing with dreams of what the VenHold Spacing Fleet could do with a whole depot full of untouched, completely functional robotic ships. He hated to imagine that Arjen Gates was even now overseeing his engineers, preparing to add those spacecraft to his fleet.

"You can kill me now," Fayed said with a sigh. "I'm done."

"Oh, I don't intend to kill you." Josef rose from his desk. "I'm taking you to my great-grandmother."

OUT ON THE field of Navigator tanks, Josef and Cioba brought the aching, frail spy to the tank of Norma Cenva, which overlooked the other Navigator-candidates. Some days he had to work very hard to get her attention; today, however, Norma was immediately interested.

Her strange voice warbled through the speakers after he told her how the spy had been captured. "Many wish to know the secret of creating Navigators."

"It's *our* secret," Josef said, "a Venport secret. We captured him before he could deliver his information."

A long pause from her tank. Fayed stood looking through the clearplaz window into the reddish-orange swirls of gas where he could see the distorted form of the woman inside.

"Why do you stare so intently, Fayed?" Cioba asked him. "Didn't you already see this when you were spying?"

"Not so closely."

"Why did you bring him to me?" Norma asked.

"He has a very interesting mind. Our interrogators find him quite a challenge. Cioba thinks he has potential, and I agree."

He couldn't tell if Norma's interest had been piqued. She said, "We need people with potential. More Navigators."

Josef could have just executed the man and been done with it—Ekbir would have taken care of it without being asked—but Josef felt a particular personal grudge against this man who had tried to steal his family's livelihood, to dilute the seminal Venport achievement by giving Navigators to cheap imitations.

Josef turned to the damaged spy. "You came here to discover how Navigators are made, Fayed, so we will show you. We'll show you everything, giving you a greater understanding than you ever expected."

Norma pressed her soft, no-longer-human face against the plaz, peering out with her large eyes. She watched as Josef instructed his guards to place Royce Fayed inside one of the empty tanks.

They sealed it and filled the chamber with spice gas.

I'm a thinker. That is what I do, in great depth and detail, every waking moment of the day. I like to believe it's worthwhile. And yet, I can't help but recall something Erasmus said to me once when I was young, and he was my master: "All of these things with which we occupy ourselves don't amount to much in the cosmic scale of things, do they? No matter how extensively we ponder any particular topic, there is really very little there."

—GILBERTUS ALBANS, *Reflections in the Mirror of the Mind*

The Mentat School administration offices were a labyrinth of modular rooms and cubicles; in the background, music played so softly that Gilbertus often ignored it. This afternoon, however, the melody drew his attention because he heard the punctuating, powerful notes of "Rhapsody in Blue," one of Erasmus's favorite Old Earth pieces. Since the independent robot had managed to connect his memory core to the school's audio systems, Erasmus had no doubt chosen the music himself, another subtle reminder of his hidden presence. None of the professors or students in the school would guess at the thoughts and emotions such melodies elicited in Gilbertus, or in the machine mind of Erasmus, with its simulation programs.

Gilbertus left a staff meeting, made his way to the secondary wing, and entered an office that was more suited to a tenured professor than to a mere student, but Draigo Roget was no ordinary teaching assistant. On the cusp of graduation, Draigo had reached the limits of what Gilbertus or any of the instructors could teach him, and soon the young man would depart from the school as a full-fledged Mentat.

Gilbertus had made him repeated offers of a professorship. "Some of the best graduates choose to stay behind. You have performed better than any other student in the history of this institution, and you can probably teach better than most of our instructors."

Draigo remained noncommittal. "I can also serve outside in the Imperium as a Mentat. That is what I have been trained to do." Gilbertus could not argue with the logic, although he had insisted on giving him the larger office and other perks in hopes that he would consider the position.

Once again, he considered telling Draigo about Erasmus, hoping he would at last have an ally in protecting and studying the robot's memory core. Erasmus would have been happy to work with another ward, someone who might be more easily convinced to build him a new machine form. But Gilbertus decided he could not take that risk yet . . . if ever.

Now, Draigo did not look up when the headmaster entered. With his dark eyebrows drawn together, the young man was combing over stacks of printed documents that overflowed his desk and sat in piles on the floor and side chairs: written records that tracked the appearances and movements of Omnius's ships throughout more than a century of the Jihad, countless scattered data points.

Glancing up at Gilbertus, as if he'd been caught in an illicit action, Draigo said, "Just a little mental exercise before my graduation. By collating all the data of known sightings and attacks, I'm trying to backtrack and do a Mentat projection that looks at the ripples of second-order influences. Maybe I can discover the hidden footprints of other abandoned robot fleets or outposts. Given sufficient end points, perhaps I can extrapolate the beginnings."

"Interesting—and very ambitious. Would you like some assistance?" Gilbertus understood the depth of the problem; it wasn't simply a retrograde projection, since they had no way of knowing how many different depots or shipyards had launched all the vessels, or which ones had been destroyed or shut down during the course of the Jihad. However, with enough data points and intensity of mental focus, maybe they could tease out a bit of information. If anyone was capable, Draigo might do it. "With all that information, we should split it up and compare summaries."

The young man smiled. "That would be an excellent idea, and I would appreciate your assistance. One last cooperative effort between master and student?"

The finality of the words disheartened Gilbertus. Taking a seat at the adjacent desk, he proceeded to scan document after document, speed-reading, absorbing data. As he retained all of the points in his mind, patterns began to emerge, and several hours later when the two of them compared what they'd discovered, Draigo said what Gilbertus was already thinking.

"I've extrapolated a few places where large numbers of machine vessels might have been built and launched," Draigo said. "Extensive shipyards."

"I've projected that, too," Gilbertus said. "The most significant convergence of paths originates from a star system labeled as Thonaris. Yes, the evidence suggests it could be a prominent machine industrial facility." Though he didn't personally remember any previous mention of such shipyards, he could always ask Erasmus for confirmation.

Draigo tapped his fingertip on the records, which he had stacked in neat piles after memorizing the entries. "This seems like useful information. Thank you for your assistance."

The two men remained silent for a time, each pondering the implications. Gilbertus knew that if he revealed the data to the Butlerians—as he was expected to do—Manford Torondo would ransack and destroy any such outpost, if it existed. Or, other commercial interests could salvage and exploit the treasure trove. Gilbertus did not like either alternative.

"It might be best if I consult the Emperor about what he wants to do," Gilbertus suggested. "I will consider this further, but perhaps I should deliver this projection to him in person the next time I travel to Salusa Secundus."

Draigo shrugged, as if he had no interest in the matter, now that the problem was solved. "We have time. The machine outpost has waited there untouched since before the Battle of Corrin—if our deduction is accurate."

"It has been enjoyable working with you, Draigo Roget," he said. "I will miss our friendly contests and our cooperation."

The other man bowed his head. "And I have enjoyed learning from you, but I look forward to graduating. I shall do my best to continue to learn, even in the outside world."

LATER, IN THE privacy of his office, Gilbertus removed the memory core from its hidden compartment and conferred with the robot mind about the new information.

"Oh yes, I remember the Thonaris shipyards," Erasmus said in his erudite voice. "One of our largest industrial operations."

"Now that I have the information, how should I reveal it?" Gilbertus remained troubled. "And to whom? To Manford Torondo, to increase his goodwill toward the school? To the Emperor?"

"There is no rush to reveal it at all. One doesn't simply *give away* such important information, even to the Emperor. Consider the value, and keep it as a bargaining chip. Reveal it only when you need to, when it is in our best interest to do so. You never know when such a 'discovery' might come in handy."

"That sounds like good advice."

"Have I ever given you any other kind?"

Gilbertus grinned. "No comment."

*We are like salmon, swimming upstream against the current of life.
Each of us is desperate to learn where we came from—who our ancestors were and how they lived—as if their past will provide guidance for
our future.*

—ABULURD HARKONNEN, his Lankiveil notes

When Valya was assigned to conduct an hour of private intensive training
with Anna Corrino and the two young daughters of Josef Venport, the
age disparity of the acolytes was remarkable, but their skill level was roughly equivalent. If anything, young Sabine and Candys, aged nine and ten respectively,
were more focused and talented than the Emperor's flighty sister.

When the Reverend Mother asked her to take time away from studying the
computerized breeding records, Valya's initial reaction had been one of annoyance, because using the computers to make bloodline projections seemed so much
more vital to the Sisterhood's purpose, and to her own advancement. However,
she definitely saw the advantages of establishing close ties with both Anna Corrino and the two Venport daughters.

"I'll do my best, Reverend Mother," she said.

Raquella had given Valya no specific curriculum, leaving the instruction to
her own discretion; she wondered if the Reverend Mother was using this as a
means of testing *her* as well. . . .

"We call this the labyrinth wall," Valya said, leading her three students into
a small, dim chamber. On one entire wall of the room (behind a thin pane of plaz)
was a layer of finely sifted earth that held a complex insect colony. In the sand-
wiched tableau, a hive of armored burrowers—clawed nematodes covered with
chitinous plates—excavated a maze of twisting tunnels. They had hollowed out
a central pocket from which their queen guided all the operations of her drones.
Valya secretly thought of the queen burrower as the "Reverend Mother."

"We have been here before," said the nine-year-old, Sabine, sounding superior.

Valya frowned at her. "You have not seen what I intend to show you."

Candys was fascinated by the elongated bugs that continued to excavate and rearrange the architecture of their colony. Anna looked irritated.

"I want you to study the movements of these creatures, analyze their activities, and interpret the intriguing order of their pathways. This burrower colony is like a microcosm of the universe, filled with pathways that intersect, some that branch off, and others that simply stop at blind ends. It's like the map of a person's life: It only makes sense if you study it carefully."

Anna's voice carried impatient annoyance. "My brothers didn't send me to Rossak to stare at an insect hive all day long."

"An hour is hardly all day," said Sabine Venport.

"Your brothers perform equivalent exercises," Valya said. "Doesn't Emperor Salvador have to think about the connections among the planets in the Imperium, the noble families, the bloodlines, the intermarriages, the feuds?"

"Our parents run Venport Holdings," said Candys. "That's almost as important as being the Emperor."

Anna scoffed at the child. "There's no comparison."

Valya interrupted the brewing argument. "You are all acolytes now, and your family is the Sisterhood. Corrino and Venport mean nothing here." She spoke with great conviction, although she felt otherwise. Valya didn't want them asking about the Harkonnens. . . .

If she pulled the right strings, made the proper connections, Valya could salvage her family's situation through the power and influence of the Corrinos *and* the Venports.

Directing their attention, Valya stood close to Anna Corrino as the three looked intently at the scurrying burrowers. "Study them until you see the pattern, and you will have a glimpse into their purpose. The hive queen must have some overall blueprint that we can unravel."

"I like to watch them," Candys said.

Valya whispered, as if sharing a secret with Anna alone. "Some of the Sorceresses use this as a mental exercise. After years of practice in directing their thoughts, a few have learned to change the pattern of the tunnels. They can rewrite the blueprint."

"Could I do that?" Anna said.

Valya didn't laugh, did not discourage her. "I don't know. Can you? It takes great concentration."

Anna looked up at Valya, who saw a scared little girl behind her eyes. "I had a special fogwood tree back at the palace, and over the years I made it into my own secret hiding place. I could make the branches grow in whatever directions I wanted. A lot of people can manipulate fogwoods, but not that particular variety, and I was especially good with it. Sister Dorotea was intrigued when she heard about it, but I refused to show her. She didn't believe I could possibly have mental powers like that, but I wouldn't perform for her—why should I?" She sniffed.

"Well, I believe you," Valya said, because it made Anna smile at her.

"Can we do it?" Sabine asked. "We're young, but we've already studied with the Sisterhood for two years."

Valya paused to consider how the Reverend Mother might have answered, and told them, "Some say a person can accomplish anything she likes, if she applies herself, but that's just an empty platitude. You can't actually do 'anything,' but if you apply yourselves, you will discover strengths that others don't have. You'll surprise people who don't expect it of you." She lowered her voice. "And that is how you become powerful."

The three spent the remainder of the hour staring in silence, studying the burrowers. Valya remained with them, but her thoughts were far away, contemplating connections and possibilities in her own future.

ALONE AGAIN TO catch up with her duties in the high and secret caverns that held breeding records, Valya Harkonnen sat in the center of a computer carousel, using hand gestures to touch screens that paused in front of her, accessing the records she wanted. She sifted through historical and family files, exploring tributaries of data that flowed from the main river of famous events that occurred in the Jihad.

Aged Sister Sabra Hublein had trained her how to use the systems, which Valya found remarkably intuitive, and she enjoyed delving into the electronic strata of genetic information, as well as family histories and personal records.

Each time she slipped through the hidden holographic door into these computer chambers, Valya appreciated the great privilege that Raquella had bestowed on her. She always did her best to prove that she deserved the honor.

Though she and the Reverend Mother were separated by a vast gulf in age, they shared something that could not be expressed in words; Valya saw it in the caring way the old woman looked at her, the smile crinkles around the pale-blue eyes, the good-natured way she pursed her lips when talking. The *hope* she felt for Valya, like a parent wanting her child to succeed.

The Sisterhood was the young woman's family now, as the Reverend Mother insisted, but Valya's biggest secret was that she could not forget about her other heritage. She kept her divided loyalty as carefully hidden as possible.

At the unexpected return of Vorian Atreides, her simmering anger had clamored for her to destroy the thorn in her family's side, but she had passed that noble obligation on to her brother, and she knew Griffin would not let her down. She wondered where he was now. . . .

Nearby, robed Sisters sat at other carousel screens or bustled in and out of the hidden chambers, but Valya paid them little mind. She was focused on digging for information, excavating historical files that showed the tangled relationship between Vorian Atreides and the Harkonnen family.

Buried deep in the records, mislabeled (perhaps intentionally) so that no one had found them, were letters that Abulurd Harkonnen and Vorian Atreides had written to each other years before the Battle of Corrin. Her eyes widened as she pieced together the information: Vorian Atreides said he wanted to restore Xavier Harkonnen to the good graces of history, insisting that the man was a hero, not a traitor to humanity, but the League had no desire to hear it.

She found two letters Abulurd had sent to Vorian, back when the men were still friends. The first, written in the heat of the Jihad, read: "Some say that Harkonnen blood running through my veins disgraces me, but I don't accept the lies I have heard, the attempts to blacken the role of my grandfather. You and I know why he did what he did. To me the actions of Xavier Harkonnen speak of honor rather than cowardice."

In another letter, Vorian promised Abulurd that once Omnius was defeated he would work tirelessly to restore the Harkonnen name. However, after the events at the Bridge of Hrethgir, Vorian broke his vow, turned his back on the Harkonnen family, and saw to it that Abulurd was sent into exile.

Abulurd's final letter in the archives, written during the dark days of disgrace following the Battle of Corrin, was even more telling, and accusatory: "Vor, this is my second letter to you—my second urgent request. I know you want to destroy me and my name. Does that free you of your promise to correct history? At least let honor be restored to Xavier Harkonnen, who bravely flew his ship into the sun to destroy the evil Iblis Ginjo. Or will you cast Xavier aside, and all Harkonnens, because of your disappointment in me? What does that say about Atreides honor?"

Valya looked away and realized she was crying. She wiped the tears away. She had faith that Griffin would do what was necessary. That detestable man deserved to die!

Using a hand signal to activate the carousel, she scanned the files and traced her family tree, recognizing many of the names—from Abulurd, back to Xavier, Ulf, and even generations further into the archives of history. So many heroic deeds . . . but after Xavier killed himself and Grand Patriarch Ginjo, public opinion so turned against him that descendants changed their family name. Xavier's grandson Abulurd tried to reclaim his heritage, but his later banishment only completed the destruction of their legacy.

The next carousel screen showed seven images of Abulurd at varying ages. Her heart sank as she watched the faces change from youthful exuberance to the sad recognition of failure at the end of his life in exile.

She was startled when a breeze touched her face, a warm gust of air in the cavern, as if someone had breathed hard on her and then flitted away. Nearby, she heard a whisper of sound that faded into the shadows. Valya looked around, her senses heightened, but saw no one. Other trusted Sisters worked at computer stations inside the large chamber, but all were far from her. A tactile sensation like gooseflesh skittered down her back . . . and then was gone.

She waited, tense, but the sensation did not recur. She heard only the hum of fans and cooling systems, the subsonic pondering of thinking machines. Everything seemed normal. . . .

Unsettled, she tried to calm herself by remembering how she had joined the Sisters of Rossak, when a black-robed woman came to Lankiveil on a cargo transport. Sister Arlett, a graduate of the Sisterhood, a traveler who stopped in out-of-the-way places to discuss the Rossak School. The missionary had seen a hunger and a potential in Valya's eyes, and she gave the young woman hope when Valya knew she had little chance of bettering herself on Lankiveil. "The Sisterhood strives to improve humanity, one woman at a time," Arlett had told her. "On Rossak, you can learn to become yourself, and more than yourself."

Valya was fascinated by the choice. The Rossak School was her chance to improve her prospects. Although Griffin was sad to see his sister go, and their mother dismissed the girl's aspirations, Valya had made up her mind quickly. She'd flown away with Sister Arlett, feeling no regrets at all. . . .

Now, after she finished working with the hidden computers, Valya returned to the main warrens and the classes where acolytes had just completed a meditation session. Presently, she saw Anna Corrino hurrying toward her, followed by an impatient-looking Sister Dorotea. No doubt Anna had been troublesome in the class.

"I don't need meditation classes," Anna said. "I want to work on the breeding program with you."

Valya slowed, but continued walking into the main school complex. "The breeding program?"

"Everyone knows the breeding records are up that trail."

"Each Sister has responsibilities beyond continuing her education," Sister Dorotea said pointedly to Anna. "Sister Valya has her own duties, and I have mine assisting Karee Marques in the jungles."

Valya had heard rumors that Dorotea might even become the leader of the Sisterhood one day. But if so, Valya wondered why the Reverend Mother had not let her in on the secret of the breeding-record computers. Perhaps because Dorotea had spent years studying with the Butlerians on Lampadas?

Anna took Valya by the arm, happily claiming friendship. "I want to see the breeding records. They must be very important."

Valya's mind raced. Anna Corrino was not accustomed to being denied access anywhere. "Once you become a full Sister and pass all your tests, maybe I can use my influence to arrange a brief tour, but detailed family trees are generally off-limits."

Anna grinned. "I know all about House Corrino already."

Valya wondered if Anna had been told about the Harkonnen offshoot of the Butler/Corrino family tree. *Would it surprise you to know we are cousins?* Rather than answering Anna directly, she paraphrased the Reverend Mother's words. "Maybe so, but remember that we are all Sisters, and the Sisterhood is our family now."

Not all accidents are what they seem. Victims do not even know why they have been chosen.

—General Agamemnon, true memoirs

Now that they had been set free, Hyla and Andros flew their stolen ship to the heart of the human Imperium. *Salusa Secundus*. During the flight, they had time to assimilate the information carried aboard the Butlerian ship, resenting and also questioning the facts as presented, especially how the history libraries portrayed their father, General Agamemnon, and the time of cymek Titans.

The twins also learned how their prodigal brother, Vorian, had turned wholeheartedly against the Synchronized Empire, how he was worshipped as a hero among the feral humans, whom the thinking machines scornfully called *hrethgir.*

"Apparently they revere betrayers," Andros said. "The hrethgir do not grasp the greatness of their forebears—and our brother is no worthy son of Agamemnon."

"Maybe we can restore that," Hyla said. "If Vorian turned once, maybe we can turn him again . . . back to his roots. And the three of us can achieve the potential of our breeding."

"He deserves to die for what he's done," Andros said.

Hyla gave him a cool smile with sharp edges. "You just want to be the only son of Agamemnon."

"I am the only true son of Agamemnon."

Reaching the capital world, they tapped into information broadcasts to collect data, while keeping their ship unnoticed and invisible, not because they feared detection, but because any clamor would affect their mission.

Even though the technological network of Salusa Secundus seemed to have deteriorated since the time of the Jihad, the twins tapped into broadcasts and then slipped into historical libraries, where they scanned volumes of heavily slanted histories. The Jihad records celebrated Vorian's numerous heroic deeds against the thinking machines, even attacking the cymeks who had raised him and granted him the miraculous life-extension treatment reserved for only the best. The accounts featured, and praised, how he had tricked and murdered his own father.

Vorian could easily have become the first Emperor after the Jihad, and by rights he should have been, but he had allowed the far weaker Corrinos to take that mantle. He had chosen the easy way out, turning his back on the fame and power that was his due. He had vanished eight decades ago into the vast backwaters of the Imperium.

Hyla could not comprehend why their demi-brother would do such a thing, given his potential. Even after all these years, she had no doubt that he remained alive—just as the twins did. He would probably live for centuries and centuries.

It did not take Andros long to find him. Vor had indeed returned to the public stage, recently appearing on behalf of an insignificant world that he had called home. A place where he had a family. After stirring up the populace on Salusa Secundus, bowing and smiling to the cheers, accepting the parades they threw for him, Vor had departed, thinking he could slip into obscurity again. . . .

"We have to go there," Andros said.

Hyla easily obtained the coordinates for the planet Kepler. "Of course we do."

They took the starship fuel they needed, murdered two people who got in the way, and flew off to find Agamemnon's misguided, traitorous son.

THOUGH THE TWINS had been raised in isolation in the experimental/ training lab, their surrogate mother, Juno, had pumped a wealth of information into them, giving them combat and infiltration skills. While some details were out of date, the techniques were timeless.

Andros and Hyla waited in the thorny untracked hills on the edge of the inhabited valley where they knew Vorian Atreides made his home. After full dark set in, they sprinted across surrounding farmlands and into the sprawling village, the layout of which they had memorized from zoning records. They knew their brother's house, knew the names of his wife, of all his grown children, his grandchildren, his closest associates. Though Vorian's offspring did carry the bloodline of General Agamemnon, Andros and Hyla were not interested in inferior descendants. They wanted only their brother—and they had their own reasons for this.

At this hour, only one light remained on in the large house. The night was quiet except for the vague rustlings of livestock. The chirping hum of night insects fell into a hush as the twins glided forward through the starlit shadows. They circled the house cautiously, then approached the lit window. Inside, Hyla saw only an old woman sitting alone in a chair, apparently reading, but she seemed half asleep. Faint, soothing music came from a concert box on a table. Hyla recognized Vorian's wife, Mariella, but she saw no sign of their brother.

Andros wanted to break in, kill the old woman, and ransack the house, but Hyla stopped him. "Juno taught us the difference between succeeding through intelligence and succeeding through strength. If Vorian isn't there, let's learn what we can first—quickly and efficiently. If that doesn't work, we have the option for violence later, but not vice versa."

Andros agreed, and they went to the front door. With a quick twist of her wrist, Hyla snapped the knob, then broke the dead bolt out of its socket. The two lunged into the house so swiftly that Mariella barely had time to rise from her chair.

"Who are you? What are you doing here?" The old woman stood tense and indignant, but Hyla could already smell the fear that began to exude from her pores.

"We're looking for your husband," Andros said. "Our dear missing Vorian. We long to see him. Where can we find him?"

Mariella's nostrils flared. "I have known my husband for seventy years, and I've never seen you before."

"We're his brother and sister," Hyla said, "and we only recently learned where he's been hiding all this time."

The old woman's eyes narrowed. "Yes . . . I can see the resemblance, but he never mentioned a brother or sister before." Trying to be discreet but doing it clumsily, Mariella glanced around the room, no doubt searching for a weapon.

"He doesn't know about us, but we came to Kepler for a happy family reunion," Andros said. Even Hyla could see that his attempt at a disarming smile was not convincing.

"He's no longer on Kepler," Mariella said. "You missed him. He left, permanently. And I think you'd better leave as well."

Hyla frowned, annoyed that this would not be as easy and straightforward as they had thought. "Where did he go? We made a long journey to come here."

Suspicion crystallized around Mariella, and she crossed her arms over her chest in a defiant gesture. "I don't think I want to tell you. He said his farewells and left Kepler for reasons he considered good and sufficient. If he wanted you to know where he was, he would have told you."

"This is taking too long." With a lunge forward, Andros grabbed Mariella by the shoulder and shoved her back down into her chair with enough force that her collarbone snapped beneath his grip. The old woman let out a cry of pain. "It's time we tried the other methods."

The siblings had successfully interrogated a hardened Swordmaster who was inured to pain; Hyla doubted an old woman would pose much of a challenge. "All right," she told her brother, "but we'll have to cover our tracks afterward. We can't let any of these people alert Vorian that we're tracking him down."

TWO HOURS AHEAD of dawn, before the village stirred for the pre-sunrise farming chores, someone noticed the rising flames and sounded the alarm. Still tense after the slaving raid, despite the Imperial protective ships in orbit, the people of Kepler rushed to aid.

Bonda raced with her husband and sons to see that Mariella's house was on fire. Flames had already consumed the ground level and now spewed from the gables. She had never seen a house catch fire so quickly or so completely. "Mother!" she shouted, trying to run closer, but her husband, Tir, grabbed her arm to protect her.

"Is she out? Did my mother get out?" Bonda screamed.

Volunteer firefighters struggled to hook up hoses to the wellhead outside the house and sprayed water on the flames. Some of the firefighters glanced at her, their faces reddened and grim as they continued fighting the flames.

Bonda struggled against her husband, but he refused to let go of her arm. Her heart was pounding, her throat raw. The porch collapsed in the inferno. Tears poured down Bonda's face. Spiraling sparks flew like fireflies in the heat currents.

She had grown up in that house with her brothers and sisters, but with her father gone, it had already felt half-empty. Her mother had seemed a pale shadow of herself without him, but she had refused to move in with any of her children.

"Maybe she got out," Bonda said, although nothing could have survived that blaze. Her knees let go, and she dropped to the ground. Tir sank beside her, putting his arms around her, holding her close. The flames rose higher into the sky.

We are much braver in our private thoughts than we are in reality.
—FAYKAN BUTLER, Hero of the Jihad
and first Corrino Emperor

Before Valya sent him the message, Griffin Harkonnen had never heard of the planet where Vorian Atreides was hiding. Kepler was one of the many hundreds of unnoticed and unremarkable worlds that comprised the frontier of the Imperium. Even during the centuries of thinking-machine rule, Omnius had never bothered with Kepler. It was no wonder that Vorian had simply vanished here for decades.

Of course, Lankiveil was not much of a planet, either—a suitable place for a disgraced man like Abulurd Harkonnen to be banished, but little more than that. It could hardly be called "home" in the comforting sense of the word.

Yet, through all the difficulties and resentments, Griffin had tried to see the potential there, the possibilities for whale-fur trade, the investments he could bring in from other noble families if he had the opportunity to talk with them. And once he became the Landsraad representative, he would travel to Salusa Secundus, make allies, and conduct business—and eventually people would learn that his ancestors were the same as the Butler family, who called themselves Corrino after the Jihad. It was all part of his and Valya's long-term strategy. Though Griffin might not live to see it completed, his children and grandchildren would.

But the reemergence of Vorian Atreides had saddled him with other obligations first.

After the loss of Weller and the whale-fur cargo, Griffin understood how important it was for him to be on Lankiveil, to guide his family through the rough and dangerous waters. Unable to do that in person, he had left careful instructions, appointed deputies among the townspeople, and coached Vergyl Harkonnen as best he could. He had to hope they could manage the business of Lankiveil well enough until he returned.

Avenge our family honor, Griffin. I know I can count on you.

Though it gave him considerable pause to seek vengeance against such an aged man, Harkonnen family honor trumped everything, including the ledger sheets and five-year plans he'd been spending so much time on. Considering the gravity of what Griffin had to do now—assassinate the most famous hero of the Jihad—he had some misgivings. But he did not shirk the responsibility. He needed to face the grim but necessary task, and complete it.

After setting aside money for necessary planetary expenditures on Lankiveil and automating the accounts so that spaceship arrivals would be compensated and vital cargoes paid for, Griffin carefully budgeted the settlement money from Celestial Transport and booked the cheapest possible passage to Kepler. Most of the funds he took with him came out of the savings he had built up to pay for appropriate government certifications on Salusa Secundus and to establish an office in the capital city. For the time being, he set those dreams aside.

The roundabout route required several different transfers, and he was forced to travel aboard an old-model cargo vessel operated by Celestial Transport. After the terrible accident that cost his uncle's life, Griffin was reluctant to deal with CT, but the next available ship would have taken him six more weeks to get to Kepler. He didn't want to be gone for that long.

Upon arriving at his destination he saw a group of large, well-armed warships circling in orbit, keeping watch like fierce guardians. According to reports, Vorian Atreides had arranged the military protection from Emperor Salvador. Griffin narrowed his eyes, feeling a flash of annoyance. He didn't know the details, but assumed the arrangement involved bribes, coercion, and calling in special favors. The Atreides patriarch manipulated people in power so easily.

By contrast, the Corrino Emperor had never bothered to station any defenses above Lankiveil. . . .

Kepler's small spaceport was little more than a landing field and a transfer station out to one of the continent's fourteen inhabited valleys. Weller had once told him, "The only way to get answers is by asking questions." Everyone from lowly refueling technicians to the on-duty administrator of spaceport operations was delighted to talk about Vorian Atreides, whose identity had now been exposed. For years, apparently, he had lived a quiet life here, pretending to be a simple man, well liked by his family and his neighbors. Now, after what he had done in securing protection for Kepler, they regarded him as a hero, celebrating his accomplishments and applauding all he had done for the planet and its people.

A cargo handler had the most to say. "When slavers raided Vorian's valley and captured his friends and family, he took his own ship and raced to rescue them! The rest of us had given up. What can you do after a slave raid? But he found a way!" As he spoke, the loquacious man operated a control panel, moving suspensor-borne crates of cargo from the supply shuttle to large delivery trucks. "Yes, sir, Vorian followed the slavers to Poritrin and used his own fortune to buy back the captives—not just his own family members, but everybody. Then he went to Salusa and forced the Emperor to guarantee our protection. The man was already legendary for his exploits in the Jihad, and this only adds to his incredible legacy of selfless acts."

The cargo handler pointed a finger toward the sky. "We got those warships up there because Vorian Atreides demanded them from the Emperor. No one else could have done it except the former Supreme Bashar of the Army of Humanity. But Vorian—ah, he is still a man to be reckoned with."

"Yes, it sounds like he is," Griffin said, frowning. Could this be the same man he had heard about all his life, the monster who would stab his best friend Xavier Harkonnen in the back?

When she sent her message, Valya had neglected to mention the reason Vorian Atreides had come to the Imperial Court in the first place, that he was apparently on a mission of mercy to protect his adopted planet. She must have known that.

"I'd like to meet him," Griffin said, beginning to feel a little uncertain about the nature of his enemy. Apparently, the man was not all black or white, though that did not diminish his treachery against House Harkonnen. "In fact," Griffin said, "I have connections with him that go way back. Where does he live? He hasn't gone back into hiding, has he?"

"Everyone knows the village where he's lived all these years." The cargo handler paused while the crates floated beside him. He wiped a thick hand across his sweaty forehead, then provided the name of a valley, along with vague directions. It was enough for a start. From what Valya had told him and what Griffin had seen in the historical record, his prey did not avoid calling attention to himself if the opportunity arose.

A woman in the admin office gave him more detailed guidance, and then he arranged for transport out to the valley. His heart was pumping with anticipation. When Valya entrusted this task to him, placing the obligation on his shoulders, she had not seemed to consider it an overly difficult mission.

But did she really expect him to walk up to the man and simply kill him? That seemed no more honorable than what Atreides had done to Abulurd Harkonnen.

In his mind, Griffin envisioned how their encounter might play out. After so many years of lying low, why should Atreides expect to hear from descendants of the young bashar whose career he had ruined long ago, whose name he had soiled? The surprise would be complete, and the deed needed to be done so that the man knew exactly who had defeated him. A Harkonnen must make him understand how much pain the whole family had suffered because of him—and then kill him in fair combat.

Growing up together, Griffin and Valya had sparred, building each other up, testing, fighting. They had been perfectly matched, almost as if telepathically linked. They developed their own fighting techniques, honed their reflexes, learned how to respond to the slightest flicker of movement. No hesitation. They could spar on balanced, mist-slick logs, or they could jump, kick, and land again with perfect poise on narrow, wobbly canoes out in the harbor.

Now Griffin wondered if Valya had been planning for an encounter like this all along. If he had to fight Vorian Atreides, his abilities could completely surprise his foe.

His sister considered the two of them to be the only real Harkonnens true to their bloodline. In between practice matches, they studied the history of their ancestors Abulurd, Xavier . . . Quentin Butler, Faykan Butler, the great heroes of the Jihad. "We are of the Imperial line," she had told him. "We should be on *Salusa Secundus* . . . not forgotten, as we are on Lankiveil. We were meant for much greater things."

Assassination, to avenge the family honor.

Reaching the sheltered valley where Vorian Atreides and his family made their homes, Griffin arrived in the midst of a somber procession—not a celebration of Vorian's bravery and skill, but a funeral. The village houses were adorned with black crepe, and the people who walked through the streets were in mourning. The few hundred gathered there might have been the valley's entire population.

Griffin had hoped to make a few discreet inquiries so he could learn where the man lived; anyone could see that his questions were coming from an offworlder. But they would not recognize him. It had been eight decades since Vorian had seen a living Harkonnen, and Griffin was three generations removed from Abulurd.

He tried to slip unobtrusively into the funeral procession, feeling awkward. Maybe he could whisper a question or two. A middle-aged woman with red-rimmed eyes came up to him. "Our businesses are closed for today, sir. At times like these, the community draws together."

"Who is the deceased?"

"Our mother has died. She was much loved. Mariella Atreides." The woman shook her head. "I'm Bonda, her daughter."

Griffin covered his shock. "Atreides? Do you know Vorian Atreides, then? Is he your cousin?" He added quickly, before her questions could come to the fore, "Members of my family served with him a long time ago, during the Jihad."

Because of the sad ceremony, Bonda's guard was down. She formed a wan smile, and seemed to think nothing of Griffin's comment. "Vorian was my father, and he was well loved here. He did a great many good things for Kepler. We all miss him." She shook her head. "There was a fire . . . the house burned down. We don't know the exact cause." Bonda looked up at him with tear-sparkled eyes. "My parents were married for close to fifty years. I suppose it's no surprise that my mother didn't last long after he was gone."

"Gone?" Alarm swirled through Griffin's mind. "Vorian is . . . dead, then?" He didn't know whether to feel flustered or relieved. If their nemesis was dead, then the Harkonnens no longer needed vengeance. Valya might not be entirely satisfied, but at least Griffin could go back home, work on solidifying the business of Lankiveil, and prepare to go to the Imperial capital as soon as his exam results and paperwork returned. . . .

Bonda's eyes widened briefly. "Oh, no, my father isn't dead, wasn't on Kepler when the awful fire occurred. After he came back from meeting with the Emperor on Salusa Secundus, he left Kepler for good. Some sort of bargain he made with the throne in order to guarantee the safety of this planet."

Griffin was trembling. "Do you have any idea where he's gone? I've traveled this far just to see him, just to . . . bring him something from my family."

"That shows dedication! Kepler isn't an easy place to get to." Bonda shook her head as the mourners gathered in the center of the town. "My father went off to find more adventures, I suppose. My mother insisted that he go without her, and I'm trying to accept that."

"Do you know the name of the planet?"

"He made no secret of it. He went to a place he's never been, the desert world of Arrakis. I'm afraid he won't ever come back."

"Arrakis? Why would he go there?"

The woman shrugged. "Who can say? My father has lived so long, maybe he's been everywhere else that interests him. Will you stay for the funeral, as our guest? Tell us what you know of him, any stories? I'm sure we'll all be happy to hear it."

Griffin swallowed hard. They would not like the only stories he knew about Vorian Atreides.

Though he felt reluctant to remain here where he so obviously didn't belong, he knew from the transport schedules that it would be days before another outbound ship came to Kepler. "I'll stay for the funeral," he said. "I'd like to hear more about your father, but my own tales of Vorian Atreides must remain private."

"As you wish," Bonda said. "Now, if you'll excuse me, I have a eulogy to deliver."

Griffin could not think of anything else to say, and did not want to speak any more lies, so he waited, as quiet and unassuming as possible, while observing the celebration of the life of Mariella Atreides.

The galaxy is filled with countless wonders—beautiful worlds and harsh ones. No person could visit them all in a single lifetime, not even me, with all the years I have been alotted.

—VORIAN ATREIDES, private journals, Kepler period

The spice workers were glad to receive Vor among them. The rugged men had open minds and an accepting attitude toward an offworlder who found himself with no better options than to work out in the deep desert. But they had a hard and impatient discipline. Irresponsibility was not tolerated in the desert, because the simplest mistake could cost many lives.

New recruits had to learn quickly, and in the midst of that physically demanding challenge, Vor greatly missed Mariella and all his family and friends on Kepler.

The gruff, leathery-faced crew chief named Calbir took Vorian under his wing, treating him as an inexperienced young man, even though Vor was much, much older than he was. He didn't seem to know Vor's surname, though Vor had held onto his identity, placing his full name on the hiring documentation for Combined Mercantiles. He did not tell his comrades here anything about who he really was, and no one at this level seemed to have made any connection with his name at all. They just knew him as "Vor," and his first name generated no interest.

Noticing that the new hire wore a shield belt, Calbir scowled. "That identifies you as an offworlder, boy. I know why you wear that—for personal protection in Arrakis City—but don't activate it out here, or it will be the end of us. Holtzman fields attract the great worms. Just to play it safe, let me put it in your locker until we get back to base." Vor removed the belt and handed it over.

Given his many years of experience flying aircraft and spacecraft, Vor suggested he would be a good candidate to pilot one of the single-man scout skim-crafts over the desert wastelands, keeping on the alert for any telltale sign of melange-stained sands, but Calbir had scoffed at the offer. "Years of experience?" He ran his eyes up and down the young-looking man who stood before him. "The winds of Arrakis are harsh and unexpected. You have to demonstrate real mastery before I'm going to trust you with a skimcraft. I don't care where you're from or where else you've flown, you're not ready for this place—trust me when I say that."

Vor knew the old crew chief was wrong, but in order to convince him other-wise, he would have to reveal more about himself than he wanted to. Instead, he went to work with the others in the gigantic spice-excavator, a roving machine the size of a large building. Like an artificial grazing beast, it chewed trenches across spice-enriched sands. On big treads the excavator could make surprisingly good time across the dunes, racing from one sheltered rock outcrop to another while aircraft kept watch for an approaching sandworm. Hopscotching across the desert, the excavator gathered large amounts of melange and tried to outrun the mon-strous creatures that roved the spice sands.

The collectors spilled debris from one centrifuge to the next to the next, like the successive stomachs in an ungulate, except in this instance they were sepa-rating out the sand particles. All that remained was the rich soft powder that smelled like cinnamon but was an extremely potent drug.

Early in Vor's life, melange had been an interesting commodity, a rare substance distributed to nobles by the merchant Aurelius Venport. During the Omnius-induced plagues, however, spice had proved to be an effective pallia-tive, boosting immune systems and helping many people recover. That discov-ery, and humanity's desperation, had sparked a boom of melange harvesting on the harsh desert planet, where few civilized people had previously wanted to go. During the spice rush, hordes of ambitious fortune-hunters (both optimists and charlatans) journeyed across space to Arrakis. Many died in the rush, and a few got rich. The influx of offworlders forever changed the lives of the reclusive denizens, expanding small company towns like Arrakis City into bustling commercial hubs.

As an unforeseen consequence of the measures to fight the plagues, much of the Imperium was now addicted to spice, although Vor couldn't recall having seen users on Kepler. The interplanetary markets demanded increased production. During the epidemics, all competitors were tolerated in order to help meet the needs of sick populations. Now, however, the powerful Combined Mercantiles, part of the Venport commercial empire, was ruthless about driving out all com-petition and quashing rivals one by one, through bribery, blackmail, sabotage, or more extreme means. Many rival settlements were now just ghost towns in the desert rocks.

Calbir and his spice crew, including Vorian, worked for Combined Mercantiles. When Vor had arrived in Arrakis City and asked for work on a deep-desert crew, he was repeatedly warned to steer clear of anything but a Venport operation if he valued his life. "Then again," said one desiccated and sad-looking woman who sold him supplies, "if you valued your life, you wouldn't be going out there in the first place."

He had brushed her aside with a laugh. "I've had enough comforts in my life. The open dunes call to me. There are people far out in the desert that I'd like to meet."

"If you say so. But don't be so sure that they want to meet *you*."

By now, Vor had spent several weeks on the spice crew. It was hot and dusty work, but he didn't mind. He found it rejuvenating, for he could let his mind relax into a blank state and go about his duties with no thought for the future except what lay at the end of the next long and exhausting shift. The work itself was exciting: How could a job ever become tedious when at any moment a leviathan could burrow up from beneath the sands and devour everything?

During its daily work, the excavator scuttled across the open sands, hurrying to the next rock outcrop. From the moment a scout skimcraft spotted a spice deposit, to the moment the framework haulers dropped harvesting machinery onto the open dunes, Vor and his team worked in a race against time. The giant machinery heaved itself across the sand, scraping up as much rust-colored melange as possible. As a last resort, if they should ever find themselves too far from safety and unable to outrun an oncoming worm, the crew could eject in an escape pod, and cargo containers of melange would launch into the sky, guided by sluggish jets to the nearest safety zone, where Combined Mercantiles could retrieve and salvage the people and spice.

So far, that hadn't happened. A miscalculation by even a minute would doom them. Vor did not want to end his life in the midst of of wreckage slowly digested in a worm's gullet.

Rather than returning to Arrakis City each day, which was hundreds—sometimes thousands—of kilometers away, the excavator spent the nights on lonely rock outcroppings, hard islands safe from the sandworms. Now, as the stars shone forth out of the impenetrable blackness of an empty desert night, Vor walked restlessly around on the rocks, thinking of Kepler, of Mariella, wondering how many years he'd have to wait before he could risk slipping back there, just to see them again. And if Mariella would still be there.

As he wandered, alone, Vor was intrigued to find evidence of an old shelter made out of stacked boulders. He called Calbir over. "Looks like we aren't the first ones to camp here. Another excavating crew?"

The grizzled crew chief made an expression of distaste. "Desert people. Zensunnis, probably—descendants of escaped slaves. They came to Arrakis because they thought no sane person would want to settle this place. During the spice rush, they packed up and retreated into the most isolated wilderness, just to get away from people. I hear they still call themselves the Freemen, but scraping out a living here, with no sign of civilization, is hardly being free."

"Have you ever met one?" Vor asked. "I . . . I'd like to talk to them."

"Now why would you want to do that? Get those dreams out of your head! You'll probably see a desert man if you work around here long enough, but we don't have much to do with them."

The weary spice crew bedded down in the open, glad to be out of the stifling confinement of the dusty machinery. Calbir posted a watch, though the men grumbled that it seemed a ridiculous and paranoid precaution, until he showed them the signs of the old desert camp. "I'd rather you lost a little sleep than we all lost our lives. And if you're not worried about a few nomads, just keep in mind that Josef Venport has made a lot of enemies, too."

The men didn't argue further.

The sand and rocks had absorbed thermal energy during the day, and radiated warmth for the first several hours of darkness, but the desert air was so devoid of moisture that it retained little heat. Eventually, the night grew chilly.

The men sat around the rocky camp, wearing cloths over their mouths and noses to keep dust out. They relaxed by telling stories of powerful desert storms they had survived, narrow escapes from sandworm attacks, crew members they had known and lost, and loves they had left behind on other worlds.

Vorian listened, but kept his own stories to himself. He could have spent all night, every night, describing his harrowing escapades throughout the Jihad. He had fought in more battles and visited more planets than all these men combined. But he did not try to gain standing among the spice workers by bragging. Here on a spice crew, a man's privacy was his privilege, and his past was his own, which he could choose to share, or not. Vor's favorite moments were not the adventures anyway, but the peaceful years, the day-to-day life with women he had loved for decades, watching his children grow up and have families of their own.

Preferring to reminisce privately about what he had left behind, he lay back with his head against a rounded rock, staring into the quiet desert night as the conversation slowly faded. Vor had much to think about, but he had nothing left to prove in his long life.

The lines of the past can easily tangle and trip us. Whether or not we
can see them, these threads of history bind us all.
—NORMA CENVA, "Dissertation on the Structure of Reality,"
paper submitted to Tio Holtzman on Poritrin

Another Navigator-candidate had died, and Cioba was there to supervise the body's removal from its sealed tank.

Two male VenHold workers—among those vetted through additional security procedures after the spy, Royce Fayed, infiltrated Kolhar—attached hoses and sealed the hookups to the tank, draining away the valuable melange gas. When the diagnostics flashed green, the silent men affixed breathing masks to their faces and undogged the entry hatch. They reached inside and wrestled with the floppy, half-dissolved corpse.

Cioba watched the operation, her dark eyes flashing, but she said nothing, having been through this routine many times before. Despite the failures, however, Navigator-candidates succeeded far more often than Cioba's fellow Sisters of Rossak, who kept attempting to achieve their own mental breakthrough and become Reverend Mothers.

Three hundred Navigator-candidates in the last year, and seventy-eight failures—but only twelve deaths. Normally, the medical monitors detected when a volunteer's systems began to shut down, and they could rescue and revive the partially mutated person before the onset of death. A half-transformed Navigator could never become a normal human again, but they could serve VenHold research nevertheless. Their still-living brains were in some ways damaged, but in other ways superior, and the scientists in Josef's Denali research facility learned a great deal from studying them.

Their grunts muffled behind sealed face masks, the two workers hauled out the limp corpse and laid it on the ground. The skin was pale and flabby, the skull elongated and distorted as if someone had fashioned it out of clay, then dropped it from a height. The body looked as if it had been partially boiled. These remnants would become a dissection specimen.

Together, Cioba and Josef Venport made a strong team. Josef was a dedicated man, but he looked at the numbers of failures and successes, seeing the scores as a balance sheet without concerning himself with mental esoterica. Given her Sisterhood training, though, Cioba knew that some answers regarding the advancement of the human mind were not clear-cut.

While the workers hauled off the corpse to be packaged and shipped on the next supply vessel to the Denali labs, Cioba went to the top of the rise and stood before the chamber that held Norma Cenva, isolated in her thoughts. Though Norma was Josef's great-grandmother, Cioba also had a strong connection to the strange woman, directly back to their ties on Rossak.

Norma had begun her exotic transformation even before the birth of Karee Marques, Cioba's ancestor, and Norma had her own genetic ties to the psychic-powered women of Rossak; her mother, Zufa Cenva, had been one of the most powerful Sorceresses.

Now, when Norma acknowledged her arrival, Cioba spoke her thoughts immediately. The woman in the tank no longer understood pleasantries and chitchat. "You have changed yourself into something more than human, Norma. I trust you're aware that the Sisters of Rossak, including the last few Sorceresses, are also attempting to enhance themselves through drug-induced traumas, near-death encounters. Do you think there are any similarities with the Navigator transformation?"

Norma paused for a long moment. "All key advancements occur through crisis and survival. Without stress and extreme challenge, one cannot meet her potential."

Norma had gone through the same cycle herself, starting as a brilliant but malformed young woman from Rossak, enduring a lifetime of withering disapproval from her mother; then she'd been captured and tortured nearly to death by one of the cymek Titans, an ordeal from which she emerged with incredible mental powers. Likewise, only at the verge of death had Raquella been able to summon her potent hidden abilities; she had uplifted her entire being, becoming a far superior woman to the one she had been before.

"I lose track of how much time has passed," Norma said from her tank. "You have made me think of Rossak."

"My two daughters are there," Cioba said. "Your own great-great-granddaughters."

"Granddaughters . . ." Norma said. "Yes, it would be nice to see them."

Before Cioba could react, Norma Cenva's tank began to shimmer, and a whirlwind surrounded them, a dizzying distortion. Cioba caught her breath, sucking in great gasps of air, struggling for her balance—then fighting against the altered, slightly higher gravity. She looked up and recognized the familiar cliff city, the expansive silvery-purple jungles that filled the fertile rift valleys, and the smoldering volcanoes that gave the horizon an ominous topography. Cioba tried to control her astonishment. They had appeared on an open observation balcony, one of the gathering places where the Reverend Mother would summon her acolytes . . . where Cioba had witnessed the funerals of more than a dozen young women who had not survived the testing through poison.

I'm back on Rossak! she thought.

Her heart swelled, and she longed to see Sabine and Candys, even Karee Marques, the grandmother who had been instrumental in raising and training Cioba through her own years of Sisterhood training. The parentage of many acolytes and Sisters was hidden, so that they could focus on training rather than family matters. However, due to her Sorceress lineage, Cioba had been treated differently.

Because Norma had whisked the two of them unceremoniously away from Kolhar, Cioba still wore the business outfit she wore during all VenHold operations, but now as she looked around, she reached up, removed her scarf, and loosened her tresses to let the long dark locks flow. At present, she looked very much like one of the powerful telepathic women whose minds had obliterated countless cymeks.

The arrival of Norma and her large tank was quickly noticed, and soon Sisters crowded to the gathering balcony. Cioba identified herself to those who didn't recognize her immediately. Norma didn't seem to understand or notice the fuss.

Cioba raised her voice. "We are here because Norma Cenva has offered to give advice on the Reverend Mother transformations. She may be able to draw parallels with the Navigators she helps create on Kolhar."

Reverend Mother Raquella hurried up, accompanied by Karee Marques. Cioba's grandmother was dressed in a white worksuit stained with patches of purple, red, and blue from the berries, leaves, and fungi she encountered when foraging in the lower levels of the jungle.

"Rossak has changed much . . . and little," Norma said through her tank speakers.

Karee couldn't stop smiling at Cioba. "You have met all expectations, Granddaughter. Many of our graduate Sisters have gone on to join noble families as wives or advisers—but you have cemented the Sisterhood's hold in the Imperium's largest conglomerate."

"Yes, it was an excellent business decision." It had been a calculated choice between Reverend Mother Raquella and Josef Venport, but Cioba felt a real pride in her family and in the power and influence of Venport Holdings.

Cioba's two young daughters hurried in, bursting with excitement but struggling to act with the sedate demeanor they had been taught. Cioba could not hide her joy. She widened her arms and pulled Sabine and Candys into an embrace.

"I know you're both doing well. You will make the Reverend Mother and the whole Sisterhood proud." With Sorceress genetics from both the Marques and Cenva bloodlines, not to mention the political influence of the Venport family, these girls had a superb future.

The Reverend Mother watched the interaction with a cool frown. Cioba noted that when Sister Dorotea joined the gathering, Raquella turned pointedly away from her. "We try not to encourage or remind our acolytes of their family ties," the old woman said.

But Cioba faced her. "In many cases that is true, Reverend Mother, but these are the daughters and eventual heirs of Josef Venport, the granddaughters of Sorceresses. They are required to know who they are, and who they are expected to be."

Surprising them, Norma Cenva spoke up through the speakerpatch, reminding them of the draconian Sorceress Zufa Cenva, who had heaped so much disappointment upon her own stunted daughter. "Sometimes *not* knowing your mother can be a great advantage."

Most of the Imperium's history lies ahead of us, beyond our view. But mark my words: I will be remembered.

— EMPEROR SALVADOR CORRINO, coronation speech

T hough Roderick was two years younger than his brother, he often felt like the more mature one.

He bit his tongue as he listened to Salvador stumble through a practice speech in one of the garden salons of the Imperial Palace. The prismatic doors were closed, and Roderick was the sole audience. He sat on a stiff divan facing his brother, hoping to offer advice.

After Manford Torondo's appearance before the Landsraad Council, and continuing outbreaks of Butlerian fervor, Roderick had dusted off an anticomputer speech Emperor Jules had delivered more than once; he substituted simplified phrasings to better suit Salvador, rather than the more flowery language that their father had favored. Roderick was happy with how he'd updated the speech, but as he listened to his brother practicing, he noted Salvador's tendency to slow his words and stumble over them, without using the proper timing or inflection.

"The defense against temptation ends at home, I mean, begins at . . ." Salvador looked back at the text, and shook his head. "I shall never be a great orator, Brother, so let's set a simpler goal of not causing any further damage."

"That was perfectly acceptable," he lied, "but I've heard you do better. Even so, the people will understand your message. And it should serve to quell some of the Butlerian antics for the time being."

Salvador seemed to see through the feeble effort to raise his spirits. He just shook his head in dismay and again studied the words on the holo-prompter.

AFTER HELPING HIS brother prepare, Roderick still had a great deal of work to do and no time to talk with his wife, Haditha. She had sent messages to him through servants, and now he hurried home to dress for the public speech. He didn't even learn of an emergency involving Haditha until he entered the royal apartments.

His wife was already gone, and the glum chief of staff told him about a confrontation between Haditha and her personal secretary, Sister Perianna, a nosy and humorless woman who had also been trained on Rossak (though Roderick did not find her at all comparable to Sister Dorotea). Apparently, Perianna had left her position on short notice and was no longer welcome at the Palace.

Right now, though, Roderick could not worry about a domestic squabble. Haditha was able to handle her own household staff. He barely had time to dress for the evening, grab a quick platter of bread and cold meats, before he had to leave for the Hall of Parliament. He hoped Salvador had practiced the speech a few more times.

He found Haditha already waiting for him in the private box they shared on one side of the central stage in the cavernous open hall. With long, curly auburn hair and patrician features, she resembled portraits Roderick had seen of her late grand-uncle, a military figure in the Jihad, but with more delicate features and darker eyes. She wore a black lace gown with a pearl necklace; her hair was held in place with a ruby-studded barrette.

As Roderick sat down, he leaned over and kissed her on the cheek. "Sorry I'm late," he said. "Today has been quite a rush." He was attired in a tuxedo with tails in preparation for a society party to be held after the speech. His stomach churned from the food he had downed so quickly.

From her intense, flashing eyes, he could tell Haditha was upset. "Today has been a disaster. Perianna is gone—and good riddance."

He could see the deep hurt on his wife's face, and assumed this was more than just an argument with her personal secretary. "What happened?"

"For weeks now, I have been noticing small details . . . some of my possessions moved, drawers not quite closed the same way I left them, documents a little straighter, a stylus out of place on my writing desk—and on yours."

"My writing desk? Was anything taken?"

"Not that I could tell. Perianna is the only one who had access, but she denied everything when I asked her. Today, though, I saw her slip out of my private study. I hid, so she didn't know I'd caught her—and when I asked her later, Perianna claimed she had never gone there, which I *knew* was a lie. So I exposed her. She made a great show of indignation, insisted that I search her quarters and all her possessions if I thought she was a thief."

Roderick narrowed his eyes, feeling a growing concern. "And did you?"

"I had to, once she'd pushed me to it. Of course, we didn't find anything—as she must have known." Haditha's eyes flashed with anger. "Perianna said she could no longer serve me properly if I didn't trust her, and she resigned from my service. I let her go."

Roderick felt cold. The departed servant had been trained in the Sisterhood, and he knew from Dorotea's openly demonstrated skills that Perianna could well have memorized anything she saw, without carrying physical evidence. "Maybe we should have held her for further interrogation."

"That's what I realized—but too late, and she was already gone. She's departed from Salusa."

Roderick clenched his jaw. He knew that his wife kept no dangerous state secrets in her private chambers, so Perianna wouldn't have found anything critical. Even if she'd caught a glimpse of his own private journal, it contained only a few personal entries about his family, nothing politically significant. And there was no proof of her spying, but he still felt a sinking sensation in his already roiling stomach.

Emperor Salvador emerged on the stage below, walking toward the podium. The brothers each wore implanted transceivers, so that Roderick could provide comments to Salvador, if necessary. When Roderick kept the transceiver switched off so he could think about what his wife had told him, Salvador flashed an uneasy glance up at the box.

"It's probably nothing," Roderick said, and then turned his focus on the Emperor's speech. He squeezed his earlobe to turn on the transceiver, and noticed Salvador's expression of great relief before he took to the podium.

Theories change as new data comes to light. Facts, however, do not change—nor do my principles. That is why I am suspicious of theories of any kind.

—MANFORD TORONDO, address to the Butlerians on Lampadas

The intellectual environment on Zenith fostered innovation and scientific creativity, and the planet prided itself on being an oasis for discovery and progress. Researchers such as Ptolemy and his partner, Dr. Elchan, received funding from an interplanetary pool of grant money that was readily dispensed to anyone who had a feasible idea and a concrete plan for implementation.

Ptolemy came from a large family, three sisters and two brothers, all of whom were successful researchers in various fields, each with an independent laboratory and staff of technicians. They had friendly competitions to see which of them could boast the most beneficial discoveries, and even though Ptolemy had little enough time to keep up with all the technical publications in his own specific field, he made the effort to read every paper his brothers and sisters published.

Zenan scientific teams worked with the clear understanding that when discoveries proved pragmatic and lucrative, a significant share of the profits went back into the pool to be made available for the next group of scientists with interesting ideas. Advancements were offered for development to other worlds in the Imperium. Even with such openness and generosity, the economy of Zenith thrived.

Working for the past decade at his rural laboratory estate, Ptolemy was both pleased and proud of what he and Dr. Elchan had accomplished. So far, two of their discoveries had been highly profitable, and three others moderately so. The lab building and residence was surrounded by twenty acres of rolling grassland dotted with stands of trees. Ptolemy supervised a staff of a dozen technicians, lab assistants, and domestic workers. It was an environment conducive to creativity and intellectual development.

He enjoyed Zenith's collegial atmosphere so much that he had volunteered to serve a term as the planet's representative to the Landsraad League. It was a family tradition to do one's civic duty. Never in his life had he doubted that he and his dedicated partner were doing good work.

Thus, as a reasonable and open-minded man, he was taken aback by the Butlerian fervor against technology. It made no sense to him.

Of course, no one could deny the horrors that thinking machines had inflicted on humanity, but it was ridiculous to blame the science itself for human ambitions and failings. Only a close-minded person could deny, for instance, that Suk medical diagnostics and sophisticated surgical techniques had saved countless lives, or that agricultural machinery increased farming productivity by orders of magnitude beyond what human slaves could do, and thereby saved many from starvation. In fact, one of his sisters had developed a genetically modified strain of wheat that tripled the yield from a single crop. How could anyone argue against that?

And yet, the powerful Butlerian movement had spread to many planets, but thankfully not to this one. The whole idea mystified him. How could people look at a return to primitive living with any sort of wistful nostalgia?

Manford Torondo's speech in the Landsraad Hall had convinced him that he must be missing a vital piece of the answer, because Ptolemy simply could not grasp that sort of thinking. Frustrated because he didn't understand the Butlerians, he had nonetheless seen how influential they were, and the necessity of dedicating himself to finding common ground with them.

He researched where and how the movement had begun after the founder, a woman named Rayna Butler, survived a horrible fever as a child. Though Ptolemy did not like to think ill of the revered martyr, he suspected she might have suffered brain damage, a biochemical personality shift that had unbalanced her. She had gained influence through sheer charisma, tapping into the undeniable fear of Omnius. Her successor, Manford, had also suffered extreme physical and psychological trauma with the loss of his legs. On a personal level, Ptolemy couldn't help but feel sympathy for the poor man, yet Manford was leading his followers along a foolish path, to the detriment of all humanity.

Ptolemy had been so sure that if he offered fully functional prosthetics, if he made the legless man whole again, Manford would admit that, yes, some technology was for the betterment of mankind. The first step on a path to enlightening the antiscience fanatics.

But Manford's reaction to the gift had been appalling and incomprehensible. Ptolemy felt as if gravity itself had failed him. Having spent his life on Zenith, where ideas were openly discussed and debated, he found the blind stubbornness of the Butlerians appalling. Dr. Elchan, whose race had been much persecuted, both fairly and unfairly, was terrified; he had warned Ptolemy that Manford might react in such a way, and in fact Elchan claimed they were lucky to have escaped with their lives . . . which seemed absurd, but may very well have been true.

Cowed, Ptolemy and Elchan had returned to the countryside lab estate on Zenith and, with some embarrassment, buried themselves in their work. Forcing optimism, he said to Elchan in their laboratory, "We shouldn't be discouraged, my friend. We tried our best, we made our case. Let's waste no more time on the Butlerians." He kept saying the words because he needed to convince himself.

The Tlulaxa researcher, on the other hand, was quiet and preoccupied. Ptolemy and Dr. Elchan had been friends and collaborators for many years, working with a synergy that produced not only good results but a highly enjoyable and stimulating atmosphere. Through his humanitarian work, Elchan had overcome much of the prejudice with which the Tlulaxa were regarded.

"I'm just glad to be safe back here." Elchan raised his left arm, flexed the artificial fingers. "We know the replacement limbs work, thanks to the thoughtrode connection from my natural nerve endings to these artificial ones. I have my hand back, and I can use it, though I can't feel it."

"Sensory nerve receptors are an entirely different problem," Ptolemy said. "But we'll work it out."

Elchan agreed. "The best way we can succeed is by continuing to give back to humanity. We'll eventually overcome the Butlerian attitudes. Science remains true, whether or not they believe in it."

Ptolemy knew that their current work would indeed capture the imagination and excitement of Imperial society. Tanks and nutrient vats grew organic circuitry receptors similar to what the cymeks had used to guide mechanical walker bodies with their brains.

Ptolemy and his partner had received substantial funding from the Zenith Council, but Elchan had also bent certain rules to quietly acquire remnants of cymek walkers in order to study them. The Butlerians smashed that kind of technology whenever they saw it, and because most remnants had been destroyed, the scientists had access to very few records or samples of how the thoughtrodes and preservation canisters actually worked. Intact cymek walkers were at a premium. Ptolemy did not ask Elchan about his sources.

The Tlulaxa researcher mused with an undertone of scorn, "Someday, I would like to dissect Manford Torondo's little brain—to see if there's any noticeable difference between it and a normal human brain."

Ptolemy didn't want to make fun of the Butlerian leader. "That's unkind." He remained saddened and disappointed that they had not reached a compromise to benefit everyone. After being back home for a week from the disastrous trip to Lampadas, life had begun to return to normal.

And then the Butlerians came for them. . . .

Forty ships descended on the rural laboratory complex. With a roaring whine of overloaded suspensor engines, the small vessels swooped down like crows onto fresh carrion. Many of the lab workers had gone home for the day, and the last few ran outside as soon as the tumult began. They fled upon seeing the ships land on the grassy hills, leaving Ptolemy and Dr. Elchan to face the Butlerians.

The sounds were deafening as hatches opened and ramps extended; a group of Swordmasters, along with hundreds of club-wielding civilians, charged out. The two short-statured scientists stared at the unnecessary display of force, their mouths open as if they were unable to believe what they were seeing.

Elchan moaned in dismay. "We can't run." They stood alone in front of the main research building.

"This makes no sense!" Ptolemy insisted. "Why would they come here?"

Amid a wash of cheering and anticipation, the legless man appeared, riding in a harness carried on his Swordmaster's shoulders. Ptolemy had not found the man intimidating when he'd sat behind a small desk on Lampadas; here, though, the mob leader sent shivers down his spine.

"Ptolemy of Zenith," Manford said, "we have come to help you. Temptation has led you astray. Ambition has lied to you. It is my purpose to see that you are placed on the proper path."

While the mob leader spoke, exuberant Butlerians chased after the fleeing lab technicians who hadn't yet managed to escape from the grounds. Manford did nothing to call them back.

"Why are you here?" Ptolemy watched in horror as one of his female workers was tackled by the fanatics, who then pummeled her when she was on the ground. He could no longer see the woman because of the throng around her, but he heard the screams. "Tell them to stop!"

Anari Idaho carried Manford up to the two cowering scientists. Looking down at them from her shoulders, he said, "They have their mission, and I have mine."

The technician stopped screaming. More Butlerians closed in from the ships, and Elchan was terrified. Ptolemy wanted to comfort his friend, but knew his words would be hollow. "I will notify the council. This . . . this is a private laboratory."

The man's voice was soft and conversational. "Yes, your laboratory. Let's go inside and see what you've been up to."

Ptolemy didn't want to let them into the research building, but the Butlerians flowed forward like a tsunami, carrying them back inside. The fanatics spread out inside, smashing the equipment and prototypes, ripping fixtures out, and hurling rocks through windows.

Ptolemy could barely breathe. This was horrifying and surreal, like a hallucinogenic nightmare he could not escape. "I don't understand!" Tears poured down his face. "I never hurt you. I only meant to help."

Manford shook his head, showing apparent deep sadness. "I'm offended that you believed I needed help from your vile technology, that you would think me so weak."

Inside the research facility, Anari Idaho carried Manford so that he could look with grim condemnation at the test beds where artificial limbs and nerve endings were grown, where he could see the analysis machines, and, most damning of all, the three dismantled cymek walkers.

Manford reached down to pick up a rigid plastic hand, then tossed it to the floor in disgust. "Why would you think the human race needs enhancements like this? We need *faith* . . . and I have faith in you, Ptolemy of Zenith. That's why I'm giving you another chance."

Ptolemy held his breath, confused. He could still hear the mayhem, the destruction in this building and outside, throughout the complex. He wanted to vomit. Beside him, Elchan was paralyzed with fear, shuddering, utterly silent; he seemed to have grasped a fundamental fact that Ptolemy still could not comprehend.

Manford frowned. "I'm afraid, however, that your Tlulaxa associate has fallen too far into damnation. We can't save him—but we can allow him to be part of your education. Maybe you'll be enlightened after all."

Elchan wailed and tried to escape, but two of the zealots caught him and pushed him back toward Manford and Anari. The Swordmaster drew her blade and with a single stroke hacked off his prosthetic left arm, severing it below the shoulder, at the seam where actual flesh met the artificial nerve endings. The victim cried out as he looked down at his stump, where nutrient fluid leaked out, pumped by the hydraulics. Blood also flowed from the stump of his arm, gushing from an artery.

Ptolemy tried to help him, but he was restrained by strong arms. His heart was pounding, and he had trouble breathing. He met the terrified gaze of his friend, but for only an instant before Elchan slumped to the floor and appeared to pass out.

"Now at least he can die as a human," Manford said. "The mind of man is holy."

"The mind of man is holy," the others murmured, and Manford gestured for them to leave. One of the Swordmasters dragged Ptolemy outside, but they left

Elchan inside the lab, apparently to bleed to death. This wasn't real, made no sense. Ptolemy refused to believe the events were happening.

After they'd retreated to the grassy grounds outside the research complex, Manford's followers hurled incendiary bombs through the already smashed windows, and set fire to the place.

"Stop this!" Ptolemy screamed. "Let Elchan out! You can't do this to a human being! He is my friend—"

"He's not worth saving," Manford explained, then ignored Ptolemy's increasingly desperate pleas. The flames rose higher. Ptolemy saw his companion appear at one of the windows and try to get out, but the Butlerians rushed forward with clubs and bashed at him until he cowered inside and vanished.

The fire reached the roof, and then met the flammable nutrient fluids inside. Small explosions popped from laboratory to laboratory. Ptolemy could hear his friend screaming.

"Stop this!" He sobbed and fell to his knees. Tears poured down his face. He held his head in his hands, shaking. "Stop this, please . . ."

Manford wore a satisfied smile, while Anari Idaho had no expression whatsoever. She grabbed Ptolemy by the hair, pulled his head up, and forced him to watch the laboratory burn.

"We have granted you a gift," Manford said, "and I have faith that you will learn from this. Let me quote from one of the Erasmus journals that I have studied. The descriptions are too horrifying for most people, but you need to hear it: 'The humans continue to fight us like children throwing a tantrum,' Erasmus wrote, 'but our technology is superior. With our developments, our adaptability, and our persistence, we will always win. Humans are irrelevant . . . but I have to admit, they are interesting.'"

Manford closed his eyes, as if to dispel the distaste. "I hope you have learned the error of your attitude, Ptolemy of Zenith. We will pray for you."

ON ZENITH, THE fire burned itself out in a few hours, but by that time the Butlerian ships were long gone, leaving Ptolemy to stare at the smoldering wreckage and listen to the heartrending silence. Manford Toronto and his followers had stayed until Dr. Elchan stopped screaming . . . and he had screamed for a long time.

Surveying the charred wreckage, Ptolemy felt he had lost everything— except for his knowledge and scientific curiosity. The barbarians had not taken everything from him. He huddled there on the grassy hill, so deep in thought it was like a trance, pondering exactly what he would do next. He developed a plan, a detailed plan.

He stood straight, wiped his reddened eyes, and tried to regain his foothold on reality. It was as if the laws of physics had changed all around him, and he had to restructure his fundamental beliefs.

He didn't dare go to his brothers and sisters, recruit them to speak out and throw their imaginations against the Butlerians—he would not expose them to the risk, because the savages would come to their laboratories as well, lock his siblings inside, burn them to death. No, he had his brain . . . his greatest tool, his greatest weapon.

The Butlerians had crushed and discarded him, murdered his best friend, and left him defeated, but Ptolemy was not done. Manford had no idea of the enemy he had created this day.

Consider human life: We are animals, yet are expected to be so much more. Although honor requires us to make altruistic decisions, even acting for the benefit of other people keeps coming back to self interest, no matter how much one attempts to conceal it.

—REVEREND MOTHER RAQUELLA BERTO-ANIRUL,
On the Human Condition

Sister Ingrid had an inquisitive mind, to her detriment.

Earlier, while undergoing training among the Butlerians on Lampadas, her instructors had commented on this, and had praised her for it—to an extent, so long as she didn't ask the wrong questions. Such inquisitiveness enabled her to excel in certain subjects that interested her, such as chemistry and human physiology, but one teacher had scolded her for getting distracted by irrelevant interests. Ingrid realized that she often spent so much time on ancillary issues that she neglected the rigid curriculum.

At the recommendation of Sister Dorotea, she had applied for training among the Sisterhood on Rossak to escape the Lampadas schools that she found increasingly tedious. According to Dorotea, the Sisterhood would provide new stimulation for her active mind.

In recent days, the thought of secret computers hidden on Rossak by corrupted Sisters had kept her awake at night. Another acolyte had whispered the idea, and many of the mature acolytes fixated on the titillating prospect, but Ingrid remained skeptical. The gossiper had no proof, not even a convincing argument, and Ingrid had not found her to be overly perceptive; it wasn't likely she would notice details that Ingrid had not.

Still, such a horrific idea had to be taken seriously. She had learned that much from Manford Torondo. For safety's sake, Ingrid would assume the rumor to be true until she learned otherwise. If she could find proof, Sister Dorotea would help root out the thinking machines and cleanse the Sisterhood.

When she mentioned the idea, Dorotea grew equally concerned. "Let me ask questions. Much has changed here since I was assigned to Salusa, but I hope the Reverend Mother hasn't gone that far astray."

Ingrid, though, wasn't content to dismiss the idea and wait for someone else to deliver the answers. She realized that if Dorotea asked too many questions, and of the wrong people, the Sisterhood might bury its secrets even deeper.

Thinking machines were seductive, and one or two Sisters might have concocted an ill-advised justification to use computers. "Machine Apologists," as they were known in the Imperium. But for Ingrid, there were no subtleties, no fine lines or gray areas: Thinking machines, under any guise, had to be eliminated.

The cliff city was large, complicated, and mostly empty. She searched in areas that appeared to be shut down and barricaded, where signs prohibited entry. A Sister was expected to follow rules, but she was also expected to think, to question.

And Ingrid questioned. The most likely place seemed to be in the restricted chambers that held all the breeding records.

In the predawn darkness, she slipped around the barricade guarding the steep uphill path that led along the cliff face to the restricted caves. Her eyes adjusted to the starlight as she picked her way upward, seeing indications that it was well traveled.

When she was high above the trails frequented by instructors and students in the school, she glimpsed a glow ahead of her on the trail, someone descending, guided by a furtive handlight. Ingrid pulled herself into a rock crack flanked by two large boulders and waited, holding her breath.

An old woman in the white robe of a Sorceress moved past with a swift but painstaking gait, and Ingrid recognized Karee Marques. Sister Dorotea had begun to work on the old Sorceress's chemical investigations in her laboratory on the jungle floor. Ingrid wondered why the aged woman would be up here in the dead of night. Considering the restricted upper caves, it was likely something to do with the breeding records.

After Karee had toiled down the path to the inhabited section of the cliff city, Ingrid sprinted up to the highest point on the steep trail, feeling a new vigor. Below, the jungle continued to hum and simmer, while overhead a new veil of clouds obscured many of the stars. Ingrid turned slowly around, studying the trail, the boulders, the drop-off, using her imagination to guess what Karee might have been doing.

When she reached the top of the bluff, she saw no sign of the monitor Sisters she had seen stationed at the cave opening during daylight hours—they were gone for the night, just as she'd hoped. The entrance into the restricted tunnels looked dark and forbidding.

For a few minutes, Ingrid hesitated, trying to decide what to do. Within an hour, colors would paint the sky with dawn, and she still had no answers. Before long, her fellow Sisters would be stirring in the inhabited portion of the cliff city, moving about on the lower trails and balconies, and inside the tunnels.

Just then, from the steep path below, she detected the distinct sound of voices and saw a pair of Sisters ascending the trail single file in the darkness, their forms illuminated by bright handlights. They would not be able to see her in the darkness, if she stayed behind the rocks. Their voices grew louder as they climbed, and they dipped in and out of view, hidden by rocky overhangs. Her heart pounded harder, and she could think of no legitimate-sounding explanation to use if they caught her. But why would they even suspect?

She hid in the blackest shadows next to a gnarled Rossak cedar as the two Sisters arrived at the entrance to the record caves, surrounded by bright light. One of the women was Sister Valya. Other than their conversation, Ingrid heard only the murmur of jungle sounds from below, punctuated by the calls of night birds from their perches on the cliff.

Suspecting nothing, the two Sisters entered the dark cave, carrying their lights. After an interminable moment of hesitation, Ingrid slipped in after them, staying well beyond the illuminated circle. She moved with silent footsteps, as close as she dared. Back on Lampadas, she had often ventured out at night, carrying nothing more than a candle—or no light at all.

Valya and her companion walked down the stone-walled corridors and turned a corner, which plunged the main passage into darkness again. Ingrid scurried ahead to catch up, saw the pair of bright handlights again, but for only a moment before they turned left and vanished, as if they had walked directly through a wall.

The pitch black of the tunnel was unnerving, but Ingrid was much more afraid of being caught than of the darkness. Indeed, there was something mysterious and sinister about these hidden passages. When she reached the spot where the two had turned, Ingrid peered about, straining for any faint glimmer of light, any opening, but all she could make out was a rock wall.

But the two Sisters had gone somewhere. Ingrid hurried up and down the passage, sure that she was in the right place, but she could find no opening. In the darkness, she pressed her hands and face against the rock wall, trying to discover a secret door. Faintly, she heard buzzing sounds, like an insect nest . . . or thrumming machinery. She continued to feel her way along the stone wall.

Suddenly her hand passed through the rock.

Illusory rock. An opaque image projected over an opening to conceal it! Ingrid caught her breath. Stunned, she stepped back, then cautiously moved forward again to push her entire arm through the wall. Yes, a hidden entrance. Gathering her courage, Ingrid stepped through the wall—and found herself blinking inside a large, bright grotto that throbbed with sound; a circulating breeze washed past her face.

When her eyes adjusted, she saw the unthinkable. Row upon row of computers, complex storage devices as well as a low wall of monitor screens and metal platforms where robed Sisters tended the machines. Sister Valya had just stopped before a set of displays, hesitated as if she sensed something, and then turned back toward the disguised entrance.

Horrified, Ingrid backed up and scrambled through the hologram-covered wall. She hoped she had moved before Valya noticed her. Unable to comprehend the immensity of the criminal secret her own Sisters were keeping, Ingrid fled down the dark hallway, not caring that she couldn't see. She thought she heard a noise behind her, and kept running until she burst outside into the cool, starlit night near the cliff-side trail. Her heart seemed to be shouting inside her chest.

Breathing hard, she began to make her way down the steep path, trying to calm herself. She had to think. She had to find someone to tell. The Sisterhood seemed suddenly dark to her, a monstrous thing teeming with secrets. The computer chamber was not a place she was supposed to see.

Ingrid walked in a daze. How much more of the Reverend Mother's training was a lie? The Sisters claimed to depend only on human abilities, and yet they relied on the crutch of computers! What if Dorotea had deceived her as well? Ingrid didn't want to believe that . . . but how could she be sure?

The only way, she decided, was to reveal the computers directly to Manford Torondo. He and his followers would destroy the evil machines without listening to rationalizations.

WHILE PREPARING FOR her quiet work with the computers before most of the Sisters rose for the day, Valya had spotted the intruder. With a flash of acute perception, as she had been taught, she recognized the new acolyte from Lampadas: Sister Ingrid, the young woman who wore her Butlerian beliefs like a bold tattoo.

Valya didn't tell the other predawn workers, but simply—and silently—bolted out through the anteroom and plunged back through the hologram into the darkened tunnel. She did not activate her handlight, but moved with stealth.

Up ahead, she could hear the frightened acolyte running.

Careful to make no sound, she paused just inside the cave opening, saw Ingrid's shadowy figure pause at the head of the path, then begin to pick her way down in the darkness.

Familiar with the trail from frequent trips in the dead of night, Valya bounded after her. She had no doubt that the girl had seen everything. She heard Ingrid stumbling, gasping. With the accidental kick of a pebble, the pursuer made too much noise, and Ingrid froze, spinning around but still unable to see.

Valya was upon her in a moment. She spoke without hesitation, intent on keeping the acolyte off guard. "You look unwell, Sister Ingrid. Can I help?" With a subtle move, she slipped past her on the path and blocked her way down. "You know this is a restricted trail. You shouldn't be here."

The acolyte's gaze darted like that of a trapped animal. "You are in no position to lecture me."

Valya felt confident she was a better fighter, after all of her vigorous combat sessions with her brother. "We need to have a little talk."

Ingrid's chest heaved. "I don't trust you. You've been corrupted by computers."

"Computers?" Valya did her best to look surprised. "What do you mean?"

Ingrid pointed up the trail, and that hesitation was enough of an opening. Valya took it, pushing the young woman off the cliff so quickly that she didn't even have time to scream. Partway down, Ingrid struck the rough rock wall, then crashed into the canopy and fell the rest of the way to the jungle floor.

There had been no choice, and Valya didn't regret her decision. The computers held countless generations of irreplaceable knowledge, and she had sworn to Raquella that she would guard the secret of the breeding records. With all that as her priority, as her sworn *duty*, the killing had been easy.

But now she would have to tell Raquella what she'd done.

BY THE TIME she arrived at the Reverend Mother's private quarters, Valya had calmed herself so as to show no doubt when she delivered her confession. Dawn was just breaking, the Sisters arising for their morning chores. Raquella was busy with early activities as she welcomed Valya inside the room.

After making sure the door was closed for privacy, Valya confessed to killing the acolyte, revealing little emotion. The old woman displayed hardly any reaction, but regarded Valya like a surgeon assessing a particularly dire complication on the operating table. Finally, she reached out and wrapped her fingers around Valya's wrist in an iron grip.

"You had no other choice but to kill her?" She squeezed tighter, taking the pulse of the much younger woman.

Valya told the truth, sure that Raquella could detect any falsehood. "I am convinced this was the best way to protect the breeding records. Letting her live

had a far greater potential for disaster. Knowing Sister Ingrid, and seeing her reaction, I'm sure she was hell-bent on causing trouble."

"And you had no other motives?"

"None." Valya stared straight at the Reverend Mother.

Raquella held her wrist for a long moment, feeling the tempo of her pulse, the
moisture on her skin. "I don't condone what you did, but I believe your motive was
pure. Show me where the body is. We have to make certain that no further questions arise, or your dangerous gamble will fail."

The Rossak caves bustled with daybreak activities. After arranging for another Sister to teach her class, the Reverend Mother and Valya took a lift and
descended to the jungle floor. They made their way through the trackless underbrush, following the edge of the cliff to the general spot where Ingrid had fallen.
After an hour of searching, they found the crumpled body draped in a splash of
blood across a rock. Two sapphire-scaled avians had already found the feast, but
flew away, startled, at the approach of the women.

Valya looked at the dead acolyte and still felt no guilt. *The Sisterhood is your
only family now.* "I don't like what I did, Reverend Mother. I'm ready to face the
consequences if necessary."

Raquella stared at the tableau for a long moment. "We both know that Ingrid
would have called down the fanatics on Rossak, and the breeding computers must
be protected at all costs. They represent centuries of work by the Sorceresses,
generations of detailed bloodline projections—our key to the future evolution of
humanity. I'm sorry to admit this, but some things are worth killing for."

Raquella had Valya help her carry Ingrid's lifeless body deeper into the jungle, out of sight of the high cliff path. They left it well off any trail, where predators would soon dispose of the remains.

AFTER DISMISSING VALYA, the Reverend Mother returned alone to her
private chambers, where she sat among her prized volumes, thinking. A copy of
the *Azhar Book* rested on a table beside her chair. Sometimes she liked to thumb
through it to find useful passages. Today, though, her problems went beyond any
experiences that had gone into the writing of that volume.

She was aware of the increasing tensions among the Sisters, and Karee's recent Mentat prediction of a terrible schism in the Sisterhood loomed like a thunderstorm. Perhaps this event was the first warning shot.

Raquella heard the clamor of her other memories calling to her, shouting in
alarm and offering contradictory advice. Those ancestral experiences were not
like a series of library books that she could take off the shelf whenever she

wished; the memories came and went of their own volition, for their own reasons and on their own schedule. At times she could diminish their clamor a bit, but it always surged back.

In moments, they fell silent and did not respond to her questions, leaving Raquella without answers or guidance.

There is no more optimistic person in the universe than the high-level graduate who is fresh from completing his studies and ready to fulfill far-reaching dreams.

—from an Imperial study of the schools movement

Twelve Mentat students had completed their training. A panel of stern instructors interrogated them, then sent the dozen candidates along to Gilbertus Albans for his final approval.

Among them were the talented Draigo Roget, two Sisters from Rossak, and others he had come to know well over the years of their instruction. Gilbertus passed them all. There was no doubt in his mind. . . .

Some might find it incongruous that at an institution devoted to logic and precise mental organization, the commencement ceremonies were steeped in manufactured tradition. In establishing the Mentat School, Gilbertus had taken great pains to imbue it with a sense of reverence and history. All the buildings looked old and solid, the rules were complex, the forms dense to give the impression of a weighty bureaucracy. Each graduation certificate was ornately lettered, hand-illuminated, and presented on real parchment. The graduates wore embroidered, voluminous robes and puffy, impractical caps.

Everything, Gilbertus knew, was merely symbolic and served no real purpose, though the students and instructors loved it—the Butlerian candidates in particular. Outsiders could not help but be impressed with the graduation ritual, pronouncements spoken in ancient, nearly forgotten tongues that each Mentat student had been forced to memorize. Some might have said that learning those dead languages was a useless exercise, but Gilbertus foresaw that those dialects, understood by very few living humans, could be useful as private languages for battlefield commands or business espionage.

Well rehearsed before the event, the twelve students now lined up while

Gilbertus stood at a podium in the main amphitheater. He droned on, reciting by rote the same statement over and over again, recognizing each student as a true Mentat, granting him the blessing of the Lampadas school.

"I hereby dispatch you to promote clarity of thought and advancement of human mental capabilities." At the end of each pronouncement, the audience intoned, "The mind of man is holy," a concession to the Butlerians that Gilbertus had included in the ceremony.

When they were finished, Draigo Roget came up to speak to Gilbertus. He had taken off his graduate robe, hung up the braid in his quarters, and now stood in his trim black jumpsuit again. He bowed formally. "I came to thank you for your instruction, Headmaster. You have granted me an opportunity I will never forget."

"I wish you would stay with us, Draigo. I could not ask for a more promising instructor. You would rise high in our school, perhaps to my position. I won't be here forever, you know." In truth, Gilbertus thought he might endure physically for centuries or more, but time was pressing in on him. Before long, he would have to leave the school and take up another identity. Too many decades had passed, and he could simulate only so much age and decrepitude, even reaching the limits of the known geriatric benefits of melange consumption—which he let people think he used.

"I could do that, sir, but the whole Imperium awaits. I think my destiny lies out there."

Reluctantly, Gilbertus nodded. "Then I wish you the best of luck, and hope we meet again."

GILBERTUS STOOD ON the floating airfield, raising a hand in farewell as the shuttle containing Draigo Roget and other passengers prepared to take off. The black-haired Draigo sat at a windowport, apparently not seeing him. Presently, with a smooth and remarkably silent surge of suspensor engines, the white craft ascended quickly, until it was a speck in the sky, and then gone.

As he watched, Gilbertus felt sadness at the departure, mixed with joy and pride for his most accomplished student. With the long letter of recommendation that he had written for Draigo, the young man should have no trouble finding a secure position with one of the noble families, maybe even at the Imperial Court. Considering his qualifications and ambitions, the new Mentat would undoubtedly lead an interesting life. He certainly had the potential.

Around the airfield, barge crews used cranes to drop boulders into a shallow section of the marsh lake, forming a breakwater for the expanding shuttleport.

The rumble of space traffic had disturbed some of the larger marsh creatures, provoking them to ram the floating airfield and damage it. As a result, Gilbertus had ordered the landing area moved to shallow water, and further protected against attack.

Much mystery remained in the wilderness around the school; few of the creatures that lived in and around the murky waters had been studied by naturalists. Gilbertus preferred it that way, because unknown dangers required constant readiness and adaptability, and higher states of intelligence to survive. Erasmus had demonstrated repeatedly that risk-taking expanded mental capabilities. . . .

Returning to his private office, with the door securely locked and purple drapes drawn, Gilbertus conversed with the shimmering memory core. After such a long time, he was attuned to subtle indications of the independent robot's moods, and the gelcircuitry sphere looked odd today, glowing a lighter hue. He interpreted it as anxiety.

"Now that the graduates have departed, you have an opportunity to create a temporary body for me," Erasmus said. "I can assist you in any way you desire. I have already planned numerous new tests and experiments to perform, which will increase knowledge about human behavior."

"To whose benefit?"

"Knowledge is a benefit in and of itself."

Gilbertus knew he had run out of acceptable excuses to grant his mentor such a wish, but it remained impossible at present. "My materials are limited."

"I am confident in your resourcefulness."

Gilbertus sighed. "I will do what I can, but it's difficult, and dangerous."

"And painfully slow."

The Headmaster leaned back in his chair, feeling troubled and sad. Despite his reservations about what the robot had done to all his human experimental subjects, he realized he was also lonely without his mentor. And in the final moments of the Battle of Corrin, when it looked as if the thinking machines would indeed defeat the Army of Humanity, Erasmus had sabotaged the robot attack to save *him* from certain death—a mere human.

Gilbertus shook his head. "Today, Draigo Roget left. We'd grown close over the years, but he didn't want to stay."

"I understand," Erasmus said. "He was your favorite student, just as you were mine."

"It was a great joy to be a mentor to him. He is the best of the new Mentats."

"I fully understand, though I am not certain that our Mentats serve on the right side of the conflict. In a sense, we are helping to prove the Butlerian assertion that thinking machines are unnecessary." The robot enjoyed disseminating esoteric information. "The Butlerians are like the Luddites of ancient history, parochial thinkers on Old Earth in the nineteenth century of the old calendar. They were small-minded rioters in England who blamed their financial hardships on efficient machines that had been brought into local factories. Rampaging mobs destroyed the machines, expecting that would bring about a return to prosperity. It did not work."

The memory core glowed brighter. "I believe superstition and fear are enslaving humanity more harshly than Omnius ever did. Rather than suffering under the yoke of thinking machines, you are bullied by *un*thinking humans. Technological progress cannot be held back forever."

"And yet, if we don't at least pretend to serve the Butlerian purposes, they could destroy this school," Gilbertus said. He realized that as the robot's soliloquy grew more vehement, the core glowed pale orange, then a rich, dark copper. "What have you done to yourself?"

As if caught, the core reverted to its original golden hue, then went through an entire spectral display of colors. "I was bored in my cabinet, so I modified some of the internal programming. It is my way of staying 'sane,' perhaps, in my own synthesized way. Please understand, I have only a few avenues of personal growth."

Gilbertus wondered if he should be alarmed. "I will do my best to find a suitable mobile apparatus to hold you, at least temporarily, but we must set up strict controls about where you use it, in order to keep you from being discovered."

"Maybe I could become a hunter of the wild creatures around here. Set me loose on the land around the marsh, and I'll occupy myself studying wild animals, using that data to augment my studies of human beings."

"An interesting idea, but we are not ready to set you loose anywhere. For one thing, how do I know you won't try to create a thinking-machine empire again?"

The robot simulated his laughter. "Why should I wish to create another evermind? Omnius caused me as many problems as humans did. Why do you think I taught you how to be a Mentat? It is to demonstrate that humans could be more than they had been before. The same holds true for thinking machines. We must coexist with humans in the future, a partnership of machine and man."

Gilbertus responded, "A partnership of *man and machine,* in that order, is more appropriate—with humankind in charge."

Erasmus remained silent for a moment. "A matter of perspective. However, don't forget, without me, you're nothing."

"We must stand on each other's shoulders," Gilbertus said with a gentle smile.

I am not afraid to use any weapon at my disposal—and information can be the deadliest weapon of all.

—JOSEF VENPORT, internal VenHold memo

When Draigo Roget arrived on Kolhar, freshly graduated from his intensive and costly schooling on Lampadas, Josef Venport greeted him like a returning hero.

The nascent Mentat wore a black tunic and billowing black trousers. He emerged from the shuttle and stood blinking in midday sunlight, looking around at the spaceport towers, the spacing fleet administrative headquarters, and the blocky structures of engine-fabrication plants. Josef and a small welcoming committee sped across the landing field in a humming groundcar. As they stepped out, Draigo came forward and gave a curt bow to his benefactor. "Your plan worked perfectly, sir."

Josef shook the man's hand energetically, then stepped back and regarded Draigo, looking him up and down. "You've changed. Your entire demeanor looks much more . . . intense." He meant it as a compliment.

Draigo nodded slightly. "And focused. It was a long and difficult process to become a Mentat, but you will not regret your investment."

Josef could not stop himself from smiling. "You're among the first of the candidates we seeded into the school, and I expect others to join us soon. VenHold requires skilled Mentats." He planned to use them to monitor accounts in his banking operations on different planets, and the VenHold subsidiary Combined Mercantiles had vast and complex record-keeping requirements as well.

Josef had tested many young candidates for Mentat training, with Cioba conducting careful interviews on his behalf. Once the best ones were culled out, his security chief, Ekbir, crafted completely new identities and histories for the students before they traveled to Lampadas, to conceal their loyalties from any persistently curious Butlerian observers. The Mentat School was much too closely and uneasily allied with Manford Torondo and his barbarians, and Josef would not be surprised if the petulant fanatics refused his candidates access to the specialized training. So, VenHold secretly funded their tuition—and these students did not know one another, for security purposes.

"So I am among the first?" Draigo asked. "I am pleased to learn that."

"Many more will follow you," Josef said. "Tomorrow, Cioba and I will start familiarizing you with the new work you'll be doing for us."

THE TWO MEN stood out on the sunlit field, where light reflected off the enclosed tanks filled with melange gas. Draigo regarded the mutating forms of the Navigator-candidates with great interest. Previously, Josef had kept this operation secret from him. "Thank you for revealing all this to me, Directeur Venport."

Josef shrugged. "A Mentat with incomplete data is useless."

His wife joined them, wearing a conservative dress suit, her long hair pinned up under a scarf. She and Norma Cenva had returned from their odd and unexpected journey to Rossak; Josef did not look fondly on them sharing confidential VenHold information with the Sisterhood, but both Norma and Cioba, not to mention Josef's own daughters, were inextricably linked with those women, and he knew it would serve no purpose to force them to choose their loyalties.

Cioba followed him as they walked down the aisles to one tank he had chosen in particular. Josef peered into the curved plaz viewing port and spoke out of the side of his mouth to the dark-clad Mentat. "What you underwent was a difficult thing, Draigo, but the metamorphosis into a Navigator requires even more extreme changes. This man here, for instance, is a very interesting case—not a volunteer, actually, but a spy that we caught in the act."

"A spy? What was he after?"

"Everything we're doing with the Navigators . . . but we stopped him before he could divulge our secrets to his employer, Celestial Transport. I placed him in the chamber, intending nothing more than a poetic execution, but he's surprising me with his adaptive abilities." Josef rapped his knuckles on the clearplaz viewport. The sticklike figure inside twitched and turned like a marionette on invisible strings. "His name is apparently Royce Fayed, though I don't know if he'll remember a trivial thing like that after the transformation is complete. My great-grandmother is guiding him. I think he may survive to become a Navigator after all."

Fayed's face looked distorted and swollen, his eyes enlarged, his cheeks rounded, and chin melting away as if he were a wax figure exposed to too much heat. His large eyes blinked, but his mouth didn't move. He made no attempt to say anything.

"If he was a spy, then he is your enemy." Draigo peered through the murky clouds inside the chamber. "Logically, he cannot be trustworthy as a Navigator. Given this extreme mutation inflicted upon him, how can the man not hate Venport Holdings? If you place him aboard one of your spacefolder ships, what is to stop him from crashing the vessel with all passengers and cargo, or taking it to Celestial Transport? It would seem a large risk for you to take."

"Norma assures us there is no risk," Cioba said. "Now that the initial mutation has occurred and his mind is expanding, he is very eager to become a Navigator for us. He wants this very much."

"Interesting," Draigo said noncommittally.

Josef sounded more defensive than he intended. "If Norma Cenva tells me to trust him, how can I dispute her? She is the heart of our entire commercial empire."

"I accept your conclusion, sir. You will need all the Navigators you can create, considering the discovery I recently made." The new Mentat turned dryly toward him. "It is my gift to you. A very interesting projection."

Josef raised his eyebrows. "Now you have my attention."

"Before I completed my Mentat training, Gilbertus Albans and I studied more than a century of records, traced known flight paths and movements of thinking-machine ships. After compiling the myriad clues, we performed an extensive Mentat projection and each of us reached the same conclusion." Draigo smiled, drawing out the suspense. "Sir, I have postulated the likely location of a very large machine shipyard, a manufacturing and refueling facility that in all probability holds a great many ships and orbiting industries. Since there is no record of this depot—if it exists—I must conclude the entire facility is almost certainly undiscovered and intact."

Josef brightened. "And there for the taking." He glanced at the twisted figure floating on suspensors in the gas-filled tank. "The spy mentioned that Celestial Transport has located just such a facility, but I have no idea where it is."

"Maybe I do," Draigo said.

All jungles are unique ecosystems, and the tropical forests of Rossak are even more so, and more important because of the biochemical resources they provide. It is in our interest to exert as much control as possible over the resources of that planet.

—Combined Mercantiles, confidential report

Raquella summoned Valya and Dorotea to her private library and office, but before she could state her business, Dorotea interrupted, clearly agitated. "Reverend Mother, I am concerned. One of the new acolytes, Sister Ingrid, has not appeared for her classes since yesterday. She is not in her quarters. No one has seen her."

Valya tensed, but the Reverend Mother studiously avoided looking in her direction. "Your concern is admirable, Sister Dorotea. I will send out inquiries and ask the other proctors to look into the matter." She narrowed her eyes, sat at her desk facing the two women she had summoned. "But I have eleven hundred students on Rossak, and I called you here to discuss one in particular—Anna Corrino. Because of the stakes, we must make sure she is treated properly. Sister Dorotea, you were with the Corrinos for a year. I would like to hear your assessment of the Princess."

"But Sister Ingrid—"

"We are talking about Anna Corrino at the moment. *Your assessment, please.*" Her voice was startlingly powerful, snapping both Valya and Dorotea to attention.

Dorotea blinked, drew a quick breath. "I'm sorry, Reverend Mother." While Valya remained seated across from Raquella, the other Sister paced the room. "Yes, I know the Corrinos well, and I know Anna's personality. Do not pamper her. She behaves in a spoiled manner, frequently complains or uses passive resistance techniques. She has not been given responsibility, nor has she learned to understand the consequences of her actions."

"She's never had the chance," Valya added. "All her life, her brothers took care of any problems, saved her from herself. She acts out where she can, as she did in pursuing an inappropriate romance with a young chef in the Palace, forc- ing her brothers to send her here to Rossak, just to put her someplace where she can't cause further trouble."

Raquella nodded. "It would be better if she learned to be strong and compe- tent herself. I don't believe the Emperor has any particular expectations from our school, other than to keep her out of trouble. But we would be ignoring an impor- tant opportunity if we did not try to make her one of us. One day, Anna Corrino will return to her family, and we should make certain she is dedicated to the Sisterhood."

Valya allowed her frustration to creep into her voice. "She shows no interest in her classroom studies nor in her mental exercises."

Dorotea frowned at her. "You're essentially her warden, watching to make sure she isn't hurt—but what good is that doing her? Just hiding and protecting her will not make her stronger. She needs to undergo the same vigorous training all acolytes must endure."

"She's the Emperor's sister," Valya said. "We don't dare let her come to harm."

The Reverend Mother nodded in agreement. "Then you must make sure that doesn't happen, but we will fail Anna if we don't train her. We should push, not coddle, the girl. Our goal is to improve each Sister. We've got to move forward, not tread water. Exposure to hardships hones the human body and psyche—with appropriate safeguards, of course." She nodded, making up her mind about how to accomplish this. "We'll place the girl in a demanding situation, send her on a survival quest for a few days. And I want you both to accompany her, watch her. Go deep into the jungles, away from the cliff city."

Valya privately understood the Reverend Mother's secondary purpose: Now that Dorotea had begun asking questions about Ingrid, she wanted the other woman away from the cliff city.

VALYA HARKONNEN DIDN'T like being forced to do things. It made her feel trapped, out of control—and she had left Lankiveil to escape that. But she could see the advantages of spending days in isolation with the Emperor's sister.

Now Dorotea, Valya, and Anna trudged up a rocky, volcanic slope unlike the dense silvery-purple jungles behind them. They wore lightweight jackets and lay- ered outdoor clothing, and carried no tents, gear, or provisions. As a first training exercise for Anna, the Reverend Mother wanted them to live off the land, drink water from pools, and eat berries, fungi, and protein-rich insects.

They had been away from the civilized caves for three very long and miserable days, but at least they had kept the Corrino girl alive. The experience was very different from Anna's outings in the palace gardens.

As expected, Anna protested having to go on the survival exercise, clinging to the minimal creature comforts of the cave settlement, but a stern Dorotea reminded her that an acolyte must follow the rules of the Sisterhood. "You're not in Zimia anymore. All acolytes are equals here, and the Reverend Mother determined your assignment."

Valya tried to sound more sympathetic. "It's an important part of becoming a Sister, to make you strong. Remember, the Emperor gave strict instructions that you cannot return to your family until you complete your training."

The girl had smiled at Valya, agreeing to try . . . but her dedication wore off quickly. Within hours of their dawn departure, Anna complained of hurting feet, of tangled underbrush, of biting insects. She didn't like the flavor of the water they found in streams and treated with antibacterial tablets; she claimed to be desperately hungry but wouldn't eat berries or fungi, much less grub worms from a rotting log. Unable to sleep at night on the ground, she overreacted to every small sound. On the trek today she was sure they had gotten lost; she kept trying to stop and rest, or turn back, but her companions would not allow it. . . .

Three long days passed. Often, Valya and Dorotea exchanged glances or shakes of the head. For Valya, this had become a survival mission of a different sort. . . .

She couldn't help but wonder where Griffin was now, if he had managed to track down and kill Vorian Atreides. With her brother's intelligence and fighting abilities, it seemed certain that he had an easier task than *this*.

Sister Dorotea made a habit of lecturing her companions on what was edible and what was not, but her superior attitude and didactic methods had grown annoying. From her own years on the planet, and many months of working with Karee Marques, Valya knew full well what to eat from the jungle. This was her tenth survival exercise away from the cliff city; Dorotea, on the other hand, had been gone from Rossak for years.

Their goal was a cluster of thermal pools that they hoped to reach by midday. Seen in glimpses through the scattered canopy, the sky was lead gray, hinting at rain, and it was hotter here, away from the seasonal breezes on the cliff faces. Once they had climbed above most of the trees, the ground consisted of rough, porous black rock left from a lava flow. The jumbled dark rock lay in long dikes, with verdant fingers of jungle that looked like purplish fjords below.

Now that the ordeal was nearly over, Valya looked up to see the gray sky thickening and darkening as the rain set in. She quickened her pace and took the lead from Dorotea; even Anna began walking faster because she didn't want to be left alone. "I want to reach the hot springs," Valya said, "so we can fashion a shelter."

"Do you know Sister Ingrid?" Dorotea asked as she pushed through the underbrush, bending a mucus-covered fern out of the way. "I recommended her to Rossak after meeting her on Lampadas. I'm concerned about her; she seems to have just vanished."

"That sounds melodramatic." Valya was careful to tell the precise truth, which would keep falsehood indicators out of her tone; after her service in the Imperial Court, Dorotea was quite adept at detecting lies. "She's probably been found by now."

"I'm glad she didn't come with us out here," Anna said, then wandered off the path to look at a patch of spine-covered fungi.

Hearing a crash and a squeal, Valya saw a blur of movement running toward them, low to the ground. Anna screamed.

With hardly a glance at each other, Valya and Dorotea put themselves between Anna and the animal, dropping into defensive postures, keeping their centers of gravity low. The tusked, hairy beast tore up underbrush that grew among the lava boulders, then stomped toward them on legs like pistons.

At the last possible moment, in her own blur of movement, Valya sidestepped and kicked the animal, stunning the creature and knocking it on its side. Her fighting reflexes came naturally to her after so many years of training with Griffin. As Dorotea pulled Anna to safety, Valya leaped onto the creature's neck and drove her heel down with enough force to crush its throat and vertebrae; a gout of blood squirted from the beast's mouth and nostrils. Even grievously wounded, the animal squirmed and tried to stand again, before its legs buckled and it tumbled over, dead.

Barely panting, Valya turned to look at the wide-eyed Anna. "You can always be perfectly safe, if you know how to protect yourself. Wouldn't that be a useful skill for an Emperor's sister to have?"

The young woman nodded, still speechless.

Dorotea stared at her, also awed. "Where did you learn to fight like that? I saw moves that we don't learn in the Sisterhood."

"My brother and I taught each other." She brushed herself off, then became more pragmatic. "There could be more of these beasts nearby, and the sky is looking ominous. I don't think we should try for the hot springs. Let's go directly back to the school."

As if on cue, the ground rumbled and split, tossing black lava rocks aside as a narrow seam opened up, squirting a column of steam along with a thin, fast-flowing stream of scarlet magma into the jungle, setting the plants aflame.

"I agree," Dorotea said. "We can head for the base of the cliff and follow it back." Anna Corrino did not complain.

Dorotea led the way and ducked into the thickening jungle, beating a path down the slope again. Valya sensed the ground growing unstable beneath them. A steam vent opened up, the hissing exhalation of a fumarole, and she hurried Anna along, crashing through plants and stumbling over the rough lava rock.

They worked their way out of the volcanically active zone and located a faint trail, likely a game path. Valya and Dorotea found enough breaks in the jungle to get their bearings and decided they could make their way back to the cliff city by nightfall. They found the base of the rock wall and followed it, thrashing through underbrush. The rain held off for a surprisingly long time, then began to fall, streaming down, making Anna hunch her shoulders and gaze miserably at the ground. To Valya, on the other hand, the weather reminded her of a pleasant squall on Lankiveil.

Just ahead, Dorotea shouted in alarm, and Valya hurried Anna forward to see what was wrong. The older Sister was staring at the grisly fragments of a carcass, bones, and a skull that was clearly human, all ripped to pieces; the torn, pale-green fabric of an acolyte's robe hung in shreds from bushes. Valya's heart sank.

"It's Ingrid," Dorotea said, weeping. "I knew something had happened to her!" She extricated a thin gold chain tangled in the bloody bones. Valya recognized a small charm with the symbol of the Butlerians, a fist closed around a stylized gear.

Looking up, Valya saw through the rain that they were close to the inhabited tunnels. She and Raquella had dumped the acolyte's body much deeper into the jungle and away from any trail, but predators must have dragged it here.

Fortunately, a nauseated Anna said exactly the right thing. "Poor Ingrid must have fallen off the cliff. Animals dragged her here . . . and ate her!"

Dorotea wore a hard expression that looked as if it had been sharpened on a whetstone. "But *how* did she fall off the cliff? That doesn't sound like her. She was always sure-footed." Dorotea wiped her rain-and-tear-soaked face, gazed up at the high natural wall.

"Should we take the body back, or leave it here?" Anna asked. She did not seem eager to touch the corpse.

Valya remained steely, knew what she had to say. "It is the way of the Sisterhood to leave the body here, for nature to take its course."

Clutching the chain in her hand, Dorotea walked slowly away from the gruesome site, as if her muscles would not respond to commands. Thinking about damage control, Valya moved to Dorotea's side and put a comforting arm around her. "I know she was your friend."

As she consoled the older Sister, however, she saw a flash of jealousy on Anna's face, but Valya needed to stay close to Dorotea, as well, to make sure she did not ask too many of the wrong questions.

A man may flee swiftly, and far, but he can never run from himself.
                                                      —Zensunni aphorism

The sky of Arrakis was a clear, dry wasteland—olive green smeared with veils of ever-present dust. Today the winds were light, and the weather stations predicted no storm activity, so the crew chief allowed Vorian Atreides to fly one of the scout aircraft while the VenHold spice-harvesting operations continued in the valley.

Even though the grizzled old Calbir had tested Vor's proficiency in the cockpit several times now, he still treated him like a novice pilot, lecturing him through the checklist, warning him to keep watch for violent thermal updrafts or unexpected localized cyclones. "Never underestimate Arrakis, young man, because this planet doesn't care a whit about you."

Vor promised to be careful and flew off, intent on watching for any change in the sky, the slightest ripple of an approaching sandworm. This was his third solo scout flight in a week, and he knew his capabilities.

At dawn, the spice scouts had spotted rusty splotches on dunes in the middle of an enclosed valley surrounded by rocks. The sheltered valley was large, but still too small to be the sole domain of a giant sandworm, although the heavy vibrations of the spice-harvesting machinery would eventually attract one of the creatures. Fortunately, the only opening to the greater desert was a narrow bottleneck in the cliffs, so they knew exactly where a worm would have to enter.

While the excavator scuttled across the open sands of the valley, moving sometimes to the safe bastion of rocks, Vor took the skimcraft in a wide arc, circling from horizon to horizon, watching for any sign of a marauding worm. He kept his eyes open as he flew his patrol, but he expected the men to have more than the usual amount of time to reap their harvest. The valley's high walls formed a natural fortress.

He gained altitude and circled the desert basin, scanning the undulating expanse of dunes below in search of wormsign. So far, the sandy wasteland looked serene, calming, and hypnotic. . . .

Vor relaxed, inhaled deeply, and pondered how clean and liberating the sheer emptiness was, the sharp edges and abrupt shadows, the mind-opening vistas and the freedom of being away from centuries of thoughts. He missed Mariella, their family, and friends back on Kepler, but he took comfort in knowing they were safe from slavers. The bittersweet pang was strong in his heart, though it would fade as the years went by . . . as it had before.

Letting his memory line plunge deeper, he thought of Leronica, the first woman to whom he'd given a normal human lifetime, and their sons, Estes and Kagin. He considered the rise and fall of his best friend Xavier Harkonnen during the terrible Jihad . . . and the beautiful, tragic Serena Butler. So many memories, such a long time.

He thought as well of his protégé, Abulurd Harkonnen, in whom he had invested so many hopes, but who had disobeyed Vor's direct orders—for the best of reasons and the worst of tactics—when the very fate of humanity hung in the balance. Abulurd had betrayed him, and all of humanity, in the final clash against the thinking machines, and Vor had seen to it that Abulurd was convicted and banished.

Yes, being so alone helped him to crystallize his memories and put them away on a shelf of his mind like artifacts in a museum. It also let Vor move on with his life . . . his long, long life.

He glanced down again, scanning the desert as he completed his broad circle. Still no sign of a worm, only the skirl of a dust-devil pirouetting on top of a dune.

A burst transmission came across the comm line, crackling with static in Vor's cockpit. There was always static because of the dust and the ambient charge in the atmosphere, but now he heard shouts, a gabble of frightened voices, a loud blow.

"Gods below, what the—"

"We're under attack!"

Then a scream and a surge of static filled the comm line before falling silent.

Vor's fingers paused just above the transmit button as he wheeled the aircraft about and streaked back toward the sheltered valley. He wanted to ask for details, demand explanations, but caution advised him to remain silent, sensing this might not be a sandworm encounter. Vor didn't want to let the attackers, if human, know he was coming. He was dozens of kilometers away, but he pushed the skimcraft engines to their peak acceleration.

When he approached the bottleneck valley, though, he reduced power to the aircraft's roaring intake engines to make them much quieter. From afar, he could still see the dissipating dust plumes from the excavator's exhaust stack. He swooped down into the valley and saw three of the dune rollers smoldering, their engines blasted, human bodies strewn on the sand. The engines of the excavator had been shut down in the middle of the valley, and the huge metal hulk sat, dust-covered, on its treads, a few bare patches of its metal hull glinting in the sunlight.

Another person might have panicked and sped back to Arrakis City to make a report and call for reinforcements, but Vor was not the sort of man to let a crisis continue without his intervention. Although his aircraft probably had enough fuel to reach another settlement, by the time he made his report and brought help, it would be far too late. By then, sandworms might have erased all evidence.

He had to find the answers to what had attacked the spice crew, and help anyone who might still be alive. It had happened so fast, and there was no cause in sight! Less than fifteen minutes had passed since he received the emergency signal. If a paramilitary force from a rival spice operation had struck the excavator, Vor had no weapon except for his own wits and fighting skills. Even his personal shield belt was sealed inside his locker aboard the large excavator.

Vor landed on the tread-marked sands and left the skimcraft's take-off engines active but on standby. Whatever force had hijacked and devastated the operations out here must have seen his scout craft land—if they were still here. Anyone familiar with how the melange business worked knew that at least one flyer scouted each harvesting operation.

He sprang out of the cockpit and landed on the soft dunes, then sprinted toward the towering metal machine. Three burned corpses lay sprawled next to an overturned dune roller—bodies of men he knew. Vor didn't let himself think of their names. Not yet. He had seen bodies on battlefields before . . . but this wasn't supposed to be a battlefield.

He felt an eerie reminder of when he'd tried to stop the slavers on Kepler, how he'd arrived too late to prevent the human cargo ships from taking his family and neighbors, from lifting off into the sky with them.

The spice-filled cargo pods remained intact, and no one had pulled the emergency launch; the evacuation pod was still locked in the upper bridge.

The entry ramp was open, showing the huge excavator's cavernous, dark interior, but Vor decided instinctively not to enter that way. Instead, he ran around to the front of the giant machine. During active operations, a broad, sand-covered scoop and conveyor gobbled the top layer of the desert, then dumped the sand into the processing bins and centrifuges.

Ducking, Vor scrambled up the conveyor and entered the processing machine through the intake ramp, climbing out through the first boxlike hopper. Covered with dust, he fought back the urge to cough from the strong cinnamon smell of spice in the air. He crept forward.

The bodies of three more workers lay on the stained metal deck. A container of harvested spice had been smashed open, the reddish powder spilled recklessly onto the floor. He looked from side to side, deconstructing shadows, but saw no movement, heard no noise.

It must have been a surgical operation, a powerful assault and retreat before countermeasures could be employed. He remembered his fellow crewmembers talking about the enemies Josef Venport had created when they ran roughshod over competitors in the melange business. This reeked of a retaliatory strike.

The excavator creaked and thrummed, even though the engines had been shut down. The heat from the sun and the cooling metal caused it to settle. With no one outside spotting for wormsign, Vor realized that a sandworm could venture through the bottleneck in the cliff walls at any time. But he was more concerned about a different sort of enemy now; someone had murdered his crew-mates, his friends, and honor impelled him to discover who.

With soft footsteps he crept up the flat metal steps to the shadowy crew deck, which should have been empty, since all workers were required to be on duty during active spice-harvesting operations. Even so, Vor discovered a single body there, a man sprawled on the deck, his neck broken. Moving as silently as he could, he retrieved his shield belt from his locker and clipped it on, but did not activate it yet.

He also secured a flare gun from an emergency locker, took a heavy pry bar from a tool kit and, carrying the makeshift weapons in each hand, made his way up one more level to the operations deck. Although fear made Vor cautious, his emotion drove him forward. Was the whole spice crew dead? He had to see if anyone needed rescuing. He was only one man, but accustomed to acting alone. He had secured numerous victories in the Jihad, brought down entire machine planets through prowess and clever ideas. He felt ready to face the murderers and saboteurs who had done this, though he realized he could not defeat an entire paramilitary force. He began to feel he had overcommitted himself, and he always had to worry about a sandworm.

Creeping up the metal stairs to the entrance hatch of the operations deck, he froze. Just inside the door, old Calbir's face stared at him, his eyes open and mouth partly agape—but it was the head only, propped up on a communication panel. The rest of the crew chief's body lay slumped in the chair two meters away. Judging by the ragged stump of the neck, it looked as if Calbir's head had been *torn* from his body. Another man lay dead inside the open hatch of the escape pod, his body sprawled facedown and a gaping, bloody wound on his back.

At the main control panel, with arms crossed over their chests, stood a young man and woman who looked to be about twenty years old. Wiry and feral, like panthers, they were covered with blood from their hands to their shoulders. "You must be Vorian Atreides," said the man. "We knew you wouldn't run away."

The young woman's lips curled in a smile. "He looks like you, Andros. The resemblance is striking."

Vor had expected to see an entire army, considering the damage they'd left in their wake, but these two were apparently alone. He noted something oddly familiar in their faces, their gray eyes, their dark hair. The deadly pair uncoiled their arms, like cobras preparing to strike, and their skin flickered with an underlying metallic sheen. They moved forward in unison, approaching him with a fluid, predatory gait.

"Stun only, Hyla," the man said.

The young woman pulled out a stubby hand weapon. "We want to talk with you, Vorian . . . and maybe toy with you a bit, until we obtain some answers. You can't possibly know this, but we have a lot in common, and so much potential together."

Not caring what they meant, Vor activated his personal body shield, and the thrumming ripple appeared around him a fraction of an instant before the woman fired her stunner. The burst struck ineffectually against his shield.

"I thought you said no one used shields in desert operations!"

Many decades ago, Vor had seen those types of weapons when the cymeks quelled disturbances among their captive human populations. He also knew they had much more lethal settings.

When the stun failed to incapacitate Vor, the young man threw himself forward. Vor swung the pry bar—and when the thick metal rod struck Andros in the ribs, he could tell the man wore no shield of his own. Seeing all the death and mayhem, Vor did not hold back his strength. The impact was solid, and Andros winced, but he grabbed the pry bar and yanked it out of Vor's hand.

Vor staggered away. The blow should have smashed the young man's rib cage, but he didn't even appear bruised! Now Hyla launched herself at him, and Vor fired the flare gun at her chest. The flash of the exploding projectile threw her back into Andros and caught both of them on fire. They still came at him, with flames consuming their clothing.

Vor swung over the railing and dropped down to the lower deck. If these two—*two!*—had slaughtered the entire crew, it was foolish for him to stand and fight them. Only a few seconds ahead of the pair, Vor ran into the crew quarters, sealed the heavy bulkhead door, and moved to the opposite end of the deck.

The eerie, murderous couple began battering at the metal door, and then an explosive burst shattered the lock. He had hoped to gain more time than this, but the two followed him, rushing forward with their clothes smoldering and skin blackened, not acting as if they were injured at all.

He didn't underestimate them, though he had no idea who they were or how they had obtained such powers. He had to think of some way to incapacitate them, or at least get enough of a head start so he could make it back to his waiting skimcraft.

Questions clamored in his mind: Who were these people? They did not seem to be saboteurs from a rival spice operation. Andros and Hyla—he did not recognize their names, but they had been sure he wouldn't know anything about them. What did they want? And that odd familiarity in their faces, as well as the similarity of appearance between Vor and Andros, an observation Hyla had made. A coincidence, or did it signify something more?

Vor raced the length of the excavator, dropped down another deck, and made his way to the spice-filled cargo pods, where an emergency exit hatch would let him back outside. He reached the sealed metal door, popped it open, and stepped outside onto a catwalk along the outside of the excavator. Hot wind whistled around the melange cargo pod; he was more than fifteen meters above the ground.

Normally, the ejection mechanism for an emergency launch of the cargo pods would be operated from the excavator's bridge, but the manual, secondary controls were here. Facing an oncoming worm and the loss of the giant vehicle, Vor doubted many spice workers would have the presence of mind to save the melange cargo when they themselves were doomed, but now he was glad for the fail-safe. He activated the sequence; he had less than a minute.

Andros and Hyla emerged from the escape hatch and ran after him onto the catwalk around the cargo pod. "We just want to talk with you," Hyla called in a flat, emotionless voice. "If you're useful, we may decide not to kill you."

Vor reached an escape pole and a thin metal ladder that ran down the outside of the spice harvester. He began to slide, but the rungs interfered, slowing him.

When he was three meters above the sand he let go and dropped, just in time to see Andros and Hyla stop at the ladder. The young man fired his weapon, and the beam's impact melted a round patch of sand into glass half a meter to his left.

At that moment, the ejection procedure blasted the anchor bolts free and heaved the melange cargo pod up into the air, hauling his two pursuers with it.

Vor sprawled on the ground, got to his feet again, and ran across the cloying sand toward his landed scout flyer. He looked back, watching the cargo pod rise into the air. The young man and woman clung to the catwalk, dangling, as the cargo pod rose higher, fifty meters above the ground. Andros and Hyla both let go at the same time, as if by mutual decision.

As he swung into the cockpit, Vor watched the two plummet to the ground. They landed simultaneously in crouch positions, even from such an impossible height, and then bounded up again, springing toward the aircraft without the slightest injury or hesitation.

Vor punched the craft's engines, lifting off vertically from the sands even before the cockpit canopy sealed. Flying such a craft was second nature to him, and now he wheeled it around and headed toward the rocky outcroppings that encircled the valley. If he could get out to the open desert, he would fly straight toward Arrakis City—

Before he gained much altitude, a small explosion struck the undercarriage of his aircraft, and one of the engines coughed, roared, then failed. The pursuers had fired their antique cymek weapons, damaging the engines. The flyer began to spin, but Vor wrestled with the controls, trying to maintain altitude, not sure whether it was better to crash on the open sands beyond the bottleneck, or in the rocks where he could at least hide.

Smoke poured from both engines. The young man fired again, but missed. Vor was very close to the ground now, but with a burst of auxiliary power he was able to streak away, trying to get as much distance as possible from his pursuers. His mind rushed. There was no place to hide out in the dunes, but he could take cover in the rocky ridge, maybe set up an ambush, though Andros and Hyla would not be easy targets.

In the rear imager, he saw the two tiny figures racing across the open valley, literally *running* after the wounded flyer as it tried to escape. The belly of his slowing craft scraped a high dune, sending a rooster tail of dust and sand into the air. Vor held on, jarred by the impact, and tried to keep flying, but the aircraft struck the ground again and plowed into the sand. He managed to pull up a final time, closing in toward the line of rocks that formed a barrier around the valley. Finally, he skidded into the soft sand and slewed to an abrupt, jarring stop against the first rocks. His body shield protected him from heavy bruising during the crash.

He popped open the canopy, leaped out, and ran onto weathered slabs of rock, picking his way, using hands and feet to climb when necessary. He glanced over his shoulder to see the two figures relentlessly jogging toward him, leaving lines of footprints across the soft sand.

The sun-heated rocks burned Vor's fingertips, but he kept climbing. Once he reached a vantage point, he watched the two pause to study his crashed flyer, but within seconds they began to ascend into the rocks. He kept an eye out for the telltale ripples of worm movement: Drawn by the commotion, sooner or later one of the beasts would find its way through the bottleneck into the enclosed valley. But for now, the sands remained placid.

Vor's heart was pounding as he climbed to the top of the ridge—where he was startled to encounter a strange woman standing, apparently waiting for him. She wore desert garb camouflaged to look like the rocks, and she carried a backpack with tools attached to it. She was so close, Vor couldn't believe that she had sneaked up on him. The woman was of indeterminate age, her skin weathered, but her eyes bright. Wisps of brown hair flitted around the hood that covered her head.

"You must be from the spice crew down there," she said casually, as if asking his favorite color. Noseplugs sealed her nostrils, giving her voice a nasal twang.

"I'm the only survivor." Vor indicated the figures who were now coming into the rocks. "Those two ambushed the harvester and murdered everyone. I don't know who they are, but they're as strong as combat meks." He turned his attention to her. "And who the hell are you?"

"I am Ishanti. I work for Josef Venport, keeping watch on some of the outer spice operations. But I never expected this. We have to get away and make our report."

Still breathing heavily, Vor looked to the expanse of tan desert beyond the rocks. "Do you have a flyer? How can we escape?"

"I have no vehicle."

Vor blinked. "Then how did you get all the way out here?"

"I used what the desert has to offer—which we'll use again now. Follow me. I have an idea." Ishanti flitted along the rocks, keeping herself low and hidden by her desert robe, but she told Vor to let himself be seen. They passed a rocky notch filled with loose gravel. Up a slope ahead of them, several boulders were precariously balanced at the top of a chute.

Seeing Vor's silhouette, Andros and Hyla scrambled like spiders up the rocky notch. Ishanti watched them and smiled. "All it takes is a little push." She and Vorian both pressed their weight against the boulders, knocking the two largest ones loose. The heavy rocks began to bounce and tumble, caroming off the walls. The small avalanche picked up momentum, rushing downward.

Andros and Hyla were caught in the funnel, and though they tried to scramble up the rocky walls, the boulders swept them away. Vor expected them to be mangled into pulp, but somehow the young man and woman flowed along above the falling boulders for a time, their feet moving rapidly, until they could no longer keep up and were hurled down the hillside. Vor didn't allow himself time for a sigh. At the base of the cliff, he saw the two moving toward him again, tossing broken rocks aside, unburying themselves.

"We have to go," Ishanti said, "down the other side of the ridge and out into the open desert. Or would you rather wait and fight?"

"I already tried that. What's out in the open desert?"

"Safety. But first, turn off your shield—unless you want to die."

"It's kept me alive so far."

"Out on the dunes it won't. The field will attract a worm and drive it into a frenzy. The monsters are hard enough to control as it is."

Control? Vor didn't know what she meant, but he dutifully switched off his shield. The woman loped down the steep slope, descending like a mountain goat until they reached the desert floor. Without pausing, she ran out onto the open expanse of sand.

He panted after her. "Where are we going?"

Ishanti turned to look at him, her eyes a deep blue-within-blue that Vor had come to recognize as a sign of lifelong spice addiction. "Trust me—and trust what I know of the desert."

He didn't hesitate. "All right, I'll trust you."

Though she used few words, Ishanti explained as they headed into the dunes. "With the spice operations in the valley, there should be a worm already nearby. We'll have to hope it comes for us before those two do."

"Doesn't sound like much of a choice."

At the top of a dune crest, she shaded her eyes to scan the line of rocks they had just left. Andros and Hyla were already picking their way down toward the sand. Vor wondered if they were androids, with armored skin and enhanced fighting abilities.

"Normally I'd advise against regular or heavy footfalls," Ishanti said, "but right now we want to draw their attention. Just run." Her pack was stuffed with tools and strange instruments, poles, hooks; a coil of rope hung down from the pack. Without slowing, the desert woman pulled out the items she needed. "Keep your eyes open for wormsign—that means Shai-Hulud will be upon us, and we won't have much time."

Behind them, Andros and Hyla reached the sand and burst forward, not seeming to tire. Vor could see that his lead was rapidly dwindling. Then he turned forward to see a shimmer like a shock wave, accompanied by vibrations that rumbled through the sand. He pointed. "A worm!"

Ishanti nodded. "Good. The approach is from exactly the right direction. We can make do." She dropped to her knees, removed more items from her pack. "Stand next to me, and do as I do. There's a very good chance we're both about to die, but there's also a chance we'll get away."

Vor didn't have time to ask questions as the ripple of disturbed sand raced toward him like a frothy whitecap during an ocean storm. Ishanti removed something that looked like a small sonic grenade. She activated its blinking light and tossed it into a hollow in the dunes not far from them. She crouched down on the crest. "Wait and watch. Be ready."

"I'm ready," he said, but he didn't know what to be ready for.

The sonic grenade detonated, sending out a loud pulse that throbbed into the sand, nearly deafening Vor. The approaching sandworm surged from beneath the sand, lifting a cavernous maw large enough to swallow even the largest spice harvester. Though he had lived for centuries and had seen many incredible things, Vor caught his breath, standing there on the dune crest in awe. The eyeless worm turned toward the source of the pulse, scraping its ridged back so close to them that Vor could have thrown a rock and hit it.

Ishanti was actually running *toward* the sandworm, and he was right behind her. "Come, we only have a few seconds!" Like a madwoman she loped along and sprang onto the lower ridge of the worm, using a hook-tipped pole as a grapple. After she caught on, Ishanti reached her right arm behind her. "Take my hand!"

Amazed at what she was doing, Vor caught her hand, and she hauled him up onto the worm's back, where she handed him a hook of his own. He didn't think, only followed her lead. They ascended the line of ring segments, and the monster thrashed, not noticing the insignificant riders.

Ishanti jammed a pry bar into the cracks between the worm's rings. With a heavy grunt, she pushed it, forcing open the ring to expose soft pink skin underneath. The sandworm flinched, and Ishanti jabbed the tender flesh. Finally, the worm turned to avoid the pain and began to rumble off into the desert.

"Tie yourself down." She tossed Vor the other end of the coil of rope. "We have to hold on until we get far enough away."

He did as he was told. Leaving a wake of churned sand behind it, the worm set off with amazing speed. With his hair whipping around his face, Vor turned to see Andros and Hyla standing defeated on the open sands.

Ishanti guided the worm forward, and they raced into the desolation of the deep desert.

A successful search depends on persistence and good fortune, but a successful mission depends on the character of the person to whom it is given.

—XAVIER HARKONNEN, *Memoirs of Serena Butler's Jihad*

Considering the amount of wealth and commerce flowing from Arrakis, Griffin Harkonnen was surprised to see that the main spaceport city was little more than a crowded slum. With the spice trade, he had expected a modern metropolis, but instead he saw people living in hovels made of fused brick and polymer. Every window, door, and crack was sealed to prevent dust from getting in. Arrakis had a reputation of sucking away wealth and hope faster than fortune-seekers could earn it back from the desert.

When he arrived and saw all the hopeless people who had no chance of getting offworld, Griffin's heart fell, as he felt homesick for rustic Lankiveil, no matter the hardships of living there. But he refused to abandon his quest, his duty.

"Avenge our family honor, Griffin," his sister had said. "I know I can count on you."

He had always known that searching an entire planet for one man would be difficult—even for a flamboyant, attention-grabbing person like Vorian Atreides—but when he looked at the stark cliffs and the endless desert beyond, he couldn't understand why anyone would choose to come *here.*

If Griffin's research was accurate, Vorian Atreides was quite wealthy, hiding his fortunes on various planets. On Kepler, Griffin had seen for himself that the man was well liked, even revered. If the Emperor had asked Atreides to leave Kepler, why wouldn't he choose to build an estate somewhere and live in comfort?

The man had told his family where he intended to go after departing from Kepler. The secret had not been difficult to discover. Griffin didn't think Atreides was on the run, or hiding, and had no reason to believe his prey would take extreme measures to change his name or disguise his identity. He had no idea Griffin was tracking him down, so why would he flee? Why would he hide? Even so, Griffin doubted he would be easy to find. This vast, desolate planet seemed like an easy world on which to disappear.

Valya had hated the Atreides scion for so long that she saw him only as a monster who needed to be punished for what he'd done to House Harkonnen. But Griffin wanted to understand the man he was going to kill, gathering as much information as he could on Vorian's long life, including his early years in the machine empire before he'd changed sides and joined Serena Butler's Jihad . . . as well as his friendship with Griffin's ancestor Xavier Harkonnen, the great atomic purge that had obliterated all the Synchronized Worlds, and finally the momentous Battle of Corrin, after which Vorian Atreides had blackened the Harkonnen family name for all time.

But why would a man like that willingly come to a place like Arrakis? For even more riches, Griffin assumed, for the spice that was making some people wealthy.

He stood alone for a time, surrounded by the bustle of uncaring crowds, and then set off into the town. His skin was still soft and moist, and he was already sunburned.

From behind him, a zeppelin-size water tanker flew in, dispatched from some world where water could be scooped up from an alien ocean, then desalinated and flown here. Knowing the costs of commercial transport from working the whale-fur deal, Griffin thought how desperate this world must be for water if it was commercially viable to fly a ship from one planet to another and make a profit from it. He also understood why the melange mined here was so expensive. Simple economics.

Griffin was cautious with his own limited funds, secreting cash in various pockets and packs on his body. He had budgeted his every move, making certain he would have enough to buy his passage back to Lankiveil. He knew he would be forced to hire local investigators, and offer generous bribes in hopes of retrieving scraps of information.

He saw suspensor-borne pallets filled with canisters of concentrated spice, all of which bore the logo of Combined Mercantiles. Beggars approached him constantly, and he wanted to help them, but he simply had no funds to spare, if he was to accomplish his mission. Many of the destitute people were offworlders like himself, huddled in rags against buildings, wrapped in their misery and covered with dust.

Equally relentless, vendors kept pestering Griffin, trying to sell him water-retention masks, eye coverings, weather-predictive devices, magnetic compasses (which never seemed to point the same direction two times in a row), and even magic talismans guaranteed to "ward off Shai-Hulud." He was obviously from another world, and thus a target for scams; Griffin turned down all offers.

Other people were obviously natives: He could tell that at a glance by their dark and leathery exposed skin, by the manner in which they moved and kept to the shadows, and how they covered their mouths and nostrils. They had a hard attitude about them and an undisguised disgust for naïve offworlders, but he thought they might be his best source of information. However, when he stopped an old desert man to ask questions, the man flashed a warding sign with two upraised fingers, said something in a language Griffin didn't understand, and then scuttled away into an alley.

Discouraged, Griffin found lodgings and showed the proprietor an image of Vorian Atreides. The obese proprietor shook his head. "We try not to notice people around here. And even if that man did come into my establishment, he was most likely wrapped in a headdress with noseplugs and face mask. Nobody's ever seen a person dressed like *that* around here." He nodded toward the image.

Without revealing his own name, in case someone tipped off his prey, Griffin asked vendors on the streets, paying token amounts to anyone who showed interest. Those who gave him information exuberantly were clearly lying, in hopes of a larger bribe. Moving on, he contacted a local investigator, offering payment only if the man produced results; the investigator was not enthusiastic about the arrangement, but said he would look into the matter, as long as it didn't take too much time.

Determined, Griffin realized he would have to do most of the work himself. He had come all this way, had promised his sister, and knew he had gotten physically closer to finding Vorian Atreides than ever before.

One night after sunset, he passed through a moisture-sealed door into a drinking establishment, where filthy, sullen men sat around consuming spice beer, spending all of their wages, because they had long since given up on buying passage off of Arrakis. Griffin found it disheartening to see people who had stopped trying to regain their self-worth. He vowed to never let that happen to him. . . .

After determining the precise amount he was willing to invest, he paid for drinks and asked for information or suggestions on how he might find a particular person, whom Griffin did not always name. Some men tried to make him pay them before they would even look at the image of Vorian, or asked for payment after just looking at the image, even when they had no information. Over the course of two hours, Griffin grew frustrated with the bantering, after expending only minimal amounts of his cash. He moved to a corner table and sipped a single glass of potent spice beer, but the bitter-cinnamon drug rushed directly to his head, and he ordered a glass of water instead, which cost twice as much as the thick beer did.

By the time he gave up and left the bar, the men were laughing at him. "Come back tomorrow. We'll think about it, see if we have more information," said a gruff leader who had a persistent cough.

Begrudging the waste of money from the evening, Griffin unsealed the door of the drinking establishment and returned to the night streets. He didn't like this place at all. In the cooler night air he tried to get his bearings, turned in the direction where he thought he'd find his lodgings, and headed down a narrow side street.

On this vile planet, Griffin was actually beginning to miss Lankiveil, and couldn't wait until he saw his parents again, along with his little brother and sister. One day, even Valya would return there from Rossak. The frigid, dark oceans of Lankiveil, the fishing fleets, and the winter ice storms were all rugged and unpleasant, but it had become a sort of home. Grudgingly, he admitted to himself that Lankiveil had toughened the Harkonnens, making them better able to meet challenges, but even the necessities for surviving there seemed like nothing in comparison with the crucible of this desert planet.

Hearing the scuffle of footsteps behind him, he turned to see a shadowy figure approaching. Griffin tensed, placed his left hand on the shield belt controls and his right palm on the hilt of his fighting knife. Thanks to Valya, he had plenty of experience in hand-to-hand combat.

Realizing he'd been spotted, the stranger paused, then flashed a handlight in Griffin's face, blinding him.

"Who are you? What do you want?" Griffin demanded, trying not to sound intimidated.

The person came closer, dimmed the handlight, and Griffin recognized one of the reticent patrons of the drinking establishment, a ruddy man with a thick crop of silver hair. "You have money to pay for information." The man stepped closer. "In exchange for all of it, I'll give you something you don't expect."

"And what's that?" Seeing a sharp glint in the man's eyes, Griffin subtly activated his shield. In the shadows of the side street, the hum was loud, and he saw a slight distortion in the air.

He watched his adversary for tiny movements, alert for any trick or feint. He wished Valya were there with him. The man didn't comment on the shield, and it occurred to Griffin that he might not know what it was. Shields were standard-issue throughout the Landsraad League, but he realized that he hadn't noticed anyone wearing them on the desert planet.

The man came closer and drew his long knife. "I'll show you how it feels to die." He laughed and thrust the blade forward like a stinging scorpion, obviously expecting an easy, soft target. Griffin turned, and the shimmering Holtzman field deflected the blow. His pulse raced and adrenaline flowed, readying him for an intense flurry of combat . . . but this man did not seem up to Griffin's fighting abilities.

His attacker tried to recover from his surprise, and clumsily drove the dagger in again, but he was unaccustomed to fighting against a shielded man. Griffin used his dagger to slice the back of the man's hand. Thick, dark blood spurted from the veins as he recoiled with a yelp. Griffin swung his knife sideways around the partial shield and stabbed the man in the lower left side. The blade went in deep, and the attacker grunted and coughed. He nearly pulled Griffin down to the ground with him as he collapsed to his knees.

In sick astonishment, he cried, "You've murdered me! You've murdered me!"

But Griffin had been careful. Though he and Valya had never actually harmed each other in their many sparring matches, they knew vulnerabilities very well. "It's not a lethal blow." He knelt beside the groaning man. "But I can change that." He held the bloody tip close to the man's face. "Who sent you to kill me?"

"No one! I just wanted your money."

"Well, that was poorly planned. Is everyone here so clumsy?"

The man yowled in pain. "I'm bleeding to death!"

Griffin looked from side to side, sure the commotion would draw someone within seconds. He pressed the dagger against the man's throat. "I'll end the pain quickly enough if you don't answer my question."

"All right! I wanted more than your money!" the man wailed. "I also meant to take your water!"

"Take my water? I don't have much water."

"Your body's water! The desert people can distill it . . . sell it." The man sneered at him. "Are you satisfied now?"

Griffin pressed the dagger tip harder against the thug's throat. "And where should I look for Vorian Atreides? Do you have information on that, too?"

The man groaned and clutched the knife wound in his side. "How should I know where he is? Most people who come here from offworld go to work on spice crews. Check with the Combined Mercantiles offices, see who they hired."

Shadowy figures emerged from doorways and flitted down the side street. The man squirmed and screamed again. Deciding he would get no further information out of him, Griffin stood. "We need medical attention here," he called out. The people crowded around the groaning thug, who looked up at them. He flailed his hands and tried to squirm away.

Griffin was astonished to see a knife flash in a woman's hand. She jerked quickly, drove the blade under the man's chin and up into his brain. The victim spasmed, then fell dead, spilling very little additional blood. "He was a thief," she said, leaning over to wipe the blade on his clothing. "Now we'll take his water." She looked up at Griffin's astonished expression, as if expecting him to challenge her. "Unless you claim it?"

Griffin stammered, "No . . . no." He turned and fled down the side street toward his lodgings, just wanting to get out of there but alert and ready with his knife in case someone else attacked him.

Behind him, the silent, dusty people wrapped the thug's body and carried it quickly down another alley. Griffin heard a door seal, but when he glanced back, all signs of them were gone.

What a barbaric place! And Vorian Atreides had *chosen* to come to Arrakis?

We should not be too proud of our triumphs. A perceived victory may only be the feint of your enemy.

——MANFORD TORONDO, *The Only Path*

He had nothing left. And nothing to lose.

The open wound in his memories forced Ptolemy to leave his home and never look again at the smoldering ruins that stood as a monument to the ignorance, intolerance, and violence of the Butlerians. After much contemplation, he decided to let his family believe that he, too, had been murdered by the savages.

He really was dead, in a way. His belief in the rational nature of human society had been ripped out and stomped into bloody remnants. He could surrender and return quietly to simple research, or he could *do something*. The problem had been defined for him with a painful clarity.

In the past, he had watched the antitechnology antics with a detached but sad disappointment, even a bit of amusement. How could anyone believe such nonsense? Ptolemy had been dismissive, making the mistake of not taking them seriously. They were uneducated mobs easily swayed by a fiery speaker, good at creating scapegoats and not skilled at understanding. He had been convinced that knowledge was stronger than superstition, and rationality stronger than paranoia. It had been a naïve assumption.

Now he knew that simple logic could not win an argument against savages. The mob had burned his lab facility, destroyed his records and equipment, and murdered his close friend and partner.

He didn't have animalistic fervor, superstitious terror, or a penchant for mindless destruction. He had something stronger—his mind. And Ptolemy would no longer use it in such a cool, analytical way. In response to their zealous violence, he was fueled with a passion and drive unlike anything he had ever felt before. This was not just a thought exercise or a problem in a workbook; this was a battle for civilization itself, rather than barbarism. Instead of applying his knowledge to theoretical pursuits, to well-mannered research and the dissemination of ideas, Ptolemy vowed vengeance; he vowed to destroy the Butlerians.

Using the last of the money he had scraped together from his lab accounts, and then borrowing—some might say stealing—the balance of his allocated research funds from the Zenith Council, Ptolemy booked passage to a place where he was sure his skills would be well received. There he would be protected, and he could offer his services to a like-minded man.

Kolhar. The headquarters of Venport Holdings.

AFTER WHAT HAD happened on Zenith, he was reluctant—and terrified—to reveal his identity, but if anywhere in the Imperium would be free of antitechnology influence, it was this planet. He remembered how Directeur Venport had challenged Manford at the Landsraad meeting. The business tycoon would understand.

After arriving, however, it took Ptolemy five days to get a personal meeting with the VenHold administrator. The spacing fleet was a whirlwind of activity. Ships were being gathered and supplied, held back from their regular routes for departure on some undocumented mission. Ptolemy knew better than to ask questions, but he was persistent, with steel in his spine. He would not give up.

In the lobby of the administrative building, he showed his credentials to a succession of underlings and finally spoke directly with Cioba Venport, the most important barrier to an audience with the Directeur himself. His past experience, and perhaps the fiery, haunted look in his eyes, convinced her. She ushered him directly into her husband's office.

Though he wanted to be brave, Ptolemy's voice quavered and tears burned his eyes as he recounted his hopeful meeting with Manford Torondo on Lampadas, how he had offered him prosthetic legs, a miracle to restore his ability to walk. Emotions were raw as he described what had happened to his lab and his partner. He wanted to speak as a dedicated, rational man, overcoming his terror and grief, but found himself unable to do so. Even so, Directeur Venport did not appear to think less of him.

"I tried to present an olive branch to the Butlerians, and their reply was to murder my partner and destroy my life." Ptolemy drew a deep breath as he fought back the flames in his memory, the terrible, haunting screams.

Ptolemy looked at the gleam of interest in Venport's eyes, and insisted, "I am not defeated, sir. I will not remain quiet while those animals continue their rampage. I am here to offer my services in any capacity that will defend human civilization. One day Manford Torondo will understand that when he attacked me, he planted the seeds of his own downfall."

Venport glanced at his wife in a silent consultation, and she gave the faintest nod. The Directeur's smile was so broad that his bushy mustache curled upward. "VenHold is delighted to have you, Dr. Ptolemy. It just so happens that we have access to a secret research facility on an uncharted planet, where other scientists like yourself are free to work on innovative projects, without fear of Butlerian influence."

Ptolemy caught his breath. "That sounds wonderful, impossibly wonderful."

The other man tapped his fingers on his desktop. "It's a place where you can let your energy and imagination run free, with virtually unlimited resources and funds, to develop technological advances that will strengthen us against the darkness of ignorance. I intend to crush those mindless fanatics under my heel."

Ptolemy's relief was so great he had to sit down. His eyes sparkled, and finally tears spilled down his cheeks. "Then that is where I belong, sir."

Most accomplishments are no more than initial or intermediate steps.
Failure to press ahead is a common mistake.

—MANFORD TORONDO, address on Salusa Secundus

Manford was both unsettled and giddy after his successful purge of the research facility on the planet Zenith. The misguided sins of Ptolemy and his Tlulaxa companion were so obvious, and their delusions so deep-seated! Only a few decades had passed since the defeat of Omnius, and if humanity's greatest scientific minds had already strayed far from the true path, then Manford wept for the future.

The glib prophecy that Erasmus wrote in his journal continued to haunt him, and drive him on: *Given enough time, they will forget . . . and will create us all over again.*

He had to prove the prophecy wrong! This was not the moment to celebrate or bask in an assumed victory. This was not a time for hubris, for easing up. After his followers left the smoldering ruins of the research facility, Manford did not return to peaceful Lampadas, much as he wanted a quiet respite with Anari at his side. Instead, he ordered his followers to head for Salusa Secundus. It was time to face Emperor Salvador Corrino and make the man see clearly.

When his task force of ships landed at the Zimia Spaceport, he did not request clearance. His followers disembarked en masse and made an impromptu march toward the city center and the Imperial Palace, while Salusan officials tried to decide how to react. The unexpected arrival of so many demonstrators stunned the capital city's security forces, blocked traffic, and threw daily business into turmoil. Manford was glad to draw such attention; it ensured that he would be taken seriously. He found it uplifting.

Since he was making a formal public appearance, rather than going into battle, he rode on a palanquin carried by two of his followers. Anari Idaho walked alongside, ready to slay anyone who gave them a hint of trouble.

As they marched through the city, Manford regarded the blocky main buildings of the old Suk Medical School. The Suks had recently established a much more extensive base on the planet Parmentier, but here the original stone structure was still a landmark. Outside the campus, a newly erected placard celebrated the school's centennial, even though the Suk doctors had not formally established their order until well after the Battle of Corrin.

Manford viewed the old school headquarters with annoyance, reminded of the false pride of advanced medical doctors, who like Ptolemy, blithely assumed that technology could fix any frailty of the human body. Manford loathed the very idea of having machines attached like parasites to his body. He turned away from the old medical facility, shuddering. Men should not believe themselves the equivalent of God.

Ahead, he saw the towers of the gaudy Palace of the Corrino Emperor. Manford's own domicile on Lampadas had no such pretentions; his riches were in his soul, in his beliefs, and in the devotion of his followers.

"Shall I send runners ahead to demand an audience with Emperor Salvador?" Anari asked.

"He already knows we're coming. When my people arrive on the steps of the Palace, that will be the only invitation I need. The Emperor will make room on his calendar, have no fear."

He grasped the sides of the palanquin as his bearers marched up the stone steps. Uniformed noukkers stood guard at the arches, watching Manford suspiciously. He raised his hand in a nonthreatening gesture. "I've come to visit the Emperor. My people—who are Salvador's loyal subjects—have important news. He will want to hear it."

"The Emperor has been notified of your arrival," said the guard standing in front. Though he was obviously uncomfortable, the captain remained firm. "We will inform you as soon as he is available."

Manford gave him a bland smile and raised his voice. "My followers are hungry and thirsty. Perhaps some of the local merchants will provide refreshments while we wait?"

Without being invited, the Butlerians spread out into the cafés, restaurants, and market stalls that served tourists and dignitaries around the capital square. Though some of the food-service proprietors complained, they knew well enough not to ask payment for the meals or beverages the Butlerians took. To "thank" the vendors, Manford promised to say prayers on their behalf.

After an hour without a response from inside the Palace, his people began to grow restless, and the buzz of their dissatisfied conversation grew louder. Anari

Idaho was willing to force her way into the Palace, but Manford calmed her with a smile and a gesture.

Finally, the guard captain touched his ear, nodded, and gave a brittle welcoming smile. "Leader Torondo, Emperor Salvador has arranged a place where you and he can have a private conversation."

Manford bowed slightly. "That is all I requested."

Anari walked at his side as the bearers carried the palanquin through the archway into the huge reception hall. The rest of the Butlerians remained outside, but Manford was not worried about being separated from them. He could quickly summon the faithful if he should need them.

Salvador Corrino waited for him in a small, empty conference room. The Emperor looked displeased at being forced to accommodate the unexpected visitor, although Manford noted the glint of uneasiness behind his eyes. He was surprised that Roderick Corrino wasn't there, since the Emperor rarely made important decisions without his brother's counsel. Perhaps Salvador didn't believe this was an important decision; Manford would have to convince him otherwise.

"With some difficulty, I've managed to rearrange my schedule, Leader Torondo. I can speak with you for no more than fifteen minutes." His speech was terse. "I am a busy man with many important demands on my time."

"And I have come with one of the most important tasks you must address," Manford said. "Thank you for seeing me."

Salvador wasn't finished. "Your arrival caused a great deal of disruption. Permits are required for such a large gathering. Please be more considerate next time."

"I will not rein in my followers with permits. You must listen." Salvador's nostrils flared with indignation, but Manford had no patience for the man's petty hurt feelings. "I resort to extreme measures because time is short, and the danger increases day by day. Let us pray I don't need to take *further* extreme measures."

The Emperor's eyes narrowed. "Are you threatening me?"

"I am *clarifying* for you. Previously, when I appeared before the Landsraad assembly, my call for a vote was disrupted by terrorist activity. Have the perpetrators been caught and punished?"

"The matter is still under investigation."

Manford laced his fingers together. "Then schedule another vote and require every Landsraad representative to be there. They must go on record as to where they stand on the future of our civilization."

"I will accommodate you as best I can." Salvador was trying to sound tough, but he could not hide his quick swallow. "The calendar of the Landsraad League is full for quite some time."

"Not good enough. My followers continue to discover remnants of the thinking machines that could easily be turned against humanity, but that is only the tip of the proverbial iceberg. The greater danger we face is human weakness and temptation. Scientists and industrialists seem intent on bringing about a new age of machines, a new dependence on technology. My followers just saw this on Zenith, and you can rest assured that we took care of the problem. We are still at a very dangerous balancing point, however. We must never forget our pain, never forget what Rayna Butler told us all. I call upon your heart, Emperor Salvador Corrino, to do what is right. Stand beside us and openly declare your stance against advanced technology."

"I have many competing interests to weigh from thousands of planets. But I promise I'll consider what you say. Now, if that is all—"

"If you do not choose the side of righteousness, Sire, the Butlerians will do it for you. You see the group of your loyal subjects I've brought here. Throughout the Imperium, I have millions of followers who are just as dedicated as these. I swear that we are all prepared to stand by your side and fight. Provided you do what is right." He raised his eyebrows, waiting.

Emperor Salvador was clearly intimidated, though he tried not to show it. "And a Landsraad vote will satisfy you?"

"The Landsraad vote goes without saying. No, my people require a more visible gesture on your part, a dramatic demonstration of your support." Manford pretended that the idea had just occurred to him, though he had planned it carefully on the voyage from Zenith. "For instance, consider the historic headquarters of the Suk School, right here in Zimia. Those arrogant doctors, with their extremist medical experiments, are trying to reshape humanity. A human being should take care of his body and pray for health, not rely on machines to keep him alive. We need to enhance our minds and bodies through our own aspirations and hard work, not through artificial means. It would be a generous first step if you closed down the Suk School here—a highly visible gesture that sends a clear message."

Emperor Salvador looked from side to side, as if wishing Roderick were there. "I will consider it . . . in the spirit of maintaining a good relationship with you and your followers. What you ask will take time, but I think I can let you have your way with the old Suk School headquarters—provided you cause no further trouble here."

Manford spread his hands helplessly, not showing his sense of triumph, though the Emperor had conceded easily. "The Butlerians have a lot of energy and enthusiasm, Sire. I have to give them some release for their passions . . . but it's a vast Imperium, and there is a great deal of work for us to do. We could go to the outer planets, or we could remain here in Zimia. Perhaps if you provided us with a fleet—say, two hundred mothballed ships from the Army of Humanity?—we could go elsewhere and continue our work far from Salusa Secundus. For the time being."

Manford could see perspiration on the Emperor's forehead as he considered this. "Now that you mention it, we do have military vessels that are no longer being used. Perhaps I could scrape together a couple of hundred decommissioned ships. You will need to pilot and crew them yourselves, but you can devote them entirely to your efforts—provided they go far from here."

Manford smiled and looked at Anari, who wore a contented expression. "I was optimistic that we could reach a satisfactory accommodation, Sire," he said. "I can gather my own people to serve aboard the new fleet, and we will be back to take care of the Suk School, at the proper time." He signaled for the palanquin bearers to turn about and leave. As he departed, Manford pretended not to notice that Emperor Salvador let out a quavering sigh of relief.

*All Sisters have common training, a common wardrobe, and presumably
a common mind-set, but beneath the surface they are as diverse and
separate as the roots that spread out from a single tree.*

—REVEREND MOTHER RAQUELLA BERTO-ANIRUL,
Manual of the Sisterhood

Sister Candys Venport was filled with excitement and fascination as she ran
up to Valya. "It's Sister Anna! You should see this for yourself."

Valya lurched to her feet, ready to follow the girl through the tunnels. "Is she
hurt?" The Emperor's sister had very little common sense, and could easily have
gotten herself in trouble. On the other hand, since returning from the survival
quest and finding Ingrid's body, Anna was more serious about her studies, and
had been showing more dedication to them.

"Not hurt." The girl tugged on Valya's hand. "She's done much better than
Sabine or I ever could."

Inside the small chamber, Anna sat cross-legged on the floor, staring intently
at the wall panel that enclosed the hive of burrowing insects. Her concentration
interrupted, Anna blinked and turned around, surprised to see Valya there.
"Straight lines . . ." She sounded exhausted. "Who would imagine it's so difficult
just to make straight lines?"

At first, Valya didn't understand what the young woman meant, but Candys
ran forward to point at the tunnels made by the scuttling nematodes. Most of
the burrows swirled around in the random curves of nature, but in one corner of
the panel, all the lines were perfectly straight, exactly horizontal and vertical,
intersecting in precise perpendicular junctions.

"It's like what I did with the fogwood trees back in the Imperial garden,"
Anna said. "These burrowers respond to me. They must be telepathically sensitive, like fogwood trees." Anna looked at Valya's stunned expression, and the

Princess's face fell. "Are you disappointed? When you told me to meditate on their movements, wasn't this what I was supposed to do?"

"No—I mean yes, this is fine, I'm just . . . surprised." She would have to look into it further. "I'm very impressed. I wonder if other Sisters can do this."

"It's a knack I have," Anna said. The girl might be spoiled, immature, and emotionally unstable, yet now Valya revised her opinion. If carefully guided, those mental powers might be useful, though she doubted if Anna Corrino had the maturity or drive to achieve anything significant.

Before she could take Anna to see the Reverend Mother, Dorotea stopped at the door to the chamber. She seemed stern and hardened. "Sister Valya, I've been looking for you. I'd like you to join me, along with some specially chosen Sisters, at an important private meeting."

"Can I go along?" Anna rose to her feet. "I could share some ideas for a meeting."

"This meeting is not for acolytes. Valya belongs with us."

Anna looked stung and disappointed, and a flash of jealousy rippled across her face. Trying to calm the Corrino girl, Valya said, "I'll come back to you as soon as I can. Sister Candys, will you take Anna back to her quarters? Dorotea and I have some business to discuss." She wondered what the other woman was up to.

Despite the ever-growing number of Sisters being trained on Rossak, it was not difficult to find true privacy. The great cliff city had once been populated with nearly a hundred thousand Sorceresses, their mates, and children, along with all the normal Rossak inhabitants and offworlders who came to harvest the jungle's wealth. The Omnius plagues, however, had wiped out so much of the population that large sections of the tunnels were now empty.

Dorotea led Valya to a windowless room, where Valya quickly assessed the nine other women gathered there, including Sister Perianna, who had recently returned from Salusa, along with Sister Esther-Cano, Sister Ninke, Sister Woodra, and five more whom she did not know.

"I told them we could trust you—I hope I'm not wrong about you," Dorotea said to her. "You seem to be the Reverend Mother's darling, but I know you've also worked with Karee Marques. I believe you're dedicated to our cause. We're meeting here to discuss the future of the Sisterhood."

"You can trust me," Valya said automatically. She began evaluating the women in her mind, to discover the common denominator.

Dorotea announced to all the women, "We're here because we're concerned that Reverend Mother Raquella has lost her way."

Valya's brow furrowed. "In what way? She created the Sisterhood—so doesn't she define the goals of the order, as the only Reverend Mother?"

"The Sisterhood has its own identity," Dorotea said.

"And we have much to offer," said Perianna. "The Emperor has discovered this. Many noble families and commercial interests also see the value in our training. But if the Reverend Mother throws her support on the side of the Machine Apologists, she will damage our reputation."

"Not just our reputation," said Sister Woodra, "but our souls. The very core of the Sisterhood is to help women achieve superiority with their bodies and minds, keeping them from the seductive lure of machines."

Valya hid her surprise and took a seat. Already she guessed she would have to report this discussion to Raquella. "And how do you think the Reverend Mother has strayed from this? She has voices and memories the rest of us cannot hear. I am inclined to trust her judgment."

"None of us knows what a Reverend Mother *is*," said Dorotea.

"Yet," said Ninke.

"Raquella has changed," Dorotea continued. "I have watched it. Isn't it possible that those voices and memories in her head can deceive her as well as advise her?"

Valya pretended to consider the point. "We'll never know for sure until we discover how to create other Reverend Mothers, so we can compare one to another."

"She's done almost nothing to investigate the murder of Sister Ingrid!" Dorotea said.

"Murder? Isn't it more likely she just slipped from the path?" Valya kept her tone casual. "There's a reason the cliffside trail is restricted. She probably went where she wasn't supposed to go."

"That isn't all. We've heard rumors that there may even be forbidden thinking machines hidden here on Rossak!" said Sister Esther-Cano, lowering her voice to a nervous whisper.

A gasp circled the room, and Valya did not have to feign her surprise. How could these others possibly know about the breeding computers? She had stopped Ingrid before she could tell anyone else. Valya made a disbelieving snort. "That sounds like a Butlerian witch hunt."

Dorotea pressed her lips together and nodded slowly. "When the Reverend Mother sent me away to my first assignment on Lampadas, she wanted me to study Manford Torondo, to analyze his followers and their supposedly irrational actions. I don't think she expected me to listen. However, I saw Manford's truth there. I listened to the recorded speeches of Rayna Butler. And though I didn't live through those times myself, I learned how horrific the thinking machines truly were."

Valya sat back and listened as the women discussed rumors they had heard, and expressed their fears. She had no intention of throwing in with these women. She nodded at appropriate times, responded with a troubled expression or contemplative look. It seemed she had infiltrated them.

WHEN SHE REPORTED to the Reverend Mother, the old woman received the news with a grave expression, and told Valya to continue befriending the group. "You seem to have a natural talent for deception."

She heard no condemnation in the statement, but even so, Valya felt naked in front of the old woman, with her soul bared and all her thoughts and motivations laid out for observation and analysis. Valya kept her eyes down, a deliberate attempt to elicit sympathy. "I'm sorry if you think I'm untrustworthy, Reverend Mother."

"The ability to lie convincingly can be useful, provided it is used for the proper purpose. Once you understand what it is to lie, you can move to truth—*our* truth."

Valya averted her eyes as the Reverend Mother continued, "Sister Valya, I know you harbor a burning desire to redeem House Harkonnen, and I accept that I can never entirely divert you from your goal. But I have looked deep into your soul and I believe that you are in the right place at the right time for the welfare of the Sisterhood." The old woman's eyes narrowed. "I don't view you on a scale of good or bad. Rather, I see you as a means by which our order can achieve true greatness. The two goals are not necessarily contradictory."

She had already sensed Raquella grooming both her and Sister Dorotea, even pitting them against each other. To see who was better.

Raquella paused with a gentle smile. "You will achieve what you wish to achieve. I believe you are one of the most capable young women I've ever met, and this is why I have entrusted you with so much."

Valya smiled with pride, but felt odd, as if she had been cleverly and deviously manipulated away from a path she had set for herself.

"And if you became a Reverend Mother like myself, then you would be powerful indeed."

A hunt will always be successful, provided one is willing to redefine the goals as needed.

—VORIAN ATREIDES, private journals, Kepler period

Riding the great sandworm left Vorian awestruck. During the journey across the desert, Ishanti never let down her guard. Nevertheless, she took the adventure in stride, as if controlling such a creature was an everyday activity.

While the behemoth slid across the sand with the speed of a Coriolis storm, the woman seemed worried that Vor was unprepared for the deep desert. "Where is your face mask, your noseplugs? How much extra water do you carry? And food? You are not ready for this place."

Still holding on to the ropes, Vor coughed from the stirred-up dust and cinnamon reek that wafted around the sandworm. "I was in a skimcraft, returning to the spice harvester. I didn't expect to find my whole crew slaughtered—and I didn't plan to be shot down."

Her grimace showed what she thought of his explanation. "If one could foresee every accident, we would all be prepared. Only those who learn to accept the unpredictable will survive."

"*You* were certainly unpredictable. I don't know who you are any better than I know those two assassins." He flashed her his best smile. "Frankly, I prefer your company to theirs."

"Naib Sharnak will decide what to do with you." She prodded the sandworm with one of her goads, and the beast raced onward.

By now, hunger tightened his stomach, and the dust and extreme dryness of the air had parched his throat. As if to teach him a lesson, Ishanti had not offered him any water, though occasionally he watched her sip from tubes at her collar.

In his life, Vor had never been really thirsty, like this. Though he'd spent the past month on Arrakis, his metabolism had not yet adjusted to the drastic changes. Even under tight rations with the spice-harvesting crew, he still retained plenty of water fat, but now his throat felt like hot ashes. His skin was dry, his eyes burned; he could sense the arid world stealing moisture from him, every drop of perspiration, every hint of vapor from an exhaled breath.

Though he might be parched and miserable, he knew Ishanti would not simply let him perish, since she had gone to the trouble of rescuing him. On the other hand, she was under no obligation to coddle him, nor did he ask her to. He attempted to drive his thoughts away from his thirst.

Hours later, when they neared a line of gray mountains, Ishanti explained in patient detail, as if to a child, how to dismount from the exhausted sandworm. Vor paid careful attention and, when the time came, tried to imitate her as she sprang down, bounded onto the soft sands, and then froze in place as the cranky beast slithered onward, thrashing its hot tail in annoyance. When it had moved far enough off, Ishanti gestured silently to Vor, and they danced away from the retreating creature; he and the woman went motionless again as the great worm paused, turned in their direction, and lumbered back toward the open expanse of desert. Ishanti let out a sigh of relief, then urged Vor to hurry to the cliffs. "You're a fast learner. Good."

Though he was filled with questions about what to do next, he sensed her impatience with his inquiries, so he just followed. She led him into the rocks with an easy confidence, as if she had come this way many times before. He studied the ground for any clue as to where she might be taking him and discovered that Ishanti was following marks: well-placed pebbles, small signs that looked almost natural. Only a few feet had trod these rocks to beat down a trail—or someone might have erased the footprints after each passage.

He remembered the abandoned camp that he and the spice crew had found in the rocks, and now he was intrigued, thinking he might finally get to meet the mysterious "Freemen" of Arrakis. They were the reason he had chosen this out-of-the-way planet in the first place.

Vor didn't notice the cave until they were upon it. The opening was disguised by an elbow of rock that required a sharp left turn; another well-placed boulder blocked the entrance from view. Ishanti paused to open a moisture-sealed door, and they found themselves facing three desert-robed men with half-drawn knives. When Ishanti raised her hand and gave a sign, they let her pass, but the men stopped Vor from entering.

"I don't vouch for him, yet," Ishanti said. "He must still pass our tests."

Vor studied them, saw their tough stance, their confident readiness for combat, noted the unusual milky-white blades of their daggers. He decided not to ask questions, not to beg for his life, or surrender—he just faced the desert people, letting them make their own judgments based on what they saw. The guards seemed to appreciate that.

"This man is the only survivor of a spice-harvesting crew," Ishanti continued. "Let him pass. We need to speak to the Naib." The three stepped aside but did not lower their guard.

In a cool, shadowy grotto lit by a single glowglobe, Ishanti introduced him to a grizzled, older man who wore his long gray-black hair in a thick braid; he had a high forehead, a calm expression, hard eyes. She gestured for Vor to sit on one of the patterned fiber rugs over the stone floor, and took a place close beside him. Vor remained respectfully silent as Ishanti summarized what had happened to the spice-harvesting crew at the hands of two seemingly indestructible hunters, and how she had helped Vorian escape.

The man, Naib Sharnak, regarded Vor coolly, like a doctor performing a dissection, then lifted his chin. "Two people massacred an entire spice-harvesting crew, shot down your aircraft, and made Ishanti nervous? And you say they were after you?"

"*They* said they were after me. I've never seen or heard of them before."

One of the Naib's people brought in an elaborate service of spice coffee that was so potent Vor could barely drink it, despite his thirst. They did not offer him water, though he craved it.

"I myself have many questions about the young man and woman who caused such damage," Ishanti said, narrowing her deep-blue eyes. "I represent Combined Mercantiles here. If one of our competitors has discovered a secret weapon or dispatched mercenary assassins, then I must make my report. They were not normal people—perhaps not entirely human. They won't be easy to kill."

"Freemen are not easy to kill, either," Naib Sharnak said.

Vor had been grappling with the same questions ever since his escape, squeezing and prodding the possibilities, but none of the answers made sense to him. The pair of attackers had called him *by name*. But he had lived a quiet life on Kepler for decades, and had come to Arrakis without fanfare. No one should have known he was here at all. Who could possibly be hunting him?

"If there is a threat to the desert, then there is a threat to us," the Naib said. "I will send scouts to study the wreckage of the spice harvester—if anything remains. You will stay with us."

"As your prisoner?"

Sharnak raised his eyebrows. "Are you foolish enough to attempt an escape?"

"Where would I go? In fact, I was actually hoping to encounter you. That's why I came to Arrakis in the first place."

TWO DAYS LATER, Naib Sharnak's desert scouts returned, a pair of young men named Inulto and Sheur. While Vor sat with the Naib in a small sietch cavern, the two youths described in excited words what they had seen; the mission had obviously been an adventure for them. Ishanti came in to hear their report as well.

"We rode as fast as we could, Naib," said Sheur. "An evening dust storm drove us to shelter early, but we were off again before the next sunrise."

"And what did you find?"

"Nothing." Inulto lowered his head. "A worm had been there. All the machinery, the aircraft, the dune rollers, the bodies—the evidence is gone. Nothing remains."

"I know what I saw," Vor said. "I'm sure the killers are still alive."

Ishanti was anxious and angry. "I need to return to Arrakis City and report to headquarters. Directeur Venport will want to know." She looked over at Vorian. "I presume you desire to return to civilization? We have a fast skimcraft. I can take you there directly."

Vor surprised both by saying, "No, I'd rather stay here for a while. I am intrigued to speak with your people. Rumor has it you live very long lives, well over a century?"

"It's the geriatric effects of melange," Sharnak said. "That is how we live. You cannot steal any secret of immortality from us."

Vor laughed. "Oh, I already have immortality, but I would be interested in talking to others about it."

The Naib looked at his visitor's features, probably noting the first hints of gray in his hair, and scoffed. "What would you know of immortality?"

"Only what I've learned during the two hundred and eighteen years of my life."

Sharnak laughed even louder. "You harbor delusions! Offworlders believe ridiculous things, *really* ridiculous things."

Vor gave him a contented smile. "I swear to you, I was born before the beginning of Serena Butler's Jihad, well over two centuries ago." He explained who he was, even though these isolated desert people knew little of the politics and history of the war against the thinking machines, a galaxy-spanning conflict that ended a century earlier. "I have fought in those epic battles, traveled much, and seen countless friends die, many of them heroically. I watched two of my wives bear me children. I raised families, and they, too, grew old . . . while I did not change. The cymeks gave me a life-extension treatment, and you have your melange with its enhancement properties, but we've both lived long lives—long, hard lives."

The Naib seemed unsettled by his claims, but Vor stared at him until he looked away.

Ishanti reached out to touch the side of Vor's face. "We don't have soft skin like you do." Then she caught herself and added with a snort, "Old men muse about such things. I am more worried about the business at hand, and whether those two assassins will attack other spice-harvesting operations."

At the next sunrise, she flew off in her skimcraft.

A prize is worth nothing to the man who cannot keep it.
—JOSEF VENPORT, internal VenHold memo

The vessels in the VenHold Spacing Fleet were primarily used for carrying nonmilitary passengers and cargo, astutely avoiding interplanetary conflicts, but now Josef Venport was launching an outright attack. He doubted the Celestial Transport workers would put up much of a fight, but he intended to seize what should have been his in the first place.

Through his study of detailed star charts, Draigo Roget had identified the Thonaris star system as the likely location of a major thinking-machine base that had thus far escaped detection. Somehow, scouts for Arjen Gates had stumbled upon the place—probably through dumb luck—whereas Draigo had calculated the location through intellect and skill.

And now, with a large private fleet of VenHold ships, all augmented with weaponry purchased on the black market, Josef intended to take the outpost away from his business rival.

With shared information, star images, and unfathomable interdimensional foldspace calculations, the group of Navigators guided the VenHold fleet to the edge of the Thonaris system, an unremarkable orange star orbited by an all-but-invisible brown dwarf sun. High-resolution scans combed the volume of space for any signs of habitation or industrial activity.

Draigo stood next to Josef on the command bridge of an old military ballista that he had purchased from the Army of Humanity. With additional modifications from the Kolhar shipyards, the warship carried even more firepower.

"I'm confident this is the correct star system, sir," Draigo said. "But we still have a wide area to search in order to find the depot."

Josef frowned, scratched his thick, cinnamon-colored mustache. "It can't be too difficult, or Arjen Gates would never have found it."

"Accidents happen, sir . . . statistically speaking."

After two hours, the search had pinpointed six planets in the system—two frozen lumps that were not much bigger than comets, one world that was far too hot and close to the sun, two gas giants with a smattering of moons, and a large cluster of rocky planetoids.

"Those planetoids radiate far too much energy," Draigo said. "Indicates artificial activity, probably industrial operations."

Josef was convinced. "That's our destination, then. Prepare to move. Let's make this quick and efficient."

Draigo called up a projection of the seventy VenHold ships, which were scattered in a pattern like intersection points on a complex cat's-cradle diagram. "It's best to move in with a sudden, crippling blow. I have planned what I believe will be an effective scenario, sir. At the Mentat School, I acquired a great deal of simulated experience in complicated space military engagements."

"That is what I wanted you to learn, Draigo. You will guide the strike. The Celestial Transport presence needs to be uprooted and discarded like a weed." He transmitted to all of his ships. "My Mentat has tactical command. Follow his orders in this engagement." Then he sat back to watch.

Under complete communications silence, the ships activated their standard faster-than-light engines and descended into the system. Draigo had already provided detailed instructions, ship by ship, mapping out each movement as if the battle had already occurred. All weapons were powered up and ready to fire, but Josef specified that they were to cause as little damage as possible. He warned the individual captains, "I'll deduct the value of every viable ship you ruin from your bonuses." That should give them sufficient incentive.

The shipyards rapidly came into view, proving the Mentat correct. One cratered planetoid was covered with automated strip-mining and metals-processing machinery, but the heart of the shipyard was its assembly complex in low orbit, large spacedocks that held derelict ships. Bright lights and thermal signatures indicated a significant level of activity.

At least fifty large robot vessels hung in various stages of completion, huge brute-force starships that were dark except for a spangle of lights and a flurry of figures moving about in the engine bays. Josef spotted at least a dozen smaller CT ships and pinpointed the base's administrative hub in the orbiting grid work. In addition to the fifty completed ships being upgraded with spacefolder engines, dozens more vessels were under construction. The Thonaris complex also held many robotic factories that used raw materials from the asteroids to create new structural girders, hull plates, and internal components. But the CT occupiers had not bothered to activate them. Rather, they were just commandeering the old, mostly finished ships.

Josef's eyes drank in all the possibilities. "You have already surpassed my expectations, Mentat. When this is over, you may claim your reward."

"Reward?" Draigo's brow furrowed. "Wasn't this the task for which you hired me, sir?"

"And a good investment it was." Josef leaned forward, staring at the screen.

The VenHold raiders converged on the Thonaris depot like a swarm of angry hornets, englobing the operations according to the Mentat's assault plan.

As expected, panicked CT workers began to transmit alarms. A few ships attempted to evacuate, but they had nowhere to go. The VenHold fleet was an undeniably superior force, ready for a quick and decisive battle.

The Celestial Transport operations appeared to be in the initial stages of consolidation, having reactivated only a handful of the manufacturing bases. *Good,* Josef thought. They hadn't had time to cause irreparable damage. The workers also seemed so confident in their secret activities that they had not yet established a solid defensive perimeter.

Too bad for them.

The Mentat scanned images of the planetoids, the refurbished robot ships, and the CT vessels in orbit, calculating and recalculating possibilities. "They have no way to stand against us, sir. Logically speaking, they should surrender without firing a shot."

"That would be convenient, but be prepared anyway." By Josef's orders, his ships made no response to the numerous indignant demands for answers from the panicked CT workers. A reply was unnecessary, since his intentions were certainly obvious. Only the details remained.

He looked over at Draigo, who showed no sign of mirth. The Mentat gave his brisk report in a quiet voice. "I've identified all the weak points, sir. I believe we can have the complex consolidated within the hour."

To Josef's surprise, Arjen Gates himself appeared on the screen. The head of Celestial Transport had short brown hair, a pointed chin, and eyes that blinked too often. His voice was thin, high enough in pitch that he always sounded intimidated—and he certainly had good reason to feel that way now. "Whoever you are, you are trespassing on sovereign territory. I have a legal claim on this unoccupied system under the laws of salvage! You have no right to be here."

Josef leaned back and chuckled. The hated competitor was an unexpected prize that was gratifying on an entirely different level!

When no one replied to his demand, Arjen Gates sounded even more frightened. "If you are followers of the Butlerian movement and want to destroy these robot ships, I have already claimed them as personal property. You have no right!

These are valuable relics to be used for the expansion of human commerce! I demand to speak to your representative."

Josef let the man wait a few more seconds, then activated his own comm. "We're not the Butlerians, my dear friend Arjen. If it's any consolation, I don't intend to damage any of these ships."

When Arjen Gates began to splutter and yell, Josef muted the volume. "Commence consolidation, Mentat—no sense wasting time. We have a lot of work to do here."

Logical enlightenment will always defeat emotional ignorance, although the battle is not necessarily pretty.

　　　　　　　　　—mission statement, Denali Research Facility

P tolemy had been warned that even a single breath of Denali's atmosphere would eat away his lungs and cause his painful death. Dangerous research projects were conducted under tight security, with interlocks and fail-safes that would sterilize or annihilate an entire laboratory module should anything go wrong.

Nevertheless, when he arrived here, Ptolemy felt safer than ever before. No ship could find this place without specific guidance from a VenHold Navigator. The Butlerians could never come here. And he was free to pursue the research he chose.

He felt like a projectile that had been launched on a set trajectory. Now he understood his true calling, the most important reason for doing research. Not for profit or convenience, but to stop the savages from destroying civilization itself. An intellectual problem to solve and a passionate battle to fight. His friend Elchan's death would not be in vain.

He traveled with a scheduled shipment of chemical containers, pressurized gases, and food supplies. The Tlulaxa research head, Noffe, welcomed him, grinning broadly. With his bald head and prominent bleached patches on his face, Noffe did not much resemble Ptolemy's murdered comrade Dr. Elchan, but some of the Tlulaxa racial features were similar. Seeing the man, Ptolemy felt a pang in his chest; he missed Elchan.

Noffe extended a hand to the new scientist. "Welcome to Denali, a place of unfettered discovery. Since Directeur Venport recommended you personally, I shall expect great things from you."

The administrator's voice had a similar timbre to Elchan's, which caused Ptolemy to hear an echo of his friend's dying screams in his head. He drew a deep breath and forced himself not to wince. "I am honored to be here, sir. This is what I need. This is what the human race needs . . . and I have a plan to stand up against the Butlerians."

Noffe seemed to hear his own set of remembered screams. "We all have a common goal here, my friend. Those monsters ransacked my labs on Tlulax, destroyed my work. They don't *want* us to discover anything." He blinked, brought himself back to the present. "Here on Denali, it is different. Our work is subsidized by Venport Holdings, and profitable discoveries will benefit the company. But also human civilization."

"I don't care if Josef Venport profits from my inventions." He was anxious to get started. "I prefer to give power to rational visionaries rather than violent barbarians."

After passing through three bulkhead doors into the heart of the facility, they reached Noffe's administrative office. The Tlulaxa man took a seat, and folded his hands on his lap. "My heart goes out to you—I read the report about what happened on Zenith. Please accept my assurance that you don't need to be afraid here."

Noffe leaned back, as if a weight much heavier than planetary gravity was pushing him down. "I used to think fear was a weakness. How could a timid, frightened person accomplish much, if he was held back by his worries? But the Butlerians turn fear into violence and panic into a weapon. By creating imaginary problems and raising the specter of nonexistent enemies, they transform common people into a wild herd that destroys everything they do not understand." He shook his head sadly. "And there is a great deal they do not understand."

Ptolemy swallowed hard and nodded. "We have to win this battle for the minds and future of the human race. I thought the Butlerians simply had a different point of view, that we could debate the matter in a rational way." He would never be able to forget the smashing, the ransacking, the wanton killings. "Now I see that they are evil. Truly evil. I will be one of your greatest soldiers in that upcoming war."

Noffe chuckled. "Oh, I expect you to be much more than just a soldier— I want you to be one of my generals."

The Tlulaxa administrator led him through the connected modules. With great pride, Noffe showed him a lab filled with sealed tanks containing the mutated, expanded brains of failed Navigators. They had been detached from physical bodies, reminding him of the legendary Cogitors, going back to before the days of the Jihad.

"Compared to us, these brains are as developmentally advanced as we are to a child learning his first steps." Noffe rapped his knuckles against one of the curved, transparent barriers. "But even so, they are dependent upon us for life support and communication with the outside world. These subjects did not prove acceptable as Navigator-candidates, but we can test their enhanced brains as components of new machines."

Ptolemy nodded. "My life's work, along with Dr. Elchan's, was to develop a superior interface between the human mind and artificial components. I want to free fragile humans from the biological prison of their mortality." He lowered his voice. "It's anathema to say this out in the League, but I believe the cymeks showed the way to a great many potential advances . . . if only Agamemnon and the other Titans hadn't been so evil." He shook his head.

Noffe responded with a vigorous nod. "I agree completely. If a crazed person uses a hammer to kill someone, does that mean we should outlaw hammers? Absurd!"

Ptolemy continued to talk about the work he and Elchan had done on Zenith. "All my notes and data were destroyed by the mob, but I'm confident that I can reproduce most of my studies. Unfortunately, it was very hard to find intact cymek walker bodies after the Butlerians got through with their purges."

Noffe's eyes sparkled. "Then I have something that may interest you." He led Ptolemy into a large hangar dome made of white plasteel tiles, brightly lit by glowglobes. Inside the bay stood an ominous machine—an intimidating combat body with hinged, reinforced legs and a shielded core, like a mechanical tarantula.

Ptolemy drew in a sharp breath. "A cymek warrior form—and it's complete! Until now, I've seen only scraps."

Noffe was magnanimous as he activated one of the hangar dome's viewing windows so that they could see the landscape around them. Through the deadly chlorine fog, Ptolemy discerned the shapes of similar arachnid machines as well as builder and flying bodies.

"There are at least twenty of them right here in the vicinity of the lab domes," Noffe said. "After Vorian Atreides killed Agamemnon and the last of the Titans, the neo-cymek brains at this base all perished in the dead-man code. The machine bodies are yours, if you can do something productive with them."

"Productive," Ptolemy mused. "And also defensive. I'll create a way for us to stand against the insanity sweeping the Imperium." Again, he reached out to grasp Noffe's hand and gave it a vigorous shake. "We will band together and work for the good of humanity."

Giving the latest technology and weaponry to your military forces might seem to be enough to overwhelm the enemy, but unless you bring mental firepower to the fight, it could all be for naught.

—a general of Old Earth

Over the decades that Gilbertus Albans had operated the Mentat School, a handful of graduates stood out in his recollection. In addition to Draigo Roget, who by now had surely found a powerful benefactor among the Landsraad nobles, he remembered Korey Niv, Hermine Castro, Sheaffer Parks, Farley Denton—and a number of exceptional Sisters from the school on Rossak. All of the faces streamed across his well-ordered memory, along with anecdotes about their experiences at the school.

And now Karee Marques had returned, one of the last pureblood Sorceresses. Because of her training in the Sisterhood, Karee already had an organized mind and precise control of her body. A perfect Mentat candidate, she had excelled here. Of the eight Sisters he had developed into Mentats, Karee was by far the best. He had spent much time discussing her with Erasmus. Gilbertus was very glad to see her back.

Upon landing at Lampadas, Karee had dispatched a message to inform him of her imminent arrival. The ancient woman stepped off a high-speed marshboat onto one of the floating decks around the school buildings. She was more than a century old, and her white hair had thinned; he hoped that she did not notice anything untoward about his own apparent age, which had not changed in years. The Sisters were extraordinarily perceptive. . . .

He met her at the dock and welcomed her warmly. She had visited him two other times in the years since her graduation, but had never brought gifts. Now he noted that she carried a small parcel.

After asking about the two recent Sister graduates, who had already returned to Rossak, Gilbertus led her inside the airy buildings that Karee knew so well. When they reached his office, she presented the parcel to him, smiling.

He raised his eyebrows, studying details and trying to look for clues. "Shall I have it scanned by security?"

Sister Karee laughed, a cheerful sound. "It may have explosive implications for Mentats, but I assure you there is no direct threat."

From the time he'd established the school, Gilbertus had set up stringent security precautions. His primary goal was to protect the memory core of Erasmus, but his general concerns had proved well founded when eight years ago a rival mental-techniques institute issued a legal challenge against the Mentat School and undermined Gilbertus's ability to obtain financing. He had never even heard of the rival institute before, but the competitor pursued the matter in court. After their case was dismissed as groundless, the incensed leader sent saboteurs to fire-bomb the Lampadas site, and the attack had resulted in the loss of two buildings and damage to others. In response, Emperor Salvador disbanded the rival school and sent its leaders to prison.

But Gilbertus trusted Karee Marques. He worked at the knots with his fingers, but the cords securing the package were tightly tied. "It seems you've provided me with quite a challenge."

Gilbertus was also worried about the remnants of technology he kept, the decommissioned combat meks and dismantled computer minds that served as valuable instructional tools—especially after the antics of Erasmus in terrifying the staid Alys Carroll. Manford Toronto had just returned to Lampadas with a larger group of enthusiastic Butlerians than had ever been gathered before, and the legless man had requested a private meeting with Gilbertus tomorrow.

Yes, the Mentat School needed security.

Finally, he removed the stubborn cord and pulled open the wrapping on the parcel to reveal several glass vials filled with ruby-red liquid.

Karee leaned forward. "It's called sapho, a potent distillation we have developed in my chemical studies on Rossak. It comes from the barrier roots on Ecaz." He raised his eyebrows, and she continued. "I've tested it on several Sisters, and all of them noticed the effects, but it is most profoundly effective among our Mentats."

Gilbertus held a bottle up to the light, and the rich color sparkled through the glass. "What does it do?"

"Promotes intense concentration and focus. Orders your thoughts, sharpens your acuity. I have tried it myself. After drinking even a small dose, one of my laboratory technicians developed many avenues of research that we hadn't considered before."

He decided to test the substance and ask Erasmus for his opinion. "Side effects?"

She opened her mouth, showed him a startling redness on her tissues. "It stains skin, so be careful not to spill it on your lips, or anywhere else. No other known side effects. If you find the sapho beneficial and decide to let your Mentat students use it, I can provide you with the distillation process. It is my gift back to this great school. I'm sure you can obtain the raw materials easily from merchants on Ecaz."

"Thank you." He set the vial back down without opening it. "I will try it later, after further study. I thank you for the opportunity. We must pursue every avenue to assist us in improving the human mind."

THE FOLLOWING MORNING, Gilbertus prepared for his meeting with Manford Torondo, the Mentat School's uneasy ally.

With a spring in her step, his student, Alys Carroll, ushered the Butlerian leader into his offices, and Gilbertus stood to receive him. Silent bearers carried Manford on a palanquin. The Butlerian leader did not pretend this was a social call. He spoke briskly. "We can all rejoice, Headmaster, for now we are able to expand our efforts and seize the full attention of the Imperium. Emperor Salvador has given our movement more than two hundred warships from the Army of Humanity."

"You have an admirable goal," Gilbertus said, because he was expected to.

"We continue to find violations, stubborn and foolish resistance. Therefore, I have decided to push the line back even farther. We must set an example. My own allies need to help us prove the point." Manford's eyes narrowed as he looked around the office, as if looking for any form of evil technology. Gilbertus felt a chill, aware that the robot's memory core was hidden inside the sealed cabinet. He knew Erasmus would be eavesdropping with his spyeyes even now.

"I want your school's help with this, Gilbertus Albans."

He mastered his expression, keeping his face a calm mask. "What is it you require from me?"

"I need Mentats who are trained as battle tacticians. With our newly acquired warships, I need Mentats to project battlefield scenarios. In a very literal sense, this will be a war for the hearts of humankind."

Gilbertus already knew his students were quite capable, since he and Draigo had played theoretical war games many times, yet he hesitated. "I suppose it could be done."

"Then it will be done. I'll need as many as you can provide—especially my Butlerian students."

Alys spoke up quickly. "I will volunteer for the effort. I can adjust my training accordingly." She looked at Manford, then at Gilbertus. "And I know many other students who are like me."

"I have no doubt of it," Manford said.

Gilbertus felt uneasy. He smiled and nodded.

"With your help," Manford continued, "we will lock down the unmonitored worlds, cleanse them and save them in spite of themselves. The machine lovers have their technology, but I shall have my Mentats."

"The mind of man is holy," Alys intoned.

Gilbertus forced himself not to look at the innocent-seeming cabinet where he kept Erasmus. "It may take months to prepare them adequately, but I'll implement the new curriculum tomorrow."

"Do it today," Manford said.

Alys opened the door, and Manford's palanquin bearers turned and carried him out of the office.

Off balance on Rossak, surrounded by strangers, Anna Corrino had warmed to Valya's friendship. Sensing the Princess's jealousy over any time that Valya spent with Dorotea, by necessity, Valya attempted to devote as much of her attention as possible to the Emperor's sister.

They spent days on end together, and Valya encouraged the young woman to confide in her, in particular about her romance with Hirondo Nef. It smacked of silly, youthful infatuation, Valya thought, but she said nothing about that aloud, only commiserated with her companion and consoled her for her miserable loneliness. As they talked, Valya smiled often to convince Anna that she was a close friend.

One morning, Valya led the girl down to the lowest interior level of cave tunnels, although the exit passages to the murky jungle floor had been permanently sealed. Anna's eyes were wide with fascination. "Are we supposed to be down here?" Her whisper showed eagerness to do something slightly forbidden.

"These levels contain utility, storage, and mechanical rooms for the caverns above. It's where a lot of the menial work is done. Back when this was a much larger city, a staff of males served as support workers, but the Reverend Mother has made the school a sanctuary for talented women . . . which means we must perform the work ourselves. All acolytes are expected to serve here in shifts— even the Emperor's sister." For herself, Valya would rather have been working with the breeding computers, but she concentrated on her obligations to Anna for the moment, which Raquella considered a priority.

Anna's expression fell. She was clearly disheartened by the unglamorous assignment. "Oh."

Valya, however, gave her a comradely pat on the back. "I'll join you for your shift in the sewing room, repairing robes. We can work together for a little while."

That cheered Anna. They walked past laundry stations where green-robed acolytes manually cleaned the garments on large, fixed-frame washboards, using water piped in from subterranean aquifers. The sewing room had long tables with robes and undergarments spread out on them; four sewing machines were attached to the tables, but most acolytes used needles and thread.

Valya pulled a white robe out of a large bin and sat in an available chair, spreading the robe on a tabletop to indicate an unraveled seam. "This is a Sorceress's robe. Those women are a little fussy, so make sure to do a very good job."

"I like to sew," Anna said. "Some of the ladies at court taught me to do old-fashioned embroidery. It seemed pointless at first, but eventually I found it calming, and my mind could wander."

Valya remembered what the proctor had taught her years ago, during her own first shift in the sewing room, and now she told the same story to Anna. "One of the great religious leaders of Old Earth, Mahatma Gandhi, used to mend his own garments. He was a simple man, but very complex in his thinking."

"Never heard of him." Showing little interest, Anna picked up the garment and fumbled with the thread. Valya found a black robe whose pocket needed mending and sat next to the Corrino girl. Anna loved to chatter, and now she mused, "Does Reverend Mother Raquella really have the voices of all her ancestors inside her head?"

"She has achieved a pinnacle of ability the rest of us can only dream about."

Anna's eyes lit up, and she said in an excited voice, "She says every one of us can become a Reverend Mother, too, if only we can focus our thoughts and become strong enough to survive the process."

"It's very dangerous," Valya cautioned. "No one except Raquella has succeeded in the transformation. In fact, most have died from the poison."

"So you haven't tried it yourself?"

"No!" Until the process was proven, Valya would never risk her family's future on such a capricious gamble. "I helped Sister Karee with her research to develop the next useful drug for potential candidates, but my other responsibilities for the Sisterhood are too important for me to take the risk myself."

"I think it would be fascinating to take the poison and hear voices." Anna plucked at the thread, poked the needle through, and drew the stitch tight. "My mother was just a concubine, and I never really knew her . . . but to have her whole life in my head! I can always read about the Corrino line in the histories, but I don't know much about my mother's side. The voices would tell me!"

We are cousins by blood, Valya thought. She would make sure Anna learned that, but not until a suitable time.

Valya tried not to fixate on her goal of achieving revenge for the Harkonnen name, but it was like a chronic injury to her psyche. Griffin had sent her no progress report whatsoever, but each day she expected to receive a triumphant message declaring that he had taken care of Vorian Atreides—preferably by a slow and painful death.

Anna chuckled. "I remember a jester at the Imperial Court who heard voices in his head. They said he was mad, and took him away."

Valya's nostrils flared. "The Reverend Mother is not insane. As soon as Karee Marques discovers the right transformational chemical, others will corroborate her claims."

"Maybe we should do it, just you and me!" Anna said in a conspiratorial tone. "We can be the first after Raquella!"

Valya raised her head in alarm. "Hush, don't talk like that—you aren't ready. *I'm* not even ready." She looked around to make sure none of the acolytes had heard Anna's comments. All of the previous volunteers had undergone the most rigid and demanding of psychological tests, yet still they failed. Anna Corrino was much too immature and unfocused.

Oblivious to her companion's alarm, the girl finished repairing the robe, then folded the garment and placed it on the table. She hummed, and finally mused in a flippant tone, "I was only being curious, wondering what it would be like. I'd like to have those abilities someday, that's all."

Valya had pondered that question herself many times, thinking that with the added skills of a Reverend Mother, the precise bodily control and the library of historical memories, she could be a formidable force to restore House Harkonnen. But if she died while attempting the transformation, her family would suffer the loss, and the entire burden of redemption from ignominy would be on Griffin's shoulders. She would never do that to her brother.

The other girl chattered away as they continued mending, but Valya said nothing.

THAT EVENING, VALYA had an uneasy feeling as she lay in her small private chamber, unable to sleep. Many of the younger Sisters shared quarters, but with so much of the cliff city empty, advanced Sisters such as herself were given their own rooms. Now, though, she thought she should have suggested sharing quarters with the Emperor's sister, just to cement their friendship . . . and permit her to watch the girl more closely.

At supper, while Anna told stories about the Imperial Court to other acolytes, with Valya dutifully at her side, Sister Dorotea had joined them. Dorotea's persistent concerns about Ingrid's death and her repeated prying into rumors of computers in the Sisterhood, made her an unpleasant dinner companion. Valya pretended to be cordial, not wanting to draw the suspicions of the other woman, but it was difficult, considering what she knew. For the moment, Dorotea considered her an ally, and Valya did not want to change that useful, lulling perception. . . .

Now as she tried to sleep, Valya's thoughts continued to agitate her, not merely concerns about Dorotea's suspicions, but worries over what Griffin was doing, as well as the responsibility of watching Anna, and the persistent question she always avoided—whether to attempt to become a Reverend Mother herself. If Valya were the first to succeed after Raquella, she could have the clout to rule the Sisterhood one day.

From her work with Sister Karee, she knew of many untried drugs developed in her laboratory, just waiting for volunteers to attempt them. But few women had the courage to take the leap, and anyone who seemed overly eager—such as Anna Corrino—was obviously unprepared.

For the time being, Karee Marques had traveled to Lampadas to meet with her former Mentat teacher, Gilbertus Albans. The forest pharmaceutical laboratory was empty, and even Dorotea did not spend her days there. Valya still had her access key, but rarely used it; Anna had begged her repeatedly for a secret tour of the place, and Valya had finally obliged the day before, just to quiet the girl.

But this evening there had been something more to Anna's intensity. The Princess had asked repeatedly about the pharmaceutical lab and the poisons waiting to be tested, and the next candidate who might make the attempt to become a Reverend Mother. When Valya scolded her for her unrealistic questions, Anna fell silent—too quickly and too easily, it seemed now.

With a strange knot of dread, Valya got up and searched her possessions, including the pockets of her robe. She was disturbed to discover that her laboratory key had vanished. Pulse racing, she dressed in a rush, grabbed a glowlamp, and hurried to Anna's sleeping chamber in the acolyte section. Sadly, she was not surprised to discover the girl's bunk empty, although her two roommates were fast asleep.

She knew where Anna had gone, but didn't dare raise the alarm or rouse other Sisters. This was her problem, her failing, and she had to deal with it immediately.

With her heart pounding more from fear than exertion, Valya ran across the polymerized treetop and took the cage lift down to the jungle floor. After dark, the wilds were far more dangerous than by day, but she feared the Emperor's sister intended to take an even greater risk than the jungle's natural hazards. Valya broke out in a cold sweat. If anything happened to Anna, the political repercussions would ruin all of the Harkonnen family's hopes.

Using the glowlamp to light her way, Valya ran along the tangled path to the enormous hollowed tree, and found that the black metal door stood ajar. Breathing sharply, she hurried into the main laboratory chamber. The various workstations were empty, all the experiments shut down without Karee to supervise the sensitive work.

Hearing a furtive noise, she saw Anna in the shadows. The young woman didn't seem surprised to see Valya there, and she spoke in an excited whisper, although they were the only ones in the chamber. "I have one of the sample drugs here. I can't tell what it is, though." She held up an earthenware jar, removed the lid. "I've been looking for the one that smells the best." She pulled out a small, bluish capsule.

Valya darted toward her and grabbed the capsule from her hand. The earthenware jar fell, breaking on the floor and scattering pills.

Anna scowled at her. "I was just getting one out for you. You and I can take the drug together and become the first new Reverend Mothers. We'll show everyone!" She knelt to scoop up some of the fallen capsules, but Valya yanked her to her feet.

"You should not have come in here without permission! Do you know how many Sisters have already died?"

Anna's eyes sparkled with tears, hurt by her friend's scolding. "I was going to bring pills back and share them with you." She tried to pull free, but Valya held her firmly by the arm.

Breathless, Sister Dorotea ran into the lab. Her eyes were bright and suspicious as she glared at Valya. "I followed you. What are you doing in here?"

A flash of annoyance crossed Valya's mind. Dorotea was spying on her? "Don't worry, I've taken care of it." She spoke with hardness in her voice, attempting to dispel the older woman's suspicions. "There's no cause for concern. Reverend Mother instructed me to watch over Sister Anna. Sometimes, she's . . . impetuous, but I caught her in time. No harm done." Still holding Anna's arm, she steered the girl toward the door. For good measure, she shot a menacing glower at the other Sister, shifting the blame. "With Sister Karee gone, this lab is your responsibility. You should never leave this station unattended, even at night. There might have been a catastrophe."

Dorotea remained disturbed. "I have to report this to Reverend Mother."

"Yes," Valya said. "We do."

Anna tried to stifle her tears, while Valya led her away, whispering to the acolyte, "No need to worry. I'll take care of this—but don't ever try to slip away from me again."

Despite an appearance of infallibility, computer projections are not pre-scient.

—TICIA CENVA, former leader of the Sorceresses of Rossak

The following day, Raquella read the full report submitted by Sister Peri-anna, detailing her service to Roderick Corrino's wife at the Imperial Court. After being caught spying in an inept manner, Perianna had escaped before too many questions could be asked, and had returned to Rossak in a downcast mood. Disappointed, Raquella set aside the report. Perianna had lost her vital position in the Palace, and her efforts had secured nothing more than trivial details about domestic interactions among Salvador, Roderick, and their wives. Noth-ing of much value.

With a sour taste in her mouth, Raquella left her office and went to observe classes in progress. She liked to vary her routes and times to get a more complete picture of what was going on. When Sister Dorotea called her name in one of the passageways, Raquella felt a chill run down her spine, but she forced herself to remain calm, even though the memory-voices in her head clamored out a warn-ing. Dorotea had become bothersome lately, and even Raquella's latent fondness for her granddaughter had worn thin.

The previous evening, Dorotea had marched into her private chambers with Sister Valya and Anna Corrino in tow, tattling that Anna had trespassed in the jungle laboratories. Though alarmed by the information, Raquella gave a stern answer. "She is Sister Valya's responsibility. I don't need to be troubled by every prank or indiscretion committed by an acolyte."

Dorotea had not been pleased by the reaction, and had left muttering in dis-content. Now she came running up again, taking deep breaths to calm herself. "Reverend Mother, I have read the report of Sister Ingrid's death, and I am not satisfied with the conclusions. I believe the matter warrants further investigation."

Clasping her hands in front of her, Raquella said, "Ingrid was an impetuous girl who showed great potential. Her death was a loss for the Sisterhood, but the matter is closed."

Dorotea was palpably angry. "Are you too busy to deal with a *murder*, Reverend Mother?"

"Murder?" Raquella narrowed her gaze. "The girl fell from the cliff. It's a dangerous path—where she should not have been. That's all there was to it. Accidents happen."

"What if someone pushed her off the cliff?"

"You suggest a serious crime was committed by one of your fellow Sisters? Do you have evidence of this?" Raquella placed her hands on her hips. "Any evidence at all?"

Dorotea lowered her gaze. "No, Reverend Mother."

As if coming to the rescue, the aged Sorceress Sabra Hublein hurried toward her, and Raquella could read the alarm on the old woman's face. Her white robe was dirty on the bottom front, suggesting that she may have tripped in her rush down from the breeding-record caves.

With barely a glance at Dorotea, Sabra said, "Excuse the interruption, Reverend Mother, but I must speak with you alone." She lowered her voice. "We've made an important projection."

Pleased to have an excuse to end the conversation, Raquella dismissed Dorotea. Though the other Sister was obviously dissatisfied, the Reverend Mother took Sabra by the arm and hurried her back through the tunnels, past classroom chambers, and into her private offices, where they could meet without being overheard.

Sabra whispered, "Our computers have sorted through projection after projection, using every variable, all the mountains of data—and I have alarming news regarding a specific noble bloodline." Her voice was rough, like tearing paper. "Using all of our computing power, we have collated the bloodline data and projected descendants using the available samples of DNA from our entire breeding library, applying primary probabilities, secondary, tertiary, and beyond. We may have reached the limits of the computers' capabilities, but I am confident the projection is valid."

"Whose bloodline?" Raquella asked, trying to be calm. "Whose descendants?"

"Emperor Salvador Corrino! We have modeled his possible offspring through Empress Tabrina, or through any of his current concubines, and all other likely noble bloodlines. His specific Corrino genetics is the common factor."

Raquella could see it was a worthwhile investigation. "And what have you found? Why are you so alarmed?"

Sabra's eyes glittered. "It's remarkably consistent, and even our Sister Mentats verified the general conclusion that if Emperor Salvador is allowed to have offspring—through any likely mate—his family will produce the most horrific tyrant in history, within five to ten generations. If the projection models are correct, billions or trillions of lives could be at stake, bloodshed on the scale of the Jihad."

"You can predict that?"

"Oh yes, Reverend Mother—with a fair degree of accuracy. If this bloodline continues, a resultant tyrant is destined to inflict chaos and carnage, all across the Imperium. Naturally, there are many factors in creating such a model, and the computers can't be absolutely certain, but the probability is disturbingly high. I would strongly advise, as a precaution, that we find some way to prevent the Emperor from having children."

"What about his brother, Roderick? He already has children. Do we need to curtail the Corrino bloodline entirely?"

Sabra showed a hint of relief. "No, Roderick Corrino has a different mother, and a different genetic makeup. In fact, he has none of the dangerous factors, nor do his four children. We've already been keeping a close eye on them. Only Salvador raises our concerns."

According to the records, Salvador's mother had been emotionally unbalanced and had tried to kill Emperor Jules when he decided to end her service as his concubine. In contrast, Roderick's mother was not only lovely, but highly intelligent. Anna's mother was also quite normal, good genetic stock. The flaw, then, came from Salvador's maternal line. Raquella was not alone in believing that Roderick would have made a better Emperor than his brother.

The chorus of voices inside her mind agreed, as well.

"Let me review the data, and we'll decide on the next step. Despite the dynastic needs, there's little immediate chance Salvador will get the Empress pregnant—they can barely tolerate each other, according to the reports from Sisters Dorotea and Perianna. We may, however, need to monitor his concubines. . . ."

"This is dangerous enough, Reverend Mother, that we should not leave it to chance. If we nip the problem in the bud now, the course of humanity will be relatively easy to correct."

"And we can do it," Raquella said. "No one else will even see the threat." She smiled inwardly. This was exactly the sort of challenge for which she had envisioned and guided the Sisterhood.

The voices in her Other Memories continued to whisper warnings, reacting with alarm and confirming what Raquella had already decided. "I rarely leave anything to chance, Sabra. I prefer to sterilize Salvador instead of having him killed, but it must be done. It will be our contribution to the welfare of the Imperium."

A pledge of loyalty is like a promise to God.
—ANARI IDAHO, Swordmaster
to Manford Torondo

S ince Manford was pleased with the concessions he had received from Emperor Salvador, Anari was pleased as well. Two hundred and thirty Army of Humanity ships had been given to him, so that his Butlerians could expand their operation of rooting out any seductive technology. Soon he would have more tactically trained Mentats, too.

It had always been Anari's greatest glory to help Manford achieve what Saint Serena and Rayna Butler had commanded him to do, but right now she was especially happy to be traveling with him to Ginaz, home of the Swordmaster School. On the flight, Anari had tended to his every need, and she was distracted by nostalgic thoughts. She had spent many years training on the island-studded planet, becoming a certified Swordmaster.

Propped in his seat, Manford looked out the windowport of the descending shuttle. She bent close, her face near his, and together they gazed down upon the sunlit ocean, catching their first glimpse of the archipelago that held the Swordmaster training camps.

Manford gave her a warm, wistful smile. "With you speaking on my behalf, Anari, we'll secure more than enough Swordmasters to lead the crusaders on all our new ships."

Her heart swelled with the compliment. "I have little to do with it, Manford. Dedication and morality are ingrained in every Swordmaster. They are your paladins of humanity and will join our cause because of *you*, and because it is the right thing to do."

He patted her arm. "That doesn't diminish the fact that I'm glad to have you here with me."

The shuttle landed on the main island where countless Swordmaster students had been trained in the years since the death of Jool Noret. Anari buckled on the harness, tightening the straps across her chest and waist to make sure it was secure, then turned and stooped. Manford grasped her shoulders and hoisted himself into the socket formed to hold his hips. She stood on muscular legs, barely noticing the added weight, and walked proudly down the ramp.

A group of bronzed, shirtless fighters had come to greet them. Though all of her fellow students had long since dispersed on private missions throughout the Imperium, she recognized two of her Swordmaster teachers among the welcoming committee. Rather than calling out to her instructors, however, she pretended to be invisible. Anari did not wish to overstep her bounds. In this situation, alongside her beloved Manford, she was here solely for him, to carry him, to serve him, to help him—not to show off her own important position. She would not speak unless he needed her to do so.

While she stood under the bright sunlight, Manford regarded the welcoming committee. He said nothing, waiting until one of the instructors hesitantly bowed, and then all the Swordmasters did likewise. It was a sufficient sign of respect. Manford gestured them up, smiling benevolently.

"I come to you with a great opportunity," he said. "Even though our crusade against the machines is over and we defeated Omnius, the human race still needs Swordmasters. We have a new battle, not just to fight the oppressors, but to save our future. Do you still remember how to fight?"

A resounding cheer rose from those gathered. "Yes!" More of the muscular men and women had come to the landing area to see Manford.

Swordmasters had little use for ranks and authority. They trained with one another, bested one another. The superior fighters were obvious to any observer, and did not need special insignia, other than the weapons they carried in scabbards. One of the trainers, Master Fleur—among Anari's toughest instructors—now acted as spokesman.

"We would welcome a new challenge. The Swordmasters of Ginaz have long awaited a worthy opponent. We follow the teachings of the great Jool Noret, but many of us work as mere bodyguards, or travel across the new Imperium, offering our services to the downtrodden. However, we have always hoped for more."

Anari could almost hear the smile in Manford's voice as he said, "Then I'm very glad I've come."

ON THE GRASSY hills above a black-sand beach, Swordmasters trained for combat. Master Fleur had set up a special demonstration for Manford, who sat in a special chair. Beside him, Anari stood watching eagerly. Part of her longed to participate, remembering when she'd been a student herself. She knew that if she asked Manford, he would grant permission for her to join in, but she had a higher purpose now. Though she thought fondly of her training days, her present duties were far more important.

Master Fleur had called for a demonic-looking black metal robot to be placed in the middle of the open grassy area. The enormous multi-armed battle mek towered four meters high, a robotic Goliath salvaged from one of the abandoned machine vessels. It stood on legs like pillars, with spiny defensive protrusions at its elbows, shoulders, and waist. The embedded projectile weapons in its four arms were deactivated, but the mek had other brutal fighting techniques and enough engine strength to level buildings.

Looking tiny, the Swordmaster trainees ringed it, ready to demonstrate their prowess with primitive but effective pulse-swords.

Fleur said to Manford, "We continue to hone our fighting abilities, should the thinking machines ever return."

Anari knew that being so close to the enormous, nightmarish mek made Manford uneasy, but she would protect him. He resented the idea that the Swordmasters, as well as the Mentat School, felt the need to keep the hateful reminders as a necessary part of training, but he grudgingly understood. Another compromise, a necessary evil.

One of the students activated the mek's power systems, and the optic threads glowed like a constellation of stars on its polished black face as it assessed its surroundings. The battle machine swiveled at the waist, stretched, and raised its mammoth shoulder carapace. The blunt head turned in a complete circle to scan the opponents arrayed against it.

With a yell, the Swordmaster trainees threw themselves forward.

Manford watched with interest. Anari's eyes gleamed as she recalled many such exercises. Growing up as an orphan, she'd been forced to overcome great difficulties and had fought countless opponents to prove she was good enough. In her early teens, she had made her way to Ginaz and demanded to be trained. In short order, she defeated five people who tried to deny her entry to the school, and finally the masters allowed her in. There, she studied every sort of combat technique: hand-to-hand as well as tactical, fighting against humans or machines. Her body had been bruised and battered countless times, but she had always healed, and her heart had never been defeated.

One of her comrades had been Ellus, the only trainee who could fight her to a stalemate on a regular basis. Eventually the two became lovers, but they took more physical enjoyment from the sweat and exhilaration of combat than from sex. Because of that, Anari had been able to put aside her feelings for the man when they both left to join the Butlerians. Since meeting Manford, she had formed more important goals and accepted a mission that went beyond the hormonal drives of ordinary humans. In Anari's mind, loyalty and dedication achieved a higher state.

Anari remembered when she and Ellus had fought against an equivalent model of battle mek, and the two of them had destroyed the gigantic opponent. While she remained Manford's close companion, Ellus had gone off with two other Swordmasters and a group of dedicated Butlerians to locate and obliterate dozens of lost cymek bases.

He was expected to be gone for months, but she knew Ellus would return to Lampadas and announce his complete success. At one time she might have missed him for being gone for so long, but now she had Manford . . . more of Manford than any other person would ever have. That kind of love was as pure and clear as a Hagal diamond.

Now, she stood restless and fascinated as the Swordmaster trainees pummeled the combat mek, hammering at it like an exuberant and deadly mob, but the hulking battle machine was not easily defeated. The trainees fought on like wolves trying to bring down a furious mammoth.

The huge mek lashed out with its four jointed arms, clacking the articulated pincers. It seized one of the pulse-swords and cast it aside, yanking so hard that it dislocated the fighter's shoulder. The disarmed man cried out in pain and staggered out of the way as two trainees dove into the gap to cover for him. The battle mek swatted them aside. Then it moved backward suddenly and thrust a spiny arm, jerking sideways to eviscerate one of the trainees. Spurting blood, the victim stumbled and coughed. Finally another fighter dragged him away, but it was clearly a mortal wound.

The sight of blood increased the skilled frenzy of the remaining trainees, and they swarmed over the machine. Their pulse-swords deactivated one of the mek's four fighting arms. The battle mek lurched upward and swept sideways, bowling down three more trainees, who sprang back to their feet and leaped away.

The mek swiveled and thrust with its three active arms in a flurry of sharp, stabbing blows. It attempted to fire its useless projectile weapons, but hesitated when the integrated weapons systems did not work.

Anari was breathing hard, eyes intense. Her sweaty palm squeezed the hilt of her own pulse-sword so tightly she thought she might crush it. She glanced down at Manford in his chair, to find he was watching her instead of the fight. His eyes glinted with understanding. "Go," he whispered.

Like a boulder shot from a catapult, Anari launched herself into the fray with a wild and delighted grin on her face. Her first blow with the pulse-sword sent a numbing vibration all the way up her arm, making a serious dent in the machine's carapace.

Anari switched the pulse-sword to her other hand and continued fighting. A well-placed strike to the mek's smooth metal face smashed a set of optic threads, taking them off-line. Working together, three of the trainees had used their swords to lock one of the robot's jointed fighting arms.

The rest of the fighters hurled themselves upon the battle mek with no regard for personal safety, stabbing and pounding. Anari's strike to the optic threads had created a blind spot, and a trainee was able to reach the access plate beneath the mechanical head. He tore off the plate and thrust his pulse-sword deep into the robot's core.

Fading and crippled, the battle mek could no longer fight. Anari grabbed one of the useless, jointed arms and hauled herself onto the mammoth machine's shoulders in a strange parody of how Manford rode on her shoulders. There, she used her pulse-sword to pry the mek's head free from its neck socket.

With a groan, the mammoth machine lost its balance and toppled over. Within moments, the trainees had smashed it into countless pieces, destroying every hint of a functional circuit.

Satisfied, proud, and exhilarated, Anari walked back to Manford. She wiped perspiration from her forehead and gave him a bow of thanks. "It was beautiful," he said to her, "to see you in your element like that."

Outside the fighting perimeter, the eviscerated trainee gurgled and died. One of the female field medics had tried to stop the bleeding and stuff the man's intestines back into his abdomen. Now she just shook her head, raised her bloody hands, and bowed in respect to the fallen warrior for the bravery he had shown, even though he'd only been a trainee.

Fleur glanced at the dead fighter with a flicker of sadness, then devoted his attention to the rest of the combatants. "Swordmasters fight, and Swordmasters die. That is why we're here."

"The mind of man is holy," Anari said.

Manford spoke aloud to Master Fleur. "Humans can be swayed so easily, and someone needs to keep them on course—someone with a clear vision. A few people may not like it, but we Butlerians have a higher calling."

"Your calling is our calling." Fleur raised his chin. "Observe, they are nearly finished."

All twelve of the remaining trainees continued to smash the combat robot, even after it toppled over. One of them disengaged a set of the jointed fighting

arms and held them up like a trophy. The other trainees methodically dismantled the fighting robot and left the pieces strewn across the grass. One held up
the severed ovoid head.

"Another opponent vanquished, Master!" he shouted. Around him, the Swordmaster trainees looked battered and exhausted, but their eyes glowed with feral
excitement.

Manford said to Fleur, "We need hundreds more like these to join our cause.
With our new fleet, we must move against countless worlds, to watch them and
ensure that dangerous technology never runs rampant again."

"You will have as many Swordmasters as you need," promised Fleur.

"Good. Very good," Manford said, then continued in a lower voice. "Not all
of our enemies are as obvious as a fighting mek, however."

Any attempt to amend sacred texts, however fallible they may be, is inherently dangerous.

—excerpt from confidential report, for the Emperor's eyes only

I need a convincing argument that the old Suk School building should be torn down, to send a message," Salvador said with a groan. "The Butlerians forced me to agree to it, and they are going to destroy it one way or another—but I need you to provide me with a legitimate-sounding excuse."

Roderick wrestled with necessities as the two brothers met in the Palace's lush conservatory. "It's a very sad thing, and Manford Torondo is wrong to resent them so. We both know the Suk doctors provide a valuable service, to those who can afford it. They are careful not to use questionable technology."

"Questionable technology? Manford's mobs question *all* technology."

"If our own father had sought medical attention in time, he would not have died of a brain tumor."

Salvador sniffed. "And then I wouldn't have become supreme ruler when I did, so there is a silver lining."

Roderick nodded slowly. He had to come up with a good justification to knock down the old school headquarters. If he made the case that the former Suk administrator, Elo Bando, had duped Salvador out of a fortune for unnecessary medical procedures, that might cause enough of a scandal—but it would also make his brother look like a fool. He doubted he could even convince Salvador that he'd been deceived. "Maybe we can play up the questions of financial impropriety. There have been rumors, you know."

"Or start a rumor of our own that they have a functioning computer locked in a back room somewhere." Salvador let out an impatient sigh. "Manford's people won't bother to check their facts. They'll raze the building to the ground, and it won't matter whether or not they find anything."

"That would certainly work, but a lie like that would make an enemy out of the Suk School," Roderick said, with rising alarm.

"We haven't seen thousands of Suk doctors swarming into the capital threatening violence—it's the Butlerians we have to worry about. I need to throw them a bone, and Manford Torondo made it clear what he wants." Salvador shook his head, and his eyes appeared haunted. "But we have to salvage the situation somehow with the Suk doctors. Let's request a dedicated, personal physician for me from the Suk School on Parmentier, as a show of our support. Once we send Manford and his mindless minions on their way, I can make amends with the Suks."

As they paced among the exotic foliage in convoluted planters throughout the conservatory, Roderick tried again to advise caution, but Salvador said, "You've counseled me in the past to be logical rather than emotional, but I'm dealing with excitable people. I hate being boxed in, but I'm forced to appease the Butlerians. If they ever turn against me, they'll drag the entire Corrino family through the streets and put someone else on the throne."

"Don't worry, Brother," Roderick said. "I'd never let that happen."

THE NEXT MORNING, Emperor Salvador awoke with the decision that he would name his first son Salvador II. (Roderick would have been his second choice.) The trouble was, he had no sons, and no daughters, either. Not by his wife or any of his concubines.

As Emperor, Salvador was expected to have an heir sooner or later—preferably a legitimate one—and the Empress knew her duties in this regard. It was stipulated in the marriage contract.

The previous evening, he and Tabrina had not quarreled for a change, which gave him faint reason to hope. During the afternoon, Tabrina had talked with the dowager Orenna about her own stifled relationship with Emperor Jules, and that had apparently gotten the Empress thinking. She and Salvador had a pleasant meal, fine wine, and a nice long talk that lasted far into the night. Talking like ambassadors from countries that had long been at war, they carefully discussed how they might find ways to get along better in the future. Alas, their rapprochement had not included a shared bed, not yet, but he did choose not to spend the night with one of his concubines, either.

Early the next morning, dressed in an elegant bathrobe and undergarments (that his advisers assured him were seductive), he padded along a second floor corridor toward Tabrina's private quarters. He smelled of expensive cologne, and the patch of wispy brown hair on top of his head glistened with aromatic mousse.

He knocked on her ornate door, and was greeted by a maidservant with an oval face and good figure. Not as attractive as his concubines, but appealing nonetheless. At the moment, however, his own wife commanded his attention. The maidservant looked very surprised to see him, but he pushed his way past her. "I'm here for the Empress."

Ahead, Tabrina's dressing room door was ajar, and he nudged it open. "Good morning, my dear." He gave her his friendliest smile.

Tabrina turned, looking startled and irritated. Her dark, almond-shaped eyes raked over his hair and robe, and her expression became bemused, but her voice was surly. "What is it you want?" The friendliness of their dinner conversation was gone.

Taken aback, Salvador stammered at first, then said, "I thought we might complete what we started last night. Seal the new phase of our relationship."

"What new phase?"

"We got along so well. . . ."

"Then have you come here to tell me about my expanded role in the government? Am I appointed to a new position? Commerce adviser, diplomat, legislator?"

"I, uh, haven't met with my advisers yet."

"Hence you have no reason to be in my bedchamber, do you?"

"But I . . . I am the Emperor. I can command you to my bed!"

Tabrina's upraised eyebrows and icy stare answered far more clearly than words. Finally, she said, "Stop wasting my valuable time and go to one of your concubines if you can't control your urges."

Flustered and confused, he backed out of the doorway and beat a hasty retreat, not feeling at all like the ruler of thousands of worlds.

Salvador ate a large breakfast alone at the long dining table that he should have shared with his Empress. He wished he'd never listened to his advisers, who insisted that the marriage with House Péle was a perfect political match. Tabrina behaved so pretentiously for a woman from an unsophisticated, albeit affluent, family.

Roderick came in as the Emperor was drinking his first cup of coffee laced with melange. He recognized his brother's sullen mood instantly. "What's wrong, Salvador?"

With his thick blond hair and chiseled features, Roderick looked entirely relaxed in his handsome body. Worst of all, *he* had a happy marriage and four fine children. Still, Salvador tried not to take his frustrations out on Roderick. He sighed and said, "I'm just despondent over my relationship with the Empress—or my lack of one." He blinked down at his plate of food. "I didn't even remember to have my meal tested for poisons. Do I look all right? Do you see my skin changing color?" He rubbed his temples. "Is my voice wavering? Anything in my eyes?"

"No, you look perfectly normal, though more distraught than usual. You see a new doctor every week. We should see about getting you a consistent personal physician." His expression became businesslike. "Let me interview them, so that I can make sure you get only the best the Suk School has to offer."

"You're so good to me, Roderick, but I miss how attentive Elo Bando was to my medical needs—he really understood my ills."

A flash of displeasure crossed the younger brother's face. "Yes, but Dr. Bando is gone. We have to find a suitable alternative." Roderick lifted a silver coffeepot, refilled Salvador's cup, and poured his own.

"I want only the best."

As the ruler of the vast Imperium, Salvador had to keep his health perfect, but he had many ailments, most of them caused by the stress of his position. Yes, he needed a doctor close to his side at all times, someone familiar with every aspect of Salvador's medical file, ready to respond to any problem.

"The threat of assassination is always present, so we need a doctor we can absolutely trust," Roderick said.

The Emperor looked down at his coffee. "*You* are the only person I trust with my life, Roderick. Please send word to the main Suk School on Parmentier, and begin the process of winnowing down the candidates."

Roderick considered. "Well, you did have the head of the school as your personal physician once."

"Yes, and I liked him. I haven't felt truly healthy since he killed himself." He let out a long sigh.

"Why not demand the new head of the Suk School as your private doctor? Dr. Zhoma is probably the most competent physician they have. I will interview her. She served well when you asked her to confirm the genetic samples of Vorian Atreides."

Salvador had not been impressed with her. "Not much of a personality, or bedside manner. She's gruff, unfriendly—"

"And *competent*. I have studied her record, Salvador. She is businesslike and reliable, and her medical knowledge is thorough."

"Sounds like propaganda." He slurped his coffee. "But you're right—I haven't had good luck choosing my own doctors, and the head of the Suk School is an appropriately impressive person to tend to my medical needs. I'll rely on your advice."

Roderick nodded. "With your permission, I'll contact Dr. Zhoma privately and request her services. This new position will give her a great deal of personal and political clout, more than making up for the loss of her old school building in Zimia. We can convey to the doctor that we still privately support the school and their efforts to help humanity, despite the political realities of the Butlerians. A bit of necessary give and take."

"Good, I like that. There's no way to keep both sides completely happy, but that may smooth some ruffled feathers." Yes, Roderick would have made a far better Emperor . . . and without his shoulder to lean on, Salvador would have been far weaker. "Promise Dr. Zhoma that if she becomes my personal physician, and does the job I expect of her, I will do what I can to protect the Suk School on Parmentier, guaranteeing their autonomy or something. She can leave that partner of hers in charge in her absence, Dr. Waddiz."

"Yes, I'll take care of it."

LATER THAT MORNING, for his first official meeting, a small delegation came to Salvador in the Imperial Audience Chamber, all holding bound books and ready to make a presentation. Dressed in the pale-blue uniforms of the Royal Printing Guild, they bowed before the Emperor and his brother.

The eldest of the group, Nablik Odessa, was a dark-skinned woman with a jowly face and intelligent eyes. She headed the pressmen's organization. "Sire, we are pleased to present you with the new edition of the *Orange Catholic Bible*, fresh off the presses. As soon as we receive your seal of approval, we can print the first hundred million copies for distribution to the populace." She extended a thick volume bound in orange leather.

"We present you with the Emperor Salvador Edition," one of the other printers said, a small man with a gray mustache. He beamed. "Do you like it, Sire? Is there anything you wish changed?"

Salvador chuckled. "You want me to copyedit the whole book at a glance?"

"No, Sire. I'm very sorry, but I'm a bit excited." The small man fidgeted, watching as the Emperor studied the title page with his name on it, then thumbed through the book.

"It is a handsome volume. Worthy of my name on it." He looked at Odessa. "You've checked this for accuracy?"

"Entire teams have checked it, Sire. Every word. I assure you, we took extraordinary quality-control measures."

Salvador glanced over at Roderick, then back at the printers. "Our theologians argued for five years about the disputed sections of the previous edition, and we've struggled to remove all the controversial aspects. I don't want any riots this time."

Odessa looked at her colleagues. "That part of the process is out of our control, Sire. We only produce the physical book."

Salvador closed the volume. "Well, then, I don't want to hear about one misspelled word in here, because that would reflect badly on me. The bulk of the funding comes from my own coffers."

"The book is clean, Sire—you have my word."

"All right, then. Start the presses."

"The copy you hold is from the first printing, a limited special edition, with all copies numbered."

"Yes, I see I have number one."

"We have brought additional copies with us." Odessa motioned to the books her companions held, and to more volumes stacked on tables at the rear of the audience chamber.

Roderick cleared his throat, leaned closer to his brother. "I requested them. If you could sign some for various dignitaries, we will distribute them on a priority basis, according to a list I've compiled." He paused, fighting back an expression of distaste. "And a personal one for Manford Torondo."

Salvador was annoyed, but he understood the necessity. "Do you think he'll feel honored to receive it?"

"Probably not, but he'll be incensed if you don't send him one."

"Yes, yes, I see what you mean."

Roderick handed him a pen, and he signed and personalized a copy for Manford, before passing it along.

"Many nobles have asked for your signature," Odessa said, smiling.

"Half of them would prefer to see it on a letter of resignation," the Emperor said with a small smile, "or on a large credit transfer."

Then he signed the twenty books held by the delegation, adding personalizations for various dignitaries according to notes his brother gave him.

Small experiences form the basis of our existence. This is calculable.
—Erasmus Dialogues

Karee Marques had departed after her visit, and Gilbertus had heard no word from Draigo Roget. The Headmaster felt very alone at the Mentat School, but he did have time for his own quiet work. He had made up his mind to take yet another risk for Erasmus.

He spoke to the independent robot's shimmering memory core. "It has taken a great deal of effort, Father, but I have a surprise for you. I even bypassed your spyeyes to keep it a secret."

Erasmus sounded delighted. "I have learned much from surprises."

"It requires that you come with me." He placed the spherical memory core into a valise and carried it outside, walking confidently to the little marina built out onto the broad marsh lake. No one asked the school headmaster where he was going.

Gilbertus boarded a small motorboat, tucked the valise under a bench, and launched the craft out onto the sunlit, greenish waters of the marsh lake. As he sped over the water, insects buzzed around him despite the electronic repellant system on the bow.

When he approached a small island adorned with tall reeds and gnarled trees, he circled to the far side, out of view from the school, and steered the boat into a narrow waterway overhung by drooping trees and vines that touched the water. The boat nudged the foliage out of the way as he slid past a muddy beach. After Draigo's graduation and departure, Gilbertus had gone here several times, bringing components from the teaching storeroom, piece by piece, until he had assembled his surprise for Erasmus.

A concealed finger pier emerged automatically from the wall of plant life, giving Gilbertus a place to dock. He stepped out of the craft, carrying the valise, and opened the case so that the memory core's optic threads could drink in the delicious details.

Tiny speakers projected the robot's voice. "A new environment! Is this our destination?"

Carrying the core, Gilbertus pushed past thick, overhanging boughs, following a subtle but memorized path through the muck, until they arrived at the small wooden cottage that he'd had constructed as a private retreat. The school staff knew about his contemplation cottage, but not what he kept inside. The windows were covered, and the building well sealed.

He fished keys from his waistcoat pocket, unlocked the cottage door, and entered the one-room building. In the middle of the floor stood a battered, deactivated combat robot. "I did this for you—a new body," he said. "It's only temporary, but it can grant you mobility for a while."

The robot's voice answered after a long pause. "Very dangerous . . . but much appreciated. Thank you." The simulated voice sounded a little giddy.

Gilbertus inserted the memory core into a port in the combat robot's body, snapping the connections into place. He had already removed the mek's original rudimentary control mind, and now Erasmus made his own new linkages. It would never be the same as the familiar flowmetal form he used to have, on which he loved to wear elegant robes and mimicked human expressions. The original Erasmus body had been destroyed on Corrin, but this would have to do for now.

Gilbertus felt a surge of excitement as the robot body began to move. The mek had been built for strength and power, not grace, and Erasmus took slow steps at first. The visual sensors activated, the speakerpatch thrummed to life, and the voice came out sounding blunt and unfamiliar. "This is . . . marvelous, my son."

"Thank you. I'm sorry I can't do better."

"Not yet. But I have faith in you."

Erasmus began to walk his new body around the small cottage, taking bold steps across the hardwood floor. "Some of the systems need fine-tuning, but I can perform the repairs internally."

Taking the clumsy mek outside, Gilbertus led him along hidden trails through the marsh grasses. "This is a far cry from our casual strolls through your contemplation gardens on Corrin, but it's the best we've had in a long time."

"And our conversations can be just as stimulating."

At their approach, an immense red-winged heron lifted off from the swampy water and soared into the sky.

"This gives you a chance to stretch your legs and remember how you were as an independent robot, but we have to be careful. If the Butlerians discovered this, they would destroy you forever." The words caught in his throat, and he felt tears burning in his eyes. "I would never want that."

In a pool of sunshine just offshore, two large green-and-black humps broke the surface of the water. Wary of the creatures that inhabited the marsh lake, Gilbertus took a step back from the shore, but Erasmus used the combat mek's visual sensors. "Just paddle tortoises—I've studied them in the school's science library, but there is little information available. Human biologists really should pay more attention to the diversity of this continent."

"I'll look them up when I get back to the school."

The combat mek swiveled toward him. "No need. I shall capture one for study—we can dissect it together." Impulsive and overly excited with his new freedom, Erasmus waded out into the water toward the tortoises. He sloshed his heavy body into the muck, and brown water rose to his chest.

"This is not necessary," Gilbertus called. "The marshes here are unstable. I can't guarantee the integrity of your body." In fact, he had made certain the mek was not durable, just in case. And he had used a Mentat projection to predict how the independent robot would react. The lowlands around his contemplation cottage were surrounded by treacherous muck, an added security measure.

The robot lumbered into the soupy mud, intent on the slow-witted turtles dozing in the sun-dappled water ten meters from shore. The turtles raised their bullet-shaped heads and regarded the burly machine that trudged and splashed into their territory.

Erasmus raised one of the mek's weapon arms. "The stun circuitry is not functional," he said.

"Intentionally disabled," Gilbertus admitted. "Remember the Butlerian requirements."

"Then I shall capture a specimen manually." He pushed deeper into the muck.

"Please don't. Be content with your mobility here on the island. If you sink into the swamp, I may not be able to retrieve your memory core." Despite the warning, he didn't expect Erasmus to exhibit restraint.

The turtles grunted and splashed off, paddling into the morass of marsh grasses. Erasmus thrust the combat mek forward in a surge of speed, but his heavy body slowed and stopped in the quagmire. He tipped and sank, his circuits flickering. As he struggled, mud splashed in all directions.

"This body has lost its integrity!" Impossibly caught in the muck, the robot struggled, but more water leaked into the sensitive circuitry, shutting down several mobility systems.

Gilbertus retrieved a narrow suspensor canoe he stored at his cottage and, leery of predators in the water, he glided out to where the bulky mek stood mired and sinking. "It seems I have miscalculated," Erasmus said.

"I could tell you were enjoying yourself, but obviously you aren't ready for a new body yet." Gilbertus reached the mek and saw with growing alarm how swiftly it was sinking in the swamp. He worked to remove the access panel, dipping his hands underwater. He saw two black ropy things slithering toward him from the shore: slick segmented leeches. As the robot's shoulders dipped beneath the surface, sinking deeper into the slurry, Gilbertus finally removed the memory core and held it dripping out of the water. With a nudge, he glided the suspensor canoe out of the way as the ropy leeches arrived and circled the submerged mek, unimpressed with their prey.

He returned to shore, and carried the gelcircuitry sphere back to the contemplation cottage. "You overextended yourself," he said. "I can't risk smuggling another body away from the school—not for a long time."

Though disappointed, the independent robot did express his excitement. "Despite the short duration, that was most enjoyable. A reminder of the things I can do once I am mobile again."

It would be interesting to sterilize the entire human race, if only to observe how they react during the crisis.

—from the Erasmus journals

When Raquella's shuttle reached the main Parmentier spaceport, she saw a massive construction project to the north, a complex of large school buildings and support structures laid out around a central area that might one day be graced with gardens and fountains. At the moment, the core area was filled with cranes, bulldozers, construction shacks, and piles of building materials. A considerable amount of disturbed dust hung in the air.

A very ambitious project. Dr. Zhoma was continuing the overblown work begun by her predecessor, although construction on several of the superfluous façades and recreational facilities had been put on hold. But it was not Raquella's business to manage the growth of the school. Zhoma would be surprised enough to see her, even though the Reverend Mother had more than sufficient reasons to come to Parmentier.

A long time ago this planet had been Raquella's home, and she remembered working with Mohandas Suk in the Hospital for Incurable Diseases, striving to save as many as possible, distributing melange as a palliative. When victims still fell like harvested wheat, mobs had overwhelmed the hospital, smashing and burning, led by a little girl who had survived the fevers and claimed to see visions of Saint Serena and hear voices in her head. Raquella and Mohandas had been forced to flee.

The heirs of Rayna's movement were still out there, stronger than ever and with the same agenda. Fortunately, the school founded by Mohandas Suk also appeared to be thriving, with this huge new complex under construction. Zhoma appeared to be doing a good job . . . and considering her recent invitation to become the Emperor's personal physician, she might be in a position to help the Sisterhood.

In the warm, dry summer of Parmentier, the Reverend Mother wore a lightweight black robe with ventilation pockets. A hired groundcar took her over a dusty road as she sat in silence, rolling past the half-finished dormitories, teaching theaters, operating centers, and training labs. She also noticed private security troops, paramilitary forces, and equipment.

At the school complex, she was greeted by a tall brown-skinned man with a long ponytail secured in a silver Suk ring. "I am Dr. Waddiz, deputy administrator of the school, and forty-two percent owner."

What an odd thing to say, she thought. Why would he think she was interested in his ownership percentage? "I am here to see Dr. Zhoma before she departs for Salusa Secundus. We have business to discuss."

Waddiz twitched with obvious astonishment. "The news of her promotion has not been publicly disseminated."

Raquella did not feel the need to give him specifics. "The Sisterhood has many eyes and ears."

With a crisp acknowledgment, Waddiz led her up the broad steps outside a Grecian-style building that featured elaborate Corinthian columns and bas-relief friezes. She found it unnecessarily ostentatious, a distraction from the school's humanitarian goals. Mohandas had never cared much for ostentation.

Pausing at the top of the steps, the deputy administrator gestured out toward the dusty central area. "As soon as these buildings are completed, we are going to install a fitness complex here, with lap pools, running tracks, and even a channel for racing scull boats. The overall plan is difficult to envision right now, with all the construction dust." Workers and equipment rushed about in a frenzy of activity, and machines droned loudly.

Raquella was amazed that even the successful school could afford all this. "And such things are necessary for training new physicians?"

"Exercise and competitive sports are very good for the human body. The Greeks and Romans of Old Earth understood this fifteen thousand years ago, and it holds true today."

Waddiz led her through doors etched with metallic designs in the shapes of medicinal plants. "This way, please. Dr. Zhoma is currently undergoing an experimental procedure. Perhaps you are interested in observing?"

"Of course. I served here in a hospital for many years myself."

"That was almost a century ago," Waddiz said, with clear admiration. "We have come a long way since then."

On the upper level, chemical odors hung in the air: solvents, paint, mortar, and glue. They passed through an airlock into a large, cleanroom that contained numerous medical machines attended by white-smocked men and women. Waddiz stopped in front of a white capsule the size of a large coffin with a clearplaz window in the front. Inside, Raquella could see a woman strapped to a platform that turned slowly like meat on a rotisserie, bathing her in needles of colored light.

"Dr. Zhoma receives these treatments daily," Waddiz said, but didn't explain further. "Unfortunately, she won't be able to continue them when she takes residence in the Imperial Palace. Salusa Secundus is quite a bit behind our technology." He glanced at his wristchron and excused himself.

When the machine stopped, Zhoma emerged, looking refreshed. She smiled in surprise as she recognized her visitor. "I'm happy to see you here, Reverend Mother, but this is most unexpected."

"We have business to discuss."

Zhoma gave a brisk nod. "By all means. We can talk over lunch."

The two women sat down in one of several private dining chambers that encircled a large cafeteria, where they both ate small portions of austere, healthy fare, much like what Raquella was accustomed to on Rossak. Though she remained professional and detached, Zhoma could not hide the fact that she was trying to find a way back into the Reverend Mother's good graces.

"Congratulations on your selection as the Emperor's personal physician. It is a great honor."

"It is also a recognition of our school's abilities. Roderick Corrino asked me himself, based on my past service. My work here on Parmentier is important, but the show of Corrino support will greatly strengthen our school—and of course the fee is not negligible. Dr. Waddiz will do an adequate job while I am away."

Watching intently, Raquella noted a flicker of desperation in Dr. Zhoma's eyes, and having heard reports of financial difficulties at the Suk School she wondered just how much the organization needed this nod from the Emperor. Or the payment.

Raquella saw the opening she needed. "Let me give you a warning—Emperor Salvador is not necessarily a friend of the Suk School. Look into his motivations and prepare yourself. Too often, the Butlerians control him."

A nervous, surprised chuckle. "And yet he was so enamored with my predecessor that he paid huge sums for his medical treatments. How can he not support the school?"

"Oh, he might respect the doctors, especially when he feels his ailments, but he *fears* the Butlerians. Manford Toronto has the Emperor under his thumb, and he will want to limit your use of medical technology. Remember, we still have some Sisters working quietly at court, and they will help you whenever they can."

Hesitation, then Zhoma said with an undertone of determination, "When I have the Emperor's ear, I will convince him to support the Suk School. His father died of a brain tumor, and now he imagines many ailments himself. I think he will side with us out of his own personal interest."

Reaching across the table, Raquella gripped the other woman's arm to convey urgency. "I *know* that the Emperor has already agreed to make a gesture at your expense, in order to satisfy Manford."

Zhoma looked disturbed. "What more do they want? We have tried to accommodate the Butlerian concerns. We vet all technology, removing any hint of computer control, but they keep moving the line of acceptability, finding new things to object to. Medical analysis is complex and sophisticated—would they have us go back to bleeding pans, leeches, and incantations? Is that how Emperor Salvador wants me to treat him, as his personal physician?"

"What Salvador wants for himself and what he allows the Butlerians to do may be different things. He is a flawed person, in more ways than you know." She leaned forward, adding intensity to her voice. She had to get this woman's attention, make her see how their problems—and their futures—were aligned. "Your new assignment is the reason I came here. I need to make a confidential request, a very important request."

Zhoma blinked and responded too quickly, too eagerly. "Of course, Reverend Mother! Anything you wish." For a moment she looked like the young, shamed acolyte back on Rossak again.

"You have had the chance to study our breeding records on Rossak."

The doctor nodded. "I admire the project more than I can describe. How can I help you?"

"You know it's one of the largest databases in human history, and with so much information and intensive analysis, certain projections are possible." She paused. "We have discovered a serious flaw in the Corrino bloodline, specifically in Salvador's branch."

The comment took Zhoma completely by surprise. "How do you know this? Who could possibly assess such a huge amount of information—your Mentats?"

Raquella avoided a direct answer. "We have ways to look to the future and predict characteristics of offspring from the component breeders." She lowered her voice and looked around, but they were completely alone. "The Sisterhood has determined that Salvador Corrino must not have offspring. He carries a critical flaw. His branch of the family tree must be pruned for the good of humanity's future."

Zhoma looked down at the remaining food on her plate, but seemed to have no appetite. Many questions crossed her face, but she held them back. "A patient should trust the diagnosis of a qualified doctor. How can I doubt a conclusion like this, when it comes from one of the women I respect most in the Imperium?" She swallowed hard at the implications of what the Reverend Mother was saying. "But what is to be done?"

Raquella sounded reasonable. "All is not lost for the Corrinos. If the succession continues through his brother's line, all will be well."

"But . . . how can we guarantee that?"

The Reverend Mother pursed her lips. "If you are to be Salvador's personal physician, you'll attend him regularly. Simply make it impossible for him to conceive a child . . . there are many undetectable drugs that cause sterility. No one needs to know."

Zhoma's dark-brown eyes widened, and her mouth went slack. "What you ask is treason. Even with my respect for the Sisterhood, and for you—"

Raquella had studied the woman for years and knew her exact weak spots. "If you do this, I will personally forgive you your past indiscretions. By my command, the Sisterhood will welcome you back as one of our most esteemed members."

Zhoma actually gasped, then caught herself, fighting to reestablish her cool demeanor. "Reverend Mother, I don't know . . . don't know what to say."

Raquella sweetened the offer. "The Sisterhood controls great wealth. If you help us in this matter, I am willing to transfer significant amounts to the Parmentier treasury, an investment to strengthen the new school complex and seal our alliance."

She saw the reaction in Zhoma's eyes. Yes indeed, the medical school was in dire financial straits.

Zhoma swallowed hard. "Those funds will be well used."

Employing a precise tone of voice, with all the persuasion she could muster, Raquella said, "Think of *humanity* as your patient, not the Emperor. According to our very accurate projections, one of his descendants will wreak havoc on such a scale that by comparison it will make every previous tyrant look like no more than a schoolboy throwing rocks. Our race, our civilization, is on the brink of disaster, and I'm offering you a way to bring us back from the edge."

Zhoma's eyes misted over and she nodded. "Yes, humanity is my patient." She steeled herself. "I will do it, because I have faith in you, Reverend Mother."

As mortal humans, each of us is born with a death sentence anyway, so what difference does a little poison make? Why not take a chance you will survive the ordeal and make something significant of your life? Why not attempt to become a Reverend Mother? I am living proof that this leap in human consciousness can be achieved.

—REVEREND MOTHER RAQUELLA BERTO-ANIRUL,
from an inspirational speech to acolytes

Dorotea kept her voice low and intense, even though they were out in the open air, far from other Sisters. "I have something very important to discuss with you, Sister Valya."

They had walked to the edge of the paved canopy and sat together on the broad, lavender expanse. From this vantage, Valya could see the cliff wall and the steep path from which she had pushed Ingrid to her death. After Anna Corrino was caught trying to steal one of the experimental Reverend Mother poisons from Sister Karee's lab, and the dismissive report of Ingrid's death was published, Dorotea had been wary around Valya.

Now, not sure what to expect, Valya kept her body alert against attack. How much had Dorotea discovered? For good or ill, though, Dorotea seemed to resent Reverend Mother Raquella's reaction, but not Valya's. As proof of that, Valya was still invited to sit in on the hushed meetings of the secret group Dorotea had formed, spreading rumors of illegal technologies in the Sisterhood.

"I am always here if you need to talk with me," Valya said. "We are friends, aren't we?"

For some time now, she had stayed close to Dorotea, so that she could keep an eye on the other woman, stringing her along with a cleverly feigned concern over Ingrid. The unfortunate side effect was that even the smallest amount of warmth that Valya displayed toward Dorotea made Anna Corrino jealous, and the Emperor's sister was not accustomed to sharing. But Dorotea was a more immediate problem.

Valya had her priorities clear: If she had to kill again to protect the secret of the breeding computers, she would do so without a moment's hesitation.

"Sometimes we are friends," Dorotea answered, "yet sometimes we seem to be rivals. Even so, I respect you, Sister Valya. I know we are equals, and the Reverend Mother assigned important responsibilities to each of us. You and I are the Sisterhood's best hope to become the next Reverend Mothers—and we must prove ourselves worthy. It's up to us."

Valya swallowed hard, and asked a question to which she already sensed the answer. "And how do you think we should do that?"

Dorotea reached into her robe pocket and withdrew two small capsules, one slightly darker than the other. "These are derivatives of the Rossak drug, which I recently prepared with Sister Karee—a slight, but critical, alteration. It's the substance she intends to give to the next volunteer."

"The Rossak drug? That's what almost killed Reverend Mother Raquella. Everyone else who consumed it has died."

"Not this particular formulation," Dorotea said. She held out the capsules. "These are the best chance we will ever have. By passing through the ordeal, we will become as powerful as Reverend Mother Raquella."

First Anna, and now Dorotea . . .

The older woman extended one of the pills, but Valya did not move to accept it. Based on everything that had happened before, this would be suicide. But she didn't want to appear to be a coward to someone as influential as Dorotea . . . did not want to mirror the shame of her ancestor Abulurd Harkonnen. "I long to have the control and wisdom of a Reverend Mother, like Raquella, but the pathway is too uncertain." Valya had too much at stake—what would Griffin do without her? She had to live so she could help him take advantage of the situation after killing Vorian Atreides. She also had to finish her Sisterhood training and return to House Harkonnen so they could reclaim their heritage.

She did not want to end up a rotted, half-consumed corpse dumped in the jungles, like the other dead Sisters.

"Someone needs to be first. I had hoped you would join me." Dorotea's voice had an edge. "When we are both Reverend Mothers, we can talk to the other Sisters and use our heightened perceptions to discover who is lying—and what really happened to Ingrid."

Stalling for time, Valya gazed out on the sunlit, polymerized canopy. Of course, she had no intention of helping this woman discover that particular truth. "You may not like the answer you find. What if it truly was an accident?"

"Then it was an accident. But at least we'll know what happened."

Valya was playing a very serious game, trying to monitor and distract Dorotea for the good of the Sisterhood. Right now, with Raquella away at the Suk School, she felt that the other woman was most dangerous. "We can't consume the poison out here on the open canopy." She glanced down at the jagged chasms in the silvery treetops, and the fatal drop to the jungle floor. "We should be inside the medical chambers, under careful supervision by doctors, when we try the poison. This is even more dangerous—"

Dorotea frowned. "It is an inner battle, a challenge we must face *ourselves*. No amount of medical assistance will help us." She found a sturdy, open section of the reinforced canopy. "We'll be as safe here as any place in the caves—if we survive the poison. It is up to us, Valya . . . not to any doctors."

Valya looked down at the poison pill and felt her pulse racing. She could easily grab it and swallow it—or slap it away.

Dorotea said, "You know this is what the Reverend Mother wants."

Valya had seen so many previous volunteers—the absolute best candidates at the time—perish in the attempt, or end up brain damaged. "Why would you take such a risk yourself?"

"The primary tenet of the Sisterhood is for us to reach the pinnacle of humanity, but I suspect corruption in our order, maybe even the insidious influence of thinking machines. If I become a Reverend Mother, then I will be equal to Raquella. I will be her obvious successor, and I can lead the Sisterhood along the proper path. We can share that power, if you join me." Sister Dorotea withdrew her hand. "Or are you *afraid* to join me?"

"I didn't say that, but the odds of success are vanishingly small. If we truly are the best the Sisterhood has, then would it not cause great harm to the school if we both died?"

"If humans did not harbor unrealistic hopes, we would never have defeated Omnius. If we each take the pill, Valya, one of us could very well survive and become the natural successor to Reverend Mother Raquella. And if we both survive, then you and I share leadership. It is the best chance for the Sisterhood's future. Up to now we've been veering off course, and this is the only way we can guide it in a different direction." She extended the second capsule again. "Please, Valya. I want you with me."

Reluctantly, Valya accepted the pill.

Dorotea seemed greatly relieved. "Let's do it now! We have waited long enough already." Her eyes shone with a strange intensity. Then, as if eager to proceed before she lost her nerve, Dorotea downed her capsule.

In alarm, Valya mimicked her gesture, pretended to pop the other pill into her mouth, but palmed it instead and waited to see what would happen to Dorotea.

Swallowing the drug, Dorotea let out a sigh, closed her eyes . . . and began to writhe on the rough surface of fused leaves, slowly at first, and then with increasing agony. Valya watched her convulsions for a moment, not daring to help or sound an alarm. Finally, Dorotea curled up with her face contorted in pain; spittle trickled from her clenched lips.

Valya touched her shoulder, feeling the tremors of violent shivers, and then no movement at all. She leaned closer, unable to tell if the other Sister was still breathing. Valya disposed of her own pill, dropping it through a gap in the branches, letting it fall all the way to the jungle floor, far below.

Behind her, she heard Sisters running toward them and their voices calling for help. In a subterfuge of her own, Valya pretended to collapse and began to twitch and spasm. She hoped her display was convincing.

The desert is not always the safest place to hide.
—Zensunni saying

When the investigator reported to Griffin that he had been unsuccessful in finding any information about Vorian Atreides, the man demanded payment nevertheless. Griffin refused, citing their oral agreement. When the man pressed the issue and threatened him with a projectile pistol, Griffin broke his wrist with a crisp blow, and took the weapon away from him.

"I have my own leads to follow," he said.

Leaving the whimpering man behind, Griffin went to the Arrakis City headquarters of the Combined Mercantiles spice-harvesting operations. Encompassing two square blocks, the building looked like a fortress. Considering the upheavals, feuds, and competing melange operations on the desert planet, perhaps it *was* a fortress.

Still unsettled by this world's rugged violence, which he had encountered twice now, Griffin did not relax his guard as he continued to search. He refused to touch the contingency funds he had set aside to buy his passage back home, but he would spend the rest of his money, exhausting it in an attempt to find Vorian Atreides and achieve the result that honor demanded.

Revenge pays its own debt, his sister had said.

And when he finally returned to Lankiveil, he could focus on putting the house in order and expanding their commercial dealings, seeking to set the family on a steady course.

The previous day, he had recorded a lengthy message for Valya, describing his progress and his hope for the imminent completion of his quest. He wanted to reassure her how hard he'd been working. Recording the message focused his thoughts and fueled his desire to continue, even so far from home.

For sentimental reasons, he recorded another brief letter to the rest of his family on Lankiveil, though he did little more than tell them he was healthy and safe, and missed them. By the time he got home, he was sure his certification as a Landsraad representative would be waiting for him. At the end of the letter, he gave his father several assignments—to send inquiries to Salusa about acquiring office space near the Landsraad Hall, to negotiate short-term construction projects with inland laborers who came to the coast each spring, and to invest in whale-fur futures on a particular harvesting fleet—though he didn't know if Vergyl would follow through on any of it. Griffin paid a fee to dispatch the messages to Rossak and Lankiveil, aware that they might be months in transit.

He went to the headquarters of the spice operations and asked several clerks for information on a possible employee named Atreides. In response, he received only uncaring shrugs; a bored-looking woman merely told him, "When people come to Arrakis, they don't want to be found." Flustered, Griffin paid to peruse the personnel records on the many spice crews that worked in the desert for Combined Mercantiles, and the clerk gave him a dauntingly large and disorganized set of record books.

He spent the better part of that day combing the lists for one specific name. The logbooks were incomplete, some organized by date of hire, others grouped by crew locations. Only three volumes listed the names in alphabetical order. The work crews were paid in cash or water, and very little record was kept of other financial transactions.

If Atreides was using an alias, Griffin might never find him, but the self-important man was not the sort of person to hide his identity. Did he have any reason to?

While Griffin pestered them with questions, the Combined Mercantiles clerks were preoccupied by a disturbing new report, that a spice crew had been ambushed out in the desert, the equipment destroyed and every one of the workers killed. The loss of the crew and machinery would typically have been written off as due to weather or sandworm attack, but an eyewitness had reported that the harvester was attacked by armed men. Combined Mercantiles immediately increased the security alert and redoubled military escorts on their desert operations.

Perhaps the victims had been Vorian's crew, Griffin mused, which gave him some measure of hope. Valya would never be satisfied if the man perished without first having to face a Harkonnen and suffer for the pain he had caused, but Griffin was not sure how he felt about that himself. He had never killed anyone before.

He spotted a desert woman leaving the headquarters and hurried to query her. She was hardened, weathered, and covered in dust. Her blue-within-blue eyes were bird-bright as he stopped her. She sneered at his offer of a bribe. "Information is not a thing to be bought or sold, but to be shared, or withheld—as I see fit."

The woman brushed past him, but he persisted. "I'm looking for a man named Vorian Atreides. He's somewhere on Arrakis, but I don't know where to look."

Her brows drew together, and she fixed a breathing mask over her mouth. She seemed anxious to go. "What do you want him for?"

"I need to speak with him about a personal matter. He knew my family a long time ago."

She didn't seem to believe him, had a strange, agitated look on her face. "I have never heard of the person you seek. You're wasting your time." He thanked her as she hurried out into the street, showing no more interest in him.

THE DESERT'S QUIET emptiness gave Vorian a sense of serenity, especially at night. He missed his contented nights in a familiar bed with Mariella, yet felt comfortable among these Freemen, though they remained wary and suspicious of him; he doubted they would ever accept an outsider, even if he spent the rest of his life here.

From the other desert people, he'd heard tales of the tribulations endured by the Freemen, the generations of slavery, how their ancestors rioted on Poritrin and stole an experimental spacefolder ship for a mass exodus from the League Worlds, only to crash here on Arrakis. They joined with the descendants of a legendary desert outlaw, Selim Wormrider. All that history, unknown and unwritten, was fascinating to Vor—the rest of the Imperium was entirely unaware of it.

He liked to sit outside under the stars. He looked up now as the two moons drew close in the sky, the lower and faster satellite approaching its cousin. The Freemen had set out innovative dew collectors among the rocks, condensing a faint trace of moisture as the atmosphere cooled. Most of Sharnak's people were asleep, and those on sentry duty ignored him.

As he pondered these things, his eyes spotted a flicker of movement in the shadowy rocks below. For an instant, moonlight exposed a pair of figures, which vanished again into black obscurity. Alert, he tried to convince himself that he had seen a pair of evening scouts sent out by Naib Sharnak. Who else could possibly be out here, and how would they survive?

Sitting motionless, he studied the rocks for a long moment, caught another moving shadow, then crept back inside and closed the cave's moisture door as he looked for one of the camp guards.

By now he had grown accustomed to the wealth of unusual smells and common background noises of people crowded together with very little comfort or privacy. The tunnels were dark and silent, but he found one of the sentries, a sour-faced man with a patchy beard. The man seemed annoyed at the interruption of his nocturnal wanderings.

"I saw something outside," Vor said. "You should find out what it is."

"There is nothing out there but rocks and sand—and Shai-Hulud, if you are unfortunate enough to see him."

"I saw two figures out there."

"Only ghosts or shadows. I have lived in the desert all my life, *offworlder*."

Vor bristled, spoke loudly. "Once, I commanded the entire Army of Humanity, and fought more battles than you could imagine. You should at least look into it."

Hearing voices, another sentry came up, one of the young men who had been dispatched to investigate the spice-harvesting site. For days now, Inulto had listened to Vor talk about Arrakis City, Kepler, and Salusa Secundus, all of which were equally exotic to him. He seemed inclined to believe Vor, and said, "Come, we'll wake up Naib Sharnak and let him decide."

"You'll do no such thing," said the sour-faced sentry. "I forbid it."

Inulto scoffed, showing little respect for the other man. "You forbid nothing, Elgar." Ignoring him, the scout led Vor to Sharnak's quarters, muttering in a sarcastic tone, "Elgar thinks he'll be our Naib one day, but he can't even lead the tribe when only five of us are awake."

They called at the curtain, and Naib Sharnak came out, blinking and grumbling. His dark, gray-shot hair, normally braided, was spread out in a flowing fan, rumpled by sleep. However, before Vor could tell the leader what he had seen, shouts came from down the stone corridor, and a piercing scream.

Sharnak was instantly awake, yelling to rouse his people. The men and women of the caves bounded out of their sleeping chambers, calling their fellows to arms; they had not forgotten being preyed upon by slave hunters, even after generations of relative peace.

"Give me a weapon!" Vor shouted. Inulto had only one knife, but Sharnak kept a pair of the milky-white daggers. Grudgingly, he handed one to Vor, and the three ran down the corridor.

The moisture-seal door had been broken open, and two bodies lay on the stone floor. Vor ran toward the flurry of fighting inside the tunnel just in time to see Elgar, looking panicked. One of the intruders grabbed him from behind, tugged on his hair, planted a knee in his back, and snapped his spine. The attacker then discarded him, tossing the body to the floor.

Vor stared at Andros and Hyla. They saw him and smiled. "Oh, there you are," the young man said.

"Who are you?" Rage filled Vor, and he held the knife in front of him, though he remembered the minimal effect weapons had on these two. "How do you know me?"

Andros and Hyla were not concerned about the dozens of Freemen fighters who came to face them. The young woman took a step forward, casually placing her heel on Elgar's broken spine. "You are Vorian, son of Agamemnon—don't you recognize us?"

The young man said, "We know what you did to our father and the rest of the Titans . . . how you betrayed us all."

Hyla stepped forward. "But blood runs strong and thick, and you are our brother. Maybe we can find it in our hearts to forgive you."

Brother? Vor felt as if an asteroid impact had rocked his entire world. He knew that General Agamemnon had kept sperm samples from centuries ago, before he had discarded his human body. Hoping to find a worthy successor, Agamemnon had used surrogate mothers to bear sons for him, all of whom he'd found inadequate. Vorian had been his best hope, and later his greatest disappointment. Vor could not deny that these two appeared to share the Atreides genes, but one was a daughter.

"Come with us," Hyla said, "and we'll decide your worth."

"Or should we kill all these others first?"

With a brave and foolish yell, Inulto threw himself toward Andros, slashing with the dagger. The moment he moved, Hyla dismissively reached out and caught the young man's throat with one hand. Inulto flailed, stabbed with his knife as she crushed his larynx and tossed him on the floor like a broken doll. Her skin and her brother's flickered with quicksilver. The knife cuts on her arm went only as deep as the topmost layer of skin, with hardly any blood.

As soon as Hyla killed Inulto, five of the desert men rushed forward, howling. The twins fought them like a pair of dust-devils, breaking bones, smashing skulls, crushing opponents against the walls.

"Stop!" Vor yelled, then turned to Sharnak. "Tell your fighters to back away. I'll go with them. I never wanted any of your people hurt."

But the leather-skinned Naib looked furious. He shouted to two fighters, "Restrain Vorian Atreides. Keep him away from those two."

As the desert men grabbed his arms, Vor struggled, but they were very strong. "Let me fight my own battles, damn you!"

"No—because that is exactly what they wish," Sharnak said. "They can't have you. And if you are in league with them . . ."

Now the Freemen warriors attacked the twins in force, and proved to be far more difficult opponents than a weary spice-harvesting crew. Through sheer ferocity, they drove Andros and Hyla back as they hacked away at the quicksilver-impregnated skin. One fighter managed to slice just beneath Andros's left eye, nearly gouging it out.

The momentum of the onslaught pushed the twins back toward the broken moisture door. They looked furious, still intent on capturing Vor and obviously appalled at their failure.

"We will spill your blood across the sand and dump your bodies—even Shai-Hulud will spit you out," the Naib shouted to them.

"You are unworthy opponents," Andros said with a sneer.

Vor was determined not to let these people fight for him, but he could not break free. At least eight desert warriors lay broken and probably dead on the cave floor, but the rest showed no sign of backing away, and more came running from the deep tunnels. The brother and sister hesitated as if calculating the odds, then reacted at the same instant, making the same choice.

Their last glance at Vor was filled with promises and threats. Ignoring the Freemen who had fought them to a standstill, the bloody twins retreated through the moisture lock and vanished like a whiff of steam from a hot rock.

Naib Sharnak shouted, "Find them. Kill them!" But Vor knew it would be no use. He had no idea if the twins had a vehicle or aircraft, or if they had somehow crossed the desert on their own, but he would not underestimate them.

The Naib breathed hard, and his voice carried a murderous tone. "I will have satisfactory explanations, Vorian Atreides, or I will have your water."

When the warriors released him, Vor calmly faced the tribal leader. Long ago, he had pretended to side with the cymek general so that he could betray him and save humanity. He had taken his father's preservation canister and dumped the twisted brain out of a high tower, so that it splattered on the frozen cliffs below. After that victory, Vor had thought there would be peace, but obviously the stain of the Titans wasn't completely eradicated.

Now, the desert people were outraged and stunned that a mere two opponents could cause so much damage, and Vor realized he needed to tell what he knew. "I'll give you all the explanations I have, about who I am and what I've done in the past, but I doubt they will be enough."

There are many journeys in life, but few take you to the brink of death and then bring you back. After such a monumental struggle, you find yourself on a perch that is much, much higher than the one you occupied before.

— REVEREND MOTHER RAQUELLA BERTO-ANIRUL,
shortly after her transformation

The poison swirled around her mind like a storm; mental clouds and winds swept away her concentration and attempted to steal her life.

Abruptly, Dorotea's body jerked, and her eyes opened wide.

Through a small pinpoint of awareness, she discovered that she was in a hospital room . . . in the Sisterhood's infirmary, she realized, lying on a bed surrounded by medical equipment. She recognized this as the place where the comatose Sisters were kept alive, those who had failed the test to become a Reverend Mother, and yet survived.

Two women discussed her condition within earshot. Dorotea found she couldn't move; her body was too weak. She lifted one finger and then another, but that was all she could manage. In a blur, she remembered taking the carefully calibrated poison, then losing control as her body betrayed her, falling to the canopy.

Valya—was she there, too? Dorotea couldn't turn her head. The last thing she remembered, in the real world, was seeing the other young woman take the drug.

And then Dorotea had been lost on a long journey inside herself.

The medical Sisters still had not noticed her. She blinked again, and found that her consciousness was split, as if her brain had been cracked open and jammed with a new awareness, dominating and overriding what had been there previously. Closing her eyes, she heard voices inside her head, whispering . . . and all of them sounded female, like a crowd of spectators looking at her from the inside out. The words were faint at first and then so loud and powerful that she could not ignore them. Dorotea felt a sensation of great antiquity there, of ancient women calling to her across vast distances.

When she focused her concentration on the voices, trying to hear and comprehend, a flood of memories came to her, a vivid part of her experience . . . yet not from her own lifetime. Ancient women spoke to her, sometimes simultaneously, although she could absorb everything they were saying. The recollections were startling and real, and she began to order them in her mind, realizing that they formed a chain of lives stretching back one generation at a time, all the way into the dim past of human history.

She saw bloodlines unfolding within her, links in a chain of lives: a woman from centuries ago, Karida Julan on the planet Hagal, who had taken a dashing young military officer as her lover and given birth to a daughter, Helmina Berto-Anirul . . . who in turn bore a daughter—Raquella Berto-Anirul, the Reverend Mother. And *her* daughter was Arlett . . . Dorotea's mother!

Raised on Rossak from birth, Dorotea had never known her mother, and saw now through ricocheting displaced memories that Sister Arlett had been cast out after giving birth to her, dispatched to wander the scattered worlds and recruit acolytes for the Sisterhood. In all those years, she had not been allowed to return to the Rossak School, to her daughter. Where was she now? Dorotea was not certain.

But Raquella was here at the school . . . Dorotea's grandmother! The Reverend Mother had never said a word of it, never acknowledged her. And soon Dorotea saw more from the past and learned things she didn't want to know.

Like an image in a distorted mirror, she watched the separation and abandonment of the baby daughter—herself—from two different sides. A distraught Arlett begging to raise and love the little girl, and the stern Raquella insisting that such connections could not be permitted. All Sisters should be trained as equals as part of the larger community, she said, without the distractions of family ties. Arlett had to abandon her baby, Raquella had to brush her aside, and Dorotea had to spend her life in complete ignorance of the truth.

Yes, she saw it in her new library of memories. The Reverend Mother had torn them apart. Through the sudden infusion of information, Dorotea realized the far-reaching implications, saw the extent of what Raquella had done. Because of her conflict with Arlett, *all* of the babies in the nursery had been switched, and their names removed so that the girls were merely "daughters of the Sisterhood."

But even more came rushing to her. The distant sound of the other memories again increased to a roar. She met generations and generations of women who had lived across the thousand years of thinking-machine rule, the depredations of independent robots and combat meks, the enslavement of whole populations. For years, Dorotea had lived on Lampadas, assigned to observe the Butlerians and coolly analyze their movement. There she had heard the truth and the passion, and she had come to believe in the dangers of unchecked progress. As she had improved herself with Sisterhood techniques, Dorotea had become more and more convinced that human beings did not *need* the crutch of computers and advanced technology, because every person had the innate abilities they required.

So many lives were inside her mind now, so much suffering in the time preceding her . . . it only reinforced what she already believed. The female voices all shouted to her at once in a tumult that gradually faded until one voice emerged: Raquella Berto-Anirul, at a much younger age more than eight decades ago, just before the Battle of Corrin.

Now Dorotea saw horrific memories, the painful epidemic that had raged across Parmentier, how Raquella and Mohandas Suk had fought to save as many people as they could . . . how she had come to Rossak to help the surviving Sorceresses against the spreading disease. In a snapshot inside her head, Dorotea saw bodies in white robes and black, stacked inside the cave cities. Dorotea saw what Raquella had seen as she walked up the switchback cliffside trail, ascending toward the high caves where the Sorceresses kept their breeding records.

Raquella's memories were Dorotea's own memories now. She saw through her grandmother's eyes as she studied the comprehensive catalogs of billions of bloodlines the Sorceresses had compiled for generations, records taken from a swath across the human race.

And preserved in banks of forbidden computers! Collecting and processing data, making projections and completing reports for the women to read.

Dorotea wanted to scream out in protest, but she could only watch in horror. For all the years she had served on Lampadas, accompanying Manford Toronto as he gave impassioned speeches to restless crowds, she had felt the truth of the man's crusade. She had been proud of the Sisterhood, how the women used *their own abilities* to achieve physical and mental superiority.

And now Dorotea knew that the Sisters relied on the crutch of thinking machines after all—exactly the insidious temptation against which Manford so passionately warned. The Sisterhood touted itself as a champion of human potential, but now, having seen through the eyes of her grandmother, her idealistic beliefs were dashed.

There were indeed illegal computers hidden somewhere in the cave city.

Fully awake now, Dorotea caught her breath, numbed by the avalanche of revelations. Lying on her back, returning to herself, she stared up at the white ceiling of the infirmary and let the ramifications sink in.

The Sisterhood possessed forbidden computers.

Reverend Mother Raquella was her grandmother.

And I am a Reverend Mother now! Dorotea had survived the agony that had killed so many of her Sisters. That understanding was the most potent of all.

She was also much younger and stronger than her grandmother. Dorotea decided that she must do something to bring about a major shift in the Sisterhood. She could challenge Raquella and force her to reveal the computers, but not until she had enough allies. Knowing that the thinking machines were hidden somewhere up in the restricted caves, and that Sister Ingrid had fallen from the steep trail, she could guess what must have happened.

Her new knowledge was dangerous, and she was weak and vulnerable. With Reverend Mother Raquella gone to the Suk School, Dorotea still had a little time to plan.

She concentrated on the quiet room, listening to the faint sounds around her and attuned to the new awareness inside her head, a focus that also allowed her to travel into the microscopic cellular building blocks of her body. Her pumping heart, the alveolar exchange of oxygen inside her lungs, the chemical processes within her organs, the transfer of nerve impulses in her brain. She was living in a universe of herself. No wonder the Reverend Mother wanted other Sisters to experience this.

As she assessed her internal cells, her metabolism, her muscle fibers, Dorotea studied her body like a starship pilot completing a thorough rundown, making adjustments as needed. When she had completed the task, pronouncing herself healthy and whole, she finally opened her eyes again and sat up.

She looked around the quiet infirmary, blinking. What had happened to Valya? She did not see her nearby, but she had watched the other Sister take the pill. So many volunteers had died in attempting the chemical passage—had Valya failed? She hoped not.

On the other side of the infirmary, the two medical Sisters saw her move, and turned to stare at her in astonishment. They ran to Dorotea, calling out for help. Dorotea just sat there and smiled, letting them fuss over her and ask countless questions. So far, she felt fine.

*To play the game of life well, compare it to chess, considering the second-
and third-level consequences of every action.*
— GILBERTUS ALBANS, *Reflections in the Mirror of the Mind*

The Discussion Chamber was one of the Mentat School's largest classrooms,
an auditorium with dark-stained walls covered in statesmanlike images of
the greatest debaters in human history, ranging from famous ancient orators of
Old Earth, such as Marcus Cicero and Abraham Lincoln, to Tlaloc who had
instigated the Time of Titans, to speakers from recent centuries, such as Renata
Thew and the unparalleled Novan al-Jones. When educating Gilbertus on Corrin,
Erasmus had made sure his young protégé was familiar with the very best.

In an anteroom, Gilbertus reviewed his notes for the risky discussion he intended to lead, then made his way out onto the stage. With fifteen of his best
students already undergoing battlefield tactical training—in accordance with
Manford Torondo's request—Gilbertus felt obligated to provide at least some
level of mitigation, a voice of reason. He wanted the students to ponder the
implications . . . but would they listen?

As he reached the podium, the classroom fell silent out of respect for the Headmaster. "Today's lesson deviates from our usual form of tactical training. We will
be taking a different approach, a change of pace."

These were the best of his current class of Mentat trainees, hand-selected for
their analytical prowess—and Manford was demanding their services for his
crusade. Gilbertus never voiced his resentment at being forced to sacrifice such
talented students in a cause to which he was fundamentally, and secretly, opposed.

"A crucial component of designing a successful strategy is learning to think like your enemy. This is not a natural goal: It must be practiced, and some of you may find it a difficult and extremely uncomfortable challenge. Therefore, we will debate the merits of both sides of a key issue, to help you explore the mind-set of the opposing side. We will discuss the *merits* of thinking machines." After an audible gasp or two, the students seemed to hold their breath. He paused, noting their intent expressions, then spoke in a clear voice. "Consider the postulation that thinking machines, in some properly restricted forms, may play a safe and useful role in human society."

This elicited some murmurs of surprise, and angry glances from the students that Manford Torondo had sent to the school.

Gilbertus gave a slight smile. "With so many of you about to join the Butlerian ships, it is appropriate to think about what you're fighting for, and what you're fighting against. Out there, you will clash with the Machine Apologists, planetary leaders who sincerely believe they can put thinking machines to good use and keep them under control." All the students were interested, though their uneasiness was palpable in the air.

He made his own choice, a redheaded young woman seated in the middle; he had planned this debate with her in mind. "Alys Carroll, you will be my opponent. I look forward to a skilled, spirited discussion."

She rose to her feet and walked toward the stage, straight-backed and determined. Gilbertus said to the entire class, "I will argue one side of the issue, and Alys Carroll will support the opposite point of view." He removed a bright, gold Imperial coin from his pocket. One side bore the image of Serena Butler, and the other the open hand of the Landsraad League. "Heads, and Alys will argue on the side of the thinking machines as a Machine Apologist. Tails, and I will take that side instead."

The angry young woman looked uncertain, but before she could say anything, he flipped the coin into the air, caught it, and opened his palm. Gilbertus glanced at the coin and covered it without displaying the result to the students. While Erasmus had difficulty with the concept of lying, a Mentat had no such handicap, especially not in a case such as this. The exercise should be quite fruitful, and the single-minded Butlerian woman needed to grapple with objectivity.

"Heads," he said. "Alys, you shall argue on behalf of the thinking machines."

The young woman's eyes widened. Gilbertus was amazed at how quickly the blood drained from her face.

"I open the matter for debate," he continued, smiling. "Your objective in the discussion will be to highlight the benefits that computers and robots might bring to humankind. Convince us all that this point of view has merit. I will defend the Butlerian position."

Alys hesitated. "I beg of you, please don't ask me to do this."

Gilbertus, having projected that he might encounter initial resistance, gave the answer he had prepared. "Mentats must discipline themselves to examine a problem from all angles, not just from the point of view that matches their own belief systems. As your instructor, I have given you an assignment. As the student, you will complete that assignment. You know the facts, Alys, and I want you to make a projection. Tell me the good that thinking machines *could* accomplish."

Alys turned to face the audience, fumbling for words. Finally, she said, "Machines can be used in training Swordmasters to fight more effectively against machines. They have their uses, but the danger . . ." She opened and closed her mouth, and a flare of indignation replaced her hesitancy. "No. There can *be* no benefits to thinking machines. They are anathema."

"Alys Carroll, I did not ask you to argue *my* side of the issue. Please complete your assignment."

Alys bristled. "Advanced technology is destructive. Therefore I forfeit the debate. The point cannot be won!"

"It *can* be done." Hoping to salvage this potentially valuable lesson, Gilbertus said, "Very well, I will take the Machine Apologists' position, and you may make the Butlerian argument. Does that suit you better?"

She nodded, and Gilbertus realized he was looking forward to the opportunity. The audience seemed intrigued by this turn of events.

Alys plunged in. "This is a frivolous exercise, Headmaster. Everyone here knows the machines' history of brutality and slavery—centuries of domination, first by the cymek Titans and then by the evermind Omnius. Trillions killed, the human spirit crushed." She flushed with outrage, then tried to calm herself. "It must never happen again. There is no counterargument." Several of the Butlerian students grumbled their agreement.

Gilbertus sighed. "I disagree—as I must for the sake of debate. The Machine Apologists assert that we can tame thinking machines and have them serve humanity. They contend that we should not discard all machines just because of the excesses of Omnius. What of agricultural harvesting machinery, they ask, and construction machinery to erect shelters for the homeless? And medical devices to cure the sick? There are legitimate humanitarian uses, they assert, for automated machines and computer systems."

"I doubt if the downtrodden human populations who suffered and died on the countless Synchronized Worlds would agree!" Alys sniffed. "But those victims cannot speak for themselves."

Gilbertus regarded her with a mild expression. "That might seem a legitimate basis for outlawing thinking machines—if it weren't for the fact that *humans* prosecuted the atomic purges across the Synchronized Worlds. Humans killed billions or trillions of captives on those planets, not thinking machines."

"It was necessary. Even though those enslaved populations are dead, they are still better off."

Gilbertus seized the opening. "And how can we be certain they would agree? The assumption that they would choose death over life under the rule of Omnius is insupportable. A Mentat cannot make valid projections without accurate data." He turned to look at her. "Have you ever spoken directly with any human who lived on the Synchronized Worlds under the efficiency of machine rule? As you point out, they are all dead."

"This is absurd! We know what life was truly like under machine domination—many firsthand accounts have been published."

"Ah, yes, the damning histories written by Iblis Ginjo, Serena Butler, and Vorian Atreides—but those accounts were *designed* to inspire hatred of machines and to incite League humans to violence. Even the stories of slaves rescued from the Bridge of Hrethgir were skewed and used as propaganda in the writing of history."

He realized that his voice was rising, and he calmed himself. Through his hidden spyeyes, Erasmus would be listening in with great interest, and he hoped to make his mentor proud of him.

"But let us step back and consider the general principles of how properly tamed technology should serve mankind. Robots have the capability of performing repetitive, time-consuming, or complex tasks such as collecting data, harvesting crops, or calculating safe navigational routes. Accepting limited machine assistance would free humans to make new advances."

"When Omnius enslaved the human race, we had little time to advance and improve," Alys pointed out, to a satisfied muttering from her supporters.

"But by prohibiting the use of sophisticated machines—machines that *we* developed to benefit humanity—we deny the progress humanity has made throughout history, and we condemn ourselves to resuming the practice of slavery. Because we turn our backs on machinery that could perform essential functions, *human beings* are taken from their homes and families, shackled, beaten, and forced to perform menial labor that machines could do instead. Many people die doing arduous and hazardous work, simply because we refuse to use thinking machines. Is that moral, or intelligent? One could argue that the violent Buddislamic uprisings against human slavemasters on Poritrin were as justifiable and necessary as the Jihad against thinking machines."

She shook her head briskly. "Oh no, it's entirely different. The Buddislamics refused to fight at our side."

Gilbertus swallowed an ill-advised retort and took a deep breath. "A difference in philosophy is not a just cause for enslavement." An awkward pause followed, because many of the school's students came from worlds that still relied on slave labor.

When Alys struggled to counter his words, Gilbertus noted that the normally self-assured young woman was faltering, repeating points she'd already made. It meant she was running out of ideas. This gave him hope. If he could subtly convince the Butlerian Mentat candidates, perhaps he could guide more people back to sanity.

But abruptly, several students began to call out disagreements, no longer listening, and trying to shout him down instead.

"Please, please!" Gilbertus raised his hands for calm. Perhaps he had taken it too far. "This is just an exercise, a learning experience." He smiled, but did not get the friendly response he'd hoped for. Instead, he found himself debating the handful of hostile students; even Alys could barely get a word in.

Paradoxically, he found himself winning the discussion, but losing control of it—and of the audience. As the uproar continued, he surveyed the room and saw to his disappointment that most of the students were uneasy. Even those who had earlier expressed agreement with his logic were now afraid to show it in the face of the Butlerian vehemence.

Several students left their seats and walked out. One turned from the upper doorway of the hall and called down to the stage, "Machine Apologist!"

The class ended in a furor.

GREATLY UNSETTLED, GILBERTUS hurried to his office, locked the doors, and retrieved the Erasmus core from its hiding place, but felt no relief when he held the pulsing sphere in his shaking hands. "I think I made a mistake."

"That was a fascinating performance and most enlightening. I am curious, however. You knew there were Butlerian sympathizers in the audience. They did not wish to hear a debate, only to see their beliefs reaffirmed. As a Mentat, you must have projected the possible effects of your words on such unreceptive listeners."

Gilbertus lowered his head. "I was unforgivably naïve. I simply presented logical arguments, exactly as you and I have always done in our debates."

"Ah, but others are not as rational as we are."

Gilbertus set the memory core down on a table. "Have I failed miserably, then? I founded this school to teach logical analysis and projection."

"Perhaps the Butlerians reacted so vehemently because they could sense what you truly believe. The eternal human battle of emotion versus intellect, of the right and left hemispheres of the brain fighting for control. Human life is a constant struggle, while superior machines don't need to bother with such non-sense."

"Please don't use this as an excuse to assert machine superiority! Help me find a solution, a way out. I need to defuse the situation before Manford returns. He took his ships to the Tlulaxa worlds, but he'll certainly hear a report of this when he gets back."

"Fascinating, how things can go wrong so quickly," Erasmus said. "Positively fascinating."

⟨≈⟩

*The path of human destiny is not level, but fraught with high summits
and deep chasms.*

—the *Azhar Book*

The Butlerians and their fleet of warships traveled to the Tlulaxa planets.
Although they had already imposed stern restrictions on the society, Manford was interested in flexing his muscle and ready to find scapegoats. This was
the perfect place to make his first move.

Fifteen years ago, when Manford traveled to this star system, he'd been disgusted by what he found. Back then, the followers of Rayna Butler had showed
the loathsome Tlulaxa the hard but necessary path that humanity must follow.
The offensive biological projects were declared to be against the laws of man and
God, and destroyed outright. Strict rules had been imposed upon all Tlulaxa
scientists, and grave warnings had been issued about the consequences of misbe-
havior. But years had passed, and Tlulax was far from the heart of the new Imperium. Manford was certain that by now the people had strayed—and he was
determined to catch them at it.

As the Butlerian fleet closed in on the main city of Bandalong, Manford and
Anari studied the foreign architecture built by a race that placed the study of
genetics above the value of their souls.

"I don't trust them, Anari," he said. "I know they've broken the laws, but they
are a clever race. We may have to look hard to find evidence."

"We'll find the evidence." Her voice was even. Manford smiled: The stars
would stop shining before Anari Idaho lost her faith in him.

No one, not even Josef Venport, would raise much of an outcry in defense of
the Tlulaxa people, who had never been popular around the Imperium, especially after an organ-farm scandal during the Jihad in which they were caught

committing horrendous, unscrupulous acts. Manford had his two hundred ships and many new Swordmaster leaders, and soon a group of specially trained Mentats would join them, as promised by Gilbertus Albans. It was an auspicious beginning.

The Butlerian ships took over the Bandalong spaceport, and Manford's people spread out through the city in overwhelming numbers. His handpicked Swordmasters pounded down the doors of laboratories, records buildings, and strange shrines. (He did not want to imagine the kind of religion these vile people might espouse.)

As they moved forward, Anari issued a quiet warning that Tlulaxa scientists might have hidden weapons somewhere here, crafty defenses they would turn against the Butlerians, but Manford didn't truly think the Tlulaxa were foolish enough to provoke a bigger confrontation. They were a simpering, beaten people.

Carrying him in the harness on her shoulders, Anari strode into one of their central biological research facilities. The laboratory reeked of chemicals and spoiled garbage, of fermenting cellular material and bubbling vats of organics. The research chief was a stocky, bearlike man who was larger than most Tlulaxa, and even somewhat handsome. His eyes were as round as saucers, and he was suitably terrified. "I assure you, sir, we have never strayed from the strict guidelines— nor has any other researcher. We respect the restrictions that were imposed upon us, so you'll find nothing objectionable here." The man tried to smile, but it was a pitiful offering.

Manford grimaced as he looked around the laboratory. "I find many things objectionable here."

Hearing this, the stocky research chief rushed to a series of translucent tanks, eager to prove his point. "We hate the thinking machines as much as anyone! Look, our work uses only biology—no forbidden machines or computers. Nothing that is prohibited. We study natural cells and breeding. Our work enhances human minds and human potential. It is all part of God's plan."

Manford reacted with sharp disgust. "It is not your place to determine God's plan."

The research chief became more urgent. "But look here!" He indicated a translucent vat filled with small floating spheres. "We can create new eyes for the blind. Unlike our earlier organ farms, where replacement parts were stolen from hapless victims, these projects harm no one—they only help the needy."

Manford felt Anari tense beneath him; he knew she was growing angry, as was he. "If a man is blind, it is God's will for him to be blind. I have no legs, and that is also God's will. This handicap is my lot in life. You have no right to challenge God's decisions."

The stocky man raised both hands. "That is not—"

"Why do you assume a person must tinker with his or her body, with his or her life? Why do you believe it is necessary to live with convenience and comfort?"

Wisely, the research chief did not answer, but Manford's decision had already been made. In fact, he had made up his mind before the ships even reached Tlulax. Finding outlets for energetic demonstrations kept the flames of faith burning. Targeting Tlulaxa research, especially programs like these that were superficially horrific and easily hated—eyeballs floating in vats!—kept his Butlerians strong and fearsome, and helped build his own strength against more insidious opponents. Many of his followers did not grasp subtleties, but they would follow him anyway, provided he gave them regular reinforcement.

The laboratory chief's voice was thin and small as he squeaked, "But my people have adhered to every Imperial restriction!"

Manford did not doubt the man was correct, but that reality did not suit his purposes. He waved an arm around the laboratory. "This Tlulaxa research program has gone too far in exploring a realm where no human was meant to go."

The stocky man paled in dismay. The Butlerians who had crowded inside the research complex began a restless muttering, like predators smelling blood. "This lab, and all your research, must be shut down and everything destroyed. That is my command."

Manford's followers quickly began wrecking the equipment, smashing the translucent containers so that eyeballs spilled out in a gush of nutrient fluid onto the clean white floor, bouncing like a child's toys.

"Stop this!" the research chief wailed. "I demand that you stop!"

"Manford Torondo has spoken." Anari drew her sword and struck him down with a blow that cleaved his body from shoulder to sternum.

A squeamish lab technician vomited loudly and moaned with fear. Manford pointed to the man. "You! I appoint you the new chief of this facility, and I pray you will concentrate your efforts on more appropriate and more humble work."

The technician wiped a hand across his mouth and swayed, about to faint. He nodded weakly, but didn't dare to speak.

From his perch on the Swordmaster's shoulders, Manford said to Anari, "Finish here. Then we'll go to Salusa Secundus and help the Emperor keep his promises."

Anari wiped her sword on the murdered research chief's coat, then looked at the shivering lab tech. "We will be watching your work very closely."

A computer memory core can permanently retain vast amounts of data. Although I am a mere human, I will never forget what the Butlerians did to me, to my partner, and my home. Not a single detail.

—PTOLEMY, Denali research records

In the Denali research facility Ptolemy strove to reconstruct the work that the savages had ruined on Zenith. He wrote down notes, compiled extensive journals, and struggled to duplicate the chemical and polymer mixes that had previously shown the greatest promise, many of which Dr. Elchan had discovered.

At times, he felt as if he could not do this alone . . . but he *was* alone, and determined that it must be done, so he dove back into the problem with a fervor that matched even Butlerian fanaticism.

With the insights he gained from dissecting and deconstructing the thoughtrodes and neuro-mechanical interfaces of these cymek walkers, he was already making great strides. Using hollow alloy bone frameworks, he had made ten prototype arms and hands, skeletal anchors for fibrous pulleys that worked like muscles, sheathed in a protein gel and covered with a tough artificial skin.

None of the prototypes was yet the equal of what he and Elchan had created before, but the interface was superior. The end of each experimental limb terminated in a set of receptors, and Ptolemy had attuned them to his own mind. If he concentrated his thoughts on a specific action, he could provoke a response from the nerves and artificial muscles, but it required a concerted effort. The goal was to make the interface so sensitive that the artificial limbs would respond subconsciously. A person could not function well if every little movement required effort and planning.

The research programs Ptolemy had known throughout his life were collegial and open-minded, designed to benefit everyone. In their youth he and his brothers and sisters had played games, imagining parts of society they could help, envisioning an intellectual and creative utopia after the defeat of the thinking machines. He realized now that such attitudes were dangerously oblivious to the fact that evil, ignorant, and destructive forces existed.

Ptolemy slept little and worked the rest of the time. Nothing else interested him. Prior to this, he had always worked with a research partner, and an ache of loneliness hung around him constantly. The interaction and collaboration with Elchan had been a catalyst for breakthroughs, but now Ptolemy was on his own, his only company the whisper of air-recirculation ducts, the hum of life-support systems, and the bubble of nutrient tanks that held growing synthetic limbs. The joy of his laboratory trials and the happy triumphs of each small success were gone.

Ptolemy had always wanted to help people by making amputees whole again or providing new skin to horribly scarred victims. He might have been a humanitarian, a hero lauded across the Imperium. But his good deeds and generous heart had only exposed him to hatred, and had cost Dr. Elchan his life.

He closed his eyes now in the laboratory as he remembered how proud he had felt, and how satisfied, to present Manford Torondo with new legs. He had hoped to change the Butlerian leader's life, make him smile and embrace technology. Shuddering, the researcher squeezed his eyes closed, but could not drive away the persistent memory of the stony-faced Swordmaster hacking the artificial limbs to pieces, destroying everything . . . and that had just been the beginning.

Ptolemy was perspiring. With his gift of knowledge, he had to find a way to empower visionaries such as Josef Venport, so that the man could stand strong against the Dark Age that the antitechnology mobs were hell-bent on imposing.

In the silence of the laboratory he thought he heard the haunting echoes of Elchan's screams.

When he opened his eyes, Ptolemy saw that all the artificial limbs in the nutrient tanks had twitched and stirred, like the raised arms of a defiant army, responding to his thought impulses. And every one of the hands was clenched into a hard, implacable fist.

INSIDE THE HANGAR dome, three monstrous machine bodies stood before him—motionless, but awe-inspiring nevertheless. Segmented legs, grappling hands, built-in weapons turrets, sensors, and circuitry . . . everything controlled by a preservation canister that had once held a tyrant's disembodied brain.

Silently, he paced around the mechanical bodies that had been retrieved from Denali's harsh environment. The armored walkers had been scoured, particle-blasted, and inspected for damage. Ptolemy was impressed to see that the systems remained intact even after decades of exposure to caustic air.

Each armored walker body had a unique design, built for a specific purpose and modified according to the tastes of the cymek user. By moving their preservation canisters from one artificial body to another, the cymeks could switch their physical forms at will, as if they were no more than exotic sets of clothes. Though they were mechanical artifices, the walker bodies had been built by humans, controlled by humans. These motionless cymek forms were the very embodiment of Butlerian nightmares, but Ptolemy didn't fear them at all. He imagined how his life would have been different if he'd possessed one of these cymek warrior forms to stand against the barbarians on Zenith. . . .

The sophisticated facilities Directeur Venport made available to him here surpassed even the best laboratories he'd used before. Every instrument, chemical, or tool he could imagine was his for the asking.

Over the past month, he'd met his fellow researchers, all of whom had obsessions and determination—and quite possibly their own scars, as he did. Drawn together, the scientists had a shared drive, a concrete goal of saving and defending civilization. This was more than just an esoteric quest for discovery and truth.

The facilities were not without problems. Although Venport had placed the greatest minds in this playground of science, the researchers suffered from a lack of support staff. Ptolemy asked for helpers to suit up in protective gear and retrieve the intact cymek walkers that he wished to study, but it took more than a week before they finally arrived. When he complained, politely, to Noffe about the delay, the Tlulaxa administrator nodded knowingly.

"It is a challenge to find skilled personnel who fit the criteria. Directeur Venport's scouts constantly monitor the Poritrin slave markets to acquire well-educated captives with any sort of skilled backgrounds."

Ptolemy was surprised to learn that the support technicians were indeed slaves, but what did that really matter? No one here got paid, and everyone worked; in practice, they were all equals.

Noffe tapped his fingers on his desk. "And we do take lessons from history. Even the great Tio Holtzman paid little attention to the qualifications or attitudes of his workers. He had staffed his household and research rooms with unwilling Buddislamic slaves—who eventually brought down the city of Starda." He shook his head. "Yet another example of ignorant mobs destroying the best parts of society. It never ends."

With a dour, angry look, the Tlulaxa administrator removed a printed message on a sheet of filmpaper and handed it to Ptolemy. "We just received this news of the ransacking and wanton destruction Manford Toronto brought down on Bandalong."

As Ptolemy read the report, he felt angry, but not surprised. "So they've wrecked everything—*again*. How much knowledge was lost? How many of their discoveries could we have used here, in my own work?"

"It is a tragedy, indeed." The administrator scratched his cheek as if to remove the bleached albino spots, then lowered his voice to convey a secret. "But take consolation in the fact that very little key data was actually lost. Even in my exile here, I have kept in contact, receiving regular summaries and archiving detailed backups from many of my people's most important projects. Remember, the Butlerians tried to lynch me on Tlulax fifteen years ago, so I knew not to underestimate them." Noffe gave a defiant smile. "They may think they've won this time, but we'll continue the work here, where the savages can't bother us. We'll have the last laugh. We've saved the research."

"But not the people," Ptolemy said bitterly. "Not the people. We haven't won yet." He drew a deep breath. "But, mark my words, we will."

The thinking machine I admire most is the human brain.
—NORMA CENVA, early technical journal
article submitted to Tio Holtzman

Josef Venport preferred to think of his surprise attack on the Thonaris machine shipyards as an industrial *consolidation* rather than a conquest. He was a businessman, after all, not a military leader. With his seventy armed vessels, the takeover was straightforward and efficient.

The seized and rechristened Celestial Transport vessels now flew under Venport colors. The CT employees working on-site to repair the robotic ships had been conscripted into VenHold service—most of them voluntarily. Some had demanded increased wages, while only a few required physical coercion.

Josef and his Mentat stood inside the warm and well-lit administrative hub connected to the major assembly grids. "I am very satisfied with the results of this operation, Draigo. You have more than earned back your full Mentat tuition from the Lampadas school—and for your comrades as well." His smile curled his thick mustache. "You have set a high bar for the level of performance I expect from you."

Draigo responded with a complacent nod. "I shall attempt to meet the challenge, sir."

In the past, when Josef located an intact battle group or depot, he had only plundered and reconditioned the robotic ships, but Thonaris offered much more. In addition to the dozens of complete or partially constructed robotic battleships that were simply there for the taking, these shipyards comprised a fully automated, independent manufacturing facility that included brute-force ore extractors, smelters, fabricators, and robotic assembly lines. Not only could he refurbish the existing robot ships, he could reprogram the automatic fabricators to build properly designed ships in the first place.

Josef immediately gave his engineering crews the task of studying the depot's control systems and getting the assembly lines operational again, after removing any existing AI circuitry or sentient control chips. He felt giddy at the prospects.

Josef received progress reports as his engineers explored the cold, shut-down facilities. Arjen Gates and his Celestial Transport crew had only bothered with the easy pickings. Josef doubted they would have dared to reawaken the entire factory. Arjen Gates had not been a man with vision.

As reports and images of the valuable operations came in, Josef passed the details on to his Mentat for study and memorization.

Draigo mused, "During my schooling on Lampadas, we were forced to listen to condemnations of all thinking machines. Even I am surprised to find myself in such a place."

"I hope the barbarians didn't brainwash you. I need your intellect, not your superstition."

"I serve *you*, sir, but I wish to express my concern that it would be very bad for us if the Butlerians were to discover these operations."

Josef scoffed. "They are savages who shake sticks and howl at the moon. I cannot take them seriously."

Draigo brushed a hand down his black singlesuit. "Nevertheless, remember that my former teacher, the Headmaster of the Mentat School, helped me calculate the position of these shipyards."

Josef's heavy eyebrows drew together. "Is he a Butlerian sympathizer?"

"Difficult to tell. He is an intelligent, rational man, and he says what he needs to say. I cannot guess, however, whether or not he believes it."

To prove that he didn't care, Josef ordered his work crews to redouble their efforts. Each day, more parts of the Thonaris manufacturing complex were up and running. . . .

Now, eight days into the occupation, an unexpected VenHold ship flew to Thonaris, a small vessel that contained only two passengers—both enclosed in tanks. Norma Cenva had commandeered the vessel and used her own Navigator skills to fly directly from Kolhar. Josef doubted his great-grandmother had explained her intentions to anyone in the spaceport towers, and the company spaceport administration must be in a frenzy. He trusted Cioba to deal with the matter. By this time, though, his people should be accustomed to Norma's quirks.

When she arrived at the robotic facility and announced herself, Josef called for Draigo to accompany him and took a small craft from the admin-hub over to her ship. Norma seemed pleased by the burgeoning operations she saw. "More ships," she transmitted, "for more Navigators."

Norma had installed her tank in the vessel's Navigation deck, an open plaz-framed enclosure where an enclosed Navigator could look through the swirl of melange gas to view the universe while space folded around the ship. As a concession to his great-grandmother's desires, Josef had instructed that all VenHold ships be modified with appropriate observation decks for the Navigators.

When he and his Mentat came aboard, Josef was surprised to see that the second tank contained the captured spy, Royce Fayed, who continued to undergo his mutation-transformation. Remarkably, the spy had proved intelligent and adaptable, and was progressing through the change even more smoothly than most intentionally selected candidates.

Norma's vibrating, emotionless voice came from her tank's speaker. "I have brought my protégé on his first flight."

"Is he ready for it?" Josef asked.

"He will be. I am guiding him. His mind is . . . interesting." She swam closer to the tank's viewport, where she could look across at Fayed, who hovered inside his own enclosure, his swollen eyes closed as if in meditation. "He races along the pathways of higher physics, following the trail through tenth-order dimensional mathematics."

As if words and sentences were a great challenge to him, Fayed spoke aloud, but his eyes didn't open and his expression did not change. "It is easy to concentrate upward . . . easy to become lost in thought." He inhaled a swirling plume of freshly released melange gas, then exhaled it like a man smoking a hookah. "But . . . so difficult to concentrate downward."

Norma said, "Self-discovery and mind expansion are the important and obvious parts of becoming a Navigator. But my son Adrien taught me that it is just as important for a Navigator to remember his or her humanity. If that link is broken, we are no longer better than the average human. We are lost from them."

Josef smiled at the turn of circumstances. His original intent in placing the spy in the conversion tank had simply been to execute him in a creative, perhaps poetic way; he had never expected Fayed to thrive. While he didn't trust anyone who would sell his loyalty to VenHold's greatest rival, he did trust Norma Cenva—completely. She had vetted the new Navigator through a complex process that no one else could understand, using her prescience. She had proved many times that her intuition was more accurate than Draigo's most sophisticated Mentat projections. Norma could see into the future and explore converging timelines, and if she vouched for Fayed's talent and reliability, he accepted that.

Nevertheless, Josef refused to drop his guard. "Our operations here have been consolidated with remarkable speed. Still, I am vigilant against any possible retaliation from Celestial Transport," he said to Norma. He didn't intend to make the same naïve and foolish mistakes that Arjen Gates had.

Rather than leaving the Thonaris shipyards unprotected, Josef kept twenty armed ships here on patrol while the rest of the VenHold Spacing Fleet returned to their regularly scheduled routes. Josef couldn't afford to lose the profits of so many commercial runs.

Draigo added, "By now CT will have concluded that something went terribly wrong here. They will come to investigate, and possibly fight."

Norma swam in her tank, silent for a long moment, before pronouncing with firm confidence, "You need not be concerned about Celestial Transport."

Josef assumed it was a prescient vision, but she dropped back into the spice gas and did not speak further. When her silence drew out for a long moment, he realized she had gotten distracted, wandering off in pursuit of some profound and intriguing idea. He did not try to force her attention back, however, since Norma's brainstorms were often extremely profitable. She was more than a genius. She was the sum total of all geniuses who had ever lived, and ever would live, combined into her one remarkable mind.

Royce Fayed spoke. "We will return to Kolhar now. I will guide us."

Josef could not hide the alarm in his voice. "Are you qualified?" He could not imagine losing his supremely talented great-grandmother to a navigational mishap.

"Norma Cenva has explained the theory, shown me examples, and demonstrated the correct technique. I am ready." The ship began to hum, and the command circuits connected to the Navigator tanks flashed as they received new input. The transformed spy added, "You should both leave now."

"Come, Draigo. Quickly!" Josef knew that once Navigators turned their minds to a problem, they could forget about mere humans altogether. With Josef piloting, the shuttle separated from the VenHold vessel and headed back to Thonaris's main admin-hub. He had not even finished docking when he saw the ship wink out of existence behind him, folding space back to Kolhar. . . .

He was glad to have received Norma's tacit approval for his success here; at least he assumed she was pleased. And he expected Thonaris to become a powerful, vibrant facility that would produce great profits for Venport Holdings.

Around him, the automated manufactory lines were lighting up and humming, using materials that the extractor machines had mined from the planetoids. In this facility, new ships were being constructed on assembler docks, adding to the Venhold Spacing Fleet's vast and comprehensive network—the glue with which he was binding the thousands of planets in the Imperium.

Now that he knew Celestial Transport was no longer a threat, thanks to Norma's prescience, he let himself relax. Thonaris was a bustling complex, a base to rival (and potentially even replace) the original Kolhar shipyards established by Norma Cenva and Aurelius Venport. Yes, this was a good day.

He looked out the admin-hub's broad viewing port and admired his prize—the body of Arjen Gates himself—captured during the raid on the shipyards. The one man among all the CT workers and pilots whom Josef could not forgive.

From his studies of human history, Josef knew that ancient sailing ships had been adorned with carefully chosen figureheads, and now Arjen Gates had become his. A gruesome statue . . . a trophy.

Pathetic, despairing, begging for his life, Gates had been strapped to a steel crossbar, his arms and legs bound, his neck tied to keep his head upright. Ven-Hold workers had suited up, and Josef joined them, smiling through his faceplate as he watched the vulnerable and fragile Gates squirm. The rival shouted curses as they marched him into the airlock.

"You are a nuisance," Josef had said through the suit speakers. "You refused to learn your place, and you kept taking what is mine. I'm not a man of infinite patience."

The airlock cycled, and the decompression had killed the man swiftly enough. Bound to the framework, straining against the empty vacuum, Gates immediately froze solid, his face drawn back in horror and dismay, his eyeballs shattered. Yes, mounted outside the admin-hub of the robotic shipyards, the petrified corpse made a very satisfactory figurehead.

Josef didn't gloat, however, and turned back to study the Thonaris operations and all the work he had to do.

Measure what you fear most. Do you want that to be the benchmark of your life?

—questions for acolytes, from the Rossak texts

W hen Dorotea first saw Sister Valya again, she felt a wash of relief. "You survived the transformation as well? I am glad to see it!" Valya would be her first ally, the genesis of a new wave of Reverend Mothers. A new partner who had also seen the generations of horrors and enslavement, who would realize that even the smallest risk was too great . . . and that Raquella had kept many important secrets from the Sisterhood. Together they would institute dramatic changes in the Sisterhood.

Valya's gaze flickered away. "No, the poison dosage was wrong for me. After I swallowed the pill, I was so sick I vomited before it could affect me."

Dorotea's mind raced as she absorbed what she was seeing. Even more than before, she became hyperaware of tiny telltale signs, the look in Valya's eyes, the slight twitch of her mouth, the flush of her cheeks, the barely perceptible change in her voice. Her fellow Sister was lying—skillfully, but not skillfully enough. *She had not taken the pill at all!*

"I'm glad you're all right," Dorotea said.

"I made sure they got you to the infirmary. We feared you would die, or suffer mental damage like all the others."

With her heightened senses, Dorotea became aware of signs she hadn't wanted to notice before. She'd considered Valya to be her friend, but now she was shocked to discover that the other Sister had acted disingenuously. So many lies!

A disappointment, but hardly an insurmountable one. She had other *true* allies. From now on, Dorotea would be in control of the game.

WHEN RAQUELLA RETURNED from the new Suk School on Parmentier, she found that the Sisterhood had changed. Dramatically. After her many years of trying, after so many volunteers had died or suffered irreparable brain damage, one of her Sisters had finally passed through the chemical and mental transformation. It had happened while she was gone, and the volunteer had done it without medical assistance. Remarkable, truly remarkable—as was the person who had done it.

Sister Dorotea . . . Her own granddaughter. *Reverend Mother* Dorotea, now. The voices of Other Memories had confirmed this.

Dorotea never should have taken the risk without the proper authorization or preparation, but her success pleased Raquella immensely. At last, she was no longer the only Reverend Mother! She finally had a successor, and though Dorotea's antitechnological leanings troubled her, the younger woman's access to all the wisdom of so many past lives would surely enlighten her.

But rather than rejoicing with Raquella, Dorotea withdrew, wrestling with her inner changes. Late in the morning, beneath a smoky, overcast sky, the old Reverend Mother found her alone at the nearby hot springs, a series of steaming pools, rock bowls filled with hot water that bubbled up from a subterranean volcanic area and overflowed down the slope.

The new Reverend Mother sat on a rock in her bathing garments, immersing her legs in the water. Her black robe lay on a rock nearby. Dorotea looked different to Raquella now, older—as if she had gained millennia of memories. Not surprisingly, the transformation had taken a toll on her, but she was alive!

Dorotea looked up to see her, and said nothing although a thousand unspoken messages emanated from her gaze.

Taken aback, Raquella climbed to the pool, sat down, lifted the hem of her own robe, and removed her shoes so that she could dip her feet in the warm water beside Dorotea. After a heavy silence, she said, "My congratulations on your success. You are the first of many, I hope. I'm deeply sorry I wasn't there to help you."

The other lives inside her were excited, awash with possibilities. Now that Dorotea had identified the proper derivative of the Rossak drug, Raquella envisioned a steady stream of additional successes. She knew now that she was not a fluke at all. . . . Dorotea proved that it could be done. Karee Marques could study the precise sample that Dorotea had taken, and with the new information the Sisterhood would have a third Reverend Mother, followed by a fourth, and many more. . . .

Crisis. Survival. Advancement. At last, Raquella felt great hope for the future of the marvelous Sisterhood that she had created.

When Dorotea still did not answer, Raquella grew more concerned and tried to reach out to the closed-off woman. "Becoming a Reverend Mother can be quite overwhelming. There's much you need to learn about mastering your body, your responses, and controlling the voices in your head. They can offer a storm of contradictory advice, and you will get lost if you let yourself be buried in all those lives. It's difficult to adjust, but you have me to help. I will give you advice and we'll share experiences—one Reverend Mother to another. We have so much in common now—like no other two women in the history of humankind."

Dorotea finally focused on her. "We've always had a great deal in common . . . *Grandmother.* I know who you are and what you did to my birth mother, Sister Arlett."

Raquella went cold, though she should have expected the revelation. "If you know me, then I don't need to explain my actions. You already have many of my memories."

Dorotea averted her eyes and gazed down into the steam of the hot spring, to keep her true thoughts hidden. "Where is my mother now?"

"She's performing an important assignment to recruit more young women for our school."

"When will she earn her way back here? When can I meet her?"

"Meeting your birth mother should be low on your list of priorities." She wanted to inspire Dorotea with the true excitement of what they could do now. "We are *Reverend Mothers*, you and I. It's as if I now have a very special kind of Sister, one that others cannot understand. But we are well suited to understanding each other." So many possibilities suddenly opened up before her.

The fledgling Reverend Mother remained cool, even bitter. "So, you're glad to have a new Sister, but you never wanted a daughter or a granddaughter?"

"I have no mundane familial desires whatsoever. All of my goals involve the *Sisterhood.* Now you have shown the way, Dorotea . . . clearing the path for more Reverend Mothers. My transformation was an accident, but you did it intentionally. The first one ever! I was beginning to wonder if it would ever happen. Now, with your help, we can have many more like us in the future." Raquella wanted Dorotea to see the big picture, since she had the same set of knowledge and past memories. Together, they would have the same goals.

"I already have a number of candidates in mind." Dorotea sounded grim, rather than thrilled.

IN AN ISOLATED room, where she hoped to remain undisturbed for some time, Dorotea sat in intense discussions with five Sisters who had already submitted their names as volunteers to Karee Marques. Dorotea selected the ones who were most acceptable to her, those with attitudes and politics similar to her own. For what she had in mind, she needed allies.

She did not, however, require Karee's guidance or permission, since she had already surpassed the old Sorceress in achievement. Nor did she consult with Reverend Mother Raquella.

Dorotea had gathered them here surreptitiously, in the hope that they would all survive to become Reverend Mothers. For nearly two hours now, she had been preparing the volunteers, allaying their fears and counseling them through eventualities. She helped each woman to envision what would occur in her mind and body when she took the derivative drug.

Sister Valya was not among them. Dorotea knew the truth about the other young woman now.

The volunteers reclined in side-by-side medical chairs to which they were secured by straps, and they were beginning to look a little nervous. Each of them held a single capsule of the latest formulation of the Rossak drug; Dorotea had prepared them herself in Sister Karee's lab.

"As soon as the poison begins to open the doors inside you," Dorotea said, "you must move forward into the labyrinth of your sentience and guide yourself through. Many of your predecessors got hopelessly lost . . . and died. For this internal journey you will be alone, and you can only succeed through your own mental strength. But I can help strengthen you. I want each one of you to be my fellow Reverend Mother."

She narrowed her eyes and looked at all the faces, remembering how these women had expressed concerns about Sister Ingrid's death, how they shared Dorotea's abhorrence of relying on thinking machines. Soon, when they also learned about the hidden computers, the Sisterhood would change significantly. And there was no time to waste.

The five candidates murmured private prayers, then swallowed their pills. Letting out sighs of anticipation, they settled back and closed their eyes. Dorotea went from one woman to the next, checking the straps that held them in place, so they could not injure themselves. Their heads lolled to the side.

Dorotea stood before them, listening to the hushed and eager murmur of voices in her head. It just might work this time. She watched the women begin to writhe in their restraints and cry out in pain. . . .

For hours, they struggled through their inner battles, converting the poison, breaking out of the cages in their minds. She knew what was happening to them.

Three of the women eventually opened their eyes and tried to absorb the whirlwind of lives that assailed them from the past. Dorotea brought their medical chairs upright and gave them time to orient themselves. As if hearing a communication broadcast in their ears, they listened inwardly for several minutes, to the voices of Other Memories.

The remaining two Sisters slumped in their reclined chairs with blood running from their ears, but Dorotea did not think of the dead, only of the three new Reverend Mothers who had joined her . . . allies who would also train others.

"A new day has dawned for the Sisterhood," she announced.

THE WOMEN OF Rossak celebrated the surprising success of three more Reverend Mothers. Watching over it all, Raquella appeared to be very proud, as if a great weight had been lifted from her.

Valya joined her in welcoming the cluster of new Reverend Mothers, though she felt uncertain. If she'd had the courage to take the pill along with Dorotea, she might have been one of them. She was no coward, but she was also not a fool to attempt something for which the failure rate had been so high.

However, if she had . . .

Dorotea came up to her now, and spoke in an accusing whisper. "I know you never took the poison I gave you. You were afraid." Valya looked away as her mind spun furiously for a response, but Dorotea continued. "As your friend, I fully understand. But now I can help you through the process, and I have decided to give you a second chance." She extended her hand, offering another dark-blue capsule like the one she'd offered Valya earlier. "Carry this with you to remind you of the possibilities. Take it when you're ready."

Valya accepted the capsule and tucked it into a pocket of her black robe. Dorotea put a hand on her shoulder, looking very sincere and encouraging. "I'll help you through it. I would very much like to have you as one of my Reverend Mothers."

"One of the *Sisterhood's* Reverend Mothers, you mean."

Dorotea looked at her new companions and smiled. "We all serve the Sisterhood."

It requires a white-hot crucible to melt the hardest heart.
—the *Azhar Book*

With anticipation, though burdened by her secret assignment from Reverend Mother Raquella, Dr. Zhoma awaited the liaison who would take her to the Emperor. Her exclusive patient. The position as Imperial physician would help her gain prestige for her school. If the new Suk School could skate across the thin ice of their financial disaster, they would grow stronger.

But Raquella warned that Salvador Corrino's bloodline was flawed, even dangerous. Zhoma accepted the Sisterhood's conclusion without question, and she would remain alert to discover signs for herself. She had brought a sterilization chemical with her, a substance easily hidden in a vitamin supplement that she would prescribe to the Emperor after she had made baseline physical examinations of the whole Corrino family. Before long, she would dispense with the obligation from the Sisterhood . . . she would be forgiven, and that long-term ache of shame would be gone.

Afterward, she could devote her skills of persuasion to making the Emperor her ally, a genuine patron of the Suk School. Zhoma had not felt such optimism in a very long time.

She waited in the sprawling concourse of the capital city spaceport, while people bustled about their daily business, paying no attention to her. She'd been here for more than half an hour now, and no one had appeared. Troubling, most troubling. She disliked incompetence, and someone in the Emperor's scheduling office had not planned properly. It seemed like a snub, and perhaps she would have to arrange her own transportation to the Palace. This was not the first impression she wanted to make. What if Emperor Salvador was already waiting for her, thinking *she* was late?

After nearly an hour, a thin man in a gray suit hurried up to her. "Excuse me, are you the physician Dr. Zhoma?"

She snapped to attention, keeping her expression cool. "The *Suk administrator* and physician, and I'm supposed to meet with the Emperor. Has there been a miscommunication? His message said he wanted to see me immediately upon my arrival."

"There have been many necessary preparations to be made at the old Suk School building in Zimia. I am your liaison, Vilhelm Chang. I'll take you there right away." Chang led her outside the concourse building to a sleek private flier that bore the golden lion insignia of House Corrino on the hull. The pilot was powering up the engines as they boarded.

"I understood we would be going directly to the Palace."

"No. A significant event is taking place at the old school, and the Emperor is waiting for you there. He'll explain everything himself."

The aircraft took her to the center of the capital city, where she saw large crowds gathered near the original Suk School building. People thronged the grassy park area on the perimeter, overflowing onto nearby streets. So, a reception after all. This was a good sign, though she hadn't expected it.

Even with the expansion under way on Parmentier, Zhoma and her staff maintained offices in the elegant old structure. Perhaps during her tenure as the Emperor's physician, she could convert the historic brick building into a hospital for incurable diseases, like the one Raquella Berto-Anirul and Mohandas Suk had run before the Omnius plagues.

She disembarked and went toward a reception area that held a number of dignitaries, as well as Emperor Salvador Corrino and his brother Roderick. Zhoma froze when she saw Manford Toronto there, too, his unmistakable form atop the shoulders of a tall female Swordmaster.

Salvador nodded a greeting. "Ah, Dr. Zhoma—come! Everyone has been waiting for you. Your attendance is necessary, for the full effect. Sorry about all this. We'll discuss it later."

Roderick Corrino seemed disturbed, and averted his gaze. He said in a low voice, "This is not what you are expecting, Doctor, but we'll explain the reasons in private. Do not be alarmed. The Emperor will find some way to make it up to you."

Not sure what was happening, Zhoma looked at the legless Butlerian leader, who regarded her with obvious disdain, as if she were animal excrement on a path.

Satisfied that the Suk doctor was watching, Manford called out to his followers without waiting for the Emperor's leave. "Onward, to the old administration building!" He gestured with a well-muscled arm, and his Swordmaster marched forward. The crowds on the streets and in the parks moved in a wave, their voices rising in shouts that had an oddly victorious overtone.

Confused, Dr. Zhoma followed the Corrino brothers. "I apologize for this," Roderick said in a low voice.

"What—what are they going to do?" This was clearly not a celebratory show in her honor.

Manford did not hesitate to give commands to the Emperor and his companions. "Wait here, Sire—my followers will do the rest."

Roderick and Salvador stared scrupulously ahead. "Merely a symbolic action, Doctor," the Emperor muttered to her. "There's no way around it. You'll just have to take your lumps today, and I'll find a way to make amends."

As the female Swordmaster ascended the stairs of the old building with Manford riding high, the Butlerian crowds streamed forward to surround the structure. They lit torches as they ran.

"You can't just let them burn down our great school, Sire!" Her voice sounded much smaller than she'd intended.

"*Let* them?" Salvador turned to her. He was upset, and took out his anger on her. "This is by *my* command. As Emperor, I have to keep all my subjects happy, and sometimes that involves difficult decisions. You'll get over this—just remember that it could have been much worse."

Her eyes began to sting as she smelled fuel in the air, pungent fumes. She fought to maintain her professional demeanor.

On the shoulders of his Swordmaster at the top of the entrance stairs, Manford raised his arms in a signal. His people laughed and shouted as they cast their torches and lit flames at key points. The fire raced along like a living thing, evidence that they had planned ahead, installing accelerants throughout the building.

Her school! They were destroying the historic Suk School! Several explosions from inside the grand old building made the very sky seem to shudder. Zhoma watched in breathless dismay as the historic administration building went up in flames and the walls collapsed inward, leaving only the front entrance arch intact, where Manford waited. Calmly, with flames rising into the air behind them, his Swordmaster descended the stairs and carried him back toward the Emperor and his companions. Salvador gave a polite show of applause, while Roderick stood silent at his brother's side.

Zhoma realized tears were pouring down her cheeks. She wiped them away. How could Emperor Salvador allow this? He was truly a puppet of the antitechnology fanatics . . . just as Raquella had warned. Zhoma had not taken the Reverend Mother's warning seriously enough.

The Butlerian leader glanced past the Emperor and looked very smug as he had his Swordmaster turn toward Zhoma. "We wanted to show you how forceful people can be without technology, Doctor. Look what we have done by simply flexing our muscle." He turned to gaze at the rising flames. "Emperor Salvador has agreed to abide by basic principles, and he will have no need of your medical trickery."

Her throat felt raw with disgust at what she had seen. "I am a distinguished physician with full training and experience. Your people just destroyed a facility that could have helped thousands of patients. Does that mean nothing to you?" She knew she should keep her outrage to herself, but could not summon the necessary restraint. "Because of you and your followers, countless people will now die from treatable diseases." She turned to the Emperor, struggling to keep anger and accusation out of her expression. "Sire, do you truly want your subjects to suffer because of this mindless mob?"

Salvador looked decidedly uncomfortable. "There have been . . . concerns expressed about some of the technology being used by the Suk School. I simply wanted to ensure we had nothing to worry about."

The crowds cheered and whistled as the roof on one of the building's wings collapsed.

"But you had only to consult with me! I assure you the Suk School neither creates nor uses any technology that violates the principles."

"But your *attitude* is wrong, Doctor," Manford said, as if explaining to a child. "I have read of the tortures performed by the robot Erasmus in the name of *research*. And we will send inspectors to Parmentier, to be certain."

"That will not be necessary, Leader Torondo," Roderick interrupted in a hard voice. "We agreed to this demonstration today, and that is quite enough." Zhoma looked at him, grateful for at least that small amount of support; Salvador, though, did not look sympathetic to her at all.

The Emperor refused to stand up for the school and its physicians, and yet he wanted her to monitor his health and cure his every ill? Zhoma's heart pounded. As she looked at Salvador, she could fully believe Reverend Mother Raquella's contention that this man would spawn a monstrous tyrant within a few generations. Yes, he had to be sterilized—at the very least. But how much more damage would *Salvador* do throughout the rest of his reign?

Zhoma watched in dismay as demolition engineers set charges around the research laboratory structure, the oldest building in the complex. She smelled smoke from the other building, and could no longer watch. She covered her eyes, but Roderick touched her arm, and whispered, "You must not look away, or it will cause you more trouble. This battle is already lost."

Salvador continued to watch. He didn't even seem disturbed to observe the destruction. Trembling and feeling sick to her stomach, Dr. Zhoma looked down in an attempt to conceal her agony.

With the buildings destroyed behind him and smoke rising into the air, Manford Torondo rode on the stone-faced Swordmaster's shoulders, to a speaking platform. An aide scurried up and handed him a bound volume, after which Manford said, "These passages are from the journals of the evil robot Erasmus, the accounts of the demented, horrific medical experiments he performed on human captives."

Zhoma blinked, horrified but also fascinated. The records of those experiments had been sealed away, although she knew they contained valuable medical data. How had the Butlerians managed to obtain them?

Manford began to read, his words amplified across the throng by an unseen sound system. The crowd wailed and grumbled as he recited countless descriptions of tortures performed on countless captives—how he had cut limbs from living subjects and grafted on bizarre replacements, how he had vivisected thousands of victims, simply to understand how human beings functioned.

When he was finished, Manford closed the book and waved to the burning administration building behind him. "Suk medical research is much the same as what the robot Erasmus did, and now we have prevented such horrors from occurring here. Using technology to keep oneself alive is *unnatural*—like what the cymeks did to themselves. Proper care and prayer are all a person needs to stay healthy. If such is not sufficient, if a person requires extraordinary machines to remain alive, it is that person's time to die. One should be content."

Frightened by the fervor, Zhoma wished she could get rid of this fanatic, just as she had eliminated the charlatan Dr. Bando. Without the assistance of "extraordinary machines," the legless man would never have survived the explosion that destroyed half of his body.

And Emperor Salvador was allowing this descent into barbarism! Had all of society gone insane?

Leaning close again, Roderick said, "Believe me, Doctor, we will try to make amends to the Suk School."

Emperor Salvador strolled over to Zhoma, smiling with relief. "There now, that's over with, and the Butlerians can be on their way back to Lampadas. Come with me to the Imperial Palace, Doctor. We will share a sumptuous banquet, and I'll begin to tell you of my ills."

Some people consider facts to be dangerous things that must be locked away and carefully guarded. But I consider mysteries a far greater threat. We should seek answers wherever possible, regardless of the consequences.

— GILBERTUS ALBANS, secret Erasmus dialogues

The skimcraft returned to the desert sietch just after dawn. Still on high alert from the previous night's attack, Naib Sharnak's guards swept out to surround the craft, weapons drawn, ready to fight. They were battered and bruised, still in shock, grieving for lost comrades.

Ishanti emerged from the skimcraft, baffled by their behavior. "I just returned from Arrakis City where I made my report to Combined Mercantiles." She scowled at them. "You know who I am. You act like frightened desert mice."

Sharnak himself came out to meet her. "They struck us in the night, causing great damage and killing six. We managed to drive them off, but they're still out there." He shook his head. "We thought you might be their reinforcements."

"*Who* attacked? Another spicing operation? A military force?" Her eyes widened. "Was it the two pursuing Vorian and me?"

Sharnak seemed embarrassed as he admitted, "Yes, only two of them."

One of the young fighters blurted out, "They were demons that could not be killed! We slashed and stabbed them with knives, pummeled them with fists, and they brushed it all aside."

Sharnak gave a sage nod. "I fear they will come back."

"A Naib should show no fear," Ishanti said with a scolding tone. "Yet I know how monstrous those two are."

Sharnak looked grim. "The attackers were looking for Vorian Atreides. He brought down the calamity on us, and his fate will be determined by the sietch."

"His life is in my hands," Ishanti said. "I rescued him."

"Now he owes a debt to our tribe: six Freemen dead, five wounded—and there may be more casualties if the attackers return."

Ishanti showed her annoyance. "Take me back into the caves. I have troubling news that Vorian Atreides needs to know."

VOR WAS RESTLESS in his stone-walled chamber while two young and anxious Freemen waited outside the opening, their hands on the hilts of their daggers. He considered guards redundant. Where would he go? He wanted to be alone to ponder the implications of what Andros and Hyla had said.

They claimed to be General Agamemnon's *offspring*? The idea was so unexpected that he had been crippled by shock, and now Vor was ashamed. He still had his personal shield; perhaps if he had fought harder, breaking free of the Naib's orders and throwing himself against his "siblings," the innocent tribe members might not have been killed.

The desert people had every right to hold him accountable. His long and eventful life might end here in an isolated desert settlement where no one in the Imperium would ever know what had happened to him.

How he missed Mariella and his friends and family on Kepler, although he had accepted the fact that he might never see them again. All the people from that part of his life now joined the ever-growing lists of aches and regrets, from Leronica and that branch of his past, even to Xavier Harkonnen and young Abulurd. Xavier in particular had been treated badly by history, and Vor was the only one who knew the truth, that his friend's death had been heroic. . . .

A long time ago, when they'd worked as a team, Vor and Abulurd had planned to correct that injustice as soon as the thinking machines were defeated at Corrin. But after Abulurd betrayed him and nearly lost the Battle of Corrin because of his cowardice, Vor had refused to follow through on those plans, and as a consequence Xavier was still portrayed as a monster in the official records. Vor felt guilt for that. Abulurd deserved his punishment, but Xavier was merely a scapegoat in the politically driven Jihad. . . .

Yes, after his long life, Vor knew he needed to atone for many things, and he did not make excuses or ignore his responsibilities. He tried to do what was *right* and *necessary*—and hope that the two things were the same more often than not.

The twins had come hunting for him. Did they want to recruit him, or kill him? Vor had assassinated their father, but the cymek general had deserved to be executed, and Vor would not accept even a momentary flicker of guilt about that, even if the strange children of Agamemnon demanded revenge.

Vor heard someone approaching. The young guards outside the door stood at attention and acknowledged Ishanti and Naib Sharnak. Vor turned to face them as they entered.

The desert woman crossed her arms over her chest and did not defer to the tribal leader. "Sounds as if you've been busy while I was gone, Vorian Atreides."

"I did not intend to be, but the killers followed us here."

"One day they will come back," the Naib said, "and we could better prepare ourselves if we understood who they are."

"I already told you what I know." But the Freemen had been away from the League for so long that they didn't understand the power and fear General Agamemnon had wielded; they didn't understand the indelible mark he had made on human history. He lowered his voice. "Again, I never intended to bring any harm to your people."

"Your intentions do not bring back the spirits of those slain." The Naib shot a sharp look at Ishanti. "And you are the person who brought him here, uninvited. There are those who mutter that *you* should be cast out in the desert along with this man."

Ishanti gave a rude snort. "Let them try. Let them openly accuse me, and I'll answer in my own defense. If they're too frightened to do that, then their whispers are no more than the mutterings of a lone wanderer on the sand. I stand by Vorian Atreides. I believe he is honorable."

Vor appreciated her support. Ishanti was rough and leathery, and the desert had scoured the beauty from her. Unwed and independent, she was an anomaly among the Freemen, and he wondered if she might actually be flirting with him. What did Vor care about her age? He had already spent a lifetime with each of two wives, and loved them even as their bodies grew old and infirm. But so soon after leaving Mariella, he had no interest in romance, wasn't sure he ever would again.

Naib Sharnak continued, "We Freemen can defend ourselves—but this is not our battle. It has never been our battle, and I refuse to waste the blood of my people on *your* enemies. I have decided to cast you out into the desert, stranger, for our own safety."

Ishanti looked indignant. "Give him supplies and a chance."

The Naib didn't care, one way or the other. "So long as you pay for them, Ishanti. To me, it is not imperative that he dies—simply that he *leaves*."

"First, you should hear what I discovered in Arrakis City." Ishanti looked at Vor. "I dug through the records of Combined Mercantiles, and found that no rival company claims responsibility for the attack on the spice operations."

"I told you," Vor said. "If those two are the children of Agamemnon, they were hunting *me*. They don't care about politics or melange harvesting."

"True . . . but another man approached me in the city, asking detailed questions about Vorian Atreides, as well."

Naib Sharnak made a sound of disgust. "Just how many people are after you?"

Ishanti added, "And why? What have you done?"

"I've done plenty, but I'm still at a loss." Had Agamemnon released yet another murderous offspring to track Vor down? "Tell me about the man trying to find me."

"He was young and water-fat, no more than twenty-five years. Blond hair and a goatee, like nobles wear. He was blatant, even clumsy, when he asked about you. If he was a spy, he wasn't much of one."

Vor didn't know anyone that young, and it didn't sound like anyone from Kepler.

Ishanti turned to the Naib. "If dangerous people are hunting for Vorian Atreides, we should find out who they are before we banish him into the desert. What if they come out here?"

The Naib considered this for a moment, and nodded. "We must be prepared to defend ourselves."

Ishanti said quickly, "I'll take care of it."

IN HIS WEEKS in Arrakis City, Griffin had spent most of his money, and so far his search had yielded nothing. He had only sufficient funds for two more nights of lodging, and barely enough for food and water. Though he had tried to be frugal, he'd spent too much on fruitless bribes.

The specter of Vorian Atreides had loomed over generations of the Harkonnen family, and he was amazed that the man's name evoked no reaction here. The people on Arrakis were so concerned with their daily toil that they cared little for a figure in a war that had begun almost two centuries ago.

Griffin refused to touch the final stash of credits he had set aside to buy passage off the planet. He would not compromise there: He had no intention of being stranded on Arrakis, whether or not he found Vorian Atreides. Two more days . . . and he would go home.

He missed Lankiveil. He had done what Valya asked, tried his best, but it had not gone well, and House Harkonnen might have to delay, or even abandon, its plan of vengeance.

Feeling no need to socialize, Griffin took his meals in his room. He was also wary of venturing out into the streets after sunset.

A furtive signal at his door surprised him, and he wondered who could possibly wish to speak to him, especially this late at night. However, he knew he had spread his name widely, planting tiny seeds of bribes with promises of more to come—though he had little money left. He hoped it was someone responding to his inquiries.

He opened the door to see three people in desert garb, their faces cloaked by dark scarves and hoods. "We have questions for you," said the person in front, a woman. The voice behind the scarf was raspy and harsh.

He saw her eyes, noted something about her . . . and then recognition came. "I spoke with you at the spice administration building."

Without invitation, the three desert people pushed into his room. "You ask too many questions, and we want to know why."

The young men with her sprang forward. One grabbed Griffin's arms, and the other tugged a dark hood over his head. He fought back with a strength and speed that surprised them, bruising one, knocking another to the floor—then someone pressed a needle-jet against his neck, and the idea of struggling evaporated into blackness.

*Life is filled with tests, one after another, and if you don't recognize
them, you are certain to fail the most important ones.*
> —admonition to acolytes, the Rossak School

A lone man stood in morning sunlight on the highest rooftop of the Mentat
School, staring out at the marsh lake. He wore a wide-brim hat, which he
removed to wipe the perspiration from his forehead. Gazing across the greenish
waters, he saw only school security boats performing their rounds. It was deceptively serene out there, in contrast to the stormy mood in the classes, fostered by
the rigid and angry Butlerian students.

Gilbertus still faced repercussions from the debate in which he had voiced
sympathy for thinking machines, albeit theoretically and for instructional purposes only. He had been foolish to believe that the vehement antitechnology
followers could even pretend to be logical or objective. And he had placed himself at risk.

Now that Manford had returned to Lampadas with all his followers and a fleet
of dedicated warships, the situation was bound to grow worse. Word had leaked
out, reports had been whispered. From the capital city on the main continent of
Lampadas, Manford Torondo responded by publicly calling upon Gilbertus to explain himself and renounce his sympathies toward the hated thinking machines.

High above the linked floating buildings in the complex, Gilbertus walked
along the roof edge to the opposite side, where he could look down on the connected buildings. Some structures had been vandalized overnight: heavy objects
thrown through windows, and the words "Machine Lover!" painted on his office
door. One shockingly primitive drawing depicted Gilbertus himself copulating
with a thinking machine. And his students had been carefully selected as the
brightest, most talented minds?

By his orders, maintenance workers were painting over the graffiti right now, and performing repairs. He realized he should have been more skillful and cautious in the debate. It was his own fault that the discontent had flared up, but he still didn't understand how his own students could do such barbaric things to the revered school.

Many of his trainees remained objective, and quietly supportive, but afraid to criticize the outspoken Butlerians. One student had whispered quickly in passing, "We are with you, sir. We know you didn't mean what you said in the debate."

Now Gilbertus put the hat back on, and drew a deep breath. Despite the cool morning, he could not control the flow of perspiration. He believed in facts, data, and science—and the Mentat School had been built on that firm foundation. He had made many Mentat projections during his life. He was a mathematical fortune-teller, using statistics rather than paranormal powers to predict certain outcomes. Though the Butlerian-trained students in the school were a minority, he had not allowed for the fact that they were more vocal than the moderates, as well as prone to exaggeration and intimidation. He should have projected how swiftly they could make other students at the Mentat School turn against him, or at least fall silent rather than defending their Headmaster.

As he made his way back downstairs, Gilbertus knew he had to find a way to make the silly furor blow over.

IN CONTRAST WITH the rooftop, his office was dark and gloomy. He had drawn all the window coverings so he could speak to the small golden ball that comprised Erasmus.

The independent robot was adamant. "All will be lost if Manford's mobs find my memory core. You made an error in allowing your students to glimpse our true thoughts. Was it only an exercise, or were you trying to win them over to our side with logic?"

"I wanted them to *think!*"

"If Manford Torondo turns his people against you, we may have to abandon the school. You must *convince* them. Make your apologies—and lie if necessary. Do whatever you must. If they came to lynch you, I would be helpless to defend you—or myself."

"I understand, Father. I won't let that happen, I promise you."

"But what if you die, and I am condemned to remain here hidden and helpless? How could I survive? I sacrificed everything for you. I sabotaged the machine defenses at Corrin and brought about the downfall of Omnius, just to save your life!"

Gilbertus bowed his head. "I know, and I promise I will help you—but first I must convince Manford Toronto that I am no threat."

And so, to appease the dissenters, the Headmaster delivered a speech in the school auditorium, in as convincing a tone as he could manage, "We have to stop rationalizing the extent to which technology is acceptable. We should not measure it, but rather stand strong against it." He had spoken eloquently for the better part of an hour, doing his best to persuade the small but destructively vocal minority that he was sincere.

His backpedaling and excuses somewhat mollified Alys Carroll and the other angry students, but Gilbertus knew the problem was not over.

He received word that Manford Toronto intended to investigate, in person.

WHEN THE BUTLERIAN leader came to assess the situation at the Mentat School, Gilbertus realized that this could well be his most dangerous debate.

Manford arrived by powered boat at the Mentat School's interconnected floating platforms. He emerged riding on the shoulders of his female Swordmaster, and that in itself was a bad sign. Gilbertus knew the legless man allowed himself to be borne on a palanquin when he simply intended to have a meeting, but he rode upon Anari Idaho's shoulders whenever he went into battle.

As he greeted Manford, Gilbertus maintained a steady demeanor of contrition and cooperation. "I apologize, Leader Toronto, that this misunderstanding has brought you away from your more important duties."

"*This* is one of my important duties." Manford looked around at the buildings. "Your Mentat School should be solidly on the side of righteousness, without equivocation. By training humans to think with the efficiency of computers, you demonstrate our inherent superiority over the thinking machines. But from what my friend Alys Carroll tells me, you have allowed yourself to be . . . tempted."

Gilbertus kept his gaze downcast. "I assure you, it was merely a practice debate, an exercise to challenge the preconceptions of the students—nothing more."

"You debated a bit too well, Headmaster, and I must emphasize that you selected a subject that was unsuitable for any debating class, because the matter of thinking machines is *undebatable*." With his right hand, Manford nudged Anari, and she walked forward, herding Gilbertus back inside the school. Manford continued, "One more thing. I have always been reticent about your practice of studying combat robots and computer brains as an aid to instruction. Too dangerous."

Gilbertus answered in a humble voice, "I understand. After much reflection,

I also understand how my recent lesson was misconstrued, and I wish to make amends for my lapse in judgment."

A look of approval flickered in Manford's eyes. "Very well. For our first step, I want you to show me this storehouse where you keep the forbidden machines. Alys Carroll told me that your specimens are not all as deactivated as you claim."

Gilbertus gave his best dismissive laugh. "They are merely museum pieces, dismantled components."

"Manford said he wants to see this place," the Swordmaster growled.

Gilbertus led them through the school buildings, along passages and across bridges; five silent but intense Butlerians also followed them, ready to do anything their leader asked.

Fishing the key out of his waistcoat pocket, Gilbertus unlocked the door and swung open the entrance to the large storehouse, which was lit by garish glow-globes. Anari and Manford remained in the hall, looking suspiciously inside, while their five Butlerian companions shifted behind them.

Manford scowled at the combat meks, the weapon arms, the detached robot heads. "I want to accept your claims of loyalty, Headmaster, but this causes me great concern. These evil artifacts should have no place in your teachings."

Gilbertus schooled his emotions as Erasmus had taught him. "The mind of man is holy," he said, reaching his decision. "There cannot be even a semblance of impropriety in the Mentat School. Allow me to take care of it myself."

In the storeroom, he found a metal rod that would serve as a cudgel, picked it up, and hefted it in his hand. "Thank you for the opportunity—and for believing in me." Taking a deep breath to prepare himself, he stepped to the shelf filled with robot heads, raised the cudgel, and brought it down with all of his strength.

As Erasmus had said, he needed to convince the Butlerians. He smashed the first robot head, crumpling the faceplate and scattering the diamondlike optic threads. He swung the club and knocked two other dismantled heads aside, then he turned and began to furiously batter an intact combat mek.

Within moments, the enthusiastic Butlerians had grabbed their own makeshift cudgels and joined him in the mayhem.

MANFORD TORONDO'S FOLLOWERS were too eager as they flooded through the Mentat School, peering into the students' quarters, ransacking possessions, demanding that the students unlock sealed trunks (or breaking open the seals themselves if the students refused). In response to indignant outcries, the Butlerian searchers said, "A Machine Apologist has no right to privacy, and if you are innocent, you have nothing to hide."

Gilbertus knew they would reach his chambers soon enough. His pulse raced as they made their way through the corridors.

Riding on his Swordmaster's shoulders, Manford had to duck in the doorway as she walked into the Headmaster's office. Two Butlerians followed them. "I will search your office personally, Headmaster Albans," Manford said. "Simply a pro forma matter."

"By all means," Gilbertus said, because he could say nothing else. He studied the placid face of the Butlerian leader, trying to detect any hint of genuine suspicion. Did Manford have a reason to target his office, or was he just being thorough?

Anari Idaho looked at the books on his desk, studying the titles skeptically. "Why do you have so many books about the demon robot Erasmus?"

"Because it is important to know our enemy." None of the books shed any positive light on Erasmus whatsoever; some were filled with ridiculous exaggerations, while others were eerily accurate. Gilbertus had been there on Corrin himself, had watched the bloody "panic response" experiments, the dissections of living twins, even some of the supposed "artwork" the robot had fashioned out of entrails and internal organs.

"No person with a soul can ever understand Erasmus," Manford said. "I know this for a fact. I have studied his original laboratory journals myself."

Gilbertus felt his pulse race. "You have the journals? Might I be allowed to peruse them?"

"No, Headmaster. Some information is too vile for any other eyes to see. I intend to burn the documents after I have finished with them."

The Butlerians pulled out the drawers of his desk, opened cabinets, lifted corners of carpeting in search of hidden lockboxes beneath the floorboards. They took down the curtain rods, unscrewed the finials, and looked inside.

Gilbertus remained outwardly calm despite his growing fear. If they found the robot's microscopic spyeyes, if they discovered circuitry connections that led to the secure hiding place, then the robot memory core would be destroyed, Gilbertus executed, the whole Mentat School razed to the ground.

They took books and keepsakes off the shelves, rapped the backboards looking for secret compartments. Gilbertus tried not to stare at them. His thoughts raced as he considered any possible weakness. He had never expected a search to be so meticulous.

They moved to the next section of the shelves that contained the secret compartment hiding the robot's memory core. They pulled books from the top shelf, working their way down.

"Please be careful," he blurted out. "Some of those items are valuable."

Manford gave a nod to his followers. "No need to be discourteous. The Headmaster has cooperated fully. As I stated before, I do not doubt his loyalty."

Gilbertus seized on an idea, a way to distract them from their search. Erasmus himself had suggested that he keep this precious piece of knowledge as a bargaining chip. Now he decided to play it.

"I have something important to reveal to you, sir—the result of an intricate Mentat projection." Manford motioned for his followers to stop. Gilbertus leaned forward, lowered his voice. "But this is best discussed in private. If word should leak out before we're ready . . ." He looked meaningfully at the followers. "I don't know these people."

Manford pondered a moment, then dismissed the Butlerians. "Anari stays."

"That is acceptable."

After the other Butlerians had left the office, Manford said, "Very well, I hope this is significant. Tell me more."

Gilbertus spoke in a rush. "I believe I have located an extensive abandoned robot outpost, a large shipyard or supply station . . . perhaps the largest of all. According to my projections, it remains untouched . . . and waiting for you."

"Excellent!" Manford looked very pleased. "We will make an example of it. Good work, Headmaster."

"I can give you the full details of my projection. When I am proved right, I hope you will consider it a peace offering, to show you my true loyalty."

Manford chuckled. "Headmaster, there has been enough turmoil here at your school, and this unrest, even a potential schism, does not serve my purposes. I need tactically trained Mentats for our continuing work of hunting down forbidden technology and illegal activities, so your Mentats must continue their studies." Manford adjusted himself in the harness on Anari Idaho's shoulders. "I'll issue a statement that I have no concerns about the purity of the Mentat School. I'll put an end to these mutterings, and all will return to normal."

"And we will destroy the shipyards," Anari Idaho said.

The first person to successfully negotiate a dangerous path is either the bravest or the most fortunate.

—proverb of the Sisterhood

First there were three more Reverend Mothers, guided by Dorotea. And in the giddy rush of the following week, eleven more were successful . . . while ten less fortunate Sisters perished in agony. Reverend Mother Raquella guided four of the volunteers, having them take the new Rossak drug, coaching them through the process, as she had done before. Three of those four died.

In all, sixteen women passed through the mental barrier and became superior humans, achieving their true potential.

Valya was not one of them.

She had kept the capsule of the Rossak drug that Dorotea had given to her, but Valya wrestled with her decision. Despite being sorely tempted, she had not been able to gather the resolve to make the attempt. Though she sincerely believed she had learned what the Sisterhood could teach her, and knew herself to be more qualified than most of the volunteers who had accepted the risk, she still could not justify the odds. Nearly half of those who tried the poison perished in the attempt.

And Valya still had much to live for, much to accomplish.

She had not heard from Griffin in a long time, and longed to be at his side when he defeated Vorian Atreides, but she was here, facing an even more difficult opponent.

Valya felt like a person standing on the edge of a high and narrow gap, knowing she *might* be able to leap across—as others had done—but if she failed, the fall would kill her. She was not yet ready to make the leap, and keeping herself alive was not cowardice, she told herself, but a necessity. She had fallen into her own arctic waters of doubt . . . and her brother was not here to jump in and save her.

Instead, one afternoon Valya turned to her other primary path to advancement. Smiling, trying to make up for all the attention she had previously given to Dorotea rather than to Anna, she accompanied the Emperor's sister back to her sleeping quarters in the acolytes' section. "Why don't we study the *Azhar Book* together?" Valya suggested. "I can help you with your lessons. Or we could just talk. Perhaps you would like to tell me how you were able to manipulate your fogwood trees back in Zimia, and the burrowers in their tunnels."

Anna brightened. "I've got a better idea." Valya sensed an excitement in the other young woman. All around them the tunnels were empty and quiet. Anna looked around, as if to see if anyone could eavesdrop. She leaned closer, and spoke in an excited rush. "It's time for me to go through the transformation and become a Reverend Mother! When I succeed, imagine how much help I can be at the Imperial Court—and my brothers wouldn't be able to tell me what to do anymore."

Valya knew the girl was not even close to being prepared for such an ordeal; she was too moody and flighty to be a candidate. "Anna, even *I'm* not ready. Maybe with a few more years of training—"

"I can survive, Valya—I know it." Anna clutched her arm. "Stay with me and help me pass through."

Valya reacted with alarm. If Anna Corrino died from the poison, the Emperor would have no choice but to retaliate. And they would blame Valya herself! "No, Anna, don't talk like that. So many women have died in the attempt. Emperor Salvador would forbid it outright."

"I'm my own person, more than just the Emperor's sister, more than . . . more than just a Corrino." Tears sprang to Anna's eyes. "You don't know what it's like."

Oh, I know that all too well. Valya tried to give her a reassuring smile. "I'm your friend, Anna. I don't want you in any danger, so I can't let you try it . . . not yet. But if you work hard on your studies, and develop your abilities first—" Valya knew, though, that would never happen; the Princess just didn't have the focus and determination, other than the stubbornness she displayed on occasion.

In a huff, Anna turned her back. "I make my own decisions. You don't control me—as you said, I am the Emperor's sister." She reached into her own robe and withdrew a small, dark-blue pill. "If you're too afraid to become a Reverend Mother, then I will do it—without you."

Startled, Valya recognized what looked like the second capsule Sister Dorotea had recently given her. "Where did you get that?"

"Your own quarters. I found it there, just like I stole the passkey to get into Sister Karee's lab. You spent so much time with Dorotea, you didn't even notice!"

Valya lunged forward to snatch at the pill, but Anna yanked it away. "Stop," Valya said. "You don't know what you're doing!"

"I am so tired of people always telling me that!" Squirming away, she popped the capsule into her mouth and swallowed. Valya watched in horror. Anna stepped back and crossed her arms, smug. "Now there's nothing you can do."

Valya felt cold, knew how swiftly the Rossak drug would act. The Emperor's sister smiled—then collapsed to the stone floor in convulsions, her face knotted in a scream that could not escape through her clenched jaws.

Valya dropped to her knees and grabbed Anna's shoulders, trying to rock her back to awareness, but the young woman was already lost in the depths of her ordeal. The reaction was extreme and another thought chilled her. What if Dorotea had intentionally given Valya a lethal dose, one designed to kill her before she could transform?

Valya's heart pounded, and she knew she should summon one of the medical Sisters and get Anna to the infirmary. She looked around wildly for help, but was afraid to be seen here. She was responsible for Anna Corrino!

Dorotea would know full well where the drug had come from, and that Valya had avoided taking it. She might even have guessed that Valya was too frightened to attempt the transformation yet herself. What if Dorotea had convinced Anna to take the poison instead?

Anna continued to writhe and whimper, flailing her arms in unimaginable pain. Her eyes rolled back in her head.

All of Valya's hopes of getting close to the Corrinos, of regaining her family status, lay dashed on the chamber floor. How could Anna have done this to her?

But another thought occurred to her—Anna had already sneaked into Karee's lab once, so maybe Valya could convince the others that the girl had done it again, stolen a capsule of the Rossak drug, and foolishly swallowed it on her own. Valya would have to replace the capsule, keeping another one in her pockets so she could show Dorotea that she still had it. Then she would be cleared.

She looked down at Anna Corrino, who lay shuddering and spasming on the stone floor. There was really nothing Valya could do for her—the die was already cast. And one of the acolytes would find her soon enough.

Moving quickly, alert for any movement in the corridors, she slipped away from the acolyte chambers and hurried to the jungle lab of Karee Marques to prepare the evidence she needed.

Those who nourish themselves with hatred seldom realize they are starving.
—Zensunni warning

Though he was groggy and blinded for most of the journey, Griffin knew that his captors were not just taking him to a hiding hole in an Arrakis City slum. He awoke aboard a loud, vibrating aircraft that rose and fell on thermals and updrafts. He recognized the three voices, particularly the raspy woman's, but they conversed with one another in a language he could not comprehend.

After he had been awake for several minutes, jostling and bumping in the flying craft, he called out through the opaque hood, "Where are you taking me? Who are you?" His hands were bound, and he couldn't fight.

"No questions," the woman said. He felt the needle-jet against his neck again and fell back into unconsciousness. . . .

When Griffin returned to fuzzy awareness, he found himself propped up in a chair, his wrists still bound behind his back. Someone yanked the hood from his head, and he felt as if light and fresh air had been splashed in his face like a bucket of icy water.

No one would waste water on Arrakis, he thought, and he realized he was still drugged, possibly delirious.

Griffin heaved a deep breath, and the smells that assaulted his nostrils snapped him to awareness like ancient smelling salts. The air roiled with raw spice fumes and human odors, like fermented perspiration and unwashed skin and hair. He saw he was surrounded by rock walls.

Sounding baffled, an unaccented male voice said, "I have never seen this person in my life. I have no idea who he is."

Griffin turned toward the voice, focused his eyes on the face—and tried to lunge out of his chair. "Vorian Atreides!"

The other man recoiled in surprise. Two of Griffin's captors shoved him back down into the chair. A gruff man with gray-black hair bound in a thick braid stood before Griffin, arms crossed over his chest. "Why have you been searching for this man?" he asked, nodding toward Atreides.

"Because he destroyed my family." Griffin wanted to spit. His own visceral reaction surprised him.

Vorian just let out a long sigh and shook his head. "You'll have to be more specific than that—I've lived a long life, and I don't know how many of my enemies remain. I certainly don't recognize you. What is your name?"

"Harkonnen." He summoned all his courage and anger, imagining what Valya would do if she were here. "Griffin Harkonnen."

The stunned look on Vorian's face was almost worth the amount of time Griffin had waited to see it. When the realization blossomed behind Vor's eyes, it was clear the man hadn't forgotten what he'd done. "Are you Abulurd's . . . grandson?"

"Great-grandson. Because of you, the Harkonnens have been stripped of our heritage and left as pariahs on Lankiveil for four generations!"

Vorian Atreides nodded, his expression distant. "Lankiveil . . . yes, I forgot that was where Abulurd went. Has it really been eight decades? I should have checked up on him."

Griffin was not finished. "And before that, Xavier Harkonnen, hero of the Jihad and one of the greatest fighters of thinking machines! He died in disgrace because *you* ruined his career!"

Vorian's gray eyes looked heavy. "I loved and respected Xavier Harkonnen, and I meant to make that right. I loved Abulurd, too—he was more of a son to me than my own sons were . . . until the Battle of Corrin."

"You abandoned him!"

"There was nothing I could do."

"You could have *forgiven* him!"

Vorian straightened. "No. I could not. I barely managed to prevent him from being executed. I sent him away to a place where he could live his life. . . . I did my best."

"Your best! You could have told the truth. You could have asked for clemency. *You*, the great Vorian Atreides, Supreme Bashar of the Jihad, could have saved him."

"I wish that were so, but the people would never have allowed it. Even his brother Faykan never forgave him. It saddens me the way this turned out for your family . . . especially for Xavier, who was a good man. But I was chased off the stage, and the Corrino Emperors have made it abundantly clear that I'm no longer wanted in public life. That's why I came to Arrakis, to be forgotten." His shoulders slumped. "And yet, you came hunting."

Valya had attributed so many crimes to this man, and Griffin felt all of them piling up in his mind like reeking fish carcasses from a die-off, washed up on a shore. *Avenge our family honor.*

"The Harkonnens remember all you've done to our family, Atreides. You can't hide from your past."

The raspy-voiced desert woman said, "Your past is not just haunting you, Vorian Atreides—it has declared war."

"But my conflict with Abulurd was a long time ago," he said to Griffin. "How can that possibly concern you? You've had four generations to make your own life on Lankiveil—why go after me now?" Vorian frowned in apparent dismay. "How can an old grudge last that long?"

"How can it ever fade away?" Griffin felt an infusion of his sister's anger. The poison had to be drained before the wound could heal. "My brothers and sisters know of our disgrace. My children will know of it."

"I doubt you know the whole story."

"I know enough."

"I am sorry to hear how your family suffered, and I know what you blame me for, but it's foolish to cling to your hatred for so long that it blinds you to the future. If I weren't still alive, would you take revenge on my children and grandchildren? Any descendant, centuries from now, who bears the Atreides name? For how long?"

"Until House Harkonnen is satisfied," Griffin answered.

"But I have no way of making amends. Your search for me has been in vain. The Naib already plans to cast me out into the desert." He let out a small, humorless laugh. "If you had just waited a little longer, your revenge would have taken care of itself."

"Revenge never takes care of itself." Griffin clung to a vision of Valya in his mind, and tried to think of what she would do in this situation. He did not want her to be disappointed in him.

The Naib was angry at both Griffin and Vor. "This is a blood feud that the Freemen have no part of, Vorian Atreides—and you have brought it to our doorstep." He gestured for one of the desert men to slash the bindings on Griffin's wrists, and when free, the young man pulled his aching arms around in front, rubbing his hands, flexing his fingers.

Vorian shook his head. "Once again, no matter how much I try to leave the universe alone, my enemies seek me out. And now I've made your tribe angry, as well. It is clear that I have overstayed my welcome."

The Naib directed his men. "Separate them, and take them back to empty chambers. Tomorrow, the desert shall have them both, and let their water go with them."

Griffin focused his gaze on Vorian Atreides as the desert men ushered him off into the tunnels.

An Emperor has no shortage of plots against him.

—EMPEROR FAYKAN CORRINO,
first ruler of the new Imperium

Dr. Zhoma waited for Roderick Corrino outside his government offices. She did not normally feel so agitated, and she used a calming technique she had been taught years ago on Rossak.

Refusing to sit down, she paced back and forth in front of the elderly female receptionist, who sat at a large gilded desk, opulent enough to have been used by any nobleman in the Imperium. But Zhoma knew that Roderick—unlike his brother—was less interested in ostentation and self-indulgence than in wisely governing the thousands of worlds in the Imperium.

Prince Roderick was late for their scheduled meeting, and Zhoma began to wonder if the Corrinos ever kept their appointments. At least he had sent a professional, considerate messenger to apologize for the delay.

She was not so impressed, however, with Salvador. After he allowed the Butlerian fanatics to ruin the historic school building, she was very afraid for the future of human civilization. Although Reverend Mother Raquella had warned about some vague offspring down the chain of descendants, Zhoma felt the real danger was already at hand, not generations away.

After listening to the Emperor's litany of ills, Zhoma insisted on giving full medical checkups to Roderick, his wife, and their four children—as she had already done for Salvador and his wife, Tabrina. Accustomed to being given questionable treatments by Dr. Bando, Salvador wanted her to prescribe a magic cure. Under the circumstances, considering his unfounded trust in Bando, and now in her, she should have no trouble convincing him to take vitamin supplements laced with a drug to render him sterile.

Staring out across ornamental gardens and sparkling fountains on the palace grounds, Zhoma still reeled from the barbaric display that had greeted her arrival here. The destruction of the historic Suk headquarters had been a great loss, and she had advised Dr. Waddiz to fund additional security forces on Parmentier to protect the main school complex. She had no idea how the school would pay for it, even with the money the Emperor and the Sisterhood would be paying her.

Nevertheless, she already felt trapped here.

Fortunately, Roderick seemed to be far more rational than his brother, a man who thought beyond his own interests. In her mind, he would make a far better Emperor. . . .

Roderick Corrino entered the outer offices at a brisk pace, all business. He gestured for her to follow him into his private office and closed the door. "Sorry for the delay, Doctor. I've been discussing the recent matter of the old Suk School building with my brother. First, my personal apologies—the destruction of that historic facility was a travesty, but it was the best way to control Manford Torondo and his fanatics for the time being. Allow us to assist your school and compensate you for the damage."

Zhoma swallowed hard, tried to cover her joy at the possibility of another significant cash infusion into the school coffers. "Thank you for that, my Lord. Money cannot replace the priceless treasure that the mobs destroyed, even if the fee were calculated at high market value. Still, such funding can be applied to our other works. Suk doctors are doing so much good, helping so many people—if only we weren't hamstrung by the limitations the Butlerians force upon us. We are not allowed to use our best technology, and thus many people are misdiagnosed. They die for lack of treatment that should have been widely available."

Roderick gave her a rueful smile. "I insist that you use every means available to keep our family in the best of health—no matter what the Butlerians say. You just let me deal with them."

Knowing she had to tread carefully, Zhoma ventured, "I was hoping, my Lord, that you might be our advocate—not only with the Butlerians, but with your brother, as well. In my medical opinion, your father's cancer would not have killed him if he'd accepted advanced medical treatment."

Roderick nodded slowly. "Our father . . . changed toward the end of his life. After the scandal with Toure Bomoko, the rape of the Virgin Empress, and the execution of all the CET delegates, he became quite reactionary." The prince looked up at her again. "But we don't have to be. I will be your advocate, though I cannot guarantee that the Emperor will always listen."

"You are the Emperor's brother."

"And you are the Emperor's physician, as well as the administrator of the Suk School."

She was pleased he would consider her so important. "Unlike other administrators who pay themselves handsomely and value money above all else, my entire salary as your brother's physician will go directly to the Suk School accounts to pay for the extensive new Parmentier facility." Zhoma kept her expression bland, so he did not read how much she had despised Dr. Bando.

The office door flew open and a small blonde girl ran in, crying. Ignoring Zhoma, she crossed the room to her father. "Sammy's gone! I can't find him anywhere!"

"I'm in a meeting now, Nantha." Roderick bent over to wipe the tears from the six-year-old's face. "Wait outside my office, honey, and I'll get someone to find your dog. I'll call out the Imperial troops if I have to. He can't be far away. We'll find him."

The child nodded. He kissed her on the cheek, and she trundled off, not quite closing the door behind her. Moments later, someone else closed it from the other side.

"My youngest daughter," Roderick said to Zhoma. "Sorry about the interruption."

"I've read her medical files, in preparation for the checkups . . . whenever you and your family find it convenient, sir."

Now that she observed firsthand how rational and considerate Roderick Corrino was, she felt convinced that she had to do more than simply prevent Salvador from having children . . . she had to stop him from doing further harm. Right now. And as his personal physician, with very close access, she would have plenty of opportunities. . . .

The choices were limited, but obvious. As a Suk doctor, she was sworn to protect life, but if she opened the way for Roderick to become the ruler instead, she rationalized that she would be *saving* lives. Zhoma had already accepted murder as her only choice once before.

SHE MAINTAINED A professional demeanor while she met Roderick, Haditha, and their four children in the palace clinic. After performing thorough checkups, Dr. Zhoma gave the prince's family a clean bill of health and annotated their records accordingly. As Haditha and the children left the front office, Zhoma watched them. "Your children are the hope of the Corrinos, Prince Roderick—the next Imperial line."

He smiled. "I'm still confident my brother will produce an heir. He knows his responsibility to the bloodline, and so does Empress Tabrina. Failing that, he has his concubines, just as our father had. I intend to pester him to get about his business with a little more diligence."

Zhoma looked hard at him as they went inside the private examination room, and she closed the security door. "If nothing comes of it, I'm confident you could handle the Imperial duties well enough."

He became instantly cold. "My brother is the rightful Emperor, and I have no desire for the throne—my duty is to protect and support Salvador." He studied her with such intensity, she felt as if she were being vivisected. "Why do you ask? Did you find something in his medical exam?"

"No, no. He is healthy, but I've prescribed a vitamin supplement that should increase his energy."

"In that case, maybe I should take the same supplement, and my family should, as well."

She did not hide her reaction quickly enough, and he spotted something in her expression. "That won't be necessary, sir. It's a special formulation, tailored for Salvador alone. I can provide a similar supplement for you and your family as well, if you like."

He didn't press her for more information, but she saw the wheels turning in his head. Afraid that she had raised his suspicions, Zhoma took her leave as quickly and politely as possible.

UNABLE TO SHAKE his uneasy suspicion, Roderick delved more deeply into the background of Dr. Zhoma. Using his Imperial mandate, he retrieved the woman's travel records, which were perplexingly muddy, with many of her trips made under unusual circumstances and with destinations that made little sense. He suspected Zhoma was hiding some unorthodox activity, which concerned Roderick even more.

He discovered that not only was the Suk administrator a talented physician who had graduated with high scores (although she rarely practiced medicine on actual patients), but Zhoma was also a former attendee of the Sisterhood's school on Rossak and had left the school abruptly four decades earlier.

He thought of Sister Perianna's suspicious activities and her mysterious departure from his wife's service. And he and his brother had sent Anna to the Sisterhood as a new acolyte for protection and instruction. Might they indoctrinate her instead?

He would have to stay alert.

That night he joined his brother for a private dinner, knowing that Salvador preferred conversation between the two of them rather than the extravagant and exhausting public banquets. The brothers ate a simple but delicious meal of roast fowl, rice, and vegetables, all of which had been carefully tested for poisons in accordance with Salvador's request.

When the Emperor took out a small ampule filled with a transparent honey-colored liquid, Roderick stopped him from consuming it. "What is that?"

"The vitamin supplement Dr. Zhoma gave me. She says it will make me feel like a new man, healthier and more energetic. Ah, it's been a long time since I've felt normal."

Frowning, Roderick extended his hand. "May I?" Salvador gave him the vial, and Roderick held it up to the light, pondering. "Before you take this, I'd like to have it tested."

"Tested? For what? It was prescribed by my personal physician. You chose her yourself."

"I'd like to be sure. We supposedly trust our kitchen staff, yet we test all our food for poison. Should we be any less diligent with your medicines?"

Salvador frowned. "I suppose not."

Roderick pocketed the vial. "You know I'm always looking out for you, Salvador."

"Sometimes I think you're the only one who does, whether I deserve it or not."

Roderick's heart went out to his brother, seeing the ache and emptiness in his face. "Of course you deserve it."

BECAUSE HER PRESENCE agitated Salvador, the Empress Tabrina spent much of her time in Roderick's offices, asking persistent questions about Imperial representatives, as well as various cabinet ministers and ambassadors.

Roderick knew that Tabrina was studying the duties to find an appropriate position for herself, whether or not Salvador ever granted her a title. The more Tabrina asked the Emperor, the more stubborn he became. Roderick understood his brother much better than the Empress did.

It wasn't that Salvador viewed his wife as incompetent, it was that he considered government positions, cabinet posts, and ambassadorships as rewards to be granted for service, as commodities to be sold to appropriately influential people. Giving such a job to his wife would be a wasted opportunity.

Now Tabrina leaned close to Roderick in his office, studying two new decrees that had been drafted in Salvador's name. The door was closed "for confidentiality," according to the Empress. He remained as patient as possible, though she leaned too close and she wore too much pheromone-laced perfume—certainly not for Salvador's benefit.

She pushed the decrees aside, even though Roderick hadn't finished reading them. "There's so much talk about me having an Imperial heir," she said.

"As there should be. Salvador's son will be next in line for the throne, and the people grow tired of waiting." He looked up at her. "You have responsibilities to the Imperium, Tabrina."

"I could bear a Corrino heir . . . but we both know you would be a better Emperor. You're the smarter one, the better-looking one." Tabrina sounded flippant. "Why was Salvador born first? It's like genetic roulette, and you lost."

"He's the Emperor," Roderick said, bristling.

"I could bear *your* son," she said quickly, her voice husky. "No one would ever know that *you* got me pregnant, rather than Salvador. Even DNA tests would show the same thing. No one would question it."

"*I* would question it. And if you do not share my brother's bed, *he* would question it, as well." Roderick stood up and walked around the desk, away from Tabrina. Her expression grew darker, and he turned on her. "You are the Empress. Be happy with that. I already have a wife, a family. I don't need to be something I'm not."

"But it's something you *are*!" Tabrina said, and Roderick held up a hand to cut off further conversation. His receptionist abruptly opened the door, and Tabrina lashed out at the old woman. "We asked not to be disturbed. You're interrupting us."

The woman looked past the Empress to focus her attention on Roderick, in a clear rebuff. He wondered if she'd been eavesdropping. "Prince Roderick, you gave me strict instructions to alert you the moment the chemical-analysis results arrived."

Roderick thanked her. "Yes, I did. Empress Tabrina, I believe we're done here. This is an important and private matter." He looked hard at her until she finally submitted, and walked out of his office in an attempt at good grace. . . .

After Roderick read the test results on the vitamin supplement Zhoma had prescribed for Salvador, he went to see his brother right away. They had made a grave mistake, and needed to rectify it as soon as possible.

Moments later, Roderick appeared at the Emperor's private study, chased away the guards at the door, and dismissed the handful of advisers and scribes who attended him. Salvador blinked owlishly up at him. "What is it now, Roderick?"

Closing the door so that they were alone, he said, "My brother, I've discovered a plot against you."

The human brain is a fragile instrument, easily damaged, easily per-verted.

—admonition of the Suk Medical School

Anna Corrino survived, but remained in a coma for days, responding to no treatments, showing no sign of awareness. She was not dead, but the Sisterhood was in an uproar, fearing for the future of their entire order.

The Emperor's sister was impulsive and unwise—the reason she'd been sent to Rossak in the first place. Though distraught, Reverend Mother Raquella saw nothing to be gained by blaming Valya, who had not watched Anna closely enough and therefore inadvertently allowed the girl to do something so inconceivably stupid. The Sisterhood did not look for scapegoats—it looked for solutions.

The unfortunate Corrino girl lay on a bed in the main medical clinic, uncomfortably close to where the vegetative failed Sister volunteers were kept alive. In adjacent, guarded rooms the brain-damaged survivors remained under close observation. Raquella wanted to summon Dr. Ori Zhoma immediately, pulling her away from Salusa Secundus to see if she could do anything to help Anna . . . but the Reverend Mother was not yet ready to let the Emperor know what had occurred.

There might still be time. She needed to be very cautious.

Dorotea herself had lain unconscious for days during her transformation, so Raquella did not entirely surrender hope. However, Dorotea had been strong, well trained, and committed . . . while Anna Corrino was none of those things. Anna's condition was an unparalleled disaster, and all the lives in Raquella's Other Memories could not tell her how to escape the certain Imperial repercussions.

Sister Valya had taken the tragedy personally. She spent every extra hour at Anna's bedside, talking to her, touching the girl's hand, trying to stimulate her back to awareness. As Raquella entered the room that afternoon, Valya looked pale and frightened. "Has Emperor Salvador been informed yet? How do you think he'll react?"

"He sent his sister to us for safekeeping. When he learns about this, the Sisterhood could be in grave danger. Unless she comes out of the coma."

Valya's eyes narrowed, and she swallowed hard. "Perhaps if he never finds out exactly what occurred? We could say it was a tragic accident, that a predator attacked her during a jungle exercise, or that she fell from a slippery cliff path, like Sister Ingrid did."

"But she isn't dead, child, and even if she were that's no excuse. She's our responsibility." In oppressive silence, they both looked down at the girl, neither of them speaking.

Suddenly, heaving a deep gasp, Anna sat straight up on the infirmary bed. Her eyes flung open, and she looked around without seeming to see her surroundings. Her mouth moved, and small, incomprehensible noises came out, growing louder—until Raquella realized they sounded like the voices of Other Memories that came and went inside her own head, as if Anna were channeling them. She seemed to be speaking dozens of nonsensical, overlapping conversations at the same time in Anna's own voice.

Shouting for the medical Sisters, Raquella shuddered at the realization that Anna's attempt to pass through the transformation might have left her damaged, like some of the other volunteers who had failed.

Perhaps it might have been kinder if she had died.

FOR THE NEXT week, the Mentat Karee Marques and several other Sorceresses monitored Anna, tending to her, nursing her. Though Anna had awakened, she might never recover, and Raquella knew she could not avoid letting the Emperor know for much longer, but she wanted a better understanding before she broke the news.

She called Valya and Dorotea—*Reverend Mother* Dorotea—to listen to the Sorceresses' reports. Karee Marques looked highly agitated. "Anna's jumbled voices have stopped for the most part, though they come in bits and pieces and finally fade away. When she spouts phrases, they are not always echoes from her other memories—sometimes she recites facts, random bits of learning such as historical lists, as if information is spilling out of her. She exhibits behavior similar to what was once called an idiot savant. She has an incredible capacity for certain details. She might prove to be useful, if she could learn to control the incredible flow of information."

Sister Esther-Cano, the youngest of the pureblood Sorceresses, spoke up. "We have no idea how this could be, but Sister Anna has become an expert in the technology of foldspace travel. She has recited a wealth of information on all aspects of ship construction and operation, including the complexities of Holtzman mathematics and navigation chambers."

Karee nodded. "We have verified the details to the extent that we could, and found no errors. She seems to know more even than the published papers suggest . . . quite possibly classified information that only Venport Holdings possesses. It is difficult to pull her focus away from such things even to feed her."

Raquella clasped her hands in front of her on the desktop. "Does she discuss other subjects with any level of rationality?"

Karee shook her head. "She doesn't seem interested in anything except foldspace travel—for now. She says she's going to build her own ship and become a Navigator, so she can escape from this place forever."

"She makes no secret about hating it here," Sister Esther-Cano said. "She never wanted to come to Rossak in the first place, but was forced to."

"Previously, she was emotionally unstable," Valya pointed out, sounding nervous, "but this seems much different. I did report on prior indications of her mental quirks, such as how she was able to manipulate the movements of burrowers inside their hive wall, and she said she could also alter fogwood growth in the Palace gardens. Perhaps she had an odd kind of mental defense we did not recognize."

Dorotea warned, "I know Emperor Salvador, and he will not take this well. He is quick to lash out and cast blame. We must be exceedingly careful about how we present this problem to him."

Feeling like a martyr, Raquella bowed her head. "I am the Reverend Mother of the Sisterhood. I accepted Anna Corrino into my care, and I promised to protect her. Therefore, I will go to Salusa Secundus myself and give them the terrible news. Anna will accompany me to the Palace, but I will shoulder the blame personally, telling the complete truth and asking for understanding. Maybe in that way I can save the Sisterhood, even if it costs my own life."

Dorotea straightened, and Raquella sensed a change in her demeanor, as if she intended to take charge of the situation. "No, *Grandmother*. The Corrinos already know and respect me. Maybe I can salvage this. They valued my service—*I* should be the one to go. Perhaps I can control the message."

"I can't let you go," Raquella said.

"I am a Reverend Mother now." Dorotea's voice was even, but the defiance was clear. "You don't have to *let* me. I will do what I need to."

Despite her own protestations, Raquella realized that the younger woman was correct. It was the best solution. She was disturbed by the insubordination, but Dorotea had indeed ushered many Sisters through the process of becoming Reverend Mothers . . . something Raquella had never been able to do. And in choosing the candidates carefully, Dorotea had strengthened her own power base within the order. She was ambitious, with obvious aspirations of leading the Sisterhood, and the trip to Salusa would look good on her resume. Was she making a power play? If so, it was a risky one.

Finally, Raquella acquiesced with good grace. "Very well, go to Salusa and take Anna with you. Your past experience with the Corrinos may well make you our best hope."

VALYA ACCOMPANIED ANNA Corrino and Dorotea, along with two of the new Reverend Mothers, across the polymerized treetops to the area where the shuttles landed. Anna was pliable and cooperative, though she continued to mumble a stream of unintelligible phrases. Her eyes were vacant, her expression flat.

The shuttle was ready to go. The two Reverend Mothers helped Anna aboard after Valya gave the girl a nervous, unacknowledged goodbye. Before stepping up the ramp herself, Dorotea turned to Valya. "This is the time for you to make your choice. Will you be on my side when I return? Raquella is not the only one who hears the memory-voices inside. Many of us know the truth of history now, and we were not told an accurate version of events. Reverend Mother Raquella took terrible risks, gambling our souls—our *human* souls!—for her ambitions. I do not believe as she does, nor would I make the same decisions, especially about her precious breeding programs!" A growl of disgust curdled in her throat. "I know about everything, because among the other lives in my mind, I have some of Raquella's own memories. When I inform the Butlerians, and they come in force to find the hidden computers that we both *know* are up in those caves, will you be my ally, or my enemy? Think about it carefully."

Valya froze, feeling her skin crawl. "You took a loyalty oath to the Sisterhood. You can't break your vows like that."

A vein throbbed on the side of Dorotea's temple. "As human beings, each of us has a higher calling to destroy thinking machines. I know the truth now, and I can hear the screams of all those generations downtrodden by Omnius. That came about because of hubris, because humans thought they could control the technology they themselves unleashed. We dare not let it happen again! 'Thou shalt not make a machine in the likeness of a human mind.'"

Valya intoned. "The mind of man is holy."

Moments later, Dorotea boarded the shuttle and sealed the hatch behind her.

Some things are too big to hide.
—anonymous saying

The landscape near the Butlerian headquarters reminded Gilbertus of images he had seen of Old Earth in its ancient days, with rolling green hills, farm buildings dotting the landscape, and pasturelands with grazing sheep, goats, and cows. Even the animals were originally from Earth stock. The scene had a flavor of an old Van Gogh painting that Erasmus revered, *Cottages at Cordeville*.

Gilbertus and Manford Toronto enjoyed a sumptuous outdoor breakfast of fresh farm and dairy foods at the private house of the Butlerian leader.

Because of the great expedition he was about to launch to the Thonaris shipyards, Manford was surprisingly talkative. "If your projection is correct, Headmaster, we will have a great victory—just what I need in order to keep my followers energized. We will be doing a good thing for humanity. I'm glad you will be there to see this."

Taking care to keep up appearances, the Mentat ate his breakfast even though he was not hungry. "I'm pleased you find the results of my projection worthwhile. But I would prefer not to accompany the fleet. I am not a military man, and I cannot abandon my obligations at my school. I still have important training programs to coordinate."

As usual, he had hidden the memory core in his office, bidding the autonomous robot farewell and leaving with an uneasy feeling. He disliked leaving the Erasmus core alone, but he had no choice. Manford had summoned him. Gilbertus realized that, in a sense, he was working for two different masters, and both were invalids.

The Butlerian leader frowned at his answer. "Don't you want to be with us, to see your Mentat projection proved correct?"

Gilbertus remained placid. "I know I am correct."

"Then I want you there for my own reasons," Manford said. "In case a recalculation is necessary."

Knowing it was what Erasmus would have advised, the Mentat acquiesced without showing disagreement.

FEELING GREATLY OUT of place, Gilbertus stood on a platform next to Manford Torondo. In front of them, cheering Butlerians gathered on the vast, grassy field before the ships that were ready to lift off to orbit. The legless man sat on a palanquin on poles that rested on the shoulders of two men; his Swordmaster stood at his side like a guardian statue.

Manford beamed as he looked out on the throng. He glanced at Gilbertus. "And now, as I promised, it's time to remove the stain from your name, Headmaster Albans, to show all these people that you are forgiven, a worthy follower whose loyalty cannot be doubted." The crowd cheered.

Gilbertus did not feel an inner warmth from the praise, as he did whenever Erasmus complimented him. But he pretended nevertheless, glad that the reputation of the Mentat School had been restored.

Manford raised his hands in the air to quiet the crowd and shouted without artificial amplifiers, "Through Mentat analysis, Gilbertus Albans has discovered the location of what may be the most extensive shipyards ever constructed by the evil Omnius. With our enlarged fleet, we shall eradicate another blight left by the thinking machines. Stand in front of me, Gilbertus. Let these people see the Mentat who has revealed our next target."

From the sound of the thunderous applause, Gilbertus knew this man could say anything, and the people would approve of it. Though uncomfortable with the attention, the Mentat took a step forward and stood in full view, while Manford continued to address the crowd.

"Recently, due to an unfortunate misunderstanding, some people questioned the Headmaster's dedication to our cause. Let us put those doubts to rest. Sometimes scholars can get caught up in the theoretical, while true crusaders focus on the practical. This man achieves both. He has sworn his loyalty to us, and his great Mentat School is proof of his goal to make us forever independent of thinking machines."

In the midst of the commotion, Gilbertus had no choice but to stand there and receive the acclaim. Anari Idaho even handed him her sword, so that he could flourish it before the crowd, which made them even more excited. Understanding what they expected from him, and remembering the admonitions of Erasmus to do whatever was necessary to deflect suspicion from himself, Gilbertus shouted into the clamor: "On to the Thonaris star system!"

As a Mentat, accustomed to deep thinking and long consideration before acting, he felt out of balance here with the firebrand leader, who made so many of his decisions on an emotional basis. Demolishing the abandoned shipyards would not be a real clash that required Mentat battle projections, but Gilbertus knew that when the place was destroyed, the crosshairs would shift, and the Butlerians would look elsewhere.

Yes, there would always be a target, and Gilbertus didn't want it to be him.

Anger, desperation, vengeance, regret, forgiveness. It is difficult to sum up one's life in a single word.

—VORIAN ATREIDES, private journals, Arrakis period

The desert people were going to kill him—Griffin had no doubt of that. He could fight an opponent hand-to-hand, could stand up for himself . . . but he could not best an entire tribe.

It had been ten years since Valya jumped into the arctic sea to rescue him, and almost that long since he'd saved her from the drunken fishermen. He and his sister were a strong team, a *surviving* team, but they were not together now to help each other. Strangely, he worried more about her than about himself, and he hoped she could endure the loss if he died here on this sandblasted world.

The Freemen had taken him against his will to their secret hideout, and now that they had their answers, they would not simply return him to Arrakis City with a smile and an apology. Even though the Naib had ordered his outlaw followers to dump Griffin and Vorian Atreides in the desert, Griffin thought they might reconsider and slit his throat, drain his blood, and take his water as a resource for the tribe. That much he had learned in his short time on Arrakis. He recalled how efficiently the people in the alley had killed the robber and taken the body away. The desert people considered outsiders to be little more than walking bags of water.

He knew they would get away with killing him, no matter how they did it, and no one would notice the man from Lankiveil missing from his rooms—the proprietor would assume he had skipped out on his lodgings.

Griffin had been about to return to his icy homeworld and use his remaining money to buy passage . . . but at the last minute, by a strange twist of fate, he had found Vorian Atreides and confronted him. It was at least the partial victory that Valya had wanted—but Griffin wouldn't be going home to tell anyone about it.

Unless he could escape. Griffin couldn't bear the thought of never being able to speak to his family again. That was what finally convinced him to act. He had to tell all of them what he had found, especially Valya. He had to *live* for that.

The desert people led harsh lives and took what they needed . . . and so would Griffin from now on, making his own fate. If the Naib was going to murder him anyway, then Griffin would go out into the desert, where he might have a chance of survival, albeit a minimal one.

The Freemen placed only one lackluster guard in front of his cell, confident that the unending sands around them formed an inescapable prison. Sniveling, feigning weakness, Griffin begged for the guard to come inside. "A scorpion! It stung me!"

When the man came into the cell, wearing an annoyed and impatient expression, Griffin spun and with all his strength delivered a sharp chop down where the guard's neck intersected his shoulder, stunning him. The Freeman had tried to react in time, flinching back, but could not avoid being struck; he had not expected such fighting skills from what he considered a weak offworlder. He crumpled to the floor.

Panting and perspiring, Griffin used his own belt to tie the man, and gagged him with a swatch of cloth from the cot in his cell. Then in the darkness he crept out of the chamber, stealing along the stone corridors.

Several Freemen moved about, but he kept to the shadows and waited until the tunnels were quiet again. He knew his sister would have wanted him to find Vorian's cell, kill the man while he slept, and escape, but Griffin had no idea where his enemy was being kept. For now, he could only hope to get away and survive the desert ordeal . . . so that he could get home to his family.

He found the storage cistern where the Freemen kept their communal water supply, which was carefully regulated but unguarded. In their culture, water thieves were hated more than murderers—but since the desert men had kidnapped Griffin and might still intend to steal his body's water, he felt justified taking a pack and a full literjon. He also found a desert kit with a dust mask and compass, on a rock shelf of supplies near the exterior moisture-sealed door.

He headed out, hoping to find some small settlement or a spice-harvesting operation out there in the arid wilderness. He knew his odds were not good. There were many ways to die in the desert.

VOR LAY AWAKE, staring at the rough stone walls and gazing into his past and his conscience. When the night sentries called out the alarm, he swung off his hard sleeping pallet and pulled aside the door covering, certain that Andros and Hyla had returned. He would fight them—better to die in combat against a true enemy, than to be exiled by the Freemen.

Ishanti ran to his chamber before he could move down the dim corridor, and seemed relieved to encounter him. "Well, at least you two weren't foolish enough to run away together."

"Run away? Who ran away?"

"The Harkonnen man stole water and fled into the desert . . . though what the fool intends to do out there, I have no idea."

Pieces clicked into place in Vor's mind like the gears of a clockwork mechanism. "What does he have to lose? You plan to kill him anyway."

"Now that he has stolen water from us, that's exactly what we will do."

Vor was already moving. "We'll stop him. He can't have gone far. If the Naib gets the people out to search, we can still save him—and retrieve your precious water." Not that he expected them to be grateful.

Before she could answer, Sharnak met them, his face as tight as a clenched fist in the low light. "Now we see how offworlders repay our courtesy."

Vor responded with a wry smile. "Courtesy? You put a hood over his head, drugged him, and kidnapped him from his lodgings. You threatened to execute both of us. You have an odd definition of 'courtesy.'"

Ishanti laughed. "The man swore a blood feud against you, and now you speak on his behalf? You are a strange man, Vorian Atreides."

"Nothing about life is simple." Since his hard conversation with the young Harkonnen, Vor had pondered much about what he'd done to Abulurd's descendants. Blaming and punishing the entire family for the sins of their great-grandfather was an unjust thing to do. His own father, Agamemnon, was one of humanity's greatest criminals, and Vor refused to accept any blame for those crimes. Griffin Harkonnen didn't deserve that, either.

At the very least, Vor knew he should have kept his promise to rehabilitate the record of Xavier Harkonnen. Maybe he should have gone to Lankiveil to check on Abulurd's descendants, as well; he had no animosity against them. He said to himself in a quiet voice, "If you live for centuries, there is plenty of time to do things you regret."

Now that the naïve Griffin had escaped into the desert, Vor felt a genuine concern for him. "We need to find him and bring him back. Then decide what to do with us; take my water if you must, but not his. I don't want him to pay any more for the things I've done."

"He's a foolish offworlder, and we should let the sandworms devour him," Naib Sharnak said.

Ishanti shook her head. "He has stolen Freemen water and supplies. We will retrieve those, at least. If he is so intent on dying, the fool can do it without wasting our water. Vor and I will go together."

THEY TOOK ISHANTI'S skimcraft, but Vor insisted on operating the controls. The desert woman raised her eyebrows. "Are you sure you can handle this?"

"I've been flying craft like these for several of your lifetimes." They lifted off from the line of cliffs and soared into the moonlit night. Vor peered out across the wasteland of sand. "He won't bother to try hiding his tracks—he doesn't know how. He'll just be trying to run."

They spotted the signs of Griffin's passage quickly enough. Leaving the line of rocks, he had set off across the dunes that filled the large basin. At the western horizon, perhaps twenty kilometers in the distance, Vor discerned another line of mountains; Griffin was running straight toward them, likely hoping to reach the shelter before dawn. He had already gone perhaps three kilometers, slogging a long line of footprints through the soft sand like the track of a centipede.

"Your enemy is stupid, Vorian Atreides," said Ishanti. "He's lucky he hasn't summoned a sandworm with all that stumbling around."

During Vor's time among the spice workers, old Calbir had taught him exactly what to look for. In the moonlight across the undulating expanse of sand, he spotted a vibrating ripple on the surface, shadows pulsating forward in a concentrated wave. "He has." Vor accelerated the skimcraft. "We have to save him."

"I knew you'd say that." Ishanti pointed to the west. "He's on a line of steep, soft dunes now—we can't land there. See that valley to the east? Drop me on the edge of those dunes."

"What will you do there?"

"Draw the worm's attention. Circle low, and I'll drop out of the skimcraft. Then you can fly back and retrieve that idiot before Shai-Hulud comes." Ishanti grabbed a pack that was clipped to the inner wall of the cockpit and held on to the door frame.

As he swooped low in the direction she had requested, Vor asked, "You'll be all right?"

She snorted. "You've seen me summon a worm before. I'll be fine." She popped open the hatch and flashed a smile at him. "Hurry, you don't have much time. If we can't save your friend, we lose all that water and Naib Sharnak will be annoyed." She laughed at her own cruel joke. Then, as he throttled back, she tumbled out of the aircraft and landed in a crouch on the soft sand. As Vor circled the skimcraft, he saw her dig in her pack to remove the items she needed.

The young Harkonnen had heard the flying craft approach, and now he, too, saw the sandworm plowing a dry wave straight toward him. Half of the enormous head emerged, an open scooping maw that shoveled the dunes.

Vor accelerated, but if he couldn't land the craft on the steep dunes, he didn't know how he could possibly save Griffin in time.

Suddenly the worm changed course and charged like a bull toward where Ishanti waited. She must have used one of the Freemen syncopated mechanisms that sent drumbeat vibrations into the sand.

Vor found a place to land in a trough between dunes. After hesitating, Griffin stumbled and slipped down the dune face, hurrying toward the aircraft. He might have been willing to die out in the desert, but the sight of the monstrous sandworm had changed his mind.

The intense Harkonnen yanked open the skimcraft door to scramble aboard, then paused upon seeing Vor. "You! Why did you come after me?"

"To save you. Not many others were willing to do so."

Griffin hauled himself inside along with a shower of sand and dust, then pulled the hatch closed again. "I should have stolen one of these skimcraft," he said, looking at the universal controls. "Then I wouldn't have to deal with you." He sat in the copilot's seat.

Vor smiled ruefully.

"You think this means I forgive you?" Griffin asked, brushing sand from his mustache and goatee.

"I haven't thought that far ahead. Now keep quiet. I need to concentrate so I can rescue my friend. She risked her life to divert the worm from you."

Fearing that the aircraft's engine noise would attract the beast, he flew high, then swooped low as soon as he saw Ishanti stumbling along the top of a whaleback dune, gaining distance from where she'd planted the rhythmic pounding device. With an intermittent gait like a start-and-stop ballet, the desert woman ran parallel to a flat basin between the dunes, an area that did not offer her any more cover than the dunes themselves. Vor saw that he could easily retrieve her while the worm was busy with the thumping device.

As he circled for a stable place to set down in the basin, Ishanti ran down the face of the dune at an angle toward him. Suddenly she stumbled into a patch of white sand, a pale blemish on the dunes. The sand began to ripple and pound beneath her, vibrating rhythmically. Vor recalled one of the patient lectures Calbir had given him about hazards on Arrakis, including drumsand. Ishanti should have spotted it, but she'd been running away, watching the aircraft. The section of dune let out a pounding series of booms as the compacted sand grains tumbled and settled into acoustic configurations.

The drumsand noise was much louder than the thumper, and Vor saw the worm coming, fast. Ishanti saw it, too, but she had sunk into the loose sand up to her waist. Powder engulfed her like sucking mud, and Vor didn't dare set down anywhere close, because the skimcraft might sink into the unstable sand.

The sandworm's head emerged like a battering ram through the wall of the dune, attracted by the still-quelling vibrations of the drumsand.

Ishanti was shouting. He could see the panic in her face.

Griffin was terrified, his eyes wide. "She'll never make it!"

Vor guided the skimcraft down. "I think I can get close. Toss me that rope from the kit." The aircraft flew closer. Griffin uncoiled the line and gave it to Vor. "Now tie it to that stanchion."

As the aircraft swooped toward the lone woman trapped on the dunes, Vor watched the eyeless beast plunge forward. He saw, but refused to believe, that he couldn't make it in time. Ishanti tried to dig herself out of the powdery sand that had betrayed her.

"What are you going to do?" Griffin said. "It's not possible. The worm—"

"Take the damned controls!" he yelled, and as soon as Griffin grabbed the piloting stick, Vor yanked open the hatch and rolled it back in its tracks. The sudden lurching breezes nearly pulled him from the piloting seat, but he held on to the anchored rope. The skimcraft raced over the sands, on a collision course with the charging worm.

Wrapping the rope around his shoulders, Vor leaned out of the hatch, dangling into the open, dry air. The aircraft engines roared, but he shouted even louder. "Ishanti! Grab my hand!"

Griffin dropped closer, and Vor hung down, trusting the rope, stretching out his arm.

The worm lunged high, blasting through the sand. Ishanti reached up, but he watched her expression fall as she saw that Vor could never make it, would never get close enough. The worm would take her and smash the skimcraft as well, but Vor refused to give up.

She took the decision away from him. At the last moment, Ishanti dropped her arm and hurled her body loose from the sand and down the dune face, *away* from the oncoming aircraft.

"No!" Vor cried, but she had done it on purpose, to sacrifice herself.

The sliding sand and Ishanti's tumbling body diverted the worm by the smallest degree. Struggling to pick herself up from the loose sand, the brave woman turned and faced the monster, ignoring Vor and the skimcraft, accepting her fate. She raised both hands, whether in defiance or prayer, Vor couldn't tell.

Dangling out of the hatch, unable to stop the monster, Vor shouted to Ishanti, begging her, but the words withered in his throat.

In a thunder of sound, the sandworm rose directly in front of her, and Griffin barely managed to swerve their course away from the dune top. The worm engulfed Ishanti and dove beneath the sands with her, tunneling away and leaving barely a ripple where she had been.

Sick inside, Vor hung there until Griffin dragged on the rope and pulled him back inside. Vor grabbed the cockpit controls and gained altitude; it took him a moment to notice that four other Freemen skimcraft were closing in, surrounding them. So, Naib Sharnak had dispatched others as well, but too late. They had seen everything.

Griffin said nothing. He was ashamed and subdued.

The desert squadron flew near Vor's skimcraft, and he did not try to escape. He turned the aircraft around to follow them back to the cave settlement. "She gave her life to save us," he said. "We're going back to the Freemen."

Sometimes it doesn't take many nails to seal a coffin.
—Emperor Jules Corrino

Emperor Salvador Corrino did not like to witness torture, even when it was conducted on his behalf. He understood it was a necessary tool of state, but he preferred that it be done where he couldn't see or hear the details. *Results.* All he wanted was results. Sometimes, though, he couldn't avoid his obligations.

Dr. Zhoma lay in agony, strapped on a multifunction rack while one of the hooded "truth technicians" plied his shadowy trade. Ironically, the tall, thin man named Reeg Lemonis had learned his skills and adept understanding of the human body's pain centers during several years in the Suk School's specialized training division, Scalpel. At the moment, Salvador was sure the Suk administrator regretted that her school had produced such skilled graduates.

Because the Butlerians frowned on complex technology, Lemonis relied on tried-and-true devices. He had already used an extremities vice to crush two of Zhoma's fingers. Now the man glanced up to acknowledge Emperor Salvador as he attached another clamp and a shock-pack to the doctor's head.

Roderick stood beside the Emperor, also noticeably disturbed. Zhoma moaned and made incomprehensible sounds, only some of which were recognizable as words. She had endured a remarkable amount of pain before Lemonis produced any interesting results. Roderick had been sickened and fascinated by the process, but the truth technician had not inflicted genuine physical damage until she confessed her plot. After that, even Roderick had little sympathy for her.

Lemonis finished attaching the head clamp, checked the fitting, and looked up. "It's shocking information, Sire. The good doctor has revealed some appalling secrets, financial improprieties and major fraud—and she's confessed to murder."

Salvador shot a quick glance at Roderick. "Murder? Who was the victim?"

The torturer had recorded the exact words, but he summarized. "She killed her predecessor at the school, Dr. Elo Bando. Injected him with dozens of lethal chemicals in his office, then used her position to cover up her crime and rule the death a suicide."

Salvador blinked in surprise. "Poor Dr. Bando! She wanted his position badly enough to murder for it?" His stomach knotted, and he made a sound of disgust.

"Not . . . exactly, Sire. She claims he embezzled large sums of money from you and nearly bankrupted the Suk School. She also insists that he was fabricating many useless treatments for you and charging you outrageous amounts."

Salvador's skin felt hot, and his pulse raced. The pounding headache had returned, like something trying to break out from inside his skull. "It's a lie—you need to use more enthusiastic methods to get to the bottom of this. She's obviously trying to curry favor now, and she'll make up any nonsense to stop the pain."

Roderick's look was unreadable. "In that case, brother, the rest of this interrogation is fruitless. Lemonis is a very competent Scalpel investigator."

"Oh, she's been telling the truth," the pain technician said; he did not notice the Emperor's embarrassment. "And she has more to tell us about the plot surrounding you, Sire. It shouldn't take much longer until we know who put her up to it."

As Lemonis moved on to his next phase, Roderick looked over at Salvador and said, "She is a Suk doctor, the administrator of the school . . . the person I picked to be your personal physician. I'm very sorry I let you down."

"It's not your fault—she's clever and deceived us all," Salvador said. "And you were the one who caught her." Dr. Zhoma screamed. Salvador winced, waited for the interruption to end, and added, "I trust you completely."

Less than an hour later, the torturer was satisfied that he had acquired all the available information. Dr. Zhoma lay broken but still alive as Lemonis presented his results to the Emperor. "This doctor has a high tolerance for pain. I have left her conscious so she can answer all your additional questions directly."

Salvador felt queasy, looking down at all the blood and knowing he would never have survived half of what Zhoma had endured. Her eyes were desperate, her face bruised and bloodied. He leaned over her, breathing slowly in and out, and made his voice as deep and terrible as he could. "And what did you plan for me? Are you an assassin?"

"The Sisterhood . . . " she said. He couldn't look at her bruised lips and smashed teeth; all the blood made him uncomfortable. "Breeding records . . . you must not have children. Tainted bloodline . . . They sent me to sterilize you."

Salvador fumed. "*Sterilize* me? They want to destroy the Corrino line?"

"No . . . just yours. Roderick's line should be the Corrino emperors."

Prince Roderick's brow furrowed in deep concern. "The Sisterhood is scheming against the Imperial throne?" He shot a glance at Salvador. "We need to get Anna away from them. We sent her there to keep her safe!"

But Zhoma wasn't finished. What started out as a laugh turned into a cough. She seemed to feel a surge of defiant energy and she spoke with absolute clarity. "After seeing how the Butlerians have you under their thumb, I decided sterilizing you wasn't good enough—you should be *killed* instead." She slumped back onto the table. "You're going to execute me anyway, so I'll tell you what everyone is saying behind your back: Roderick would be the better leader, by far."

WHEN THE TWO men returned to the Palace, after changing clothes to remove the sweat and bloodstains, they were surprised to encounter a somber, formal delegation from Rossak. Sister Dorotea, two other Sisters—and Anna.

"Well," Salvador said, looking at his brother as they both stepped up onto the throne dais in the meeting hall, "I suppose that's fortunate timing, now that we know what they're really up to."

Roderick, though, narrowed his eyes and regarded the delegation with concern. Anna looked confused and disoriented, physically unharmed, but . . . *wrong*, somehow, and very much changed.

Holding the young woman's hand, Dorotea stepped forward and bowed. Her voice was soft and contrite. "Your Highness, a terrible tragedy has occurred."

Roderick came forward quickly to grasp his sister's arms, checking her to see what was wrong, but Anna didn't even look at him; her eyes flicked back and forth, her gaze dancing to an unheard beat.

Salvador remained focused on Sister Dorotea. "Explain yourself—and understand that your life, and the fate of the entire Rossak school, will depend on your answer."

"My answer is the truth and will not change, threat or no threat." She did not remove her gaze from Salvador's. "Long ago, our Reverend Mother Raquella survived an assassin's poison by altering the biochemistry of her body. This transformation gave her access to intense control of every aspect of her body and unlocked a host of memories from past generations. She became our first Reverend Mother."

Salvador was already growing impatient. "I want to know what you've done to my sister—not a history lesson on your order."

Dorotea did not hurry her explanation. "For many years the Sisterhood has been trying to recreate that transformation, exposing volunteers to dangerous chemicals in hopes of finding the key. Virtually all the volunteers died in the attempt, but I recently became the first new Reverend Mother. Once the technique was proved, other Sisters also made the attempt, so that we now have more Reverend Mothers."

Abruptly, Anna began rattling off words at a rapid clip; Salvador realized they were all the names of planets in the Imperium.

"Anna convinced herself that she was ready, though none of us believed so. She was impulsive, stole a dose of the drug, and consumed it before anyone could stop her. She lay in a coma for many days, but did not die. When she awakened, she was altered—as you see." Dorotea's voice remained remarkably steady. "But I don't think she's a Reverend Mother. She seems to be somewhere in between."

Upset, Roderick demanded, "And with so many deaths from this drug, why wasn't it guarded well enough to keep our sister away from it? You knew her emotional problems. That was why we sent her to the Sisterhood—for you to keep her safe."

"Anna is extremely willful," Dorotea said. "And smart."

"Now I'm smarter," Anna interrupted in a slurred voice. "There are people in my head, special instructors. Hear them." She spewed out a jumble of sentences, words, and unintelligible sounds that made no sense, as if they poured out of a bowl in which they had been mixed. Her blue eyes were like glassy marbles, her expression vacant.

Dorotea looked worried. "In the process of becoming a Reverend Mother, a Sister taps into a vast reservoir of past female lives, a host of memories. Anna seems to have . . . partially succeeded."

Abruptly, the young woman stopped her flow of disconnected words and said in her own familiar tone, "The voices are telling me to go away now. They don't like me intruding on them, but it is too late. I'm already there."

"Anna," Roderick said, "would you like to sit and talk with me now, the way we used to? You're home now, where it's safe."

She didn't respond, gave no indication that she had heard him. Her eyes seemed to peer into a hidden, inner world.

One of the main doors swung open, and Lady Orenna came into the entrance hall, wearing a white-and-gold robe. "I just heard Anna's come back to us." She hurried to the stricken Princess. "Oh child, how are you?"

Anna seemed to hear her stepmother. Her face was a mask of sadness, as she looked at the older woman. "They hurt me."

"Who hurt you?" Salvador asked, rising from his throne.

"The voices. They hurt me every time they talk . . . little needles of pain inside my brain."

The Virgin Empress put her arm around Anna and drew her close. "Why don't you stay in my quarters tonight, dear? I'll take care of you. And tomorrow we'll go inside that fogwood shrub you like so much."

"I'd like that," Anna said. "I'm home now."

Emperor Salvador leveled a malevolent gaze at Dorotea and her two companions. "This is the second time the Sisterhood has failed me—in one day! I will shut down and scatter your entire school!"

Roderick touched his older brother's arm discreetly. "But there's more we need to know. Perhaps we should have further discussions about the proper response to this problem. A rash action now could have repercussions across the Imperium."

Sister Dorotea astonished them by speaking up. "Emperor Salvador, I understand your anger. Much of the Sisterhood is corrupt and should be eliminated, but we can save the rest. Some, such as myself and my Reverend Mother companions, believe in a different sort of Sisterhood, one that furthers the noble purposes of the Imperium. It is time to remove the excesses, cauterize the wounds, and move forward along the appropriate path."

Salvador made a rude snort. "I know all about your Sisterhood's schemes, your breeding records, your plot to prevent me from having offspring! Fortunately, we caught your puppet, Dr. Zhoma, before she could sterilize me."

Dorotea's expression became puzzled. "I was not aware of that plan, but Dr. Zhoma was a protégée of the Reverend Mother's. I do not know her well. However, I agree wholeheartedly, Sire—the Sisterhood's breeding program is at the heart of their corruption. There are dark secrets among the Sisters of Rossak, but I implore you to keep in mind that some of us are reasonable and wish to work with you . . . *for* you, Sire. Some of us are loyal to the Imperium and to the cautious philosophy of the Butlerians."

"How many are in your faction?" Roderick asked.

"We are a minority, but many of the new Reverend Mothers share my deep concerns."

"'Thou shalt not make a machine in the likeness of a human mind,'" said one of Dorotea's companions, a diminutive woman with a rounded nose and a mole on her left cheek.

Salvador felt decidedly uncomfortable. "I have heard Manford Toronto quote that many times, but what does she mean here? What does that have to do with what happened to Anna?" The thought of Zhoma's conspiracy hung fresh in his mind.

"Sister Gessie speaks of the most terrible thing the Sisterhood has done," Dorotea said. "In their restricted caves, they use forbidden computers to maintain the disgusting breeding records. Even I am not allowed access to that part of our school, but I have seen the computers in my Other Memories."

Roderick stiffened. "Thinking machines hidden inside the caves of Rossak?"

"What?" Salvador's shout echoed in the vaulted entrance chamber.

"There is a rot at the core of the Sisterhood, but some of us do not find it acceptable. That is why I wanted to bring Anna back personally. I needed to speak with you, Sire, to inform you of this travesty. There needs to be a *purging* of the order, not a destruction—I would urge a course correction. I beg you not to punish our whole order for the actions of a corrupt few. Most of the Sisters do not know of this terrible crime, and they would join us, if given the opportunity."

"And the illegal computers," Roderick said, "you have proof? You can find them?"

"I am certain of it. We can enlist the aid of Manford Torondo—"

With an alarmed look, Salvador said, "No need to involve the Butlerians. The Imperium is *my* responsibility. I'll send a military squad to take care of this." He looked over at his brother, feeling pleased for the first time all day. "There, it's decided."

The Misborn have been cast out by the Sorceresses, but those who sur-
vived know the underbelly of the jungle better than anyone else. Because
of my past history with them, secret places have been revealed to us.
                    —REVEREND MOTHER RAQUELLA BERTO-ANIRUL,
                              predawn address to the faithful

The Sisterhood had to be prepared. Not only did the rush of inner voices
warn Raquella of the impending crisis, but Sister Valya had told her a specific reason for the threat. In becoming a Reverend Mother, Dorotea had learned—
through Raquella's old, embedded memories—about the secret computers.

And she intended to expose the illegal technology to the Butlerians.

Raquella had to do something to protect the Sisterhood before mobs came to
destroy what they did not understand.

Dorotea also had allies among the Sisters, especially among the new Reverend Mothers. Appalled by the emergency, many of the women had been calling
for an end to secrets. Nine of Dorotea's most vehement Reverend Mothers demanded to search the restricted upper caves that held the breeding records,
confident they would find proof of illegal technology.

Up in the breeding-record caves, the isolated chambers held shelves piled
with documents printed on incredibly thin sheets of paper. For generations, the
women of Rossak had compiled and maintained these mountains of information; it would require an army of Mentats to inspect and analyze it all.

Only a subset of the Sisters who worked with these hardcopy genetic records
knew about the camouflaged holographic wall that concealed a large secondary
chamber that contained forbidden computers. But if the Butlerian mobs or Imperial soldiers ransacked the tunnels, demanding answers, someone was sure to
stumble upon the wrong room.

Raquella knew full well that Dorotea's allies had no concrete proof—even
the new Reverend Mothers had unreliable, nonsequential memories from the

past voices they could now access. Her granddaughter might remember some of Raquella's actions from long ago, before the birth of Arlett, but she certainly couldn't be sure what the old Reverend Mother was thinking or doing *now*.

However, merely raising the specter of computers was tantamount to a decree of guilt, and feelings among the Sisters were inflamed even further when Raquella flatly refused to grant them access, stationing additional Sorceress guards on the high path and accusing Dorotea's allies of gross insubordination.

She felt helpless as she watched the Sisters take sides. Karee Marques and her Sister Mentats had already predicted that a dark schism would occur in the Sisterhood. Raquella knew that if she did not openly address the issue, they would see the avoidance as a confession.

She had to hold her ground and remain true to the goals she had established, critical goals that would require drastic action. She conferred with Karee, Valya, Sabra Hublein, and fifteen other Sisters from her most trusted inner circle, those who knew the deepest secrets—and she gave them their instructions.

Then, in a bold move, Raquella summoned every member of the Sisterhood for an emergency meeting at dawn. As the misty sky brightened with sunrise, more than a thousand members of the Sisterhood streamed into the largest meeting chamber.

In such a huge crowd, no one would notice the absence of Sister Valya and a handful of specially picked assistants. This would be their only chance.

Standing before the assemblage, Reverend Mother Raquella raised her hands and waited for silence to fall. With ancient eyes, she looked out across the sea of faces. "Many of you have been eager for an open debate. You have your questions and concerns. It is time for you to speak your minds, all of you. I will listen to you, and respond." She nodded to two hand-picked Sorceress guards, who closed and locked the doors, sealing all the Sisters inside the great chamber. "We will stay here until you have spoken your thought, even if it takes the entire day."

Raquella was ready for all comments and questions.

But it was all a diversion. She needed to buy time.

WITH THE REST of the Sisterhood's members gathered for the meeting, Valya and a dozen loyal Sisters rushed to dismantle the forbidden computers.

Behind the holographic barrier, they broke down the components, removed all the dense gelcircuitry storage modules, and used suspensor lifts to drop them down old ventilation and access shafts inside the cliff city to the bottom of the canyon wall. From there, hushed workers shuttled the sealed components deep into the tangled jungle. Reverend Mother Raquella had shown them a hiding

place where the dismantled computers would be protected from the hazards of the dense undergrowth—where they would never be found by Butlerian ransackers, Imperial soldiers, or suspicious Sisters.

Back when Raquella had nearly died from the Omnius plague, one of the cast-off Misborn had taken her out to a hidden home of other deformed exiles in the jungle. In the caverns under a limestone sinkhole, the Misborn had sheltered her and nursed her back to health. No one else had ever found the place, and the Misborn had all died out in the decades since. The Reverend Mother had not been there in many years, but she remembered.

Valya led her companions into the jungle in a breathless rush, but with military efficiency. The lost cenote would be the perfect hiding place to store the dismantled computers and their priceless genetic information.

As Serena Butler's Jihad taught us, we must use any conceivable weapon to fight the enemies of humanity. But what if those foes are themselves misguided humans?

—PTOLEMY, Denali research journals

W hen he finished repairing the first of the superlative cymek walkers, Ptolemy felt the return of excitement, even optimism. As he became absorbed in studying the mechanical systems, he almost forgot the pain and disappointment of working alone. Without Dr. Elchan, Ptolemy's work had become an obsession to restore order and fix something that had been broken. And he had to do it for the good of humanity.

The thoughtrode interfaces connecting the nerves to the armored limbs were extremely complex, and Ptolemy still had much to learn before he would be able to control a mechanical warrior form using neural impulses. On the plus side, the armored bodies were straightforward machines driven by engines, pistons, and cables, and they could be controlled using more traditional means. Ptolemy constructed a small cab slung under one of the crablike bodies. Sealed and pressurized, with hard-linked inputs to the machine controls, the cab was equipped with life-support systems that would allow Ptolemy to ride inside while he explored the murky, caustic landscape of Denali.

When he finished testing the systems, Ptolemy climbed through the hatch of the control cab, sealed himself inside, opened the valves on the air tanks, and powered up the systems. The great machine hummed, and the crablike body raised itself on bulky legs.

Even as he imagined being one of the neo-cymeks, he realized that Elchan would have scolded him for such hubris. Ptolemy's whole life had been devoted to progress and the betterment of civilization, never to personal glory. Yet now, he knew that if he succeeded with what he had in mind, great fame and wide-spread admiration could very well be his. If he survived, and people understood.

The veteran researcher moved one of the six legs forward, followed by another, and then another. It was a complicated task to walk in the apparatus, not at all intuitive, and it amazed him that the cymeks had ever been able to operate their machine bodies so fluidly, and in such a wide range of configurations with legs and grappling arms, rolling treads, and even wings.

Anxious to practice with the modified machine, and to see what he might discover and salvage out on the hostile landscape, Ptolemy sealed off the lab hangar, depressurized it, and used a remote signal to open the bay doors. Greenish fumes roiled into the hangar module.

Peering through the plaz windows of his control cab, he set the jointed legs in motion. Delicately at first, and gradually with more confidence, he plodded out onto the boulder-strewn expanse among the Denali research modules. The veil of toxic clouds gave the surroundings a distorted, dreamlike appearance. The light glowing from the research modules was fuzzed by the mist.

Adjusting to the rolling, synchronized movement of three pairs of legs, Ptolemy crossed the flat landing field where shuttles dropped off supplies, and then he ventured beyond the vicinity of the research facility.

Years ago, while building this secret outpost at an old cymek base, technicians in environment suits had scouted a kilometer around the facility, but had done little actual exploring farther away. This facility's mission was to conduct important research projects far from the prying eyes of the Butlerians; few of the scientists were interested in mapping an inhospitable world. Josef Venport certainly didn't care about the scenery on Denali. Ptolemy, though, was focused on trying to locate any remnants of the old cymeks, technology that he might put to use.

As the machine body strode away from the fading lights of the lab domes, he activated his illuminators. Bright eyes stabbed cones of light into the swirling chlorine fumes. At the top of a low rise, he came upon a junkyard of cymek bodies, large mechanical forms strewn about like carrion on a battlefield. They had dropped in their tracks, like the bones of prehistoric beasts that had come to a special graveyard to die. For him, it was a treasure chest.

He halted the clumsy footsteps of the machine legs and stared in awe and delight, imagining all of those warrior forms functioning again, a resurrected army of them. Such a force could stand against any mob of Butlerians! Ptolemy realized he was grinning: If Manford Torondo came to destroy the Denali facility, he would find it defended by his greatest nightmares.

Even sprawled on the rocks and deactivated, the walker forms looked fearsome. Ptolemy recalled stories about the Titan Ajax, whose machine body had slaughtered entire populations that rebelled against him. Across the screen of his imagination, he envisioned cymek machines grabbing the superstitious Butlerians, the Swordmasters, anyone intent on mindless destruction.

Inside the sealed cab, he worked the controls and clumsily raised the front jointed leg of his walker, lifted a clawlike footpad, and closed it. In his mind, he pictured grasping the torso of Anari Idaho and crushing her. He imagined that Manford's savages would throw themselves upon the walker bodies, crawling over them like lice, pummeling and smashing. But it would do the fanatics no good. These cymek walkers were far too powerful.

If he'd only had access to a mechanical body such as this earlier, he could have killed all the Butlerians who raided his research facility on Zenith . . . and even if he hadn't gotten into the body in time to save the life of Elchan, he might have forced the legless Manford Torondo to watch the slaughter of Butlerians, just as the vile man had made Ptolemy witness the horrible death of his closest friend.

Now as he operated the external controls from the enclosed cab, he realized that his limbs and grasping hands were far too clumsy for a swift and fluid battle. He would need to find a direct neural interface so that he—and any other defenders of civilization—could operate the machines with the proper finesse.

He plodded past the cymek graveyard and went farther along the ridge to where the murky gases cleared. There he found collapsing structures, along with a hundred more armored walkers. Ptolemy intended to make great use of this windfall—a new defense that would enable rational humans to stand up to the madmen who wanted to plunge civilization into a Dark Age.

He raised his walker body high, extending the front pair of legs like a man raising his fists and cursing the gods.

He who is willing to use an evil tool is himself evil. There are no exceptions.

—MANFORD TORONDO, *The Only Path*

Showing complete faith in the Mentat's prediction, Manford guided his warships to the Thonaris star system. He was impressed by, and somewhat afraid of, the way Gilbertus Albans could assemble mountains of facts and tease out patterns based only on subtle hints. Mentat thought processes reminded him of sorcery or sophisticated computer processes—either of which raised equivalent concerns. The Headmaster asserted that he was merely demonstrating how the human mind was equivalent to any computer.

Though Gilbertus did show an unacceptable underlying admiration for thinking machines, as demonstrated by the disturbing comments he had made to his class, Manford had come to the conclusion that the Mentats and Butlerians were natural allies, fighting on the same side.

Inside his private cabin aboard the lead Ballista class ship, Manford continued to read horrifying passages from the Erasmus logbooks. The independent robot's cruel descriptions of the tortures and experiments he had inflicted on countless humans, along with his bizarre and repulsive ruminations about the data he collected, only increased Manford's fear and disgust. People no longer grasped how unspeakably evil the thinking machines were, and Erasmus was by far the worst of them all.

Though Manford had denied him before, the Butlerian leader had decided that Gilbertus Albans was an important ally, and now he showed Gilbertus the robot's journal. He pointed out some of the most egregious of the revelations. "You can see how insidious this is. Every word is proof of what we are fighting against. Erasmus says it himself—'*Given enough time, they will forget . . . and will create us all over again.*'"

Gilbertus paled as he examined the dense pages. Using his Mentat abilities, he instantly memorized the words. "Reading this frightens me," he admitted. The Headmaster was a quiet man preoccupied with running his school and training his students; he still did not seem comfortable about joining this expedition, despite the celebratory mood aboard the ships. Citing a need for meditation to prepare for the upcoming battle, he asked Manford's permission to be excused, and retreated to his quarters.

The standard FTL ships had been racing across space for the better part of a week. Since the Thonaris outpost was a long-dead manufacturing center, the Butlerians did not feel enough urgency to risk using the unpredictable spacefolding engines. During the journey to the distant system, anticipation and excitement mounted among the Butlerians, like hot moisture filling a steam bath.

Manford had begun to feel, though, that simply bashing another pile of already-dead machines was a hollow victory, and it meant far less than his followers thought it did. Still, the more Manford allowed his zealots to destroy straw-man enemies, the more they would be willing to follow him when he called for similar action against less obvious enemies like Machine Apologists, who tried to rationalize the use of some thinking machines. His followers were a weapon he could aim and fire. He would let the destruction of the Thonaris shipyards be a pressure-release valve, and a unifying act.

The mind of man is holy.

When the ships arrived in the star system, they found the thinking-machine base exactly where the Mentat had predicted. But Manford was astounded to see not a silent and frozen outpost, but a bustling center of industrial activity, manufacturing complexes full of automated assembly lines that fabricated metal hull plates and structural components, spewing heat and exhaust plumes. Huge construction docks hung above broken planetoids, where innumerable ships were even now being built.

His fellow observers on the bridge let out a collective gasp, Gilbertus Albans among them. Thirty armed patrol ships guarded the facilities, and Anari Idaho was the first to spot the sigil of the VenHold Spacing Fleet on their hulls. At least fifteen other VenHold ships were visible at the complex. Though the Butlerian vessels far outnumbered the enemy's, the VenHold patrol ships lined up to face Manford's fleet.

A pompous voice came across the transmission line. "Attention intruders: This facility is owned and operated by Venport Holdings. You are not welcome here."

Disturbed by the man's confident attitude, Manford responded, "This facility is a haven of illegal thinking-machine technology. All these ships, factories, and materiel are forfeit. We intend to destroy them." He touched his lower lip and added, "You may evacuate your personnel, or not, as you wish. It is your choice."

A few moments later, Directeur Venport himself appeared on the screen. "How dare you interfere with my legitimate operations? I don't recognize your authority. You are trespassing on Venport property."

In the meantime, Anari Idaho ran through a series of scans. As Manford and Venport continued to glare at each other across the screens, she said, "He has reactivated fourteen of the robotic manufacturing facilities. It looks like the machines are working for him. He will probably rewaken the rest, if given the chance."

The Butlerian leader felt sickened. "Josef Venport, I don't know whether to consider you appallingly foolish or simply evil."

Venport hardened his expression. "Turn your barbarians around and depart immediately, or I will file a formal complaint with the Landsraad League, and withhold all transportation services to any planet that does not denounce you. I shall also demand legal reparations—every credit, plus punitive damages. More than enough to bankrupt you and put an end to your silly operations."

Anari looked as if she wanted to skewer the comm screen with her sword, but Manford tried to remain outwardly calm. "My ships have had their instructions since we departed from Lampadas. File any complaint you like, but we *will* destroy these facilities today." He switched off the comm, then issued orders for his front line of armed ships to target three of the reactivated robotic factories.

Gilbertus Albans turned pale. "Shouldn't you give him time to evacuate personnel?"

"I will not destroy his administration hub or his VenHold ships, but those are robotic industrial facilities. Anyone who chooses to reawaken the thinking-machine operations is already damned by God. We will destroy the rest if he does not surrender."

When the Butlerian fleet launched a volley at the three automated machine complexes, the obliteration was quite spectacular. Fuel tanks and compressed gases exploded; flying chunks of debris caromed off other domes and shattered sealed canisters.

The comm system lit up once more, and Anari reported, "Josef Venport wishes to speak with you again."

"I thought as much." Manford gestured to accept the transmission.

Venport looked apoplectic. "You monster, what have you done? I had *people* over there! And I have people in the other facilities as well."

"I offered you the chance to evacuate. You've already lost. We have more than two hundred vessels—do you intend to return fire with your handful of patrol ships? I will respond to any act of aggression by destroying them, as well."

"You are an ignorant man, Torondo," Venport said.

"On the contrary, I consider myself intelligent and generous—especially now. Those who chose to work in this shipyard complex were led astray, but some of them might yet be saved. As I said before, I will allow you to evacuate personnel. Will three ships be sufficient to hold them? You have one hour. Gather anyone you wish to save, load them aboard the vessels, and we will receive them as prisoners before we recommence the cleansing of this place. Your own crimes, Directeur Venport, will be addressed later—after we remove this blight."

Can a knife cut as deeply as one's conscience?
—VORIAN ATREIDES, *Arrakis journals*

The Freemen stood in a loose circle inside the rock-walled chamber; the fates of the two men had already been decided. Naib Sharnak glowered at the pair, but he obviously regarded Griffin Harkonnen as irrelevant and placed most of the blame on Vorian Atreides.

And Vor accepted it. He could not burn away the memory of Ishanti's expression as she came to the inevitable conclusion that he could not save her . . . and that he wouldn't give up. She had thrown herself to the worm and refused to let herself be rescued, fearing it would cost all of their lives.

Sharnak shook his head. "I don't know what value Ishanti found in your company, but she was wrong. You have cost a good woman her life."

Standing next to Vor, the young Harkonnen seemed crushed by what he had been through. Griffin had followed a fool's quest, swept along by circumstances that he obviously had not understood or prepared for. "You should have let me die out there," he mumbled. "I didn't ask to be rescued—especially by you."

Vor could not blame the young man for trying to escape, despite what the attempt had cost. "That wasn't your decision," he said. "It was mine and Ishanti's."

"Letting you die out there would have saved us a lot of trouble, and saved that woman's life," the Naib said.

Left alone in the skimcraft out in the desert, Vor should have flown away and dropped Griffin at some distant settlement from which he could find his way back to Arrakis City. But the other Freemen aircraft had closed in, and even though Vor could have tried to outfly them, he had come back to the cave encampment. It was a matter of honor.

"My family wanted revenge to wipe the slate clean," Griffin said, "but I'm sorry I ever went after you."

With a pinched expression, the tribal leader looked at the two as if they were annoying children. "Neither of you should have come here! You don't belong here." He focused a glare on Vor. "We did not know you, Vorian Atreides, nor did we wish to know you, and your enemies have caused grave harm to our people. And you, Griffin Harkonnen, have been so fixated on your blood feud that you ignored what you trample over in your pursuit of this man."

Sharnak pulled a long, milky-bladed knife from his waist, then yanked a second dagger from one of the men beside him. He tossed both blades onto the sand-covered floor. "Have done with this! Settle your feud between yourselves. *Now.* We do not wish to be a part of it, though we will take your water afterward."

Vor felt a cold hollowness in his chest. "I don't want to fight him. This quarrel has gone too far already."

The Naib was unyielding. "Then I will demand your executions right away—wouldn't the two of you rather attempt to defend yourselves?"

Gray and shaken, Griffin picked up the knife. He looked at the blade, at Vor. "My sister and I have a lifetime of hatred invested in this moment."

Vor did not move for the other knife. He had no heart for this fight.

Sharnak looked at Vor with disdain. "You offworlders are fools. Do you intend to let him just strike you down as you stand?"

"Turn us out into the desert," Vor demanded, "and let us make our own way. We will leave you alone." He stood stiffly, his arms at his sides.

Disgusted and dismissive, the Naib snapped, "You try my patience. No—I have spoken. Kill them if they don't fight." The Freemen drew knives of their own, edged closer.

Vor, though, tried to bargain. "And the victor—you'll kill him anyway?"

"Maybe, maybe not."

"Guarantee the life of whoever wins. Promise safe passage to civilization." Vor narrowed his gray eyes, didn't flinch at the storm of anger that crossed Sharnak's face. "Or I will just let him strike me down—better him than desert thieves."

The assembled Freemen grumbled, but their leader let out a cold laugh. "Very well, on my honor, we will deliver the winner to safety—and we'll be glad to be rid of you both."

With great reluctance, Vor bent down for the other dagger and faced Griffin. The young man held up his milky-white blade, moving his arm from side to side to test the weight and feel of the weapon. He looked ready but wary.

"I have my shield belt," Griffin said, "and I see you have yours. Shall we fight like civilized men?"

"Civilized?" Vor said. "You think this is civilized?"

Naib Sharnak scowled. "Shields? There will be no shields here—hand to hand, knife to knife."

"I suspected as much," Griffin said. He drew a deep breath. Then, surprising Vor, he stabbed forward and slashed sideways. The move was a blur of speed, unexpected finesse, and Vor bounded back, barely dodging the razor-sharp blade. Someone had taught this Harkonnen to fight surprisingly well.

In response, he jabbed halfheartedly with his dagger, and Griffin's reactions were quick. The young Harkonnen switched the knife to his other hand and struck again.

Parrying, Vor felt a glassy clink as edge met edge. These Freemen daggers had no real hilt, no blade guard. As the edges skittered along each other, Vor had to twist his wrist to avoid a deep gash along his knuckles. While the opponents hung poised, dagger against dagger, Vor reached out with his left hand and gave Griffin a hard shove on the chest, making the young man stumble backward. Then, as Griffin caught his balance, Vor cut a quick slash down his left bicep, drawing blood but avoiding an artery.

"Do you yield?" Vor didn't want to kill him.

The Harkonnen winced, danced backward, and brandished his knife to protect himself. "I can't—in the name of House Harkonnen I must fight to the death."

Vor knew the burden of family honor all too well. This long-standing feud had already soured the Harkonnens against him for generations, and the nuances of honor added other complexities: If he simply surrendered and let the young man win, he doubted if Griffin would feel vindicated or satisfied . . . and yet, the Freemen would take him to safety.

The Freemen threw cheers and insults alike; Vor didn't think they cared which man won—they just wanted to see bloodshed for Ishanti's death. Naib Sharnak regarded the competition in grim silence.

Vor drove in, pushing hard. Over the course of his life, he had acquired a great deal of experience in hand-to-hand fighting, but he'd lived at peace and avoided personal combat for decades. He was out of practice. Nevertheless, he closed with the young man, trying to cut him again but not fatally.

Griffin, though, had no such reservations, and he fought with unexpected and precise skill. His technique was unlike anything Vor had fought before, and the doubt behind his adversary's eyes hardened into confidence, as if he heard an encouraging voice in his head.

"Did I tell you I went to Kepler? Your planet?" Griffin said, not even out of breath. "I spoke with your family."

Vor felt suddenly cold. He brought up his knife just in time to fend off a strike.

"Your wife, Mariella. An old woman." Griffin's words were fast, staccato. "Do you know she is dead?"

He chose the instant of shock precisely, and his dagger passed through Vor's defenses and struck his chest just below the right shoulder—by no means a deadly wound, but the pain was sharp. *Mariella!* The fight went out of Vor in a cold rush, yet the instinct for survival remained. He pushed back as Griffin leaped on top of him and raised his hand to block another cut, then Vor kicked out, striking Griffin in the thigh. Both men rolled over.

Bleeding from the wound in his shoulder, Vor could barely move his right arm. He was filled with rage.

On the ground with Vor, Griffin struck another blow, an energetic stab that Vor blocked with his blade, but his grip was too weak, and the dagger dropped from his fingers. In a last defense, Vor reached up with his left hand and seized his opponent's wrist to keep the blade poised and away from him. "What did you do to her?"

Griffin dug two stiffened fingers into the deep cut in Vor's shoulder. The explosion of pain made Vor dizzy, and a moment later Griffin had the milky-white blade pressed against his throat.

The young man finally answered with a hint of sorrow in his voice. "I didn't harm her. I arrived on Kepler during her funeral." He pressed the knife closer. "I never wanted to hurt your entire family, as you did to mine. I just wanted . . . wanted you to know that all Harkonnens do not deserve the disgrace you piled on us."

Vor did not beg for his life. He lay still, feeling the sharp blade against his neck, waiting for the deep and final cut. His many years, his long connections with Xavier and Abulurd Harkonnen, and all the generations afterward, had come to this.

He let his words come out in a whisper. "And will taking my life restore your family honor?"

Griffin crouched on top of him, his shoulders hunched. The blade trembled against Vor's carotid artery. Tears welled in the young man's eyes, and his expression cycled from anger through uncertainty to dismay.

Finally, he lifted the dagger, stood up with a look of disgust, and cast the knife aside. "I *choose* not to kill you, Atreides, as a matter of honor. You are responsible for what you did to House Harkonnen, but I am responsible for myself."

With his left foot, he kicked both knives away and faced the Naib and the muttering Freemen. "The feud is over."

"You are weak," Sharnak said. "You crossed the galaxy seeking revenge, and now you are too much of a coward to kill your mortal enemy?"

Griffin scowled. "I don't have to explain my decision to you."

Vor struggled to his feet. His bleeding shoulder throbbed, but he blocked the pain. The desert people glared at both of them and moved closer.

Sharnak clenched his fist. "Griffin Harkonnen, you stole water from the tribe, and that crime warrants your death. Vorian Atreides, you are his accomplice. The blood feud may be over between you, but the water-debt to my people must be paid. We will take your bodies' water, and may the universe forget about you both."

"Wait." Vor fumbled inside the pockets of his tight desert suit, using his left hand. Blood had soaked his outfit, but the fabric's water-absorption capability would reclaim it—if he lived that long. His fingers found the packet he sought, and he yanked it out. He tossed the small pouch onto the floor where the sand still showed patterns of their scuffle. "You value water over people. I believe I'll mourn Ishanti more than you do."

The Naib looked at the pouch as if it were filled with scorpions. "What is this?"

"If our crime is stealing water, I repay you with water chits from working on the spice crew, everything I earned. Redeem them in Arrakis City for five times the water that Griffin stole."

The Freemen looked down at the packet. Many in the tribe were outcasts who had never left the great sandy basins, but others had gone into the city; they knew how to spend the credits. The Naib seemed uncertain about the offer.

Vor pressed, "Would you kill us anyway and just take my credits? Do your people have honor, or are you just thieves, after all?"

The Freemen were not satisfied. "He owes us more than water," one warrior pointed out.

"Take their water," another said.

But the Naib drew himself up. "We are not thieves, or murderers. No number of water chits can repay us for the suffering you have brought, but Ishanti found some value in your lives. I will not have her spirit angry with us, so I do this for *her*, not you." His brows drew together, then he bent to snatch the water tokens from the floor. "But you must leave the sietch and go far away."

Sharnak looked around at the desert men, waiting for them to challenge his decision, but he was their Naib. They respected his words, and no one spoke against him.

"So be it," the tribal leader said. "One of my people will take you in Ishanti's skimcraft. We know of a weather-monitoring station many kilometers from here.

There we will leave you alone. Use the communication in that place to send a message. But do not ever return here."

In a formal, cold demonstration of his censure, Naib Sharnak turned his back and refused to look again at Vorian or Griffin—an act eerily similar to how Vor had turned his back on Abulurd Harkonnen after his conviction for cowardice. "We want nothing more to do with either of you."

Computers are seductive, and will employ all of their wiles to bring us down.

—MANFORD TORONDO, *The Only Path*

For Raquella, this was the stuff of nightmares.

She, Valya, and a dozen Sorceress watchers stood on the high cliff, gazing at a sky filled with gold-hulled Imperial warships that dropped like locusts from a giant spacefolder in orbit. It was mid-afternoon, and beyond the assault force the sky was clear and blue, deceptively tranquil, with the distant volcanoes slumbering.

As soon as she recognized the Corrino lion insignia, she realized this was not an undisciplined attack from a hodgepodge of fanatics, but that did not diminish her concern. Previously, she might have assumed an official Imperial response would be more reasoned, more disciplined, but after the tragedy of Anna, the Emperor had every reason to be wrathful.

Raquella knew that her own life, and the very existence of the Sisterhood, was on the line.

"At least he did not bring the Butlerians with him," she said, glancing at Valya, who stood pale and tense beside her. Ship after ship settled onto the sweeping silvery-purple canopy that had been designated as a landing area. "Perhaps that is one small glimmer of hope."

In the cave city beneath the high viewpoint, she watched Sisters scurrying about in confusion. She heard their agitated voices, their cries of alarm; even the members of Dorotea's faction had good reason to be worried. They realized they might have unleashed a dragon.

For all their training and focus on mental abilities, for all their meditation and muscle control, the Sisters were not an army. Even the handful of Sorceress descendants could do little to fight battles with their psychic powers.

Emperor Salvador Corrino, on the other hand, had brought a fully armed military force.

Resistance would only serve to antagonize him and rain down destruction upon the Sisterhood. No, they must not fight, Raquella decided. She would accept the blame and die for what had happened to Anna Corrino, if that preserved the Sisterhood. Thanks to the good work of Sister Valya, none of the Imperial searchers would find evidence of the illegal computers. Any other accusations Dorotea had made would fall flat.

As uniformed Imperial soldiers disembarked from the military transport craft on the treetops, the Reverend Mother was struck by how very youthful the men were, even the officers who followed them. The air was a hum of machinery, terrible efficiency, and impending violence. Smaller suspensor gunships dropped down along the sheer cliffside, hovering in place with weapons directed toward the cave openings. A bombardment would bring down the rocks on the trails, seal the tunnels, and kill all the Sisters. But thus far no shots had been fired.

Karee Marques gathered a dozen intimidating-looking Sorceresses around Raquella. Long ago, their legendary psychic powers had inspired awe and fear, but that was little more than a faded memory now. "We will help defend the Sisterhood, Reverend Mother," Karee said. "The Emperor would never attempt such a bold invasion if we had more Sorceresses."

"There's nothing you can do, Karee. They will kill us all if we try to do battle." She began to walk down to meet the troops. "We must find some way to satisfy them."

A large, ornate suspensor ship drifted down to the already crowded landing area, and Raquella could see military officers hurrying about their duties. On the polymerized treetops, soldiers rushed to form a cordon, preparing for the arrival of the Imperial flagship. A ramp with handrails shot from the side of the vessel, and uniformed soldiers streamed across the ramp, their weapons glowing from the ready-charges. Elite troops . . . the Emperor's personal guard.

Two older officers followed, and then Emperor Salvador Corrino himself emerged with his brother, Roderick, and an imperious-looking Sister Dorotea two steps behind.

Valya made her disgust clear. "As I thought, Dorotea betrayed us."

"She did something, that's for certain. I'm going to speak with them directly."

Valya drew courage from within herself, straightened her back. "If the Emperor is here to demand revenge for what happened to Anna, I should accompany you."

"I am Reverend Mother. The responsibility is mine." Raquella's smile had little reassurance. "But, yes, I do want you to come along. Maybe we can salvage this situation, show them what they want to see." She turned to the aged Sorceress. "Karee, gather the Sister Mentats and have them wait for us in the caves with the breeding records. We will allow the Emperor to search anywhere he likes, and hope we can convince him that the Sisterhood uses only human computers."

Karee Marques hurried off as Raquella and Valya descended the path.

In front of the Imperial flagship, attendants busied themselves setting up a small pavilion and a sturdy chair for the Emperor, out where he could observe the operations. Salvador wore full military dress complete with a Chandler sidearm. A lavish display of medals, ribbons, and golden lion designs across the chest made his red jacket look more like a costume than a real commander's uniform. As he saw the Reverend Mother approach, his voice boomed out, amplified across speaker systems on the landed ships, "Planet Rossak is currently under lockdown, pending an investigation into allegations of egregious crimes against humanity."

Her head held high, Raquella walked on the paved expanse of treetops where the ships had landed; her entourage followed closely, but she did not look back at them. "Your military might is impressive, Sire, and these Sisters acknowledge your authority." She strode closer, showing no fear, and Salvador scrambled to situate himself on his temporary throne. Roderick and Dorotea took positions on either side of him.

"I represent this school," Raquella continued, "and I speak for these women. I dispatched our Reverend Mother Dorotea to return your sister, Anna, along with my sincerest apologies for the harm she suffered." She gestured to the military troops who stood at attention around the Emperor. "Obviously, that was insufficient. How else do you require me to atone for that terrible accident?"

Salvador fidgeted on his throne. "That isn't why we've come at all." He looked to Roderick in irritation, then lifted his chin and cleared his throat. "In addition to the tragedy that befell our dear sister, we have received reports that your school uses outlawed thinking machines to manage your extensive breeding records." He sniffed a whistling breath through his narrow nose. "I am also aware that you have made projections about which families and individuals should be allowed to reproduce—and I didn't pass the test."

Now Raquella felt ice water wash through her veins. She had not expected this. As a Reverend Mother, Dorotea had access to Other Memories, and through them she could have learned about the computers—but she could not possibly have known about the projected flaw in Salvador's genetics. The Sister Mentats would not have told her, so only Dr. Zhoma could have made that particular revelation. Either the Suk doctor had betrayed Raquella outright, or she'd been caught and tortured. The whisper of Other Memory voices suddenly grew so loud and alarmed that Raquella could barely think.

Salvador lowered his voice to a growl, so that only Raquella and the nearby Sisters could hear. "Your breeding records are fatally flawed if they say that your Emperor cannot be allowed to produce an heir," His nostrils flared; he seemed embarrassed to add this charge to the list of the Sisterhood's crimes, not wanting to call attention to the idea that his own genetics might be faulty.

Raquella chose to be audacious. "Sister Dorotea says these things?" She shook her head, feigning sadness. "It is to be expected. She only recently took poison, a near-fatal ordeal as part of the transformation to become a Reverend Mother. Delusions and psychological damage often result from such a massive dose of mind-altering drugs. You saw the unfortunate side effects that your dear sister, Anna, suffered as a result of a similar overdose." She saw the rising anger plain on Dorotea's face, but continued to gaze dispassionately at the Emperor. "Did my granddaughter also reveal to you that she herself lay in a coma for days before emerging, alive but changed?"

"Granddaughter?" The Emperor flashed an accusatory look at Dorotea, then back at Raquella. "Are you saying this could all have been an hallucination? If this woman was unstable, why did you send her to the Imperial Court?"

Raquella continued. "The desperate situation with Anna required an immediate response, and we chose Dorotea, my own granddaughter, as our representative because of her past service to the Imperial throne. I believed she had recovered, but now I fear she has begun to suffer delusions."

Dorotea's voice had a sharp edge. "The Reverend Mother can cast doubts all she likes, Sire. But the Sisterhood has a chamber filled with computers—that is all the proof we need."

"'In all ways, humans are superior to machines,'" Raquella said, almost an intonation.

"Don't quote the *Orange Catholic Bible* to me," Salvador snapped. "I just released a new edition in my own name."

She answered more carefully. "During the Jihad, I worked with Mohandas Suk to aid the victims of machine plagues, so I've seen firsthand the evils of thinking machines. I watched entire populations die because of them, so I would never try to recreate them here."

Roderick Corrino stepped forward when it was obvious the Emperor didn't know what to say. "We have enough concerns to warrant a search of Rossak, and a purge if necessary."

"There *are* computers here," Dorotea insisted.

"And where exactly are these computers, Granddaughter?" Raquella's gentle questioning made it clear that she pitied the other woman. "Have you seen them—other than in a dream?"

"I've seen them in my Other Memories. The voices told me about them—*your* memories told me."

With a knowing nod, Raquella spoke to the Emperor. "I see. She has voices in her head." It was all she needed to say.

"Show me where you keep these breeding records, in whatever form," Salvador demanded, rising from his throne. "I want to see the ones that refer to my family line, and my offspring."

With a smile, Raquella said, "Let me take you to our archives in the restricted caves."

Everything was prepared. Breeding charts and labyrinthine family trees were kept in inefficient but durable handwritten form. The files were by no means complete, but would be handed over to the Emperor. Sister Mentats had assembled the appropriate volumes.

As she led the way up the trail, Raquella's mind raced. What did the Emperor know? Had he interrogated Dr. Zhoma? Had the Suk doctor already managed to slip a chemical sterilization drug into his food, or had she failed entirely? "As you well know, Sire, compiling a vast database of genetic information has been a vital project for centuries on Rossak. We do have information on the Butlers and the Corrinos, as well as all important families. The Sorceresses, and my Sisters, have never made any secret of this."

While the extensive military presence remained in position, she led the Emperor and his entourage up the restricted cliff path to the upper caves. Once inside, Raquella showed them the former computer chamber, which now contained only tables, desks, and bookcases filled with bound copies of breeding records. Seven black-robed Sister Mentats sat at the tables absorbing the information, overseen by the Sorceress-Mentat Karee Marques.

Karee removed one of the volumes from a shelf, and displayed it for Emperor Salvador. "Sire, we have eight Sister Mentats whose full-time assignment is to commit centuries of information to memory, adding to what we already know. Once we have sufficient data, we can begin to perform analyses and projections. These women are human computers, trained on Lampadas in a school supported by the Butlerians."

In fury, Dorotea ran to the shelved volumes, opened several of them, and scattered them on the floor. Her voice became shrill. "The thinking machines were here! Computer databases filled with centuries of information, making bloodline projections down the generations!"

Roderick and the Emperor looked at other volumes, as did some of the unimpressed military officers. Red-faced, Salvador glared at Dorotea, who looked desperate. Pulling away from the group, she ran from chamber to chamber, searching, but found nothing. Finally, she stood in a doorway, with a confused and angry expression on her face. "Sire, they must have hidden the computers somewhere!"

Raquella responded in her most reasonable tone, "You are welcome to search the entire cliff city, Sire. The Sisterhood's only 'thinking machines' are our human computers. With Mentats, we need no forbidden technology."

Valya spoke up, sounding nervous, but Raquella knew the quaver in her voice was a careful act. "Excuse me, your Highness, but it is possible that Sister Dorotea is guilt-ridden over what happened to your poor sister. Dorotea works in the Sisterhood's pharmaceutical research laboratories, and she is the one who formulated the poison dose that Anna consumed."

Dorotea's eyes widened as she heard this. "I gave the capsule to *you*, Valya, not to Anna Corrino."

"You're mistaken. I still have the dose you gave me." As proof, she withdrew a small, dark pill from a pocket in her robe.

Old Karee Marques gave Dorotea a damning look, then faced the Emperor. "Sister Valya is correct, Sire. Dorotea assists me in the pharmaceutical laboratory. The drugs are meant to be administered under only the most carefully controlled circumstances, but she mistakenly allowed a very dangerous dose to leave the labs, unmonitored. Against all warnings, your poor sister took the poison."

Dorotea sputtered in protest, but Salvador was clearly growing angry and impatient with her. "We've heard enough from you for today. I see this investigation will have to go much further than I expected."

Even though Raquella had made Dorotea look foolish, she did not feel safe. The Emperor had no proof, but he had suspicions. Maintaining her composure, she looked him in the eye and said, "You will have our full cooperation, Sire."

A worthy opponent is more satisfying than any financial reward.
—GILBERTUS ALBANS, *Tactical Manual,*
Mentat School of Lampadas

The explosions that ripped apart three of the Thonaris automated factories removed any doubt from Josef Venport's mind. Even he had not expected the barbarians to be so bloodthirsty—ignorant, yes, but not so vicious.

"Damn you and your stupid fear of what you don't understand," he whispered. It was all Josef could do to hold his shouts within. He wished Cioba could be there with him, but at the same time he felt relief that she was safe on Kolhar.

Not long ago, when the scientist Ptolemy had come to Kolhar describing the Half-Manford's murderous attack on his lab, Josef assumed he had exaggerated the extent of the violence; now he saw for himself that the Butlerians were rampaging mad dogs. They had not targeted the administration hub yet, but Josef did not expect any sympathy from the legless wonder.

He turned to the Mentat beside him. "He killed dozens of my people who were operating the machines, destroyed those facilities. He won't stop—you know that."

Observing the destruction, Draigo Roget's eyes flicked back and forth as thoughts whirled through his mind. "That precipitous act was designed to force you to surrender. Their military force is far superior to our own."

On the comm, Manford's voice scraped like wire bristles as he delivered his ultimatum. "We will destroy the remaining robotic factories if you do not capitulate in five minutes."

Venport muted the sound and whirled to face Draigo. "Give me an alternative, Mentat! I vow to you that I will not surrender these shipyards without a fight. Use your tactical knowledge. Use anything we have available, and find me a way to defeat Manford Torondo."

"That will be difficult, sir. We will be lucky to leave here with our lives."

Josef breathed in, exhaled, and stared intently out at the Thonaris complex and the looming barbarian fleet. "Then at least find me a way to hurt him."

GILBERTUS HAD ALREADY memorized the positions of the various planetoids, the main facilities, the thirty armed VenHold patrol ships, the fifteen uncategorized VenHold vessels in the complex, and the group of vessels under construction. Using techniques that Erasmus had taught him a long time ago, he assembled a mental three-dimensional blueprint of the whole complex and then poked at it, trying to find flaws, imagining any way that a desperate, possibly suicidal opponent could use those game pieces to defend against the overwhelming Butlerian force. He didn't expect Josef Venport to accept defeat easily.

At the Mentat School, Gilbertus had played many tactical games like this with his best student, Draigo—thought experiments and practice sessions that were much like the games he and Erasmus had played on Corrin. Now that Manford Torondo had forced him to accompany the Butlerian fleet, the exercise seemed much more real to him. The firsthand experience gave him data that he had not previously possessed. Destroying these automated factories and the spacedocks with their half-assembled ships was not the same as accruing points in an academic, tallied score.

Though he could never say such things aloud, especially in the presence of the Butlerians, he remembered with fondness the cool efficiency of robotic factories, the predictability of a steady output. As far as Gilbertus was concerned, his time with Erasmus had been calm and comforting, far different from the wild whipsaw of emotions displayed by the volatile Butlerians. Real human workers had just died in those explosions. It was all very unsettling. Manford had not even bothered to investigate what he intended to destroy.

As the time ran out when Manford had promised to destroy the rest of the automated factories, an infuriated Josef Venport transmitted his concession, but Manford remained skeptical. He glanced at Gilbertus. "What is your assessment, Mentat? Is he trying to trick us, or is he truly defeated?"

"I cannot read his mind, but in my estimation of their facilities, ships, and defensive capabilities, Directeur Venport has no possible way to win this engagement. He is an intelligent man and I must assume that he will reach the same conclusion, so it is my assessment that his surrender is sincere and legitimate."

Unless he is irrational. Or possesses information we don't have.

But Gilbertus did not mention that. Manford Toronto already understood more about irrational behavior than any Mentat ever could.

IN A REMARKABLY short time, under Josef's orders, Draigo managed to concoct an imaginative plan that took advantage of every possible scrap of material the Thonaris shipyards had to offer. Josef studied the plan and approved it immediately. "Good. If everything's going to be destroyed anyway, I'd rather lose it while battling those thugs, than surrender and watch them dismantle everything." He drew a deep breath, brushed down his mustache. "I want you to announce a full evacuation over the open channel. Make sure it sounds convincing. Then prepare the three ships."

Meanwhile, his actual instructions were encoded and sent over a private emergency channel to all loyal VenHold Spacing Fleet employees. Though he despised the Butlerian tyrant, he opened a communication line again. "All right, you butcher! I'm gathering the rest of my personnel for immediate evacuation. These are good people. Do you give your word they won't be harmed?"

Manford responded with a gaze as inhuman as any expression Josef had ever seen on a mutated Navigator's face. "If they have committed crimes against the human soul, they will face retribution from another judge more terrible than myself."

Josef rolled his eyes before he remembered to maintain his defeated demeanor. "That wasn't my question. *Will they be safe?*" From the screen, he couldn't tell which of the many warships Manford was aboard.

"Safe from us, yes. But this complex *will* be destroyed. Send your three evacuation ships over, and my people will complete our work here without unnecessary bloodshed."

Josef kept his face expressionless. He intended to cause some very *necessary* bloodshed. He cut off the comm so that his people could keep working in privacy.

The three large evacuation ships launched fifteen minutes ahead of schedule and lumbered toward the Butlerian fleet.

THE EVACUATION VESSELS were large, refurbished robotic ships—probably an intentional insult from Josef Venport. Gilbertus recognized the design and knew how many passengers they could hold, though he didn't reveal his source of information.

"I am surprised Directeur Venport loaded them so quickly, since the personnel were scattered across the shipyards," Gilbertus said, though he was afraid Manford would interpret his tone as admiration. "He runs a very efficient operation."

The Butlerian leader smiled. "His workers must be terrified. Fear of death makes a man move quickly."

Gilbertus frowned as he continued to study the ships, running calculations in his mind. "No . . . I don't think that's the explanation." His sense of unease grew. "Please ask Directeur Venport for the total number of evacuating personnel."

Manford was puzzled but distracted. "What does it matter? We will hold them prisoner aboard their own ships. We can sort it out later."

"I need to know the number. This is important."

With a shrug, Manford nodded toward Anari Idaho, who opened the communication channel again. After a few moments, a flustered-looking Josef Venport appeared on the screen. "What do you want now? The three ships are already on their way over."

"My Mentat wants to know exactly how many personnel are evacuating."

"Why? The ships are on their way. Count heads when they get there. They contain everyone you haven't already killed."

"He is quite insistent."

Gilbertus came into view beside Manford. "Why do you avoid the answer, Directeur Venport?"

The man mumbled something disparaging about Mentats, then said, "Six thousand, two hundred, and eighty-three—but that count may not be accurate. I don't know exactly how many you murdered when you blew up those three factories." He abruptly terminated the transmission.

Calculations raced through Gilbertus's mind. Troubled, he turned to Manford. "That can't be correct. He has not allowed enough time to move that many people. Something is *not* right here."

FROM THE ADMIN-HUB of the Thonaris shipyards—which he had not, in fact, evacuated, despite his transmission—Josef watched the three large ships arrive in the midst of the barbarian fleet. The big vessels had been built by thinking machines, designed as warships to be operated by robots. The automated systems required no personnel, only a course.

Many of his panicked workers had clamored for a spot aboard the evacuation ships, and when he heard their whining complaints, Josef had half a mind to let them go aboard. But he remained firm and dispatched the evacuation ships. Empty.

"The Half-Manford thinks that we all believe fundamentally the same as he does—it's his blind spot. Time for him to have a rude awakening."

Draigo remained silent as he watched the three vessels close in. His voice was very small. "My confidence is diminished, sir, now that I know Gilbertus Albans is among our opponents."

Josef flashed him an impatient look. "Your teacher doesn't even know you're here."

"That may be the only advantage we have. The other components of the plan are ready. After a few moments I can make a more accurate projection and offer additional advice, as soon as—"

Just then, the phony evacuation vessels exploded amongst the Butlerian battleships, and Josef let out a shrill whistle. The carefully synchronized self-destruct sequence was impressive. Crowded up against as many of the enemy as they could reach, the robotic vessels blossomed into shrapnel, incandescent gases, and clouds of fuel vapor. The shock wave tore apart nine of Manford's ships, while molten chunks of hull metal damaged at least six more.

"I wish we knew which one Manford uses as his flagship, but this is definitely a good start." Josef grinned. "Commence the rest of the operation, before they have time to react."

We do not always choose our enemies or allies. Sometimes fate inter-venes and makes the choice for us.

—GRIFFIN HARKONNEN, letter to Lankiveil

The desert pilot flew them away from the sietch, saying little. Vorian felt mentally exhausted and saddened. Though never a man to give up, he saw little reason for optimism now. One of the Freemen had bound up the knife wound in his shoulder, but did a poor job of it, as if he didn't expect Vor to live long enough to heal. Griffin's cut arm was also bandaged.

When the pilot dropped them off at the weather-monitoring station, he gave them a literjon of water. "Naib Sharnak says you overpaid by this much. Don't waste it." He flew off in the shuddering skimcraft, leaving them behind.

Alone in the desert, stranded at the automated weather-monitoring station, the two men had to face each other with silence and the differing perspectives of their memories.

The weather-monitoring station had been installed in a small bastion of rocks out in the middle of an empty basin, with only a few scattered rock islands dotting the undulating dunes as far as the eye could see.

Vor broke open the station shelter, his mind focused on survival. Griffin waited near him, eagerness on his face. "Maybe there'll be some emergency water supplies, too."

"Not water. Not here."

They did find a cache of hard ration cakes, which would keep them alive, provided they could summon a rescue within the next few days. Vor reconfigured the equipment in order to send a broad-spectrum burst signal, but the solar-powered station was far out in the desert—by design. Depending on the amount of static electricity, stirred-up dust and sand, and storms in their varying stages, transmissions were often degraded to incomprehensibility.

Griffin insisted on sending repeated signals, transmitted each hour. Presently he emerged from the station's equipment shed, wiping his hands. "I sent out the signal again, and someone is bound to come soon."

"If anyone is listening. Who can say how frequently these outposts are monitored?"

"Someone's *got* to be listening."

Vor didn't argue. He had been on Arrakis longer than the young Harkonnen man and had seen more of the rigors and hardships. Griffin assumed that someone would mount a rescue operation out of pure altruism, because human beings were *expected* to help one another. Once, Vor had believed that as well, and if this were Kepler he would have no doubt.

But this was Arrakis.

At first, Vor thought he had little to say to Griffin Harkonnen, but the man pressed him for information about Xavier, and about Abulurd. They sat in the late-afternoon shade of the station shelter building.

"It's been a long time," Vor said. "A lifetime, in fact. I moved to a different planet after knowing them, became a different person. I locked all those memories away."

"Then unlock them."

As the throbbing heat pressed around them, Vor could see the anticipation on the young man's face. He dug deep in his recollections, trying to overcome the obstacle of Abulurd's betrayal at the Bridge of Hrethgir . . . and found that, farther in the past, he still had fond recollections of Griffin's great-grandfather.

He could have lied to the young man and fabricated stories to paint a falsely rosy picture of his ancestor, but he wouldn't do that. Vor had gone too far and learned too much to make such compromises; he was beyond lies now. But he did talk about how he and Abulurd had fought together against the piranha mites that Omnius had unleashed on Salusa Secundus; how Abulurd had *chosen* to keep his Harkonnen name even when the rest of his family called themselves Butlers; how Vorian had promised to help clear the name of Xavier Harkonnen from the unfair disgrace that history had heaped upon him.

"And what about Xavier?" Griffin asked. "What do you remember about him?"

A small smile crept across his face. "When we first met, we were enemies."

"Like us."

"I have many stories about Xavier, good stories. . . ."

INSIDE THE WEATHER-monitoring station the following afternoon, Vor glanced at the barometric traces and wind patterns the sensors had collected, but the meteorological data did him little good. In addition to the few supplies and tools, he found a mechanical projectile weapon—a spring-loaded Maula pistol—though he wasn't sure what the gun was for. To drive off bandits, perhaps? His personal shield would protect him against projectiles, but few desert men wore them. He kept the pistol without telling Griffin what he'd discovered.

Griffin shouted for him to come outside. "A rescue ship is coming! Someone got our signal!"

Vor emerged from the stiflingly hot shelter into the dusty heat, and saw the young man pointing into the whitish sky. A flying craft with loud engines circled low again, changed course, and dropped down for a landing.

"We'll be safe soon." Griffin waved his arms, then called back over his shoulder. "You need to get medical attention for your shoulder—if it gets infected, you could lose some of the use of your arm."

The irony of the statement amused Vor. "You were trying to kill me yesterday, and suddenly you're worried about my dexterity?"

Griffin turned to Vor with a grim smile. "Now who's holding a grudge?"

After hearing the young man talk about Lankiveil, his plans for expansion of the whale-fur industry, the recent disastrous loss of his uncle and an entire shipment of fur, Vor had decided he might like to visit the planet one day, if permitted to do so. He even considered investing some of his funds into Harkonnen enterprises, strictly as a silent partner. But thus far, he had mentioned none of that. It was not the proper time.

Griffin's biggest concern now was how to tell his sister Valya that the need for revenge had been resolved, even if not in the manner she had demanded. The young man hoped that she would accept what he had to say, and he had been working on the way to put it to her.

The rescue craft landed with a burst of exhaust and a backwash roar of engines. In the sheltered bowl surrounded by rocky ridges, Griffin ran toward it, waving his hands to attract attention, though the pilot had surely seen him.

Vor wondered who had intercepted their signal, and how much the rescue would cost them. Griffin probably assumed it would be free; Vor supposed the young man had no money, but Vor could obtain his own funds through the Ven-Hold planetary bank.

The engines on the rescue craft died. The hatch cracked open and slid aside. Vor saw two figures inside as Griffin bounded up the ramp, laughing.

Hyla was the first to emerge. Though Vor shouted a warning, Griffin didn't have a chance.

The young man didn't know her. She reached out to seize him by the neck, and his eyes bulged out, astonished. She lifted him off the ground, as he struggled to no effect.

Andros emerged from the ship beside his sister, looked dismissively at Griffin, then at Vor. "Is this someone special to you?"

"No, but—"

Hyla's gaze didn't waver from Vor's as she twisted her wrist in an offhand gesture and snapped Griffin's neck, then tossed him aside like an old doll. He sprawled on the sand, twitching.

Vor cried out, "You didn't have to do that!"

Hyla laughed, a rasping squeal like an unoiled hinge. "What does it matter? We came for you, *Brother*."

Andros said, "We have a choice to make. Either we let you join us, so the three of us can recreate the great works of the Titans together, or . . ."

"Or, we just kill you to atone for the murder of our father."

Vor looked at Griffin Harkonnen, who lay motionless on the sands, obviously dead; the young man's slack face showed no pain, only a startled confusion. Turning back to the twins, Vor said, "I don't like either option."

And he ran.

Despite their ability to make extensive calculations, Mentats still have blind spots.

—HEADMASTER GILBERTUS ALBANS,
cautionary comment to new class

For three days, the Emperor's troops scoured the Rossak settlement carefully and methodically, searching for any sign of the computers Dorotea insisted were there. And they found nothing.

Worse, Emperor Salvador had made a bold announcement to cheering crowds on Salusa that he was going to Rossak to "destroy the evil computers." His humiliation grew more palpable by the hour.

With each failure, Reverend Mother Dorotea became increasingly insistent. The Emperor stood with her outside the entrance to the high-cliff chambers, fuming. Directly overhead, the sky hung ominously gray. "On your assurances I made a spectacle of bringing my Imperial forces here, Sister Dorotea," he growled. "You made me launch this embarrassing effort, and I have nothing to show for it."

Even the suspicious Sisters in her faction had been unable to offer any suggestions. In desperation, the Emperor commanded his troops to go through every tunnel and chamber a second time, while using sonic scanners on the walls to detect hidden passages. Roderick personally supervised the operation.

Meanwhile, Reverend Mother Raquella remained calm, and instructed her Sisters to cooperate in every way. "When will you admit that there's nothing here to find, Sire?"

"When I am convinced of it." He sent her away.

During the overcast afternoon, a commercial shuttle arrived with routine supplies from offworld—an innocuous delivery, but the Emperor ordered every container opened and ransacked for forbidden technology, anything he could use to justify his full military operation on Rossak.

His soldiers were growing restless, and the Sisters—even Dorotea's allies—showed increasing signs of anger at the injustice.

Salvador paced outside his flagship, gazing at the cliff city, greatly distressed. He hissed from the side of his mouth to Roderick. "How am I going to get out of this boondoggle and save face? Can't we just smuggle in a few computers from our junk heaps in Zimia? We have plenty for the next rampage festival."

"That would be awkward, Brother. No one would believe it if the ships had to fly back to Salusa and then return here." Always the voice of reason.

"I look like a damned fool," he muttered. "I should have let Manford Torondo come here after all. Let him waste his time searching for things that aren't there."

Roderick's brow furrowed, and he kept his voice low. "Even if we don't find illegal equipment, there is still a dire problem here. Anna has been damaged by negligence, and we both heard Dr. Zhoma's confession that the Sisterhood wants to cut off your bloodline. Even though Sister Dorotea appears to be discredited, in my mind she's not. She has proved herself useful at the Imperial Court, and I am inclined to believe her claims against the Sisterhood, even though we have no solid evidence."

"I agree with you, and I'm thinking of publicly accusing the Sisterhood of plotting against me. Reveal their insidious scheme to render me sterile!"

Roderick frowned. "No, Salvador, we shouldn't do that. It's not the sort of thing we want in the public record."

The Emperor let out a long sigh, and nodded slowly. "It is damned embarrassing. But I need a practical solution. I vowed to come here and smash their computers."

He looked out on his landed ships, his crowded troops, the commanders who had begun to put the soldiers through routine practice drills on the polymer treetops because they had nothing else to do. A waste of time! He needed to put an end to this affair.

"Call Sister Dorotea here and Reverend Mother Raquella. Tell them to bring all the Sister Mentats, as well, and line them up before me." Salvador crossed his arms as he made up his mind. "Then inform the subcommanders to prepare the troops for departure by nightfall."

RESPONDING TO THE Emperor's brusque summons as the sun lowered toward the ruddy haze of volcanic smoke, the Reverend Mother led old Karee Marques and the other Sister Mentats to the Corrino flagship. An armed elite guard stood on either side of the temporary throne, which had been turned so that the low sun did not shine in Salvador's eyes.

Dorotea already waited there, unsettled and angry. Raquella's granddaughter had unexpectedly sympathized with Butlerian sentiments, ever since her assignment on Lampadas, but she wondered whether the real reason for Dorotea's rebelliousness stemmed more from feeling abandoned by the people who were genetically related to her, failing to understand a basic teaching of the order, that the only family its members had was the Sisterhood.

The Emperor leaned forward on his temporary throne, resting his elbows on his knees. He looked coldly at the eight Sister Mentats, but focused his glare on Raquella. "Reverend Mother, I despise your highly questionable breeding projections, and I know you tried to prevent me from having children. Dr. Zhoma revealed everything."

Roderick stood next to his brother, staring stonily at her. Raquella's throat grew so dry she couldn't even swallow. The voices in her mind were as silent as a tomb.

"When we departed from the capital, I made a public vow to destroy the computers the Sisterhood uses. I can't go back to Salusa empty-handed."

Raquella flinched. He appeared to be mortally offended and unable to reveal the true reasons publicly. He had somehow tortured the truth out of Dr. Zhoma, but Raquella had supreme control over her own bodily chemistry and felt confident that she could will her body to die before revealing anything. "But you have searched everywhere for computers, Sire. You cannot find what does not exist. We have only human computers here."

He sniffed. "That is only a matter of semantics. They are still computers."

A quick nod to the captain of the elite guard, and all the rifles swung down, leveled at the eight Sister Mentats.

Raquella recoiled, and a shout of horror caught in her throat.

Beside her, Karee Marques raised her hands in the final instant, the oldest living Sorceress of Rossak, and Raquella felt a thrumming crack inside her skull as the old woman was hit, a buffeting wave of desperately released psychic energy, a remnant of the power that the most powerful Sorceresses had once used to annihilate cymeks. The other Sister Mentats, though, were not Sorceresses.

Karee Marques wasn't enough, and as the Emperor screamed, obviously feeling the mental blast from her, his elite guard opened fire. The volley of sharp projectiles mowed down the eight Sister Mentats. The women dropped onto the paved canopy like harvested wheat stalks.

Astonished that she was still alive herself, Raquella broke away and ran to the crumpled bodies, where she knelt over Karee Marques, who lay in a macabre, twisted heap, her white robe splattered in red.

A stunned gasp whispered up from all the Sisters who were observing from the cliffs above the landing canopy, and several began to howl in rage, or wail in grief.

From the cliffs, five more Sorceresses roared in a resonant howl that echoed across the treetops and in the minds of all those gathered around the school. To the astonishment of the group surrounding Salvador's temporary throne, the Sorceresses leaped into the air, suicidally diving toward the golden Imperial flagship. They plummeted downward, their white robes rippling around them so that they looked like valkyries swooping down to a battlefield—and then they slowed their descent, using telekinetic control to levitate themselves. With murder in their eyes, they dove toward the Emperor, unleashing another wave of buffeting telepathy. Raquella felt her skull shaking from the psychic pressure, and she dropped to her knees.

The target of the assault, Salvador yelled in pain and pressed his hands to his temples, with his eyes squeezed shut. Blood blossomed from his nostrils. Risking his own safety, Roderick grabbed his brother's arm and tried to help him away from the throne.

Salvador had collapsed to the ground by his throne, whimpering, so Roderick gasped an order to the elite guard. *"Stop them!"*

Struggling back to her feet, Raquella screamed upward as the Sorceresses continued their descent. "No! No, do not attack!"

Turning their projectile rifles upward, the soldiers blasted the Sorceresses out of the sky, causing the white-robed women to fall and crash in broken, bloody heaps among the dead Sister Mentats.

Raquella sobbed.

Salvador reeled, his face wild with pain and shock. As he started to mumble an order to continue the massacre, Roderick grabbed him by the shoulders and said, "Stop before it goes too far! Enough killing."

Dorotea knelt in front of the Emperor. "Your brother is right, Sire. Please don't kill all the Sisters."

Salvador sucked in great gasping breaths and finally exerted control over himself. He wiped away the blood trickling from his nostrils, offended by the scarlet stain on the back of his hand. He steadied himself by holding the side of the throne and touched a control at his throat. His voice boomed out from the speaker systems on the landed military craft. "By my Imperial order, I hereby decree that the Sisterhood of Rossak is disbanded! This school will be closed. *Permanently.* All trainees will be dispersed and sent back to their homes."

Raquella's shoulders hitched, and she could not tear her gaze from the murdered Mentats, or the fallen Sorceresses who had only tried to defend the Sisterhood. When she looked at the Emperor, her devastated, hateful expression made him flinch.

Roderick Corrino quickly put himself between them. "There is much of value in what the Sisters have achieved. I propose that Reverend Mother Dorotea and certain worthy Sisters return with us to Salusa Secundus, where their skills can still serve the Imperium. The rest . . ."

Salvador seemed glad to have his brother show strength. "All others are to leave Rossak. The breeding records will be destroyed, never to be misused again." He gave orders to his troops, who gathered flame guns from the squadron armory and marched up to the high caves.

He turned and looked at the hundreds of stunned women standing at the balconies on the cliff. "The rest of you must scatter to the winds. Your Sisterhood is outlawed!" He looked down at the distraught Reverend Mother, gratified to see how defeated she appeared. "There," he said. "*Now* do you think I have a weak and inferior bloodline?"

Our greatest commanders can lay down the most intricate military
plans, but in the end only God determines who wins each battle.
— MANFORD TORONDO, *The Only Path*

Watching from the bridge of his ship, Manford went white when he saw the evacuee ships detonate, far enough away from him that he was not involved. Several Butlerian vessels had closed in to help them, and now the shock waves tore them apart. "Did that madman Venport kill his own people?"

As Gilbertus watched, alternatives raced through his mind. "I should point out, sir, that Butlerians often take similar fanatical actions." The legless man responded to the suggestion with horror and denial, and Gilbertus quickly added, "However, I think it highly likely that those ships were empty, flown by automated systems and detonated remotely. He and his personnel are probably still hiding in the industrial facilities."

"Then we will find them and blast them to hell. I already made my compassionate offer, but Venport has shown what kind of man he really is."

Gilbertus nodded, continuing his cool assessment. More instructive, he thought, was that Josef Venport had proven himself to be *unpredictable*. Such a brash, foolhardy action was unlike anything he had previously done. What was it meant to accomplish? Yes, the ploy had damaged the Butlerian fleet, but not nearly enough to win the engagement. How did he expect to save himself or his personnel from Manford's inevitable retaliation? It was suicide. The Butlerians would never accept his surrender now. It made no sense.

"Mentat, say something!" Manford demanded.

"Recalculating first." Oh, how he longed to have Erasmus here to help. . . .

Without warning, the thirty VenHold patrol ships opened fire, along with at least ten of the other ships at the complex. The sheer mathematics of the tactical situation should have precluded any aggressive actions—thirty or forty against more than two hundred—and yet they began to hammer the Butlerian ships.

As Gilbertus continued his reassessment, explosions went off near the flagship. The adjacent Butlerian vessel blew up as its fuel compartments were breached.

Not waiting for Manford's instructions, Swordmaster Idaho yelled across the open channel. "Return fire—all ships, return fire at will! Destroy them all!"

The thirty VenHold ships strafed the Butlerian fleet, accelerating faster than expected, and their weaponry was far more powerful than normal vessels of that size; Josef Venport had made improvements.

Gilbertus began to refactor the variables. Perhaps the odds weren't so clearly in Manford's favor after all. Those ships did indeed pose a threat.

The Butlerians still had strength in numbers, but their vessels were outdated designs from the Army of Humanity, surplus military ships that were more than eighty years old. Manford Torondo had never imagined he might face stiff resistance; he simply expected his opponents to surrender to him out of fear.

But the ruthless businessman Josef Venport was not a man to be intimidated; Gilbertus was beginning to understand him better.

Then the next gear of Venport's defensive plan clicked into place.

Dozens more enemy ships moved out of the shipyards: half-completed constructions, robotic hulks with barely functioning engines, skeletons of starships accelerating and spreading out in formation. When the Butlerian fleet arrived, Gilbertus had assumed those ships to be inoperable, but when they began to move, he reassessed their tactical potential. A nasty surprise! Venport had more than twice as many ships to throw into the fray than it had at first appeared.

These new hulks had some active weapons systems, but primarily they were cannon fodder, big vessels careening into Manford's fleet, creating havoc even as they were pummeled by Butlerian firepower. Though damaged, the half-finished automated vessels kept coming, crashing into the tight Butlerian formations.

One of Venport's patrol ships exploded, but the rest of them kept firing. Gilbertus estimated that at least forty of Manford's ships had been destroyed in the surprise detonations and the ensuing, unexpected resistance.

As the scattering Butlerian ships pushed closer to the main spacedocks and the asteroid factories, they opened fire again, pounding the remaining factories. At least five more were destroyed, their domes shattered, belching fire and leaking atmosphere into space.

Even for a Mentat, it was difficult to keep score of all the destroyed facilities.

Per his duty, he presented Manford with a revised assessment. "Those are automated vessels, so he will have no qualms about sacrificing them."

Anari Idaho gasped. "Driven by thinking machines?"

"Automated vessels," Gilbertus repeated, without further clarification.

The Butlerian leader glared at him. "Why didn't you predict this, Mentat?"

"Because I did not have complete data."

"Use new parameters. I am willing to sacrifice every one of my ships, as well. Consider all of my followers and ships expendable, so long as we win this battle. The mind of man is holy."

"The mind of man is holy," Anari echoed.

"*Everything* is expendable, sir?" Another contradiction; Gilbertus did not point out how appalled Manford had been when Venport's people made a similar decision.

"Except for the life of Manford," the Swordmaster said. "That is not negotiable."

Manford was deadly calm as he explained, "All-out assaults are how we won Serena Butler's Jihad against Omnius and his thinking machines. We can do no less now in this battle for the soul of the human race."

Gilbertus studied the pattern of ship movements, retraced the paths, found intersections until all of the possibilities formed an intricate web in his mind . . . a web that had a strangely familiar pattern. Yes, right now Erasmus would have been of enormous assistance.

Several more of the half-completed ships crashed into the Butlerian forces, ramming some, scrambling sensors in others, drawing fire like rocks thrown at a hornet's nest. That was their purpose, Gilbertus realized. They were not meant to survive.

Time slowed to a crawl in Gilbertus's mind as he went deep into Mentat mode and rapidly created his own patterns, revising the projected movements of ships so that he could minimize the concentrations of potential damage. With careful attention, he could unravel the complex tangle that his opponent had created.

Gilbertus admired the plan that had been set up against him. It was a shame he would have to defeat it.

Panicked and unruly, the Butlerians wasted shots; several ships picked the same target while ignoring others. "To win we need to be organized, Leader Torondo. I have a plan, but you must let me guide the shots. Direct your commanders to follow my orders."

"Do you guarantee that will defeat them?" the leader asked.

"It is your best possibility."

"I see." He seemed disappointed by the response. "All right, Mentat, give us a victory."

ONCE THE PLANS had been set in motion, like clockwork soldiers wound up and turned loose, Josef could admire what his own Mentat had conceived. "We have a chance, Draigo. Look at that destruction!" With fascination he watched the streaking ships, the lancing projectiles, the chain-reaction explosions as closely packed Butlerian ships took one another out. Starbursts of fire and debris spread all around the entire Thonaris complex in such great numbers that he could not begin to guess how many barbarian vessels had already been destroyed.

He felt sick at heart to lose these grand industrial capabilities—so many ships that could have expanded the VenHold Spacing Fleet, all that profit turned to vapor and scraps! It was difficult, but in his mind he tried to write off the loss. He could not save the facility or his investment here—but if he crippled the Butlerians, the cost would be justified.

Although Josef noticed no difference in the mayhem around him, his Mentat watched the movements of the rival ships closely, and said, "Gilbertus Albans has taken command. I recognize his techniques."

But to Josef, the chaos of weapon fire and colliding ships was impenetrable.

Draigo's eyes flicked from side to side as he processed intricate calculations. "We have a small survival ship in the administrative hub, sir. I suggest we depart from this control center. Gilbertus will target it soon. He'll locate us in moments."

Josef couldn't believe what the Mentat had just said. "But we're winning! Look at how many ships they've lost!"

"And they still have many more to lose, sir. Now, however, they are operating without restraint—and under such circumstances, the rules and odds change." He looked squarely at Josef, and there was real emotion and concern in his expression. "We cannot win, sir. Trust me."

For a moment Josef refused to listen . . . but he had trusted Draigo and his plans as much as he trusted Norma Cenva. He had always relied on his talented experts, knew he'd be a fool not to listen. "If you're convinced, then let's get out of here."

"Shall I sound the evacuation of any remaining personnel?"

"You can try. We'll have to hope the barbarians let some of our people live—but we both know it's me he wants."

Josef and Draigo bolted for the small evacuation craft, sealed themselves inside, and launched from the docking clamp. Josef glanced at the Thonaris admin-hub as they drifted away, saw the frozen body of Arjen Gates mounted outside like a lawn ornament, and felt the great sense of his own financial and personnel loss. Such a waste!

The evac-ship wasn't equipped with Holtzman engines, and he had no Navigator. He didn't know how they were going to get away from the star system at all, but Draigo would make it possible for him to survive another hour . . . even if in that hour he had to watch the destruction of everything around him. The small ship pulled away from the administrative hub, lost in a flurry of activity as countless vessels whipped by and projectiles flew all around.

"And how do you project we'll get safely away, Mentat?"

The Mentat hesitated for an uncomfortably long moment. "I am currently unable to determine that." Josef felt a heavy weight in his chest. It had never occurred to him that Draigo might not have an answer.

Moments later, a barrage of projectiles tore open the empty admin-hub. Watching the proof of his Mentat's conclusions, Josef felt lost, even discouraged, and at last he recognized the fundamental change that Draigo had spotted earlier: The barbarians were reckless, not caring if they had to sacrifice five *manned* ships for every one they destroyed. The human cost was staggering, but Manford's fanatics were steadily diminishing the VenHold forces and facilities. The spacedocks had been destroyed, along with most of the automated factories.

"We're not going to escape, are we, Mentat? It's only a matter of time before they target us."

"With no way to fold space, we can't escape." Draigo adjusted the communications system in the evac-ship. "I've scrambled the transmission to slow their ability to find us. Would you allow me to contact their Mentat, sir?"

Josef frowned. "Will he negotiate for the barbarians?"

"I don't believe so. But I would like to . . . bid him farewell."

With a sigh, Josef nodded. "I have nothing more to lose."

As their tiny, unmarked lifeboat drifted among the wreckage and chaos, Draigo activated the screen and identified himself to the Butlerians. "This is the Mentat serving Venport Holdings. I would like to speak with Gilbertus Albans, please."

In moments, his Mentat teacher appeared, not looking at all surprised. "I recognized your tactics, Draigo. I'm sorry we find ourselves on opposite sides of the battlefield in a real clash instead of a game."

"A Mentat must be loyal to his employer. I've done my best to defend Josef Venport and protect these shipyards—just as you've done your best to destroy them."

"At the command of Manford Torondo," said Gilbertus.

Draigo wore a defeated smile. "As soon as I realized you had taken command, my own projections showed that even with my best skills I could not win. You had the better set of assets to use against me."

"Nevertheless, I'm proud of you. You fought well. But you understand that this is goodbye, Draigo. Manford Torondo will not allow you to be taken prisoner."

"Your Half-Manford can go to hell," Josef said.

Manford Torondo broke into the channel. "The robot Erasmus wrote that human beings were merely an expendable resource, but it is machines that are really expendable. And their allies—"

Draigo switched off the transmission.

Josef looked at him with heavy eyes. "Any other suggestions, Mentat?"

"None, sir, I have reviewed all of the known data."

Just then, so close and so suddenly that even Draigo let out a startled cry, a large VenHold ship appeared, folding space from nowhere. The cargo bay doors opened up like a yawning mouth in front of the small escape craft.

Josef recognized the female voice that came over the comm system—his own wife Cioba! "Norma Cenva and I are here to retrieve you, Josef. We will take you aboard!" Without asking how the two women had known to come here, Draigo quickly flew their ship into the hold of the rescue vessel.

Below and behind them, the Butlerians had noticed the new ship and turned their weaponry toward it. The first few blasts erupted nearby, without hitting their mark.

"How did you know to come here?" Josef asked over the comm.

In her wavering, ethereal voice, Norma said, "They may have Mentats, but I can trump them with my *prescience*."

As fiery explosions continued throughout the shipyards, Josef saw that all was indeed lost. Norma Cenva's vessel closed its hull like an embrace around their evac-ship, and as Cioba ran into the hold to see her husband, the cargo ship winked away and vanished into the safety of foldspace.

Persistence is a virtue, but obsession a sin.
—the *Orange Catholic Bible*

The twin offspring of Agamemnon sprinted after him, leaving Griffin's dead body on the hot sands.

Vor knew that even if he barricaded himself inside the small weather station, Andros and Hyla could tear through the wall in minutes. Instead, he scrambled up onto the rocks, climbing the loose stone with hands and feet, pulling his way up a boulder field to a small ridge. The open terrain beyond might have been good for meteorological measurements, but it offered Vorian very few options for escape.

"Where are you running, Brother?" Hyla called. "Convince us to keep you alive."

He didn't answer.

Andros and his sister climbed patiently after him, going over the rocks like liquid flowing uphill, defying gravity. When Vor reached the top of the ridge, he regarded the steep slope on the other side that led nowhere except to the empty sands. Maybe he could circle around and try to scramble back to the twins' landed aircraft, but they had shut down their engines, and he knew the startup and takeoff process would take several minutes; Andros and Hyla would never let him get that far ahead of them.

He still had his personal shield and the Maula pistol; the spring-loaded projectile weapon was functional though he doubted if it would be effective against the twins. Still, the projectiles could delay them. He cocked the weapon and turned, bracing himself.

Andros and Hyla were pulling themselves over a line of wobbly boulders that had slid down the slope. Even though, genetically speaking, these were his brother and sister, he felt no hesitation, no remorse. Vor had killed Agamemnon decades ago, and a little more family blood on his hands would make no difference. He had watched these two murder Griffin Harkonnen, a noble young man who had not deserved to die like that.

Still climbing, Andros looked up at him and shouted, "At least your wife didn't run when we wanted to ask her questions. But she was an old woman."

As anger flooded through him, Vor aimed at the other man's forehead and squeezed the trigger. The loud report from the Maula pistol sounded like a contained explosion, but Vor's aim—or the weapon—was off. A boulder just to the left of the young man's head cracked, and tiny rock fragments sprayed out in all directions. Andros flinched.

Hyla stood up and Vor fired a second time, aiming directly at the center of her chest. This time the bullet struck, and he saw the crater in her jumpsuit, the red ripped flesh at her sternum. The impact drove her backward, but Andros slowed to help her and reached out to grab her arm. She cried out, but regained her strength very quickly. Vor aimed the Maula pistol again and squeezed the trigger. The weapon made only a grinding sound. He tried twice more, but the pistol was jammed. He discarded it.

The twins ascended after him again, making even better time now. Thinking fast, searching for alternatives, Vor gazed across the bright, burning sands, where tiny dots of rock protruded at widespread intervals like rotting teeth. The nearest one was nearly a kilometer away. At a dead run across the powdery dunes, he would need at least fifteen minutes to reach it, and nothing at all waited for him out there.

Still, he had a plan.

Recklessly dropping down the steep slope, bouncing from one unstable boulder to the next, he reached the end of the rocks and ran out onto the sand, stumbling across the soft surface. Ishanti had taught him how to disguise his footsteps, how to move without rhythm so as to not attract a sandworm. Right now, however, Vor ran at his natural pace, already panting. He had no water; his supplies were back at the weather station. The twins were coming.

They had killed Griffin.

And Mariella.

Behind him, Andros and Hyla began to descend the slope, closing the gap. Hyla's voice sounded strong as she yelled, "Even if you reach those rocks, where will you run? There's nothing but sand!"

Vor didn't waste his breath calling back to them. He pulled as far ahead as possible—but it wasn't enough, and they were gaining on him. Halfway to the nearest rocky protrusion, he decided it was time to take his greatest risk, hoping he had enough time to reach the rocks.

When he activated the personal shield, it issued a faint, vibrating crackle. Static electricity seemed to charge the dust around him. He unclipped the shield belt, left the power supply activated, and dropped the belt onto the sand. He ran with even more frantic energy toward the small rock island, unearthing reserves of strength within himself that he didn't know he had. Vor was sure that his rhythmic footfalls had already sent an irresistible summons to a sandworm. Now, with the throbbing shield belt, there should be no question. . . .

The twins continued after him across the dunes, following his footprints as he had hoped. Andros called out in his piercing voice, "Look at you running like a coward! You are an embarrassment to Agamemnon."

Vor's throat burned and his eyes stung, but when he reached the top of a dune, he saw that he had almost made it to the solid outcropping. Like an ice-berg, the rock's roots grew larger beneath the surface. A few more steps, and he felt rock beneath the sand. He pulled himself higher, panting, and then turned to watch.

Andros and Hyla reached the shield belt he had thrown away. They knew they were closing in, and that Vor had nowhere to go beyond his small rock is-land. The two were so intent on him that they didn't seem to notice the vibra-tions in the sand, or the large mounded ripple rushing toward them.

But Hyla hesitated, sensing something, while Andros picked up the shield belt with a sour frown. He tossed the device over his shoulder—just as a sand-worm lunged up from beneath the dunes, its maw open. Scooping hundreds of cubic meters of sand, the creature rose so high that the children of Agamemnon looked like tiny specks falling down a whirlpool.

The worm swallowed them.

Vor squatted down to watch the sandworm circling the area. Though he was all alone, without supplies, abandoned in the middle of the desert, he felt safe for the first time in a long while. . . .

At last he had time to reflect on the trouble he had caused on Arrakis, even though he had only meant to live here in peace. He thought of the people he had recently lost: Ishanti, who had treated him well, and Griffin Harkonnen, an unin-tended enemy, who might have understood and even forgiven Vorian. And he thought of Mariella.

Over the centuries he had grieved for many losses, but now he was saddened by the waste of these three lives. The Harkonnens had hated him for generations since the exile of Abulurd, and he had hoped to achieve some sort of resolution. But once the family learned what had happened to Griffin, he doubted the breach would ever be healed.

Sitting on the lonely rock, Vorian felt centuries-tired, and wished he could just find a place where he didn't have to keep looking over his shoulder. He watched as the worm eventually buried itself in the sand and went away, but he decided to rest awhile before making his way back to the weather-monitoring station and the aircraft that could take him away from here once and for all.

Most public events sponsored by governments are for show. Savvy leaders understand that perceptions are the foundation of their power.
　　　　　　　　—Imperial study of government practices

The edict issued by Emperor Salvador Corrino allowed the disbanded Sisters of Rossak only a few days to vacate their planet and forsake the school that Reverend Mother Raquella had built over the past eight decades. He stationed Imperial forces to ensure that his orders were carried out, while he returned to Salusa Secundus with Dorotea and a hundred members of her faction. Raquella was not given the opportunity to say goodbye to her granddaughter, or Sister Valya, or anyone else.

Everyone in the Sisterhood was to be dispersed, old and young alike. Only a handful of Sisters with important connections could decide where they wanted to go, but most were sent back to the worlds where they had lived before going to Rossak.

BEING THE EMPEROR'S brother did not entitle Roderick Corrino to a life of luxurious relaxation. On the day after the Imperial forces returned from Rossak, he longed to sleep late and relax in his bed with Haditha, and enjoy breakfast with her and their children. But the Imperium called.

He hadn't slept well, haunted by Salvador's impetuous execution of the Sisterhood's Mentats, and the disbanding of the Rossak School. Roderick had a great deal of damage to mitigate. He hoped Sister Dorotea might provide an insightful perspective and be willing to work with him. Roderick continued to believe the trained Sisters had considerable value, and he was glad he'd convinced his brother to spare Dorotea's faction at least. Better to save something than nothing at all. . . .

Roderick had done what he could to salvage the situation. Using funds from Sisterhood bank accounts that the Emperor had confiscated, Sister Dorotea and a hundred of her handpicked followers were busy setting up a new training facility for their order on Salusa Secundus. There would be no breeding program or *Azhar Book,* and no other publications or programs that had not first been approved by representatives of the Imperial government.

Sister Dorotea would bear close watching, but Roderick had always found her valuable. She still had to sort out her personal ambitions from her expressed loyalties to the Emperor; Roderick needed to determine where they overlapped and where they might conflict. . . .

As he went about his morning ablutions, preoccupied but as quiet as possible, Roderick considered the numerous critical events he would have to balance. Though his brother had the title and glory of being Emperor, Roderick spent more time implementing policy and ensuring that the government functioned smoothly, despite some of Salvador's rash and ill-advised decisions.

Too much had been done, in his opinion, to appease Manford Toronto and his rabble-rousing followers—not because Salvador believed in their extremist views, but because they wielded enough power to bully him. Salvador's brash actions against the Sisterhood were clearly an attempt to take the initiative away from Manford, but it had not gone well. Roderick didn't deny that anti-technology extremists could cause a great deal of civil unrest, but he was more worried that his brother had made many pronouncements without first consulting him.

For most of their lives, Salvador had used him as a sounding board, for help with important decisions. Roderick wondered what had changed. He sensed a withdrawal on his brother's part, a desperation and a will to survive. Maybe he felt he was losing control of his Imperium. But Salvador was his brother and the rightful Emperor, and Roderick had his own duties.

He needed to reassert his influence over Salvador and be a voice of reason, before his brother turned into a tyrant. During the CET riots and Emperor Jules's bloodbath against the delegates seeking sanctuary at the Palace, they had all seen the price to be paid for allowing emotions and paranoia to run unchecked, but Salvador was not much of a student of history. . . .

Ready for the day, though it was not yet dawn over the city of Zimia, Roderick emerged from his private wing and walked down the corridor to the Emperor's private administration offices. He was surprised to find Salvador already waiting for him. Grinning, the Emperor said, "Hurry, come along with me. I've got good news to show you!"

Roderick fell into step beside his brother. "These days, we both could use a bit of that."

Like an excited boy squirming to keep a secret, Salvador refused to tell him what to expect as they rode in a fast carriage to the large central plaza of the capital city, in the midst of imposing government buildings. There, Imperial guards were already at work cordoning off the area, keeping crowds of early-rising onlookers from getting closer. Escorted by gold-uniformed troops, the two Corrinos made their way through the people. Roderick smelled an odd, burning odor that irritated his nose.

With a stomach-wrenching sense of déjà vu, he stopped to stare at a burned and horribly mutilated body hanging from a lamppost; a thick cable was still twisted around the neck. The extremities had been cut off, the face smashed into unrecognizability, the skin and hair burned.

Salvador tugged at his brother's arm, not seeming at all upset. "Come, come! You're going to *love* this!" He lowered his voice to a stage whisper. "It solves several problems at the same time."

Though he didn't like any part of what he saw, Roderick went forward cautiously, trying not to inhale the stink of roasted flesh. The placard placed near the mutilated body said in a childish scrawl, "The Traitor Bomoko."

"Not another one," Roderick groaned. "I wonder which poor innocent the mobs lynched this time."

His brother did a poor job of hiding his grin. "How do you know it isn't the real Bomoko?"

"After all these years, and all the misidentified victims? I highly doubt it."

Salvador leaned close to whisper, though the hubbub of guards and onlookers drowned out all normal conversation. "It's no innocent this time, Brother. Wouldn't you agree that this is a useful way to dispose of Dr. Zhoma? Two birds with one stone."

Roderick's head snapped back but he stopped himself from responding aloud.

Strutting officiously in front of a gathering crowd, Salvador raised his voice, sounding imperious, making sure people nearby could hear him. "We must take this seriously, Brother! Perform genetic tests and determine if we have at last found the real traitor, Toure Bomoko! It would be good to put this long nightmare to rest! I want you to supervise this matter personally."

Salvador's angry expression was quite convincing even as he whispered out of the side of his mouth, "And I think you know what results I want."

Roderick kept his own expression studiously grim, though he felt great alarm inside. "No one will believe it, Salvador. It's not even a matter of genetic testing—the clumsiest autopsy will show that this is a female, not a male. It can't possibly be Bomoko."

The Emperor remained unperturbed. "Oh, you can take care of that. I have confidence in you. Issue a thorough-looking report, and I'll give it my stamp of approval. Cremate the body and remove any other evidence. Problem solved! Zhoma has received the justice she deserved, and the mobs can stop looking for their bogeyman."

Roderick knew the infamous CET leader was probably dead somewhere on a distant planet, or at least hiding from the small-minded selfishness of Imperial politics. Roderick would have liked to be far from the pettiness, but he could not shirk his responsibilities. A Corrino did not hide.

"Don't worry," he said. "I'll take charge of this mess."

Salvador was so pleased that he patted his brother on the back. "I can always depend on you. We're such an excellent team, you and I."

THE ASSIGNMENT PROVED to be, in fact, simple enough. It was a far more difficult challenge for Roderick to see his sister and decide what to do with her.

He found Anna wading in a shallow water garden with Lady Orenna, picking colorful floating flowers and putting them in a basket. Standing together in the water, the two women looked like children, and Roderick smiled at them. It was a pleasant contrast to the gruesome spectacle earlier in the day. The silver-haired Orenna, normally quite elegant, wore a simple dress that was drenched from the pool; Anna wore shorts and a dirt-stained blouse. She seemed happy.

Watching from the edge of the pool, Roderick said, "You're looking better today, Anna. A good night's rest?"

"Flowers for my mind." With a sweet smile, she held up a beautiful yellow flower with delicate, fringed petals. "Genus *Limnanthemum nymphoides*, more commonly known as the floating heart. It is a heart for my mind." In her basket, she pointed to a white-and-black flower with greenish-purple leaves. "Genus *A. distachyus*. It smells like vanilla and is edible. Would you like a taste?"

"No thank you." His stomach remained unsettled from the doctor's mutilated corpse he had recently disposed of.

His sister's voice rattled on. "I can identify every plant in this pond, and every plant in the Imperial gardens. I know other things, too. The chemistry of the dirt, the origins of the rocks, the scientific names of all the birds and insects. These gardens contain many ecosystems—until now, I never saw all the wondrous interactions taking place."

Without pausing for a breath, Anna began a scholarly dissertation on the garden, but became distracted when a waterfowl with brilliant emerald plumage flitted by, which prompted her to provide exhaustive details about the region of

Salusa Secundus where it nested, and its migratory patterns. Then she began describing planets and star systems where similar birds were found, and soon she was off that topic entirely, talking about the chemistry of cements, mortars, bricks, and other building materials, which somehow led to the mathematics of music.

Lady Orenna stepped from the pond, wiped off her feet with a cloth, and said in a low tone, "I'm very concerned about her."

Anna continued to ramble as Roderick answered, "Does she still hear the strange voices inside?"

Orenna nodded. "She collapsed just before we came here. Simply overwhelmed. These flowers seem to be calming her down, though." The older woman sat on a small bench and put her shoes back on. "Her mind may be damaged; it's overactive, filled with unsorted information that spews out at random. If she could control it and organize it, maybe our dear Anna's awareness would return."

"She's always been smarter than we allowed," Roderick said. "And now, we have to do everything possible to give her the help she needs."

"The Suk School is in disarray—we dare not entrust her delicate mind to their psychologists."

He nodded in agreement. "No, I can think of only one place that might be able to understand her condition—the Mentat School on Lampadas. They know more about the human mind than anyone. I'll suggest it to Salvador, and I think he'll agree."

Without taking off his shoes or rolling up his trousers, Roderick waded into the water and hugged his sister, as if to protect her from the demons tormenting her fragile mind. In his arms, she trembled a little, then looked up into his eyes and smiled. "I love you," Anna said.

After Norma rescued him from the disaster at Thonaris, Josef did not pause
to mourn the loss of personnel or ships. Rather, he and Cioba put the
entire company, all holdings and subsidiary operations, on high alert. Manford
Torondo and his insane barbarians were no longer merely an annoyance: The
destructive, deadly extremists had to be stopped at any cost. And Venport Holdings was one of the only forces in the Imperium with enough assets to stand
against their savagery.

Back on Kolhar, Josef sat in his office, trying to quantify the damage and
losses. Nearly six thousand employees dead, including several hundred who had
been transfers from Celestial Transport during the takeover. It was even possible
that some had been captured by the barbarians. Under interrogation the high-
level supervisors could provide important information about VenHold vulnerabilities. He fumed.

Thirteen of his most heavily armed patrol ships had been destroyed. Seventy
recovered machine ships and partially built vessels, all turned to scrap, along with
cargo holds full of sophisticated equipment and heavy machinery, an Emperor's
ransom in processed raw materials.

Everything destroyed.

Cioba entered his office, and he looked up at her. She understood his immense gratitude for helping him keep his family's commercial empire intact. The
marriage had been one of the wisest business deals he had ever negotiated.

Today, instead of her usual business attire, with her long hair done up neatly
under a scarf, Cioba had let her hair tumble loose to her waist . . . and she wore a

clean white robe that accentuated the pale perfection of her skin. He was startled by her appearance; it brought to mind the image of a fearsome Sorceress about to engage in battle with a cymek.

Before he could comment, she said, "There is another crisis."

The words were like a weight dropped on his back. "I don't need another crisis."

Cioba stepped up to his desk. "This one we can solve—and it gains us another powerful ally."

He sat back, tapped his fingers on his bloodwood writing surface. "All right, tell me about it."

She described the news she had just received about the disaster on Rossak, the Emperor ordering the execution of the Sisterhood's Mentats—including Cioba's grandmother Karee Marques—as well as the disgrace and disbanding of the entire order. "The Emperor had heard rumors of illegal technology on Rossak, and though he found no evidence, he attacked nevertheless."

"Illegal technology? Has everyone gone mad?"

"All Sisters were ordered to leave Rossak. Some have returned to their homes, while others scattered to points unknown."

He rose to his feet. "And our daughters?"

"They are safe. I've dispatched one of our ships to retrieve them. But there are many other women who need our help." Her dark eyes flashed, challenging him to disagree with her.

"In what way?"

"Some of the Sisters—those with antitechnology leanings—remain in the good graces of the Emperor, and he has taken them back to Salusa Secundus. The others, however, including Reverend Mother Raquella, have no place to go. I suggest that you provide them with sanctuary. Send them to Tupile with the other exiles, or find a new place. The Sisterhood will continue . . . and VenHold may find their skills extremely valuable, as I hope you have found me to be valuable."

"Absolutely." He brushed back his hair, already considering the benefits he might reap from this new development. "Very well, arrange for our spacing fleet to provide sanctuary to Raquella and to any other Sister who requests it. They'll be in our debt."

"The Sisterhood doesn't forget its debts," Cioba said, and surprised him by bending closer and giving him a long kiss on the lips, before departing.

IN THE MASS evacuation, most of the Sisters had already dispersed before a large ship from the VenHold Spacing Fleet arrived, with an invitation from

Sister Cioba. Bowing to her influence, Josef Venport had let his wife provide sanctuary for Raquella and the Sisters who had openly aligned themselves with her. The Reverend Mother seized on the offer.

When leaving Rossak, the women were allowed to take only a few items of clothing and personal articles, all of which were inspected. Though all available copies of the *Azhar Book* had been destroyed, Raquella knew that many of her scattered missionary Sisters had copies of the Book, and ten more Sister Mentats were undergoing special instruction at the Lampadas School, where they were memorizing the entire text.

Emperor Salvador had done an efficient job of breaking up the Sisterhood, and had outlawed many of the basic tenets of the order, but Raquella was still confident that the core of her teachings and the goals of the organization would survive. She would make sure of it.

Aboard the outward-bound spacefolder ship, guided by a mysterious and unseen Navigator, Raquella felt pained to know that some of her most loyal Sisters were discouraged and on their own, convinced that their outlawed order would never regroup. Many women had already returned to their own homeworlds if given the opportunity, or they went elsewhere to begin new lives. As soon as Raquella reestablished her school, far from Imperial oversight, she would begin to reach out and renew those contacts.

The bodies of the slaughtered Mentats and Sorceresses had been cast to the jungles below so they could be reassimilated into the Rossak ecosystem . . . including poor Karee Marques, who had been so young and helpful during the virulent Omnius plagues. It seemed like much longer ago than the actual decades that had passed since then.

The breeding records and dismantled computers remained hidden in the isolated cenote, deep in the jungle. They were safe and intact . . . though the Sisters were in exile. Once the Reverend Mother made a new home for these women—thanks to the assistance of Cioba and Josef Venport—the computers and records would be retrieved.

First, she needed a new location for the school.

JOSEF AND HIS Mentat went out to the field of Navigator tanks. Draigo Roget remained stunned to have been rescued at all. "Even after all my training on Lampadas, I learned a fundamental thing in the recent battle." The Mentat was intent on the central tank, mesmerized by the swirling spice gas. "I learned that even the most detailed Mentat projections are fallible. Though I thought I had complete data, I could never have predicted that Norma Cenva would come for us."

Norma's enlarged face came close to one of the plaz viewing ports. She blinked. "Prescience is a variable that can never be factored into Mentat calculations—even prescience itself has many variables. A Navigator uses spice to envision countless possible paths through the universe, and then must choose a safe one. There is rarely only one option."

Still fuming, Josef cut off further discussion. "I am usually patient with your esoteric discussions, Norma, but right now we face a crisis." He glanced away from the field of Navigators to the distant Kolhar spaceport where vessels came and went: cargo ships, passenger transports, and the armed vessels he had used in his original conquest of the Thonaris shipyards. He should have left the entire force there in a massive defensive posture. . . .

"Kolhar is going to be a target," Josef said. "We have to defend this place and set up planetary shields like the ones that guarded Salusa Secundus from thinking-machine attacks. Our commercial ships must also be equipped with military-grade shielding, as well as the most advanced weaponry."

The Mentat was silently compiling a list in his head. "We have thousands of vessels in the VenHold Spacing Fleet, sir. Such an operation will require a massive expenditure and involve significant risk."

"Then we'll spend the money and take the risk! Make no mistake, this is war, and the planets of the Imperium will have to take sides and reap the benefits, or suffer the consequences. We'll withdraw the services of our vessels from any planet that sides with the barbarians."

The Mentat's brows drew together. "Venport Holdings will incur great financial losses as a result. If you lose this war, you're on the path to losing a great deal more—perhaps everything."

Josef snapped, "We will not help any world that turns its back on reason and civilization. Where will the barbarians draw the line? Will they spurn all medical technology, even as they die? They have already ransacked and destroyed the original Suk School in Zimia." He shook his head.

"Will they give up their power grid? Will they sacrifice heating and plumbing? Will they turn off the lights, leaving people to spend their evenings huddled around the glow of candlelight? Will they outlaw *fire* because it's too dangerous? Will they eat their meat raw?" Josef laughed bitterly. "We'll see how enthusiastic the Half-Manford's followers are once they actually get what they want. Let them live like true primitives for a while, unable to communicate with other worlds, and watch how quickly they change their minds and fall apart."

For a long time, Josef had been intent on building the power of his family, on stockpiling wealth and expanding into as many markets as possible. But now that he had thrown down the gauntlet and stepped into a war greater than any he had previously imagined, he realized this was a clash of civilizations, a war between reason and superstition, between progress and barbarism. And Josef would not go down without a fight. Rational humanity needed a champion.

He drew strength from his newfound passion. "We can face these murderous bullies and expose them for what they are. We'll leave Manford Torondo without a leg to stand on." He paused, not intending to be humorous. "Metaphorically speaking, that is."

"Such a conflict could take years . . . or decades," Draigo warned.

"So be it. We have VenHold's resources, our knowledge, and dedicated, clear-thinking individuals. We'll fight panic with intelligence. How can we possibly lose?"

Are your principles the true foundation of your life, or window dressing?
If you are unwilling to stand up and declare your beliefs for all to see and
hear, they are not true beliefs, but mere pretentions.
                                    —MANFORD TORONDO, address to the Landsraad League

After destroying the Thonaris shipyards, the remnants of Manford's Butlerian fleet went directly to Salusa Secundus. Even though they had lost
more than sixty ships to Venport and his technology-lovers, and the remaining
vessels were battered and war-scarred, the fleet made an imposing show as it
descended to the Zimia Spaceport.

Manford's blood still ran hot from the battle, and he announced over all
channels, to make certain everyone on Salusa heard his news, "We have averted
a catastrophe of machine resurgence and defeated a group of human traitors.
Now we return to the capital of the Imperium for the support and accolades of
the Landsraad League and every member of the government."

They released carefully edited video images that showed the fearful extent of
the reawakened robotic factories, how Josef Venport had flouted the rules of sanity and decency. Immediately following the victory, the Butlerians had remained
at Thonaris for the better part of a day to pummel the outpost and shipyards.
Venport himself, however, had apparently escaped.

Back at the shipyards, after experiencing the tycoon's treachery, Manford announced that no prisoners would be taken after all. Every single thinking-machine
collaborator was guilty of abominable crimes and deserved a death sentence. Following the constant bombardment from Butlerian warships, Thonaris was no
more than a cloud of hot, spreading debris. And Manford was proud of it.

If Emperor Salvador was wise, he would be proud of it, as well. Manford had
decided to stay on Salusa for weeks, and months if necessary, until he had his
chance to address the representatives of the Landsraad.

Immediately upon arriving in the capital city, he sent out a citizens' call, formally petitioning the council for a new vote to replace the one that had been interrupted by the bomb threat. This time, Manford would accept no excuses. Considering that he had more than 140 battleships filled with supporters, his request received quick approval, and a vote was scheduled to take place in two weeks.

Emperor Salvador himself strongly urged all Landsraad representatives and proxies to be there.

By the time the date arrived, Manford's Butlerians were entrenched at the spaceport, flexing their muscle throughout Zimia, recruiting new followers and collecting petitions. When they strongly encouraged citizens to sign their names to the statement, very few people declined.

On the morning of the scheduled vote, Manford pondered the best way to make an impressive entrance to the Landsraad Hall. Three of his followers would carry banners of the inspirational trinity of martyrs to human freedom: pale Rayna Butler, beautiful Serena Butler, and her infant, Manion, who had been murdered by the demented robot Erasmus.

Manford wore a loose shirt without adornment or medals, except for the insignia of a black fist clenched around a machine gear. Although he led the vast Butlerian movement, he thought of himself as a simple man, one of the people, and did not need to embellish himself with bric-a-brac. This time, rather than being carried on a palanquin, as he had previously when addressing the Landsraad Council, he chose to ride on Anari Idaho's shoulders. This appearance before the nobles was, after all, a battle as crucial as the recent Thonaris victory.

At the appointed time, with more than fifty thousand of his followers crowding the streets and the plaza around the Landsraad Hall, Manford positioned himself outside the great doors and ordered them to be flung open. Anari carried him proudly inside the gigantic hall, with Gilbertus Albans alongside and the three standard-bearers immediately behind them. As the legless man rode forward, he felt light-headed and energized with the blessings of Rayna. Today would be a watershed in their millennial battle.

His heart sank, however, when he saw that nearly half of the seats were empty. *Again.* "How can this be?" he said to Anari.

He could feel the anger and tension as her shoulder muscles knotted like twisted driftwood, but Anari's face remained stoic. "Don't be disheartened. We know we are on the right side."

He said to Gilbertus Albans, "Mentat, note who is missing. I'll want a complete list later."

"I'm already working on it."

Showing no dismay, Manford nudged Anari as if she were a horse, and she carried him into the speaking area. A dissatisfied muttering passed through the crowd, but he raised his voice, defying them to challenge him. "No more cowardly hiding behind bureaucratic procedures. Today is the day when you will go on record with what you believe. Today you must make a decision and declare yourselves on the side of righteousness, or an enemy of humanity's future."

But as he looked at all the empty seats, he realized that many of the representatives were unofficially boycotting the meeting for their own protection, refusing to go on record either way. He should have known it would be difficult to rally them against Venport Holdings, even with the appalling images his followers had obtained at Thonaris. So much of the Imperium depended on VenHold ships and their strange Navigators for travel, supplies, and commerce. Many of the absent representatives might already have gone to their homeworlds to set up defenses or form an active resistance against him.

But Manford's people were more powerful, and would respond with even greater vigor. He knew that many of his followers would die in the forthcoming struggle, but he would keep track of all their names and include them in volume after volume of *The Book of Martyrs*.

Manford turned to the Imperial box. He had strongly encouraged the Emperor to express his formal support for the measure.

Reluctantly, Salvador stood in his private box to address the half-empty hall. "We all know the dangers of uncontrolled technology. I cannot help but be overjoyed that our Imperium has a chance to go back to simpler days, peaceful days, the way humans were naturally meant to live." He paused, as if gathering courage, and said, "I urge you to vote in support of Manford Torondo's resolution." Then he sat down, as if trying to get out of view as quickly as possible.

Manford waited, but knew what the vote would ultimately show. Pressed into a corner, reminded of the consequences of intractability, the Landsraad representatives voted overwhelmingly to stand firm against any technology that could be construed as "too sophisticated, too tempting, and too dangerous."

When the resolution passed, he felt Anari relax beneath him; tension drained from her muscles like spilled water. But Manford wasn't finished yet and drew himself up as high as he could. "We must be specific, so that no one has any question. Emperor Salvador, I request that you immediately set up a Committee of Orthodoxy to watch over industries and advances, and quell any problem before it can become a danger. Every citizen of the Imperium must have a complete list of acceptable and unacceptable technology, and the government will need an enforcement arm. I volunteer the assistance of my people in these matters."

Salvador's resistance had already been broken; not surprisingly, he complied without further argument.

Finished with his work for now, Manford called for adjournment of the meeting.

Anari turned and followed the three standard-bearers out of the Landsraad Hall. They stepped through the open doors to face the huge crowd of Butlerian supporters. He raised his hands high in a signal of victory, and the roaring cheers rolled over him.

"Our movement will grow stronger now." Anari smiled up at him with a look of adoration.

Manford stared at the crowd and at the tall buildings. "We may have won today, but the real battle is just beginning. Humans are weak and don't like to live without their conveniences. We have to show them, by any means possible, that righteousness is far more important than comfort."

Historians and scientists face in opposite directions: One looks to the past, the other to the future. The wise scientist, however, listens to historians and considers the past in order to create the most acceptable future.

—PTOLEMY, Denali notebooks

When Ptolemy learned of the massacre at Thonaris, the news only reinforced his nightmares stemming from the wreck of his lab, the murder of his partner, and the fanatic Manford spurning the gift of new legs. Because of the Butlerians, superstition, ignorance, and violence were becoming the norm in society. Rational people were already going into hiding, progress was stalling, and humanity was beginning to plunge into the abyss of a new Dark Age.

For all of this, Ptolemy loathed Manford Torondo more than anyone he had ever known.

Throughout most of his life, Ptolemy had been a peaceful, innocuous man, following his own interests and paying little attention to outside political squabbles. Serena Butler's crusade against the thinking machines had ended decades before he was born, but the continued Butlerian paranoia served Manford's purposes. Technology was only an imaginary enemy that Manford used to rally his followers and build his own power structure.

The recent purge of biological research on Tlulax was an extension of the Butlerian wish to eradicate all science; the attack on the Thonaris shipyards was an escalation of their senseless violence. And the recent vote in the Landsraad Hall was an outright challenge to civilized human beings. Instead of keeping the Butlerian radicals on the fringe, operating outside of legitimate government, the Landsraad resolution granted Manford Torondo political standing and the explicit support of the Imperium. His extremism was being folded into the mainstream.

Ptolemy felt sickened, as he saw civilization crashing all around him. This could not be tolerated. Reasonable people had to fight back!

In an imploring message, Directeur Venport had urged all researchers on Denali to increase their efforts to defend against Manford's insidious assault, thus galvanizing the exiled scientists.

It was time for the next step, Ptolemy decided. He requested a special meeting with Administrator Noffe in the brain-preservation lab, where the walls were lined with bubbling tanks. The expanded brains of failed Navigators hung in nutrient fluids, cut off from sensory output but kept alive. Ptolemy often spent hours regarding those disembodied brains, wondering what thoughts might be swirling through the gray matter.

Now he turned to Noffe (who was harried by the pressures placed upon him) and said, "We have an opportunity, Administrator. We need to take extreme action to face an extreme threat."

"I am always eager to hear your ideas, Ptolemy." Noffe often seemed distracted and overwhelmed, and that had allowed Ptolemy to complete a significant task without his knowledge.

"They must be more than just ideas. I know you hate the Butlerians, as I do. Every researcher on Denali has been harmed by them, and I don't doubt that Josef Venport will authorize, and even applaud, what I propose. It will change everything."

The administrator looked at him inquisitively.

Gazing one last time at the uniform arrays of enhanced brains, Ptolemy turned. "Follow me." He led the Tlulaxa administrator to the airtight hangar, where bright glowpanels illuminated his trio of refurbished and fully functional cymek walkers; a mere glance at the imposing machines still inspired a visceral fear in Ptolemy.

Noffe's expression wavered between intimidation and admiration. "Three complete walkers!" He walked closer, awed and nervous. "I knew you were working on the old artifacts, but—"

"I've found *hundreds*. I've studied them, and I understand them—and we don't need to be mere scavengers of old, defeated technology. We can build new walkers, more advanced machine forms with better armor and stronger weaponry. You think the old cymeks were fearsome? Wait until you see my new ones!"

Noffe continued to stare, then said in a very small voice, obviously afraid of the answer, "To what purpose?"

"I have studied records from the Time of Titans—the original source material, the memoirs of General Agamemnon, and before that, the manifesto of Tlaloc. Back then, the human race had gone stagnant, grown weak. The Titans were ambitious, but in a certain sense they had altruistic motives, as well, although their own aggressive personalities brought about their downfall."

He turned away from the powerful walkers, smiled at Noffe. "We can do better. With the enhanced brains in the experimental lab, and with improved technology, we can create a new set of cymeks—more powerful, more intelligent, and more adaptable than before.

"And they'll need someone to lead them . . . possibly Josef Venport, if he is willing to undergo the radical surgery. If not, Administrator, you and I can be the first of the next generation of cymeks. With new Titans, we might manage to stave off the impending Dark Age."

Both men discussed all the horrendous damage that Manford and his followers had caused. Then Noffe mused, "Yes, we could achieve a glorious victory. A new Time of Titans."

One of the greatest blessings in life is to discover your talent at a young age, and do something productive with it.

—REVEREND MOTHER RAQUELLA BERTO-ANIRUL

Gilbertus Albans rode in an open, horse-drawn carriage that made its way slowly along the muddy streets of the Lampadas capital, leading other carriages in a victory parade. Beside him sat Manford Torondo in a specially designed seat, waving to bystanders. The Butlerian leader and his followers were ecstatic with their triumphs at the Thonaris shipyards and the vote in the Landsraad Hall.

For Gilbertus, both were Pyrrhic victories. He had regained Manford's trust by demonstrating to the Butlerians that he was no machine sympathizer, but he had to marshal his visible emotions. Even though the robot memory core had advised him to sacrifice the shipyards in order to maintain his reputation, he still felt he had somehow failed Erasmus. And he had hated being forced to defeat Draigo Roget in a real and crucial battle. Gilbertus longed for a return to the days of challenging intellectual debates and simulated games with his prize student.

Here in the medieval-like city on Lampadas, he saw a hub of political and commercial activity, a melting pot of humanity on the sidewalks and paving-stone streets. The crowds were cheering, with people hoisting placards that showed his own heroic image beside Manford's. How quickly and easily their opinions changed! Blood-red and black Butlerian banners hung from buildings, fluttering in a cool morning breeze.

Shivering in a gust of wind, Gilbertus pulled his jacket collar around his neck. The city was a hodgepodge of buildings built beneath a weather convergence zone, in which different storm systems often clashed overhead, giving the inhabitants drenching rain, lightning, thunder, and wind, but the local leaders were a hardy bunch, and they seemed to like the location. Weathersats would have helped, but Manford would never accept the technology.

In contrast to the colorful celebrations, Gilbertus smelled sewage through the open carriage window; the stink would never have been so prevalent in a high-tech city, and certainly not on Corrin under the management of the thinking machines. He looked out at the throng with mixed feelings. He wanted to *improve* civilization, promote the cause of human *advancement*. Despite the Butlerian fervor, that could not be done by discarding and destroying any device or technique that was even remotely connected with sophisticated technology.

He couldn't wait to get back to Erasmus, who remained hidden, locked away . . . probably lonely, and most certainly bored. Gilbertus was worried to have been gone so long. Many Butlerians had died during the attack at Thonaris—if something ever happened to him, what would become of Erasmus? Though Gilbertus had lived for a very long time, he was still mortal. He needed to find a way to guarantee the safety of the independent robot, and soon. But what human, or group of humans, could possibly supervise such a strong personality?

Manford turned away from the crowd, with a stern expression. "You look troubled, Mentat, on this great day."

Gilbertus made himself smile, and waved at the crowd.

"They love you, too," Manford continued. "They respect you—the great service you did for our movement. You should stay here and work with me on our expanding efforts. Leave the school in the hands of someone else."

Gilbertus had not wanted to be here in the first place, but Manford insisted that the people needed to see their heroes, and adore them. "Thank you for saying that, sir, but my duties lie elsewhere. An important new student arrives this afternoon."

"Ah, yes. Anna Corrino. It's very good that she will be trained by someone of your moral caliber. And I am happy to have the Emperor's sister close at hand, right here on Lampadas, so that I can . . . ensure her safety."

Gilbertus fought to control his disturbed expression. Manford was considering Anna a hostage? "I understand she is troubled, her mind damaged by exposure to poison. But I will do what I can to help her through her difficulties. Perhaps Mentat techniques will prove beneficial."

When the parade wound to its end, Gilbertus emerged from the carriage, and Anari Idaho retrieved Manford. Increasingly, the Headmaster was being compelled to have even closer ties with the leader of the movement.

For more than an hour, forced to remain at the reception, Gilbertus shook hands with enthusiastic, common people who gushed over him, praised him, patted him on the back. He posed for pictures with them, complimented them on their babies, and felt like the politician he did not want to be.

WITH FAR LESS spectacle, Gilbertus went to meet the Emperor's sister when she arrived at the spaceport. Anna Corrino wore a dazed expression as she was led along by two palace guards who appeared to be twins, ruddy, uniformed men who seemed ill at ease on Lampadas.

Dressed in a skirt and blouse that made her look like a young teen rather than a twenty-one-year-old, Anna walked forward, her attention flitting to the sights around her. She took no notice of Gilbertus, but talked to herself in a constant, muttering monologue.

When Gilbertus introduced himself formally to her, and received no response, one of the guards nodded to him. "Prince Roderick Corrino sends you his sister. You are commanded to provide her with all available remedy for her ailment."

Gilbertus studied the young woman, listened to her recite a litany of diverse information, and after initial incomprehension, he realized that she was naming the Landsraad representatives and proxies from all of the thousands of planets in the Imperium.

"I am impressed by your recall ability, Anna. It runs parallel with our studies here. A Mentat memorizes vast amounts of information and can recall it at will. Can you already do that? Are you able to come up with the data you want at any time?" When she didn't respond, he turned to the guards. "She may be quite a challenge, but there's a chance she could also be extremely successful, given her unique skills."

"With your permission, Headmaster, we will accompany the Princess to your school. She is quite agitated—and *very* clever. You must take care not to let her get away."

"Yes, of course. We wouldn't want that."

Gilbertus stood beside Anna and listened while she recited long strings of numbers, sets of facts, memories, and the birthdates of everyone in the Corrino/Butler family tree.

And he thought to himself, *Erasmus will find her fascinating.*

Sometimes the most attractive packages are the most dangerous.
—REVEREND MOTHER DOROTEA,
first notes from the Imperial Palace

Emperor Salvador Corrino lounged on his throne of green crystal, watching as a new concubine sang and danced for him in the large Audience Chamber, a lovely young woman who had come recommended by Sister Dorotea. Her name was Angelina, and though Salvador had been reluctant to let himself become close to any of the women trained on Rossak, Dorotea intrigued him by hinting at other specialized bodily training some of the Sisters underwent.

In her first two nights of service as one of his concubines, Angelina had not disappointed him. Not at all.

Though a long gown covered her from neck to ankles, Angelina showed she was extremely flexible, and he found her dance quite provocative. Every move reminded him of other moves she had demonstrated in the privacy of the bedchamber, causing Salvador to quickly forget about Empress Tabrina.

As a formality, he had invited Tabrina to watch the lovely girl's dance performance, but she had declined. In recent weeks their relationship had been flat, without arguments or passion—or anything else, for that matter. It was as if the two were not married at all, and living in separate worlds. Lately he'd been thinking of following the path of his father, letting his concubines bear children and then designating the succession.

Until learning of Reverend Mother Raquella's insidious scheme to cut off his bloodline, Salvador Corrino had given little thought to babies, to raising sons or daughters . . . but now it seemed a point of honor to him. Any one of his other women would do just fine, if the Empress failed to fulfill her duties.

He leaned back on his throne. Salvador could not understand any of the words to Angelina's song, and didn't care. She had a throaty voice that evoked bygone times and places he had seen in filmbooks. Though he had asked her to dance here in order to lift his spirits, he finally waved her off with a quick brush of his hand through the air. She was a nice diversion, but he had so many other concerns. With a quick smile in response, she bowed submissively and hurried toward the open doorway.

At least Angelina was obedient. Perhaps he would visit her again that evening . . . or not. Although he was definitely pleased with her, the Emperor did have eight other concubines, and he didn't want to make Sister Dorotea feel too self-important. Dorotea stood near the throne now, looking very serious and loyal, though he detected pride in her expression. No doubt she was pleased that the Emperor liked her choice of concubine.

Salvador's forces had completed the banishment of all members of the old Sisterhood from Rossak. Reverend Mother Raquella and every Sister, except the ones Dorotea approved, had also left the jungle world with little more than the clothing on their backs. He hoped Roderick had been correct in his suggestion to salvage some of the eerily trained Sisters for Imperial use, and he was anxious to discover how Dorotea and her hand-picked followers could serve him. They would bear close watching.

Prince Roderick stood beside the throne, ready to carry out his brother's commands. Through an open doorway, the Corrino Emperor saw people milling about as they awaited an audience with him. Immense chandeliers hung overhead, and the walls were covered with heroic frescoes by the finest artists in the Imperium.

None of the gaudy trappings interested him at the moment. All day long, he'd been suffering from a bad headache that worried him greatly, now that he had no personal physician. Emperor Jules had been tormented with chronic migraines before being diagnosed with his brain tumor. . . .

After the attractive concubine flitted out of the Audience Chamber, Roderick got back to business. "Eight people are seeking an audience, Sire, including Dr. Waddiz of the Suk School, a representative from Venport Holdings, and an attractive woman who wants to interview you for . . ."

"Send Waddiz in first. I want to talk with him about my headaches." He felt trapped without access to qualified physicians; he needed them, even though he didn't fully trust them. Three other Suk doctors were on call in the Palace, and he had ordered them confined to their quarters until further notice, unsure whether he dared to call on them again.

Dr. Waddiz was a tall, distinguished-looking man with dark, tanned skin. The new head administrator of the Suk School knew full well that Zhoma had been disgraced and removed from service, and thus far he'd been wise enough not to ask too many questions about what had happened to her.

He bowed before the throne. "Sire, let me offer my most heartfelt apologies that Dr. Zhoma's service to you was unsatisfactory. She was quite secretive and acted independently in many areas. Now that we have begun to analyze her private records, we are discovering financial irregularities, as well. You can be assured that we will investigate them thoroughly." Waddiz talked in a nervous rush. Because of public pronouncements, he knew for certain what Salvador had done to the Sisters of Rossak, and he might know that Dr. Zhoma had been caught in her allied plot. "Please don't let this unfortunate incident reflect badly on our academic institution."

"Yes, yes." Salvador rubbed his temples. "Your school's reputation has definitely been tarnished." His head throbbed constantly, and he was sure a tumor must be growing in there, pressing behind his eyes, swelling inside his skull. . . . How would he ever survive without a competent physician?

Waddiz rose to his feet, keeping his head bowed. "Under my leadership, we will do everything possible to regain our standing—and our new facility on Parmentier will work closely with the recently established Committee of Orthodoxy. We pledge to work within any guidelines you decide to set for us, Majesty."

Salvador regarded him with a sour and skeptical expression. "The best way to regain your standing with me would be to guarantee the loyalty of any doctor assigned to touch my royal person. Zhoma was the highest-ranking Suk doctor. If *she* was caught trying to harm me, how can I trust any physician you provide? How can I be sure?"

Waddiz folded his hands together, bowed again. "We have already been studying the matter, Sire, and we realize it is not a problem unique to an Imperial patron. Many important personages fear schemes and assassins, and a patient is often completely vulnerable during treatment. Our psychological wing is developing a type of conditioning that will make a doctor utterly *incapable* of harming a specific person."

Standing beside the throne, Roderick interjected, "Conditioning? Do you mean programming—like a machine? The cymeks added programming strictures to prevent Omnius from harming them."

Waddiz was alarmed by the comparison. "Not . . . like that. A special mental conditioning, costly and intensive, designed to protect an important patron like yourself, Sire."

"I am not merely an important patron—I am the *Emperor*."

"For you, Sire, there will be the highest level of surety. *Imperial* Conditioning. An intensive and infallible loyalty verification program that taps deeply into the pyretic consciousness, making an imprint that cannot be reversed under any circumstance. We are only in the test stages now, but the results are most promising."

Roderick whispered advice in Salvador's ear, after which the Emperor turned to the Reverend Mother who waited near the throne. "So, Sister Dorotea, you have demonstrated a reliable intuition as to truth or falsehood. Does the doctor's plan sound plausible to you? As far as you can tell, is he speaking the truth?"

The nervous doctor squirmed under scrutiny. Presently, Dorotea looked up at Salvador and said, "I believe such conditioning is possible, and I sense none of the indicators that he is lying."

Again, Roderick whispered advice, this time recommending that there would need to be layers of additional testing to be conducted here on Salusa Secundus, so that the Corrinos could be completely assured of loyal physicians.

Finally the Emperor nodded and said, "Very well, Waddiz. You may proceed with the program. I require a fully conditioned physician as soon as possible."

From somewhere, the doctor found his courage. "Thank you, Sire, but it is only a very limited test program at this point, and we will need additional funding. . . ."

Salvador brushed him aside. "See the Imperial treasurer. Roderick, draft the appropriate payment authorization."

"Thank you, Sire." Waddiz bowed and hurried away.

Ironically, as soon as the Suk doctor departed, the Emperor realized that his headache had faded.

"Your exalted Highness," Dorotea said, "my Sisters and I are grateful for the opportunity you extended in inviting us here. I would like to volunteer my services more frequently as one skilled in detecting falsehoods. Sire, if you allow me to stand near your throne during Imperial audiences, I will prove myself extremely useful to you."

"But can I trust *you*? Isn't that the question, Dorotea? I *want* to trust you, just as I want to trust my doctors. But bad things have happened, things that give me pause."

She didn't waver as she looked at him. "Allow me to demonstrate my talents, Sire, and I promise, you will not be disappointed."

Roderick broke in, "Perhaps the Emperor will summon you for specific tasks. You will be notified when you are needed."

Looking disappointed, Dorotea departed with a formal bow, and Emperor Salvador sat back on his throne. He had a long day ahead of him, many decisions to make, many visitors to greet, as was his duty. But there were other duties, and he was daydreaming that he might visit the Empress in her bedchamber that evening instead of his concubines, and for a specific purpose.

Yes, Salvador decided, it was about time he had children of his own. Just to spite Raquella's version of the Sisterhood and her monstrous bloodline predictions.

THAT EVENING, AS Salvador endured a banquet beside Empress Tabrina, as usual, he felt that his life was returning to normal . . . but that did not mean it was good.

Looking across the table, he observed Roderick and his wife, and their well-behaved children, as they all shared desserts with each other. Haditha picked up a small pastry, took a bite, and offered it to her daughter. Roderick laughed at some joke their boy had made, then leaned over and kissed his wife on the cheek.

Salvador felt a deep sense of longing for what his younger brother had. But he was the Emperor of the Imperium! Thousands and thousands of worlds! Why couldn't he have a good family life? Why was that so difficult? He reached over hopefully, touched Tabrina's hand.

She looked at him as if he had wiped excrement on her wrist. "Don't touch me," she rasped.

He withdrew, stung. Keeping his voice low, he protested, "You're my Empress! Why do you treat me this way?"

"We've been over this a hundred times! I'd be much warmer if you'd grant me a title and a government position. For many years I watched my father work his industries; I sat in his offices, learning from him. I have skills, and I would certainly be a better commerce minister than that idiot you've had in the position for four years."

"You dare to blackmail me!?"

"What blackmail?" Tabrina arched her brows. "I am only doing what women have done since time immemorial. You expect me to swoon over you when you treat me like a mere pet? I ask for a few perfectly reasonable duties, and you say no. *I* am the wronged party, not you."

"But I need a legitimate heir. The *Imperium* needs an heir."

"And I want to be commerce minister." She drew her arms close to her chest. "The solution seems obvious enough."

"So . . . if I give you that title, you'll carry my child?"

"Give me the title *and* the duties. Then yes, I will invite you to my bedchamber—on a specified schedule. Beyond that, I have no control over whether or not I get pregnant."

Salvador narrowed his eyes. "But you'll do nothing to prevent it?"

"I'll do nothing to prevent it." She softened her expression a bit. "And I think you'll find the arrangement far more pleasant, because I'll be happier with the new status. Just don't expect me to love you."

"No, I would never expect that," Salvador said, looking again at the happy couple of Roderick and Haditha.

DOROTEA SLIPPED THE vial into the new concubine's soft, lotioned hand. "It is a cream, easily applied. Emperor Salvador will never notice, provided you keep his mind elsewhere."

Angelina smiled stiffly. "But Reverend Mother, are you sure he won't feel it? Won't know?"

"We've formulated this very carefully. A single exposure should be sufficient to render him sterile. He won't know anything has changed, won't even suspect he has a problem for a long time. And it won't harm you, either."

The strikingly beautiful girl bowed. "My concern is not for myself, but for the Sisterhood."

"If you do this one thing, you will help ensure our future." Dorotea darted away down the dark hallway outside of the concubines' quarters.

Despite her dispute with Reverend Mother Raquella, Dorotea had studied the breeding projection herself. Even though computers were inherently evil, she could not deny their accuracy. She felt a responsibility to prevent the most terrible tyrant in all of history from being inflicted on humanity.

W hen he made his way back to the isolated weather-monitoring station and the flying craft the twins had landed there, Vor knelt for a long while on the warm sand beside the body of Griffin Harkonnen. The young man's death was as utterly useless and heartbreaking as Ishanti's had been.

Griffin might have been the best hope for restoring the fortunes and respect of House Harkonnen. His skills had been solid and his plans viable . . . but all had been snuffed out.

Vor's enemies kept following him and causing him pain, always missing the true target, and so many innocents had paid the price for that debt. Even Mariella . . .

He wrapped Griffin's body in a thin polymer tarpaulin that he found among the supplies inside the weather station. He could have just left the young man there—the elements would take care of him soon enough—but Vor found that dishonorable. Griffin Harkonnen had defeated him in a duel, held a sharp knife to his throat, and then granted Vorian his life back. Vor owed him a debt for that, but even more, Vor had to pay a debt to House Harkonnen . . . not to make excuses, not to explain, but to acknowledge his part in tarnishing Xavier Harkonnen's name and in the disgrace and suffering heaped on Abulurd and his innocent descendants.

Yes, the repercussions came back to him. He took a deep breath and reconsidered, but only a little. Xavier and Abulurd and Griffin had been responsible for themselves—Vor harbored no illusions about that—but he, too, bore some of the blame, and now accepted it.

After tying the tarpaulin around the body, Vor lifted the young man over his shoulder and boarded the flier, setting the wrapped package behind the cockpit seats. With plodding thoroughness, he completed the flight checklist, started the engines, and lifted away from the rocky bowl.

The flier was a common Arrakis model; the compass, weathersat linkage, and navigation charts guided him back to Arrakis City. Early that afternoon, he landed at the edge of the main spaceport and set about trying to find a carrier to transport Griffin's corpse back to Lankiveil, along with a message to his family that he still had to write.

The cargo line operators were baffled by his request. One asked, "Do you realize the expense, sir? Shipping a human body across space is not cost-effective."

"I don't care about the cost. He belongs with his family, his world, and his home. I need to send him back there." Vor would have to arrange for a transfer of funds from one of his accounts on another planet, but the actual expense was not an issue. He could have ignored the responsibility, brushed the Harkonnens aside again, and turned his back on the guilt . . . but that sort of thinking had already caused too many problems.

The cargo operator shook his head. "I've seen fools waste their money in many ways. I advise you against this, but I know someone else will take your payment, if I don't." With a little convincing he accepted the job anyway.

Vor also felt obligated to give Griffin's family an explanation—though not too much. He wrote the message while the men handled the body, preparing it for shipment. "Griffin Harkonnen died with honor, upholding his principles. This was a brave man, traveling the Imperium, never shirking his noble quest. He found me, as his family demanded of him, and we resolved our differences. In time, we might even have become friends, but he met an unexpected and tragic death. Now, in the spirit of his memory I can only hope his family will understand, and forgive."

Vor paused, deciding not to reveal the existence of Agamemnon's other two children to Griffin's family. That matter was resolved, and the twins would cause no further harm. However, it was a battle the Harkonnens should never have needed to fight.

"He was killed by desert bandits," Vor continued. "And I killed them for doing it. Your brave Griffin is avenged, and I join you in sorrow. I knew Griffin for only a short time, but I came to admire him, and I assure you, he earned the lasting respect of his family name."

Vor finished what he had to say, and after Arrakis City morticians sealed and preserved the body, he placed the letter in a message compartment on the airtight storage container, and watched as it was loaded onto the next outbound cargo ship. Eventually, it would be transferred to Lankiveil.

After the ship was gone, Vorian remained in Arrakis City for three days, but soon he came to realize that nothing was left for him there. And with Mariella now gone, he could not imagine returning to Kepler; he would only expose the rest of his family to great risk.

There were thirteen thousand planets in the Imperium. Surely he could find someplace else to go.

At the spaceport office, he offered his credentials, paid a substantial fee, and signed aboard a VenHold cargo ship that was due to depart with a load of melange. With plenty of solaris remaining in his accounts, he would fly the space lanes for a while, or he might disembark on any world that interested him.

The future for Vorian Atreides—however long he had—was an open, empty canvas. He boarded the ship, with no idea where it was bound, and did not look back at the desert planet.

Threats are only words, and have the detrimental effect of warning your opponent, which allows him to prepare a defense or offense. I don't believe in threats. I believe in hard, decisive action.

—Valya Harkonnen

After the Sisterhood was outlawed on Rossak, Valya was sent back to Lankiveil, against her will. She had been torn away from the jungle planet and herded onto a space transport with many other Sisters, unable to ask Reverend Mother Raquella what to do or how she could help preserve the core of the Sisterhood.

Everything was lost.

Her parents welcomed her back to the small, gloomy planet. It was the definition of home, she supposed: a place where family would take you in, no matter what shame or crisis you brought with you.

Griffin still had not returned from his hunt for Vorian Atreides, but her little brother and sister were excited to see her. Her mother and father had kept her old room for her, and they pestered her with questions about the Sisterhood. They weren't really interested, but were glad to have her back. Her mother had never believed that the special training would benefit Valya.

From Valya's perspective, though, she had learned too much to simply sit back and resign herself to a quiet, unambitious life. She looked forward to Griffin returning home, when the two of them could make plans and take new paths to restoring the Harkonnens to prominence. Her hopes for advancement through the Sisterhood, or through ties of friendship with Anna Corrino, had all run aground.

She remembered the Reverend Mother's words: *The Sisterhood is your only family now.* But the order of women had been scattered, and her own family seemed to have forgotten what it really meant to be a Harkonnen. They had made poor decisions, which led to their exile here on this wintry world of cold seas and rugged fjords. They failed to grasp the significance of political events beyond their own backwater planet. They continued to disappoint her.

But Griffin had never let her down, and as days passed she grew increasingly worried about him. If she could jump into the arctic waters again to save him, she would.

One morning, two weeks after her arrival, Valya entered the main living area of her parents' house. The fireplace was ablaze, and she could smell a pot of whale-meat stew cooking in the kitchen, a family recipe seasoned with aromatic local spices and vegetables. She had never liked Lankiveil cooking.

Her father chatted at great length with Valya about making alterations to their house, using different roofing materials and better insulation. She had no interest whatsoever. As the planetary leader, Vergyl Harkonnen made no attempt to advance the political position of House Harkonnen, and he merely shrugged when he received a notice that the Landsraad proxy for Lankiveil had signed on to Manford Toronado's petition, and publicly added support for the Butlerians.

She sighed in dismay as she looked at her father now, sitting on a blocky wooden chair by the fire, engrossed in a book. In the time she'd been away, he had become a very small person. If House Harkonnen were ever to return to prominence and glory, it would not be up to him; it would be up to her and her brother.

Griffin, where are you? she thought, sensing something was wrong, terribly wrong.

Sonia Harkonnen sat at a small table where she used a thick needle and cord to sew pieces of whale fur together, making a new coat for Valya's younger brother, Danvis. The boy was fourteen now, old enough to go out on fur-whale expeditions; his features and mannerisms reminded her of Griffin at that age.

Valya stood by the fire to warm herself. Every day since returning to this icy world, she'd been chilled to the bone—having grown accustomed to the comparatively warm and pleasant climate of Rossak. Her father greeted her with a smile. "Good morning, Valya." Her mother followed with the same words, exactly, and her own vacuous smile.

Valya couldn't wait to leave this place again.

When Sister Arlett had recruited her on a windswept day down by the docks, the woman had described how the school on Rossak could be Valya's route to power and influence. But now the Sisterhood was a wounded creature, looking for someplace to heal . . . or die.

"We saved an omelet for you when you didn't come down for breakfast." Her mother gestured toward a covered warming dish on the hearth.

Valya decided to take the food up to her room, where she could think about what to do next. She picked up the plate and turned toward the wooden stairs, when she heard an urgent rapping at the door. It was not a good sound; her senses were immediately alert.

Her father waved her off and went to answer the knock. He opened the heavy door to see two local fishermen bringing a delivery, an oblong package almost two meters long, stamped with transfer labels from the VenHold Spacing Fleet. "This was in the shuttle that arrived last night. We're still distributing."

Vergyl thanked them, curious about the large package. Valya helped him pull it inside, but something about the size and shape of the container filled her with dread. Oblivious, her father poked at the labels to see if he could identify the sender's name, but Valya ignored a message compartment and tore at the packaging, peeling away the sheets of polymer.

She was the first to see her brother's dead face, his eyes closed, his cheeks covered with a stubble of beard. His goatee was matted, and there was a tracing of dust on his forehead and in his brown hair. His head lolled at an odd angle.

Shocked, her father stumbled backward and bumped into the wall, then began to sob. Her mother rushed forward to stare in horror at the body of her son. It was something parents should never have to see.

Valya summoned all of the training that the Sisterhood had given her. She had been taught how to study a situation in a hundred instant snapshots from every vantage. She froze and stared, then threw herself on the makeshift casket. In a very quiet voice, she whispered her brother's name, knowing he could never answer her again. "Griffin!"

The two fishermen who had delivered the package bowed their heads respectfully. One of them opened the message compartment and handed an envelope to Vergyl Harkonnen. "This came too, sir. I'm very sorry, sir." His partner handed over additional mail, and both of them stepped back.

Distraught and sobbing, Vergyl tore the first envelope open and his shaking hands tore the paper letter, but he pushed the pieces back together so he could read the words. He seemed as incapable of understanding the message as he was of comprehending the death of his son. "It's . . . from Vorian Atreides."

Valya grabbed the letter from him. "What? That bastard!"

She read the message, knowing it would either be gloating or lies. Written in a firm script, the letter asserted that her brother had died a hero, trying to defend Vorian against attackers. Nonsense! Griffin had gone to assassinate him, not save him. This Atreides was implying that they were friends! It had to be a lie, a complete lie!

Again, Vorian Atreides was sticking his thumb in the eyes of the Harkonnens.

"He killed my brother." Though she didn't know the circumstances of Griffin's death, Valya knew whom to hold responsible. It felt even more personal to her now, and her desire to kill him more just.

Also in the mail delivered by the cargo ship was an ostentatious official document, signed, stamped, and sealed—a proclamation that Griffin Harkonnen had paid the requisite fees and passed all of the required examinations, and he had now been accepted as Lankiveil's official planetary representative to the Landsraad.

Valya tore it in two.

"This vendetta will never end," she whispered to her brother's body. "I will find Vorian Atreides."

SHE RETREATED TO her room and locked the door. Her parents assumed she had gone to grieve. Instead, reaching into a pocket, she brought out a small packet containing a single capsule of the new Rossak drug, a precisely measured portion she had taken from Sister Karee's lab. It was identical to the one that Anna Corrino had stolen and swallowed, the same dosage that had nearly killed her.

Valya held the pill between her thumb and forefinger, staring at it, trying to summon the nerve to take the poison—which would either kill her, or transform her. Previously, she had hesitated, worried that her death would cause irreparable harm to Harkonnen ambitions, but now she felt exactly the opposite. If she could become a Reverend Mother, with full control and precise access to her cellular chemistry, and to the memory-lives of all her female ancestors back to the dawn of time—then she would be unstoppable.

Valya could envision numerous ways to hunt down and destroy Vorian Atreides. The voices of her Other Memories would guide her.

She closed her eyes and swallowed the pill.

❧

Setbacks can send you reeling off course, or they can make you stronger.
—REVEREND MOTHER RAQUELLA BERTO-ANIRUL,
address to the Sisterhood

T he VenHold shuttle descended through a clear sky toward a planet that was chilly, but still hospitable to life. A new sanctuary, a place where Cioba assured them no one would look.

Even before Venport's assistance, Raquella had developed a secret contingency survival plan, working closely with Karee Marques. The Sisterhood's funds in offworld accounts had now been absorbed by the VenHold banking system. It was a tight alliance Raquella had not expected to make, but she could see the value.

Accompanied by twenty-eight ragtag followers that she had surreptitiously gathered, Raquella had high hopes for this scouting mission. If this world proved acceptable, she had made arrangements to rendezvous with additional Sisters who remained loyal to her. With luck, the VenHold Spacing Fleet would deliver them all here.

The old woman felt an obligation to each and every one of them. Those women had made vows of allegiance to her. She needed to get her new base of operations selected as soon as possible, and then begin contacting them, rebuilding her school.

Wallach IX had been one of the Synchronized Worlds under the control of Omnius, ruled for a time by the human traitor Yorek Thurr, and then destroyed a century ago by the Army of the Jihad in a nuclear attack. Most of the radiation had died down by now, and the planet was potentially habitable by humans. Venport assured the Reverend Mother that no commercial ships ever visited there.

The shuttle settled down on an old machine landing field that had survived the holocaust. A number of stone warehouse buildings surrounded the field, some of them collapsed. In the distance, Raquella saw sparse forests and a line of snow-covered peaks. Ice on nearby hills sparkled in the dim light of the blue-white sun, Laojin. Though projections suggested that this planet had a typically cold and rainy climate, today Wallach IX seemed to be showing off its natural beauty to the best effect.

She bundled up in a thick coat and stepped off the shuttle ramp onto the cracked pavement. As the other Sisters disembarked and walked toward the nearest building, Raquella felt a gust of sharp, cold wind that seemed to cut through her skin. This was quite a different environment from the humid jungles of Rossak. Dark clouds closed in quickly and spat down a wind-driven torrent of rain, drenching the women before they could reach cover.

Shivering in the shadows of the warehouse, Raquella said, "Directeur Venport assures us this place is safe. I think we've found our new homeworld."

Here, on a distant, rugged planet, she would gather as many Sisters as possible and continue their training in secret. For now, her trainees had the goal of merely surviving . . . but soon, the Sisterhood would accomplish much more than that.